I am privileged to dedicate my first novel to my beautiful wife Peggy. I could not have accomplished this without her love and support. She is my guiding light.

I would like to thank Mike and Edythe Kirby. As avid SF fans and my very excellent friends, their insight and imagination has been invaluable. I truly appreciate their gentle manner when telling me something didn't pass muster.

To my father and mother who inspire me in ways I am still exploring.

To my friends and family who refrained from telling me that I was full of crap; thank you with the fullness of my heart.

Unabridged First Edition
Authors Number 31/104

ISBN 0-9777235-0-X

http://charleslesher.com/

Printed in the United States of America
Writers Cramp Publishers

"Where knowledge ends, religion begins."
Benjamin Disraeli (1804-1881)

Evolution's Child

Lunarian Declaration of Independence

April 1, 2060

Occasionally in the course of human events, it becomes necessary for one people to dissolve the political bonds which have connected them, and to assume among the governments of Earth and Space, the separate and equal station to which the Laws of Nature entitle them. A decent respect to the opinions of mankind requires that the causes which impel them to this separation be declared.

We hold these truths to be self-evident, that all life is sacred, and that human beings in particular are endowed by nature with certain unalienable Rights, Freedoms, and Responsibilities. To secure these, governments are instituted among humanity, deriving their just powers from the consent of the citizens, that whenever any form of government becomes destructive of these ends, it is the right of the people to alter or to abolish it, and to institute new government, laying its foundation on such principles and organizing its powers in such form, as to them shall seem most likely to effect their safety and happiness. Prudence, indeed, will dictate that governments long established should not be changed for light and transient causes; and accordingly all experience hath shown, that individuals are more disposed to suffer, while evils are sufferable, than to risk all that they value by challenging the forms to which they are accustomed. But when the political decisions invariably revels a design to subject them to absolute despotism, it is their right, it is their duty, to throw off such government, and to provide new guards for their future security. Such has been the patient sufferance of the Luna Colonies; and such is now the necessity which constrains them to alter their former systems of government and throw off the shackles that they would extend across the vastness of space.

When the first Luna Colonies were established, many different governments and private corporations provided people and treasure towards the effort. As such, each claimed dominion over that which they created. But in the years since no single governing body has sustained support from all of the various interests, rather the individuals rights and freedoms have been subjugated to the whims of corporate and bureaucratic decisions, much of which cannot be construed in any way to maintaining the security, safety and happiness of Luna's citizens. The right to own property is trampled daily by the arrogant belief asserting 'all that exists within belongs to the company', in effect enslaving the men and women who live, work and call it home. We consider this the latest way of packaging slavery and will not participate any longer. The refusal to allow the formation of Laws with a Legislature to write them and a Justice system to uphold them has caused great hardship among the people of Luna. Justice carried out across the miles by individuals having never set foot on Luna produces more harm than good, even when performed in good faith. Lunarians live in an atmosphere of abuse and neglect, with no immediate representative government to attend to their grievances and guard against infringements of their liberty. We find, in all good consciousness, that we cannot tolerate this any longer.

In every stage of these oppressions we have petitioned for redress in the most humble terms: Our petitions have been answered only by injury. Collectively, the world's governments and corporations, many whose character is marked by acts which define tyranny, are unfit to govern a free people. They have been deaf to the voice of justice and of consanguinity.

We, therefore, as lawful representatives of the Luna Colonies, do, in the name, and by authority of the good people of these Colonies, solemnly publish and declare that these are, and of Right ought to be, Free and Independent; that they are Absolved from all Allegiance to Earth's governments, and that all political connection between them and the Colonies, is totally dissolved; and that as Free and Independent, the Colonies have full Power to levy War, conclude Peace, contract Alliances, establish Commerce, and to do all other Acts and Things which Independent States may do. And for the support of this Declaration we mutually pledge to each other our Lives, our Fortunes and our sacred Honor.

21st Century Timeline

Abigail Katee O'Neil 10/15/99	1999	
	2000	Pres: *George Bush*
	2001	9/11/01 WTC destroyed
	2002	US invades Afghanistan
	2003	US invades Iraq
	2004	
	2005	
	2006	
	2007	
	2008	US attacks Iran
Space Station is militarized	2009	Pres: *John Edwards*
DNA Base Sequencer (DBS)	2010	
	2011	
	2012	Coalition of Christian Citizens elect
ISS defeats ICBM attack	2013	Pres: *George Farcain*
Type 3 superconductors are discovered	2014	US repeals the Bill of Rights
First magnetoplasma thruster	2015	
China establishes Shennong	2016	President Farcain assassinated
9/11/01 Houston nuked	2017	Pres: *Isaac Higgins*
Powsat beams energy to Earth	2018	**North American Federation** (NAF)
	2019	Rising sea levels top **1 foot**
NAF and EU establish Taurus Colony	2020	EU invades South Africa
Japan establishes Kyoto	2021	American Church of Christ established
Japan establishes Ishikawajima	2022	ACC rally's 1.5 million against genetics
	2023	NAF outlaws all genetic research
NAF establishes Aldrin Station	2024	EU establishes New London
	2025	Pres: *Calvin Hobbs*
S Korea establishes Hyundai Shipyards	2026	NAF builds 1st orbital battlestation
China establishes Far Point Mine	2027	Rising sea levels top **2½ feet**
	2028	China, EU build battlestations
	2029	Pres: *David Hanson*
Shennong absorbs Ishikawajima	2030	NAF outlaws all biotronic research
Japan builds battlestation	2031	EU restricts biotronic research
India establishes Darpur Mine	2032	
EU establishes Purgatory Deep Hole	2033	United Nations bans human testing
	2034	British hospital bombed (117)
China establishes Mingun Mine	2035	Federation outlaws football, boxing
Calconn presented to the world	2036	Chinese Unification
Nell Goddard 1/15/37	2037	Pres: *Mark Bertrand*
Expeditions to Mars and Asteroids	2038	NAF hospital bombed (53)
	2039	Japan admits to UN violations
Rising sea levels top **6 feet**	2040	Japanese genetic clinic bombed (21)
Israel builds battlestation	2041	Pres: *Elijah Henry*
After 40 yrs NAF leaves Iraqi oil fields	2042	**Islamic Brotherhood** (IB) forms
Lindsey Davenport 10/12/43	2043	Elijah Henry forms Reformation Party
	2044	ACC joins Reformationist Party
China begins selling arms to the IB	2045	Japanese Hospital bombed (191)

	2046	IB attacks Israel and is rebuffed
World condemns IB	2047	China brokers the Saudi Accord
	2048	Rising sea levels top **16 feet**
India lays keel for the ISS Shakti	2049	Pres: *Scott Lennon*
1st Lunarian visor mass produced	2050	IB builds Mogadishu spaceport
	2051	IB buys battlestation from Hyundai
Lunarians produce first Zettasphere	2052	
Fair Access becomes world law	2053	Pres: *James Johnson*
First permanent Mars colony	2054	IB annexes Sudan
Lazarus Sheffield 4/17/55	2055	
	2056	Korean biotronic program exposed
PR Dugan killed at Far Point	2057	Pres: *John Paul*
	2058	IB invades Ethiopia
First asteroid colony	2059	South Korean president assassinated
April 1 - Luna Independence Day	2060	North and South Korea become one
	2061	IB establishes Al Fahad on Luna
	2062	Federation's Great Revival begins
Treaty of Independence	2063	Rising sea levels top **32 feet**
	2064	
Rock of Ages diverted from Earth	2065	World drought kills tens of millions
	2066	Scientific research stops within NAF
	2067	IB annexes Libya and Algeria
Republic establishes Summerhaven	2068	Reformationists restrict internet
Trans Lunar Highway completed	2069	
	2070	Turkey withdraws from EU, joins IB
	2071	NAF opens first reeducation camp
Tempel Dugan 10/31/72	2072	Rising sea levels top **45 feet**
Luna's genetic program exposed	2073	Korea allies with IB
Religious radicals call for Luna's death	2074	
Republic establishes Prattville	2075	Al Fahad grows slowly over 15 yrs
Luna Councilman Chi Lin assassinated	2076	IB begins expansion of Al Fahad
	2077	NAF declares martial law
Republic establishes Scottsbluff	2078	
ISS Shakti discovers life on Titan	2079	IB declares war on India (Food war)
Bombings begin all across Luna	2080	Rising sea levels top **56 feet**
First bomb destroys a Lunarian farm (0)	2081	China allies with IB against India
Abby survives assassination attempt	2082	
3 bombings in Shennong (19)	2083	Commodore Bakr arrives buys SMT
Mine sabotage in Darpur (3)	2084	Kahfah Road completed
6 bombs, June 15, Black Friday (255)	2085	
Central Highland convoy hijacked (6)	2086	Al Fahad exceeds 250,000
3 bombings during the year (26)	2087	SMT begins modifying convoys
Prattville water reservoir contaminated	2088	President John Paul dies at 92
7 bombings during the year (102)	2089	Pres: *Matthew Newsom*
2 bombings during the year (12)	2090	Rising sea levels top **64 feet**
3 bombings during the year (46)	2091	Kashmir Agreement ends India war
4 bombings (39) and LCH (451)	2092	

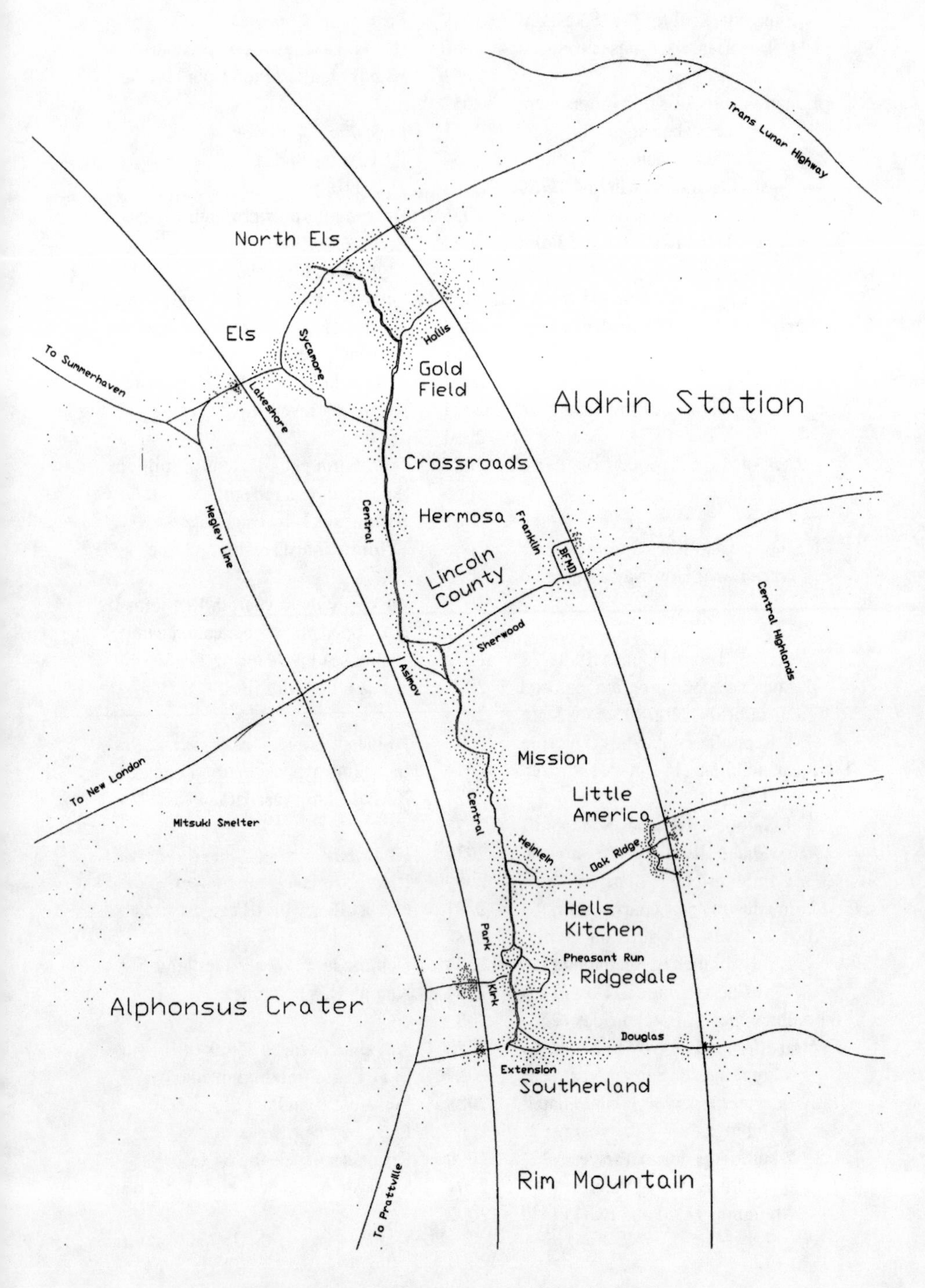

Boroughs and Commonways of Aldrin Station

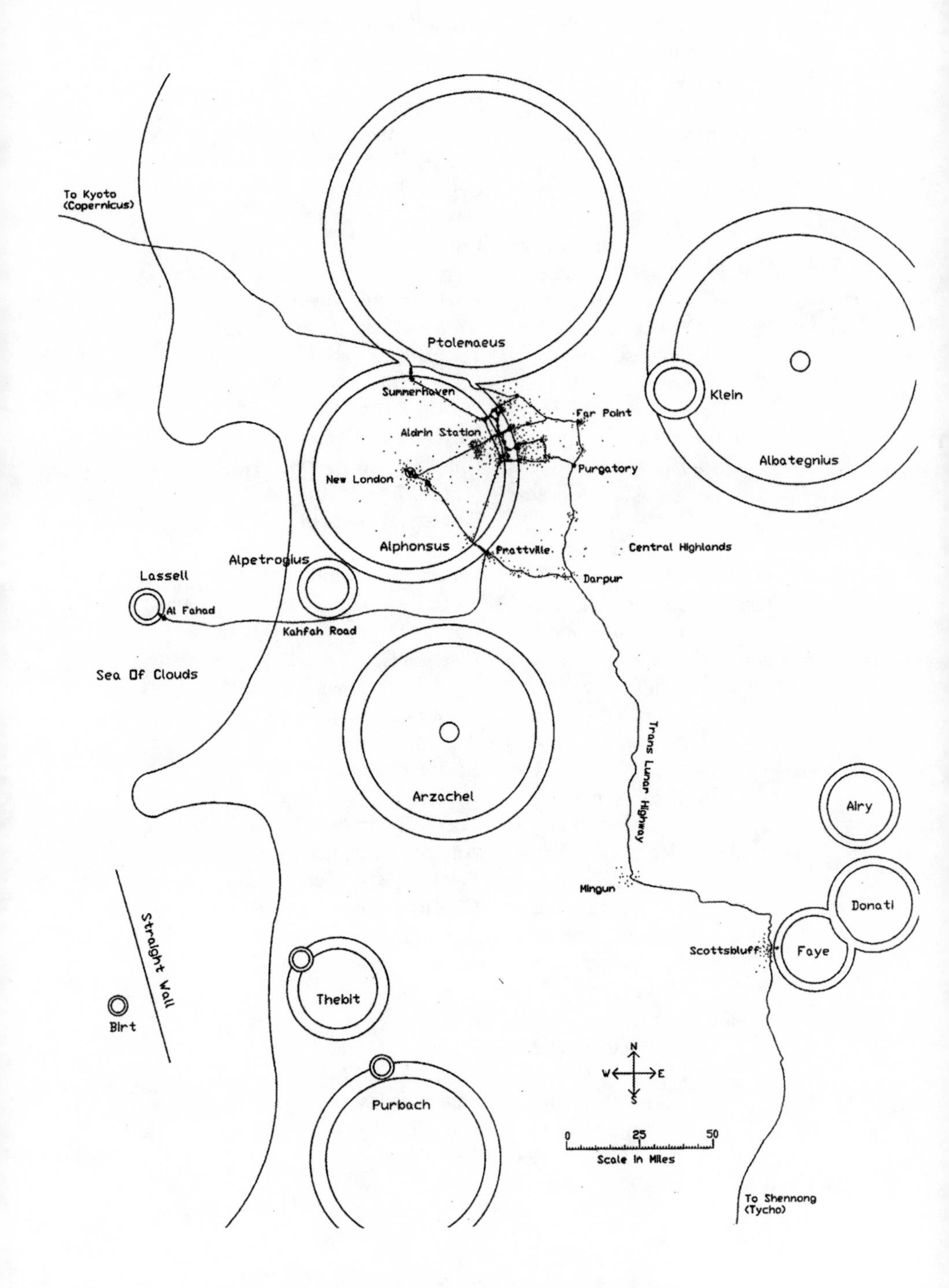

Republic of Luna: Four Craters Region

Cast of Players

Charley Company
Captain Kitajima Osaka
Master Sergeant Susan Hackling
Doctor Howard Grady
Senior Lieutenant Tempel Dugan
Lieutenant Tatiana Tushar
Sergeant Consuela Navarro
Sergeant John Kipper
S.I.T. Angel Lopez
S.I.T. Samantha Odegaard
Officer Lei Cheung
Officer Brice Guyart
Officer Jason Piqualow
Officer Karl Svensson
Officer Corazon Montano
Officer Karyl Stormberg
Officer Zoey Tanaka
Officer Alonzo Tushar

Main Players
Senior Analyst Lazarus Sheffield
Captain Lindsey Davenport
Pilot Nell Goddard
Councilman Abigail O'Neil Dugan
Security Chief Corso Dugan

Other Players
Propriety Officer Zechariah Hargrove
Elizabeth Turner Dugan
Officer Krystin Dugan
Officer Skylor Dugan
Lucas Dugan
Katee Dugan
Captain Ben Dugan
Officer Jason Harman
Officer Larz Harman
Councilman Zachary Taylor
Councilman Yang Lee
Security Chief Chen Zhi
Lieutenant Huang
Sergeant Lin Kai
Officer Meili

Islamic Brotherhood
Mohammed Basayev
Commodore Nassah Bakr
Commander Ghafour
Major General Abdel Salam Arif
Defense Minister Hasin bin Aunker
Captain Mustafa Malik
Havildar Anwar Jafa
Dalal

Background Players
Ohio Senator Elijah Hanley
Tara Dugan
Officer Odessa Simpson
Officer Dana Monroe
Officer Joey Parker
Chief Engineer Jerome Hargrove
Major Mallory Higgins
Lieutenant Hugh O'Reilly
Lieutenant Meyers
Director Lee Chin
Serena, Florence, and Tatum Dugan
Conrad Dugan, Arnold Kirltenko, Leopold Calatrava, Brandon Dugan, Bayne Bjorkman, Nate Dugan, Perri Calatrava, and Dallas Dugan
Anita Salazar
Justine Harman
Nicole Dugan
Lori Schumacher Dugan
Antonio Pellegrini
Winthrop Grubber
Constance Haig
Claressa
Suzy
Lee Fong
Sarah
Alan
Susan
Isaac Crenshaw
Mary Stephens
Con Renolds
Dueler

"Fear of things invisible is the natural seed of that which every one in himself calleth religion."
Thomas Hobbes (1588-1679)

Genesis

The volcano had been shaking for months, gentle warnings of the violence to come. Many of the birds and animals had long since abandoned the forests that blanket the mountain, instinct overcoming habit as the very ground beneath them trembled. The wandering bands of hominids are no exception, the last leaving just days before the eruption.

For countless centuries these tribes have roamed the rich valleys around the volcano, hunting and gathering from nature's abundance. They call themselves the People and will come to be known collectively as Homo heidelbergensis. Their anatomy exhibits many of the characteristics of modern humans. Over tens of thousands of generations, brow ridges recede while foreheads expand and skulls bulge to accommodate an ever increasing brain size even as their faces narrow and features sharpen. They are strong and well proportioned, more powerful than modern humans. Largely hairless, what shows of their sweaty dark skin glistens under overcast skies as they stride confidently through the hardwood forest away from the awakening giant.

From the open spaces between the forest trees, they can see the flank of the mountain many miles away, its summit hidden behind a dense mass of dark clouds. The air hangs heavy on the tribe, damp and filled with the promise of a thunderstorm. The men carry fire hardened spears and heavy clubs while the women are burdened with rough hide bundles filled with tribal possessions and whatever food they have. Coarse cut leather clothing hangs loose from their waists and shoulders, worked by the women using teeth and tools until supple. Thick calluses cover the soles of their feet. Not a single adornment graces the tribe.

Ur isn't the largest or the strongest among them. But at twenty years of age, he has established himself as one of the best stone workers in the tribe, able to find beautiful blades within the depths of a rock. Ur is also quite fluent in their rich spoken language. It is his skill at telling the ancient stories that draws the People to his fire in the evenings, his counsel they listen to most often. His mate had been taken by a water demon the season before. She had been heavy with child and slow that day. Ur had watched helplessly as the beast dragged her into the water and ripped her apart. The dark stain spreading across the surface of the normally placid river was a sure sign that she had surrendered her spirit, that he would see her no more.

Omon, the tribe's leading hunter and brother of Ur, had thought it wrong to leave the forests of their birth. That the Great Spirit would spend His anger with a few storm clouds and all would return to normal. That leaving would only make Him take notice of the tribe.

Ur felt different. The old stories told of times when the Great Spirit had destroyed the forests and everything in them. They spoke of fire spirits so powerful that the rocks themselves burned. Of smells that sucked the life spirit out of the People. But these stories were only whispered deep underground in total darkness to escape the attention of the Great Spirit. These were not tales to be told openly, and would not be spoken of now.

By strength of personality, Ur convinces the People to move north towards the tribe's winter hunting grounds. It is there that the Great Spirit provides them with caves that give shelter from the freezing rain and deep snow of the dead time. Perhaps they will protect the People from His anger as well.

The eruption begins mid morning of the fourth day. Ur, close to the front, hears someone call loudly from the long line stretched out behind him. Turning, gazing through the gaps in the dense foliage, he watches with growing fear as the Great Spirit rises above them. He stands atop Spirit Mountain pulling the surrounding clouds upward in a mighty explosion. A few seconds later His voice washes over the People with the loudest sound they had ever heard, throwing them to the ground, shaking their world like a feeding hyena.

The great hardwood forest shivers and moans around them, sharp cracks punctuate the fearful cries of the People as the weakest among the mightily oak trees succumbs to the violent quaking. To the tribe, it seems to go on forever and when it finally lets up, they behold a new sound, a deep throbbing rumble that doesn't go away. Seeping through this primal sound, Ur hears crying children and women beginning to drone in their incessant funeral wail, fear and confusion gaining momentum with each passing second.

His arms flailing wildly, leading a small group, Omon rushes forward along the stunned column towards Ur, exclaiming loudly that they should have stayed, that they had made the Great Spirit very angry by leaving. That Ur was wrong.

Rejecting this, Ur argues vehemently that the People must now hurry. To stay would mean surrendering their spirit. Omon will not see reason and turns his back on Ur to confront the frightened faces of the People. With a single blow from his club, Ur crushes his brother's skull, his body collapsing in a heap at the feet of his mate. She falls on the twitching carcass screaming her indignation, tears streaming down her face. Several of Omon's followers add their voices to hers, and the sounds coming from the rest of the tribe rises sharply. Many had liked Omon but the events of the day leave them confused and fearful.

It is at that precise moment that the ground beneath them once again heaves even more violently, pitching them to and fro with abandon. The sight and sounds of shattering trees and falling limbs gives the tribe the impression the entire world is disintegrating around them, coming apart at the seams. Even before the ground stops moving, Ur proclaims loudly that the Great Spirit is speaking to them, commanding them to flee. Why else would he force Ur to release Omon's spirit? Why else would he destroy their home? Ur pushes his tribesmen forward, away from the towering apparition rising ever higher above Spirit Mountain, leading his people away from the dying paradise. A few stay with the body of Omon, his woman, two young children, and an old hunter, never to be seen again.

Luckily, the pyroclastic flow is away from them, as is the high altitude prevailing winds. The People have no inkling of the devastation being wrought on the other side of the mountain as hundreds of square miles of dense hardwood forests are utterly destroyed. In one horrible instant, several neighboring tribes are wiped out in their entirety. Falling rocks and dense ash claim more lives.

Fighting back shear panic, Ur encourages the tribe to greater and greater speed. The smaller children are picked up and carried. Many of the elders can't keep up and are left behind. The Great Spirit defeats the sun spirit plunging the land into foreboding darkness. Just as foretold, burning rocks, some as big as a man's fist, begin to fall around them. Screams of the hurt and dying are barely heard above the steady rumble of the erupting volcano. The tribe is now running in blind panic through heavy twilight. Many fall and curl into the fetal position, whimpering pitifully while they wait to die. The People leave almost half their number behind on that fateful day, the weakest of mind and body, those least able to survive.

Long after the bombardment stops, the Great Spirit continues to shower them with a dusting of ash, not enough to kill but enough to elicit terror. It soon blankets the land and the People like a perverted snow storm and the late afternoon temperature dips below 40°F, sending a chill through the tribe. Those who have hoods pull them up to shelter their faces from the ash. They cast fearful glances back towards the almost invisible mountain. From dark depths, the Great Spirit glitters like hot coals and his voice is a distant thunderstorm that never stops.

Far into the night Ur leads his tribe away from the Great Spirit, able to see just well enough to avoid tress and bushes, always keeping the flickering red glow to his back. More than once he stops and waits for stragglers to catch up, groping through the darkness and the falling ash. Some simply disappear in the confusion. Once separated from the tribe, they have little chance of survival. Long after midnight he finds a dense blackberry thicket. Squirming under the ash heavy brambles, the tribe huddles together for a few hours of sleep.

Just before dawn the ground shakes violently once again, jerking everyone awake. Within minutes Ur has them on the move. Mid morning he comes upon a female weeping over the body of a child. She is covered with ash masking her features beyond all hope of recognition in the dim light. Yet her distress is clearly marked by the path of her tears, deep grooves in the crusted ash that streak her face in a single vertical line, one under each eye. Her hair is a solid mass plastered to her head. Almost in passing, Ur grabs the woman and pulls her roughly to her feet, telling her loudly that she must come or surrender her spirit. Without understanding his words, the women gives one final sorrowful glance to the mound of flesh that had been her son, slings a small leather pouch over her head, and falls in with the People. Her head bowed, she never looks back.

A few hours later the bone weary travelers ford a shallow ash-choked stream and start across a vast plain, each step taking them further away from the land of their birth. The men know of this great ocean of grass but no one has ever dared venture far out upon it, always keeping Spirit Mountain well in sight. Behind them, He can still be dimly seen through the light haze of falling ash, a dark entity with a flickering red heart, driving them out of their ancestral home.

The men form an envelope around the women and children protecting what remains of the tribe. The People, now numbering just over a hundred, make good time on the relatively flat prairie. The sky hangs heavy over them, keeping the sun spirit at bay as they trudge through the perpetual twilight.

That evening, nearing exhaustion, the People make camp at the edge of a broad shallow valley. Tired and hungry, they eat what they have and huddle around small fires for warmth and protection. Talk is muted. Even the sound of children is absent. The newcomer tries to lie down close to some of the other women but several of them hiss and strike out, driving her away. Ur motions for her to come to him. As she approaches he notices for the first time that something is different about her, the way she walks and her bearing. But he is exhausted. He pats the ground beside him and lays back, almost instantly falling asleep. She snuggles up against him sharing a pack for a pillow and stares out into the darkness, munching on a piece of dried meat and a few stale nuts retrieved from her pouch.

Hours later, on this, the blackest of all nights, a juvenile leopard, only recently cut loose by his mother, creeps towards the sleeping people. He has not eaten in many days but worse still, has not slept for even longer, devastating for an animal that typically sleeps twenty out of every twenty four hours. His species is small and he, not yet full grown, weighs less than two hundred pounds. Under normal circumstances he would never consider attacking the hominids. But today isn't normal.

The young cat can detect no movement around the flickering fires. Exhaustion, hunger and inexperience overcome his fear of these creatures and he senses that a swift snatch and run will net a sorely needed meal. Slowly he advances, his belly never rising more than an inch from the ground. Around him the ash has all but stopped falling and the only sound is the occasional rumble of thunder somewhere in the distance. Coiling his legs beneath him, his eyes grow large and remain steadfast on the small body of his target. With a final wiggle he pounces, sprinting across the last few yards in a rush of muscle and fang.

Instantly awake and without thinking, the young woman grabs Ur's spear and meets this specter of death just feet from his goal. Coming in from the side, she catches the lithe killing machine by surprise and jams the wooden shaft into his eye, instantly breaking his charge.

With pain shooting through him and his vision shattered, the leopard roars his frustration and anguish as he twists away from this unexpected adversary. A second later, the big cat is gone and the camp erupts in confusion and fear.

The mother of the child pulls the frightened boy to her breast and comforts him, rocking him gently in her arms, her eyes returning again and again to stare at the tall stranger with wonder. The woman stands, feet wide apart, defiantly facing Ur and the tribe. Slowly, calmly she hands him the spear, her mouth speaking unintelligible gibberish.

Some in the tribe want to drive the stranger out but Ur resists. Taking a flaming branch, he walks to where drops of blood lead into the darkness and the enormous paw prints scar the ground. The ash holds many in perfect suspension, letting him see the size of the beast that had stalked them. The woman's footprints are there as well and he quickly grasps the details of the attack. This woman has driven away a demon of the night. He brings her to his fire, ignoring the grumbling of the others. He returns the spear to the stranger before finding sleep once again.

By dawn the ash stops falling and a warm clean shower greets the People. As the rain washes away the grim from the newcomer, Ur is surprised to see how different she is, her fine hair is a soft brown instead of coarse black, and her skin is many shades paler than his. Around her neck hangs something shiny. She returns the curious stares of the People with a calm steady gaze, evidence of inner strength. He is astounded that she can not speak properly, her words utter nonsense! He has never met anyone who did not know the words of the People! But even so, he learns her name is Avalyn, a word that means spirit protector.

Slowly, hesitantly, the People resume their trek, only now the men's eyes scan the tall grasses around them, pausing to listen every few yards. Several of the more experienced hunters run ahead hoping to jump game before the noise of the tribe has time to spook it. Midmorning they down a small deer and a pig an hour later. After thanking them for surrendering their spirit, both are consumed raw by the tribe, their bones shattered to get at the fat rich marrow inside. It is mid afternoon before they see the face of the sun spirit. Many of the tracks the People have left in the thick wet ash will be frozen in time, baked by the sun into a hard stone-like mass, preserved for the ages.

After many days of travel the Great Spirit can still be seen behind them. Shifts in the upper atmospheric winds occasionally bring the tribe more ash but not nearly the quantities as before, just enough to drive them on. Avalyn begins to learn the words of the People and every evening Ur teaches her more. The other women are reluctant to accept her and the men see only another female, even though she carries a spear and hunts. Ur takes her on the fifth night. She shows him pleasures he didn't know existed.

From the beginning, the women distrust Avalyn. They are unaccustomed to a female doing the work of a man. The first to offer friendship is the mother of the boy that had been the leopard's target. Avalyn begins to help her in her traditional duties of tending fire and cooking, the preparation of hides and clothing making. Even as Avalyn learns the ways of the People, she teaches the women of things she was taught as a child. From her foraging trips she brings back a verity of herbs and spices to the surprise and delight of everyone. Her use of bone needles and simple patterns rapidly change the way clothing is made. This involvement does not go unnoticed. As time passes, the activities around the evening campfires become more efficient, easing the burden on the women of the tribe. Avalyn becomes one with them.

Even so, as days become weeks some of the People begin to talk of turning back, returning to familiar forests and lands. One night Ur has a dream, a vision in which he leads his tribe to a place of abundant food and safety, a place where the Great Spirit smiles on the People. The next morning Ur tells his fellow tribesmen of his vision. By force of will born of deep belief, he convinces them that the Great Spirit has spoken to him, promising them paradise at the end of their journey. He ruthlessly drives the tribe onward across the seemingly endless plain, convinced of his own vision, confident in his conviction that the Great Spirit has something more in store for his People than death.

One evening while watching Ur carefully put a new edge on a hand ax, Avalyn asks to see his flakes, the chips and fragments of any useful size that he generates every time he works a stone ax or scraper. The tribe knows of only three places where tool stone exists, all of them at the base of the volcano they had just fled. The obsidian the tribesmen now possess has become precious beyond belief.

Puzzled, Ur unfolds the leather and lets her look. Leaning over the treasure, Avalyn quickly sorts through the fragments, moving them around until she finds one to her liking. Holding it up, she asks Ur if she can work it.

Ur looks at the flake and back at this strange woman. Smaller than his palm and rather thin, it was marginally big enough for him to have kept. Too small to make a hand ax, it would serve as a fragile scraper at best. Yet, he is glad he has it. He refuses.

But Avalyn is persistent and with reluctance he finally gives in. Sitting cross-legged by the fire, she produces a small antler tool from her pouch, well worn at both ends. Smiling at Ur, she cradles the small chip in a piece of leather and begins to work it. Applying pressure skillfully, chips smaller than a fingernail soon litter the ground around her. Other men come to Ur's fire to watch Avalyn. They have never seen a women work stone and it fills them with wonder.

Nearly symmetrical, the finished object has a blunt tang at one end, coming to a point at the other and bifacially sharp along both edges. The men pass it around looking at the strange miniature. Barely the length of his thumb, Ur asks her of what use is so small a blade?

In answer Avalyn does a very strange thing. She cuts a long thin slice from the leather in her lap and pops it in her mouth, chewing vigorously. When Ur and the rest of the gathering grunt in amazement she laughs and fetches his spear. The tip, sharpened by fire hardening and scrapping it to a point, had been damaged that very morning. The fragile hardwood had split and would require shortening by almost a hand.

Deftly Avalyn carves away at the damage, chewing the leather strip in her mouth as she cuts a V shaped hollow in the wooden shaft using Ur's hand axe. She takes the stone point from Ur and does a trial fit. Not satisfied, she carves some more until the point fits snugly within the notch. Taking the hide from her mouth, she wraps the wet leather tightly around the base of the tip where it fits into the notch, expertly pulling it taunt before tying it off. Holding it over the fire well away from the flame, she roasts her creation, drying the leather and making it shrink and tighten right before their eyes. With one final test wiggle of the installed point, she declares it complete, handing the modified spear back to Ur.

He instantly recognizes its advantages. In complete amazement he presses Avalyn for an explanation. All she will say is that she was taught how to do this by a great hunter.

Over the next few days Avalyn demonstrates how to make spear points and fasten them securely. She also introduces new ways to work stone, what would come to be known as the Levallois technique of shaping a point before shearing it from the core. Avalyn gives the gift of knowledge. She is no longer just another female in the minds of the men. The People look upon her with new eyes.

To mark the passage of days, Ur ties a knot into a thin strip of hide each morning. On the sixth day, when the number of knots matches the number of fingers on his hand, he loosens them all, ready to begin the process anew after a day of rest.

The tribe continues north over the great savanna, the pace slow, the daily routine comfortable. Armed with stone tipped spears, bands of hunters regularly roam far from the main column bringing back meat and hides to the evening campsites. Every night after the meal the People would gather to listen to the ancient stories. Occasionally, Avalyn would speak of where she came. Over time, her stories seep into the tribe's mythology; new words, new ideas, and new knowledge add spice to the mundane even when they are hard to believe.

Weeks turn into months and still they trek onward. The People grow tired of the constant travel and some begin to talk again of turning back. But Ur will hear none of it. Over the last few days Avalyn has pointed out the increased number of birds in the skies overhead and in the number of predators at night. She thinks the Great Spirit is telling them they are nearing their goal.

That evening a lion snatches a boy child that strayed too far from the fires. The wailing of his mother keeps everyone awake far into the night until finally Ur comes to her and strokes her head, telling her that the death of her firstborn had been for the good of the People, that the Great Spirit had need and had taken the boy to be with Him but that He would give something in return. The woman takes little comfort in his words.

The next morning Ur breaks with routine and doesn't let the tribe relax even though it is the sixth day, insisting they forgo rest and push onward.

That afternoon, with the sun hanging low in the western sky, the tribe comes to the edge of a great valley. At its bottom flows a river the likes of which they have never seen. Like a mighty serpent, it undulates back and forth across a broad fertile flood plain. In the distance, great herds of beasts are scattered amongst the trees and across the grass covered meadows. Birds screech at them and insects buzz about their ears. Ur's nostrils flare with the fragrant aroma of lilacs and cherry blossoms. Around him the tribe marvels at the beauty of their new home.

Ur comes to the woman who had lost her son the night before and spreads his arms wide indicating the rich valley that lay before them. In a voice that all can hear, he reminds her that the death of her boy was not in vain and prays loudly to the Great Spirit, beseeching Him to be kind to her young son, thanking Him for the generous gift of paradise. He promises that the story of the exodus and of the boys sacrifice will be told and retold until the end of time. Ur is hailed as a great prophet, one who speaks with the spirits.

Jubilant in their good fortune, laughter fills the camp of the People as they dance and cavort about blazing bonfires. Spits of freshly killed meat hang low over the hot coals of the cooking pits and wet hides are rolled in tight bundles and piled close by to dry. Gourds of sweet spring water and ripe fruit spice the evening meal and not even the roar of hungry lions pacing just outside the fire line, can keep the celebration in check. Seldom has the tribe partaken in such a feast. The People rejoice in the land given to them by the Great Spirit.

Content in his accomplishment, Ur sits on his leather blanket padded by the rich green grass of the meadow, well within the radiance of the fire, eating and watching the merriment with Avalyn at his side, her pregnancy not yet showing.

****

Downwind, three hundred yards away on the crest of a low hill, hidden amongst the trees and tall grass, three figures watch and listen. A gentle breeze carries the odor of cooking meat, inciting anger within the largest and oldest of the group. He growls and slams his hunting club down on the grassy loam, swearing to the spirits of his ancestors that this sacrilege will not go unpunished. His companions bare their teeth and vigorously bob their heads in agreement. They are much younger and have not yet fought in tribal war, but they have heard the stories a hundred times. Both are anxious to prove themselves to the Gods, to have tales told of their deeds.

Motioning with his spear, the old warrior leads the trio away from the camp of the invaders, down into the fertile valley that had been his species home for the last eleven thousand years. It wouldn't be the first time he has defended the sacred hunting grounds and it wouldn't be the last.

"It is always better to have no ideas than false ones; to believe nothing, than to believe what is wrong."
Thomas Jefferson (1757-1820)

Exodus

The intersection is an island of light in a sea of blackness. It had rained hard only minutes before and is still sprinkling making the worn blacktop shine under passing headlights. This time of night the buildings along the roadway are in darkness and even the streetlights away from the intersection are off, mandated by the government to save energy.

The semi is full of lettuce, radishes, and onions on their way to market. During the summer months the deliveries are made at night trying to minimize heat damage. The driver has traveled this route many times and doesn't think twice about barreling through the green light at full speed.

Weighing over thirty times as much, the impact has little effect on the truck or its trailer, they keep going straight never in danger of jackknifing. But it sends the little white sedan spinning wildly across the intersection to wrap itself around a metal pole. The truck driver brings his big rig to a stop and jumps out, sprinting back to the car.

As he runs towards it, the smashed car bursts into flames. Within seconds it is completely engulfed. No one could survive the inferno. He throws his hands up protecting his face from its intensity and retreats.

"Oh dear God!" the man wails, pacing back and forth, tears streaming down his cheeks eerily reflecting the roaring flames.

"You can't help them now," an old woman says from behind him. "All we can do is pray that God has mercy upon their souls."

"Them? How many are in there?" the driver asks tearfully.

"I saw two," she replies, "but there could be more."

"Oh dear God!" the man repeats moaning.

"Mommy? Are they in heaven now?" the little girl is only five or six and should have been in bed.

"Yes Sarah, they're the lucky ones because God decided he wanted them. There's no pain or hunger or anything bad in heaven and the streets are paved with gold. Praise Jesus!" the young mother says to her child.

"I've called the police. They should be here any minute," another man says. He stopped his car when he saw the collision occur ahead of him. "I was following her and she had a green light," he says looking accusingly at the truck driver.

"What? I had the green light, I'm sure of it," the driver responds through his tears, fear and doubt creeping into his mind.

A police car with lights flashing pulls up and blocks traffic. The officer gets out still talking on his secure network portal and walks over to the gathering.

"I had the green light!" the driver blurts out.

One of the men in the crowd shakes his head. The policeman glances at him and back to the driver, "Is that your truck?" he asks.

"Yes but I had the green light!" the driver says through his tears. Within the flames he glimpses the remains of a person sitting in the driver's seat and begins to openly weep.

"Take it easy. Come over here and have a seat." He takes the truck drivers arm and guides him to his cruiser, opening the rear door for the shaken man. "Now... tell me what happened."

More patrol cars pull up and cordon off the intersection. A fire truck carefully maneuvers between them leaving room for the ambulance that's on its way. It will be many hours before this choreography of death finishes, its players well practiced in the art of picking up the pieces.

****

"...unto you my brothers and sisters! Turn and read with me at First Corinthians 11:14.... *Doth not even nature itself teach you, that if a man have long hair, it is a shame unto Him?* Can it be any plainer than that?! God doesn't want men to have long hair! It shames Him! Pray with me and support my bill with your votes and we will right this ungodliness!"

Feeling as if he had just drifted off, the sudden explosion of light and sound from the flat screen hanging on the wall jerks Lazarus awake. He had tossed and turned the night before, too excited to fall asleep, passing the time listening to Joseph argue with his wife in the apartment next door. But he eventually drifted off, and the alarm comes too soon.

It's a crisp autumn morning and the desert chill nips at his cheeks and nose, invading his small apartment through the only window. It is cracked with a triangular piece missing, duct tape and cardboard the only thing holding it together and the weather out. He retreats under the blanket, pulling it over his head.

Angry thumping on the wall precedes Joe's voice, "We're trin' to sleep over here!"

Lazarus groans and slides an arm from the warmth just far enough to grab the remote off the floor next to the bed, pushing the volume down. Movement catches his eye. Several roaches scurry across the kitchen counter away from the light. More disappear under the refrigerator.

He pulls his arm back beneath the covers, a shield of sorts against the bright and cheery colors emanating from the rather large flat screen. Having a vid this size is one of the perks of working for the government. His alarm is tuned into *Good Morning Lord!* which usually isn't so political this early on a work day.

As one of the leading fundamentalists within the Reformation Party, Ohio Senator Elijah Hanley is a vocal advocate for a more literal interpretation of the Bible. This morning he has managed to get time on the most watched early show in all the Federation. Just what Lazarus needs his last morning on Earth, a good shot of hardcore Christianity.

With that thought, Lazarus throws back the blanket and swings his feet out of the narrow bed. Sitting there in his boxers, he looks around. He will not miss this dreary one room apartment.

Ancient cabinets support a chipped and stained countertop. He can't even guess what its original color was. A relatively new coffee maker sits upon it and a faded mirror is fastened to the wall behind the sink in lieu of a window. None of the upper cabinets has a door, his few plates, mugs, and glasses in plain sight on the dusty shelves. The apartment's small refrigerator never worked and the stove has only one element that still gets hot enough to use for making tea. Lazarus has never even turned on the oven, not wanting to cook for himself, finding it cheaper to eat at the company cafeteria most of the time.

Beside the narrow bed is a battered dresser with three of its four drawers still functional. A lamp minus its shade sits on top amidst the stains and scratches. An overstuffed chair is next to the window, the fabric of both armrests worn through exposing dirty cotton stuffing. At some point in its history, its footrest moved in and out by pulling a lever. Now it's locked halfway, permanently invading the room and forcing Lazarus to move around it or bang his shin. In the corner behind the chair is a pile of unwashed clothing. Beside the chair is a small wooden table that started out as patio furniture many years before. Shelves made of cinder blocks and unfinished boards are stacked against the wall underneath the flat screen, sparsely filled with pictures, books and other things. Above the shelves in the wall next to the vid, someone had neatly carved *Made in China*. The words catch the flickering light from the screen, attracting his eyes like flies to a rotting apple.

Behind the kitchen is the bath, its door gone when Lazarus moved in and he never bothered to requisition another. He wouldn't have gotten one without expending more effort than it was worth.

He strips off his boxers and sits on the throne, its bowl stained a dark brown, the wooden seat cracked and worn. That either was once white is beyond imagination. How many butts have sat here? The apartment complex is at least fifty years old and it isn't hard for Lazarus to believe this is original equipment. He has grown accustomed to the sound of trickling water the toilet constantly makes. The fact that it works at all is a tribute to paper clips and human ingenuity.

Lazarus leans forward resting his elbows on his knees and watches the vid through the permanently open doorway.

Senator Hanley is a pudgy old man, mostly bald with a ring of white hair around three sides of his head just above his ears and an immaculately trimmed beard. He is never seen in public without a white shirt, a thin black tie, and a long black overcoat that extends to his ankles. The Senator always chuckles good-naturedly when a reporter calls him Modern Moses, but he never corrects them. Lazarus thinks he looks more like a black-clad Santa with his rosy cheeks and belly laugh. But it isn't joy the Senator wants to bring to the children of the world.

"I tell you my brothers and sisters, the increase in violence in our cities, the crop failures all across the Midwest, the hurricanes pounding our shores, are all signs of His displeasure! We are falling away from God and must find our way back before it's too late!" The Senator waves his index finger under the nose of the camera, punctuating and personalizing each declaration.

Lazarus picks up the roll of toilet paper from the floor next to him and starts to count out a strip of six squares. Shaking his head, he pulls two or three times what he normally uses and folds it neatly into thirds, wipes and flushes, glancing at the swirling mass making sure it went down and not out onto the floor. He pauses, listening for the inevitable hydraulic thump in the lines as the waste disappears and the bowl starts to refill.

Squealing loudly with each twist, he gingerly cranks open the leaky shower faucet. Stained with decades of hard water and suffering from a steady drip, every morning he fears it will break. Repair would take weeks if not longer.

But he manages one last time and waits with his hand under the flow until the frigid stream begins to grow warm. Four apartments share the water heater with his the only single occupancy, another privilege of working where he does. But since he's up early this morning, several hours before any of the others should be awakening, he sets the temperature high.

Ignoring the smell, he climbs into the shower pulling the curtain shut, letting the steaming hot water cut him adrift from the rest of the world if only for the moment. Going against government mandates, Lazarus stands under it much longer than usual, enjoying every drop and wasting the desert's most precious resource. There will be a fine added to his monthly utility bill for the extravagance and he couldn't care less. With reluctance he turns it off.

The bathroom sink has long since fallen into disrepair. Throwing the towel over his shoulder, he walks out of the bath and goes the few steps to the kitchen sink. The stained metal has seen better days. Only the cold water tap works and it's slow to drain. Years of hard water and corrosion have left the sink battered and bruised.

Squinting into the faded mirror, he smears a bit of bar soap on his hands and lathers his cheeks and chin. The single blade disposable razor is a few weeks old and he must push hard, making his skin tingle at the edge of pain. Accustomed to its smell, he splashes cold water on his face and looks at his reflection in the mirror.

At just under six feet, Lazarus isn't what anyone would describe as athletically gifted. And to make matters worse, he has spent most of his adult life sitting in a comfortable office chair manipulating a touch panel or immersed in Virtual Reality, first as a programmer and later as an analyst. Over the years, he tried to keep in shape the old fashioned way, going to a gym twice a week, sweating it off like his father and grandfathers before him. It was just dumb luck that he has never had a major illness or been injured enough to need a doctor. As a child he had developed a distrust of the medical profession from a mother who didn't even like taking aspirin for a headache, preferring instead to use the healing power of prayer. As a result, at age thirty-five Lazarus sports an excess of body fat in comparison to the average citizen. Not grossly overweight but enough to make him suck in his belly and tell himself to throw in a few extra workouts, which he occasionally managed to do, usually right after a particularly gluttonous weekend.

After graduating near the top of his class at Devine Institute of Technology, he received a lot of attention from several top software firms. Yet he selected the Department of Homeland Security in spite of the poor pay and long hours. His father had been a field officer for DHS. He kissed his family goodbye one morning and never came home. Lazarus, who adored his father, was only ten at the time, the oldest of three rowdy boys and a little girl in diapers. Over the next several days he was told many times that his father was a true hero, someone noble who had sacrificed his life in defense of God and country. As a child, his father became larger than life, representing all that was good and just in the world. As the boy grew into a man, it coalesced into a hard inner core that made it very difficult for him to accept compromise, where mediocrity by intent was a sin.

But his father is only part of the reason he chose DHS. As a young idealist, he convinced himself the best way to protect freedom was to be one of those who decide when to abuse it. However, as he learned the job he found he liked the power it gave him. His friends and neighbors treated him with respect and looked up to him. When they came to him with problems, Lazarus always did his best to help, accepting money and favors in return. Lazarus never considered anything he did to be criminal in any way. It's simply how his world worked.

Eleven years after becoming a widow his mother remarried. At the time his youngest brother was still in high school and Lazarus in the middle of his college education. A few months after that, his new stepfather moved his mother and brother to Portland chasing a job. The three of them live there still. Lazarus tries to make a point of talking with his mother at least once a month just to keep in touch but the interval has grown considerable in the last few years and he can't remember the last time he spoke with Elijah, his youngest brother. They haven't been close since Elijah returned from juvenile reeducation.

The reservations for the Athens vacation had been made almost two years before and paid for under an installment plan. The travel agency had taken care of everything including getting the appropriate travel permits, greasing the palms of the right officials just another part of the overall expenditure. Rachel and Courtney were supposed to share the adventure. But that had ended twenty-two months before on a dark and wet Scottsdale intersection, a single lapse of judgment snuffing out their lives in an instant. Their deaths became just another data point used in the battle to outlaw manual driving.

Sometimes late at night Lazarus dreams he's with his wife and daughter. Upon awakening, still under the influence of the dream, he's gripped by the overpowering realization they didn't really die, that it's all been some kind of horrible mistake. After all, he had just been with them, Rachel laughing while she brushes Courtney's long blond hair or the two of them baking cookies or playing word games. Sometimes the dream contains only Courtney, he teaching her how to ride a bike or put a jigsaw puzzle together. Plainly, there's something inside Lazarus that wants to believe in life after death. And it's these times when it's not the least bit interested that there's not a single iota of real evidence for it. He knows his standing within the community would be in grave danger if his failure to believe in the afterlife became generally known. Lack of faith is something he learned to hide from everyone at an early age. Only Rachel had known his true beliefs and even then it was whispered softly in the dead of night with few words, never in public.

A few months after the accident, Lazarus considered canceling the flight to Greece, and went as far as to broach the subject with a representative from the agency. He was politely informed that his travel arrangements were nonrefundable. It was all in the contract he and Rachel had signed.

Just as well. The truth is, planning this trip was the last big thing that he and Rachel had done together and he simply couldn't bring himself to cancel it. Now that the time is at hand he feels that somehow, this is how it was meant to be. He doesn't care that it doesn't make sense. He just knows it feels right.

Pouring a bit of bottled water into a cup, he swishes his toothbrush around before brushing his teeth. It's been months since he last had toothpaste. It's simply too expensive. He would rather put his money into toilet paper or save it for his trip.

He has planned for weeks what to take with him and packed and repacked it many times. In his bag are his Bible and a well worn copy of Robert Heinlein's *Time Enough for Love*, the only thing he has that belonged to his father. The hundred and twenty year old novel is on several government watch lists but hasn't quite made it onto the illegal category yet. The Commission on Morality hasn't completely dealt with out-of-print fiction, books not readily available to the general public, but it's only a matter of time.

Besides a simple hygiene kit, he takes a minimum amount of clothing preferring to buy new as needed instead of lugging old ones around. Tucked into Heinlein's novel are several photos and a packet of aging longhand letters, fading ink on brittle paper. The only other items are a brand new Achilles Sports baseball cap and an old style headset, the same as thousands of others currently popular with the younger crowd in and around Athens.

Pulling on fresh boxers and jeans, he throws his bed sheets together in a semblance of order and sits upon it with his back against the wall, pulling his feet off the cold floor. He picks up the remote and turns up the sound. Senator Hanley has been replaced by a different speaker.

This man has on a buttoned down dark blue business suit at least two sizes too big and an orange tie bright enough to make Lazarus' eyes water. A small mouth and receding chin hide behind a large beak-like nose that dominates his narrow face, a thin dark mustache almost invisible under it. His eyes dart about restlessly under greasy black hair, never looking at the camera for long. His shrill voice grates on Lazarus's nerves. "The government of the North American Federation doesn't need to be so intimately involved with the length of hair of its citizens!" he hisses, "For too long have we stood by and watched our freedoms slip away, one little bit after another until they are practically gone! We don't need to be told how long our hair should be! Some things are better left up to individuals..."

He watches in fascination as the mediator of the debate interrupts the smarmy little man, the lack of respect obvious. "Thank you, Senator Hanley and Professor Gladstone, for taking your valuable time this morning to join us in the No Spin Zone, the only place you get all the facts and nothing but the facts, so help me God… I invite all of you watching to do your patriotic duty and cast your vote now. This is, as always, an unofficial poll, but rest assured, Washington is listening!"

Lazarus laughs again, only now it's a mirthless sound, devoid of any joy. It's tempting to blow off voting this morning but old habit wins out. Besides, it wouldn't do to change even the smallest thing. You never know what will tip them off.

He uses the remote to quickly cast a vote. As soon as his selection is received, the totals appear on his screen as a simple bar graph. Lazarus ignores them and keys in his personal account information. Moving quickly through the menus, he sets up a scheduled action for next week, signing over his two year old Honda to his sister's old man.

With a kid and an underachieving husband, she's in dire need of a car, so he gives his, an act that would certainly rouse suspicion if DHS learns of it too soon. His other maneuvers have been more subtle, leaving his telescope at his brothers, a box filled with family mementoes at his sister's, books and electronics scattered among his few friends and coworkers. Everything else he simply leaves behind. His apartment, the Christian News Network, and vid clubs will all grind to a halt when the money stops coming in.

Logging off his personal account, he signals for a cab. He recalls the last time he saw Mary and her family. She had made him his favorite meal three nights before, a pasta recipe heavy with faux cheese and tomato sauce, his last good meal.

Lazarus hadn't confided to anyone of his intentions, not his brother, not his sister, not his friends, no one. The less they know the more likely the authorities will leave them alone. He feels momentary panic at the thought of putting them in danger not of their own making, knowing what can happen if the wrong people get it in their heads to dispense justice. But he has no choice, there is no other way. He must leave.

****

It is a well worn fact that knowledge is power. But to exercise power, one must be able to leverage knowledge. In ancient times generals stood on opposing hilltops directing their legions by messengers, flags, or other crude signals. In the modern era they use Virtual Reality and the World Wide Web, the electronic battlefield where a war of words rages 24/7, where the casualties are not only measured in lives but in the destruction of truth, the rewriting of history. Just as with any human invention, the net can be used just as effectively for the advancement of evil as for good. As a tool, it is undoubtedly the greatest communicator ever devised by mankind, unsurpassed in its ability to spread knowledge, both true and false. Every nation of the world contributes to the network. The nodes of the web that lie within the European Union, Australia, and the Collation of African People are largely unencumbered by local laws, but within the Federation, China, Islamic Brotherhood and across most of Southeast Asia, the network is state owned and strictly controlled.

Lazarus was drawn to the web at a young age and even now when pressured to pick his specialty, will claim an expertise in programming search engines. Pressed for more he will expound upon the need for network security and his experience in data acquisition, stopping short of admitting he sometimes operates outside of Federation law. In other words, he began his career with Homeland Security as a government hacker, a common soldier in the never ending battle where the smallest bit of information gleaned from an enemy's website the only precursor to a bombing or kidnapping, both home and abroad.

As his expertise grew, so too did his reputation as a stickler for detail. It is on his interpretations of seemingly random bits of data, that actions have been taken where men died. He knows this and accepts the responsibility, not hiding behind the fact that he simply passed the information up the chain of command and was not an active participant in a decision that ended someone's life.

But that is only part of the story. Over the years Lazarus worked himself up the ladder of success within Homeland Security taking advantage of every course and training camp available to him. Among them was a heavy dose of psychology which he applied to interrogating suspects. He became known for his ability to elicit information using drugs instead of torture. Now, after many years of constant effort, he ranks among the best interrogators in DHS.

All in all, Lazarus has made himself into a top echelon operative within the Department of Homeland Security. But that achievement also made him ineligible for field duty. The Director has forbidden any of his Senior Analysts from participating in the apprehension of suspects or wasting their time on stakeouts. He prefers they do the job they are best suited for, getting the information out of the most hardcore terrorist or cracking a tough firewall, things Lazarus has proven to be very good at.

Following the untimely death of his wife and daughter, Lazarus threw himself into his work. It was one of his internet data mining algorithms that had first began to compile the disturbing facts surrounding the Brotherhood's activities over the last three months. An email slip, a loose comment during a low-encrypted internet transmission, money moving in and out of the world's financial institutions, and many others, coalesced into a mosaic of information that painted an ominous picture of something big building up.

One of Lazarus's responsibilities was coordinating the electronic tracking of radical elements within the Brotherhood. Three weeks ago all hell brook loose. Not only did bank traffic spike erratically, but known players started dropping off the map at an alarming rate. In the past, an increase like this always preceded a major event. But neither Lazarus nor any of his colleagues had ever seen this level of activity before, and assuming they had identified only a small portion of the actual totals, the shear volume makes any final prediction extremely ominous. The team's official guess is that as many as a hundred thousand men could be involved, a number based not in fact but in speculation. Lazarus personally thinks it is a low estimate, that the total number of men suddenly not where they were the day before may approach a quarter million. After all, in a religious empire of over two billion citizens, the Brotherhood claims their Army is a billion strong. In reality, the Muslim Empire can field perhaps two million trained soldiers and another five million irregulars.

It doesn't surprise Lazarus when the warnings are not well received. Once informed that the NAF was probably not the target, any motivation to act, and therefore risk, evaporated like the morning dew after an Arizona sunrise. After all, their prime concern is the safety of NAF citizens (their own skins), not risking the wrath of the Brotherhood for the godless Lunarians (somebody else's skin).

The one thing generally agreed upon by Lazarus and his fellow Senior Analysts is whatever is happening is proceeding at breakneck speed. The whole tenor of the information coming out of the Brotherhood has changed radically over the past three months and none of them likes the sound of it.

****

Arizona in late October is beautiful. The sun is well over the horizon but the chill is still in the air when Lazarus emerges from his apartment. Outside his door is a small sandy courtyard surrounded by three story buildings filled with apartments just like his. Tumble weeds grow along the walls adding a splash of green to an otherwise drab scene. The building directly across from his has three broken windows, two of them repaired with cardboard and tape. The third gaps open. At one end of the courtyard a potbellied barbeque is bolted to a pipe buried in concrete. He doesn't recall ever seeing anyone use it. The sidewalk is shattered with whole sections missing, more of a path beaten into the sand than a true walkway. He takes care not to trip as he walks to the parking lot.

The waiting cab is white with a crude sketch of Calvary hill on its door, the words Christian Cab Company below. Lazarus hears the back door unlock as he reaches for the handle and climbs into the cab.

"Where to?" the cabbie asks over his shoulder.

"Gateway Airport, Global Airlines."

"No bags?"

"Just my carryon," Lazarus replies settling back in the worn bench seat. The cab is neat and clean but at least ten years old, a lifetime for a vehicle in its occupation.

As the cab pulls out of the lot, Lazarus looks east towards the Superstition Mountains. The sky above them is packed with towering dark clouds back lit by the risen sun while directly overhead the sky is blindingly blue, typical of the intense localized storms that sweep across the Sonoran desert in the fall.

"Shouldn't be much traffic this early in the morning..." The cabbie says and proceeds to tell him all about rush hour and the horror he endures every day. Lazarus lets him speak, staring out the window without hearing a word.

They quickly navigate out of the neighborhood and onto a six lane surface street. This is an older section of the city, many of the buildings need paint and the roadway is rough, full of potholes. Watching the shabby shops and fading strip malls go by, Lazarus feels a knot form in the pit of his stomach wondering if this is his last ride though his city. He takes a deep breath and rallies his resolve, his hand unconsciously rubbing the bristles of his crew cut. He knows this is his only choice. His only regret is that Rachel is not with him. Yet, in a way she is. He closes his eyes and can almost feel her beside him offering silent encouragement. His heart aches that she isn't there. But even as her memory fills him with sadness, his destination instills a sense of adventure like he has never known before. This is how the Pilgrims must have felt when they boarded leaky wooden ships and set sail across the Atlantic, or settlers when they packed everything they owned into Conestoga wagons and headed west.

"Friday and Saturday is the best, taking home all those drunks whose cars won't start..."

The cab enters the onramp and accelerates towards Interstate 10, the whine of the electric motor rises in pitch as it comes up to speed. They are almost alone on the wide ribbon of concrete. Maintenance crews, working on widening it even more, have the inner lanes segregated using concrete barriers. Trucks and a few other vehicles share the freeway in near perfect silence.

"You couldn't pay me to trade my cab in on a new model..."

Now the scenery goes by quickly, giving Lazarus just fleeting glimpses of the passing structures and signage along the industrial corridor between Phoenix and Tucson to the southeast. Lazarus runs his hand over the top of his head willing his body to relax, the short bristles of his crew cut rubbing like a stiff wire brush against his palm. His worried frown has become an almost permanent feature over the last several months, something he vows to work on every time he notices.

"Kids nowadays show no respect..."

It's only a short trip to the airport from his apartment but the cabbie makes it seem much further. Located at the intersection of Interstate 8 and 10, Gateway International Airport is the Southwest's regional hub and services over a hundred million citizens yearly. Half hypnotized by the city flashing by and with thoughts of Rachel and his little princess, Courtney, filling his head, Lazarus doesn't notice when the cab cuts back across the lanes of traffic and climbs the airport's entrance overpass. He suddenly finds himself swinging in a great arc above I-10's sixteen lanes of traffic. Below him, the freeway is a ribbon of concrete threading through an endless city as far as he can see. He has a momentary pang hearing his daughter ask sweetly, *Daddy, are we up*, a game they played while her young mind sought to relate action with words.

"...Where you headed?"

Descending from the heights of the overpass, the cab eases into the sparse traffic funneling in from the south and west. The first checkpoint comes and goes unobtrusively as the cab passes through a short tunnel where MRI scanners hammer into every nook and cranny looking for anything out of the ordinary, comparing the results to the millions of previous scans collected from this public facility. His identity is secured from the chip in his hand and checked against the Federation Criminal Database. Finding nothing of import, the cab is allowed to proceed.

"Never been outside Arizona myself..."

As the vehicle passes through the open spaces surrounding Gateway's main terminal, Lazarus can see the arriving planes hanging in the crisp morning sky like toys. The road cuts directly across all three east-west runways, tunneling below them all. To his left, a huge Airbus Maximus lumbers through the sky in what appears to be slow motion, touching down just as his cab dips into the well lighted passage below the runway. By the time the cab emerges from the other side, the giant plane is gone. The road curves away from the tunnel in a steep bank. To his front is the bone-white bulk of the terminal and the silhouettes of planes clustered around the outlying gates.

"Damn politicians talkin 'bout putting in a second airport..."

The pride of Arizona, the terminal's main construction is an enormous building that fills the horizon as the cab approaches. Its roof reminds Lazarus of a giant circus tent that drapes and swoops over huge metal support columns hundreds of feet tall. It covers a square mile of real estate and is made from manufactured spider silk, the strongest fabric ever devised.

"Too much vote'n if you ask me..."

Traffic has increased the closer they get to the airport and is at its peak as they enter the shade of this great canopy. The main artery, nine lanes wide, drops incoming travelers along a concrete and glass canyon that runs straight through the heart of the airport for over two miles. The outside lanes on both sides are reserved for stopping and unloading passengers, the inner lanes for through traffic with the fastest at the very center. The cab darts across traffic and takes the place of another even as it vacates its spot at the curb. It comes to rest a short distance from Global Airlines main entrance.

Lazarus swings the door open.

Twisting to look over the front seat at Lazarus, "Total come too ninety-six thirty-five. Don't worry about payin', it's already been deducted from yur account," the cabbie says.

Lazarus hands the man a ten and two fives, "God be with you."

The man beams, "Thanks! God bless you Sir and a pleasant journey!" He's used to fares not answering questions but getting a tip is special.

Clutching his small bag containing everything he values materially in the world, Lazarus steps out and looks around, half expecting to be confronted by airport security. A steady succession of vehicles squeezes into curbside openings as quickly as they become available. As one pulls out a new one takes its place in a tightly choreographed dance of disembarkation. Further down busses disgorge their riders. Even with the heavy traffic, the passenger drop-off area seems tiny in the vastness under the canopy.

Lazarus moves through the crowd towards the main information screen and stops in front of it, quickly scanning the display until he finds Global Airlines Flight 119. It's on time in Gate 4B. So far, so good.

Turning quickly, Lazarus almost collides with an old man and his wife. They had stopped behind him to read the screen. They are wearing typical Federation attire, the man a twenty year old black suit, white shirt and tie. His wife is in a plain brown dress that covers her from chin to ankles and a matching scarf.

"Forgive me. I need to look where I'm going," Lazarus says to the man.

Very few of those around them even notice the exchange. Most prefer to keep to themselves, their eyes never wondering far from what's right in front of them, wishing nothing more than to remain an indiscriminant particle amidst the homogeneity of humanity. Bright clothing is almost completely absent and the women all wear scarves covering their heads.

Putting his arm around his wife, the old man responds, "No harm done. God be with you, brother." The woman gives Lazarus a shy smile, the wrinkles at the corner of her eyes deepening into canyons. But he can't miss the twinkle that still burns within the expressive blue orbs. She must have been a beauty when young.

Lazarus hesitates and returns the smile. Looking at the man he says, "And with you, brother," he replies respectfully, moving around the couple and heading for the security screening area. Now isn't the time to attract unwanted attention.

Fashioned to look like dark sunglasses, Federation security personnel in cobalt blue uniforms are the only people within sight wearing VR devices. Decades earlier, during the Great Revival in '62, pious politicians enacted laws under the Freedom of Information Act forbidding all unauthorized access to the World Wide Web and gave themselves control of the manufacture, distribution and usage of the devices that provided it. It became a felony to possess an unlicensed web portal and every good American knows that breaking the law is a sin. As a consequence, the travelers sharing the terminal with him this morning are bare faced and introverted, avoiding even looking at each other let alone the armed men strolling among them, weapons slung across their backs and strapped around their waist.

Well inside, he approaches the backend of the lines feeding into the airport security scanners. He picks the shortest one and takes his place, shuffling forward. Like his fellow citizens, Lazarus avoids eye contact with the nearby guards and is glad to see the line moving so quickly. He cut the time tight on purpose but that's not what makes him run his hand over his head, time after time. He isn't exactly afraid of flying. Flying just makes him jumpy, that's all. Rubbing his crew cut charges his courage like a capacitor sucking up voltage, a habit he picked up years earlier. Most times he doesn't even know he's doing it.

The security scanners are in thirty foot tunnels that each passenger must navigate to go deeper into the airport. Upon entering, the tiny biotronic chip embedded in his left hand is queried. It promptly provides Lazarus's personal information which is fed into the security database, the FCD, where his prerecorded and approved flight plans are accessed and verified as a match with his current activity. Meanwhile, powerful olfactory sensors identify and categorize substances on him and his clothes down to parts per million, and a bank of MRI scanners sweeps over him many times looking for anything unusual inside his body or belongings. Finding nothing out of the ordinary, authorization is maintained for his entrance into the airport terminal. The entire security process is complete by the halfway point in the tunnel. If authorization had been lifted, such as would happen if the Director had caught on to his plan, large steel doors at each end of the tunnel would close only to be opened by armed police.

Lazarus doesn't hurry. It is heavily instilled in the populace to move slow but steady through the security tunnel. Between commercials and the infomercials embedded within vids, Federation citizens have seen it done properly hundreds of times and practically everyone gets it right the very first try. For those who stop or worse, go too fast, there is airport security, those minimum wage bastions of society, waiting in the wings to flag them out of line and route them to a holding area where it will be instilled upon the unlucky traveler the importance of maintaining proper procedures.

The sides of the tunnel glow with a tranquil pink, specially designed by DuPont to calm a troubled psyche. Lazarus walks slowly down its length, sure that this is where his journey ends. Sweat beads up on his forehead. He swipes at it with his sleeve. The automated tracking and surveillance system recognizes his body's nervous signals but attributes them to his known phobia of flying, something he is counting on. Upon emerging he allows himself to be swept forward with his fellow travelers.

Just when he thinks he has made it past the checkpoint, a heavyset Hispanic security guard with a thick black mustache beneath the dark lens of his visor, steps in Lazarus's path, taking him by the arm and saying, "Sir, please come with me." The man expertly plucks Lazarus from the line of people, watching him intently for the least sign of resistance.

Shock and dismay flash over Lazarus, "Is there a problem officer?" he asks as the guard separates him from the stream of passengers, a few of whom glance fearfully at the enfolding scene, their furtive looks make it clear they are glad that it wasn't them as they pass from sight, never looking back.

His other arm is suddenly put in a vice just above the elbow and he twists around to give this second officer a startled look. That he cannot see the men's eyes behind the visor only feeds his fear. The two guards guide Lazarus away from the flow of travelers into what appears to be a waiting area. The second officer points at one of several chairs lined up against a wall and orders gruffly, "Sit!"

Lazarus obeys.

He is sure that something has gone terribly wrong, that he isn't going to be permitted to leave. He rubs his hand across his crew cut, gathering resolve and calming his fears. He must maintain a clear head if he has any hope.

He watches the Hispanic officer, fascinated by the man's twitching mustache as he talks rapidly with someone online. Nodding affirmation, the man abruptly turns and walks towards Lazarus, the portion of his face visible below the visor is a hard mask that reveals nothing.

Lazarus convinces himself in those few seconds that he is about to be arrested. Everything he knows about reeducation flashes through his mind. Fear fills him and he struggles to maintain his composure. If this was how it was to be then he would not give them the satisfaction of seeing him squirm!

"Thank you for your cooperation, Mr. Sheffield. It is procedure to check the travel permits of any Homeland Security officer leaving the Federation. I hope that we didn't delay you too much." The guard's words say one thing but his tone another.

Confused but relieved, Lazarus regains his wits and stammers, "No, not at all." The man escorts him to the security area exit.

Lazarus glances back once finding the guard still standing at the checkpoint staring after him as he disappears into the cavernous terminal, alone amongst the multitude.

Bewildered and elated by his good fortune, Lazarus follows the signs, taking escalators down several levels before finding the maglev subway that will take him out to Terminal 4. He stands and waits patiently for the next train. The crowd is so thick by the time it arrives that he has no choice but to move with it as it surges forward when the doors open. Lazarus doesn't bother trying to find a seat, but stakes out a territory and remains standing clutching a cold stainless steel rail, his bag slung over his shoulder, sinking once again into anonymity. He ponders what exactly had happened back there. Never in his experience, limited as it is, has a suspect been snatched and released so quickly, therefore, he must not be a suspect.

He tempers his elation at reaching this conclusion with a heavy dose of pragmatism. Any mistake now will result in some very bad things happening to him and the chances are that he would simply disappear, that his family would either never know his fate or be told some plausible lie and paid money.

The acceleration is smooth and almost unnoticeable. Infomercials flash by on the walls outside the cars windows. One is selling a Hawaiian time share and another is pitching the spiritual insight of Reverend Gausault's newest book, *When Angels Speak*. As the train comes to a stop, the standing passenger's shuffle forward packing ever tighter, impatiently waiting for the sliding doors to activate. They aren't even fully open when the first traveler squeezes out followed closely by the horde. The crowds are something Lazarus has lived with his entire life and deals with stoically. He knows nothing else.

Riding the escalator back to the surface, he reevaluates what just happened. What had really changed? He now knows with absolute certainty that the Federation is keeping tabs on him at this very moment. But he knew this long before the incident at the checkpoint. He concludes he is being played. DHS agents must be following him to see who he contacts, waiting for him to lead them to others before arresting them all. He shudders, feeling like a mouse under the cold glare of the cat, a sentiment shared by most Federation citizens at one time or another. He reminds himself that as far as he knows, the vacation story is intact.

The escalator dumps the throng into a large circular room with its periphery containing a number of airline gates. Gate 4B is bustling with activity as Lazarus approaches.

Finding a seat, he sits down and calms himself. Glancing at his watch, he sees he has less than thirty minutes before his flight. He couldn't have timed it better.

Looking around he spots a small Old-Mex style citizen's lounge among the terminal's coffee shops and eateries. Normally he would never dream of drinking in public but today isn't normal. He finds it easy to convince himself that one last cider wouldn't hurt anything, no telling when he would have this chance again. Besides, it's traditional for him to have a drink right before getting on a plane. He gets up, slinging his bag over his shoulder and makes for the cantina. Several people are sitting inside on stools and around the tables. The dark wooden bar is tended by a young brunette with bored eyes appropriately dressed in a formless turtleneck sweater and a scarf. Stepping up to an open section, he waits for her to acknowledge him and says, "Jack's Hard Cider, three fingers, straight up."

She nods, sets a shot glass on the counter, snatches a black labeled bottle from under the bar and pours the drink right in front of him. Sliding it across the bar she says, "forty-two-fifty."

Lazarus shakes his head, marveling at the cost of things in the airport, and hands her a hundred. "Give me a refill in ten minutes and keep the change."

The young woman smiles, "God bless you. Try a basket of our complimentary popcorn." She hands him a small plastic container heaped with yellow and white kernels.

Picking up the drink and accepting the basket, Lazarus walks over and sits at a table that looks out onto the terminal floor, in plain sight for all to see that he has nothing to hide. Bringing the small glass under his nose, he lets the aroma of the liquor fill his nostrils. Taking a generous sip, he holds the fluid in his mouth briefly, anticipating the fire that would come. Swallowing, he can feel it burn all the way down, going off like a bomb when it hits his empty stomach. He leans back letting the harsh elixir relax him from the inside out, munching a handful of the popcorn, glad for something in his stomach besides the lighter fluid he had just drank. If this is Jack then he's the Pope!

He watches several flights arrive at the various gates within his view, disgorging their passengers and collecting more. He had always found entertainment in people watching, especially in airports. Parents with children move through the terminal like mother hens guarding chicks, or in one case, a mother bear guarding her cub. Business men in suit and tie try to elevate themselves above the herd ignoring the fact they are the herd. Many travel alone. Lazarus divides them into two groups from the way they interact with others, eager to be pleasant or conversely, shutting everyone out. Couples cling to each other while larger groups behave like a school of minnows darting about.

Lazarus looks up giving thanks to the young women as she sets his second drink on the table. Taking the empty glass she says in the monotonous tone of endless repetition, "God be with you." It sounds like a single word the way it rolls off her tongue.

"And with you," Lazarus replies by rote, letting his eyes wander back to the people in the terminal. He notices something unusual about the man walking past in front of him. He thinks back and tries to remember where he had seen him before, realizing that the man has walked past at least twice. Once means nothing, twice understandable, but three times starts the warning bells ringing in his head.

As inconspicuously as he can manage, Lazarus watches the man. Medium build, brown hair cut short, clothes that simply merge him into the surrounding crowd. If he were any more nondescript he would be totally invisible. His luggage, pulled along behind him, is virtually identical to hundreds of others. He makes a beeline for the information panel, stopping and looking intently up at it, his back to the cantina. Turning abruptly, the man walks directly towards Lazarus.

Picking up his drink, Lazarus takes a sip, letting action cover his nervousness, concentrating on the man's approach with his peripheral vision. With as little concern as he can muster, Lazarus casually shifts his vision and focuses directly on the man. For an instant their eyes meet and Lazarus is filled with certainty that the man is shadowing him. He has seen it done plenty of times and knows the routine almost as well as this field agent. But therein lies the heart of the matter, Lazarus has never actually been to the field. His participation as a DHS Senior Analyst was always early in the process identifying the target or later after the suspect was in custody. He finds it much different to be the target. His heart races pounding in his ears. It's all he can do to maintain his composure.

But instead of arresting Lazarus, the man walks right past him and enters the shady interior of the bar. Now he is behind Lazarus which sends a chill down his spine. Resisting the temptation to turn, Lazarus rubs his head and takes a deep breath, relieving some of the tension building within him, allowing his brain to deal with the situation. He cautiously looks around at the people he can see, knowing that field agents are never alone. Teams consist of at least two agents and as many as six, depending on the operation.

With intense relief Lazarus hears the announced arrival of Flight 119. He gulps down the dregs of the second shot, feeling the warmth of the cider flow through his body like mercury in a thermometer on a hot afternoon. He stands using his peripheral vision to watch the man at the bar who remains oblivious that Lazarus is leaving. Slinging the bag over his shoulder, Lazarus leaves knowing that if he is to succeed in getting aboard this plane, he must stay cool and play the part of a man going on vacation. If he's right and not just letting his imagination run amok, then the normal procedure would be to watch the quarry and record his every move, waiting for that fatal flaw that tips them off, the slightest bit of information they feel will make their case. Obtaining court evidence is simply a matter of time. Sooner or later everyone who has something to hide gives it up. Just keep watching.

Lazarus pops a couple of mints, specially designed to mask the smell of cider, and makes his way to the embarkation point. He ends up well back in line. From this position he can see the giant Airbus Maximus parked outside on the tarmac, distinctive with its double row of windows. Simultaneously servicing both the upper and lower floor of the Airbus, double-decker walkways extend out from the terminal to the planes front and rear exits. Walkway windows reveal a seemingly endless stream of people leaving the colossal aircraft. The big planes can haul over eight hundred people anywhere on the globe and this one arrived fully loaded or close to it. Lazarus looks around him trying and failing to estimate how full his flight was to be. A quick glance back at the lounge did not reveal any sign of the man, but that doesn't make him feel any better.

The disembarkation process is orderly with wide corridors roped off separating arriving passengers from those waiting to board. Lazarus is amazed at the seemingly endless flow of humanity exiting the plane, but finally it dwindles to nothing. An attendant steps forward and directs the people in the front of his line to proceed to the checkpoint. Again Lazarus is awash with the feeling that he was going to be stopped, that this was as far as he was going to get.

"Please move forward sharply. We have a lot of people to get aboard." The attendant looks bored as she walks up and down the line urging compliance. Most ignore her but a few fearfully do as asked. Those are the ones that Lazarus notices. Those are the ones that have the fear of God in them.

As Lazarus approaches the checkpoint, he runs his hand over his head repeatedly feeling the sweat begin to build up. Waiting his turn, he passes his left hand over the reader as he shuffles by. His seat number and name flash onto the screen.

"Please take the steps to your left and proceed to the second floor, Mr. Sheffield," the young female flight attendant says to him with a stone face. Seeing his unease she asks, "Is there something wrong?"

"No, nothing is wrong. I just don't like flying, that's all. Not to worry. I fly often and it's always this way," Lazarus says honestly, trying to disarm her concern with a smile.

"Just the same, I will keep my eye on you," she responds with a twinkle in her eye.

Good, Lazarus thinks to himself. He wants this to be remembered.

He glances out the walkway windows and is alarmed by how far off the ground he is. Turning away, he concentrates on the carpet at his feet and the back of the person in front of him, keeping to the center of the corridor, thankful to have people on both sides. He swipes at his hair, front to back in one long motion, and moves with the crowd.

Stepping over the crack separating the walkway and the plane, Lazarus catches a glimpse of the tarmac far below and feels a shiver slide down his spine. But it passes quickly as he moves deeper into the planes voluptuous interior. Two narrow access aisles service the rows of seats splitting them into three parts, the largest in the middle. The layout makes it seem more like a flattened auditorium than the world's largest aircraft.

"Take this aisle to row forty, Mr. Sheffield, and seat H is then to your left half way across," the attendant informs him.

"Thanks," Lazarus says.

He finds his row, stuffs his bag into the overhead storage and shimmies down the seats until he comes to H. A man, his wife, and their child are in the seats beyond his and it isn't long before a young man in a business suit takes the seat to his right. Lazarus buckles the lap belt and lays his head back, listening to the gathering throng.

This isn't his first time on an Airbus Maximus but that doesn't stop his amazement at the sheer size of the craft. It seems even bigger from the inside. He listens to the drone of people finding their seats. Behind him he hears a woman exclaim in a loud whisper, "How can this machine possibly fly with this many people! It don't seem natural!"

"This is just the top level. There are five hundred more seats below your feet!" A man drawls in response.

"Dear Lord! Don't tell me that!" she almost shrieks.

"Calm yourself, woman! Put yourself in God's hands and everything will be just fine!" is the man's stern response.

Lazarus shuts out the noise, thinking about the life he is leaving behind, his family and friends, and a culture he fondly despised. He will miss them immensely but reminds himself that he isn't dying, just moving. There is always the possibility of seeing them all again.

The plane lurches forward as it is pulled away from the terminal. For safety reasons and to minimize fuel usage, airport tugs pull them all the way to the takeoff staging area before detaching. In spite of his phobia, Lazarus wishes he had a window seat. But that would be out of character. He is almost directly in the middle of the plane, seven seats and an aisle to his left and eight seats and an aisle to his right.

He knows how to deal with the discomfort of being treated like cargo. Withdrawing from the herd, he retreats into his imagination. After all, it is only a couple hours to Athens. To his surprise, he dozes off.

****

Athens International Airport is just as crowded, if not more so, than Gateway. Thousands upon thousands of people scurry to and fro under the shelter of its enormous roof. From this single complex a plethora of big planes hauls tourists in and out in vast numbers while smaller planes, trains, and ships spread them out across the Upper Mediterranean.

Lazarus walks off his flight and moves casually along with the other passengers, stopping at the nearest information board looking for a specific departure. Letting his eye run down the list he quickly finds what he is looking for, the next flight to Heavens Gate.

Turning suddenly, looking past the dozens of people passing between them, he locks eyes with the man from the bar who quickly looks away and continues to walk briskly down the terminal.

Stunned by the suddenness of the encounter, Lazarus realizes he must follow. It is the only exit from this section of the terminal. Gathering his courage he strolls down the long access tunnel taking his time just as if he were on vacation. Moving at the speed of his fellow travelers, his gaze caresses the exquisite wall murals, huge affairs that stretch unbroken down the long tunnel. This is as close as he is going to get to the Acropolis, or the Parthenon, or to any of a hundred other ancient masterpieces. Places that he and Rachel dreamed about seeing.

Emerging from the tunnel, Lazarus looks left then right. Stretching as far as he can see in each direction is what appears at first glance to be an ancient thoroughfare, the facades of shops and stores that line both sides a capitalistic imitation of a 600 BCE Greek city street but much wider. This den of confusion is the world famous Athena's Marketplace, a tourist trap of mammoth proportions.

The area directly in front of each establishment is cluttered with tables filled with merchandise and people are everywhere, pawing through the goods outside the stores, roaming the isles inside and more form a constant stream moving in both directions down the imaginary street. To Lazarus, it looks like the biggest and oldest flea market he has ever seen. Everything has a used and tattered feel to it, as if it truly has been here a long time. The affect is diminished by the spider's web of struts and rafters holding up the ceiling far overhead. Hanging from the rafters are modern green signs sporting white letters in several languages, pointing the way to other gates, ground transport, and luggage carousels, one of only a few reminders that this is an airport and not just another mall.

It is the last big tourist weekend of the fall season and Lazarus stays well within the flow of people, swept along like flotsam on a river of humanity. The predominately Asian horde paws through merchandise packed along its banks, gleefully haggling with the locals to get the best price. To his left several small electric trams ease their way through the crowd, their bells dinging warnings for people to clear a path. A thousand sounds fill his ears, practically impossible to distinguish anyone speaking from just a few feet away.

Lazarus discreetly tries but fails to catch sight of the agent following him. The throng is just too thick. Walking at the speed of the crowd, Lazarus spots the entrance to his gate. He keeps going for another hundred yards before he finds what he is looking for. A small plaque on the wall beside the entrance identifies the restroom as A157E. Under the pretext of researching his vacation, Lazarus had determined that there is only one functioning camera focused outside and none inside. He's counting on the Greek's lackadaisical approach to security.

People converging on the public bathroom have created a traffic jam at its entrance. Lazarus moves into the center of this scrum, shuffles forward, and enters the room. He is carried along with the crowd heading for the stalls in the back. Without a clear cut line, he picks one and waits impatiently for it to open, edging closer with each man that exits.

When it's his turn, he enters as soon as it's clear, shutting the door and sliding its bolt tight. Ignoring the smell, he removes his backpack and hangs it from the hook on the inside of the door. Bending down, he slips off his shoes, instantly losing almost four inches of height in the process. For the last few weeks he has established an elevated height by wearing these shoes exclusively, just for this moment. In place of socks, he is wearing soft soled slippers of a style currently popular in Europe with the younger generation. His blue jeans are next, exposing a pair of baggy shorts underneath. He transfers his cash money quickly from his pants pocket to the shorts. Unzipping his bright red jacket, he slips it off revealing a dark blue tank top and arms covered in designer tattoos, the type that will wash off with a little soap and water.

Reaching inside his bag, Lazarus puts the hat on backwards before sliding his headset over it. This device was state-of-the-art when it was new, but that was thirty years ago. It's now considered low tech and backward which is precisely why it is so popular with young Europeans. Its lack of modern high tech features give the wearer a certain amount of anonymity by their very absence, not to mention it completely obscures the top two thirds of his face behind a dark shield. Unlike a modern visor which lazes directly into the wearers eyes, the image Lazarus sees in this headset is projected on the inside of the shield and he watches it like he would an ancient television. His costume adjustments have been carefully considered to fool the prying eyes of the scanners for just a few minutes, all that he will need if his plan is to succeed.

Removing the copy of Heinlein's Time Enough for Love, the book disappears into his pocket, stuffing his shoes, jeans and jacket in its place. He hides the backpack behind the toilet.

Lazarus tears off several sections from the roll of toilet paper and stuffs it into his mouth. Chewing carefully, he works the paper into a long narrow blob that fits behind his lower lip extending out into his cheeks, breaking up his jaw line, making it difficult for the facial recognition software to identify him. Lazarus has transformed himself from a rather stuffy conservative into a radical teen.

He exits the stall and merges into the stream of people leaving the bathroom. Seconds later he's back in the markets main corridor surrounded by people. In less than a minute he has changed his height, posture, the color of his shirt, and covered his hair and most of his face behind a low technology mask, a trick he learned from watching countless training vids describing in great detail what worked and what didn't as suspects try to stay one step ahead of Homeland Security. Looking back and using the primitive magnification features of his headset, he sees the man from the bar positioning himself at the bathroom exit, well within the limited range of a receiver. He grins wondering how long the man will wait before going inside to see for himself that Lazarus isn't there, that his bug was behind the toilet, not on it.

Navigating the river of people, Lazarus soon spots what he is looking for, a large exquisitely crafted statue of the Greek goddess Athena standing on a raised dais behind a long line of white marble columns marking the front of a massive stone temple. The crested helm of the figure towers over twelve feet above the crowd, her face serenely beautiful for the Goddess of War. Armed with shield and spear, the deity's right breast and arm is wrapped with a blood-red snake-trimmed aegis cloak adorned with the monstrous head of a Gorgon.

Beyond the columns, wide steps invite tourists upward to an inner sanctuary where, it is self-proclaimed, only the best merchandise is made available. Hidden speakers play classical Greek music and female hawkers, dressed as sirens, call out to the mass of people passing by, enticing them to enter the Temple of Athena and see for themselves the quality of the merchandise inside. Lazarus appreciates the irony.

Moving up the stairs, Lazarus is assured by the nearest hawker that he will not be sorry. He smiles and nods. Upon entering the shop, he glances at the time projected at the bottom corner of his headset. If his calculations are correct, the last of the employees of Athena's Temple should be finishing their dinner break. He quickly moves through the store picking out shoes, shirt, a pair of pants, and a small overnight bag, all in perfect harmony with the Asian tourists that frequent Athens. He grins when he finds the packaged deal consisting of boxers and matching socks. So far everything is exactly how it appeared when he was researching the mall on the network, even down to the blue, green, and white Mediterranean tourist shirt.

He takes his items and lays them on the counter. In a rack close by he picks out a pair of dark sunglasses, remarkable in their imitation of a Federation visor. He lays them down next to his other items. The touch panel pops up with the price listing and a voice informs him, "That will be three-hundred-fifty-one euros."

"Are you kidding? I want to talk to the manager," Lazarus states, knowing he must haggle or risk drawing unwanted attention to himself.

"Certainly, one moment please," the voice answers.

Lazarus takes the time to look around. Tourists, most of them Asian, far outnumber store employees who are easy to spot by their flowing Greek robes of one color or another. He sees several people who might be a Federation agent but no one stands out. He must assume his deception has worked.

"Sir, may I help you?"

Lazarus turns and looks down at the little woman standing behind the counter. She is short, thin, with dark hair pulled tightly back into a bun making the expanse of her forehead stand out. Wearing a white robe with gold belt pulled tightly around her waist, she gazes steadily at him, ready to do business.

"Yes, I hope so. I want to purchase these items but the price seems excessive to me. I think two-hundred-fifty euros is a fair price," Lazarus states.

"For you it would be, but for me, the Temple would lose money. We cannot stay in business long if I do that," she answers clearly bored with a conversation she has had in many forms time and again.

"You won't stay in business if you don't sell your merchandise either. What about three-hundred even? I think I can stretch that far," Lazarus responds, acutely aware that he is wearing baggy shorts, slippers, fake tattoos and a headset that marks him as a rebel. But not when he speaks, he doesn't have the language to pull it off with a local.

The woman looks at Lazarus, her steadfastness never wavering in the face of this unseen stranger. She knows the man is not what he seems. He obviously is a trying to look the part of a teen in some self conceived fantasy. But he isn't the first to do that. After all, the motto of Athens is that whatever happens here stays here. "Very well, you have a deal, three-hundred plus tax for a total of three-hundred-forty-one euros." She rings up the sale before Lazarus can blink. When he still hesitates she adds, "The Union must get its cut. There is nothing I can do about that."

Lazarus shrugs and doles out three-hundred-fifty euros cash money while the woman puts his items in a bag. "So why is the Goddess of War the mall symbol?" He instantly wishes he had kept his mouth shut.

The look of amused tolerance flashes across the woman's face then is gone, once again all business. "Athena is not only the Goddess of War but also the Goddess of weaving, pottery, crafts, and the patron deity of Athens." she replies.

Picking up a brightly colored cigarette lighter from a countertop basket filled with them, he asks, "Then this must fall into crafts?"

"No, that is a fire maker. It falls under the War category," the woman answers.

"Oh," he replies unsure if she is serious. He replaces the lighter and continues, "I would like to change. Is your dressing room in the back?"

Without asking why, she turns and points, "The door on the left. Someone is using it but they shouldn't be long."

"Thank you," Lazarus accepts his change, picks up the bag and walks deeper into the store, aware of her eyes following him. To his right is a second door which is obviously not the dressing room. Lazarus busies himself outside it by looking at racks of garments, noticing when his salesperson becomes busy with other customers. Minutes later the person in the dressing room exits and still he waits feigning interest in a rather frilly shirt. Finally it happens. The last two employees finish their dinner and exit the second door, laughing about something as they return to work. With smooth skill as if he has done it a thousand times, Lazarus slips through the door without even touching it, making sure it clicks shut behind him. His heart pounds in his ears.

He finds himself in a warehouse. To his right is a paper strewn desk, a computer touch screen peeking out from the mess. The rest of the room is filled with boxes and racks of clothing on hangers. Discarded packing and shipping material is shoved into a big pile near a large rollup door. Lazarus breathes a sigh of relief when no one is in sight.

The employee bathroom is a closet equipped with a toilet and sink. Lazarus uses his forefinger to clean his mouth of paper. Next he removes the headset and strips to bare skin before washing the tattoos from his arms, turning the sink black with the water soluble ink. He swirls the water, watching the blackness spiral down the drain before putting on his new clothing, tucking in the shirt and lacing up the shoes. Using another paper towel, he folds it carefully and wets it in the sink before inserting it into his left upper cheek. A second towel mirrors the first, blurring the outline of his high cheekbones, giving his face a round full appearance. The water soaked paper should escape notice in the MRI scans he will encounter, at least for a while.

Sliding Heinlein and his headset into the new overnighter, he stuffs the shorts, shirt and slippers into the empty shopping bag and hides it among the many boxes destined for recycle. Slinging the strap of his new bag over his shoulder, his second complete changeover is done in less than two minutes.

Lazarus unlatches the rollup and pulls upward. The rattling sound shatters the quiet making him look over his shoulder at the mall door uneasily, half expecting someone to walk through it.

Perched precariously on a narrow ledge three feet above the concrete tarmac, Lazarus pulls the door back down. Outside the massive building, he can see trucks backed up to various loading docks. Here and there people and machinery move about keeping Athena's Marketplace stocked with goods. Lazarus jumps off the ledge and begins walking along the outside of the mall, doubling back in the direction he has come from.

The concrete tarmac in front of each dock is heavily spotted with oils and tire rubber. Avoiding the worst of the mess, Lazarus moves as fast as he dares. He passes under several of the giant rigs, their drivers too busy to take notice of him. Finally he decides he has come far enough. Approaching the next trailer, he cautiously peeks into the gap between it and the storage room beyond.

A man and a woman are working inside unloading the delivery. Lazarus listens for a few minutes, keeping well out of sight of either of the two people. The woman is double checking items against a handheld computerized list as the man expertly wheels them off with a hand dolly, rolling out stacks of boxes with each trip into the trailer, calling out what they contain to the woman while he makes a neat pile in the center of her floor. Lazarus cannot understand what they are saying and assumes they are speaking Greek. But it is obvious to him that the two know each other or perhaps the Greeks are just a very friendly folk. Laughter and a pinched butt cheek tell him that there is more here than simple horseplay.

He leans casually against the wall next to the trailer until it becomes quiet inside. Listening carefully for several more seconds, Lazarus pokes his head slowly into the room. Seeing nothing, he hoists himself up and worms through the small gap, immediately moving behind the recently stacked boxes. Only then does he hear them. From behind the door to his left comes the unmistakably vibrant sound of two human beings having passionate sex, the woman being particularly enthusiastic. Seems they know each other pretty well.

Lazarus quietly moves past and down a short hallway, stopping to listen at the door near its end. He concentrates, categorizing what he hears, calculating the most opportune time to exit. Taking a deep breath, he squares his shoulders and opens the door, moving through it like he belonged.

The shopper closest to the door has her back to him and only one other person in the store looks up but immediately turns away, anxious to not get involved. Lazarus keeps moving away from the door appearing to anyone seeing him for the first time as simply another tourist, one of perhaps thirty in the store. No one else pays him the slightest heed.

Lazarus picks up a miniature Parthenon as it would have looked in 400 BCE and marvels at the detail in the piece of colored plastic. Putting it back, he casually meanders his way out of the store and back into the flood of people, staying within the protection of numbers as much as possible. From this safety, Lazarus passes the restroom where he had made his first change of clothing. Outside he spots the agent talking to a woman, slight with dark hair and pastel clothing, her features unremarkable, a perfect match for the man. Lazarus tries to memorize them both.

Even as he watches, the woman shrugs, saying something which makes the man swear in frustration, unheard from this distance but obvious in its intensity. He knows just how much trouble they will be in when they report to their superiors they had lost him and is counting on them delaying until they are sure he is gone. Just thirty minutes more is all he needs.

A second later the irresistible surge of people passing down the center of the avenue sweeps Lazarus beyond sight of the agents. He looks around at the gigantic mall. Built almost thirty years earlier, Athena's Marketplace is billed as one of the great wonders of the modern world. But in a land of ancient learning and mankind's first democracy, this is but a hollow reminder of what once was. He pities the travelers who fly into Athens and never make it beyond this tourist trap. Lazarus shakes his head with regret when he realizes he had just described himself.

He turns into the access tunnel leading to his gate with very little time to spare. Moving purposefully, Lazarus goes to the ticket console and places his hand on the pad.

A pleasant female appears on the screen in front of him, "How may I assist you this morning, Mr. Sheffield?" She has perfect inflection but is not human. AI's been doing these types of tasks for many years and yet most citizens dislike talking to them. Lazarus is no exception.

"I want to purchase a round trip ticket to Heavens Gate, outbound on Frontier Flight 701 and returning in three days on Flight 1205."

"I am sorry sir but Flight 701 is full. May I offer you some alternatives?"

"No. I'm invoking DHS591 Section 9, Paragraph 34B of the International War on Terror. Use account number 119186722 to pay the penalty for bumping someone off a flight," Lazarus orders, his voice ringing hollow and fraudulent to his own ears.

"Very well, please hold…" The face is replaced by a mountain stream, its sights and sounds intended to be soothing.

As the seconds drag on, he stares blankly at the screen without seeing it. Lazarus struggles to keep his emotions in check, vainly resisting the tendency of his thoughts to wonder beyond the moment. Because of his position within DHS, he knows he is authorized to make this purchase, and the number is for a personal offshore account that shouldn't attract attention until he is well away, but at that moment his plans seem foolish and transparent. His nerves tighten and from somewhere deep within grows the conviction that this is the end, he will never leave…

Each second an eternity. He rubs his hand over his head calming overstressed nerves and gathering courage.

Abruptly the face reappears and says, "I have debited your account eight-thousand-four-hundred-fifty-eight euros. Is there anything else I can do for you?"

AI's aren't curious, they just run their programs and if he stays within certain parameters then warnings will not be raised. And so far, Lazarus hasn't done anything that hasn't been done thousands of times before by agents of the Federation, the European Union and even the Islamic Brotherhood. Hopefully, by the time anyone notices, he will be long gone.

"No," he says hoarsely, "That will be all," not bothering to make nice. What would be the point?

By the time he has secured his boarding pass, the gate is busy exchanging one group of passengers for another. The newly arrived Stratoliner empties quickly in comparison to the Airbus. Lazarus notes the strained faces and laborious movements as they walk past just a few feet away. The sudden emersion back into high gravity makes them seem to be in slow motion.

As his line begins to move, he quickly puts down the thought that he's going to make it knowing that nothing could jinx him faster than overconfidence. Rubbing his hand over his head for the hundredth time, he keeps a tight rein on his emotions, managing a weak smile for the young flight attendant at the boarding checkpoint. He has come too far to blow it at this late stage, reminding himself once again that he is embarking on a vacation, something to be enjoyed, not dreaded.

As the line advances, he hears an angry voice back at the checkpoint, "What do you mean, my seat has been taken?"

"I'm sorry sir. There is another flight this evening and I'm sure you can get on it." And bump one of its passengers to a later flight, a disturbance in the spacelines master schedule that will take many hours to dampen out.

"Why can't I take this one? Fifteen minutes ago I had a seat and now I don't? What gives?" The man asks irritably, unwilling to believe this is happening. He needs to get to Heavens Gate before that or he will miss his shuttle.

Lazarus glances back, sincerely hoping that his little maneuver isn't going to cause too much trouble, seeing only the tip of the iceberg. Besides, it's not as if he had a choice. The man and the attendant are still arguing as he moves out of earshot.

It's a short walk down the tunnel to the spaceplane. Only then does he begin to relax, bizarrely amused that all he owns is an out-of-print sci-fi novel and an out-of-date headset. He came into this world with nothing and he's leaving it the same way.

Lazarus uses this thought to calm his frayed nerves continuing to play the part of just another passenger looking for their assigned seat. He ignores the flight attendant as he enters the spaceplane, wiping sweat from his forehead with the back of his hand as he shuffles past her. She thinks nothing of it, used to people being nervous boarding her flights. After all, they are on their way to space, many for the first time. He finds his seat and stows his meager belongings.

Leaning down as though looking for something beneath his seat, Lazarus pulls the paper out of his cheeks, stuffing the soggy mass into a hollow where with any luck, it would never be found. Straightening, he begins buckling himself in, his fingers fumbling with the unfamiliar four point harness. Finished, he rubs his bristles again and divides his attention between observing the activity outside his window and watching the stream of people go by inside, heading deeper into the Stratoliner.

Near the end of the procession, Lazarus is stunned. No! It can't be! His eyes grow big as saucers and his face flushes as he watches the women nod pleasantly to the flight attendant. Removing his sunglasses, he confirms that the not so distant profile under the bright blue scarf is Rachel's. How can that be!

Turning towards him, she moves purposefully down the aisle, looking at each row marker as she passes.

His thumping heart threatens to pound out of his chest the closer she comes. Lazarus can't take his eyes off her. It's Rachel! And the closer she gets the more surreal it becomes. His mind blurs as memories flood his consciousness making him see something unreal.

Stopping at his row the women gives Lazarus a puzzled look, "Am I wearing the Emperor's clothes again?" she asks innocently, looking down at herself.

In an instant the spell is broken. Lazarus shakes his head to clear it and really looks at her for the first time. He sees a very attractive woman looking inquisitively back at him, but she is definitely not Rachel.

"Please forgive me! For a moment I thought you were someone else," Lazarus stammers and unconsciously wipes a hand across his buzz cut. Coal black hair peeks out from under her scarf and a form-fitting sky-blue blouse reveals deep cleavage as she shoves her carryon into the overhead, expertly securing it under the bungee net.

"Don't sweat it… I rather like having that effect on a man!"

It must have been the scarf. Rachel wore them often in the hot desert sun. And blue was her favorite color. He drops his eyes to black hip-hugger stretch pants and matching black deck shoes. All in all, she is sensibly attired for a journey involving freefall. But this woman fills it out nicely.

"Looks like a full plane today," the lady remarks as she slides into the aisle seat next to Lazarus, her eyes quickly sizing him up. …long narrow face and high cheekbones… probably Native American...wearing a wedding band…a small Christian cross hangs from a thin gold chain around his neck…an aura of suppressed fear and sadness... Having taken in more than one stray in her time, this one peaks her curiosity.

"I believe you're right," he responds, nervously licking dry lips that taste of paper, his tension inching upward. He watches out of the corner of his eye as the lady begins adjusting and buckling her four point harness. It's only then that Lazarus notices that hers is different. The upper portion is actually two straps that cup her breasts before meeting at her midriff. It takes a second for him to realize that her harness is specifically designed for a full busted woman, supporting her body without crushing her chest. And it looks down right sensuous on this lady.

Reaching up and grasping his own strap he also realizes these are much more comfortable than the heavy canvas lap belts used on the Airbus. Come to think of it, the seats are better too. Lazarus settles back in the luxurious padding. Without conscious thought he strokes his crew cut and returns to people watching, wishing they would hurry yet dreading the thought of what was to come. He sighs when the hull door is finally shut and sealed, his worry shifting from being caught to actually going. Only at that moment does he allow himself to believe that it is possible to simply walk away from the Federation, again seeing only the tip of the iceberg.

With a lurch the spaceplane moves away from the terminal, pulled by an airport tug. The flight attendants take this time to quickly run through the obligatory safety presentation, pointing out the exit ports, floatation devices and emergency beacons. Lazarus doesn't pay much attention. It only makes him more nervous to think about useless escape plans while shooting through the sky at thousands of miles per hour.

Lazarus wipes the sweat from his upper lip with his shoulder and tells himself to relax for the umpteenth time. The pretty lady gives him an encouraging smile which Lazarus returns halfheartedly.

The powerful tug pulls the spaceplane across the tarmac, putting it in line with the other aircraft waiting for takeoff, shepherding it in time and space towards a very narrow launch window. When it is their turn, at one end of a long ribbon of concrete, the tug releases its hold and scurries away just as the pitch of the Stratoliner's hydrogen turboprops increase. The spaceplane smoothly begins its rollout, picking up speed down the runway.

Acceleration pushes Lazarus deep into the padded seat and he feels the rotation as the nose rises, sending the craft hurtling skyward. A few seconds after liftoff, the wheels tuck away with a clank felt through his feet and butt, giving Lazarus a start, his heart still threatening to burst out of his chest. He doesn't notice the rivulet of sweat that runs down his cheek next to his ear.

Lazarus grips both armrests, knuckles turning white, his head hard back against the headrest, yet his eyes remain locked on the scene enfolding out his window. He hates heights. His knees grow weak just climbing a ladder. But he regulates his breathing and watches intently as the ground quickly recedes.

Lazarus concentrates on the view, not his perspective, using the incredible detail spreading out before him to push down and ignore his fears. The ascent path of the Stratoliner gives him a good look at Athens. The city stretches for miles under the late autumn sun, its trees forming an urban forest, its roads and structures partially hidden beneath the green canopy. Rising sea levels have blurred the line between land and sea. Numerous buildings are flooded with only their rooftops showing. Others are completely submerged. But even so, Athens is relatively unscathed. When dikes and levees proved ineffective, many of the world's coastal cities were abandoned.

As the spaceplane banks into its trajectory, he catches a fleeting glimpse in the distance of the Acropolis and the Parthenon, mythical architecture from the dawn of civilization.

As the avenues and buildings disappear into minutia, the city itself becomes a mottled swatch of color bordered by the blue of the Mediterranean along one side and the many shades of browns and greens of the Greek peninsula on the other. The ship shudders and Lazarus feels the brief sensation of weightlessness as the hydrogen turboprops give way to the magnetoplasma thrusters.

Mountain climbers reaching the summit of Mount Everest, five and a half miles above sea level, can see the curvature of Earth's limb. It is so slight that many think it an optical illusion. Lazarus soon realizes he too can see the curvature over the Mediterranean, only it quickly becomes more and more pronounced as the seconds tick by. He wills his muscles to relax, his breathing to slow and stabilize, forcing his vital signs under marginally better control. His efforts do not go unnoticed by the lady next to him.

As Earth dwindles, the first bright pinpricks of stars appear. The sound inside the spacecraft reflects what is happening outside, the sudden pitch change as they break the sound barrier and later, the gradual fade to silence as the outside air pressure drops to zero, leaving only the low throb of the ships thrusters to comfort the passengers.

From his window seat Lazarus can't take his eyes off the sight enfolding below him. Earth's mountains and seas dwindle to a mosaic of browns, greens and blues, cloud systems become great white smears across the vast landscape. The higher his perspective, the more fragile the atmosphere shrouding Mother Earth appears. And strange as it seems, the less he fears.

Eight minutes into the flight, a chime softly rings out, "Welcome to space, everyone! We just exceeded sixty-two miles."

Lazarus feels like cheering but holds his tongue.

Still the acceleration doesn't stop. The long sleek spacecraft keeps its nose pointed up long after the blue sky is replaced by the diamond-studded black-velvet of space.

Twelve minutes into the flight, the Earth is a giant globe spread out below him, only partially seen from his window. Around it, the steady light of a hundred thousand stars burn brightly. More stars than Lazarus had ever seen on even the clearest desert night.

"Your first time?" his neighbor asks.

Lazarus reluctantly turns away from the spectacle of the incredible shrinking Earth and looks at her. She smiles as their eyes meet.

"First orbital flight, I just don't like flying," Lazarus returns the smile while shaking his head. A bead of sweat rolls off his forehead and into an eye causing him to blink and rub.

"There really isn't anything to be afraid of. Statistics show that space travel is far safer than going by any ground transport," she replies.

Still shaking his head, "It's not that I'm afraid, just aware. In an automobile if you have a flat tire or the motor shorts you call roadside service. Out here that would be difficult!" Lazarus chuckles nervously.

"But not impossible!" the women points out. "My name is Lindsey Davenport."

"Lazarus Sheffield," he responds.

Lazarus doesn't notice her slight hesitation as she files away his name, "How far are you going?" she asks shifting in her seat against the steady 1G acceleration to look squarely at Lazarus.

"Heavens Gate… And you?" Lazarus responds out of politeness.

"Aldrin Station, Luna."

"Really," Lazarus is torn between asking her about Luna and watching the incredible display outside his window. Curiosity won out for the moment, "What do you do?"

"I worked as an Engineer for MetCal, but not anymore," Lindsey says. It's obvious that she doesn't have his attention. She is talking to the back of his head. He can't keep from staring out the window. "I plan to run for President and turn off the sun at night. That will save a bunch of money and extend the life of the sun."

Fascinating but Lazarus couldn't care less right then. He turns and glances in her direction, smiles and nods, not having heard a word of what she said.

It is at that moment that freefall besieges them. The Stratoliner is suddenly ghostly still without vibration or any sense of movement. Lazarus feels the weight leave him just as if he were falling.

His only other experience with freefall had been unpleasant, but thankfully, brief. He and Rachel had taken a suborbital to Fiji for their honeymoon and he had puked on the way there. He had managed to avoid a repeat on the return trip but the damage was done. Freefall is something Lazarus had dreaded since he realized he was going off planet.

Just as he had predicted, his body is telling his mind they are plummeting from a great height. As far back as he can remember Lazarus has had serious nightmares about falling. As a child they terrified him. As he grew older he came to terms with the dreams but they still haunt him. And why is it called freefall? It's as if you are continuously falling. He had even heard an orbit described as a controlled fall around a planet. These thoughts only antagonize the underlying phobia buried in Lazarus's psyche.

His eyes grow wide and his stomach rises in his throat, his head spins and his face turns ashen. His inner ear delivers one message, his eyes another. The longer he sits, the more it seems as if his head were being drawn elastically upward. His sense of time stretches out before snapping back abruptly. The sound of children, first crying then squealing with delight, comes from the rear of the aircraft. A few seconds later nausea threatens to embarrass Lazarus once again, to bring up the Jack Daniels he shouldn't have indulged in. He grabs an air sickness bag and prepares for the worst.

Seeing Lazarus's discomfort escalate, Lindsey raises her arm, signaling the attendant that her neighbor needs some extra help.

Lazarus eagerly accepts the air sickness pill offered by the pretty attendant floating above the aisle. As he bites down on the nipple of the juice bottle, he tips it back just as he would have done back on Earth. Assuming incorrectly the reason for the amused look on the attendants face was his discomfort, he takes grim solace in the fact there are several passengers who need the barf bags in spite of the little pills.

The chime sounds again as one of the attendants prepares to address the passengers, "My name is Lee Fong, Sarah is the pretty one. We will be your flight attendants today. On behalf of Frontier Flight 701, let me welcome everyone aboard. We are currently on schedule to dock with Heavens Gate in 42 minutes, weather permitting." He chuckles at his own joke. "Seriously folks, if Heavens Gate isn't in your travel plans, you need to let one of us know immediately. We will be glad to help you into a parachute and shove you back out the door."

Lindsey keeps a wary eye on Lazarus, not wanting a surprise if he suddenly needs to puke.

"For those of you staying, we will periodically make orbital corrections, that is, we will turn on the thrusters now and then as we make adjustments on our way to Heavens Gate. We will warn you when this is going to happen by turning on the Fasten Seat Belt sign and sounding the acceleration alarm." He demonstrates by blinking the sign a few times and giving the acceleration klaxon a short burst. "Please immediately return to your seats and fasten your seatbelt. Take your time, you will have one minute." Lee Fong chuckles again.

"Connecting flight information can be obtained using Frontier Spaceline magazine located in the seatback in front of you or at www.frontier.spaceline.org. Thanks again for selecting Frontier Spaceline, your gateway to the stars!"

The pretty flight attendant, Sarah, is already serving refreshments, floating about handing out drinks and snacks. Lee Fong demonstrates his freefall prowess by soaring from one end of the cabin to the other, snagging a headrest, flipping over and landing smoothly on his feet, standing on the forward bulkhead like it was a floor, his arms crossed and a big smile on his face. He receives a mixed reaction from his passengers. A few laugh and applaud, some smile, most simply ignore him.

With his freefall induced nausea gone, fasting has left Lazarus famished with only the flight snack in sight. This turns out to be more fruit juice and a package of cashews. Lazarus bites gently on the nipple, savoring the sweetness that shoots into his mouth, mixing pleasantly with the rich oiliness of the nuts. The flavor burst lingers on his tongue long after he swallows, savory and delicious.

Seeing how much Lazarus is enjoying the cashews, Lindsey offers hers to him, "I'm not going to eat these. Would you like them?" she offers, seeking to widen the conversation.

Lazarus looks up from the small bag and falls under the influence of her riveting gray eyes. "Yes, thank you. These are very good," he responds taking them from her, reluctantly dropping his gaze from her face.

"Freefall affects taste buds in a good way," Lindsey says, pleased this handsome young man has accepted her hospitality.

"That seems to be the only good thing about freefall!" Lazarus shakes his head, popping another nut into his mouth.

"Oh, believe me, there are loads of fun things to do in freefall!" Lindsey says with a wistful grin, staring straight ahead, ignoring Lazarus when he looks inquisitively at her.

"That sounds like the voice of experience," Lazarus comments. When it becomes obvious she was not going to elaborate he continues, "Have you spent a lot of time in freefall?"

"Enough," she replies, "I worked in the Hyundai Shipyards for a while and spent time on Taurus." Hyundai Shipyards is an enormous facility where the largest space structures are manufactured and Taurus is an industrial colony specializing in solid-state electronics and satellite production, each located at the Earth/Luna Lagrange points L4 and L5, respectively.

Smart and beautiful, Lazarus is suddenly feeling a little out of his league. "I'm a desk jockey. Not very exciting, I'm afraid," he volunteers.

Raising her eyebrows Lindsey responds, "Excitement is a human quality that has only a weak dependence on physical surroundings. You would be surprised at how many boring people are in unusual and romantic occupations and how many exciting people do mundane everyday jobs." She leans over conspiratorially, her sweet breath hot on his face, "My first husband was a taxi cab driver. By far the most exciting man I've ever known!"

Lazarus is stunned when she actually winks at him! He can't help smiling, feeling a little more at ease with this beautiful and unusual woman. Her openness and self-confidence is magnetic and those eyes...

"There must be something about being a desk jockey which excites you," she purrs the very picture of innocence, mouth puckered, head tilted down slightly, she gazes up at Lazarus though long lashes looking for an answer. "Come on, tell me what it is," she insists softly, intimately, pulling the truth out of him.

The religiously correct answer involves God and duty but staring into those gray orbs only a few inches away he realizes this woman isn't asking for a recital of the slogans and sound bites that dominate Federation politics. Instead she is probing for the very essence of where he places himself within society and the world.

"You don't mess around do you?" Lazarus asks.

Her dimples become slightly more pronounced, "Life's too short for that," she replies batting her eyelashes.

But after a lifetime of denial he is reluctant to provide any real information, even to so charming an inquisitor. "Well… I guess I just like tilting at windmills." He settles for a vague half truth, a trick his father had taught him at an early age and one that has worked well throughout his career.

Knowing exactly the physical effect she is having on him, Lindsey laughs softly and lets him win this minor skirmish, "Oh! A modern day Don Quixote! Or perhaps you are just doing God's work?" nodding at the cross hanging on the outside of his shirt.

"Perhaps. With God, one never knows," he says with a cynical smile. He rubs the small gold cross before tucking the necklace back out of sight.

"I thought all Christians had a direct line to the Almighty?" her flippant tone makes it clear that she thinks this a ridiculous concept while at the same time reflects a deeper unspoken question that bores to the heart of his beliefs.

Lazarus squirms under her penetrating questions, "Can we change the subject?"

She puckers her mouth in disappointment, "Ok. Then tell me why you needed to bump Mr. Hamlin off this flight?" she asks watching him intently. The dilation of his eyes and sudden increase in breathing signals that she had hit a nerve of a different sort.

"That was your friend?" Lazarus blurts out, buying some time, thinking furiously, caught off guard yet again by this remarkable woman.

"Friend? No, not really, he's a Metcal employee I have been working with for a short while. What you did will cost him money but they pay well so he can afford it," Lindsey states flatly, making Lazarus squirm. "So tell me, what desk jockey can requisition a seat on a Stratoliner at a moments notice?"

Lazarus bows his head, "I'm sincerely sorry for that. Perhaps you can give me his address and I can send compensation to him later?"

She shakes her head in mock frustration, "Oh, don't worry about that and stop changing the subject and answer the question…" she pauses before continuing, "If you will not tell me how, then tell me why you are in such a hurry to get to Heavens Gate?"

Again, she has tied him in knots, asking pointed questions that he really doesn't want to answer. Gazing into her eyes he decides to be truthful, "Actually Heavens Gate is not my final destination, I want to go on to Luna," Lazarus says so softly that she can barely hear him.

Lindsey rewards him by leaning over even more, sliding her arm under his and squeezing, "See, that wasn't so hard… any particular place? Luna contains well over a million citizens," she says, her eyes never leaving his face, measuring and probing for the slightest sign of lying.

"Aldrin Station," Lazarus replies, the only Lunarian city he could think of at that moment. It's an instant decision that will prove to have far reaching effects.

"What are you running from?" Lindsey asks not giving him time to come up with a better story.

"No, it's nothing like that," Lazarus denies much too quickly, "This is strictly a vacation. I simply want to see an underground city with my own eyes and this is the only way I will ever do it. Homeland Security would never grant my request for a Luna visa. This is the only way I will ever see a Lunarian city," he says, losing what little remains of his enthusiasm in this conversation.

Lindsey knows that the best lies have their feet firmly grounded in truth but lets it drop for now. Looking down at Lazarus's wedding band, "Is your wife going to meet you at Aldrin Station?" she asks. Once again the sweeping changes in his physiological factors tell her she has hit yet another nerve. It also tells her that this man planned on never returning.

Lazarus sits quietly staring straight ahead, wondering how the conversation had gotten here, of all places. Looking wistfully out the window, he turns back to Lindsey before speaking. "My wife died two years ago," he says twisting at the wedding band, "I wear this just to keep all the women at bay." He grins wanly at his own halfhearted attempt at humor.

"I'm so sorry…" Lindsey says softly. Putting two and two together, she continues, "You thought I was her. When I boarded the plane, you thought I was your wife."

Startled, Lazarus stammers, "Only for a moment!" This woman is driving him nuts.

"You must have loved her very much," Lindsey declares. The silence extends for a few seconds, "You are going to love Aldrin Station!" she exclaims, granting him a change of subject.

Lazarus grabs it eagerly, "What's it like? I've seen every National Geographic vid, played net games set on Luna, and I swear I've read everything I could get my hands on," which isn't very much. The Federation discourages its citizens from being curious about so different a society. Without exception, the games are even worse, designed to vilify Lunarians. They are terrible sources of knowledge for anyone seeking truth. That leaves only the NatGeo vids, which by the time Federation censors get done with them, are of little value, depicting Lunarian cities as dark subterranean caverns deprived of sunlight and stripped of humanity, the implication of hell never far from the surface

"You poor thing!" Lindsey shakes her head, "Then you know nothing! Lunarian cities are bubbles of air carved from solid rock that contain life in all its complexity. There are forests and meadows and complete ecosystems copied right down to the bacteria in the soil. Luna is a place of light and life that is diametrically opposite to what the Federation would have you believe."

"What about the Lunarians?" Lazarus asks, feeling like a kid in a candy store.

"To be sure, they are on the defensive, threatened by an enemy not willing to negotiate." She notices Lazarus tighten up, "Over the last decade Luna has become an armed camp with everyone contributing to the common defense, just as Israel has been forced to do for the last hundred-fifty years and for pretty much the same reasons. Islamic jihad is a constant companion, mostly aimed at the hospitals and clinics that provide the genetic treatments the Lunarians have come to depend on."

This is a subject Lazarus is well acquainted with. As he worked himself up the ladder of success within the Department, it was his job to identify and oversee the closure of many outlaw clinics within the Federation. Another bullet on his resume he isn't particularly proud of.

He pushes these thoughts aside and reluctantly realizes that he must take his turn at the zero-G toilet. He knows roughly how they work but this would be his first time actually using one.

"Please excuse me for a moment." His little mini adventure has an auspicious start when he unbuckles his harness and promptly floats upward bumping his head loudly on the overhead compartment.

"Here, let me help," Lindsey offers reaching out to steady Lazarus, her touch sending delightful shockwaves through his nervous system. She makes sure he gets into the aisle safely and locks eyes briefly with the attendant.

Watching Lazarus awkwardly make his way, the attendant moves forward to assist. "May I offer some advice?" the male attendant politely asks Lazarus.

Banging his left arm into the back of one seat and his right leg into another across the aisle, Lazarus manages to stop without help from the attendant.

"Imbecile!" exclaims a young man in a British accent. He is setting in the seat Lazarus's leg had hit, an angry scowl twisting his handsome face.

Hooking a toe, almost by accident, under the seat, Lazarus collects himself before answering. "Please excuse my clumsiness."

"Bloody unlikely!" the young man spits out and turns away, dismissing Lazarus as an annoyance, one that he wished would go.

Stifling an angry retort, Lazarus ignores the young man and addresses the flight attendant floating in front of him, "By all means, I could use some advice right now."

The attendant has a small badge pinned to his breast, the name Lee Fong superimposed over a partial silhouette of the Earth, the sun peeking over its horizon, Frontier Spaceline in smaller block lettering across the bottom.

Playing the diplomat, Lee Fong says pleasantly, "No harm done, Mr. Basayev." But the lad pays him no heed, refusing even to look up.

Shaking his head in amazement at the overt display of rudeness, Lee Fong looks back at Lazarus, "Don't try and touch every seat as you pass. That tends to throw you off, start you spinning. Just push off gently and sail to where you are going without touching anything." He demonstrates by letting a tube of cashews go, sending it slowly from his right hand towards his left. Halfway there he reaches out and lightly touches the corner. The tube immediately starts to spin out of control.

Lazarus nods, "I get the point." Grasping the seatbacks on each side of the aisle, Lazarus pulls himself forward striving to imitate the grace and smoothness that Lee

Fong and Sarah demonstrated earlier. He realizes that he's going in the right direction but has a slow forward summersault that he's powerless to stop. Upside down and closing on the galley wall at the front of the cabin, Lazarus begins to panic. With a great deal of skill, Lee Fong brings Lazarus to a safe stop, laughing at the grateful look on his face.

"Better, but it still needs work!" Lee Fong tells him grinning ear to ear. "Gently," he repeats. "A little push or pull goes a long way in freefall."

Lazarus nods, "Thanks," as he fumbles with the door latch. Every movement sends him off in a new direction. Simply standing still becomes an impossible task.

"Hook your toes," Lee Fong says pointing to the loops found on virtually every surface. "That's what these are for."

Lazarus gives him a sheepish grin and mutters his thanks again.

Coming closer to Lazarus, the flight attendant asks softly, just between the two of them, "Are you ok with using the facilities?" his meaning unmistakable.

Lazarus nods with more confidence than he feels at that moment. "Sure. No problem."

"Press the call button if you need help," Lee Fong says, fervently hoping Lazarus wouldn't. He doesn't want a lavatory cleanup on this flight. Some of the stuff always gets on you no matter what, and he has a date waiting for him at Heavens Gate.

Zero G urinals use air flow to replace gravity. A six inch transparent tube extends out of the restroom wall, curves downward and runs to the floor. A hole in the side of the tube gives a man access and airflow inside carries the fluids away, arrows point in the direction of flow. Even in space it's not a good idea to piss into the wind.

Toe and hand holds encourage a close encounter with the urinal's opening. Lazarus can feel the warm touch of the air inside the tube as he positions himself. A small strategically placed sign is impossible not to read while standing in such intimate contact with the urinal. It explains the importance of cleaning up any escaping droplets and the location of high absorbent wipes to do the job, if necessary. He didn't even want to think about using the toilet just to his left. He hoped his starvation diet over the last couple of days would get him beyond freefall before that became necessary.

Finishing his business without a single drop escaping, Lazarus looks around. Towel dispensers take the place of a lavatory. One contains wet wipes, another soapy wipes and a third dry towels.

While cleaning his hands, Lazarus looks at his wedding ring and knows it's time to move on. But no matter how he tugs and twists it will not come off. He smears more soap from a towel on his finger and tries again. Twisting and turning, he's sure he's about to dislocate his finger when it finally slides over his knuckle. He carefully cleans and dries it, putting it safety into an inner pocket in his jeans, one with a Velcro seal.

Looking in the mirror, Lazarus reaches up and touches the cross. The lack of gravity has set it free. As it floats around his neck, the tiny cross bumps against his chin trying to escape. Very carefully he lets his fingers find the necklace's tiny clasp, opens it, and slips the thin gold chain off his neck. This follows the ring into the inner pocket.

Wiping his hands one last time, he stuffs the towel into the recycler. Lazarus feels strange, almost naked, without the jewelry. It's the first time they have been off his body for years. He can't nail down an exact number, but at least ten.

Emerging from the washroom, Lazarus is relieved to see that Lee Fong had gone about his business. It gives him a little confidence that the experienced spacer hadn't thought it necessary to stay close. Moving slowly, he manages to get back to his row without mishap.

As she helps him into his seat, Lindsey immediately notices his red traumatized finger where the wedding band had been and the missing necklace.

As Lazarus fumbles getting his harness refastened, he expects her to start with the questions again. He's relieved and strangely disappointed when she remains quiet.

Several times during the flight the acceleration klaxon sounds, sending passengers scurrying back to their seats. In one case, an attendant has a passenger, a teen of small stature, tuck into a fetal position. A gentle push propels the girl gracefully down the aisle to the waiting hands of the second attendant who smoothly deposits her into her seat. On one occasion, the thruster fires for over three minutes as the Stratoliner makes orbital adjustments to match it with Heavens Gate.

Located in a near perfect circular orbit just over a thousand miles above sea level and in the Earth-Luna plane, Heavens Gate serves mainly as a passenger transfer point. The small amount of non-biological outbound cargo, rendezvous with freighters in much lower orbits and transfer payloads across the vacuum of space without the need of elaborate orbital structures. Going the other way, earthbound shipments are packaged within heat shields, decelerated by an orbital mass-driver, and plunged through the atmosphere to well established drop zones. Humans, on the other hand, need Heavens Gate, coming and going.

Supporting only a small permanent population, Heavens Gate contains a large casino hotel and several restaurants in addition to harboring spaceline support personnel. A steadily rising number of tourists come here to enjoy freefall and it has become somewhat of a honeymoon status symbol. For many Earthmen, this is as far into space as they will ever get. But in reality, Heavens Gate is just a way station with the vast majority of man-rated constructions much further out in geosynchronous orbit and beyond.

Lindsey retrieves the Frontier Spaceline magazine from its pocket on the back of the seat in front of them. The magazine is a thin flexible touch screen with a wide variety of flight information available through it. With a few taps of her finger Lindsey obtains a live view of the station as the Stratoliner draws near.

Lazarus leans over to see better and reaches out. But before touching the screen he asks, "Do you mind?"

"Of course not," Lindsey responds moving the screen to better enable him.

Lazarus touches the construction icon bringing up a rough schematic of Heavens Gate showing the body of the station as a double-walled cylinder with ten feet of lunar regolith packed between the inner and outer walls, forming the main radiation shield. Shown in bright yellow, a thin layer of Aerogel thermal insulation blankets the inner surface providing an almost impenetrable barrier to the extreme temperatures of space. Touching one of many vid icons, the interior of the station pops up filling the screen with color and crowds of people having fun. This certainly doesn't appear to be the den of iniquity the Federation proclaimed it to be.

Reverting back to the live view, they watch as the approaching station grows from a bright spot on the screen into a dull metallic tubular shape hanging motionless in the void of space. From the Stratoliner's direction of approach, the structure appears at an angle. The end facing them is a shallow dome with its edges rounding smoothly into the sides of the cylinder making Heavens Gate look like an over-pressurized aluminum can on the verge of bursting. Stubby appendages protrude from the body of the station at various points like nails driven partway into a log. Antenna and power receptors sprout here and there adding a fuzzy clutter to the structure.

Lazarus doesn't get a sense of scale until he realizes that another Stratoliner is docked to the station, held fast by one of the stubby extensions. It looks like a child's toy airplane, dwarfed by the bulk of the station.

Another quite different spacecraft comes into view as they approach. It doesn't have the aerodynamic outlines of an atmospheric craft. It is made up of an open framework of beams and girders enclosing a squat solid section. Instead of minimizing the frontal area, this vehicle maximizes it.

"I believe that's our ride," Lindsey says, indicating the screen with a tilt of her head.

The section that Lazarus can clearly see seems to be a cluster of long slender tanks strapped together. But the bulk of the spacecraft remains hidden behind the station.

Since its inception, Lazarus had been a big fan of Luna Central, a Federation sitcom loosely based on the actual organization. He put up with bad acting and hateful scripts just to catch an occasional glimpse of spacecraft or learn something of Lunarian technology. He knew he couldn't risk using his resources to gain this knowledge, that any sudden interest along those lines would raise flags and questions he couldn't answer.

From this poor source he learned the shuttle is composed of two parts, a pressurized Lander containing life support equipment and the TLM or Translunar Module, which is nothing more than a set of ultra-high efficiency magnetoplasma thrusters whose sole function is to provide constant acceleration during the voyage. Once Luna orbit is obtained the two vehicles uncouple, the translunar module to remain in orbit while the Lander ferries the passengers to the surface under its own power.

Lazarus is surprised at the speed with which the station grows on the screen. Seemingly at the last moment the thrusters vibrate to life, again pushing Lazarus down into the seat padding, bringing the ship almost to a stop in space, at least in relation to the station. Much more slowly, the sleek atmospheric craft closes with the orbiting station. Outside his window, Lazarus can see the stars rotate as the spacecraft rotates, positioning itself for the docking. But inside multiple cameras seamlessly maintain his view, keeping the station motionless in the center of the screen.

As Heavens Gate fills the screen to overflowing, one of the extensions elongate, its end gapping open like a moray eel in search of dinner, it reaches out and closes around the fuselage of the spaceplane. Lazarus feels a bump and hears the solid sound of metal against metal indicating the electromagnetic grapplers have found their mark. A whirring vibration fills the cabin as the mechanical safeties screw down, signaling the end of the docking maneuver. The Stratoliner is now physically part of the station.

A soft chime sounds through the cabin, "Welcome to Heavens Gate. Please remain patient for just a few more minutes while the crew checks everything out. We wouldn't want to open the door to vacuum!" Lee Fong chuckles one last time.

Looking around the cabin Lazarus watches as most of the passengers unbuckle, retrieve their luggage and start moving towards the exit. Many are clumsy, bumping and jostling each other, chuckling at their own inexperience, excited to be here. It is easy to pick out the veterans, they move with grace and skill.

Lindsey puts her hand on his arm stopping him from unbuckling, "Might as well relax, could be awhile. The first time I flew here they had us waiting for over an hour while they fixed something. Never did find out what. Besides, our connecting shuttle isn't scheduled for departure for three hours," Lindsey informs Lazarus. "There's a nice java shop inside. Do you feel up to joining me for a cup?" Lindsey asks smiling, noting that he seems to be handling freefall better than most.

Lazarus does feel comfortable, if not confident, that he isn't going to spill his guts but isn't sure if Lunarian Java is a wise move. "I don't know about the coffee but I would be happy to join you," he says, returning her smile, strangely thrilled that she wants him to stick around, to accompany him into the station.

"Good!" she responds enthusiastically.

"I need to get my ticket for the shuttle first. Perhaps you could spare the time to accompany me?" Lazarus asks hopefully.

Lindsey laughs, "There isn't a ticket counter or agent. The only way to get a ticket is through Luna Central's passenger service website. You do have a visor, don't you?"

"Yes, of course, in my bag," Lazarus answers.

Lindsey unbuckles and floats into the aisle. Hooking her toe under a loop she opens the overhead and takes down her bag first, and then what must be Lazarus's bag. She hands it to him and quickly buckles back into her seat.

Lindsey stifles a giggle when he pulls out his antiquated headset. State of the art several decades ago, it still works but just barely. With pleasure, she removes her visor from an inner pocket of her bag and slides it on. It molds itself into her ear channels, and fits snugly across her face covering her eyes. This is the first time she has worn her visor since arriving in the Federation over six weeks earlier. In the States the only authorized civilian use of the web is through government licensed portals using touch screen technology many decades old. For her, putting on the visor is the signal she is going home.

She tries to link with him but the old headset is not equipped to handle modern protocols. "Go to lunacentral.luna," she directs him. She watches as his hands flail about.

"Got it," he says triumphantly.

The face and shoulders of a cyberspace AI personality appears before him and asks politely how it can be of assistance. It could be either male or female, Lazarus cannot tell which in the blurry image presented in his headset. But it sounds female.

"List the availability of passage on the next Lunar Shuttle," Lindsey responds.

The information appears within their VR as a seating chart.

"You're lucky. There are still seats available…" she selects two together next to a window designating one as hers and the other as being purchased. "Go on. This is where you pay for your passage," Lindsey tells him.

Lazarus nods and with a few jerky hand motions, downloads his financial information into the site.

"I am sorry Mr. Sheffield, but passage is denied," the AI says.

"Why?" Lindsey asks.

"Federation authorities have indicted him for failure to obtain the proper visas and have requested his return on the next available flight."

Lazarus is horrified and dumfounded. He had counted on them not to be so efficient. At that moment he doesn't know what to do so he does what comes natural, he runs his hand over his close-cropped hair and forces his mind to relax and think.

Lindsey seizes this golden opportunity. "Under the Lunarian constitution, Lazarus can stake claim to the Freedom of Movement. His crime has not harmed anyone and he has the right to go where he pleases," she volunteers knowing full well what this AI's response will be.

"To do so he must reject his Federation citizenship and apply for Lunarian. Do you, Ms. Davenport, sponsor him in this?"

Lindsey sits back and looks intently at Lazarus, his peculiar headset making it impossible for her to see the upper half of his face. She has him right where she wants him, "So… what do you think? You want to become a Lunarian?"

Lazarus struggles to control the emotional rollercoaster of the last few seconds. In planning his departure, he didn't let himself dwell on the things he had no control over, never believing he would get this far. His comrades in the Department of Homeland Security are just too good at their jobs. He left knowing it's a one way trip, final destination unknown. When imagining what kind of people he would meet along the way, never in his wildest dreams did it ever occur to him that a beautiful woman would magically appear. It's almost as if she were waiting for him.

He wonders briefly why she is doing this, but frankly, he doesn't care, just that she is. He sees what he wants to see within Lindsey, humor and kindness and patience and a willingness to risk that far exceeds anything Lazarus has ever experienced. He's in awe of her at that moment, wishing only to be given the opportunity to prove worthy of her trust in him.

"You would sponsor me?" Lazarus asks softly, hardly daring to breath. "You don't even know me."

Almost flippantly Lindsey responds, "It's not that big of a deal for me. On the other hand, for you this is huge. Do you even know what you will be expected to do?"

"I must pass the Immigration Aptitude Test and a physical," Lazarus croaks, his voice harsh with barely contained emotion.

"And a freehold. Would you accept Dakota hospitality until you decide?" she asks.

There are times in a person's life where a single decision, contemplated for only an instant, completely changes the path of their lives. "Yes, of course, I would be honored!" Lazarus responds not daring to believe what is happening.

"It's settled then!" She can see that nothing else matters to Lazarus at that moment. Lindsey chuckles, "You didn't fool me for a second with that vacation story. I suspect the Federation would skin you alive if they got their hands on you. It only makes sense if you are running… immigrating. With a Lunarian citizenship you may someday even return and visit your family. Without it you're dead meat," Lindsey reinforces her claim. Addressing the website personality she says, "Yes, I will sponsor Mr. Lazarus Sheffield in his application for Lunarian citizenship."

"Your sponsorship has been recorded and Mr. Sheffield has been granted provisional Lunarian citizenship pending his successful completion of the standard requirements. His passage to Aldrin Station has been secured. The shuttle will depart in three hours and fourteen minutes."

Lazarus can hardly believe it. He never imagined it could be this easy or painless. It seems all he had to do was ask. He begins to understand one of the basic tenants of a free society, that it cannot withhold its freedoms from anyone, even those that wish to harm it.

"Lindsey, I can't thank you enough! I will never be able to repay your kindness!" Lazarus is stunned. His emotions, already raw from the last three months, are stressed to the breaking point.

"Like I said, it's no big deal, really. You're the one that will bust your ass getting up to speed. Have you ever even been in a vacsuit?"

Lazarus shakes his head, "No, but I have extensive training time in environmental contamination suits and they're similar to a vacsuit."

Lindsey chuckles, vowing to find out why a desk jockey would have training in environmental contamination suits, "That's debatable but the fact remains that you will need to be fully fitted and qualified in the Lunarian version before you can even take a walk on the surface."

"Oh yes, certainly!" Lazarus would agree to just about anything at that moment. Nothing was going to stand in the way of Lunarian citizenship!

With a clank the Stratoliner's door disengages and swings open. "Be sure to collect all personal items before leaving. Watch your elbows and knees during disembarkation. Do not leave your luggage unsecured while in the station." The message softly repeats, over and over, with a few seconds pause in between.

Lazarus removes and returns his headset to his bag, maneuvers out of the seat, and joins Lindsey in the aisle without mishap, something he hardly notices in the magnitude of the moment. Smiling her congratulations, Lindsey gracefully propels herself towards the exit, leaving Lazarus to admire her from behind. To his credit, Lazarus does better, only ricocheting once.

He doesn't try to keep up with Lindsey and soon discovers he is the last to leave. Beyond the Stratoliner's open door stretches a long tubular corridor, its far end clogged with departing passengers. Lazarus manages to keep to the center, more or less, reaching out to brush the walls as he slowly traverses the tunnel.

His mind races and he can't rid himself of the feeling that this is all a dream. That he will awaken to find himself alone in his dreary apartment, stuck in a job that no longer holds value, in a culture that makes him hide his true identity and live a lie.

But already he has come further than he had dared hope was possible. After all, he is entering Heavens Gate! Never has a name been more apropos! Plus, thanks to Lindsey, he is on his way to Luna in a few hours with the very real possibility of citizenship where before there was only a vague plan with few details. He quells the surge of euphoria by reminding himself that provincial status is not full citizenship, and that he has not yet attained his goal, not by a long shot.

The other passengers are gone by the time Lazarus emerges from the tunnel into a small sunken courtyard, its depth maybe three times his height and its breadth not much bigger than that of the airlock. Fastened alongside is netting which to Lazarus, looking up at it, seems remarkably similar to the climbing rigs found on an old three-mast sailing ship, square openings sized for human hands and feet. It extends in a taut straight line up and out of the courtyard before attaching to another net perpendicular to it. As any recent arrival from Earth will do, he orients himself with the net as his floor. Movement within the small section of sky above him catches his eye but before he has a chance to look closely, his thoughts are interrupted.

"Thank you for flying Frontier," a bright-eyed young woman says as he clears the airlock and gains his footing. Floating effortlessly within easy reach of the net, she is holding out an odd dumbbell shaped item for Lazarus to take.

Seeing his confusion she quickly explains, "This is a Personal Maneuvering Unit or PMU. It will help you get around while you're here." It's something everyone learns about when they go through the mandatory classes that true tourists take. She glances over her shoulder at Lindsey who shrugs.

Lazarus misses the exchange but accepts the device.

Lindsey chuckles. "It's an aerosol. Use it when you can't reach something to push against," she explains patiently turning so he can see the PMU clipped to her belt. "Everyone gets one, not just the rookies. They would have talked about them in orientation if you had taken it."

"You know very well why that was impossible." His frustration deepens as Lazarus fumbles around clipping the PMU onto his belt in imitation of her. In the process he releases his bag which promptly spins away.

"Sir!" the attendant exclaims as she quickly retrieves the errant luggage.

Without realizing what he had done, Lazarus has released his foothold on the webbing and is now floating in midair. When the attendant returns his bag, she expertly gives him a slow spin. Reaching out he can't quite touch the net as it passes by, over and over. Stretching out his foot doesn't bring him any closer. He suddenly realizes he has no way to move forward or back! Or to even stop spinning! Just inches from the net, he is stuck! He watches helplessly as the world leisurely turns around him.

Lazarus retrieves the device he had only just clipped onto his belt.

"Look at the PMU and think about the physics of what you are doing," the attendant instructs him. "Remember, force equals mass times acceleration. You are just another satellite obeying the same Newtonian laws as every other body in orbit," she struggles to keep her amusement in check. It happens all too often that people show up with inadequate training, skipping or daydreaming through the classes. Even after only a few months on Heavens Gate she can recall more than one Federation visitor who after messing up, would pray loudly for God to come save them, but inevitably it was a Lunarian that had to stop the wild spinning before they hurt themselves or someone else. Even though the PMU has sensors that limit how fast someone can spin, occasionally they must take away the device altogether and assign a person to stay with these individuals while they are on Heavens Gate, inevitably a short and unpleasant visit for this hapless traveler, but cruel amusement for those who adapt.

"Why not just grab me?" Lazarus asks irritably, losing his good humor and getting a little peeved at the smirking young lady. He is not in the habit of being the butt of a joke. Worse yet, he can feel the first twinges of space sickness returning.

"That won't help you when you do it again. Everyone goes through this at some point. You would be surprised at how many do it in the first few minutes!" she says openly smiling, giving up the pretense that this is not entertaining.

Lazarus ignores the churning of his stomach and the slowly spinning world and concentrates on the PMU. The hourglass shaped device has a small nozzle at one end, is heavily padded at the other, a comfortable hand grip in between with a power dial in easy reach of his thumb. Figuring to curtail his next screw-up, he sets this to its lowest setting.

"You trigger the PMU by squeezing," the attendant volunteers.

Glancing out, Lazarus catches Lindsey grinning wickedly as she watches him slowly twist in space, her visor hiding those amazing gray eyes. He refocuses on the task at hand, trying to remember the mechanics of motion he studied years ago while in high school. For every action there is an equal but opposite reaction. Referencing the nets, he gauges his plane of rotation as best he can. Extending his arm straight out in that plane, he squeezes off a couple of seconds worth of thrust. The PMU hisses and he flexes his arm muscles against its force, noting that his rotation slows considerably. A few more seconds of thrust proves too long and actually starts him rotating in the opposite direction. Quickly he flips the PMU over and gives it another very short burst, coming to a stop, more or less.

"Hey, this isn't so hard," Lazarus proudly exclaims until he looks over at the attendant and sees that he has stopped upside down in relation to her.

She couldn't care less about Lazarus's orientation, having lived in Heavens Gate long enough that she doesn't think about her environment in terms of up and down anymore. She recognizes people no matter which way their heads are pointing.

She smiles at Lazarus, "Very good, sir! You will do fine with a little more practice." Looking at Lindsey as she passes her on the way out of the courtyard, "Maybe you can stick with him while he's here?" she suggests with a knowing look.

"Humph!" Lindsey huffs but grins, "Come on, Mr. Sheffield. Let's go get that java."

Still thinking about physics, Lazarus places the PMU against his side just under his ribcage, understanding now what the padding is for. He squeezes off a couple seconds of thrust, pleased when he moves, without much rotation, towards the webbing. Grabbing the net with his free hand, he pulls himself gently towards Lindsey. It reminds him of scuba diving off the coast of Australia, only without the bulky air tank.

"This gadget might actually be fun!" he informs her, returning it to his belt. The two sail smoothly along within reach of the webbing, heading out of the courtyard. With disconcerting suddenness, they go from the confines of the small courtyard to openness beyond his wildest imagination. His eyes grow wide with panic, his heart pounds in his chest, and sweat spews from his pores. He is falling into an abyss. Fear sends his head spinning and stomach churning at the sight of the stations vast interior. In danger of fainting, he gropes for the net, clutching the nearest thing to solid he can find. A whimper escapes his lips.

Lindsey is at his side, "Are you ok?" she asks, real concern etched across her face.

Lazarus uses the webbing to reorient his mind and by strength of will, begins to gain control over his fear. "Yes, I'm fine," he says gripping the net with both hands, concentrating on its fine weave. "Just give me a minute. I wasn't ready for this view!" Slowly he brings his body under control, letting his brain acclimate to the incredible vista that is Heavens Gate.

Glancing at Lindsey, "You did that on purpose," he accuses her.

Nodding, "You're right. I wanted to see how you handle yourself."

"How'd I do?"

Lindsey smiles, sensing his vital signs already returning to normal, impressed by the control her newest friend displayed. "Passed with flying colors!" Perhaps he has the right stuff.

It doesn't take Lazarus long to realize the video in the online magazine didn't do Heavens Gate justice. The stations central volume is open with one end dominated by the sun and the other capped like a gigantic tin can. The interior buildings vary in height and extend inward from the walls creating a jumbled uneven surface on the inside of the massive cylinder. Courtyards form deep wells of light and shadow while the flat sections seem to be covered in vid projections, sometimes working together to form a single enormous picture inside the cylinder, other times they are a chaotic tangle of independent images. The entrances to the various establishments are well marked by signs of every color, shape and orientation, blinking and pulsing to their own rhythm, advertising the many splendid things available inside to the fortunate traveler.

Webbing, similar to what he and Lindsey are using, stretches within the volume at strategic locations and at different angles, from points all along the periphery, never intruding far into the central open space. Several more stretch from one end of the station to the other, also staying close to the buildings. The webbing ripples and pulses with reflections from the surrounding lights and videos projections, giving the illusion of motion.

But the heart of the station is completely unobstructed, reserved for winged flight. The entire center of the massive cylinder is clear air at just below Earth-normal sea-level pressure. To fly, all one needs is a pair of aerodynamically sound wings strapped to their arms. It seems as if everyone has a different design. There are wings in every color and style. Sizes ranging from the length of a man's arm to four or five times that. Some are made of fabric, others with artificial feathers, and still more are plastic. Some are utilitarian strap on wings while others are full costumes incorporating a theme, birds, dragons, insects and even pterodactyls readily apparent.

The flyers seem to be everywhere, soaring to and fro. The large eagle-like wings are the fastest. About ten of them in tight formation are on an oval path the length of the station, their speed astounding and the ability to swoop into a turn thrilling to watch. Lazarus can hear their wings stroke the air and feel its breath on his cheek as they pass just a few feet from them.

But nearly everyone uses smaller more maneuverable wings. With these, a person can dart about like a hummingbird. Many are designed to fold against the body to reduce drag when not being used for thrust. Out in the center, a group using these wings is playing a game of Freeball, twisting and cavorting around a huge sphere, bigger than any two people in height, each team working to push it past a goal.

The flyers wear visors of one style or another, combining the freedom of flight with the infinite potential of virtual reality's three dimensional graphics.

The atmosphere inside the station reminds Lazarus of a bustling ice rink or even better, a busy Colorado ski resort. People come here to play and have brought every gadget and device they could dream up to help them do it. Mankind had finally found a way to fly and is enjoying every minute.

The buzz of voices and squeals of laughter fill Heavens Gate, reverberating off the many angles in this strange zero-G Aspen in space. Lazarus can't help but grin, amazed at the ingenuity he is seeing, caught up in the party atmosphere.

"Is that the sun?" Lazarus asks averting his eyes from the brightness at the far end that lights up the interior of the space station like a giant floodlight.

"Mirrors reflect sunlight into the station. That end is actually pointing away from the sun," she responds.

"Incredible! This is better than Las Vegas!" Lazarus exclaims in amazement.

"I wouldn't know, never been there," Lindsey says grinning. She finds it strangely compelling watching Lazarus stumble forward in his run to freedom. It's like watching a baby take their first step, or say their first word. She can see why Lunarians enjoy sponsoring immigrants, its very satisfying helping another in their pursuit of happiness. But that is not the only reason she is doing it. Lindsey senses more to this particular citizen than meets the eye. Not everyone has the ability to bump a paying passenger off a spaceflight and Lazarus did it casually. Until she knows the whole story, Lazarus is her new pet project.

"Uh huh…" Lazarus stammers gazing in wonder at the vibrant scene, delighting in the shifting images and complex panorama, his fear nearly forgotten.

Moving slowly forward once again, the pair comes up on one of the lengthwise web corridors. "Let's stop here," Lindsey says grabbing the net and letting her legs swing around, hooking a foot and gracefully coming to a stop.

Lazarus imitates her as best he can but his foot slips through the webbing. Luckily, his other foot doesn't. He rebounds slightly and has to stop himself from going back the way they had come. Mastering freefall is not going to happen in the few hours he will experience it on this trip.

She removes her visor and slides it into her pocket careful to fasten the Velcro restraining strap. "Don't worry about freefall, just stick with me and you'll be fine. But the first thing we need to do is get you a real visor. That TV screen you call a headset runs on vacuum tubes, doesn't it?" she asks not expecting an answer. Pointing she says, "We can get a visor there. Let's enjoy the view along the way, shall we?"

Lazarus smiles back, "Sounds good to me."

Lindsey's beauty strikes him yet again, the shape of her lips, her fine complexion, and the shimmering black hair held in check by the blue scarf. And when she looks at him with those eyes, his heart skips a beat. He's drawn to her like a fly to honey, something he's unaccustomed to feeling. But he's cautious sailing in unfamiliar waters and fearing he may be misinterpreting her signals. After all, fornication is a serious offense within the Federation, instilled into its citizens from a very early age. He would never be so bold as to make sexual advances. Yet he enjoys the moment in all its complexity.

The two push off together at about the speed of a fast walk back in Phoenix. Lazarus, still smiling, spreads his arms like a victorious prize fighter, joyous in his newfound freedom, his fear of falling almost fully submerged.

"Nice to see you relax and enjoy yourself," Lindsey says as she reaches out and pulls him to her, holding him tight with one arm around his waist. He drops his arm about her shoulders just as she weaves her leg past his crotch and hooks her toes on his ankle. The two sail Heavens Gate as one. Like dancers on a stage, Lindsey leads and Lazarus follows, only just beginning to appreciate the intricate waltz of freefall.

"Relax and let me pilot." Lindsey says right before she grabs the webbing abruptly changing their trajectory, sending them soaring across free space toward the small shop she had indicated.

Lazarus shuts his eyes briefly feeling his stomach churn but quickly regains control. Lindsey swings her free leg making them rotate with just enough angular velocity to be facing backward when they hit the webbing.

She giggles as he gropes for a hand hold. "Relax," she repeats using the rebound to swing them through the circular front door.

Inside is a world of accessories, most of which Lazarus couldn't name. Wings of every shape and size flutter from one wall, racks seem to hover in mid air filled with merchandise that Lazarus doesn't recognize. His eyes seek out those things he's familiar with, clothing in one section and another devoted to PMU's, some as large as a scooter.

"Greetings. Can I help you find something," a disembodied female voice asks softly.

"Greetings. Yes, we need a visor. Nothing elaborate, just something solid for a new immigrant." Lindsey responds.

The lights flicker and dance around a nearby rack. "We keep an assortment of visors here," the velvety voice says.

"Thank you..." Lindsey guides Lazarus to the rack before releasing her hold on him. Looking over the selection she picks up a silver and black model. "Here, try this on." She hands it to him.

Lazarus takes the device and fits it over his eyes, maneuvering the flexible earpieces over the tops of his ears, around the pinna, and deep into his ear canals. It feels wrong, putting pressure at the most peculiar places inside his ears and against his face.

"The Razors come with a free fitting," the voice observes softly.

"Of course. How much?" Lindsey asks.

"Our basic Model CS130 is $2149.99," the silken voice responds. "But we can also provide you with a CS190 for $8949.99 or a CS160 for $5749.99. Both the CS160 and CS190 cover the standard spectrum. The CS190 uses an Archstone interface."

"Let's go with the CS160," Lindsey responds without hesitation.

Lazarus is stunned. That's a huge chunk of his cash.

"Charge it to my account," Lindsey says.

"No!" Lazarus blurts out, "I can pay for it myself," he says a little more calmly. He pulls his money out of his pocket.

"Put that away. You don't pay until the fitting is complete," Lindsey says amused.

"Are you sure I need a visor?" Lazarus asks.

"Trust me on this, you do!" she replies.

The fitting is over in less than a minute and the modifications to the device only slightly longer, not enough time to really look around. His new visor emerges from the depths of the display case. He picks it up, sliding it smoothly into place. The Razor molds itself to his face enclosing his eyes completely, creating an almost perfect blindfold, and the audio inserts fit comfortably into his ear canals blocking all sound. Yet, Lazarus can still clearly see the store and hear Lindsey.

"How does that feel?" she asks.

"Fine," Lazarus responds. He isn't thinking about the clarity of the image or the comfort of the fit. He is still coming to grips with the fact that he just spent more than half his funds. He's oblivious to the technology he uses so casually, unaware and uncaring that his new visor's sophisticated visual sensors provide live video of his surrounding to microlasers which irradiate this data directly onto his retina. Marvels of solid-state electronics, these coherent light producing nano-machines are suspended within a thin film deposited on the inside of the visor in front of each eye, forming a grid containing over a quarter million tiny lasers.

He's clueless about the visual sensors built into his visor, the end result of 175 years of progress in optics and solid-state electronics. Smaller than a grain of rice, these micro-miniaturized digital camera systems are shapechangers. That is, these tiny marvels maintain focus by physically expanding or contracting depending on the applied voltage, adjusting not only the focal length of the miniature telescope, but the size and shape of the optics inside. Using the same piezoelectric property, the device changes the shape of each miniscule lens, adjusting the convex-concave configuration as needed to keep an image focused on the electromagnetic receptor grid at its base. Lazarus is unaware that he can now see the electromagnetic spectrum from the infrared through visible light and beyond to ultraviolet if he wished, or link to another visor or any public sensor, or any of the more than two thousand other features accessible from his new toy. But he is aware of the young lady suddenly standing next to him.

"Oh!" he turns awkwardly to face her. "Who are you?"

"My name is Helen. I am serving you today." It's the soft spoken voice. Only now she has a face with smooth regular features, a head shaven clean of all hair, and clothes fashioned for comfort and utility. The woman is totally non-threatening and helpful, the perfect combination for a salesperson.

Lindsey smiles and puts on her visor, "That's better! You're one step closer to becoming Lunarian!"

Lazarus retrieves his change from the dispenser and looks at Lindsey. "Didn't you just put on your visor?" he exclaims.

She chuckles, "I did! The reason you don't see it is that internal sensors pick up my facial expressions and broadcasts this information to other visors, including yours. Your visor simply overlays your live feed with my transmission, effectively making my visor disappear. There isn't any magic here, just a simple set of graphic calculations performed at mind-boggling speeds…" She senses she has lost him.

Lazarus swallows hard, "This is better than anything available in the Federation."

"Better than anything on Earth," Lindsey corrects him, "even the Chinese."

"It's not perfect, though. I can still see your visor when you move your head around."

"That's done on purpose. It lets you see who is wearing visors and who isn't." Lindsey turns her head side to side causing a ghostly outline of her visor to fade in and out. "Don't worry, in a few days you won't even notice. Right now it's much more important for you to become familiar with using the Lunarian virtual control panel. If you'll allow me, I'll link to your visor and demonstrate."

"By all means, show me," he says.

Lindsey chuckles, "This is demo mode," she says. "It duplicates your visor settings in mine and gives me control of both."

Looking down he sees Lindsey's hands where his should be. Watching her, he immediately realizes that her hand gestures are mirrored by the movement in front of him. In the virtual world, her hands and arms have taken control of his visor and he has become a spectator. She gives him a moment to get used to the idea.

"Ok, the first thing to learn is to turn the control panel on and off. Observe."

Lazarus watches as she rolls her hand counterclockwise in a graceful twisting action. Suddenly a ring of 2D pictographic icons appear about his waist, flat like they are lying on a table. She repeats the movement and the icons vanish. "Now you try it," she says.

Lazarus brings his hand in front of him and emulates her motion. The icons reappear.

"The icons you use most frequently are arrayed to your front. All you need to do is look at one and move your hand down. Subtle hand movements will do. No need to go swinging wildly about," she grins. "Or you can touch the icon if you want. That works too… The pictograph of the satellite is your internet portal. Right beside that are the search engine, visor settings and link monitor icons."

"What's a link monitor?" Lazarus asks.

"It shows you how many citizens are linked to your visor," she answers.

"It's a number two. Does that mean there are two other people linked to my visor right now?" Lazarus asks without understanding.

"Sort of… It's you and me. Look, there are over two hundred icons and we have a long flight ahead of us. Let's study the ones you find interesting then." Lindsey says.

"Great idea," Lazarus says nodding. "This is similar to what I've used. I should be able to catch on quickly." What he doesn't elaborate upon is his amazement at the clarity of the graphics or the speed at which they are manipulated. After only a few seconds, he appreciates his new visors total control of sight and sound.

Lindsey files that away with the other information. Not every Federation citizen is allowed to use the internet.

"Let's go then," she takes his arm and loops her leg with his, skillfully pushing them off, sending them soaring gracefully across the shop and through the entrance portal.

If he would notice, the interior of the station looks different now. The most obvious is that he would no longer see any of the visors on the people around him. And the advertisements strewn across the interior of Heavens Gate are more distinct, their sounds clearer, and their colors sharper, but only if he would take the time to look at them. In the same way, distances shrink. He can now make out the eagle flyers even at the far end of the station, but only if he stares. The fact is, he has forgotten he is wearing a visor, so perfectly does it meld to his face and ears while supplying him with a flawless reproduction of his physical surroundings. But exploring this marvelous device will come later. Right now all he can think about is Lindsey.

"I will never in a hundred years be able to repay your kindness," Lazarus says hoarsely, intensely aware of her tit pressing against his side and her hip wedged against his bulging crotch. He is having thoughts and desires that hadn't surfaced since Rachel.

"You're not in my debt. You don't owe me anything. I did what any thinking and compassionate Lunarian would have done. I helped someone who needed help," she says softly, her leg expertly putting pressure in the most delightful of places.

"Do you know what you are doing to me?" Lazarus asks softly, losing his inhibitions as if he were shedding a heavy burden, long suppressed desires pushing them roughly aside. Millions of years of evolution flood his brain with the chemicals of sex. He is acuity aware of her body intertwined with his.

Bating her long eyelashes and knowing full well the turmoil she is creating, "Oh… I have a pretty good idea," she purrs.

Lazarus looks outward at the spectacle of people flying, trying and failing to use them as objects of distraction. "Lindsey!" is all he manages to say.

Pointing at the casino hotel, Heavens Crib blazoned in colorful displays across its front facade, its huge entrance revealing crowds of people inside playing slots and freefall craps. "I stayed there my first trip up, had some time to kill waiting for my ride." Looking impishly at Lazarus, "That's when I joined the club!"

"Joined what club?" Lazarus asks hoarsely, his brain frying under her constant administrations. He has problems focusing on her words.

"Freefall sex, silly! There's nothing that compares with it in Earth's gravity!" Lindsey smiles, her gray eyes limpid pools of sexual attraction inviting him to dive in. "Why do you think this place is so popular? It's not the food!" she adds in a low husky feminine voice, her breath hot on his cheek, her body pressed against his.

He pushes back. Sexual energy from the hard spike between his legs surges through him, pounding against his brain like a hurricane lashing the Florida coastline. He can stand it no longer, Lazarus pulls Lindsey into a full embrace letting his lips engulf hers, forgetting where they are in the heat of the moment. Her arms encircle his neck and legs wrap his waist, focusing even more pressure on all the right places. His blood boils, matched perfectly by the furnace burning inside of Lindsey.

From somewhere in the vastness of Heavens Gate a voice calls out, "Get a room!"

Breaking the kiss and gasping, "I'll take that as a yes!" Lindsey reaches out and grabs the webbing, expertly swinging them towards the Crib's front entrance without even slowing down. She will take enthusiasm over experience any day!

****

The Data Acquisition and Control Center (DACC) of the FBS Yorktown is long and narrow, it's lighting dim and shadowy. Six variable-G hammocks, each cradling a pair of massive titanium rings, are mounted down the middle of the room. The rings allow the ships onboard artificial intelligence to optimally position the officers cocooned inside to withstand accelerations in any direction. Strapped into the hammocks, wearing standard deep blue NAF Naval vacsuits, are the DACC officers currently in command of the battlestation. The virtual reality designed into their helmets bulge over their eyes giving the scene a strange bug-eyed monster flavor, like futuristic fly's trapped in a giant spider web. Used primarily as backups, consoles run the length of the room and various medical and system support LCD's cover every surface within the DACC. Beyond the six officers, a single non-suited man, dressed in the blue uniform of the NAF, floats quietly in front of a softly glowing workstation, his feet tucked firmly under Velcro strips.

With a simple motion of his hand Lieutenant Gilmore retrieves the visual information available on the spacecraft just leaving low earth orbit (LEO) and does a preliminary check on its registered flight plan. "Sir, I have an outbound freighter. Request permission to interrogate," he says to the watch commander.

"Proceed Lieutenant," Admiral DyGoon replies. The admiral likes DACC duty. It keeps him in touch with the inner workings of the vast battlestation and her place in orbital space within the fleet.

"Aye Sir!"

The Lieutenant initiates a very tightly encrypted communication laser which daisy-chains through a constellation of seven forward observation satellites, none bigger than a briefcase. The minisat closest to the freighter sweeps powerful MRI beams over the spacecraft, the equivalent of a sonar ping in Earth's oceans. The returns that pour in from other nearby minisats and the battlestations own sensors are processed by powerful computers onboard the Yorktown resulting in detailed information concerning the manifest, passengers and even the condition of the freighter itself. The entire exercise requires less than thirty seconds.

"Nothing unusual to report, Admiral. Standard heavy-lift freighter, cargo is mining equipment and foodstuffs. Destination is Cullman, Luna. Only the pilot aboard, no passengers."

"Where, pray tell, is Cullman?" the Admiral asks.

The Lieutenant pauses while performing a quick search, "A small outpost in Herschel crater, at the northern edge of the Four Craters Region."

"Very well, Lieutenant, carry on."

The Admiral is much more interested in finding the Shenyang, China's newest Bayonet class battlestation. They have been playing a high stakes game of cat and mouse for over a week, each battlestation trying to maneuver her minisats to find and maintain track on the other. Freighters half an orbit away doesn't merit more than a few seconds of the Admiral's valuable time. Evolution's Child continues uneventfully on her low energy flight path to Luna, scheduled for moonfall in three days.

"The idea of God was not a lie but a device of the unconscious which needed to be decoded by psychology. A personal god was nothing more than an exalted father-figure: desire for such a deity sprang from infantile yearnings for a powerful, protective father, for justice and fairness and for life to go on forever. God is simply a projection of these desires, feared and worshipped by human beings out of an abiding sense of helplessness. Religion belonged to the infancy of the human race; it had been a necessary stage in the transition from childhood to maturity. It had promoted ethical values which were essential to society. Now that humanity has come of age, however, it should be left behind."
Sigmund Freud (1856-1939)

Lunar Transit

Few other passengers are evident as they approach their gate. Lindsey has Lazarus in the now familiar lovers lock and doesn't appear willing to disengage any time soon. Not that he wants her too. In fact, he can't remember the last time he felt so good. Having discarded the weight of a lifetime of deception and denial, he vows to be worthy of this woman. For the first time in his life he feels truly free, like a hawk riding desert thermals a thousand feet above the desert floor.

Even though Lazarus had managed to keep up with Lindsey, he knows it would take months before he could hope to match her skill in freefall. He marvels again at the grace and prowess this remarkable woman demonstrated over the last few hours. He will always remember her face floating above him, framed by coal black hair set free like a modern day Medusa, legs wrapped tightly around him, breasts rippling pleasantly with her every thrust, those gray eyes boring into his as she brought them to a simultaneous climax. He grins, feeling a stirring in his groin.

Lindsey glances at him, "If you keep that up, people will think you're crazy."

"Maybe I am, just a little," Lazarus says his smile fading, his passion tempered with a degree of guilt about making love outside of marriage, an echo of past lessons driven home by unremitting repetition that sex is something dirty, to be performed in the dark of night for the sole purpose of procreation and is a sin in any other circumstance. Certainly not just for fun! Sex is a serious activity for a specific purpose within a marriage and should not be perverted by making it cheap entertainment. At least that is what the Church hammered into every citizen, including Lazarus, starting from infancy, abstinence the battle cry against an evolutionary drive millions of years in the making.

Lindsey tilts her head inquisitively at Lazarus, "You come from a world of lies and illusion. It's all right to be a little crazy. Just don't go overboard with it." She senses the change in his demeanor, a touch of remorse and self-reproach. It's filed away as something to deal with later.

Lazarus is aware of the fallacy of abstinence, privileged by virtue of his position within Homeland Security to have access to Church records all across America. As a young Assistant Analyst, he compiled the number of marriages involving women under the age of eighteen. From there, it was a simple matter to cross reference childbirth in these marriages, finding virtually all of them giving birth seven to eight months later. In practically all cases the child was classified as premature with no complications. The Federation's official position of zero teen pregnancies among the Christian majority is grossly in error. Instead, he determined that two out of every seven girls become pregnant before their eighteenth birthday, resulting in arranged marriages with no hope of divorce under the current system of laws.

This is just one of many such factual anomalies he came across in his career that made him conclude that contrary data is purposefully kept fragmented and studies that would pull it together are routinely suppressed by the Federation. He never bothered his superiors with his findings. Instead he filed them away within his own mind and deleted any real records, self preservation the great decider. But such knowledge is corrosive and became a major factor in his decision to flee his country. He just couldn't, or wouldn't, play the game any longer.

Lindsey maneuvers them towards an apparent hole in the skin of the station, its diameter at least twice her height. Several people float out of it just as they come to a stop at its edge.

"Are you ready?" she asks.

Lazarus nods and Lindsey guides them into the hole, down a short tunnel to emerge outside the hull of Heavens Gate. They seem to be suspended with nothing separating them from the vacuum of space. Lazarus grits his teeth keeping an iron grip on his fear, sliding his free hand over his short cropped hair, concentrating on the shuttle less than a hundred feet in front of them. He struggles with his phobia finding it easier to maintain control rather than regain control. Being prepared for the experience certainly helps but it's more likely due to the fact that Lindsey is gripping his arm and he would rather die than look weak or frail in front of her.

Dominating the scene, the translunar shuttle rests edge on at the end of one of the stations many appendages, a squat disk with a tangle of struts, tanks, and tubing peeking out from below. Small free-flying robots scurry about the vessel completing final inspection and detaching lines and hoses. These quickly snake back into the station, not leaving anything to flap around during the coming departure.

He shifts his gaze to the incredible beauty of the stars that frame the shuttle, each a vivid dot of light without any twinkle and even the dimmer ones shine true in untold millions creating a luminescent fog marking the center of our galaxy. At his back, the immense curving expanse of Heavens Gate seems so tiny when compared to the vastness of the cosmos.

"You handled that nicely," Lindsey says, impressed with the mental toughness and tenacity she senses within him.

"Thank you... The stars are truly magnificent!" he hasn't yet realized his visor is bringing everything he looks at more sharply into focus. Lazarus reaches out, banging his hand into the invisible material of the portal. "What is this?"

"Duraglass, a fully-transparent non-reflective ceramic," she answers.

"This would be considered magic by our ancestors," he says.

"It's more likely they would mutter some unintelligible mumbo jumbo and start a new religion. Our ancestors were very inventive when explaining things outside their knowledge."

Lazarus finds her criticism strangely disturbing, "Yes, I suppose you're right. I'm just not used to hearing religion ridiculed so openly."

She looks sharply at him, "I am not ridiculing the need for ignorant savages to believe in gods. But I am ridiculing modern humans for believing in those same gods in the face of real answers."

"I didn't say I don't agree with you. It will take a little time for me to adjust to things being discussed so… freely," he responds.

It didn't take you long to set aside the Federation's sexual code of ethics… but she doesn't say that. Instead she says, "I know that Lunarian society is quite different from the Federation... Are you sure you want to go through with it? There is still time to go back." The question hangs between them.

Lazarus swallows and turns his gaze back to the stars, drinking in their beauty, not feeling the least bit of space sickness and his fear of falling completely absent. He's satisfied and whole for the first time in years. "This is where I belong, I can feel it in my bones," he responds.

"Well then, you better prepare for some rather radical changes in your life." She pulls at his arm, "Listen to me."

They embrace and she wraps her legs around him.

"When things pile up on you I want you to remember that you can always come to me… We might even talk once in a while," she purrs seductively, rubbing the tip of her nose on his.

Gazing into those remarkable gray orbs, he finds that he is not alone anymore. Oddly, this releases a sense of humor, "Did you know that the ancient Greeks believed those stars were milk spilled from the tits of the Greek god Hera. The story goes that Zeus, the king of the gods, tricked Hera into nursing Heracles whom she didn't like. Discovering who he was, she pulled him from her breast, and a spurt of her milk formed the smear across the sky that we still call the Milky Way."

Lindsey chuckles, "In fact, I have heard the story, but where did you learn of it?"

Before he can answer, their conversation is interrupted by a lazy drawl from behind them. "That's gotta be most godfors'ken ship ever kludged together. A Winnebaga with a thruster up its tailpipe," says the voice.

Lazarus and Lindsey break their embrace to confront the newcomer. Hovering at the mouth of the observation portals access tunnel is an old man dressed conservatively in a dark gray jumpsuit. His close-cropped white hair surrounds the gleaming dome of his bald head. A bushy white mustache hangs in a sweeping arch below his nose almost hiding his mouth and extending down his jowls past his chin. The leathery skin is covered in wrinkles and tanned dark by a blazing sun. He's without doubt, the oldest individual Lazarus has seen since boarding the Stratoliner back in Athens. But there is no missing the lively twinkle in his eyes or the emotion that animates his face with an incredible range of expression. This old man loves life.

"I hesitate to ask what a Winnebaga is. But I assure you, this ship is well designed for what she does. What more do you want?" Lindsey responds giving the old man a smile, "Where you see a collection of hardware, I see the fruit of many hours of dedicated labor. There is not one unneeded pound in her design. There's beauty in simplicity."

"Humph," the old man snorts, "What's'zit you engineering types call it, the KISS principle? Keep It Simple Stupid? Yes….Well… Nutin' beats travlin' first class, if you ask me."

"The shuttle isn't bad. Maybe a little crowded but we'll be comfortable. Besides," Lindsey continues, "unless you are some big corporate weenie with keys to the company yacht, this is the only way to get to Aldrin. Why waste your breath on something you can't change?"

Huffing like an old male lion on the plains of Serengeti, the old man chuckles dryly, "Darlin' I' been do'in that ma whole life… but you'r right, why waste energy. It's a freighter and we're the freight… Name is Isaac Crenshaw but you young'ens can call me Izzy," he says nodding in the customary Lunarian greeting.

"Lindsey Davenport," she responds with a nod in return.

"Lazarus Sheffield," he extends his hand. The wrinkles on the old mans forehead deepen into fleshy canyons even as he accepts the gesture. Lazarus immediately starts to pump sending them all into motion. By necessity, handshakes are different in freefall where one simply grasps, squeezes and releases, without actually shaking the other persons hand. That is, if it's done at all.

"Whoa!" Isaac exclaims with another deep throated chuckle, stabilizing himself with hands and feet.

Lindsey laughs magnifying his blunder.

"Sorry," Lazarus mutters with embarrassment.

"Its 'aw right. No 'arm done. So where you folks headed?" Izzy asks as things settle down. "Don't tell me, let me guess, y'all are immigratin'?"

"I've been a citizen for many years. I'm going home," Lindsey says.

"How 'bout you?" Izzy asks Lazarus, picking up on the body language of these two people like an open book.

Lazarus feels Lindsey hug him tighter, snuggling up against his side, waiting for him to respond. But in his world a person doesn't willingly reveal truth to anyone, let alone strangers. He hesitates, shrugs and says, "I'm waiting to see how the story ends."

"Ain't we all?" Izzy laughs. "What 'bout you sugar, what freehold stakes claim on you?" Izzy asks bluntly, not bothered in the least that these two are not a couple, even though they certainly act like one. Maybe they just didn't realize it yet. It happens.

"Dakota," she replies finding the old gentleman charming in a rustic sort of way.

"Fine freehold… solid traditions…" Izzy says nodding approvingly. His eyes gleam mischievously, "Hell, y'all ain't gonna believe this but Abby and I go way back." A chuckle erupts from deep in his belly and his eyes glaze over as they stare into the past. Jerking back to present, the old man laughs again and slaps Lazarus hard on the shoulder forcing Lindsey to steady them against the Duraglass, "Hell boy, who'd furget ol' Izzy?"

The flight announcement interrupts the conversation, "Passengers are now free to board Trans World Flight L95 bound for Aldrin Station, Luna." The three of them float up and out of the portal and head for the gate, joining the gathering throng entering the boarding tunnel. MRI scanners sweep over them, identifying who they are and where they are going, looking for anything out of the ordinary or out of place.

At the end of the tunnel waits a rather petite fight attendant, "Welcome aboard," she says hovering effortlessly just outside the shuttles airlock door. She is wearing a Trans World fight uniform consisting of loose grey slacks and a white blouse with TWS monogrammed across the left pocket. Her light brown hair is cut short in what Lazarus is quickly concluding is the popular style. After glancing down at something projected within her visor only she can see, she looks back up at Lazarus and smiles, "Mr. Sheffield, you are in row twenty-nine, seat A. To your right and six rows down. It's the window seat." Looking at Lindsey she adds, "Miss Davenport, you are also in row twenty-nine, seat B, right next to Mr. Sheffield." She's one of those individuals whose cheerful exuberance polarizes the people she meets into either like or dislike, with very little middle ground.

Looking around the interior of the shuttle Lazarus feels he's entering the proverbial padded cell, only much larger. Every surface is upholstered like a vintage hotrod. From the entrance, the room curves away in a large circular space, the far side partially hidden behind a smaller enclosed room in its geometric center. Seating is arranged radially like spokes in a wheel. The ceiling is high and curved like a dome seen from the inside. Dim lighting, just enough to see by, gives the interior a somber serious feel.

Many of the windows, evenly spaced along the outer wall, have simple shades drawn down over them. The few that are open look like holes cut into the side of the spacecraft because of the lack of any reflections from their surface.

The shuttles central room is split down the middle by a well lit passageway going all the way through, one side containing the lavatories and the other the galley. Microwave ovens, food storage cabinets and emergency supplies, including light-weight survival bubbles, line both sides of the passageway. The two seats reserved for the crew are tucked out of the way, one at each end with an unobstructed view of half of the cabins interior.

Floating above the aisle, Lindsey expertly maneuvers them through the shuttle looking for row twenty-nine, making for the seats closest to the outer hull, next to the window. She pushes Lazarus playfully into his seat, taking the one next to him. Lazarus finds it much easier this time to adjust and buckle the harness and then moves to help Lindsey adjust hers, but only succeeds in making her nipples hard under the blue blouse.

"Thank you, kind sir. I couldn't have done it without you!" she says playfully.

"My pleasure," Lazarus responds softly. He pushes aside all thought of sinfulness, telling himself that something that makes him feel this good can't be bad. But it still nags at him.

Isaac installs himself in the seat next to Lindsey and a middle aged lady wearing a pastel purple sweater eases into the seat just beyond him, right next to an interior brace, also well padded, running from floor to ceiling. Three more seats on the other side of the column complete row twenty-nine.

The seats are wide and comfortable, more like Lazarus's over-stuffed recliner back in his apartment, but once in them he finds it impossible to see the people in other rows because of the high seatbacks. The four of them are in their own little world. They listen to the murmur of passengers as they enter the shuttle and settle in, but the sound seems strangely distant, as though apart from them.

The baggage quickly disappears beneath their seats held there by a bungee net. Lazarus experiments with positions, laying back a little and seeing how his feet would tuck under the seat in front and his head extend over the feet of the person behind him. His window faces Heavens Gate and thus, doesn't afford much of a view yet, just a dull featureless gray expanse curving away in all directions. He can see the portal they had been in just a few minutes before, packed with people waiting to see the shuttle depart.

The dark-haired angry young man from the Stratoliner is one of the last to board. He settles into an interior seat one row in front of Lazarus and Lindsey, not giving anyone more than a sullen glance. The man is one of the few Lazarus has seen aboard Heavens Gate that didn't appear to be having a good time. Maybe it was something he ate. Lazarus makes a mental note to keep an eye on him.

The outer airlock door closes with a thump. A few moments later the inner door swings shut with a clunk, the male attendant noisily dogging down the safeties.

From near the shuttles central room the petite blond addresses the passengers. "Good day everyone, on behalf of your crew, let me welcome you aboard Trans World Flight L95. Your attendants on this flight will be Alan and my name is Susan. We will be departing shortly so if your destination isn't Aldrin Station, Luna, now is the time to speak up. We will begin serving a meal as soon as we are underway." The other flight attendant glides through the passageway to the other side. They both proceed to strap into the seats just inside the galley, giving each of them a good view of their side of the passenger cabin.

Lazarus is startled when the acceleration klaxon sounds off, followed quickly by a soft whirring that fills the cabin. A clank and a sharp sideways jolt rocks the shuttle as the station releases it, supplying a little push in the process. Lazarus grips his seat then looks out his window and is amazed to see how far the shuttle has already separated from Heavens Gate. Even as he watches, the station grows smaller. Very gently, almost imperceptibly, the shuttle rotates, taking Heavens Gate out of his line of sight.

A minute after the warning, Lazarus feels a very gentle acceleration push him down into his padded seat. It builds slowly until it reaches one-sixth Earth normal, the same as Luna normal, where it holds steady. A quiet almost imperceptible throbbing accompanies the acceleration. Lazarus isn't sure if he is actually hearing it, more feeling it in the seat of his pants.

"Nice to have a little weight back," Lazarus says with relief.

"You telling me you didn't like freefall?" Lindsey asks lifting her eyebrows inquisitively.

"It has its moments!" Lazarus responds grinning. "Where is the pilot on one of these anyway?" He asks looking down the aisle and past the column at the flight attendant, the only clear route his eyes can take in the confines of the shuttle.

Lindsey says in a bad Mexican accent, "Pilot? We don't need no 'steenking pilot!" she giggles. Seeing the puzzled look on Lazarus's face, "It's a joke from an old vid... Never mind." Putting on a more serious face, "There's no human pilot on a shuttle but I'm sure we have a very good AI."

"Folks don't pilot out here. A computer sits this mustang and we're just 'long for the ride." Izzy adds not unkindly.

"So there's no one onboard who can fly this tin can?" Lazarus asks looking past Lindsey at the old man. His lined sun-weathered face looks like it would be more at home on an Arizona ranch than a shuttle on its way to the moon.

"That's a big affirmative, good buddy. All we have are flight attendants. A pilot would be dead weight, one more payin' customer left behind. Let me tell you, it was a rooster fight to get them to put two flight attendants aboard," The old man rasps, his voice scratchy and well used. "Besides, if somethin' went haywire out here, we'd just sit tight and wait for Luna Control."

"I would appreciate it if you didn't discuss all the things that could go wrong," says the lady on Izzy's far side.

"Humph," Izzy grouses, "I'm Izzy Crenshaw and these two love birds are Lindsey and Lazarus."

The lady shakes hands with Izzy, who grins indulgently, then leans forward to better see past him, "Mary Stephens. Pleased to meet everyone," she says. Mary looks to be in her mid sixties, perhaps twenty-five or thirty pounds overweight with a round face and dark eyes. Her collar-length brown hair is fashioned in a serviceable square cut contained under a fine fishnet. Conservatively dressed, Mary is obviously out of place aboard the translunar shuttle, like a fish out of water.

Mary continues in an apologetic tone, "I don't mean to be a trouble. It's just that I don't understand a lot and it makes me very nervous to think about what's just outside that window. Better I not think about it."

Lindsey seems the most surprised by the comment, "What you don't know can kill you out here, Mary."

"Oh dear!" Mary says in a panic. "I told Christopher that I shouldn't come!"

"Easy there, Lass!" Izzy reaches out and takes Mary's hand, turning his back to Lindsey, "Where 'xactly you goin? Christopher yur son?"

Mary nods affirmative, "He talked me into coming to see him. Says I will love it. Well, I don't love it!" Her lower lip trembles ever so slightly.

"You ever been in an airplane, Mary?" Izzy asks her.

"Yes, many times. So don't try and tell me it's the same 'cause it ain't. There's air outside the windows of airplanes and I can see the ground!"

"Yur right, space is different," Izzy says rethinking his approach.

"I was raised on Ford Farm. It's a beautiful 14th century farmhouse situated about eight miles east of the city of Plymouth in southwest England. I don't know about all this high technology. I tried to tell him I was too old to make this trip but he wouldn't hear of it… This last summer was bloody horrible... Lost everything and nowhere to go… In my family for generations…"

Mary likes to talk and Izzy doesn't seem to mind, listening patiently, finding her life story remarkably interesting just as he does most everyone's.

Lazarus and Lindsey sit quietly listening to the gentle chatter around them, arms entwined, and shoulders snuggled close, the same position that teens developed a hundred fifty years ago first in drive-ins then in the vid theaters.

Lazarus wonders how many of these passengers would choose to remain at Heavens Gate if they knew what he suspects. He had to admit, even to himself, he only has suspicions, nothing truly solid. In his line of work you seldom get solid verifiable facts. He wishes he could have trusted the Director and the President to come clean with the Lunarians. But they don't even do that with their own citizens.

He mulls over once again the chain of events that has led him to this point. It isn't just one but a series of things that has stripped him of his enthusiasm and belief that he was working on the side of good. He loves his country but hates what it has become. The intolerance, the lies, the hypocrisy, and the greed make it impossible for him to trust anyone. Too often his best efforts had gone unheeded and innocent people left to suffer horrible deaths, only then getting a proper reaction from Homeland Security while the mass media played up the terror angle. The final straw was his superiors choosing to do nothing to warn the Lunarians of impending disaster, a selfish decision that promises dire consequences for millions of people, perhaps the entire world. His face reflects the magnitude of his burden.

"I see the smile is gone," Lindsey says softly, her tone warm and intimate, just between the two of them.

Looking at her, everything that has happened floods back and Lazarus can't help but grin. He squeezes her hand affectionately. "Please excuse me, Lindsey. I was just thinking of the sorry state of affairs back in the Federation."

"Which sorry state is bothering you?" she asks.

Lazarus looks into Lindsey's shining gray eyes and bows his head breaking eye contact, a frown furrowing his brow.

"What is it?" Lindsey asks again. "Come on, spill it. What's on your mind?"

Lazarus has a brief moment of panic. He isn't quite ready to start talking about the Brotherhood. He searches his mind for something else to say that she will believe. He decides to make it personal and steer away from the political issues.

"As a child I endured long hours of bible study and as an adult the government pounded into me that sex outside of marriage was a major sin. On the church wall behind the pulpit is the biblical passage from Mathew 15. *For out of the heart proceed evil thoughts, murders, adulteries, fornications, thefts, false witness, and blasphemies. These are the things which defile a man.*"

"To equate lying, stealing and killing with sex is ridiculous. You don't actually believe in the death penalty, do you?" Lindsey asks. When he hesitates she adds, "Do you think someone deserves to die for having sex?"

"No, of course not..." Looking up in confusion, he hesitantly asks, "Why…" and can go no further.

Lindsey knows instinctively the unspoken details contained in that most-complicated one word question. "Because you needed it," she says simply, truthfully. "Are you sorry?" she asks, watching his reaction for any signs of regret.

The question hits him like an electric shock. Lazarus looks into her eyes and squeezes her hand almost to the point of hurting her, "Oh my, no! Some how... You hit the nail on the head, Lindsey. I needed to break the mold and you did just that. I feel hope for the first time in ages. No! What you have given me is much more than just sex!"

"Easy tiger. Things are a little different on Luna. Lunarians don't have the same sexual constraints as the Federation. Sex is something that brings us together, not something that separates us." Sensing confusion within Lazarus she adds hastily, "Don't get me wrong. The manner in which a Lunarian conducts their sexual activities is critical. But realistically, there is only one rule. As long as everyone concerned is in agreement then pretty much anything goes."

"Reverend McCarthy claims the Lunarians condone rape, incest, and sodomy. Is he right?" Lazarus asks.

Lindsey knows exactly what he is referring to. During her brief final stay on Earth she had witnessed a blossoming of animosity within the NAF citizenry directed towards the Lunarians. Made to look like factual documentaries, vid shorts exaggerate the cultural differences between the two societies. The worst she had seen utterly vilify the Lunarians, making them out to be ungodly pagans who worship Satan and have sex orgies all the time. The worst of the worst are the twenty-eight McCarthy videos containing the biggest lies, exaggerated and repeated to the point of absurdity. What's more, Lindsey never heard anyone make a serious rebuttal or challenge the weak evidence they put forth as unequivocal proof. The vids had deeply disturbed Lindsey at the time, a feeling that lingers still.

"Rape means at least one party was forced against their will to have sex and incest means at least one partner was too young to make an informed decision. Either situation could result in the Lunarian General Council voting for expurgation. And much of what the good reverend calls incest is the fact that Lunarians don't hide sex from children or fill them with lies. They believe that knowledge is the key to making good choices in ones life, not ignorance or wishful thinking. And education starts in childhood..." Lindsey explains patiently.

Seeing the look of doubt on his face, she changes tack, "Look, Reverend McCarthy is the worst kind of liar, using just enough fact to hook his listeners into believing something hideously wrong! None of his so-called documentaries reflect reality. They are designed to control and manipulate you, not to educate you. No, Lazarus, completely the opposite is true. If a Lunarian commits rape, the person that was raped, as well as the family, friends and associates of both individuals involved, decides the punishment of the person that did the raping, up to and including expurgation. The laws are really quite simple, letting the people most intimately involved have the most say while allowing any citizen to express their opinion. The only hard and fast laws in the Republic define how evidence is collected, analyzed and preserved. Everything else is flexible, decided by interested citizens on a case by case basis in open court. It's the same for murder, theft, and fraud. Literally any action taken by one party that causes harm to another can be adjudicated before the General Council." Lindsey says.

"What is expurgation?" he asks, unfamiliar with the term.

Lindsey pauses and takes the plunge, "It's the total wiping of a persons memory. They must learn to walk and talk all over again. But this penalty is given for only the most heinous crimes. The last time was almost ten years ago."

He's surprised that he hadn't heard of this before. Perhaps the Federation is completely unaware that the Lunarians have this capability. Well, he certainly isn't going to be the one to tell them.

"So someone could get… expurgated… for stealing? That seems a little harsh!" Lazarus says.

"Does it?" Lindsey responds, "Expurgation requires a supermajority. If that many fellow citizens think you need a total head job, then just maybe you're not a very nice person."

"What about homosexuality? Others besides McCarthy speak of the promiscuousness of the Lunarians," Lazarus points out. "Leviticus 20 verse 13; *If a man also lie with mankind, as he lieth with a woman, both of them have committed an abomination: they shall surely be put to death; their blood shall be upon them.*"

"Again I ask you, do you think someone deserves to die for having sex?" Lindsey replies.

"No!"

"Then how about for blasphemy or speaking ill of the Church?" she presses. "Does someone deserve to die for not believing in the ridiculous ideas underlying Christianity?"

"No! Absolutely not!"

"Then you must tell me how a man raised in the heart of the Federation can be so liberal minded. I thought they would have squished any semblance of freethought from you long ago?"

Lazarus sighs and lays his head back, maintaining his gaze into her remarkable gray eyes. He finds it strangely exciting to talk with someone so openly of things he never before dared to discuss. He starts slow but quickly warms to telling his story.

"You're right, I read the bible every day from kindergarten through college graduation, whether I wanted to or not. I know well the bizarre and strange tales that form the foundation of Christianity, the creation story of Adam and Eve, Noah's Ark, Moses, the Passover and many others. As a young man, I found the more I studied the bible, the more confused and revolted I became. I also learned that my teachers didn't like answering questions, not the hard ones anyway. Even as a youngster, I found their answers vague and non-satisfying. It was when I pushed for better ones that my true education began."

"I was in third grade when I persistently asked my teacher why God put the tree of knowledge in the middle of the Garden of Eden if He didn't want Adam and Eve to find it. Was God laying a trap for them? Granted, I disrupted the classroom with my unwavering insistence on attaining a reasonable answer, but I really wanted to know. Didn't God realize they would head straight for it once He told them not to? That incident landed me a months worth of remedial classes after school…" he sighs, "Later that same year I asked the schools spiritual advisor why God killed so many innocent people during the Passover. Why didn't God cut out the middleman and just appear before the Egyptian pharaoh instead of killing the oldest sibling in every family that didn't smear lambs blood on their front door. And why did God make it rain frogs? None of it made any sense to me. I was positive that an all-powerful God could have made it perfectly clear to the Pharaoh what He wanted without the need for the ten Egyptian plagues or anybody dying. Well… they didn't see it that way."

"This time my tenacity earned me a trip to the headpaster's office where I waited while mom and dad were called down to the school. Mom didn't say anything during the entire meeting, simply sat there and stared at me. Total guilt trip! But dad was obviously angry from the moment he walked through the door. Only later did I learn that he was forced to forfeit a day's wage to the school board. For my part, I received a week's suspension, another month in remedial training and two hundred hours of community service under the direct supervision of Pastor Marsh, the history instructor at my school. Needless to say, I learned my lesson…"

"But that doesn't explain how you know of Greek mythology and your attitude towards religion… Tell me about this true education you received." Lindsey says.

"It began that evening when my dad came home from work. My first lesson was all about the mechanics of deception and misdirection. I learned very quickly not to openly question the authority of the Church but to simply say the right things and do as asked. A few months later, when I was ready, dad showed me the secret hide-a-way in the floor of the family's tool shed and explained its use. It wasn't elaborate, nothing more than a few loose floor boards with a shoebox space below. But through it passed treasure more precious than gold, as far as I was concerned. Books!"

"Books? You mean hardcover paper bound books?" she asks.

"Yes! But not just any books, outlawed books! If I were caught with them…Well, let's just say I would be in some serious trouble."

"So your father put books in this hole?" Lindsey asks. She can sense he is telling her the truth, but it's so bizarre.

"I don't know if it was ever him personally." Lazarus shakes his head, "All I do know for sure is that a different set of books would miraculously appear within days after I finished the last."

"How would they, whoever they are, know when you were done with them? Or what books should be next?" she asks in wonder.

"I left questions, sometimes several pages of hand written questions. The books that answered them were never far behind. A few weeks at most…I read constantly in the confines of that little shed, consuming everything that was placed under the boards. Some I even read twice. It was the single most precious gift that Thomas Oliver Sheffield ever gave to me, and it continued long after he was gone. I never did find out who or even when the books were exchanged. Better I not know than try to hold back the secret if caught."

Thomas Oliver Sheffield is his father, a name that she can google later. But for now she wants to know more about his unusual education, "What authors can you remember?" she asks.

"Oh let's see… There was Twain, Stevenson, Paine, Ingersoll, Plato, Kafka, Bruno, Thoreau, Melville, Darwin, Einstein, Aristotle, Homer, Defoe, Keats, Mann, Steinbeck, Hemingway, Rand, Dickens, Vonnegut, Woolf, Orwell, Jefferson, Faulkner, Fitzgerald, Shakespeare, Asimov, Hawking, Shelly, Lee, Kipling, Sinclair, Machiavelli, Odegaard, Poe, Rousseau, Johanson, Sagan, Wells, and Heinlein. There were more, many more, too many to count. But in each new set of books was always at least one textbook, well worn and highlighted. I studied astronomy, physics, biology, human psychology and of course, religion. These proved harder to understand yet even more exciting, their contents giving me answers to questions I didn't even know existed before reading them. The more I learned the greater became my appreciation of just how much there is to know. Over time I was able to find more substantial reasons for my childhood skepticism of church dogma, even if I had to keep it to myself. It was enough to know the truth, or at least as much as was available to me."

"Remarkable!" Lindsey says, "Tell me more about your father. Where did he go?"

Lazarus sits quietly for almost a minute, "He died when I was ten," he finally says, "KIA… killed in action. I really don't know any more than that. And believe me, I've tried. I could find nothing in the official records beyond a posthumous medal he received declaring him a Hero of the State. Everything surrounding his death was marked as Top Secret and I didn't need to know."

Another piece of useful information, "I'm sorry for your loss. It must have been hard. Do you have any siblings?"

"Two brothers and a sister. I'm the oldest. My mother lives in Portland… After dad died, I shared the gift of books with them, trying to do for them what had been done for me. But even though I was cautious, it wasn't enough. When I was a senior in high school, my youngest brother Elijah rebelled against the teachings of a particularly harsh instructor. He compounded his mistake by quoting a passage out of the Diary of Anne Frank. The school authorities pressed him for two days straight to tell them where he had learned of it. He finally convinced them that he had found it on a new website not yet restricted. It was plausible because these websites crop up as fast as they can be shut down. But dad wasn't there to stop them and Elijah was sent to a camp for wayward boys outside Albuquerque. He came back six months later a total zombie. He couldn't put a sentence together, or play ball, or even climb a tree like he had done before. But the worst part is that none of his inner fire remained, totally extinguished. In its place, a child-like zeal for spouting religious platitudes, all curiosity smothered under the oppressive hand of state sponsored truth…" Lazarus says with bitterness in his voice "I never again talked with my brother about the secret place or the books. For me Elijah died that day, driving home a very harsh but valuable lesson. Never get caught, and I never was."

Lindsey shivers, his tone sending a chill down her spine. Three decades earlier, she had gotten out just before the Federation became a theocracy. What must it have been like to grow up in such a repressive state? She hopes to never find out. "Do you have any kids?" she can see him tighten up at this question.

He pauses before speaking so quietly that Lindsey had to turn up her visors volume to hear him, "I was married to a beautiful woman I met in college. We had a daughter… she was killed in a traffic accident two years ago with my wife..." his voice trails off.

Lindsey squeezes his hand, "I'm so sorry…"

Lazarus changes the subject, "When I was a kid I blamed Jihad for my father's death, probably because everyone else did. It motivated me to study religion. I was amazed to learn of the extensive overlapping between Judaism, Christianity and Islam. I found that these three religions share the same prehistory and claim as their own the same ancient prophets. I guess religions build upon those that came before, just like civilizations... But what it all boils down to is whether you believe their holy books are divine or not. Did God write them or did men? And if men did, why should we believe anything they say? Judaism is the oldest religion dating back into the time of the Greeks and Egyptians. It thrived during the Iron Age relying on trade and agriculture and war. Their Holy Book is the Old Testament or Hebrew bible, one of mankind's oldest surviving books. It contains an incredible history of the Jewish people, their kings, their wars, their ambitions, and their vengeful God."

"Why do you believe god didn't write it?" Lindsey asks. She wants him to talk about whatever he wants to talk about, his choice of subjects very revealing.

"The first five chapters in the bible are collectively known as the Torah by the Jews and the Pentateuch by the Christians. I was taught in bible study that these chapters, Genesis, Exodus, Leviticus, Numbers and Deuteronomy, were written by Moses while under the direct influence of God. This wasn't a matter of debate, it said so right in the Holy Scripture itself. Deuteronomy 31 verse 9; *And Moses wrote this law and delivered it to the priests.*" Lazarus says then smirks wickedly.

"What the church doesn't want anybody to know about even today is that there are scientific studies that show this is not true. When you analyze the writing style found in the Torah you can categorize the usage of words and phrases that prove these five books had at least four distinctly different authors, several of which penned other sections of the bible as well. This is just one example of the hypocrisy and downright fraud found in religion."

Lazarus is letting the words flow having never dared speak like this to anyone before. He finds he enjoys it immensely. Like a thirty year old virgin suddenly finding sex, he wants more.

"I educated myself on the origin of the bible from a purely intellectual viewpoint to counterbalance my indoctrination in Christianity. The five books of the Torah are only a part of the Tanakh or Hebrew bible. In addition, the Nevi'im contains eight and the Ketuvim has eleven for a total of twenty-four books. These twenty-four books are the same as the thirty-nine found in the Protestant Old Testament, but with a slightly different organization and numbering scheme which no one has any idea why but seems to me to be definitive proof of the editing of ancient publishers. Makes you wonder what ended up on the cutting room floor!" he chuckles.

"The sources of the other chapters in the Old Testament are shrouded in prehistory and the ultimate identities of their authors impossible to determine. But beginning sometime in the 6th or 7th century BCE, the scribes of King Josiah of Judah began writing down the stories of the Jewish people including the important chronicles about Abraham, Moses and Solomon. Many of the stories bear striking similarities to even earlier ones of the Canaanites, Hurrians, Sumerians and Phoenicians. Hebrew itself is based on the older Phoenician language. This is further confirmation that the true origins of these ancient writings come from men, not God or even divine inspiration. They are simply one society picking and choosing ideas from an earlier one and molding them to their own ends."

"Very true," Lindsey says. "Plagiarism run amok!"

Lazarus chuckles, "Then the bible was said to have been faithfully copied from one generation to the next by a profession whose sole purpose was the accurate reproduction of religious texts. But the truth is, many versions came into being as generations of scribes and scholars couldn't help but make changes, some slight and almost imperceptible, others more sweeping where entire books were included, excluded or simply rewritten. We will never know what these changes were or when they were done or by whom. Wars were fought over whose version was more holy. The losing texts were literally burned, right along with their supporters. Far from being the immutable word of God, the bible that we have today is the survivor of many fierce battles."

"The problem of maintaining accuracy within the bible was further exacerbated when these writings were translated from the original Hebrew into other languages. For instance, in the 3rd century BCE the Egyptian pharaoh Ptolemy II Philadelphus asked seventy-two Jewish scholars, six scribes from each of the twelve tribes, to translate the Torah into Greek for inclusion in the Library of Alexandria. According to the legendary account found in the Letter of Aristae they were all kept in separate chambers yet seventy-two days later they all produced identical versions. While this story sounds implausible, it shows how seriously the Jews took the process. This particular translation is called the Septuagint, derived from Latin septuaginta, the number 70."

"What about the New Testament? As a Christian nation, isn't the Federation more reliant on it?" Lindsey asks.

"Yes, but never forget that the Old Testament is part of the Christian bible. Fundamentalists use the complete bible to find justifications for what they do," he says.

"Where did the New Testament come from?" she asks. "Who were its authors?"

"The New Testament suffers the same problems as the Old Testament. It's well known that the books of Mathew, Mark, Luke, and John were not written by them but came into being several centuries after their deaths. The other twenty-three books of the New Testament were also written by various authors, but proving who they are is impossible. There is no contemporary cross references that has survived. There are some historical records found in the Roman archives but precious little else."

"Centuries after the death of Jesus, what books should be included in the New Testament was bitterly fought over just as it was in the Old Testament. Each sect had there own biblical canon they considered the scared word of God and again, it is the survivors of this religious tug-of-war that is today known as the New Testament. The Book of Enoch, the Gospel of Mary, the Gospel of Judas, and many other writings didn't make the final cut. Why? …I couldn't begin to tell you… I have never understood how anyone could seriously consider this disjointed collage as the sacred word of God. It's simply a collection of short stories that loosely follow a theme. It's written by men, edited by men, produced by men and marketed by men, all to the detriment of mankind."

"Is the Qu'ran written in the same way?" she asks.

"Not really. The Qu'ran is much better edited than the bible, better organized and to the point with fewer contradictions as well."

"Have you read it?"

"Certainly, that's how I started my education, by reading the Holy Qu'ran from cover to cover. What I found shocked me. I learned that Islam embraces most of the events documented in both the Old and New Testaments but with significant changes. Islam even claims the well known biblical characters Adam, Noah, Abraham, Moses, Jesus, Mary, and John the Baptist as Holy Prophets. This seems to be another instance of a religion building on the ashes of an older one. One of the biggest differences, as far as the Christians are concerned, is that Muslims are only willing to acknowledge that Jesus was one of many biblical prophets, nothing more, certainly not God or the son of God. They claim Mohammed is the last and greatest prophet, the only one they need pay any real attention to. His teachings form the basis of Islam, and like the Jews and Christians, Muslims believe that their sacred book, the Holy Qur'ân, is the literal word of God."

"Islam's version of the divine revelation is nothing more than a heat and hunger induced hallucination. After living in a desert cave for a month, Mohammed's mind takes him on a journey to heaven where God tells him a story. Upon his return, God sends the archangel Gabriel who whispers in his ear the text of the Holy Qur'ân. Muslims want to believe that Mohammed was illiterate and couldn't read or write. They claim the Qur'ân is Mohammed's only miracle. It reinforces their notion that God wrote it."

"There's no evidence that Jesus could read and write, either" Lindsey says.

"True. The only thing both Christianity and Islam agree upon is that Jesus and Mohammed both heard voices which indicate schizophrenia or some other mental illness…"

"Several years ago my job required me to become even more familiar with Islam. Normally, citizens are discouraged from any curiosity concerning another religion but practicality forced some leniency for a select few. I was shocked at the discrepancies between what I read as the Federations official version of Islam and what I remembered as a boy reading in the shed. The hand of God must have come down and rewrote vast sections of the Holy Qur'ân. What other explanation could there be?" his words heavy with sarcasm.

"What job allowed you this access?" Lindsey asks.

Lazarus turns white as a ghost realizing he had just slipped up.

"Relax… I know you must have a very good reason for immigrating. Tell me what it is beginning with what you did for the Federation." When he still hesitates she continues, "After all, you are going to have to tell somebody sometime. Do you want it to sound like a first time presentation with no practice at all?"

Lazarus's frowns, "I don't feel comfortable discussing this in public."

Lindsey shakes her head, "If you're going to be a Lunarian you must learn that public and private have different meanings than you are accustomed too."

His frown deepens, "Yes, of course…" he is distinctly uncomfortable. The fact she is right does little to relieve his anxiety.

She presses forward knowing it's necessary, "Look, you're used to being watched wherever you go in the Federation, right?"

"Sure," he replies.

"The Lunarian system is the same only the data is available to everyone, not just government officials. The flow of information goes both ways. The Law of Full Disclosure gives every citizen access to all things public, including all individual, corporate, and governmental dealings. Only agreements made in public are considered valid under the law. Total visibility! Keeping secrets will only buy you trouble. The only exception is when the Republic is in jeopardy and even then is it permissible to maintain secrecy for only a limited time. As soon as the crisis is over, all records must be made available to the public."

"The Law, as I understand it, seems to put everything in public domain, every discussion, every meeting, even conversations between friend's falls into the public domain. What is privacy to a Lunarian?" he asks.

"It has the same definition here as it does in the Federation. Privacy is simply the courtesy extended from one citizen to another to leave each other alone. For instance, we have been granted privacy by our fellow passengers. Any one of them at any time has the right to watch us, listen to our conversation, and even join in if they are so inclined. But they don't because they have given us privacy…"

"…but this is public transportation," he interrupts.

"When are we not in public?" she retorts. "When we are at work? No! On the street? No! At home? Maybe, but only if you live totally disconnected from the rest of civilization. Privacy is the state of being apart from others and as such it's more about an individual's pursuit of happiness than a separate constitutional right. If you want to become a hermit, that's your choice. Just don't expect someone else to finance the endeavor. Besides, you must know that true privacy suffered a quick death over a century ago in the opening rounds of the Age of Information."

"Not true! Data mining is tightly controlled," he responds.

"Sure it is, by the Federation! The shear volume of their laws concerning privacy astounds me, all supporting the flawed goal of maintaining State and Corporate secrets. Don't you know you invite corruption when the flow of information is all one way? Those in power become more powerful at the expense of the citizenry. The average working stiff cannot stand against the Federation once they label him a terrorist."

Lazarus is stung by her observation. He knows first hand the power of the federal government having personally complied electronic evidence that convicted forty-three men and a women of information theft. These had been the real hard core offenders, hackers and programmers who illegally accessed financial, medical, and corporate data without permission, passing it on to the highest bidder. Now she is telling him that this information is openly available to anyone on Luna.

"But shouldn't a company be able to reap the rewards of internal research without fear of competitors riding their shirttails for free?" he asks.

"That's not a privacy issue. That's patent infringement and the LFD provides for full compensation within a time limit. But again, it's to everyone's advantage if all records are public, everything from the raw research results to the marketing plans. How can a company produce something if they cannot show a logical progression of knowledge? How can a pharmaceutical lab create a finished formula without a history of research and testing? Please tell me how a widget maker can market a new and improved widget without having records of the designs progression? There must be a litany of meetings and computer data and partnership agreements and impromptu discussions that show they actually did the work. Keep in mind that a separate record is generated every time a person accesses public records. Even a bad solicitor can easily prove the widget design was stolen by simply viewing the act of stealing itself. How can anyone sustain any criminal activity if their every move is public knowledge?"

"I can see I have a lot to learn," Lazarus says.

"More than you know, lover…" he blushes and she smiles, taking the edge off her gentle reminder of their relationship. "Now that you understand there can be no secrets, tell me why you're here..." she purrs, her breath hot on his cheek.

The internal struggle plays out across his face, yet he doesn't feel threatened. It's as if he's known her much longer than just the past few hours. Sex has a way of doing that. But it still seems traitorous to be telling Lindsey any of the many things that concern him. Long years of training and loyalty are hard to throw off, even with such a beautiful inquisitor as Lindsey.

Being this close to Lazarus, Lindsey can monitor his vital signs at least as well as an old fashioned lie detector. His visor relays heart rate, sweat production and eye movement to her, making it a physical impossibility for him to lie. Whatever it is that he thinks he knows, he considers it important enough to turn his back on everything familiar and embrace the unknown, this much she is certain of.

"Ok, let's begin by you telling me your occupational details," she says.

He hesitates, "I'm a programmer." Lying by omission is still lying.

Lindsey looks intently into his eyes, just a few inches from her own, "And?" She watches the last wall crumble.

He sighs and runs his hand across his hair, realizing he must speak the truth to this lady, "I'm a Senior Analyst for the Department of Homeland Security. My job is to gather and analyze data from a wide assortment of sources and incorporate it into presentations that the Director uses to brief the President and the Joint Chiefs."

Well, this is indeed interesting. "What kind of data?" Lindsey asks.

"Pretty much anything pertaining to the War on Terror," Lazarus replies.

"You mean the religious conflict between Muslims and Christians?" Lindsey asks.

"That may be more accurate but if I ever referred to it that way I would not only lose my job but I would wake up and find myself in a reeducation program somewhere in the frozen north. Director Dempsey doesn't mess around when it comes to his senior staff," Lazarus responds.

"So, you are a Senior Analyst for the DHS. Doesn't that make you an agent?" she asks.

"No not at all, more of a technician. I specialize in interviewing suspects and am not too bad at covert data mining. I'm part of a team, just one of many working towards a single goal, trying to determine who, what, when, and where."

Lindsey has no doubt the team were all men. The Lunarians have known about this group for some time, but Lazarus is the first defection from its inner circle. He's the highest ranking NAF official to ever defect, a bonus that he's in DHS. As a Senior Analyst, Lazarus will answer many questions, a process that has only just began.

Something substantial must have rattled his cage hard to make him take this drastic step. Now she is really curious. Lindsey snuggles up to him, squeezing his arm, willing him to lock eyes with her for several seconds, "Let me guess, you picked up on a pending terrorist attack and the NAF refused to tell the Lunarians anything. Is that about right?"

Lazarus is stunned. "Am I that easy?"

The little-boy look on his face makes her chuckle. "So tell me, what have you discovered that is worth risking your life for?"

It deeply disturbs him that she can see through him so easily, even after a lifetime of hiding his lack of religious conviction right under the nose of Homeland Security. Sighing, he rubs at the bristles of his hair before continuing, "Something big is happening within the Brotherhood. People have been falling off the radar until they're simply isn't anybody left. I've never seen this level of participation before!"

"What do you mean, falling off the radar?" she asks.

Frowning in concentration Lazarus continues, "Homeland tracks approximately four thousand individuals connected with radical fundamentalism within the Brotherhood. Their communications and public appearances are scrutinized in an attempt to understand what is happening. If possible, we bug networks and use spyware to penetrate computer records. I believe we even use old fashioned spies to watch some of them when we can. Follow them around and even become friendly."

Lindsey nods her understanding and motions for him to go on.

"Three months ago these individuals began to disappear without a trace. One day they were there, the next gone. No more network traffic, no more bank expenditures, their apartments empty, their jobs abandoned. There're just gone! Vanished!"

"Who are these people? What do they do?" she asks.

"DHS tracks all the upper echelon in the government and important military figures and most of these remain accounted for but there are a few notable exceptions. In particular, the Defense Minister, Hasin bin Aunker and Major General Abdel Salam Arif are both unaccounted for. They are considered high risk and extremely dangerous in the West. When these two disappeared, the entire NAF military raised the alert level a notch and it's stayed there ever since."

"But the majority of the four thousand are male, between the ages of eighteen and forty, and members of at least one of the fifteen or so known fundamentalist splinter groups. All of them have received military training by the Brotherhood at some point in their past. We believe these are the soldiers who carry out whatever plan the Minister or General come up with." Looking deeply concerned Lazarus says softly, "To have so many disappear is unprecedented!" His tone sends a shiver up Lindsey's spine. "It could mean as many as a hundred thousand men are unaccounted for."

Lazarus sighs and continues, "It's also a general belief among Homeland agents that the Brotherhood has completed a nuclear program which produced an unknown number of weapons. We haven't the faintest idea where they are."

"Well… you are just full of good news, aren't you?" Lindsey says softly. "That doesn't sound like a terrorist attack to me, more like an invasion."

"I totally agree. We picked up conflicting indicators of the target but everything points off-world. Hyundai's shipyards, Taurus or somewhere on Luna, We just don't know! Since the Federation has extensive interests throughout Luna and orbital space, I managed to convince Director Dempsey to inform the President of my concerns. I thought for sure President Newsom would tell the Lunarians. But the prevailing attitude in this administration is to stay out of it. Don't get involved."

Now that she has him talking he wouldn't shut up, "...But they are involved! Federation media consciously portray Lunarians as villains and monsters. It's not terrorists that most citizens fear, it is Lunarians. Everything from gamers to hard core action vids has Lunies as the bad guys and it's starting to have an effect on the country. Members of my own family have beliefs that have no basis in reality. They have never met a Lunarian but that doesn't stop them from hating and fearing them."

Lindsey nods in agreement, "You're right about that. I was concerned at the level of hostility when people found out I was from Luna. I'm glad to be leaving."

"It's just like Hitler's Jewish propaganda leading up to the Second World War!" A frown creases Lazarus's forehead.

"Relax" Lindsey sooths. "It doesn't do any good to stress out. How, exactly, did you plan to tell the Lunarians of this wonderful news?"

Sighing deeply he says, "I thought I might speak to a councilmen."

"So you're just going to dial up a Council member on the public net when we get there?" she asks smiling at the hubris of his plan.

"If I must," he replies. "Actually, I never thought I would get this far... I left this part of the plan to ad hoc. Perhaps I should start with the police department. I must find someone who will give me five minutes."

Lindsey frowns, considering what she knows of Lazarus. A self described desk jockey fighting on the side of good, but with a Don Quixote complex. He doesn't seem afraid to stir it up, speak his mind, typical of a man with convictions. Something about him is special, a naïve bravery that pushed him to jump off the ledge without ever knowing what's at the bottom. And he's a Senior Analyst. That alone might be enough.

"What makes you think the Lunarians will listen at all?" she asks softly looking at him intently.

Returning her gaze steadily, Lazarus says firmly, "Someone will listen! They must!"

She leans back pondering her options. If she helps Lazarus and he turns out to be a quack she would be embarrassed and possibly labeled unreliable by some. But if he has new information about an imminent attack then many Lunarian lives could be spared. Her pride is worth the risk.

"Do you know of Abby Dugan?" she asks.

"Yes, of course. Any school child knows of her," Lazarus responds with astonishment. "She's Luna's most famous Lunarian."

"I can't promise anything but I may be able to get you your five minutes. Corso Dugan is her son and he's also Aldrin Station's Security Chief," Lindsey says.

Lazarus stops and stares in amazement at Lindsey. "You can do this?"

Smiling at his astonishment she says, "Don't look so surprised. I'm a Dakota citizen and have the right to ask. The worst that can happen is they say no."

Something in the way she says it makes Lazarus realize the risk she is taking. "No, Lindsey... The worst is a Lunarian city crushed by a nuclear bomb...In any case, it looks like I owe you again. Thank you!"

"No promises Lazarus. Abby may be too busy to see you herself... For now, settle back in your seat and take a nap or go online. I will rejoin you in a few minutes. No matter what, we still have a long flight ahead of us and I plan on sleeping as much as possible."

"I couldn't sleep right now."

"Then read a book," she turns to face front.

Lindsey's hands blur as she expertly routes a call to Luna. She is again mindful of the increase in quality of the graphics as she logs into the Aldrin Station network, struck by how much sharper and more lifelike these images are in comparison to what she had seen while on Earth.

The seat in front of her disappears and in its place materializes the head and shoulders of a smiling middle-aged grandmother, dark hair peppered with gray, laugh lines around the eyes and mouth that testify to a healthy sense of humor, the very personification of kindness and understanding.

"Greetings Lindsey!" the apparition says brightly.

Lindsey smiles warmly in return. "Greetings Magi, how are you?"

"Fine, Lindsey. Did you enjoy your time on Earth?" Magi asks, the two second lag as the signal travels to Luna and back is barely noticeable.

"Some, but to be honest, I'm glad it's over. I'm ready to come home," Lindsey says. The image smiles affectionately in response, "Magi, is it possible to speak with Abby or Corso right now?"

"Corso is unavailable but I can check with Abby," Magi responds. "It may take a few minutes," she says and shrinks into an icon.

Lindsey nods and initiates access to the Republics main database. One of Luna's national treasures, the database resides on a vast array of zettabyte (10^{21} bytes) memory spheres dispersed throughout the Republic. Zettaspheres are data storage devices of enormous potential. A Zettasphere one inch in diameter will easily contain the equivalent of all of mankind's written works thousands of times over, all the books ever written, all the articles in all the journals and newspapers ever printed, endlessly copied. A single Zettasphere the size of a grain of rice will store over ninety years of audio/video from a security camera, two of them will store a person's life as viewed through a visor.

The key property of these extraordinary little gadgets is that once data is written to them it can never be changed. The only way to alter information contained in a Zettasphere is to destroy the sphere entirely. Yet, the data recorded on it can be read an infinite number of times. Zettaspheres are the key technology making the Law of Full Disclosure possible.

Within these tiny pieces of silicone and calcium resides not only the accumulated knowledge of the human race, but the historical record of its recent past. For the last half century, every camera, every sensor, every computer, every visor and electronic device has contained Zettaspheres. It's on this widely dispersed network that data is collected and permanently stored. Every store, classroom, and casino, every interview with every doctor, teacher and mechanic, every instrument in every hospital, factory, and amusement park, every meal ordered in a restaurant, every business deal and discussion, every walk in the park, every use of transportation, every security camera, and every visor from all across Luna have permanently recorded the events they witness, all of it designated as Public Records and accessible via the Lunarian network. For detailed knowledge of practically any event, scholars, policemen, or anyone simply interested enough to notice, are not limited to a few prejudicial passages written by the winners or losers, they are not left to make sense of a litany of witnesses each attesting to something slightly different. They have audio/video information recorded during the incident itself to help them determine what really happened. A single citizen wearing a visor can provide all the evidence needed. It's a rare case that hasn't any viable vid data. Everything is recorded somewhere.

Lindsey occupies herself with catching up on the news while she waits. She had been getting the Federation approved version of events over the last several weeks, filtered by network commentators and reporters who haven't the vaguest notion of

Lunarian society and couldn't care less. They typically oversimplify the underlying issues if they bother to present them at all, slanting the reports to imply the Lunarians deserved whatever had happened to them. Events are selected more for their shock value than historical significance and are presented out of context in small audio/video bites overlaid by verbal interpretations which are rarely checked for accuracy or questioned by the citizens who view them. It sickened her to listen to the spin these political hacks put on these bloody events.

The bombings had started almost a decade ago but are still considered newsworthy, for the graphic images alone, if for nothing else. Shock and awe sells web time and that is the name of the game in the Federation, as long as it doesn't violate the religious viewpoint of the current administration. Showing a little hell vested on the Lunarians seldom did.

The Republic of Luna doesn't work the same way. There aren't news agencies, per se, or a cadre of talking heads telling everyone what to think. Instead it's the government's responsibility to preserve the facts as accurately as possible and provide its citizens with the opportunity for each individual to view the material for themselves at a time of their choosing. It's the citizen's responsibility to interpret any deeper relationships on their own or in groups. Lunarians pride themselves on their capacity to analyze the enormous amount of data they routinely collect, then make up their own minds if something deserves notoriety or not. A standard set of sophisticated tools have evolved over many years and by using them Lunarians can quickly gather data on a specific person, place or thing and determine its overall economic, political or biological health. The various ways to group data is limited only by human imagination, driven by the widespread use of visors and powerful computers running search programs.

Lindsey is shocked by the increase in the number of violent incidents on Luna and in orbital space in just the few weeks she has been gone. Bombings, sabotage and assassinations have become almost commonplace, all attributed to Islamic extremists when the perpetrators can be identified, which is seldom. The Brotherhood is always careful to maintain distance from these acts, claiming they had nothing to do with them, appalled at the loss of life and property, always offering aid to the victims and their families. It's always rejected.

A cold shiver slides down her spine when Lindsey reviews the vid of an incident in Hells Kitchen almost two weeks earlier. A bomb had exploded in a busy mall killing three, wounding twenty–two, and damaging the habitat beyond repair. She had eaten there many times. She begins to cry when she realizes she knows one of the dead, a young man barely out of puberty and the son of a colleague.

The news vid freezes and shrinks to an icon, replaced by the image of Magi. "Excuse me Lindsey but Abby is ready to see you."

Lindsey gathers herself before facing Abigail Dugan. Abby's green eyes belie her smile, she doesn't like having her time wasted and will not hesitate to let Lindsey know about it if it came to that.

"Greetings, Lindsey," Abby says.

"Greetings," she replies.

"How was Earth?" Abby asks her, pushing a loose strand of platinum hair into place.

"Intense and worrisome, I'm afraid. Let's just say I'm looking forward to home and don't intend to leave again for a very long time. But that's not why I called you. I met someone on my trip back I believe you need to talk to. A defector named Lazarus Sheffield. He's a Senior Analyst for the Department of Homeland Security, a member of the Directors inner staff. He claims to know about an Islamic nuclear program and speaks of the disappearance of Hasin bin Aunker and Abdel Salam Arif," Lindsey says.

This got Abby's attention, "Does he know where they are?" she asks.

"No, I don't believe so. He also mentioned four thousand others that have vanished with them and the possibility of many more, perhaps a many as a hundred thousand," Lindsey responds.

"And you want me to meet with him?" Abby asks.

"He's defecting because the Federation won't open up and tell us about this impending attack. Quite admirable, actually. Beyond that, I think he offers unique insight into the situation. He may or may not have critical information but he's a remarkable young man, Abby. Worth your time."

Abby raises her eyebrows looking intently at the younger woman for a moment. "I'll meet with him but he's your responsibility. Learn what you can… There'll be someone at the spaceport when you arrive."

"My responsibility? You mean until we get to Aldrin Station, right?" Lindsey asks.

"No, I mean stay with him. Earn his trust. Mentor him. You say he's a Federation Senior Analyst? It's highly unusual for the NAF to let someone like that out of their sight, let alone defect. This is a situation I want to keep a tight rein on." Abby pauses looking intently at Lindsey, "You sponsored him and got laid. It seems to me that you are already half way there."

Lindsey doesn't even bat an eye, realizing that Abby is multitasking, reviewing the public data available from Heavens Gate even while talking with her. "It's traditional to get laid your first time in freefall. Besides, it's not everyday that I meet such an adorable virgin."

"Um… he's cute but I don't know about adorable," Abby says with a smile.

"Who will meet us at Aldrin?" Lindsey asks.

Abby shakes her head, "Don't know yet. I'll make it a surprise. I know how much you like surprises."

"I'm scheduled at the clinic on arrival. I can't take Lazarus so someone will need to hold his hand for a few hours," Lindsey says.

Abby already knows about the appointment, "Done," she responds, "Good job, Lindsey!" she nods and vanishes.

****

This is round trip three-hundred-nine for the lunar freighter Evolution's Child, christened by her first captain eighteen years ago in honor of his favorite girl band. Since then she has had many pilots, some signing on for a few years, but most only lasting a few dozen voyages. The ship isn't much to look at, an open framework of massive titanium beams powered by four of the new Pratt and Whitney Peta thrusters. Born in the airless vacuum of space, she will never feel an atmosphere.

Hyundai's orbital shipyards had just completed the fitting. The Peta Model PW2090's are fourth generation magnetoplasma thrusters, each rated at 181,000 pounds force. Together they effectively raise the freighters payload capacity to almost a half million pounds mass. It seems a crime to have less than thirty thousand aboard for the engines shakedown voyage.

Clustered amidst the thrusters are the propellant tanks and a single high capacity fuel cell. The phenomenal efficiency of the new Pratt and Whitney engines make the large twenty year old fuel tanks overkill for the relatively short routes between LEO and the lunar surface. But with full tanks, and depending on payload mass, Evolution's Child is capable of going anywhere in the Earth-Luna system and back again without refueling.

Above the tanks, within the protection of the titanium superstructure is a ten foot high pressurized cylinder containing just over twenty-thousand cubic feet of human living space. Known as the pilothouse, it is home for the freighter's current pilot, a single small airlock its front door, and a railed catwalk encircling the cylinder its front porch.

Massive titanium I-beams segment the catwalk vertically, supporting the cargo bay that is beyond the pilothouse. The ships hold is an open spider's web of girders, struts, and braces, packing it more art than science, requiring skill with a mass scale to balance the payload to the force of the thrusters. Designed to be reconfigured with each individual shipment, the bay itself can be modified to accommodate any shape and size, securing and stabilizing the mass of the cargo within the volume. The current consignment doesn't come close to filling this space.

Evolution's Child is built rugged, both locomotive and boxcar of the late 21st century, able to pickup and deliver cargo to the surface of the moon. Six massive shock-absorber landing-legs surround the engine compartment and extend up past the roof of the pilothouse, each at an angle keeping them out of the Pratt and Whitney's exhaust. They give the ugly little ship a beetle look, its meager cargo secured to its back by a few ratchet straps.

With a flip of her hand, Pilot Nell Goddard initiates the link with Luna Central, "LC, this is Evolution's Child. Standby for trans-lunar injection in T-minus one minute," she says.

The image of a man appears before her, the collar of his white shirt unbuttoned and sleeves rolled up. He's familiar to Nell from her last trip yet they both refrain from small talk. That's the way of things when doing business in space. Keep your mind on what's important or you will not last.

The two-second round trip is just long enough to notice but not long enough to be a nuisance, "Roger, Evolution's Child. You are go for trans-lunar burn. We show you at orbital insertion in T-minus seventy-two hours seven minutes twenty-two seconds. Have a safe transit."

"Roger that, Evolution's Child out," Nell responds and brakes contact. The controller vanishes, "Emcee, you are free to initiate the programmed burn," she informs the autopilot. Emcee is a very primitive AI with limited resources, but she always does what she can to make her pilots life easier.

"You got it, Nell!" Emcee responds as programmed, "Thirty seconds to ignition!" The voice has a prepubescent quality that makes it difficult for an outsider to say if it's male or female.

With a subtle flick of her wrist, Nell takes the movie off pause and settles back. The image grows until it fills her visor, immersing her in one of the Harrison Ford oldies. Nell is a film buff, not unheard of for those who sail the vast distances of space. She is looking forward on this trip to viewing the latest additions to her collection, the enhanced VR versions of some of her favorite flat screen classics.

After almost three years running this route, Nell is a veteran spacer. Her mind tunes out the acceleration warning klaxon and handles the three G's acceleration stoically. Only after the burn is complete does she momentarily turn away from the movie to check her position.

Right between the white lines! Nell grins in self congratulations before giving her attention back to Harrison.

****

While Lindsey is absorbed in making her call, Lazarus grants her privacy and decides to explore the net with his new visor. He uses the opportunity to gather information on Lindsey, requesting a general background check. By the sheer volume of data, it's obvious that there are many others who share the name Lindsey Davenport. By adding Lindsey's face, his search engine is able to drastically reduce the amount while increasing the degree of certainty that it was hers. If he had her DNA profile, a retinal scan or fingerprints he could have reduced it further and increased the confidence level even more. But this will have to do.

Lazarus creates a summary using a familiar program. …born in Columbus, Ohio on October 12, 2043… Forty nine years old? He would have guessed thirty at most.

Grandmother was the technician who first measured Type 3 superconductivity… mother was a history professor at a community college when Lindsey was growing up but lost the position during the Great Revival in 2062, as did the majority of women in positions of authority. Died last year of unspecified causes… father still alive and resides in a retirement community in Cleveland... her only brother, Harley Davenport, killed in 2062 while serving in the Marine Corp somewhere in the Middle East. That was near the end of forty years of Federation occupation. That had to hurt.

…June 2062 Lindsey relinquished Federation citizenship and immigrated to the Republic of Luna, coincidence? …received a Bachelor of Science in Mechanical Engineering from the University of New London in 2067 and followed that up with a PhD in Materials Processing from the Stephen Hawking Institute of Technology in 2070… joined Metcal soon after graduation and stayed with them for twenty-one years… long list of places, responsibilities and accomplishments attributed to her while with Metcal, all of them off-planet…. Captain, Lincoln County Police Department, 22nd Metro Division?

A chill runs down his spine. She hadn't mentioned she's a police officer! Lazarus finds it ironic that his first instinct is to fear considering his only job since completing school was DHS. He isn't accustomed to being on the other side of the law and it disturbs him.

Lazarus continues reading the summary, finding comfort that all of her accomplishments are engineering in nature. Near the bottom he scrolls through a list of articles and professional papers she has written over the years finding only one with a general enough content code for him to try reading. All the others had technical values of seven and above. As a general rule, Lazarus didn't read anything with a tech value over five and this one was rated only three. Lindsey had written it for Science Weekly, an EU network magazine devoted to promoting science education among the general population. He touches its icon.

"Please select how you would like it read," a voice says.

"No… that won't be necessary. I will read it for myself," he replies.

"Very well," the voice responds.

The document appears before him and he starts reading.

Science Weekly, Vol 1547, Issue 37148, 104
Republic of Luna, Editorial Section
[DOI: 101.1216/science.309. 37148.104]
Thursday, September 8, 2072
L. Davenport, BS, PhD, PE

The Impact of Superconductivity on Human Technology

Introduction: What separates mankind from every other species that has ever existed on planet Earth? Speech? Many animals communicate but none as efficiently as man. Intelligence? There are other creatures with large brains encompassing many complex adaptations but none with the abilities of ours.

Opposing thumbs? Walking upright? These can be found in other species. I don't believe there is one single reason for the success of Homo sapiens. Rather, it is all of these characteristics converging and manifesting within us something that truly separates our species from all the rest; our ability to manipulate the environment through the imaginative application of technology. It gave our ancestors an edge in the fight to survive and continues to this day. Our technological evolution has defined who we are every bit as much as our biological evolution. It allowed us to adapt to ever changing environments and situations that would have killed us otherwise. Ice ages and volcanoes, floods and droughts, locusts and epidemics, and today the vacuum of space, have all been conquered by humanity with the aid of technology. Yet, there is one thing that made the rise of man possible ...Fire. Stone, bone, and wood implements may have preceded it but none can argue that fire is unquestionably the greatest tool that mankind ever obtained. It is impossible to conceive of a world without fire.

We have been refining our use of fire from the very earliest days of our species existence. Fire probably started out as a means of protection, a weapon used to keep predators at bay and aided in the never ending quest for food. We will never know the exact circumstances surrounding the discovery that fire could be harnessed, that something so frightening could be exploited to improve quality of life instead of harming it. But that only adds to its mystique. At some point we began cooking our meat, contributing to the success of early man in many ways. It broke down protein aiding digestion. It killed unwanted and dangerous parasites making them healthier. It preserved food making it possible to save for that inevitable rainy day.

Fire not only cooked our foods but smelted our metals. It allowed our ancestors to put down the stone axe and take up a bronze, and later, a steel one. Its discovery is the single defining event in the history of technology without which we would never have risen above Stone Age hunter-gatherers. And still we push the boundary of fires influence. In modern times we have learned to control it in many forms. In the chemical rockets that first opened space, in the guns and bombs we periodically unleash on one another, in coal, nuclear, and fusion power plants that has provided us with electricity at different times, in the combustion chambers of 20th century cars, trucks and airplanes, in the refineries and factories that produce the goods we consume today. Almost anywhere one looks in manufacturing, fire, or the manipulation of heat energy, is an integral part of the process. The revolution in human affairs that started with fire shows no signs of letting up. From simple beginnings, its effect has impacted humanity like no other.

Coming in a close second is reading and writing. Without writing there can be no mathematics. Without mathematics there can be no science. Without science we don't have civilization. Until writing was invented and evolved, the wisdom of man was passed from one generation to the next by word of mouth, a notoriously unreliable way to communicate. The earliest known writing is of gods and other tales that we lump together under the banner of religion. Only later did merchants use writing and the emerging discipline of mathematics to keep track of goods and services. In the beginning, religion embraced writing using it to gather power unto itself. For many cultures, only the priests knew how to read and write. But for all its power, religion could not stop the accumulation of knowledge once started. Books became the repositories of knowledge both secular and religious. Writing necessitated the invention of education and the quest for truth began in earnest. Over the next eight thousand years the alphabet evolved from crude scratches in clay to the versatile symbols we use today. The written word is a voice that speaks to us from the grave. Is it coincidence that the first writings coincide with the biblical age of the Earth? Who can say, but as a tool of man, writing ranks as one of the most significant in human history.

Beyond fire and writing are many ideas and inventions that have revolutionized humanity to varying degrees and durations. The wheel, money, religion, metallurgy, domestication of plants and animals, wind power, steam power, nuclear power, computers, electricity, and gunpowder are only a few that changed the world of man.

A strong case can be made linking the development of new materials to the technological progress of mankind. Swords and plows could not be invented until bronze became available. Concrete in ancient Rome allowed the Romans to build astounding structures. Steel, aluminum and thousands of metallic alloys ushered in the modern age. But in a society dominated by technology, what is the pre-eminent invention of the 21st century?

Nanotechnology has opened a door into the realm of the very small allowing solid-state manufacturing, one atom at a time. Combined with biology and genetics, nanotechnology has been instrumental in curing most of the diseases and maladies plaguing mankind. Solid-state electronics have allowed computers to become ever more powerful, CPU operating speeds are in the tera-hertz range and Zettaspheres give mankind the capacity to store all the events of a human life in a space the size of a grain of rice. On a larger scale, man has taken the first shaky steps off his home world, colonized the moon and orbital space, and sent his machines to explore the far reaches of the solar system. Replacing nuclear and coal electrical generation, power satellites concentrate solar energy and beam it down wherever it is needed, anywhere on Earth. No one doubts that all of these inventions have profoundly influenced mankind in their own way. But there is one material that makes all of them possible, that touches every aspect of 21st century technology, revolutionizing the manufacturing of our machines, and affecting the way citizens live their daily lives. The single event that made much of our modern world possible is the discovery of Type 3 superconducting materials.

Background: Superconductors are materials that offer zero resistance to the flow of electricity. In other words, a superconductor will not get hot as more and more electricity is forced through it, thus, eliminating energy loss over distance. The phenomena was first observed in 1911 by Dutch physicist Heike Kamerlingh Onnes after he had cooled mercury to 4°Kelvin (-452°F, -269°C), the temperature of liquid helium. To witness the phenomenon in pure mercury, it was necessary for Onnes to come within 4 degrees of Absolute Zero, the coldest temperature that is theoretically attainable. By experimentation he discovered other materials would also exhibit superconductivity, each at its own point known as the transition temperature, or T_c. His research into superconductivity won him a Nobel Prize in 1913.

Twenty years later, Walter Meissner and Robert Ochsenfeld would discover that superconducting materials will energetically repel a magnetic field. This phenomenon is known as diamagnetism but is often referred to as the Meissner effect.

In the decades that followed, other superconducting materials were discovered such as niobium-nitride, vanadium-silicon, and an alloy of niobium and titanium, to name a few. But there was a problem. It seemed every scientist had a hypothesis to account for the phenomena within a particular material, but none were able to provide a single unifying theory that spanned all the compounds. What worked for one superconductor unraveled with the next.

To make matters worse, in the 1980's a second type of material was found to exhibit superconductivity. Alex Müller and Georg Bednorz, working at the IBM Research Laboratory in Rüschlikon, Switzerland, created a brittle ceramic compound that superconducted at the highest temperature then known: 30°K (-405°F, -243°C). These became known as Type 2 superconductors. But a unified theory of superconduction seemed even further away.

Research into Type 2 materials continued into the next century as more and better superconductors were devised, each striving to push the transition temperature ever higher. The world's first superconducting power transmission lines were put into place in the last decade of the 20th century and in 2010, the highest T_c attained by any Type 2 was achieved, 191°K (-116°F, -82°C), a temperature easily maintained using liquid nitrogen. But it wasn't until the discovery of Type 3 materials that the use of superconductors became widespread.

Type 3 Superconductors: In late summer 2014, the first Type 3 superconductor compound was discovered by accident at a weapons research facility in Livermore California. While looking for the next generation of high explosives, the research team at Sandia National Laboratories knew they were onto something when several micrograms of the material detonated prematurely. The explosion severely injured one person while destroying the high-pressure oven they were using to cure the sample. They quickly learned that the material must be kept away from the atmosphere. A few weeks later the most junior scientist among them was fleshing out the property tables on the new explosive when she tried to obtain the resistivity of the material. At first she thought her equipment was malfunctioning until she realized she was measuring superconductivity. Zero resistance. Before the day was out she had determined this new material had a transition temperature of a remarkable 307°K or 92°F. They had stumbled upon one of sciences holy grails, a true high temperature superconductor. I know this story is true because that junior scientist was my grandmother.

The complexity of the manufacturing process required to obtain Type 3 superconductors and the shear number of ingredients in the recipe translated into twenty-two years of intensive research before an acceptable theory emerged that described what was occurring within the material. But that didn't stop anyone from using the new discovery, jumping on the bandwagon long before the inherent dangers were identified and dealt with. What followed was a series of blunders that killed or injured many innocent people. It wasn't long before the general public had decided that the new superconductor was more trouble than it was worth.

The military community named it SuperX and it soon replaced RDX, a high explosive historically used in attack rockets, land mines, shape charges and a wide assortment of military projectiles. Where RDX demonstrated a high degree of stability in storage, SuperX detonated when exposed to gaseous oxygen. But the tremendous increase in potential energy more than made up for its flakey nature. Pound for pound it was the most powerful chemical explosive ever devised by man.

Because of the risky nature of the material, by the end of the 2020s most research being done on Type 3 superconductors were occurring on the moon or in orbit, isolating it from the public and driving a burgeoning off-world economy. On January 4, 2036, a research team working at the Bohr High Energy Collider (BHEC) in conjunction with the University of Luna at Aldrin Station released the results of seven years of experimentation. With the report they unveiled Calconn, a Type 3 superconductor having the highest transition temperature of any yet found (413°K, 284°F, 140°C). They got around the extremely explosive nature of Type 3 materials when exposed to air by cladding the cables and wires with a proprietary polymer, itself a marvel of materials science and engineering. This coating provides a self sealing shield around the unstable material inside, yet allows workers and technicians to safely install the cable in both commercial and residential applications.

Needless to say, Calconn was rigorously tested by the world's laboratories. The cable proved itself against fire, physical abuse, and virtually all types of chemical attack the terrestrial scientists could dream up without a single failure. Within a year, the first Calconn refinery began delivering cable to an energy starved Earth. Yet it took nearly ten more years before the public fully accepted it. By then Calconn was synonymous with Type 3 superconductors in the minds of the average citizen. Many still don't realize that other formulations exist.

Of note, in 2046 China established the Institute of Advanced Materials, a front for them to develop their own Type 3 superconductor without interrupting the flow of material from Luna. They didn't feel comfortable depending on a non-Chinese source for a commodity that had become so critical to their economy, a sentiment shared by many other nations. Three years after coming online, the plant met its end in a spectacular explosion that could be heard over a hundred miles away and left a crater almost a half mile wide, effectively signaling the end of serious efforts to compete with Lunarian made Calconn. China never reported how many were hurt or killed that day, but the incident effectively ended any serious challenge to Lunarian Calconn. The world grudgingly accepted Luna for the exclusive manufacturing of the volatile superconductor. Over the intervening decades, the Lunarians always made sure Calconn prices were kept low, carefully cultivating Earth's dependence.

A half century later, an average of forty giant spindles of Calconn superconductor cable are produced in Lunarian refineries every day, along with a vast assortment of smaller gage wire and other specialty items. Each spindle forms the core payload of a Product Delivery Module or PDM as the locals call them. The outer shell of a PDM is duel purpose, serving as both mass-driver projectile and later, as the atmospheric reentry vehicle. To begin their journey PDM's are catapulted into lunar orbit using a mass-driver whose key components are made of Calconn. Once in orbit they are caught and herded into transports by robotic tugs employing powerful electromagnet fields and propelled through space by magnetoplasma thrusters, both technologies heavily reliant upon Calconn. About every two weeks, a heavily loaded transport breaks orbit and delivers its accumulated cargo to one of three LEO stations, each with its own mass-driver, a twin of the unit that launched it off the moon. At the appropriate time, the mass-driver decelerates each PDM, plunging them through Earth's atmosphere using the original packaging as the reentry heat shield. A large synthetic silk parachute softens final touchdown, itself sold for a small fortune in the markets of Earth.

Besides its high T_c, Type 3 superconductors have other advantages over Types 1 and 2. Type 3 never reaches current saturation, maintaining its superconductivity at extremely high amperes instead of breaking down like the others, their resistance going from zero to infinity in a blink of an eye. What actually does happen within the molecular structure of a Type 3 superconductor as more and more current is pumped through it is the subject of cutting edge research as the end of the 21st century approaches. Space itself distorts under the stress of the incredible energies contained in such a small volume. Today our scientists are only just beginning to obtain a glimpse of future possibilities, but just as before, it doesn't stop them from exploiting these discoveries.

For many years Type 2 superconducting electromagnetic coils were used to accelerate particles in the world's supercollider's such as those at Fermilab outside Chicago, CERN in Switzerland, BHEC outside Aldrin Station, and many other smaller units supported by various universities and governments. The highest energy facilities were constructed in tunnels shaped in gigantic rings and could push the velocities of their particles to within a hairs breadth of the speed of light. But these were enormous machines that required the power of a small city to reach these energy levels. Calconn greatly reduced both power consumption and size of the resulting particle accelerator. The scientists studying high energy physics suddenly had a new toy to play with, one that even the humblest university could afford. As the 22nd century approaches, this is the new horizon that promises the stars.

Conquest of Space: Even without considering its titillating future, a strong case can be made supporting Calconn as the most influential material of the 21st century. The change in technology was so dramatic, so complete, that historians use the notation preCal to separate everything that predated the use of Calconn. Many have started to present the current era as the Calconn Age. This fact may be best known by the technical people who keep the electricity flowing and industries humming, but as of this writing virtually every citizen on Earth and Luna knows what Calconn is. It touches everyone every day in ways they may not even be aware of. Calconn based electromagnetism and magnetic field generators retooled human technology just as steam and copper-based electricity did in their time. Everything electric became smaller yet faster, stronger, more efficient, when using Calconn in place of copper, aluminum, or gold conductors, from the largest power cables all the way down to the micro circuitry found inside a computer chip. Practically from the start, every major industry clamored for Calconn based electronics and machinery. After that first decade, the demand far exceeded the supply and has for half a century, spawning an endless number of industries aimed at scratching that itch.

Once the public got over their fear of Calconn, it required less than twelve years to completely replace the copper-based electrical power grid that had built up over the previous 150 years. Transmission line losses dropped to zero and power generation efficiency, along with the items that used the power, jumped many orders of magnitude. Overnight the global power system went from barely sustaining growth to having a tremendous overcapacity simply by redesigning with Calconn. Smaller and more powerful electro-magnets gave maglev trains enormous load carrying ability. Electric motors gained efficiency and power while shrinking tenfold in size and weight allowing the dependence on oil to plummet. Calconn made it possible to create biotronic implants with such high efficiency and low power requirements they operate on the micro-voltage available within the human body. By every measure Calconn revolutionized human technology. It provided the means to shape our environment like few other materials have.

But it is the impact on the aerospace community that many point to as the most revolutionary aspect of Calconn. Immediately following the discovery of Type 3 superconductors, Pratt and Whitney and General Electric collaborated in a crash engineering program to design the first magnetoplasma thruster using Calconn. To say that they were successful is like saying the sun is hot or the cosmos is large, but in all fairness, their job was relatively easy. The idea of a magnetoplasma rocket has been around since the middle of the 20th century, but it wasn't practical because of the massive weight of the cryogenic support equipment necessary when using Type 1 or Type 2 materials. That mass disappeared when they designed the same nozzle using Type 3 superconductors. But that is only part of the picture. The magnetic fields produced within the first prototype were much stronger than expected, far exceeding the sum of the individual contributions from each coil. They learned that by clever design of the superconductive coils they could create feedback resonance that greatly amplified the strength of the resulting magnetic field. Even in the first full scale thruster, they strove to ensure that the physical geometry of the coils were in harmony with the frequency of the electrical energy coursing through its Calconn veins. In doing so, they created a magnetic field more powerful than anything that had come before, succeeding beyond anyone's wildest dreams.

It was the spectacular results of their endeavor, not the ease with which it was achieved, that sparked the aerospace community in particular, and all of humanity to one extent or another. Indeed, the reported specific impulse of the new thruster caused many scientists and engineers to declare that it must be a misprint, a mistake in reporting the data. Specific Impulse, or I_{SP} as it's known in the mathematical equations of spaceflight, is simply the rockets exhaust velocity. Multiplying I_{SP} by mass flow rate calculates the rockets thrust. The Space Shuttles main rocket engines had an I_{SP} of about 450 m/s and achieved high thrust, over a half million pounds at peak, by having enormous flow rates over a very short period of time. The pumps that supplied fuel to the shuttles hungry motors could empty an Olympic sized swimming pool in a matter of seconds. On the other hand, ion electrostatic thrusters are just the opposite, low thrust over a long time. Designed for deep space missions where it didn't matter if it took years to get there, ion thrusters had I_{SP} of 30,000 m/s but with fuel flow rates so low that the thrust this produced was less than 1/50th of a pound of force. An ion thruster could run continuously for months or even years on just a few pounds of fuel thus making it much more efficient than any chemical rocket motor, as long as time wasn't a factor.

But the newly designed Calconn-based thrusters jumped far beyond anything ever attained in a laboratory or in a computer simulation, easily obtaining an I_{SP} of 11.5 million m/s, or 3.8% of the speed of light. Combined with a mass flow rate of just over 5 grams per second, these first generation magnetoplasma thrusters produced almost 14,000 pounds force.

Less than two years after the start of the program, the first Type 3 magnetoplasma prototype was completed and installed on a military fighter airframe. The pilot took his aircraft to 132,000 feet and Mach 15 before he stopped accelerating. He flew at the boundary between Earth and space for one complete orbit. The achievement roared through the aerospace community like a raging wild fire. Mankind suddenly had one of its hallowed dreams in hand, easy access to space.

For the last half century engineers have been refining that first magnetoplasma thruster design. The latest generation is a solid-state electromagnetic nozzle culminating almost sixty years of research and experience. The heart of these devices is a million degree ball of plasma, its electrons stripped away in the intense heat of radio-frequency excitation and ion-cyclotron resonance, producing massive amounts of electricity which is fed back into the Calconn coils of the thruster thereby creating the strongest electromagnetic field ever measured. The plasma ions are accelerated at 3.5 Petameters per second squared attaining velocities approaching half the speed of light and producing thrusts upwards of 180,000 pounds force.

Conclusion: At the turn of the century my grandmother regularly flew in an old style atmospheric jetliner between New York and London. It would take 120,000 lbs of hydrocarbon fuel to make the 3500 mile journey, burned in only a few hours. Today that same weight of hypergolic fuel allows a magnetoplasma thruster to operate for over 200 days at maximum thrust, easily taking those same passengers to Mars and back several times over.

Very few things in the history of man's technology have had the lasting effect of fire but Calconn may prove to be its equal in the centuries to come. There seems little doubt that the discovery of Type 3 superconductors will be viewed as a turning point in the evolution of our species. Without it we would still be limited to planet Earth, never colonized Luna or Mars, never sent our robot miners to Saturn or Jupiter. To all those living comfortably in the modern world it seems inconceivable that, but for due diligence by my grandmother on that fateful day in 2014, you may never have even been born. Many believe that without the relief the colonization of our solar system has brought, that humanity would have suffered much more at the hands of population pressure and global climate change. Perhaps human civilization would have collapsed entirely. Food wars, the loss of ecosystems, rising sea levels, and many other catastrophic events may have proven to be too much to overcome for a species limited to a single planet. It is one of life's great ironies that it was a military project that saved Earth from that fate, that something intended to kill has brought so much good.

Mankind's journey to space began when our ancient ancestors first looked up in wonder at all the pretty lights in the sky. At an ever increasing speed, our species has grown cognizant of the universe and our place within it. We have conquered planets and explored the far reaches of our solar system, looked inward at the makeup of matter and outward at the incredible expanse of the cosmos. Yet many citizens have the opinion that we will never go further, that mankind must be satisfied with inhabiting just one solar system, that the distances between stars are just too great. Looking back at the history of our technological evolution, it is clear we develop the tools and skills we need only after we need them. Why should star travel be any different?

"Checking up on me?" Lindsey asks with a smile after he discards her article.

With a start Lazarus realizes Lindsey has completed her call. He had been so engrossed in her whitepaper that he hadn't noticed when she finished. "What did you find out?" he asks.

"Abby will have someone at Aldrin Station when we arrive."

"Will she met with me?" he asks unconsciously holding his breath.

"Maybe. Let's just take it one step at a time, ok? If there's one thing I've learned, it's not to push too hard, especially Abby."

"Sure... Ah... Lindsey? I noticed you're a police captain. I thought you told me you're an engineer." Lazarus says looking intently into her gray eyes.

"Luna is forbidden under the Treaty of having a standing militia of any kind which includes a professional police department. Instead, every able bodied citizen is a member of the reserve and is expected to serve eight weeks out of the year on police duty. My rank is Captain. I expect you will eventually join the reserve and be given rank and assignments." Lindsey replies. She glances at his vital signs and asks, "This isn't a problem is it?"

"No, not at all, I want to participate! Where I'm from the Federation discourages a person from taking an active part in society. They entertain and distract with a wide assortment of venues, net vids, sports, and politics are the three biggies. They would rather people go about their business without showing any interest in worldly affairs. Only one citizen in five votes and the Reformation Party hasn't lost an election in my lifetime. Do the math. Those in control will not allow anyone to upset the status quo." He shakes his head, "What you're telling me is that Lunarians are required to participate?" he asks.

"Let's just say participation is encouraged but the way a citizen does it is up to them. No one is forced to do anything." Lindsey says.

"I like that..." Lazarus says nodding. "The article you wrote for Science Weekly is fascinating. Do you really believe Calconn will prove to be as influential as fire?"

Lindsey smiles and shrugs. "Only time will tell. But it makes for a good article." When Lazarus seems dissatisfied she continues, "Yes Lazarus, I actually do think that Type 3 superconductors will be one of the technologies that carry humanity for many centuries. That's why I did the piece."

"What do you think will be the motivation to invent a star drive?" Lazarus asks. "There isn't any propulsion research intended for star travel being conducted right now within the Federation and I would know if there were any. I received regular briefings on every black project the Federation has, even those conducted on remote test ranges."

"Really, we must discuss them during our trip. It will help pass the time... I agree with you on the subject of research. The Federation isn't currently involved with any basic science to my knowledge and hasn't been for many decades. There's no profit in it. China, the EU and even the Islamic Brotherhood have only limited corporate financing of targeted research geared towards making money, not basic research into some pie-in-the-sky scheme such as star travel with very little hope of even covering its bills. All the really good science is coming from Lunarian labs in orbital space or on Luna itself. But the motivation will not come from money considerations or failing resources. It will be the threat to personal freedoms that will drive mankind to the stars." Lindsey says.

When Lazarus looks unconvinced she continues, "Look at history. The need to be free motivated the American founding fathers to declare independence over three hundred years ago. They wanted to be free from the tyrannical whims of King George sitting on a throne across the sea. Not to mention, free of the Church that supported him."

"America was founded on Christianity for the betterment of mankind," Lazarus says.

"That's Federation crap. Read the words of these men and you will quickly learn they believed in separating Church and State. They knew that mixing religion and politics threatened individual human rights, and that's exactly what happened after the Reformation Party gained power... Don't take my word on it, find out for yourself. You have access to many things that you didn't before. Take advantage of everything!" she says with a grin.

His face lights up. "Excellent idea! Could you show me how? And recommend some books that will help me learn about Luna? History, politics, family values, or anything else you deem useful?"

"Sure…" she links her visor with his and logs into the ships library. "You will find what you are looking for here. Select the delivery style…I prefer informal, either the fireside chat or park bench… and the book… the ships AI will do the rest."

Lazarus frowns, "Can I just read it myself?"

His question surprises her, "Sure you can. Select self service then the book."

"Thank you!" he says, amazed at the completeness of the list. It seems as though every book ever written is on the list. He's eager to explore this new horizon.

"Before I go to sleep there's one more thing..." Lindsey says.

"What's that?" Lazarus responds on cue.

"At risk of repeating myself, let me stress once again that you must always be honest and open…with every Lunarian, not just me. Lying is never an option. You have admitted being very good at hiding your true feeling and beliefs, and I can understand why... But you cannot allow that part of your former life to continue. If you hope to meet Abby, don't even think about lying or withholding information. That would be disastrous to your chances of citizenship. Lunarians despise the dishonesty of secrets and respect a person for being true to themselves and the world around them."

"To thine own self be true," Lazarus says. "And it must follow, as the night the day, thou cannot be false to any man."

"Hamlet, Act 1, Scene 3," Lindsey says completely caught off guard. "Why am I surprised you know Shakespeare?"

"That's the first time I've dared utter those words! It feels… incredible!" he looks at Lindsey with excitement. A cloud of worry flashes across his face, "Is there any subject I should avoid?"

She shakes her head, "Freedom doesn't tell you what subjects are permissible. Everything is open to debate. Lunarians will discuss anything at anytime with anyone. But let me warn you right now, most are not shy about expressing their opinions on religion, or the Federation, or the Islamic Brotherhood, or anything else." Lindsey says with a wave of her hand for emphasis. "So if you think I've been hard on you, let me tell you, you haven't seen anything. Just be prepared to defend whatever positions you take."

"I look forward to it," Lazarus says eagerly. "There is so much inside of me that cries for release!"

"No! I hadn't noticed," Lindsey smiles at his enthusiasm, "I'm sure we all will benefit from your opinions. But for now, just stop sticking your hand out. That's bad manors on Luna. You see… the majority of Lunarians have this thing about touching. So until you get a feel for how it works, don't touch anyone unless they offer first. OK?"

"I understand they don't like to shake hands, but you're saying avoid all touching?"

"That's exactly what I'm saying, just until you get to know someone, or they give you permission. Lunarians do so much vid conferencing that it's become traditional to avoid all physical contact. For the same reason, it's considered bad manners to remove your visor during meetings." Lindsey pauses and adds, "There will be many things that you will not understand at first. Just give it time and keep an open mind. Most of them will make sense eventually."

Lazarus looks at this beautiful woman, her face just inches away, and says, "If

Lunarians have even a fraction of your kindness, than the Republic of Luna will be a paradise."

Lindsey stretches the few inches between their lips and gives him a gentle but firm kiss, her taste lingering long after parting. "Flattery will get you everywhere," she purrs.

Those gray eyes bore into his, her breath warm and smooth in his nostrils, the fragrance reminiscent of a fine wine or an exquisite orchid. The stirring in his groin attests to the ability of this woman to excite him. The journey ahead looks very pleasant, very pleasant indeed.

"When I do good, I feel good; when I do bad, I feel bad. That's my religion."
Abraham Lincoln (1809-1865)

Charley Company

It's Halloween and Club Rio is packed. Non-reflective blackness on walls, ceiling and floor form a backdrop of deep-space within the large room. At the far end of this artificial black hole, the dance floor and stage appear to float in a bubble of light that pulses and ripples with every color of the spectrum.

With heads tilted back at an absurd angle and arms extended as though reaching for the ceiling, dancers undulate in total unison, like a kelp forest in high seas. They fill the dance floor and spill out among the nearby tables. Pounding bass and the haunting echo of the drums pull the dancers into the music's spell, their closely packed bodies sway sensuously with the rhythm.

Above them across the full extent of the clubs flat black ceiling, spins the awesome majesty of the universe. It's perspective is a ship flying at enormous speeds through the cosmos, passing galaxies like sand flowing through an hourglass, curving around one gigantic swirl only to plunge headlong into the billions of stars contained in the next and soaring past an enormous black hole at its center, its event horizon defined by hundreds of stars being pulled apart in a gigantic spiral of doom.

Beyond the dancers, on a raised stage, a four man band in garish skin-tight orange and purple jumpsuits, belts out their version of a heavy metal classic, filling the dance floor and most of the club with a soul-jarring guitar riff. The bands singer leaps high into the air as he wails, twisting and cavorting, making the most of Luna's gravity.

The two guitarists are playing Light Sabers, instruments that are all but invisible until a note is played, then pulsates in multicolor rhythm to its own sound. Made of a special Duraglass alloy, only the titanium strings are visible when it's silent. But with the slightest strum, the body of the instrument is infused with color and intensity in cadence with the song. Sound and color merge, sometimes harsh and violent, other times smooth and subtle, expressing the will of the musician through music.

Behind the guitarists the drummer hovers high above the stage, his drums floating in a great arc about him. They too pulse with color at each impact, complimenting the guitars with a driving undercurrent of both sight and sound.

Far from the dance floor, a pool of light marks the clubs main entrance, illuminating the nearby tables and the end of a long dimly lit bar. Some patrons sit at barstools while others stand, sharing the polished stone bar top. Bartenders rush about assisting customers and filling orders from the hustling servers. Glass shelves along the back wall of the bar are filled to capacity with an assortment of alcoholic beverages, more than half from Earth. A shot of authentic Black Label Jack Daniels whiskey imported from Tennessee or Smirnoff vodka from Moscow will cost a half days pay at the mines.

Past the bar several low-G snooker tables are the center of attention. Laughter and the occasional sharp crack of ball-to-ball contact penetrate the nightclub between songs.

Tables and booths make up the majority of the clubs main floor, each packed with the young and not so young of Aldrin Station. Tabletop candles cast a flickering dusky light over intimate conversations deciding this night's sleeping arrangements or some juicy bit of gossip, a human close-order-drill evolved over many generations.

Without exception, everyone in the room wears visors. It's common to never take them off. Although Lunarian visors come in many shapes and sizes, most are standard Razors, a silver bar that extends from ear to ear with a single thin black stripe along its horizontal center. But regardless of the model, these devices have one unifying feature, they all have sensors that pick up on the wearers underlying facial expression and broadcast this information to other visors rendering themselves invisible. Other than removing your own visor, the only way to tell if a person is wearing theirs is the occasional ghost of its outline purposefully shown, a fleeting glimpse of its form as they turn their head or sip a beer.

In the midst of this chaos, a server, one of many in Club Rio this night, skillfully maneuvers around the dance floor, weaving through the crowded tables, heading purposely for a booth near the back. She is showing a lot of skin in a tight fawn-colored costume with a large white fluff-ball doing a poor job of covering her butt cheeks. Above her short-cropped brown hair is a pair of large floppy ears that stand straight up.

Arriving with a smile, the sever places the full tray on the table and leans down, showing the tab and more than a little cleavage to the young man sitting closest to the end. He glances at the total and passes his left hand across the scanner embedded in the ticket, authorizing transfer of funds while enjoying the view.

"Outstanding costume, Suzy," Tempel says, their visors automatically linking making it possible hold a conversation over the music. He's tall and lanky with broad shoulders, typical of his generation. All five brothers are heavier, but at twenty, he's still deciding how much muscle to put on.

"Thanks!" she replies making her ears flap, "I'm a Playboy Bunny!" Suzy bumps against the table as a man jostles her from behind, quickly excusing himself. "Wow! What a crowd!"

"I don't know what a playboy bunny is but I do love Halloween," Tempel says.

Samantha reaches across in front of him, grabs a plate, and begins filling it with deep fried soymeat from Suzy's tray. Her fingers are quickly covered in barbeque sauce. Tempel and Sam have known each other for all of their young lives, their families interwoven all the way back to great grandparents who arrived in Aldrin Station on the same shuttle. For twenty years they have shared classrooms and teachers, friends and family, they even wear each others clothing on occasion. Everyone thinks they will marry but this remains to be seen.

Sam leans toward Suzy, "All of Luna is celebrating Tempel's birthday. Didn't you know?" she says before licking the sweet rich sauce from her fingers.

"You don't say! And I thought it was Halloween or something." Turning back to Tempel, she smiles. "How old are you?"

Tempel grins back and says, "Old enough."

"He's twenty," Sam replies for Tempel.

"Twenty is a good age. But so is forty-eight. Let me know if you need anything else," Suzy winks at the handsome young man before easing back into the crowd, bunny tail swishing in time with the beat.

Their U-shaped booth is one of many extending out from the pitch black wall of the night club. Its raised position gives its occupants an excellent view of the dancers, stage and most of the clubs main floor.

Around Club Rio's many tables and booths, off-duty officers sip their beverage of choice and relax, unwinding from the drudgery and dangers of their patrols, chatting and laughing among themselves. Men and women alike have short-cropped hair or no hair at all and very few are less than six feet in height. Most wear utilitarian stretch jeans, body hugging pullover T-shirts and deck shoes designed to provide firm footing on the polished stone walkways and ramps of their city. The colors vary across the room but those at this table are black right down to socks and shoes.

Brice and Odessa are down at the far end of the booth trying to tickle each others tonsils with the tips of their tongues. Oblivious to everything except each other, Odessa is running her hand inside his shirt and across his pectorals. Next to her, Jason is earnestly talking with Consuela, who is unsuccessfully trying to look interested. Beyond them, Kipper leans forward snagging two beers, handing one to Karyl before taking a swig of his. He makes a big production of laying his arm across the back of the seat behind her before snuggling close. Corazon and Tatiana have their heads together in deep conversation, the newly arrived beers ignored for the moment. Across the table from Tempel, Tatiana's twin brother Alonzo is exchanging smiles with a dark haired shortimer several booths over.

Sam leans against Tempel, pressing a breast firmly into his arm. "Happy Birthday!" her lips brushes his ear, her breath the sweet scent of barbeque. Tempel playfully licks a spot of sauce from the corner of her mouth, making her grin.

Alonzo slips out of their booth, heading for the dark haired girl. Sam nudges Tempel and nods her head at Alonzo's back.

"Lover boy's at it again!" she says playfully, her lips brushing his ear, her breath caressing his cheek.

Alonzo and the girl lock eyes as he approaches her table. He leans over, their noses almost touching, and says something causing her to laugh and shake her head vigorously. The young Lunarian says something more and she casts her eyes down and slides over making room for him beside her.

Tempel grins, taking another pull off his beer and nuzzles Sam's ear, "Who?"

She turns her head pushing back against Tempel, her lips caressing his as she talks, "Shortimer working at Far Point. Tatiana has met her. Don't know her name." she ends the conversation with a kiss.

When used by a Lunarian, shortimer is a rather derogatory term that refers to the people sent up from Earth for a month or a year. Most shortimers tend to keep to themselves. There isn't any law against them being in a Lunarian bar on a Saturday night, but it is unusual.

Tempel is intensely aware of Sam's warm body pressed tightly against his, her scent engulfing, her lips soft and warm. Time slips by.

Immersed in loud music and Sam strumming his senses, Tempel remains oblivious to the exchange that starts near the east entrance when two armed men enter the club.

"Excuse me, all weapons must be checked in at the bar," the clubs doorman calls out. The cut of their clothing mark them as shortimers and their visors are dark goggles that bulge over their eyes and don't transmit the wearer's facial expressions. These are not the graceful sweep of a Lunarian Razor or the dark shades dominant in the Federation. Rather, these visors are a Brotherhood design known collectively as bug-eyes.

The two men ignore the command and continue as if they hadn't heard, unlikely in this section of the establishment. The volume near the entrance is not much louder than elevator music. Unless they are deaf, they heard.

The doorman signals for help and several bouncers armed only with non-lethal stunners converge and intercept the men before they get far. "Stop immediately…" Mac addresses them from behind, his hand resting on the butt of his stunner, making sure these intruders know he's there, "you must check your weapons or leave." Several bartenders pause watching the exchange, resting their hands on more firepower stashed under the bar. Each stunner projectile is a self-contained capacitor that discharges its energy upon impact, a traumatic but non-life threatening event for the unfortunate target, receiving a powerful physical blow just as they are electrically zapped, disrupting nerve and muscle function.

"We will be here only a short time," growls the older man in a heavy accent, a shortimer with salt and pepper hair and matching beard. He misses nothing, fully aware of where the players are in this little drama, the one at his rear, another on his right, and others behind the bar, his mind weighing the odds and automatically making a plan.

"That's fine but you will still need to check your weapons," Mac insists.

The younger of the two has continued to sweep the inside of the club and has fixated on the dance floor or perhaps the stage just beyond. He sneers, leans over and says something in an unknown language to his companion who responds with a single syllable grunt.

Turning away from the bouncers blocking his way, the older man leads them to the end of the bar closest to the entrance. Sliding his sidearm out of its holster, he lays it on the bar top.

"Left hand please," a female bartender commands from the other side. "We need it to establish ownership."

Like some giant insect, his bulging visor stares at the woman, his demeanor cold and threatening. With a sneer he complies, placing his left hand beside his weapon, palm down fingers splayed.

She ignores this blatant attempt to intimidate her and monitors the sensors beneath the bar as they collect personal data, associating it with the disrupter. "Mustafa Malik, welcome to Club Rio. You can pick up your gun on the way out. Can I get you a drink, compliments of the house?"

Without responding, Malik turns away, motioning for his younger companion to take his place.

The man doesn't attempt to hide his loathing, pulling his weapon from its holster in a show of quick-draw prowess, making the bartender step back and the others reach for their stunners.

But before things reach critical mass, Malik growls, "Anwar!"

The young man laughs, flips his weapon end for end, and lays it on the surface of the bar. With exaggerated slowness, he splays his left hand next to it, palm down.

The bartender, clearly not amused by the taunting challenge, nevertheless, does her job, "Anwar Jafa, welcome to Club Rio," she says stiffly as the sidearm disappears under the bar. "You can pick it up on your way out. The first drink's on the house."

"Later," Jafa replies, a disturbing promise in his tone. He flashes white teeth in what might pass for a smile at a rabies convention, turns and follows Malik deeper into the nightclub. Just as Malik foretold, the sound near the entrance is not very loud, but as they penetrate the infidel's lair the volume soars upward dramatically until it overwhelms any chance to talk normally. Jafa steels himself against its power, yet the noise grates harshly against his Middle Eastern sensitivities. Allah be Praised, this is not music!

****

A few minutes later, feeling safe within Club Rio, and distracted by each other, no one at the table sees the fight start. The band falls silent causing Tempel and Sam to break their kiss. People are making room for the combatants, forming a wall of humanity about the center of the dance floor.

Alonzo is down on his back, his visor hanging from one ear, a stranger sitting on his chest slamming his head repeatedly against the stone floor. The girl stands just beyond them, horror and fear twisting her pretty face, meekly submitting to another older man gripping her arm at the elbow. Both men are half hidden behind Brotherhood visors that do not transmit their facial expressions, the bulging devices giving them a strange alien appearance.

No one among the on looking Lunarians know what the fight is about, but even so, many of them are quickly realizing that this shortimer is pounding a fellow citizen and more than a few are starting to press forward demanding loudly that the attack stop.

By that time Tempel is out of the booth and heading for the dance floor. Moving with speed and power, the young athletic Lunarian stretches out vertically and plants his shoulder into the side of the man straddling Alonzo, knocking him off and sending them both rolling in a tangle across the polished stone floor. By the time they stop, Tempel has the man in a death grip, one twist and he could separate his spinal column between the 4th and 5th cervical vertebra, silencing him forever.

The man struggles in his grip but soon realizes he's in big trouble. He gasps and grits his teeth trying vainly to somehow hold his own even as the obstructed blood flow turns his face above and below the visor crimson.

Just as suddenly as it started, the club bouncers put a stop to the fracas. "Tempel! Let him go!" Mac says laying his hand on the young warriors shoulder.

Surprised by how quickly he became willing to kill, Tempel relaxes his hold and rises leaving the shortimer gasping on the floor at his feet, rubbing his neck and only beginning to appreciate his pounding headache as blood surges within his brain.

"What's going on!" Mac demands.

Tempel shrugs and growls, "Ask him," without taking his eyes off the shortimer.

Instead, Mac turns to the older man and says, "Malik, you have worn out your welcome. Gather up your comrade here and leave."

Malik looks strangely pleased as he observes the group spread out behind Tempel. Sam and Tatiana are kneeling beside Alonzo who is telling them he's fine, to stop babying him, all the while blood continues to flow from a nasty cut on the back of his head. Young Jafa is rubbing his neck but standing, glaring at Tempel.

"Cheryl, give these gentleman back their weapons... empty," Mac says. "Then I will walk you to the door."

Malik couldn't care less about being ejected from Club Rio, and when Jafa starts to speak, he raises his hand to stop him. "We have what we came for... Anwar, see to Dalal while I retrieve our weapons." His heavy accent is almost a purr as he walks to the bar where Cheryl has placed the two empty guns. He slides one into his holster. Returning, he hands the other to Jafa. "Peace be upon you," he says to Mac, bows in mockery to the other Lunarians, then leads them out the way they had come. The girl follows a few steps behind the two men, her head down in submission.

Once out of Club Rio, the three move swiftly toward Steinway Avenue. Once well away Jafa turns to Malik, "*The one they call Tempel must be one of them. Only a spawn of Satan could do that to me!*" He speaks in the ancient Aramaic dialect of Nabataean, a language seldom heard since the 7th century and only sparingly in Aldrin Station over the last few months. They are reasonably sure that the infidel's have not translated it but they are cautious, speaking it seldom and even then, using special code phrases to further confuse the meaning of words.

"*Indeed,*" Motioning for the girl to walk beside him, he continues his fast pace as she scrambles to catch up. "*Tell me Dalal, what have you learned?*"

"I agree with Jafa. The man I danced with is one and Tempel is his leader. The others I am not sure of but I believe they are as well." The fear has evaporated from the young woman but subservience remains. She knows that dancing with the infidel pushed the boundaries even for an undercover operative, but it was all for Allah. "They call themselves Charley Company," she is straining her merger low-G ability just to keep up with the two men.

"*Charley Company...*" Malik mused. "*Allah may yet smile upon us...*" He has heard mention of special units but never anything concrete, just disturbing rumors of advanced technology. But where there's smoke, there's fire. As Malik mulls this over they emerge from Steinway Avenue and find themselves once again among the infidels. Here in the North Courtyard of Brooklyn Mall, they are passing a small sidewalk café.

A block stone façade surrounds the classic dark wood of the front door, symmetrically positioned between two large windows, the name La Bruschetta boldly painted on the wooden beam that spans all three. An old-fashioned menu displays in the left window, an arrangement of nuts, cheese and chocolate the other. Fastened to the stonework, replica oil lamps flicker from each side of the entrance and a bright red awning tops everything.

Outside the front door, rough-hewn cobblestones and a series of planters define the extent the sidewalk café intrudes on the main plaza. Small round tables, with matching red tablecloths and attended by comfortable high-backed chairs, are scattered across the patio. A small planter overflowing with live flowers adorns the center of each table. More oil lamps glimmer atop metal posts adding to the old-world ambiance of the café.

"Come, let us stop here and have a cup of fine Lunarian coffee," Malik says in English. He changes direction leading them towards the tables. An ad hoc plan is forming that will send shockwaves through the ranks of Charley Company. He switches back to Aramaic, "*Let us see what Allah has in store for us.*"

Malik selects a chair that puts his back against the stone wall with a clear view of Steinway Avenue.

Magi makes note of their exchange, placing the conversation in its entirety into a growing database in an effort to eventually decipher this new language. But without a proper cross reference to a known language, she has very little chance of reaching that goal anytime soon. It is not the first time an archaic dialect has been used in this way.

****

Mac glances at Tempel as the three shortimers leave, "That was some tackle. Where did you learn that?"

"Captain Osaka," he replies, shaking off the adrenal effects of the encounter.

Mac chuckles, "I should've known!"

Tempel kneels beside Tatiana and Alonzo. She has managed to stop the blood using a bar towel but Alonzo still looks in bad shape. He had taken several hard blows.

"How you doing?" he asks his friend.

"Never better," Alonzo responds. Reaching up for Tempels arm, "Give me a hand," and begins pulling himself up.

"I don't think that's such a good idea..." Tatiana says even as the young man stands, still holding the towel against his head. Others see for the first time the extent of blood that has soaked the back of his shirt and stained the polished stone floor beneath him.

Mac frowns and orders "Lay back down Alonzo. Medical Response Team, report to Club Rio immediately."

Despite his repeated assurance that he's fine and a steadfast refusal to lie down, they finally persuade the young warrior to sit at a quiet table near the east exit in the quietest section of the nightclub. Charley Company gathers around him. Cheryl fusses behind the bar, staying close and keeping an eye on the proceedings.

Several club patrons step forward to offer assistance, one of them an off duty MRT medico. "Let me take a look at that cut, Mac," the woman says as she moves around behind Alonzo. Looking under the bloody towel, "The bleeding has stopped but you will need a repair surgeon to close it." Moving around to his side, she turns his head to face her, pulling down his cheeks, gazing into his eyes, "You are suffering from a mild concussion. But if you take it easy, you should be fine."

"So... was she worth it?" Brice asks after reviewing the start of the fight as recorded from Alonzo's visor.

Alonzo glares at him.

"Can you believe that Alonzo let a pretty shortimer set him up for a sucker punch?" Corazon asks, also having replayed the vid. Grinning at the look Alonzo gives him, he shrugs, his body language saying that facts are facts.

"On the up side, at least she was pretty. Most of them look like they shaved their ass and are waking backward," Brice says to a mixed review. A few chuckle at his crude joke but most ignore it.

Upon receiving a call, Consuela turns away, heading back towards the booth not seeking privacy, just a place to talk uninterrupted. Only Jason makes note of it.

Tempel listens to the banter and watches as a cleanup disk, glowing red with avoidance lights and less than a foot in diameter, scurries across the dance floor collecting the blood and other biomaterials. Before it's finished, the band starts to play and things begin to return to normal. It would have been much the same if Alonzo had been killed. Tempel pushes those dark thoughts aside. Making up his mind, he turns to his companions and states, "It's been a long day. After Alonzo is taken care of, I'm going to take off, catch a bite, then get some sleep."

"Mind if I join you?" Sam purrs, her eyes speaking louder than her words.

Tempel grins knowing he wouldn't get much sleep if he agreed, finding the prospect appealing, but before he can reply...

"Not me! I want to party!" Brice declares, "SuperNovA has a new shark that I want to check out. Who's with me?" Brice looks around the group. SuperNovA is another nightclub fashioned after a Vegas casino, all glitz and bright lights, instead of hard rock and shadows.

Turning to Tatiana, Corazon asks, "What about you?"

"I think I will go with Alonzo then hook up with Karl. I'll see you tomorrow at roll call," she responds, shutting the door on anything more. She and Karl have become hot items recently, cutting down on the time spent with other friends.

"Tell that big Swede he's the luckiest man alive," Corazon says with a grin. Not in the least surprised but he would be lying if he said he wasn't disappointed. He turns back to Brice and says, "I'm in!" Corazon never lets one rejection spoil his entire night and SuperNovA is one of his favorite hotspots. He need never sleep alone.

Snuggling up next to Odessa, Brice asks, "An hour or so at the tables, then my place?"

She grins and nods. "Sure, why not. I love kicking your ass right before I kiss it and make it all better," she coos, her smile softening her words and earning a hearty chuckle from the others. They all know Brice talks a good game but pretty much everyone pounds him in any serious competition not involving brute force.

Kipper and Karyl both shake their heads when Brice looks at them, "Sorry, something has come up that needs tending." Karyl grins mischievously, tightening her hold on Kipper.

Over at the booth, well away from the discussion, Consuela is still deep in her own conversation and without saying a word to anyone, gets up and walks through the club away from the group and out the west exit. Again, Jason is the only one to notice. He figures the call must have been from Joey Parker. The two of them are pretty tight nowadays, something Jason isn't particularly pleased about.

"I'll tag along," Jason says, suddenly wanting to get drunk.

"Great!" Brice exclaims and asks Tempel, "Why not eat at Lucifer's Diner? You and Sam can walk with us on our way to SuperNovA."

Tempel shrugs, "Fine with me."

"Sure, why not," Sam imitates Odessa perfectly, receiving smiles and grins from everyone including Odessa herself.

They are interrupted by the arrival of MRT. Without any fanfare, the medicos walk the injured man out to the waiting ambulance, Tatiana at his side. They already know the story and the extent of his injuries and waste no time in getting him on his way to the hospital. By morning he will be good as new without even a scar to show for his carelessness.

****

Emerging from Steinway Avenue, Brice and Odessa leads the small group of friends across the North Courtyard. They swing wide of a tall three-level stone fountain and make a beeline for an eatery on the other side of the square. It has a striking holographic sign on its roof just above the entrance featuring a red devil complete with horns and a forked tail, making stabbing motions with his pitchfork towards the words, *Lucifer's Diner, Fine Dining with a Flare.* Flames dance about the devil's feet and his head turns to look down upon those passing by, eyes flaring briefly as he flashes a fang-filled smile before turning back, stabbing once more at the message. The basic sequence repeats for every citizen, but never twice in the exact same way.

The air in the Courtyard is damp, brimming with the scent of flowers and other greenery growing in elaborate planters and in neat little gardens scattered across the broad expanse of polished stone. Laughter and loud boisterous talking echo within the subterranean plaza set to the background sound of gently falling water.

Brice catches sight of two teen girls sitting on the low stone wall of the fountain dangling their feet in its water, giggling over something. One of them is his cousin, Emily, who he really doesn't want to see right now. Adults and children of all ages freely move about the courtyard, laughing and enjoying each others company. Only the three shortimers pay the group any attention. Tempel notices them from across the courtyard sitting at a table outside La Bruschetta having coffee and staring.

"Later!" Brice calls over his shoulder on his way past Lucifer's. Then he, Odessa, Jason and Corazon are gone, disappearing into the mall.

The interior of the diner is long and narrow with an entrance at each end. The entire space between consists of windows that look out upon the courtyard and a white countertop stretches along the entire length of the opposite wall. On the customer side of the counter is a perfectly straight row of backless stools, their bright red round pads supported by a single silver tube bolted to the floor. Polished aluminum paneling under the countertop reflects the stools like a mirror. On the working side of the counter are matching white cabinets, flanking an open window equipped with a wide sill, where food is passed from the kitchen. More aluminum paneling covers the exposed walls. A swinging door at one end leads from behind the counter back to the kitchen. Supplies and other diner paraphernalia are neatly scattered about, close at hand to facilitate serving the customers.

A row of booths runs along the front wall, their white table tops just a few inches below the windows. Red imitation leather bench seats are reflected in polished aluminum paneling that extends along the wall below the windows. Each table has its own old fashioned salt and pepper shakers and paper napkin holders, pushed against the wall and partially reflected in the paneling.

At one end of the diner is a hand painted mural depicting a scene from an old vid, a young man wearing a black leather jacket straddling a motorcycle, his feet firmly planted on the ground, his arms crossed over his chest, and a wave of black hair falling down in front of his eyes. A cigarette dangles from his lips and its smoke curls about his head. Behind him are more bikers and their leather clad women, some astride motorbikes while others aggressively stand with feet spread wide, hands on their hips or crossed over their chest. Their expressions are defiant as if challenging the onlookers to a fight.

The other end contains a door leading to the washroom and along side it a smaller mural showing the bikers cruising two-by-two down a narrow blacktop highway stretching across a flat desert, hair flowing back in the wind and their expressions much more serene.

"Greetings Sam, Tempel. What can I get for you?" The tall thin man behind the counter asks them as they come in.

Sliding onto a stool, Tempel replies without bothering to look at a menu, "Greetings Lou, chili and a beer and don't be stingy with the onions."

The man smiles, Tempel always orders chili and a beer when he comes here. "You got it. And for you, Sam?" he asks.

"The same," she replies. The aroma of fresh cornbread wafts from the kitchen. "And a slice of cornbread," she adds.

Lou smiles and nods, turns to the open window and calls out, "Lucy, two chilies hold the peppers, extra onions and cornbread!" He picks up a tall glass and places it at an angle beneath the tap before pulling back on the slender handle. Beer slides into the glass smoothly building up a head by the time it is full. He sits it down and repeats the process, placing the two beers in front of his customers. Reaching under the counter he adds a squirt bottle filled with honey and a platter of butter. Nothing beats fresh baked cornbread smothered in butter and honey.

Behind them, beyond the windows of the diner and across the courtyard, the three shortimers pay their tab and leave the sidewalk café heading directly towards the diner.

Beyond the fact they are speaking a language Magi can not interpret, there is something more that makes her cautionary programs increase their level of warnings. Extrapolation shows her that a confrontation between Tempel, Sam and these strangers is likely.

"Tempel, Sam, you have company coming in at your twelve. The same people that beat up Alonzo," Magi says even while she is notifying the closest police patrol.

Realizing that they will not arrive in time, Magi calls to Brice, Odessa, Corazon and Jason, "Stop! You must return to North Courtyard immediately at best speed."

Without asking why they turn and head back, only then questioning her.

Tempel and Sam link to the diner's outside sensors and watch as the three make their way across the courtyard. It's obvious in the men's demeanor that they have someplace to go while the girl hangs back. They rise from their seats and walk to the door, "Keep that chili hot, Lou. We'll be right back," Sam tells the man behind the counter who looks puzzled by the turn of events. The two Lunarian warriors step out of the doorway keeping their backs to the diner watching the shortimers approach. The woman stops at the fountain taking a seat on the wide stone wall around its perimeter not far from Emily and her friend.

As the men draw near they slow and separate putting about ten yards between them. Jafa, the younger of the two, locks his gaze on Tempel, hate for this particular infidel boiling in the depths of his soul. "Are you prepared to meet Allah?" His hand is poised over his sidearm like a cobra ready to strike.

Jafa appears to be in his mid-twenties with dark Mediterranean features partially hidden behind the strange visor. He is several inches shorter and many pounds lighter than his older companion, Malik.

Temple steps away from Sam giving them both a clear field of fire and bracing him with Jafa. "There is no god, you superstitious fool! But if it's death you seek, then you came to the right place," he responds boldly, immediately seeing the desired results. Jafa's anger grows until he can barely contain himself. Behind the shortimers he senses the approach of Odessa, Brice, Jason and Corazon.

"We got your back!" Brice says scanning the expanse of the courtyard and beyond looking for anyone that may try a long range shot. They see only Lunarians scrambling to get out of the line of fire. But the mall's arboretum stretches a thousand yards and is filled with good hiding spots that can be used by a sniper to shoot from. The four fan out focusing their attention away from the confrontation looking for the slightest energy signature or movement.

Sam and Malik stare at each other across the intervening distance. Beneath his bug-eyed visor, the older man's lips curl into an ugly scowl that matches his aggressive body language. He is much shorter than she, built heavy and near the ground, with close cropped salt-and-pepper hair and a matching scruffy beard that is more salt than pepper. His weathered skin leaves little doubt that he has been around the block more than a few times.

Both shortimers appear confident, hands loose over their sidearms. Across less then twenty feet of smooth polished stone, the young Lunarians face down the two off-world assailants, hands hovering over holstered weapons.

The four stand tense, poised before the gates of death.

"Hold it right there!" bellows a male voice. Emerging from Steinway Avenue, a small police patrol in tan and black uniforms races across North Courtyard coming up behind Malik and Jafa. "At ease! If anyone moves they will answer to me!" the Lieutenant in command thunders as he comes to a stop behind the standoff.

Tempel recognizes the voice without seeing him. Lieutenant Hugh O'Reilly, a DNA sequencer in his civilian life, has grown up in one of Dakota's many residential habitats. Influenced by a grandfather born and raised in Ireland, he has come to cherish many of his mannerisms, cultivating them into a brogue that would pass muster in any pub in the British Isles. He's shorter than Tempel but easily masses over two-hundred pounds of bone and muscle. With the Lieutenant is Sergeant Skylor Dugan, Tempels older brother, and Dana Monroe, his cousin. Joey Parker, a friend he has known all his life and also a member of Dakota freehold, rounds out the small patrol. Here, in the heart of Lincoln County, it's not surprising to have so many Dugans represented in local law enforcement. As one of the founding families of Aldrin Station, the Dugan clan is a large close-knit family with many ties to the community.

O'Reilly has been kept abreast of the situation through Magi. She linked him with the nearby sensors which provided real time information of the rapidly evolving situation. He moves to flank the confrontation, directing his officers to spread out, their weapons already drawn, effectively placing the two strangers into a potentially deadly kill zone. Within seconds of O'Reilly's arrival, the two aggressors know it would be suicide to draw.

With the situation stabilized, O'Reilly accesses both men's bioID chips. He's careful to keep out of his officer's line of fire as he approaches the older man, "If it isn't Mustafa Malik. What brings you in from the Highlands?"

Malik scowls sullenly, knowing that his chance for a kill is over. "*May Allah grant me one wish, to kill you repeatedly throughout eternity,*" he says calmly in ancient Aramaic. Even he is intimidated by the sudden appearance of these policemen, guns drawn, obviously more than willing to cut him down if he weren't careful. The voice of the infidel grates against his nerves.

O'Reilly peers intently at Malik, sensing cold indifference. "Speaking in an unknown language is bothersome but it will not affect the aim of my officers."

"Officers!" the man spits this time in English, "Bah! You are nothing but vigilantes! I don't expect justice from such as you."

O'Reilly's voice takes on a hard edge. "What you can expect is to die if you draw your weapons." The lieutenant pauses, looking intently at Malik, fully expecting a retort.

When Malik scowls and remains quiet, he turns to the younger man, "Anwar Jafa, you have been here less than a month and already getting into trouble. Let me give you a piece of advice, don't hang with this loser!"

"We have done nothing!" Jafa says, furious that they have been thwarted. He too realizes that he will not be able to kill the hated infidel today. He tells himself that it is only a matter of time, Allah will see to that.

"It's not so much what you have done, but what you have in mind to do," O'Reilly says.

"Since when is thinking a crime?" Jafa asks. "I thought that in a democracy" the word rolls off his tongue under duress, "a person was free to think what they want?"

"That is true, you are free to think what you want but this little confrontation is a little more than just thinking," O'Reilly responds, moving to come up behind the two.

Malik remains calm not offering any resistance. He is acutely aware of the guns covering him, and is convinced they are looking for the least excuse to open fire. He crosses his arms making it obvious that he is keeping his hands away from his weapon. Jafa follows his lead and does the same, his facial muscles twitching with suppressed anger.

O'Reilly nods and slips both men's sidearms out of their holsters. Motioning to Skylor Dugan, the lieutenant gives him the two disrupters, "By law I must request that you both provide authenticity to the official video. It is your right as a non Lunarian citizen living in the Republic of Luna to refuse, but you do so at your own risk," he pauses, waiting for some response. A sullen silence is his answer. "I didn't think so. Sergeant, take Parker and escort these gentlemen and their lady friend over there out of Lincoln County. Oh, and Sergeant, if they give you any trouble, shoot them."

Skylor nods, "Aye! You heard LT! Let's move out!" he motions to the men with his sidearm.

A little grin comes to the face of Malik as he realizes that the incident is over. There is not a doubt in his mind that if the situation were reversed he would kill these arrogant Lunarians. But he relies on the restrictions within their own laws forbidding such an obvious solution to their problems.

Officer Dana Monroe sighs and holsters her weapon. "Tempel, you guys are supposed to be having fun, relaxing after your shift."

"This is what we do for fun!" Brice says from behind him. "We also steal candy from babies and trip old people when we can find them!"

O'Reilly doesn't need to look at their bioID's, as members of Lincoln County PD he personally knows each and every officer. But he is still required to complete an incident report and like so many others down through history, the lieutenant doesn't like doing paperwork. With a sigh, his hands flash as he begins filling out the online form. Starting with those nearest him, he moves left to right, pulling data from the officer's bioID and dropping it in the appropriate places.

Senior Lieutenant Tempel Dugan, 22nd Metro Division, Charley Company, 845396380

Sergeant IT Samantha Odegaard, 22nd Metro Division, Charley Company,

841593378

Officer Brice Guyart, 22nd Metro Division, Charley Company, 846700215

Officer Odessa Simpson, 22nd Metro Division, Echo Company, 841497162

Officer Jason Piqualow, 22nd Metro Division, Charley Company, 841667910

Officer Corazon Montano, 22nd Metro Division, Charley Company, 847177623

"Before you leave I want each and every one of you to complete your individual authentications," O'Reilly says. Authentication is a legal process whereby the data recorded by a citizen's visor and/or public sensors is verified and submitted to Magi for inclusion into the permanent record.

Several groans are heard among the six officers.

"Don't make me come looking for you! Magi, inform me of anyone not finished in the next thirty minutes." His glare is enough to insure that there will be no slackers.

"Aye Lieutenant O'Reilly, will do!" Magi responds, heard by everyone.

"Ok Tempel, we're out-a-here. Don't forget, your people must finish the authentications!" With a wave of his hand the two policemen move quickly across the courtyard and disappear down the corridor, intending to meet up with Skylor and Parker somewhere not far ahead.

****

The locker-room is loud and boisterous as LCPD prepares for shift change. The space is large, providing for hundreds of police officers to don uniforms or vacsuits. Steam roils out of the showers along one side as the men and women ready themselves for the days work. Charley Company is but a small portion of this chaos.

Just minutes before first call, the ramp is packed as it always is at this time, but everyone moves swiftly and confidently without any pushing or shoving, each officer proceeding at the same fast pace. The four hundred men and women swarming around him are all dressed in the tan and black of the Lincoln County Police Department, the bright blue patch on his right shoulder further identifies him as a member of 22nd Metro Division. Emerging from the ramp into the parade grounds, Tempel makes his way to where his unit is gathering, taking his place at the left front of the formation, and begins counting heads. As senior lieutenant, it's his job to make sure everyone is present or accounted for.

"Sam, where are you?" he asks when he notices she's not present.

"I've been called to a meeting with Abby. I'll see you after roll call," is her immediate response. They don't bother casting an image to each other, staying with audio only for this brief conversation.

"Captain, Sergeant Odegaard is absent but accounted for," Tempel reports.

"Thank you, Lieutenant!" Kitajima responds sharply from the group of captains just emerging from the battalion offices onto the parade ground.

Tempel senses anger, but doesn't have time to dwell on it.

As the officers take their places at the head of Luna's finest, they bring each company to parade rest, hands locked behind their backs, feet shoulder-width apart, sidearms holstered and eyes looking straight ahead. Following ancient tradition, the eerie sounds of a bugle begins to echo across the subterranean cavern calling them to assembly.

Before the last note fades into silence, Commander House's adjutant calls forth across the parade ground, "Attennnnntion!" The sound of four hundred boots striking stone and hands slapping holsters explodes in a single thunderclap that reverberates up and down the man-made stone cavern, putting vivid punctuation to the buglers' call.

At least half of these officers will spread throughout Lincoln County relieving the patrols currently on duty. Others are scheduled for training, expanding and honing their various abilities. Still others are scheduled for guard or escort duty. This scene is duplicated in each of the city's ten boroughs as the shift changes. Security Chief Dugan has mandated that ten percent of the population be on uniformed duty at all times while the remainder of the population keeps their weapons close to hand.

Roll call sounds along the line of companies, "Charley Company, all present and accounted for!" Captain Kitajima Osaka calls out in his turn.

A minute later it's finished, more of a formality than necessity, and the assemblage is released to begin their assigned duties. Keeping Charley Company at attention, Kitajima does an about face, "Column Left! Harh!" he barks.

In near perfect unison, each officer snaps a sharp left turn while remaining at attention.

"By Twos, Forward.... Harh!" Kitajima barks out. The two squads move out with Master Sergeant Hackling calling cadence from a position near the rear. Kitajima keeps pace alongside, marching the company off the parade ground and through a short corridor just wide enough to walk three abreast.

They emerge in the central level of the well-used practice warren. Here is where the battalion conducts most of its practical simulations, everything from target practice to combat maneuvers.

"Double Time! Harh!" The column begins a long winding run along a track around the perimeter of the huge space, each officer leaning forward, balancing traction with acceleration. Kitajima sets an unusually strenuous pace even for lunar gravity, challenging them to stay in formation while maintaining speed. Although the officers of Charley Company are physically fit, they are soon covered in sweat.

Thirty minutes later, "Company... Harch!" The formation slows to a march virtually all of them gasping for breath. Kitajima leads them off the track to a grouping of tables used as a classroom.

"Company... Halt!" Kitajima barks, "Fall out and find a seat!"

The officers break ranks obeying the order even as they recover from the workout.

Kitajima walks past the tables, turns and faces the company. "At Ease!" he says, officially bringing the company to order. These young men and women have remained silent and attentive not knowing what's wrong, just that something is bothering their Captain this morning. "A few hours ago several of your comrades risked your mission!"

Every eye is locked on the Captain and no one dares move a muscle.

Coming to stand where he looks down at Tempel he continues, "I have reviewed the security tapes from North Courtyard and I am shocked!" Kitajima barks directly at him. "Lieutenant Dugan, did you know who that was?"

"No sir, I had never personally met Malik before last night." Tempel responds.

"He's on the watch list, as is Anwar Jafa. It's your job to know! They were just about to chew you up and spit you out!"

"Excuse me Captain but I can take them in a fair fight," Tempel defends himself.

Kitajima moves cat-quick to stand looking down at his senior lieutenant, almost daring him to flinch. "Lieutenant Dugan, Malik has survived two gunfights that I know of," he says quietly, "How many have you?"

Tempel's suddenly wishes he had kept his mouth shut.

"Answer me, Lieutenant!" Kitajima growls.

Tempel is now sitting at full attention. "None Sir!" is his response.

Kitajima moves down to Jason, "How many gunfights have you participated in, Officer Piqualow?"

"None Sir!" he echoes his comrade. After witnessing Tempel's tongue lashing, he wants no part of Kitajima this morning.

Kitajima looks out among the assemblage, "Has anybody here ever been in a gunfight…..Speak up!"

"No Sir!" is the unanimous response.

He moves further down the platform glaring out at the young faces staring back, "All of you are fully qualified SWAT members but none of you have been bloodied… I fear that until you personally participate in real combat, you will not fully appreciate the point I'm making."

Kitajima stops in front of Brice, glaring down at him. "When you deployed at North Courtyard you faced outward. Why?" he asks.

Brice looks out of the corner of his eye at Jason.

"Don't look at him, just answer the damn question! Why did you face outward and put your backs to Malik and Jafa?"

"We didn't know if there were any others in North Courtyard or out on the arboretum that would back them up," Brice responds.

"Besides, we had two against two," Jason adds.

"That's my point!" Kitajima bores in, "When you come up against any enemy, but especially an unknown enemy, you must threaten them with everything you've got and be willing to back it up! There is no place on a battlefield for sportsmanship! That line of thinking will get you killed!"

Kitajima looks down at Corazon, "If you can get behind them, do it." He moves on to Jason, "If you can shoot first, do it. Find a weakness and exploit it with overwhelming force! It's the only way to stay alive! Work as a team! Together you are much stronger then Malik! But if you voluntarily split your forces you weaken yourselves, inviting trouble!"

"This confrontation was the result of a bar fight. Are you saying they should have gunned them down?" Consuela asks bluntly.

Kitajima stops in front of Sergeant Navarro, "No sergeant, that's not what I am saying. You are less likely to need to kill someone once they come to the conclusion that any aggression on their part would simply be suicide. I am talking about taking the situation far beyond mutual assured destruction. Make the confrontation as lopsided in your favor as physically possible. By leaving the front door even slightly ajar, you were inviting them to kick it down! If someone is threatening to harm you or your comrades you must view them as hostile and treat with extreme prejudice! Failure to do so will eventually cost you your life! And those of your friends! Look around you. Your comrades depend on you for support and mutual protection. If you're dead you cannot fulfill that duty!" He turns and moves back to center stage, "Is That Clear!"

"Aye!" is the unified and conditioned response from Charley Company.

Kitajima glares around the assemblage, fourteen of Luna's finest young men and women, and slowly nods. "I sincerely hope that it is! But I doubt it! Knowledge of this type must be paid for in blood! No one paid the price! No one died." His gaze passes form one officer to the next finding determination and courage in the young faces, wondering who will be that first casualty.

"We have a new mission for today," Kitajima announces in a much calmer voice, satisfied they have absorbed the lesson as best he can teach it.

Lunarian citizens throughout the Republic spend at least eight weeks out of every year on active duty, fulfilling the roles of peacemakers and law enforcement within their communities' police departments. Years ago there was talk about reducing the time but instead, with tensions running so high, Charley Company, along with many other companies, has had their time increased substantially. Besides, the training and experience make them superior citizens, more rounded and better prepared for the harsh realities of the 21st century, not to mention, keeping them all actively engaged in the defense of the Republic of Luna.

Every citizen has continuing responsibilities within the security structure somewhere. Off-duty simply means a change of clothes, not a change of attitude. Luna in 2092 is an armed camp, well aware of the hatred brewing on not-so-distant Earth, having felt the wrath of religious extremists on many occasions.

The situation makes for some interesting relationships. An officer may serve under someone within the department's chain of command and yet be that person's supervisor in their civilian jobs. It is an unwritten law that the PD chain of command, when invoked in civilian life, takes precedence. But it is considered bad form to throw their rank around while wearing street clothes. It's never done.

Special Weapons and Advanced Technology is one of the choice assignments within any PD, only very special citizens need apply. These young men and women are trained to use the latest gear and techniques. Charley Company is one of several SWAT teams in Lincoln County PD's 22nd Metro Division, each are organized into two squads containing a lieutenant, a sergeant, a sergeant-in-training and four officers.

"Red squad will deploy outside along Cannery Row with Blue as backup. Your job will be to clear personnel and cargo coming off the tin cans before it enters the city." A few groans greet the announcement. No frontline unit likes customs duty and these young Lunarians sees themselves as the tip of the spear, even if they have no combat experience. Kitajima doesn't bother sugar coating the assignment, he doesn't like it much either. "Tempel, you are excused from this assignment. But for the rest of you, I want you keep your eyes open and your mind on your duty. This latest rash of bombings could be the start of something bigger! So look sharp people!"

"Captain?"

"What is it Brice?"

"Can we wear the new suits?"

"Negative, standard vacsuits only," looking out at the company, "Any more questions…We reform at oh-nine-hundred on the parade ground. Dismissed!"

The company remains motionless for a fraction of a second and then explodes into action. They had a free hour to kill and didn't want to waste a single second. Everyone except Tempel, that is.

Tempel watches his comrades leave. A few look curiously at him as they pass but even Brice knows better than to say anything.

Kitajima comes and stands close by Tempel who raises his eyebrows. "You are to report to Magi for special assignment," Kitajima says.

"Magi, what have you got for me," Tempel asks as the last young officer vacates the area.

Having waited for Tempel to initiate the conversation, the image of Magi appears before him standing only a few feet away, as visually real as Kitajima but physically only digital data that he can never touch. Her soft brown eyes and dark hair streaked with gray neatly pulled back in a bun, is a familiar sight.

Since Magi exists only in the digital realm of computers, the AI could present itself using virtually any appearance, but historically it has always been feminal. From the beginning, Magi has used the results of morphing a group of female elders into a single person, a visual average that makes her quite beautiful and very grandmotherly. It also uses the voiceprint composite of these same women to speak with, giving Magi a truly unique character, one that any citizen recognizes and trusts instantly.

"Abby wants you and Sam to report to Hawking Spaceport for escort duty." Magi communicates with them through their visors. But that isn't the only means she has to talk with citizens or they with her. Developed before visors were perfected, the Republic contains a network of public interfaces with speakers and microphones built into them. These tiny devices use reflective wave technology to accurately transmit a full range of sounds. Not only are these tiny sound generators included in every scanner, but more are built into businesses and restaurants, in corridors and airlocks, in conference rooms and even baths. All of which are only a part of a vast interconnecting system that extends across Luna and throughout orbital space.

The element of Magi that Tempel could touch is dispersed over many CPU's, each the culmination of a century and a half of continuous research and development into solid-state integrated circuits. From the beginning, computers were modularized with a motherboard at their center. These early machines contained single-thread CPU's able to perform only one instruction at a time in a plodding linear fashion. It wasn't long before engineers began putting more than one CPU on a single motherboard, more than one motherboard within a single computer, and linking many computers into gigantic arrays, using software to divide the computation among the different processors. They realized the more threads they have working on a given problem, the faster they obtained answers. The first multi-thread CPU arrived well before the turn of the century. Time after time, what started in the realm of supercomputers became standard in the next generation of hardware. In 2034 the Lunarians developed the first Infinite-Thread CPU. Since then, ten's of millions of ITCPU's have been manufactured, the latest employing multi-dimensional crystals using quantum spin characteristics as their digital building blocks. Others are older and less advanced by this benchmark with their own unique set of qualities, but for the most part, an ITCPU found in Dakota warren works just as well as one found in any rover, or farm, or pizza parlor, or science lab, or visor.

With every ITCPU there is at least one Zettasphere, bringing together computing power and storage capacity unmatched in human experience. Zettaspheres already hold almost a half century of Lunarian history, including the visor recording of every citizen who ever wore one. All across Luna, audio/visual data is constantly recorded and archived for future generations, everything from security scanners to bakery ovens, from the temperature sensor on a shower to the CAD program on a workshop lathe.

Taken together, the ITCPU's and Zettaspheres compose the universe of Magi's existence but not who she is. Magi is so much more than just an extensive network of processors and memory spheres. Originating seven decades ago as a simple voice activated communications network, the AI has grown with each new generation of Lunarians. From the start the software was able to learn from its interactions with humans, and that ability has matured into what many believe is true machine intelligence. Within Magi's kernel, algorithms have evolved that imitate human response not only in the audio/visual interface but in the underlying patterns of emotion and thought, giving the program the illusion of being human. Magi emulates the mind of man.

But to truly understand Magi, one must first understand threads. A thread is not something you can hold in your hand or even confine within one specific piece of hardware. Instead a thread is a copy of Magi capable of independent decision making and adaptive growth that can operate wherever it finds CPU capacity. As such, a single thread will freely move from place to place throughout the network like a ghost in the machine.

Theoretically, the number of threads operating within the network is infinite. Yet, reason dictates there must be a practical limit, but it's a large number they are far from reaching. Currently there are over eighty million threads operating across Luna, most assigned to equipment controls, security sensors, machinery and a copious number of other devices, both large and small. Like the cells within a mighty beast, they all communicate with each other, letting the whole know the condition of the one.

While servicing Lunarian technology is important, it's the people who make Magi who she is. Before they are even conceived, citizens are assigned a thread that stays with them their entire life. All across the network, these citizen versions of Magi preferentially interact, synchronizing data and helping maintain consistency when interfacing with humans. This constant exchange of information between threads is an orderly and dynamic process creating a single entity perceived as Magi. *E Pluribus Unum*. Out of many, one.

In 2092 Magi permeates life on Luna. Over the last seventy years, as the software became more capable, it was given an ever increasing amount of responsibility within Lunarian society. Now that several generations have grown up with Magi, few question that a software program should play such a central role in their lives. Under the guidance of medical specialists, Magi controls the intricate details of bringing male and female DNA together to create offspring with the desired traits. Later during pregnancy Magi monitors the health of the growing fetus and mother, and after birth Magi is the babysitter, teacher, friend and confidant for their entire life. As an individual grows, Magi provides everything from the morning wakeup call, to supporting school projects, to analyzing the structure of their subterranean cities. Magi is the secretary and the maid, the kitchen helper and the farm worker, the banker, the doctor, and their friend. No Lunarian is ever truly alone. But in the final analysis, Magi is still a program and not alive in any biological sense, although many believe otherwise.

"Abby wants you and Sam to meet a Federation defector, a Mr. Lazarus Sheffield. Lindsey is bringing him in and will hand off to you. They will be arriving on Trans World Flight L95 at eleven-ten. Not only is he the first Federation runner in over a decade, he was a Senior Analyst in the Department of Homeland Security," Magi continues, "You and Sam are to take Mr. Sheffield out to lunch. Abby wants you to use your own judgment as to what questions to ask. Just keep him talking. Depending on his answers, Abby has scheduled a meeting with him at thirteen hundred hours."

Tempel shakes his head as if to clear it, "Wait a minute Magi, Sam and I are taking this guy out to lunch?"

"Aye," Magi says cheerfully. "Sam will meet you at the terminal."

Kitajima shrugs, "I'm sure Abby has reasons for giving you point on this. Don't let her down."

"I won't."

"This is the time when humans have begun to sail the sea of space."
Carl Sagan (1934-1996)

Aldrin Station

Trans World Flight L95 is continuously tracked from the moment it separates. Orbital and ground based sensors scan the craft many times as it crosses the void between Heaven and Earth, probing for the slightest abnormality. Six hours into the flight, Lazarus sleeps through a brief freefall as the thrusters shut down and the shuttle flips 180° before starting them back up, decelerating at standard one-sixth G the rest of the way to lunar orbit. Luna Central oversees the shuttle's orbital insertion, the undocking from the Translunar Transfer Vehicle and the subsequent deorbit of the Lunar Lander, with minimal input from the onboard flight attendants.

Lindsey gently shakes him, "Lazarus, wake up. We are preparing to land."

Lazarus claws his way to consciousness, feeling comfortable in the laidback overstuffed recliner. He yawns and stretches, "Thanks. I must have fallen asleep reading."

"You did... almost twelve hours ago. I've never seen someone sleep so hard!"

The descent to the surface is quiet and smooth right up to the point the AI cranks up the Landers main thrusters twenty minutes out of Aldrin Station. The sound increases to a deep resonant throbbing vibration that runs up Lazarus's spine like an electric current. The flight trajectory is designed never to exceed three G's but it seems like more, much more, to Lazarus, pushing his stomach down around his ankles. He grips his armrests and gazes out the window willing his body to relax as the stark lunar landscape whirls by at an alarming rate.

Micro-satellites continuously track the descent, never breaking contact, repeatedly illuminating the shuttle with long range MRI. Satellite and ground based sensors pick up the return signal, forwarding it to powerful computers for analysis.

Luna Central flight controllers and the defensive cannon emplacements strung out along the top of Rim Mountain, monitor the shuttle when it appears from over the horizon, its thrusters flaring with energy as it decelerates on final approach. Its path into Alphonsus crater is from the north, right over the small town of Summerhaven. Powerful scanners swept the craft time after time, collecting a mountain of data, among which is detailed information on the shuttles structure, her passengers, and her cargo. The scans are quickly and carefully compared to the thousands of other shuttle flights stored in the database, all the while the cannons keep their crosshairs on the spacecraft. No unusual anomalies are found and the shuttle is allowed to continue unharmed. Duty officers in three different command centers relax letting their systems fall back to standard recon mode, looking for meteorites or terrorists threatening the Alphonsus crater complex.

Lazarus can see surface installations inside the crater as the shuttle slows. The vibration reach's a crescendo as the AI brings the ship to a stop, hovering a hundred feet above the ground before slowly settling down towards Luna.

Almost imperceptivity, the shuttle comes to rest on the spaceport pad and the thrusters fall silent. The sudden quiet sends a shiver through Lazarus and his stomach does a little flip but settles back nicely. Slowly he releases his grip on the armrests and relaxes, not realizing until that moment how tense he had become the last few minutes. He feels momentarily lightheaded and dizzy, a common reaction to the wild gravity swings he just experienced.

It does nothing to stem his euphoria. He made it! He's on the moon!

Lazarus retrieves his small bag from under the seat and looks at Lindsey in triumph. "I can't believe I'm really here!" He can hardly hold still, his hands fidgeting and restless. He's ready to explode. "I can't believe I got away."

Lindsey smiles at his enthusiasm, "But you did and you are." For her, it felt good to be home but she can't imagine what it must be like for Lazarus. She recalls her own first arrival years before and finds the memory faded and distant. She promises herself that she will find the vid and refresh her memories. After all, it was a big day for her as well.

Most of the shuttles passengers are out of their seats and heading towards the exit. Both flight attendants wait next to the airlock door, anticipating the arrival of the ground transports. Lazarus and Lindsey are content to remain in their seat talking quietly.

Izzy and Mary had talked extensively during the flight, laughter frequently punctuating their conversation and now the two are old friends. Izzy stands, collecting their baggage and other items. Before leaving Izzy turns to Lazarus and Lindsey, "You younguns' have a great life! And don't except any wooden nickels!"

"Peace and happiness for you as well," Lindsey responds looking puzzled. It's obvious she doesn't have a clue what a wooden nickel is or why they shouldn't accept one.

Mary laughs loudly and waves as the two join the other passengers waiting in the aisle for the ground transport to arrive.

Lazarus's expression transforms from excitement to apprehension as if a switch had been thrown. "Are you sure you can't tell me who's meeting us?" he asks for the third time, running his hand over his head.

"I told you, I don't know who Abby is sending. But you can be sure it will be someone you can trust." Taking pity on this earthman so far from anything familiar, she continues, "Relax," she pats his arm reassuringly, "as long as you're truthful, you will be treated with respect."

"Well, I've got to admit. This is a better plan than the one I was going to use," Lazarus says.

"Of course it is," she replies squeezing his arm for emphasis. "Things are different on Luna. Don't be judgmental when something you don't understand hits you upside the head. Keep in mind that the Lunarians have been living here for over sixty-five years," Lindsey says, repeating some of her advice.

His eyes glow with excitement and he smiles nervously, "Yes, I remember."

Lindsey likes this part of Lazarus very much. The headfirst way he handles his fear, the blind courage to make this attempt to help people he never met.

"Lindsey, whatever happens I want you to know how much I appreciate everything you've done." He smiles from ear to ear, thinking again about the hours they had spent together in freefall. "I will never be able to repay you for the generous way you have helped me. I'm forever in your debt."

Lindsey returns his smile, "There you go again, with that debt crap. Get it through your head. You don't owe me anything." She had enjoyed his company. And once she had gotten the whole story out of him, found out about the information he was carrying, it was her duty to make sure the right people heard him. She leans over and kisses Lazarus, communicating her feelings much more effectively than mere words.

They linger over the kiss, only breaking when a sharp bump and the clatter of metal ringing against metal announces the arrival of ground transport. The light over the airlock changes from red to green signaling a good seal has been made and that breathable air awaits them on the other side.

The male fight attendant un-dogs the inner airlock door and swings it open. Stepping into the chamber and out of sight, he unlatches the outer door, opening it with a clank. An attractive young woman accompanies him back into the shuttle, "Welcome to Aldrin Station. Please proceed to the back of the transport. I can only take about half of you. There's another transport right behind me that will take the rest." She moves gracefully aside smiling and welcoming each passenger to Aldrin Station as they move past.

Lazarus starts to rise but Lindsey reaches out and restrains him. "Let's wait for the next one. It shouldn't be long."

Lazarus relaxes back in his seat, content to spend even a few more moments with Lindsey. "Sure. I'm in no hurry," a lie instantly recognized by Lindsey.

"What did I tell you about lying?" she looks at him expectantly.

"Are you serious?"

"Yes, absolutely I'm serious. Little lies grow into bigger ones... If someone asks you how you are feeling, tell them the truth. If you tell someone to have a nice day, mean it. Otherwise keep your mouth shut. The small lies will contaminate you just as quickly as larger ones," Lindsey says.

Lazarus nods, "I shall make every attempt to tell the truth, no matter how painful."

They watch as the transport quickly fills and the shuttles airlock doors close once again. Lazarus can partially see the now filled vehicle from his window. Four giant balloon tires support a scissor mechanism that brings its passenger cabin to the level of the shuttles main airlock. As he watches, it moves away from the ship, lowering the cabin as it goes. Then it turns and is gone. Behind it a second transport takes its place, raising its cabin and inching forward. With another sharp bump and the ringing of metal, the magnetic grapplers lock onto the shuttles outer airlock.

Lindsey rises and leads Lazarus to the exit, nodding pleasantly to the flight attendant as she passes. She picks an empty pair of seats near the back leaving the window for Lazarus.

Scanners sweep across the passengers and their baggage. As before, nothing unusual shows up and clearance is issued to proceed to the terminal at Aldrin Station.

The surface transport moves quickly over the compacted regolith roadway. There isn't much to see out of the small window but Lazarus has his nose pressed close nonetheless. Rim Mountain dominates the horizon. Above it, bright pinpoints of stars are set in the blackness of airless space. He can see part of Earth directly upward but not well enough to recognize a landmass. Looking forward from his window, Lazarus studies the spaceports main airlock as the transport approaches. Like a monstrous storm drain, it protrudes out onto the craters floor from the side of the mountain. The outer door is just large enough to accommodate the transport. Smoothly the vehicle slows to a stop just inside. He can see the sides of the airlock just inches from his window. A moment later the door behind them closes and an atmosphere explosively fills the small volume around the transport. The passengers hear the inside airlock door open with a clank. The transport accelerates out of the chamber and starts down a long tunnel. Everything out his window becomes an indiscriminate blur giving him a distinctive feeling of speed.

"How far do we go in this tunnel?" Lazarus asks.

"It's about a half mile, I would guess," Lindsey responds.

He shakes his head. "That puts, what, a mile of rock over our heads?"

"Something like that. But never forget this is Luna. Everything, including the mountains, weighs only twenty percent of what they would in Arizona," she adds with a mischievous smile.

"Why doesn't that comfort me?" Lazarus states dryly "Twenty percent of big is still big," he points out, returning her smile.

The passengers are not even aware of the transport going through a whole series of airlock doors, each opening just long enough to let the moving vehicle pass before rapidly closing behind it. The system never has more than one door open at any given time. The last opens out onto the expansive main floor of the Stephen Hawking Interplanetary Spaceport. It slows smoothly to a stop alongside several other transports.

The attendant waits until a green light comes on over the airlock door before opening it, "Please follow the yellow markings on the floor to customs. Thank you for flying Trans World Spaceline."

The passengers exit down a ramp to the floor of the terminal. Lindsey links her arm with Lazarus as they descend. Initially, his feet slip, as though he were on ice, his weight insufficient to give him his usual traction on the polished stone floor. Lindsey shows him the Luna shuffle, pushing off with both feet at once, hopping instead of walking. Letting her lead, Lazarus learns a small amount of grace by the time they cover the fifty yards to customs. He's relieved when he finds a workable rhythm. He recalls the ancient black and white films of the first men to walk on the moon, Neil Armstrong and Buzz Aldrin. They may have invented the Luna shuffle but Lunarians perfected it.

****

Even though Hawking Spaceport services forty-one pads, it's not particularly crowded this morning. The domestic flights have lines, but very few travelers are in the interplanetary area, coming or going. Flights to Shennong and Kyoto announce eminent departures. Children chase one another in the waiting area and Tempel can see a group of young Lunarians having a beer in an adjacent lounge, killing time before their flight.

Well armed police officers are stationed at good defensive points around the periphery overlooking the main airlocks. More are standing close by customs as passenger bioID's are checked one last time.

Tempel crosses the terminal and stops where he can see the transport loading area and waits. He is wearing the black and tan of the LCPD, a single gold bar in his lapel designating his rank of lieutenant. The bill of his hat is pulled down shadowing his visor, a police issue silver and black Razor that molds to the contour of his face. All of the people around him are wearing visors of one form or another. It's common on Luna to see ordinary folks going about their everyday tasks wearing the devices. And those that don't wear them have them nearby, in a bag, belt clip, breast pocket or worn around the neck like a piece of jewelry. Tempel is never seen in public without his on and he isn't alone in this practice.

A few minutes later the incoming lock cycles open and the first of two transports enters and parks. Tempel watches as small groups of recent arrivals emerge and follow the marked path towards customs.

"Which one?" Tempel asks Magi even as a second vehicle enters and parks beside the first.

"He is not among the passengers on the first transport," Magi responds as the ramp slides into place for the second vehicle. As the passengers start to emerge she says, "That is him, coming down the ramp beside Lindsey." Lindsey is locked arm in arm with the shortimer, making sure the man doesn't fall. Magi puts a virtual flood light on him while placing the others around him into near darkness.

Tempel maintains his distance while watching the pair closely, granting them a moment more of privacy. The man is wearing a hideous blue, gold, and green tourist shirt, dark blue trousers, a brand new visor, and a small bag slung over his shoulder. His gait is clumsy, what one would expect for someone right off the boat. His shoes slip on the polished stone floor of the terminal.

The man appears to be about thirty-five with a typical high-gravity build, chunky by Luna standards and not especially tall, light brown almost blond hair cropped short making it nearly invisible in the magnification he's using. The shortimer's most striking feature is his deep blue eyes which shift about uneasily. Several times he nervously runs his hand over his head. His gaze repeatedly returns to the armed police officers stationed in the terminal.

"Lindsey has sponsored him and helped setup the meeting with Abby," Magi responds. "She has submitted a record of their conversation onboard the shuttle. I have prepared a summary. Would you care to experience it?" Magi asks.

"Aye, thank you Magi" Tempel responds.

"My pleasure."

The conversation recorded by Lindsey's visor is replayed through his at sixty times normal speed, giving him complete understanding of an hours worth of dialogue in a minute. It's from her perspective, as though he were sitting in her place beside the shortimer listening to him ramble on about religion and some other nonsense concerning the Brotherhood and nuclear weapons. The fact that Lazarus works in the Federation's Department of Homeland Security raises red flags. He trusts the Feds about as far as he can throw Luna.

****

Lazarus and Lindsey are slower than most other passengers moving through the arrival area. It's easy to spot the rookies, they move like they are learning to walk all over again and Lazarus is no exception. He restlessly looks around as he tries to master this crazy way of walking, noting the armed guards. He's uncomfortable in this strange place, yet excited and yearns to see everything. The terminal does not seem that different from other airports he has been in, an open space stretching several hundred yards on its long side and less than half that in width, counters and offices arranged throughout in an open design, people moving about at a leisurely pace. Its calm compared with Athens and Athena's Marketplace. The thing that is strangest to him is the ceiling, its sky blue and glows like a mid-summer Arizona afternoon. Its shape eludes him and he can almost imagine he's standing beneath a cloudless desert sky.

Falling in line, they wait, watching as, one by one, the passengers in front of them go through customs. Lindsey precedes Lazarus passing her left hand over the glowing amber reader. Following her, Lazarus repeats the procedure. He's now officially on the moon!

Lindsey gracefully reclaims his arm keeping him steady as they move forward. He glances nervously at a nearby police officer, his visor letting him see the young woman's face, shadowed by the bill of her hat pulled down low. She doesn't look old enough to be packing a pistol.

"Greetings, Tempel," Lindsey says as they emerge from customs, nodding pleasantly to the strikingly handsome young man waiting for them. Taller then Lazarus, he is lean and muscular, and wearing the same uniform as the officers stationed around the terminal.

"Greetings, Lindsey," he tips his head in response.

Turning she says "Lazarus Sheffield, let me introduce you to Senior Lieutenant Tempel Dugan."

Lazarus starts to extend his hand, quickly recovers and nods his head in a clumsy imitation of the Lunarian custom, "Very pleased to meet you Lieutenant. Please, call me Lazarus."

The man is several inches taller than Lazarus but probably weighs less, despite his broad shoulders. His close cropped hair or no hair at all appears to be the dominate Lunarian style for both men and women. Tempel's movements are fluid and powerful which Lazarus attributes to being born into this environment.

Tempel returns the gesture, "Greetings Lazarus. How was your trip?" he asks.

Lazarus frowns, thinking this is a very youthful escort. He's suddenly worried that no one will take him seriously. But at least it's a Dugan. Pushing down his fears, he tells himself to simply take this one step at a time. "Pleasant but I'm famished. I haven't eaten a decent meal since Phoenix!" She said to be truthful.

Lindsey laughs and adds, "Spaceline and food should never appear in the same paragraph, let alone right next to each other."

The three of them turn and start across the terminal with Lindsey maintaining her hold on Lazarus, helping him learn to cope in the light gravity.

Ignoring her humor Tempel asks, "What would you like to eat? We have a couple hours to kill before your scheduled meeting with grandma Abby. My orders were to take you out for lunch."

Lazarus can sense that this isn't exactly what the young man wants to be doing. But he feels much better knowing Abby had sent her grandson to meet him.

"Yes…Well…" Lazarus's train of thought stumbles as any mans will when a particularly sensuous woman is walking directly towards him. Tempel glances sideways at Lazarus, knowing full well what is going on and curious as to how this earthman will handle it. Lindsey grins, not threatened in the least, watching the show with interest.

Her beauty renders him speechless. With skin the color of honey, her high cheekbones, arching brows, and full lips are exquisitely proportioned around piercing blue eyes. Shaped in the perfect hourglass, she is wearing a pair of black skin-tight stretch Levi's and a white low-cut pullover that draws attention to her unrestrained tits. They sway hypnotically and nipples, hardened by rubbing against the fabric, dare him not to stare. There's something fluid in her movements that he puts down to living in low lunar gravity. Nearly half a head taller than Lazarus, her blond hair is cut even shorter than his. A holster rides low on her wide hips, the butt of a weapon clearly visible. As a lawman, Lazarus has learned to both rely and be skeptical of first impressions but the effect this woman has on him is immediate and overwhelming. He's instantly aroused, his face turning beet red with embarrassed.

The four meet and stop, still in the common area of the terminal, forcing the sparse traffic to move around them like a cluster of boulders in a streambed, "Lazarus Sheffield this is Sergeant Samantha Odegaard," Tempel introduces, mildly amused by the earthman's struggle to maintain his composure.

"Greetings Mr. Sheffield, it's truly a privilege to meet you," Sam says and smiles. Then much to everyone's amazement, she offers her hand.

Delighted and instantly at ease, Lazarus gives her a broad smile and accepts, "I assure you, the pleasure is mine… Sergeant!" he responds. Her hand is warm.

Samantha laughs before releasing him, sending little jolts of electricity through Lazarus. She has grown accustomed to eliciting this reaction from shortimers, but this is her first Federation runner. "Please, call me Sam," turning to Lindsey, "Greetings Lindsey. I hear you won't be going back."

Nodding and still grinning, Lindsey responds enthusiastically, "Aye, the next time I feel Earth's gravity will be too soon!"

"Are you going to join us for lunch?" Sam asks her.

"No, I have some things I need to take care of. I will leave you to get acquainted with Lazarus. He has led a very interesting life."

"Wonderful! I can't wait to hear all about it!" Sam turns back to Tempel and asks, "Have you decided on where we are to eat?"

Tempel shakes his head, "Not really," he responds.

"What's your favorite restaurant, Lindsey?" Lazarus asks, wanting very much for her to stay with them, hoping to tempt her with food.

"Depends on what you want to eat. Breakfast is excellent at Milligan's Café. Lunch… either Mighty Macs or Lucifer's Diner. Savannah's serves a mean fauxsteak but if you want a view nothing beats The Surface Cafe," Lindsey responds. She loves Lunarian food and has long since tried all the best places in Aldrin Station.

"Which one is closer?" Lazarus asks hoping to lure Lindsey to stay by making it a fast lunch.

"Hungry, are we?" Sam laughs, a sultry feminine sound that caresses his ears. "Lucifer's Diner is closest, right next door. We can be there in minutes. But Mighty Macs isn't much further and it's in Brooklyn Mall. What do you want to eat, burgers at Macs or a chili at Lucifer's."

"Take him to Macs and show him the North Courtyard and the mall. He'll love it!" Lindsey says to Sam.

"A burger sounds good!" Lazarus says looking intently at Lindsey, willing her to stay. "Are you sure you can't join us?"

"I'm sorry Lazarus…" her eyes look past him and her voice trails off. Surprise followed by annoyance flashes across her face.

Lazarus turns to see a tall dark-haired young man approaching, his smile wide and welcoming and aimed at Lindsey.

"Lindsey darling, I wanted to be waiting when you got off the transport but was held up. Please forgive me!" He brushes past Lazarus to embrace her, his lips targeting her mouth.

Lindsey halfheartedly returns the embrace, turning her cheek to his lips, "Greetings Dwayne. You shouldn't have bothered."

Dwayne simply chuckles and says, "How quickly we forget." Turning to Tempel and Sam he says, "I told Abby that I would be more than happy to meet Lindsey and our guest but she insisted that you do it."

Tempel looks at Dwayne and says, "I can't imagine why."

Dwayne chuckles again, the sound grating on everyone's nerves. He turns to Lazarus, "You must be the shortimer everyone is talking about."

Lazarus is miffed but unruffled. "Lazarus Sheffield… and you are?"

Again the man laughs, "Dwayne Taylor, grandson of Councilman Zachary Taylor," he says as though it should mean something.

"I have no idea who that is," Lazarus responds. In those few seconds, Lazarus learns as much as he wants about Dwayne Taylor, grandson of Councilman Zachary Taylor. This yahoo's attempted familiarity with Lindsey troubles him deeply. Remembering Lindsey's warning that things are done differently on Luna, he ruthlessly suppresses these unfamiliar emotions until he has time to think. But regardless of the reasons, Dwayne rubs Lazarus the wrong way.

"Zachary Taylor was the first Lunarian." Dwayne stares at Lazarus for a moment. "You have much to learn."

"As do we all," Lindsey says sharply, looking intently at Dwayne. "DT, I have personal business and Lazarus is having lunch with Tempel and Sam. So if you will excuse us…"

Her dismissal finally cut through his facade of friendliness and his expression hardens. "As you wish… I have a few things to discuss with you," he returns her stare. "Call me at your convenience." Without looking or acknowledging anyone else, he turns on his heels and departs the same way he came.

"Well that was… unpleasant," Sam says looking at Lindsey.

"Don't look at me that way. He has a charming side," Lindsey responds. "Or at least he did."

"So does a crocodile if you can avoid his teeth," Tempel chuckles softly shaking his head, "I still can't figure what you saw in him, Lindsey."

Ignoring Tempel, Lindsey steps close to Lazarus and says quietly, "Don't sweat it. Tempel and Sam will take good care of you and I will see you later," she looks in his eyes and gives him another short but firm kiss that lingers long after their lips separate. Her actions speak louder than words exactly how she feels and for whom.

Lindsey nods to everyone and moves away leaving Lazarus to stare after her, suddenly feeling very alone. Taking a deep breath he turns and smiles, "She's quite remarkable."

Tempel looks slightly disgusted but Sam chuckles and says, "Yes, Lindsey is special. How did you happen to meet?"

Looking up at the beautiful Lunarian, Lazarus thinks back, finding it strange that it seems so long ago, yet it was only yesterday. "She had the seat next to mine on the Stratoliner coming out of Athens."

Sam smiles, "Love at first sight! How romantic!" Before Tempel has time to inject a cynical remark she continues, "Well, come on. Let's go get some food in you," she says taking Lazarus by the arm much as Lindsey had done, but Sam is the better part of a half foot taller than Lazarus making him tilt his head back just to look her in the eyes. He didn't mind a bit.

Tempel, Sam, and Lazarus exit the terminal using Steinway Avenue. Shops and offices line both sides of the wide corridor and the group stays in the middle moving with the sparse traffic. Lazarus is getting better at the lunar shuffle but every once in a while his muscles try to do it the way they have been trained from birth and he stumbles or slips.

Each time Sam grips him tightly preventing him from falling. When she sees his frustration she says, "Don't worry. You'll get the hang of it."

"He won't as long as you're holding him up," Tempel says.

"Is this your first time off-planet?" Sam inquires, ignoring Tempel.

"Yes, unless you count Luna Central," Lazarus replies.

Tempel turns to look at the earthman, "What do you know about Luna Central?"

"I watched it on wedcast. It's about the only source of information Federation citizens can get regarding the Republic of Luna," Lazarus responds.

"Are you talking about net vids? Entertainment?" Tempel shakes his head in disbelief, "You need to get that right out of your brain. No vid produced for mass entertainment on Earth can come close to the real thing, especially a Federation vid describing Lunarians!"

"You are undoubtedly correct Lieutenant, but it's all I had," Lazarus says with a shrug. Sam smiles and squeezes him a little tighter.

Tempel looks at him in disgust. Using an entertainment vid for education is beyond his comprehension.

Emerging from the mouth of Steinway Avenue, Lazarus finds himself in a horseshoe shaped alcove containing a beautiful courtyard, a magnificent colonial style fountain at its center. The fountain uses a French pineapple motif but is designed for low gravity and is much taller than its Earthly cousins. Its descending bowls are farther apart giving the water time to attain speed before splashing into the next lower pool. It flows with a strange slow motion, as though it was filled with molasses instead of water, something only a shortimer would notice. Yet, its sound is comforting to him in ways he cannot explain.

Along the three sides of the courtyard are various shops and eateries, some standing independent of the alcove's stone wall while others are partially or fully built into it. To his left is a small storefront dedicated to selling visors and other network devices, its wide front windows advertising the latest features. Beyond is the wood and stone façade of an Italian style sidewalk café, its patio filled with tables and chairs. To his immediate right is a vacsuit retail outlet, beyond that a micro brewery, a bakery, and some kind of general merchandise outlet. Music, laughter, and flashing lights spill from a kid's gaming area across the courtyard.

Against the far wall is the brightly lit front windows of a familiar type of eating establishment, a flame-dancing devil on its roof, pointing his three pronged pitchfork towards the name of the joint, *Lucifer's Diner, Fine Dining with a Flare!* Lazarus is taken aback when Lucifer turns and looks directly at him, the eyes flaring as though possessed by his namesake. Lazarus grins at his knee-jerk reaction to the symbol, immediately appreciating the irony of its existence in this place.

Here and there situated between the shops he can see more corridors similar to the one just traveled, leading to places he cannot imagine but eager to explore. Lazarus breathes in humid air, fragrant from an abundance of neatly manicured flower gardens scattered all across the courtyard. Beyond the shops and courtyard is an expanse of grass. Upon it a group of young people play a game, jumping high into the air and throwing a small ball to a teammate or at a net located twenty feet up at each end. Their calls echo across the distance as they soar high, testing themselves against their friends.

Lazarus grins with excitement. He could never have imagined a place so beautiful and full of life. He looks beyond the courtyard, beyond the game, beyond the alcove, and sees what appears to be a forest. Craning his neck to catch a glimpse of what lies ahead, he stumbles as Sam changes course to take him there. They weave in and out among the people, most of whom pay them little attention.

"Is this Brooklyn Mall?" Lazarus asks as they make way for a fast moving covey of laughing and squealing children, none more than five or six years of age.

"This is the North Courtyard. It's just a small part of Brooklyn Mall," Sam says. Giving the ball players plenty of space, she guides him out of the courtyard and to the edge of the terrace, presenting him with the most amazing vista Lazarus has ever seen.

Brooklyn Mall is a massive vaulted cathedral sheltering a manmade paradise. Before him lies acre upon acre of mid-latitude hardwood forest, manicured and maintained in perfect condition. It extends farther than he can see. From his elevated vantage point, Lazarus looks down upon a picturesque valley of gently rolling hills without any flat and level ground in sight. It's relatively narrow where he is, widening considerably as it falls away from him and curving to the right concealing what lies beyond.

Here too, the upper surface of the habitat glows in perfect imitation of a blue sky on a summer afternoon, adding greatly to his perception of openness. The luminosity fades as it extends down the walls, disappearing entirely about fifty feet up. From there down, the walls look like a cliff face. It's as if he were on Earth standing on a hill looking down at the bottom of a canyon containing a well kept park, not a subterranean city on the moon.

Massive trees dot the landscape, their leaves shimmering and rustling in the breeze while birds flitter about their great limbs. Not far below and to his left he can see a small pond under two particularly large trees, their uppermost branches towering over Lazarus. A noisy stream runs out of the pond and down the slope away from them, its path marked by boulders and thickets of flowering shrubs, bushes, and reeds.

Small birds and squirrels chatter and cavort in the treetops and across the perfectly manicured lawn. Light filters gently through the forest canopy giving the grassy parkland a lazy afternoon cast. A rain shower had just finished and the humid air smells fresh with just a hint of fragrance. Lazarus tries unsuccessfully to catch a glimpse of the far wall, prevented by architecture intentionally designed to provide mystery to the vista, places where his eyes cannot go, tweaking his imagination like a maestro directing an orchestra.

To his right more shops and restaurants extend the terrace another hundred yards along the wall, their roofs covered in lush grass and flower gardens. Here and there between the shops, ramps slope upward providing easy access to these upper areas. As with all Lunarian architecture, there is not a straight-line or sharp corner in sight. Everything is curves, one element flowing smoothly to the next, carved from a single block of stone.

Turning back to the forest, Lazarus lets his gaze linger. He can see paths winding away from the terrace down into the valley, leading to an assortment of benches and tables overlooking other gardens most with their own water feature. One area is swampy and choked with cattails. Another has a pond with a single massive jet of water dancing a hundred feet high. Further away through a gap in the trees and well down into the valley, Lazarus spots a gazebo silhouetted on the crest of a hill. The beauty is breathtaking.

"Tempel, why don't you go ahead and get the burgers while Lazarus does a little sightseeing?" Sam waits patently for Lazarus to get his fill of the view.

"Aye," the young Lunarian responds.

"Totally awesome!" Lazarus declares, touching his cheek, "I can feel the sun on my face… How's that possible?"

Sam is amused by the reaction of the earthman to her city, "The lighting matches solar radiation minus the more deadly frequencies… Where are you from, Lazarus?" she probes gently.

"Valley of the Sun…just outside Phoenix, Arizona. Typical high desert, scorpions, sunshine and blue skies," Lazarus answers never taking his eyes off this amazing underground world. It's more spectacular than he had imagined. Reality always is.

"Scorpions! There is a region along Central Commonway between Hermosa and Crossroads that our biodiversity engineers has designated high desert. After you have settled in, perhaps you would allow me to take you there. I would be very interested in your opinion," Sam says.

"I look forward to it!" Lazarus says, "And to exploring Aldrin Station. I want to see everything,"

"Then you shall," Sam replies.

Lazarus glances back at the North Courtyard. He had taken Rachel to visit Mesa Verde during a summer vacation, one day spent on something that requires a lifetime to understand. The Native Americans who made those cliff houses would feel right at home here.

Sam guides him down the terrace past several shops towards a small food court. Burnished stone tables occupy the edge of the terrace close to the grass and well under the shade of an enormous tree. The tables service Mighty Mac's Burger Barn along with Little Italy Pizzeria, Starman Coffee Plantation and several more businesses that are out of sight due to the strange curvilinear design inside the mall.

"Is this one ok?" Sam asks.

As way of answering, Lazarus pulls out and holds one of the metal-framed chairs. Sam, amused by the earthman's quaint manners, smiles and sits down. No one had ever done that for her and she finds she rather likes it.

"Lunarians use stone like we use wood and metal on Earth," Lazarus observes, running his hand over the glassy smooth surface of the tabletop as he takes the seat next to her.

"The quarrying process polishes and seals the surface. The beauty inside the stone can be stunning," Sam slides her finger along a scarlet slash of color running the length of the tabletop. "This is a metal-bearing ore and the color depends on the metal. Needless to say, it makes beautiful furniture and habitats excavated from it are highly prized," Sam's voice captivates Lazarus. "My family works high energy excavators and makes furniture on the side."

"How do you make a chair out of stone?" Lazarus asks.

"The same way you make a chair out of wood, very carefully," Sam responds smiling. "But we make tables, benches, and countertops, mostly."

"So you must know a lot about excavating?" Lazarus asks.

"Not as much as Tempel. If you have technical questions, he's your guy," Sam states.

"I'm fascinated with Lunarian habitats. Nothing like them has ever been created in the long history of man!" Lazarus says, excitement making his eyes sparkle.

"You're not going to call us cavemen or Neanderthals?" she asks.

"No! Definitely not!" he says. He looks up just as Tempel sets a tray heaped with food down in front of him.

Tempel raises an eyebrow, "I wouldn't say man has a long history, at least not in any true sense of geological time. All two hundred thousand years is nothing but an instant in the 4.5 billion years of Earth history." He sets down in front of Sam and Lazarus plates heaped with fries and a burger.

"There's much I don't understand, especially concerning Earth history and evolution. It wasn't taught in school while I was growing up and books about it are banned," Lazarus says before taking a big bite of burger. His face lights up with enjoyment as he starts to chew.

Sam frowns and wipes her mouth with a napkin, "And the citizens allow this?" she asks incredulously.

Lazarus swallows and nods, "The citizen's vote on which books to ban, as well as the punishment for those caught reading banned books."

"I find that hard to believe. It must be rigged by the government! Why would anyone choose ignorance over knowledge?" Sam isn't equipped by her society to understand this concept. To her, raised from infancy to respect and understand the guiding principles behind science and mankind's quest to understand the cosmos, it's inconceivable for someone to turn away from any idea. Ideas are to be examined closely and only set aside if they are found lacking merit. Under no circumstance should any idea be suppressed simply because it fails to fit into their previously accepted version of reality.

Lazarus talks around a bite, "No one chooses ignorance. Federation citizens are just people but they are given very little choice in what beliefs are acceptable. And when a person actually buys into the whole religion thing, it leaves no room for anything that contradicts it. They are right and everybody else wrong."

"You say they. Are you not among these citizens? Don't you profess the same beliefs?" Tempel asks.

Lazarus looks steadily at him for a long moment, swallows and reminds himself that he must drop his deception and be totally honest, finding it hard to set aside something that's been such a major part of his life. He licks dry lips before answering, "No… I don't... I searched for it as a kid but all I found were broken shards of clay where there should have been diamonds."

"That's… sad," Sam says softly.

Tempel looks at her with exasperation before turning back to Lazarus, "What's that supposed to mean?"

"It means that even as a child I questioned the logic of an omnipotent God creating a defective Adam and Eve, and then blaming them, and the rest of mankind, for his own mistake. Or how a Christian can reconcile turning the other cheek and an eye for an eye?"

"Humph" Tempel huffs, clearly not impressed.

"Which books are banned?" Sam asks between mouthfuls of burger and fries.

Lazarus chews and thinks for a moment, "It would be easier to tell you which books are allowed. The banned list is enormous. I think the authorities can find something wrong with any book if they look hard enough and usually someone already has."

"What punishment is given for reading them?" Sam asks. Over the last three decades, there has been a dearth of Federation citizens immigrating and her exposure to these strange ideas limited to intellectual discussions.

"Depends on what book and who catches you. Best case is a fine but worst case is a nice long vacation at a reeducation facility."

"That doesn't sound so bad," Sam says innocently.

Lazarus stares at her for a moment, "I would withhold judgment if I were you. I've spent a significant amount of time inside them and it isn't pretty." Lazarus turns away, ashamed in that instant of the number of reeducations he had personally been involved with. Speaking as if every word is being pulled from his throat, "As a Senior Analyst in DHS, I interrogated suspects… Sometimes that included physical torture, sometimes drugs… Specialists would come in and do… other things… When they were done the suspect would be taken to one last room. A few hours later, when they come out… they're another person… they've been reeducated…"

Sam puts her burger down and doesn't touch it again. The horrified look on her face is almost comical to Lazarus. He begins to understand in that instant how naive the Lunarians are to what's happening on Earth.

Tempel glances up to see if Lazarus was stretching the truth and goes back to eating, filing the information away. He finds it hard to generate any sympathy for Federation citizens. They made their bed and now must sleep in it.

"What happened to them inside the room?" Sam asks.

Lazarus shakes his head, "I didn't need to know…"

After a moment, "Why would you be a part of that?" Sam asks.

"It seemed like the right thing to do in the beginning, but it changed. At first the suspects were limited to terrorists or violent criminals. But in recent years, I participated in more and more cases involving citizens whose crimes were more political in nature. Many of them were only guilty of not reporting for duty after being drafted. They just didn't want to do their six years. Others simply questioned the government or the religious patriotism promoted by the government, too loudly… I grew to hate my job…"

His voice trails off and Lazarus continues to eat in silence, no longer tasting the meal, thinking about reeducation, thinking about his brother. He blames himself for what happened so long ago. If he had it to do over again, he would be more careful in the way he handled Elijah. And he wouldn't have selected DHS as a career. But he can't go back. Realizing he has finished the burger, he looks up into Sam's startling green eyes.

"Why didn't you quit?" she asks.

"No one quits DHS…" he returns her stare levelly.

"You did," Tempel says.

"That's right, I did," Lazarus says. He sighs and lays his napkin on his plate, "Very tasty. I now understand why Lindsey likes Mac's."

Sam nods and continues to stare at him.

Tempel pushes his tray back, "Stop at the Plantation for coffee?" It's one of his favorite places and he figures he should be able to enjoy himself while listening to this earthman's hard luck story.

Nodding in agreement, Sam asks Lazarus, "Are you a tea or coffee drinker?"

"I enjoy them both, but a cup of tea does sound nice." he replies feeling like he's laid his soul bare. Never has he spoken so openly about his job, not even with Rachel.

"I hope you saved some room, Lazarus. They have a pastry that you must try," Sam wipes her mouth with a napkin. Looking sideways at the earthman she asks, "Lazarus is an unusual name. Where does it come from?"

"My dad told me I was named after the hero in a science fiction novel written in the mid twentieth century, but I have my doubts. Lazarus is the name of two people in the Bible, the man Jesus raised from the dead and a character in one of his parables. Since they named my brothers Saul and Elijah, and my sister Mary, it stands to reason that Lazarus was chosen because it's a biblical name." Lazarus responds.

"Whatever the reason, it's charming!" she says.

Listening to the two of them talk, Tempel lets his eyes drift over each person within sight. The tables service a number of eateries and concession stands at this end of the mall. The merchants appear to be doing a slow but steady business.

A middle-aged couple is sitting at a nearby table eating and talking quietly. Three boys are placing an order at the Pizzeria. A man sits alone on the far side eating and surfing the net. Others are passing along the sidewalk or one of the many paths into the arboretum. It isn't crowded but it also isn't empty. Life fills every nook and cranny.

"What's an agent for Homeland Security doing here?" Sam asks.

Lazarus hesitates and Tempel turns to stare at him, linking with his visor, reading heart rate, perspiration, and all the other polygraphic indicators, looking for the slightest appearance of deception.

"I'm not an agent, only an analyst, and I'm immigrating…" Lazarus pauses and sighs deeply, running his hand over his head, "I'm running away from a situation that has become intolerable for me. I no longer believe in my government, my job, or my life… The NAF has information that indicates the Republic of Luna is in grave danger. Since sending troops or an envoy is out of the question, I'm the next best thing," Lazarus says seriously.

"Whose idea was that?" Tempel asks.

"Mine," Lazarus responds. "You see, I believe you are about to receive the next big hit from our mutual friends, the Islamic Brotherhood." Lazarus hesitates again, "Can I assume this lunch is being recorded?"

Tempel and Sam look at each other as if to say, what? Are you kidding? Sam smiles hesitantly at Lazarus, "Of course. All business is a matter of public record. That's the Law."

Tempel continues to watch Lazarus for signs of nervousness or deceit. "Why do you think we need help? The Republic can take care of itself."

Despite the amazing architecture they are sitting in, life is harsh on the moon and always has been. A Lunarian grows up fast in mankind's high frontier or doesn't grow up at all. In the beginning before deep rock excavations were possible, the young suffered the highest mortality rate of any group. Living in a vacuum is a very unforgiving environment to raise kids. Accidents happened all too frequently.

But the group that now holds that distinction cannot be classified by age, gender, or occupation. Their deaths are the result of sectarian violence. Outside of their holdings, Lunarians are tolerated as a necessary evil by most earthmen, as pure evil by some. Rumors of bounties and contract killings abound, gunfights have become commonplace and people simply disappear.

Born into this situation, the Dugan children began handling weapons as soon as they could hold one steady. Tempel was nine when he recorded his first perfect score in the family's gun range. By the time he was eleven he could outdraw his brothers and sisters and cousins, all except Ben.

Patrick Dugan taught his children that carrying a gun is a responsibility, not a toy or an adventure, and if he ever caught any of them playing loose with it, he'd take off their backside with his belt. None of his kids ever lost any hide. Duce drilled into them early and often that gunplay was a last resort, used only when every other avenue had been exhausted. Taking the law into their hands is something done cautiously. But if necessary, then do it with cold precision and skill. Tempel often wonders what Duce would make of the current state of affairs on Luna. He has no doubt that if his father were alive he would approve of his being a SWAT lieutenant in the police department, a leader of warriors.

"I'm sure you can take care of yourself. But there will be serious consequences if even the tiniest mistake is made," Lazarus says to Tempel. "You see… I have reason to believe the Brotherhood is going to detonate a thermonuclear device somewhere on Luna."

A cold silence falls over the table. Tempel's lip curls into a silent snarl and his eyes harden. Samantha sits and stares numbly at Lazarus, trying in vain to put this information in perspective, failing again to comprehend how any human could do such a horrible thing.

"I don't understand why they want to hurt us. What have we done to them to make them hate us so much?" Sam whispers, breaking the silence. Even with the level of violence escalating, a lifelong commitment to reason makes it difficult for her to believe such a horrendous event could occur.

Lazarus frowns, "You won't find any logic to the madness. Religious fundamentalism, whether it's Islamic or Christian or Jewish, displays amazing tunnel vision. A few misguided individuals convince others that it's the will of God and everyone falls into lockstep. Like a bunch of lemmings."

Sam looks blankly at him, "What's a lemming?"

"Huh? Oh, it's an extinct rodent that lived in the Arctic tundra. They would periodically follow one another over the edge of a cliff or into the ocean committing mass suicide, one of nature's more straightforward ways of keeping their population in check." Lazarus looks thoughtfully at her, "If war is nature's way of thinning out Homo sapiens, then religion is its grand enabler."

"You speak of nature like it's a person. Don't put human qualities on something that's simply a chain of events, a series of processes. Isn't that what religions do with God, make him up in the image of humanity?" Tempel asks.

Lazarus looks at him and nods, "True, very true. But they claim it's the other way around. Man is supposed to be created in the image of God."

"I fail to see the difference," Tempel says.

"You still haven't explained why they want to kill us," Sam insists.

"According to Islam's leading clerics and imams, Lunarians are genetic monstrosities, an aberration in the eyes of Allah. This places you at the top of the list of nonbelievers to be dealt with," Lazarus says to Sam, a slight frown creases his brow. "The Holy Qur'ân tells them it's their duty to either convert nonbelievers to Islam or destroy them."

Sam looks at him like he has grown horns, "But the citizens don't take them seriously… Do they?"

Lazarus bows his head and fiddles with his napkin, "I quote from the Holy Qur'ân 47:4. *When you meet in battle those who disbelieve strike off their heads after you have bound them fast in fetters.* All Lunarians have been soiled by genetic science which means that conversion is impossible in this life. They believe that for God to pass judgment on you, they must kill you. It's their way of calling court in session. And if they should be killed while doing the work of Allah, they are promised paradise in heaven for all eternity… Mohammed's version of paradise reflects his 6th century bias and includes plenty of wine, food, and sex with beautiful little girls and boys. 78:31 *As for those who guarded against evil there awaits them a triumph, orchards and vineyards; and blooming young maidens…* 76:19 *Sons of perpetual bloom shall go round waiting upon the believers…* Blooming young maidens refers to little virgin girls and sons of perpetual bloom are little virgin boys. I'm sure I don't need to explain why virgins are included in paradise. The Hadith expands the promise to include a sex market where the virgins are on display for the believer to choose from."

"Regardless of why they want us dead, nothing comes or goes in Aldrin without passing through heavy security. A cockroach couldn't get by! Let alone a nuke!" Tempel says. Like the rest of humanity, he believes the sensors and scanners that monitor the movement of goods and people guard against this possibility.

"Aren't the reports of bombs getting through accurate?" Lazarus asks hoping that perhaps this was a fabrication or exaggeration of the government controlled mass media. It wouldn't be the first time.

Tempel stares at the earthman for a moment, "Citizens must be helping them." he finally admits.

"I don't know that much about Lunarians but I do know the Brotherhood. I have no doubt they are in the final stages of something major. I just don't know what or when," Lazarus says with a frown.

"Do you have any supportive evidence or must we simply take your word for it?" Tempel asks harshly.

"I couldn't bring anything with me for obvious reasons but some of the evidence can be regenerated." Lazarus leans his forearms onto the stone tabletop and looks intently across at Tempel. "I will help your network people as much as I can."

"Point us in the right direction, so to speak," Tempel says, suspicious of anything Lazarus may direct them to. Even if he's sincere, Tempel is skeptical that this shortimer could teach Katee and Lucas anything about hacking the World Wide Web!

"I'm not a politician, Tempel. What I know is that over the last three months Homeland Security acquired overwhelming evidence of something big coming down, encrypted emails, network conversations, and security tapes on more than a few suspects. But the biggest single issue is the four thousand or so Brotherhood soldiers that are not where we expect them to be any more!"

Frowning but with all his attention now focused on Lazarus, "What do you mean, they're not where you expect them to be," Tempel asks gruffly.

"My department kept track of all known and suspected fundamentalists. These are the guys who do the dirty work, blow up schools, terrorize resorts or assassinate the local news anchor. The real cream of the crop!" Lazarus says. "Well... three months ago these scumbags started dropping off the radar, disappearing without a trace. The Brotherhood's Defense Minister, Hasin bin Aunker and Major General Abdel Salam Arif are missing too. Do you know who they are?" Lazarus asks.

Sam face turns ashen and she glances at Tempel whose expression remains stiff and unchanging. "We've heard of them," she acknowledges.

"Don't expect any help from the Federation. They will not honor the Treaty of Independence. The most you can expect is neutrality. They will stay out of it!" Lazarus says.

"That's all we ask! If the Brotherhood wants more martyrs, then we will accommodate them!" Tempel snarls.

Sam can see that Tempels outburst disturbs Lazarus. She decides to change the subject. "As I understand it, you requested a meeting with Abby? Why Abby?" Sam asks raising her eyebrows.

"Lindsey helped me, but Abigail Dugan is famous even in Arizona." Lazarus looks down at his hands, "She has a reputation for fairness." He looks puzzled, "It's not like you have a central government. I can't ask to speak with the President! You don't have one!"

"The will of the people is the only government we need," Tempel says.

"But a government provides for the common defense and the Republic doesn't even have a military," Lazarus states in amazement.

"A standing militia of any kind is prohibited under the Treaty. But every able-bodied citizen serves part-time on a police reserve unit," Sam says.

"Then who decides what needs to be done and enforces the decisions?" Lazarus asks.

Sam sighs, "We all do. The freeholds conform to the majority rulings voluntarily. To defy the Council guarantees sanctions by the rest of Luna. If it's one thing we have a good grip on, it's that nobody survives on Luna without a lot of help. Isolation means death."

"No man is an island," Lazarus says. He loves the fact that he can now say these things in normal conversation without fear.

"Exactly as Mr. Dunn intended..." Sam says. "A half-century ago, the men and women living on Luna figured out that the only real security they could expect was from their own hand. Every aspect of their existence had to be brought under tight control, right down to the air they breathe. The system that evolved from this basic survival need is the freehold, whose primary purpose is the economic security and physical safety of its citizens. We are the first true democracy. Leaders are voted on, projects are voted on, everyone has a say in everything, if they choose too. You will find that Lunarian politics are big time entertainment but believe me, it's a responsibility that every citizen takes seriously, even the kids. We belong to LCPD, 22nd Metro Division. Every borough in the city has its own PD. They in turn fall under the jurisdiction of Aldrin Station's Security Chief."

"What about the non-Lunarian settlements?" Lazarus asks.

Sam shakes her head, "Non-Lunarian politics are complicated. Four different countries have military bases on Luna and over one hundred and fifty corporations maintain private security forces. The Lunarian Law of Full Disclosure applies only within our holdings. The habitats in Little America, and the facilities of other nations, claim privacy and are not part of Luna's network. We have very little control over what they do." When Lazarus looks slightly lost she continues, "Little America is an enclave east of Hells Kitchen on the outer edge of the city, home for 95% of the shortimers within Aldrin Station. They don't like our visors so there are many places we are not allowed to go. We don't know what goes on in there."

"So a large crate could be delivered, let's say, to a facility somewhere far away from here, brought in overland and would not pass through a Lunarian inspection point?" Lazarus asks.

"There are many landing sites. Freighters are designed to take cargo where it's needed," Tempel says. "But nothing as big as a nuke could get past the orbital scanners, even out in the boonies," he says with complete conviction.

"And every crate is scanned?" Lazarus asks.

Sam nods, "Yes, many times." Frowning thoughtfully, "I still can't understand why they want to nuke us. It makes no sense!"

"For the same reasons they bomb us now!" Tempel says angrily, concluding this entire discussion is a colossal waste of time, "Come on. Let's go. We still have time for coffee at the Plantation."

****

Tempel leads the way setting a fast pace, cutting straight down the central grassy meadow beneath the massive trees. His path soon has them moving along the edge of a babbling brook. Lazarus admires the towering trees with their limbs stretching towards the sky blue ceiling far above. Flowers, shrubs and fruit trees thrive in well maintained plots scattered throughout the valley. Birds and squirrels cavort in the treetops and the buzz of a honey bee attracts his attention.

"The trees here are magnificent!" Lazarus says with an awed shake of his head.

"We have taken great care in selecting the very best genetic strains and they grow very fast in Luna's gravity," Sam responds holding him tightly, continuing to help him learn to moonwalk.

"What kind are they?" Lazarus asks, gazing at the incredible panorama around him. This is the vision that defines the Lunarian way of life, not the tunnels or corridors, but the beauty that confronts him here.

"These are Ash trees native to Europe," Sam says. "According to Norse legend, Igdrasil is the Ash Tree of Existence with its roots in hell and limbs spreading across the universe. At its foot is the Kingdom of Death where the Three Fates sit, the Past, the Present, and the Future. Seasonal changes represent various events, things suffered, things done, catastrophes, stretching through all lands and times. As the story goes, an eagle rests on the highest branch of Igdrasil to observe all that passes in the world, whilst a squirrel constantly runs up and down its trunk to report those things that the eagle may not have seen. Serpents twine round its limbs and from its roots flow two streams, the knowledge of things past and the knowledge of things to come. According to legend, man himself was formed from the wood of this sacred Ash tree."

"That makes as much sense as the biblical version of creation," Lazarus says.

Sam notes his sincerity, nods and says, "They are equally absurd."

The valley widens considerably as they move downhill and around the curve. Seen in the gaps between trees, a tall cliff face starts to come into view ahead of them. It isn't coated with the luminous blue sky but is bare stone, craggy and irregular with horizontal striations sculpted into its face, the floor slopping up sharply at its feet. Predominantly Sedona red, it is mottled with browns, pinks, and many other earth tones. A few more steps and Lazarus realizes it's not simply a cliff, but a massive column that extends to the ceiling far above. To him, it looks like an enormous butte at home in Monument Valley, Arizona, only bigger.

As they continue downhill still following the small stream, the canyon flattens into a broad plain with the column at its center. The trees here are further apart with knee high prairie grass instead of the manicured Bluegrass found in the upper reaches of North Canyon. Around the base of the column, before the floor slopes up to meet the vertical face, are more shops and a picnic area with a decent sized swimming lake. People are everywhere, but it's far from being crowded. Lazarus estimates maybe a couple hundred are within his sight. If this was in the Federation, that number would be in the tens of thousands. To him this place is nearly empty.

Lazarus pulls Sam to a standstill, gazing in rapt wonder at the cathedral-like expanse. Tempel continues a few paces more before stopping and turning back. From the rock face high above, a waterfall begins its descent towards a small pond which, in turn, spills down the sloped surface in a white water cataract to the much larger body of water. The fall creates a fog that partially shrouds the foot of the column and half the lake. Even from this distance, he hears splashing and peals of laughter.

Between him and the lake, several dogs sprint across the open meadow in great bounds, disappearing into the tall grass only to reappear as they leap again. A moment later they flush out several large animals. Lazarus can hardly believe his eyes as a group of deer break cover and move rapidly away, powerful legs sending them soaring high and far, white tails flashing in the ceaseless light of Luna.

"What is this place?" Lazarus asks his voice barely a whisper.

"Central Commons," Sam says.

"How big is it?" he asks staring at the top of the column, finding it difficult to judge its scale.

"At its peak, the mall is 600 meters high and Central Commons alone contains just over two square kilometers." Tempel answers.

"I'm sorry, but can you put that in English units?" Lazarus asks.

Temple glances at him. "Just under 2000 feet and about 500 acres," he says.

Looking up in awe, Lazarus says, "2000 feet! No wonder I feel small. Are all habitats like this?" he asks.

Sam shakes her head, shedding the feeling of dread that had descended over her during the previous conversation. "This is a mall. It's about nature and entertainment."

"Malls are designed to give us a little more headroom. Grandma Abby says they remind us we come from a planet," Tempel adds.

A screech overhead draws his attention, "Is that a hawk?" Lazarus asks.

Sam glances up, "Peregrine Falcon."

"There are predators here?" Lazarus asks.

"Some. Don't worry, there isn't any big enough for you to worry about," she says.

Shaking his head in disbelief, "Luna is full of surprises. Why's the mall shaped this way? Can I assume the giant butte in the center is holding up the roof?"

"It's structural if that's what you mean. All habitat geometry is designed to withstand the enormous pressure from the mountain above. They are, in reality, bubbles of air in a vast sea of stone," Tempel says.

Sam feigns surprise. "Very poetic," she says.

"Thank you," Tempel responds. "Four of our largest excavators worked on this for six months just to rough it in."

"It's quite remarkable," Lazarus says. To his left and right are two more wide valleys similar to the one they are standing in, their walls sculptured to look like the steep sides of canyons, an illusion not lost on Lazarus. He cannot see very far down either because both curve, but one appears to go uphill and the other downhill.

"I must keep reminding myself that all of this is man-made. In fact, the very air we are breathing is manufactured and the soil artificial. The plants, the insects, and the animals are all selected. How do you manage all of this?"

Sam chuckles and pulls Lazarus to get him to move as they talk. "Let's get under cover before it rains." She leads him across the broad expanse of grass towards a covered picnic table not far from the base of the column.

Looking up, Lazarus is hit by a wave of dizziness and quickly drops his gaze. He steps under the canopy just as a warm rain begins to fall.

Running his hand over his head, Lazarus gathers himself. "Everything is so clean, no smog, no pollution of any kind," Lazarus says. He remains standing gazing back up the valley they had just come from, its distance hazed by the rain shower. The air is fresh and sweet to his flared nostrils, full of the smell of damp foliage. A rainbow graces the distance.

"What do you know about the habs?" Sam asks.

"Well, I know they're in the form of a disk standing on edge," he says. "Why not use a sphere? It's been known for millennia that the most efficient use of space is a sphere."

"The rock pressure would crush a sphere. It simply couldn't hold up. The basic habitat design is actually two disks intersecting along their centerline, creating an X. The cross-section of each disk is elliptical, not rectangular. Even here in the mall you can see the inward curve in the vertical walls," Tempel explains, pointing and gesturing for emphasis. "It's the same design the ancient Egyptians used when they built chambers under their pyramids."

"I don't understand," Lazarus says.

"The deepest chambers and passageways used a step or terraced design to withstand the tremendous overhead compressive loads. Each successive block layer was hung over the space a few inches until the two sides finally joined high overhead, in effect, creating an arched ceiling. We use the same shape only ours is smooth, not stepped."

"That's amazing! How do you decide where the habitats should go? How big they can be?" Lazarus asks.

"The size, orientation and distribution of all excavations are obviously interrelated and must be carefully controlled," Tempel lectures him. "Any miscalculation weakens the city and could cause a collapse."

"I seem to remember that's happened before," Lazarus says, raising his eyebrows emphasizing the question in the statement.

"Sure it has!" is Sam's quick response. "We study all the major and minor incidents in school. The Hampton Bay collapse was the largest; it killed over a hundred people."

"You needn't worry, earthman," Tempel says. "There hasn't been a collapse in over forty years. Hampton forced a major re-write of the design simulation. Every known factor has been incorporated into the sim. Not only is the outer envelope designed to maximize support, but the inner structure as well. The floors, ceilings, walls and ramps inside the habitats are designed to distribute the outer load. It's a lot safer now."

"Is there a master plan for the entire city?" Lazarus asks.

"Of course there is… DREMS incorporates the shape of habitats, transportation and utility corridors, even plumbing tubes. The mountain itself undergoes extensive SQUID evaluation looking for fractures or fault lines…" Sensing his ignorance, "S-Q-U-I-D stands for Superconducting Quantum Interference Device. It maps extremely small variations in the mountains magnetic field to identify cracks and stress risers within the rock, before they becomes cracks… The point is that all of these influences are factored into any proposed new excavation no matter how small," Tempel says.

"Dreams?" Lazarus asks.

"D-R-E-M-S stands for Deep Rock Excavation and Maintenance Simulation," he answers.

"Can you show me or is it classified?" Lazarus asks.

"Classified? DREMS is on the public net. Everybody has access to it." Temple glances at Sam and shakes his head before linking with Lazarus. In a rapid series of subtle hand movements he brings up a three-dimensional image floating in the air between them.

The mall fades to the background as Lazarus stares in total fascination at the slowly turning multicolored model. In exquisitely fine detail, it shows the twenty mile section of Rim Mountain that contains the city. Most of the habitats, and their interconnecting commonway's, lie within a central band at roughly the same elevation as the surface outside the crater. The clustered habitats of all eleven boroughs are color-coded and identified with tiny letters only clearly readable when he looks right at them. If he lingers for a moment on a specific hab, detailed information concerning ownership and usage displays itself.

A half mile below the boroughs, at the elevation of the crater floor, is another band containing far fewer habitats but with a complex network of large and small tunnels. The habitats on this lower level are smaller and much further apart.

A third level of habitats is grouped in small clusters above each borough. Within each group are one or more large habitats. He stares at one of these. The information that appears before him identifies it is a reservoir.

Tunnels connect the three levels, some large and well defined within the image, others are wispy threads almost invisible.

Tempel speeds up the images rotation. The quality of the graphics astounds Lazarus. As a Senior Analyst he had access to the best simulations the Federation had to offer but this is better than anything he has ever seen or imagined possible.

"The upper level is our water reservoirs and some agricultural habitats. The central level is where we live and the lower level is waste recovery and bulk transportation. Currently, there are 1173 habitats, over seventy miles of commonway's and three hundred miles of primary and secondary service tunnels below the city. The sewer system alone has a thousand miles of ancillary tunnels, some big enough to walk in but most are the size of your fist. The excavators are kept constantly busy burrowing more. This is only a small fraction of the sim data. Here is where we are," Tempel says. A bright pinprick appears within the central level.

Tempel circles a group of habitats, his finger leaving behind a glowing trail that slowly fades away, "This is Dakota warren."

Lazarus is puzzled, "Please, define a warren for me."

"A warren is a group of habitats daisy-chained together that share the mechanicals needed to keep us eating and breathing. Usually they have a short interconnect corridor between the individual habitats but sometimes they are butted up rim to rim. A big warren, like Dakota, has habitats spread out vertically and horizontally." Tempel says.

Reaching out, Tempel pulls the image, magnifying it to take a closer look at Brooklyn Mall.

It's as if he is no longer in the mall but instead high above it soaring down through the rock of the mountain, falling towards the habitat, its detail rapidly drawing closer. Lazarus reaches out and grasps Sam's arm staggering slightly.

"Take it easy Tempel. He isn't accustomed to using our net!" Sam scolds putting her arm around Lazarus to steady him.

Tempel replies with a dry chuckle but slows down and brings them to a stop hovering over Brooklyn Mall's Central Commons. Below them are three individuals standing next to a covered park bench. The rain soaked grass catches the light, reflecting back at them like diamonds sprinkled across the lawn.

Lazarus suppresses his fear of heights by repeatedly telling himself that this isn't real, that he isn't hovering in midair a hundred feet up looking down at these people. He suddenly realizes that the three people are them. He hesitantly waves his arm out in front like a blind man looking for obstacles. The action is eerily reflected below. He resists the urge to look up.

Sam recognizes his discomfort, "We are accessing the mall's public sensors and seamlessly integrating real-time video with DREMS."

"If this is a dream, then please don't wake me," Lazarus says glad that she's there to distract him.

Lazarus had grown up around computers and electronics, yet he realized long ago that one of the sacrifices his country had made as they clung ever tighter to Christian religious beliefs was that of change. He knows that no new technology has developed within the Federation for over fifty years. What little there was came from foreign countries and imported at great expense. Some call this lack of innovation stability, but Lazarus knows it for what it is; stagnation.

Of all the classified reports he had read over the years, not one mentioned this advanced state of technology. The Lunarian computer system had to be crunching data at a tremendous rate to provide them with such high quality video, better than anything he had seen or heard about anywhere on Earth let alone in the NAF. He concludes once again that this is something the Federation must have purposefully kept this from him and the other Senior Analysts. He files the omission away with all the others.

Even as Lazarus mulls this over, Tempel takes them back the way they had come, arriving over the food court, looking down at the people eating. Three adolescent boys are sitting at the same table they had so recently vacated, eating pizza. Tempel moves in close bringing Lazarus and Sam with him. It seems as if they are standing right next to the table, listening to their horseplay, seeing every expression as clearly as if they were actually present. The boys are wearing visors and one of them turns, looking right at Tempel.

"Something wrong?" he asks.

Tempel shakes his head and says, "Nope. We just want to wish you boys a nice lunch." He nods to them and departs.

Back across the mall they soar, this time staying beneath the massive limbs, weaving around the tree trunks. Lazarus is starting to really enjoy the ride by the time they reach their destination, back at the flesh and blood versions of themselves standing patiently beside the picnic bench.

Tempel brings Lazarus to a standstill inches from himself. It's like looking into a mirror. Lazarus can see every pore, every hair, every twitch of his mouth, more clearly then if he were in his kitchen back in Arizona staring into the ancient mirror behind the sink getting ready for work. He can't resist reaching out, watching his hand disappear into the chest of the image in front of him. He hears Sam's musical laugh, pulling him back to something real.

"Scanners throughout the city are available to anybody at any time but the malls are covered in great detail. This is where we come to play," Tempel says.

With a grand wave of his arm Tempel sweeps their images away, scattering the millions of tiny pixels like dust in the wind until nothing remains.

Lazarus looks around slightly dazed and confused. He sees a man and a woman a short distance away, standing and watching them. Sam is holding on to his arm, looking intently down at him.

"Are you alright?" she asks, concern showing on her face.

Lazarus nods and gives her a big smile, "Who are those people?"

"They are the people that are monitoring our conversation," she replies. When Lazarus looks even more confused, Sam adds, "They are the composite results of morphing forty-seven men and women into a single couple."

"I don't understand," he says.

Sam responds by walking over to the woman. She nods a greeting and asks, "Constance, do you mind?"

The image nods.

"I would like you to meet Mr. Lazarus Sheffield," Sam says.

The face and countenance of the figure before them morphs smoothly into the features of a heavyset woman with shoulder length brown hair and a hawkish nose.

"Greetings… Constance Cassidy," she says tipping her head politely.

"Lazarus Sheffield, pleased to make your acquaintance," Lazarus responds hesitantly and nods in return.

"Constance works with Tempel and if I don't miss my guess, you are keeping tabs on him, isn't that right?" Sam asks, the grin on her face reflects the mischief she's causing.

Constance stares back at her, "Actually I find this earthman fascinating. All this talk of nukes and terrorists is exciting." Looking at Lazarus, "Now, why don't you get on with it?" With a nod, she melts back into the composite, removing herself from the conversation.

Lazarus abruptly reaches up and removes his visor. Sam and Tempel exchange glances, keeping theirs on. "If you don't mind, I would like to see Aldrin Station with my own eyes." The composite image of the watchers unnerves him and he feels better simply ignoring the fact they are being so closely watched by so many.

"It's your choice," Tempel says then leads them away from the picnic area.

Lazarus looks at Sam and asks, "Doesn't it bother you to know you are being watched all the time?" Her visor makes it hard for him to hold a conversation.

"First, it's not all the time. We have had privacy up until now, haven't we? And second, why should I mind? I never even think about it." Sam says.

"So… when is it not ok to spy on someone?" Lazarus asks.

"It's simple, earthman. Never link with someone in their home without their permission and never stalk them when they're in public. If you follow those two rules you'll be fine. Don't, and you'll have trouble." Tempel says.

Lazarus looks at him with a rather puzzled expression, "I have a lot to learn."

Tempel glances back. This earthman may actually know how ignorant he is, a point in his favor.

Lazarus asks. "There is something that is really bugging me. What happens if we suddenly lose integrity in this habitat? All the air leaks out catastrophically?" Lazarus asks.

"Unless you can breathe vacuum, you die!" Tempel says over his shoulder. He points to a nearby airlock leading into a merchant's backroom. "The locks you see throughout the city are set up to minimize air loss. They are programmed to automatically close when they sense a pressure drop. Once shut, the pressure must be equalized for a main lock to freely reopen. Don't get caught on the wrong side of the lock!" Tempel says.

Seeing his confusion, "It's a joke," Sam says.

"How do you know which is the right side?" Lazarus asks.

"The emergency lights above the airlock will come on. If they are red, get on the other side before the lock closes. If they are green, just sit tight," Sam informs him.

"Sounds simple enough, but what if both sides are red?" Lazarus asks.

"Kiss your ass goodbye!" Tempel says then points again to the merchants lock. "There are many rooms with air tight doors. Find one and get inside. If the door has already shut, override it but get inside quick."

"Don't worry. We haven't had a major incident in years," Sam says, grinning.

They move around the pond, across the expanse of grass and continue downhill.

"This is the East wing of Brooklyn Mall," Sam says.

Lazarus is really starting to enjoy the walk. It requires a completely different rhythm to stroll in one sixth of your birth planets gravity but Lazarus is getting better. Tempel leads them off the path and across beautifully maintained grass to the Plantation, a quant French-style sidewalk café on the terrace abutting the mall's East entrance. There isn't an alcove here, just a small grouping of shops that look down upon the arboretum.

Weaving around tables, the three pick a spot close to a lush garden with a miniature waterfall splashing into a small pool completely surrounded with ferns. The air has a damp, humid smell. Tall broadleaved plants shade the café. The house lights are low and a thick Asian carpet softens the mall sounds. To Lazarus, it seems like he has entered yet another little world.

A tall lanky lad with broad shoulders comes over to take their order. He immediately notices that Lazarus isn't wearing his visor.

"Mocha Sanani," Tempel says.

"Ambrosia with honey," she looks at Lazarus and adds, "Double that and add a couple of Blackberry Rolls."

"Ambrosia?" Lazarus asks.

"It is a white tea from south China that we have grown on Luna for over fifty years. It's very good with honey and blackberries," Sam says.

"Sounds wonderful," Lazarus says. Rachel had liked tea. He leans back in the comfortable chair and relaxes. The chair is warm and soft and the sound of the water soothing. A yawn escapes before he can stop it.

"When are you due?" Tempel asks Lazarus.

"Due what?" Lazarus asks.

"Sleep... When was the last time you slept?" Tempel asks.

"I had a long nap on the shuttle. I'll be fine." Lazarus says.

Sam laughs and says, "Jelag!"

Tempel nods knowingly, "It will take a while for your system to adjust to the lack of night and day."

"I don't understand why Lunarians don't use Universal Shiptime," Lazarus states, "Why not dim the lights half the day like spacecraft?"

"Only civilian spacecraft do that, mostly because it offers them a measure of control over their passengers. Military ships use the same twenty-four hour schedule that we do," Tempel says pointing up at the clock above the pastry counter visible through the open door of the café. "The twenty-four hours is divided up into the three shifts you see, red for first, green for second, and blue for third, each eight hours long. Some people still use morning, noon and night but it doesn't mean much. A long time ago they tried dimming the lights at night but it turned out to be a colossal waste of effort. There is not one single reason why one shift should be singled out for sleeping and not another. We leave it up to the individual to pick when they should be sleeping!" Tempel explains.

"The words tomorrow or today or yesterday don't have much meaning here, do they?" Lazarus says.

"Sure they do. A day is still twenty-four hours just like it is on Earth. We just don't have a nice neat twelve hour light and dark cycle here. Even if you're on the surface, a lunar cycle is fourteen days freezing darkness and fourteen days of blazing sunlight. It's simpler to have all of Luna work off the same time," Tempel says sipping his coffee.

"I think you like explaining things to Lazarus," Sam says grinning at Tempel.

Tempel blows her a kiss. Turning back to Lazarus, "Most people adjust their sleep cycle to fit with the people they work with. I only need about four hours sleep in every twenty-four."

"That might take some getting used to," Lazarus says shaking his head. "I personally need at least six hours or I'm not worth much the next day." He nods his thanks to the waiter as the young man deposits a steaming mug next to the prettiest pastry he had ever seen, a perfect spiral of dark purple set in pie crust.

Tempel grunts wondering if any earthman is worth his O2 regardless of how much sleep they get, "The meeting with Abby won't take long. After that you can get some sleep."

Sam peals a chunk from the side of her pastry and pops it into her mouth with pleasure.

Lazarus nods and takes another sip. Sitting the cup down, "I can't tell you how much I am looking forward to meeting your grandmother. You may not realize how famous she is on Earth. In some circles she is spoken of with Einstein, Darwin and Hawking! Her white paper on biotronic DNA manipulations is the definitive work on the subject," Lazarus says, his voice betraying his excitement.

"I thought the Federation didn't allow any science in school, especially genetics?" Tempel asks.

Lazarus sits quietly for a moment before answering, "Who said I learned about her in school?"

"Humph… did you learn about her on bathroom walls? Or maybe you hacked into our websites?" Tempel didn't believe for an instant that it was possible to get past Magi but there is much that is freely shared with anyone who asks.

"In a way… Your websites are monitored closely and when something new is posted it was my job to read its content. Right before I blocked everyone else from it," Lazarus says.

Tempel looks intently at him. Without his visor on, he doesn't have access to Lazarus's extended vital signs, but he can still measure heart rate, blood pressure and sweat. He's sure Lazarus is being truthful but seems to be deeply bothered by his admission, more than the crime seems to warrant.

Sam looks concerned but before she can say anything, Lazarus raises his hands in mock surrender, "I was young and idealistic and convinced myself I was working on the side of good," Lazarus says. He drops his eyes and rubs his hand across his head. "It's not something I'm proud of but Lindsey stressed honesty above all else. I will not hide or avoid the things I have done."

"Good advice," Tempel says.

"We are not here to judge you, Lazarus," Sam says.

"You seem to be doing that yourself," Tempel says.

Lazarus sighs and runs his hand over his head again "You have learned much about me and my family. Please, tell me about yours."

Tempel is a product of an open society where the flow of information defines freedom. To be branded a liar is one of the worst things that can happen to somebody, their opinions, and they themselves, are rendered irrelevant. It never occurs to him to lie or avoid the truth. "My family is typical," Sam grunts but keeps quiet. "Grandma Abby met and married Patrick Ryan Dugan just after Aldrin Station was founded back in 2024. I never met my grandpa. He was buried under a thousand feet of rock nineteen years before I was born but all of us have heard the stories of how PR and Abby met, married, and changed the world."

"I, for one, believe your grandparents did change the world," Lazarus says. He shakes his head and continues, "It must have been tough in the beginning. They had to invent or re-invent equipment and ways of doing things as they went along. Nobody had ever lived in a vacuum before."

"Except in the space stations, the little ones when they were figuring out how to do it. But you're right, living on the moon was something completely new. Aldrin Station started out as a group of inflatable shelters exposed on the surface, the facilities were limited, construction techniques primitive and practically everything had to come up from Earth. But sometimes I think the stories are exaggerated."

"I wouldn't bet on it," Lazarus exclaims. "From the engineers I've met, I can attest to their arrogance. The good ones possess the hubris to believe their designs must be the best, simply because its there's. I'm sure that most, if not all, the equipment the colonists brought with them must have needed massive redesign when confronted with the reality of living on the moon."

Tempel nods, "You have a point. PR came to Luna as a mining engineer. After screwing around with the way excavation was done back then, he came up with the first high-energy disrupter feedback circuit. His basic design has been refined but hasn't changed much since then. It's the single invention making deep-rock Luna habitats possible. Before grandpa, excavations were done using explosives and impact tools with men and machines manually clearing the debris. I can't imagine that!" Shaking his head, "All grandpa did was take advantage of the technology around him. He was highly motivated at the time by the overwhelming need to get everyone underground. It's dangerous to be on the surface too long. Eventually your luck runs out... It was later that Smith and Wesson turned equipment designed for deep rock excavations into a weapon." He pats his holstered disrupter.

"How does disrupters relate to deep rock excavations?" Lazarus asks.

Tempel frowns and looks at him for a moment wondering if Lazarus was pulling his leg. "Both weapons and excavators are coherent high-energy electromagnetic beam generators. When the beam strikes surface atoms, it ruptures the bonds holding them together and releases even more energy. This starts a chain reaction that spreads to adjacent atoms. A properly calibrated excavator can maintain this as long as the cloud of displaced atoms is removed. The process attains its highest efficiency in complete vacuum when the resulting plasma gas, called blowoff, is dispersed away from the cutting area. Therefore, vent tubes are the first things cut when excavating a new hab or tunnel," Tempel explains.

"If the sun is angled just right, a person out on the surface can see a haze along the crest of Rim Mountain above a major excavation. They may even see a rainbow. The mountain contributes just enough extra gravity to slow down dispersion of the blowoff gases rising from the surface vents," Sam says.

Lazarus nods, "I've heard government environmentalists and church leaders comment about the pollution the Lunarians are creating. Moon pollution! Do you buy into that?"

"It might become a problem," Tempel admits, "but nobody knows. We don't like venting the blowoff into Luna vacuum any more than they do but right now it isn't feasible to do anything else. There isn't any doubt that the amount of matter found in a square meter of vacuum above the surface of Luna is increasing, and no one can predict with any certainty what it means."

Tempel pauses taking a sip of his coffee, watching Lazarus enjoy a piece of pastry. "In a perfect vacuum there aren't any bits of matter floating around. Luna is exhausting thousands of tons of atomized material at each excavation site. Multiply that by hundreds of sites and you end up with some very large numbers. Some are advocating condensing useful elements out of this witches brew, but the cost is too high for what you get. It's simpler and more profitable to mine ore for what we need."

"I look forward to hearing about the details but right now I'm more interested in learning about your grandmother and the rest of your family." Lazarus shifts the subject back to the person he believes has the most say in his future.

Sam grins into her tea.

"Actually, she's my great grandmother. She was born in 1999 in Kansas City. One of the youngest to graduate with two PhD's from one of your old American schools, MIT I believe it was called. In 2024 she volunteered for the US Space Command and was the doctor on the mission that founded Aldrin Station. As one of the original settlers, she helped set up the city's first hospital and the first biotronic research program. She's still involved in biotronics and is an active professor at the University of Luna. Her lectures are always attended by thousands, sometimes millions."

"That's amazing, still teaching at ninety-three!" Lazarus says. "What about your father and mother? Brothers and sisters?"

"My dad, Patrick Ryan Dugan, was Abby's youngest child. Everyone called him Duce. He married my mom, Elizabeth Anne Turner, a few months before my oldest brother Ben was born in 2060. Liz then had Stone in '62, Patrick Ryan III or Tray in '64, Maggie in '65, Krystin in 67, Skylor in '70 and Alex in '71. I was last, born Halloween 2072."

"Impressive. In the Federation, families must pay for the privilege to have more than one child," Lazarus says. "The government calls them fines but the result is that only the rich have large families. I can't wait to meet your parents."

"You have been extended Dugan hospitality, so you will undoubtedly meet Liz but Duce disappeared surveying the Central Highlands in '86," Tempel says staring straight ahead taking another sip of coffee.

That puts Tempel at fourteen or fifteen years old when his dad didn't come home. Lazarus doesn't push, knowing what it's like to grow up without a father.

It hasn't taken long for him to tire of looking at their visors instead of their eyes. He slips his back on while Tempel talks, noticing for the first time that his surroundings sharpen and colors appear more vibrant with the device. Staring at the little waterfall, he clearly hears every splash, but the sound reverts to background noise when he looks away. Turning his head, Lazarus stares at the waiter inside the café, suddenly being able to observe his interaction with another customer as if he were standing next to them. The man turns and looks at Lazarus who hastily breaks eye contact and concentrates on Tempel. He isn't sure what just happened.

"Liz's family, the Turners, belong to Humboldt freehold over in Mission. When she married Duce she kept her maiden name and honored her new husband by accepting his as well, Elizabeth Anne Turner Dugan. This seems to be catching on with my generation. It makes for interesting names among our womenfolk."

"Just the women? I thought Lunarians were all about equality?" Lazarus says.

"That's what I've advocated all along, the men should change their name too." Sam says.

"How many kids did PR and Abby have?" Lazarus asks.

"In all, he and Abby have four kids, nineteen grandkids, fifty-seven great grandkids, and four great-great grandkids, so far."

Lazarus leans back in his chair and says, "It sounds like I'm going to have a heck of a time keeping it all straight. What about you, Sam, what's your family like?"

She smiles, "Not nearly as interesting as Tempel's, I'm afraid!" Turning to Tempel, she says, "We need to be going."

Tempel nods, gulping the last of his coffee.

They walk a short distance and approach Brooklyn Mall's East entrance. Unlike the North entrance, there aren't any shops or courtyard here, just the massive airlock doors thrown wide open.

Lazarus stops and turns to take one more look at the mall. It's so beautiful, it doesn't seem real. They have moved downhill since they entered from the North Courtyard so he's looking uphill. In reverse symmetry with the North section, the East widens and curves away from him, preventing him from seeing Central Commons. Tree leaves glisten with raindrops as their great limbs sway in the breeze. People walk the paths under the massive trees enjoying the day. Laughter floats across the distance. Being here makes Lazarus feel good.

Tempel waits impatiently but Sam motions for him to relax. She smiles at Lazarus when he turns to follow them out of the mall. They move down a wide straight corridor for several hundred yards, and emerge into another massive space.

At first Lazarus thinks they have entered another mall. Overhead is the same sky blue and giant trees dominate the landscape. But this space is different, a ribbon cut into the stone where the mall was a bubble. It's a forest as far as he can see in both directions, foliage gently swaying in the breeze.

They emerge upon a broad ledge at least twenty feet up one side. To his left and right ramps lead down to the grassy floor below. Directly in front of him is a rail-lined overpass extending straight and flat to a matching entrance on the far side. Scattered along its length are ramps that lead downward. Carved into the stone during the initial excavation, some of its surfaces are polished while others are left rough.

Instead of going down, Tempel leads them well out onto the bridge and stops at the rail. The floor recedes as they move away from the wall towards the center of the span so they are high above it when they finally stop. This gives Lazarus a marvelous view but causes his stomach to twist. He keeps back from the rail and gathers himself. The trees towering over the bridge are not Ash like those in Brooklyn Mall. Below them, like sidewalks or some other strange pathway, two strips of some dark material pass beneath the bridge, curve around the massive tree trunks, and disappear into the distance. Through the trees, several hundred yards away, Lazarus can glimpse another stone overpass composed of a series of arches that remind him of a Roman aqueduct. Staring at it for a moment, his visor zooms in until Lazarus can see people on the bridge.

Grass carpets the ground and everywhere he looks are small manicured gardens of flowering plants and shrubs adding splotches of color to the scene. Perhaps a hundred feet distant is a stand of cherry trees in full bloom. Stone retaining walls and numerous other landscaping details create a park-like atmosphere.

"Is this a commonway?" Lazarus asks.

"Aye, this is Asimov Commonway. It extends about two miles in that direction and less than a half mile in the other." Sam says.

"This isn't the only commonway is it?" Lazarus says.

"Asimov is only a small loop that services the west end of Lincoln County. Our meeting with Abby is about twenty minutes away. We will take the slidewalk to Central then to Sherwood." Sam says. Sensing his wonder, "The trees here are Sycamore, Elm, Yew, some Chestnut and a variety of fruit trees."

"Do they have a Norse legend attached to them?" Lazarus asks.

Sam smiles and tilts her head, "Maybe… but if they do, I don't know about it. There are many species of birds, insects and small mammals that make their home here. We can use them to make up our own legend."

"Count me in. I've always wanted to start my own religion…"

Movement attracts his eye and he looks up. Soaring silently far above the tree tops at high speed is what appears to be a long sleek train. When he continues to stare, the parallel lines of its rails come into focus stretching out of sight in both directions. He realizes that instead of riding on the rails, this train is suspended from them. Such technology! Lazarus flushes, suddenly feeling like a Neanderthal trying to make sense of a Stratoliner.

The train's gone an instant later leaving Lazarus to wonder if he imagined it. No, it never made a sound but the rails are still there if he looks hard enough.

He drops his gaze back down to earth, "It seems like a lot of resources have gone into making and keeping things pretty. Who pays for all the extras?" Lazarus asks.

"What extras?" Sam asks, puzzled.

"Well… moving people from point A to point B don't require forests," he says nodding at the nearest tree, "or cherry trees," shifting his gaze to the colorful pink flowers in the distance. The longer he looks the more distinct the tiny flowers become. He even begins to hear the bees buzz among the branches and catch a whiff of cherry blossoms.

Tempel frowns, "Are you saying you prefer staring at a blank wall whizzing by, or the person's head in font of you, like we see on vids of people riding the New York subway? The increase in size doesn't add much to the cost of excavation and Magi takes care of maintenance."

"Why wouldn't you want beauty into your home? Who wants to live in a dungeon?" Sam asks genuinely perplexed. "Luna didn't come with trees and green grass. We make every cubic foot of dirt including the bacteria and nurture every tree, shrub and blade of grass or they won't exist at all."

"There are mechanical scrubbers to clean our air but nothing beats trees for doing the job right," Tempel says. "Biodiversity is very important to us."

"I think I just redefined what I consider extras," Lazarus says with a weak grin. His gaze carries down the commonway, taking in the vibrant expanse. A few pedestrians move on and off the slidewalk or simply zip along its surface, quickly disappearing around the nearest bend or behind some particularly dense foliage. He understands.

"You have created something unique and special here. You should be very proud," Lazarus says softly. He looks down, watching as several people pass under the overpass. They are standing on a small disk which moves along the path. "You don't expect me to travel on this carnival ride do you?"

"Carnival ride? I'm not sure what a carnival ride is but slidewalk's are how we get around. It won't hurt you. If you can stand then you can use a slidewalk." she points down to a collection of small octagonal disks, each about twenty-four inches across, strewn along the edge of the slidewalk below them. It reminds Lazarus of a disorganized little parking lot off the main highway. "Those are drifters. Just step on one and Magi will activate the maglev technology built into the slidewalk directly beneath it raising the drifter about an inch. To move forward, shift your center of mass forward, same with left and right. To move faster, shift more of your balance in the direction you want to go." When he still looks dubious she adds, "Just move your weight closer to the edge."

"How do you stop?" Lazarus asks. It's one thing to know how to get it going, but as far as he is concerned, it's much more important to know how to stop.

"Simply center your mass," Sam responds.

"Magi will not let you get hurt," remarks Tempel.

Lazarus doesn't know who Magi is but that's not important right now. He looks down at the drifters scattered about where others have left them, "What about rules of the road?"

Sam grins, "Good questions. Traffic obeys the right hand rule. East bound traffic uses the south slidewalk and conversely, west bound uses the north slidewalk." She points to the two wide roadbeds. "Magi will not allow you to travel the wrong way on a slidewalk or run into someone else."

"How do you move larger goods around?" Lazarus asks.

"There's a network of tunnels below the city for truck convoys. The commonways are for people," Sam explains.

As they stand on the overpass, several citizens have linked a number of drifters together and are sharing conversation as they travel. Not far behind them come six children, each perhaps eight or nine years old, weaving in and out among themselves and laughing. Lazarus hears someone from the group say, "You kids mind your manners!" as they pass beneath. The children laugh and speed away.

"Where you're from doesn't have slidewalks?" Sam asks, seeing how Lazarus is absorbing everything, like a dry sponge plunged in water.

"Nothing like this!" Lazarus exclaims. "Some of the larger airports and spaceports have moving walkways but not slidewalks." Lazarus shakes his head. "The Federation can't seem to get past the automobile. Everyone still has to have one or two, even after the cost of hydrogen has gone through the roof."

"What did you expect after burning all the fossil fuel?" Tempel growls revealing strong feelings on the subject. "Do you realize that over eighty-four million barrels of crude oil and nine million barrels of natural gas were pumped out of the ground daily? 365 days a year? For almost a hundred years? It was all burned! What could they have been thinking about? It wasn't the future, that's for certain! What a bloody waste!"

"I personally have never even been inside a petroleum powered vehicle," Lazarus responds defensively, "Besides, it wasn't a total waste. It allowed us to build the infrastructure we needed to get to space."

"I've heard the justifications, I just don't buy them!" Tempel shot back, "It could have and should have happened much sooner. Too many people were making too much money to stop the burning! Luna doesn't have any naturally occurring hydrocarbons so alternatives come to us at great cost. Robotic freighters from distant Titan come in at regular intervals but are not nearly enough to fill the demand. What I find particularly loathsome is you build shrines to the idiots who profited from the biggest rape of resources in the history of mankind!"

"Politicians build shrines to each other. I didn't have anything to do with it," Lazarus responds.

"Of course you didn't," Sam says. "But it was your government."

"And what about the climate change it caused?" Tempel continues, "Earth's intense weather can be directly tied to the release of greenhouse gases. It has resulted in famine, drought, and the rise of sea levels have created 2 billion refugees. If orbital powersats weren't supplying energy to freshen sea water, civilization would have collapsed long ago." He shakes his head, "Your Presidents must have had their head up their collective asses not to do something about global warming when they had the chance!"

"Most of that happened before I was even born," Lazarus says.

"That's a copout which does nothing to solve the problem." Tempel retorts.

"What would you have me do?" Lazarus asks. "I can't fight the Federation."

"Here's an idea, why don't you run away and leave it for someone else to fix!" After a moments silence, Tempel nudges Sam, "Come on, let's go! We don't want to be late!" He leads the way down the nearest southbound ramp letting his anger boil away. It's unreasonable to blame this one earthman for the sins of a planet but some things are better felt instead of analyzed.

"Don't let Tempel's passion harm you. He realizes it's not your fault anymore than it's his," Sam says taking Lazarus by the arm and following.

Reaching the bottom of the ramp, Tempel steps on a drifter with no hesitation and slides out about ten feet and circles back, waiting while Sam and the earthman descend the ramp and join him. He is still angry but now is not the time or place for further discussion.

"Magi, pull together a double for us, will you?" Sam says, sensing the distress rise in Lazarus as they approach the edge of the slidewalk.

Two of the eight sided plates rise off the surface and assemble into a single platform, the common edge almost disappearing. It slides over silently and stops right in front of Sam.

Sam steps confidently onto the arrangement with practiced ease. "Come on Lazarus, you ride with me," she commands.

Lazarus hesitantly follows, expecting the assembly to wobble as he put his weight on it but finding it rock solid. Sam slides her arm inside of his, steadying him until he can get his sense of balance on the now moving platform.

"The first time might be a little tricky," she says squeezing his arm in a motherly fashion. "Let Magi control the drifter, you just let her know where you want to go."

Lazarus glances over at Tempel, wondering just how much animosity he will encounter within the Republic. Mankind continues to do many despicable things, preemptive wars, political assassinations, and torture, all in the name of national security or ideology, and he's right, the global environment is in shambles. The melting of the polar ice caps and the subsequent rise in the ocean levels, the terrible increase in storm intensity and massive shifts in climate, have led to widespread starvation and food wars. How can he possibly defend such atrocities?

Sam eases them out onto the slidewalk with Tempel bringing up the rear, picking up speed until they are moving along at a leisurely five mph, about the speed of a brisk walk. As Lazarus gains confidence, Sam increases their speed. Magi smoothes out and prevents jerkiness when an arm is swung or a head turned. It isn't long before Lazarus relaxes and really begins to enjoy the ride, his second in the last half hour.

"This is exhilarating!" Lazarus exclaims. "How fast can we go?"

Sam chuckles, "On a good day with no other traffic around you can achieve about twenty mph."

"If you want to go somewhere fast, take a maglev train. They top out above a hundred." Tempel adds from just behind Lazarus, a spot he can catch the earthman if he falls. He may not like it but Lindsey gave the earthman hospitality and he will not be the one to dishonor her word.

"I can't wait to ride in one!" Lazarus responds.

As they move along the commonway, Lazarus lets his eye wonder among the trees, glad to have the steadying influence of Sam's arm in his. The designers and architects of Aldrin Station knew the value of keeping mystery in the vistas presented to the inhabitants. Moving down the slidewalk, they pass through a variety of environments, each unique. Some are lit up in bright afternoon sunlight, others in the overcast of an impending storm. Some are crowded with hardwood trees while others are dominated by orchards. Many have roses and other flowering plants set in manicured gardens. Most of the commonway is carpeted with soft green grass and highlighted with colorful shrubs and plants. But there are a few places that are polished stone cathedrals with very few plants, glorious in their simplicity. One section contains strange twisted stonework that surrounds the passing traveler like something out of Dante's Hell.

More than once Lazarus observes squirrels running across the grass or playing in the branches of a magnificent tree. Sparrows, parrots, hummingbirds and many other species flicker about adding a spectacular flash of color, movement, and sound to the environment. Hummingbirds are especially plentiful and bee hives are evident in many places.

"This is quite beautiful," Lazarus says softly. "I have never seen so many roses!"

Sam nods, remembering something Abby once said, "We should always take the time to stop and smell the roses."

"Very good advice," Lazarus responds.

But at twenty years old Sam has spent her entire life in and around Aldrin Station and New London. At that moment she yearns to see more, to give herself something to compare this with. She glances at Lazarus with just a touch of envy. At least he had the courage to leave Earth and everything familiar.

Tempel and Sam maneuver out of the main flow of the commonway and brings them to a standstill. The drifters settle to the floor. Lazarus does well enough for his first time, just a little wobble.

"Well done!" Sam tells him with a grin.

Tempel grunts. After all, it was Magi that deserved praise if anyone did. She had done all the skilled work. This bozo had simply managed not to fall off.

"The feminist agenda is not about equal rights for women. It is about a socialist, anti-family political movement that encourages women to leave their husbands, kill their children, practice witchcraft, destroy capitalism and become lesbians."
Pat Robertson (1930-?)

Abigail Dugan

Upon exiting the commonway, the three make their way down side tunnels and corridors, branching first left then right, finally coming to an airlock off a small service corridor. Tempel passes his left hand in front of the security panel and the heavy airlock door slides open.

On Earth his sense of direction was impeccable. Rachel had proclaimed more than once that he had an iron nose that always pointed north. But here, in a subterranean city under a mountain on the moon, Lazarus is completely lost with no chance of retracing his steps even if his life depended on it. He's in an underground world where many of his normal visual cues are absent and too many passages simply look the same. Lazarus struggles to suppress his anxiety and trust these two young Lunarians, but he is completely dependant and that makes him uneasy.

Giving Lazarus a comforting and encouraging smile, Sam stays beside him as they enter the room, "Relax, this is just a meeting between two citizens, that's all."

Tempel glances at Sam and shakes his head, "He isn't a citizen yet."

It's obvious that Tempel doesn't have a good opinion of shortimers. Sam reserves judgment, sensing something inside this earthman that warrants her attention. Besides, she likes and trusts Lindsey and if she thinks Lazarus is worth the trouble then he must have something.

The interior is stark and utilitarian containing a cold metal table and matching chairs. An oil painting of a full Earth hangs on the wall, the blues and browns of his home planet providing the only color in the room.

"You must wear your visor during the meeting with Abby. Do you have a problem with that?" Tempel asks watching for even the most subtle reaction. He detects only a rising excitement, the type he would expect of someone in this position.

Lazarus sighs and nervously runs his hand over his head, "No, of course not," he responds. He had forgotten he was wearing one.

Satisfied, Tempel leads the way through a second inner airlock and down yet another dim corridor, coming to a third air-tight door. This one opens on Abby's office.

His first reaction is amazement. The room isn't uniform in size. Instead it's shaped like a pear, one end larger than the other, and its floors, walls and ceiling smoothly transitions from one to another without clear-cut borders. Lighting comes from luminous film deposited on the ceiling and upper walls, soft and pleasant casting few shadows. Dominating the large end are eight intricately carved stone chairs, their seats and backs lightly padded. They surround an oblong stone table that is low and massive. A silver tea service sits upon it. Pale streaks of gold and tan with the occasional slash of scarlet, form a distinctive layered pattern across the tabletop. This same pattern continues in the room's floor and walls, and onto a large desk on the other side of the office. An interactive picture frame hangs in an arched recess behind the desk. Filled with ancient books, bookshelves are carved in the wall on each side of the recess extending many feet in both directions. All the major pieces of furniture were carved from the mountain when the room was created, the beautiful stone polished to a fine sheen and left in place never needing to be rearranged. Typically Lunarian, the room and its built-in furnishings have no sharp edges. Instead it employs a flowing design that doesn't separate the chair from the floor but makes each an extension of the other.

The four people inside arise from their seats as Lazarus enters. One of them looks familiar… He suddenly realizes it's Lindsey. But her beautiful hair is gone! All that's left of her mane of raven delight is short black stubble, not much longer than a week old beard. She gives him a quick wave and a smile of encouragement which he returns nervously.

"Mr. Lazarus Sheffield," Tempel says stepping aside "This is Doctor Abigail Dugan."

His confusion instantly deepens. This beautiful woman bowing her head to him is much too young to have been born last century! The other women must be Dr. Dugan, but even she looks too young.

Abby nods to Lazarus in the Lunarian custom, "Greetings, Mr. Sheffield."

Lazarus nods awkwardly, "Ah… Greetings, Dr. Dugan."

"Welcome to Dakota," she says warmly.

Lazarus gathers himself knowing he has only one opportunity for a first impression. "It's my very great pleasure and honor to meet you, Dr. Dugan. I appreciate you granting me this interview," he finishes in a firm voice. Lazarus knows that Abigail Dugan is ninety-three but the women in front of him couldn't be past forty!

Abigail Dugan lights up any room with her presence. Her platinum hair is pulled back in a charming little-girl ponytail, yet she exudes an air of calmness and maturity that transcends her apparent age. Her broad full lips poised to smile belie the wariness in her green eyes. She instantly enchants Lazarus just as she has many more worldly men than he.

Abby nods before indicating the older woman with a wave of her hand, "This is Magi, our AI. I thought you would be more comfortable if she joined us."

Lazarus is stunned. Magi is the AI? And she is standing right in front of him. Never in his wildest dreams had he thought the Lunarians had the capability to project such a splendidly accurate image of someone who never existed, right down to shadows and wisps of hair waving in the room's ventilation. This only adds fuel to his growing confusion. Abby, who is ninety-three, looks thirty something and the AI, who could look any age, looks like a well aged grandmother. Magi's kindly brown eyes gaze steadily out from an age-lined face and her dark hair peppered with gray is neatly pulled back in a bun. None of it makes sense to his reeling mind.

Abby pauses letting Lazarus assimilate, well aware that nothing like Magi exists on Earth and it's her personal opinion that there should be. She feels strongly that if there was, many of Earth's problems would simply vanish.

After a moment, she presents the man stranding next to her, "This is Aldrin Stations Security Chief, Corso Dugan."

Corso Dugan is a ruggedly handsome man. His dark skin reflects African heritage and his sharp features could be chiseled out of solid rock. Gray eyes and coal black pupils glow with an inner fire, in stark contrast to his ebony skin. There isn't a hair on his head and tiny black ear loops in the shape of a viper eating his tail firmly grip each lobe, the only adornment Lazarus can see. Muscles ripple and bulge along his arms, shoulders and across his chest, stretching the tight pull-over shirt to the point of failure. This man exudes confidence and invincibility.

Besides that, he looks to be in his mid thirties! The oldest son of a ninety-three year old that looks thirty-five! Lazarus feels his head spin as the point is driven home of just how different these people really are. He struggles to get a grip on his emotions, more than a little intimidated by this turn of events.

Lazarus feels the intensity of his stare from across the beautiful stone table, "Tell us again, Mr. Sheffield, what brings you to Luna," Corso says in his deep voice, never one to beat around the bush.

With a physical rush he realizes what must be going on. This meeting, these people, the entire event must be taking place in cyberspace. Of course! That would explain everything. He almost reaches up to remove his visor. He stops just in time remembering he had been told to keep it on during the meeting. Nonetheless, he relaxes, glancing at Magi as if her image represents proof.

"Corso! Where's your manors!" Abby scolds gently. "Let's sit and have some tea. There is always time for tea, isn't there Mr. Sheffield?" she says indicating with a flip of her hand which seat he was to take. Abby picks up the steaming teapot and fills two delicate cups, placing each in a matching saucer. Sliding one to a spot in front of Lazarus she asks, "Do you take anything in your tea, Mr. Sheffield?"

"Ah… No… Please, call me Lazarus," he responds, flashing back to a little Chinese restaurant over on Seventh Ave, not far from his office at Homeland Security. It seems a lifetime ago. How did she know he liked tea? Probably just a coincidence, he decides. But how could she serve him tea if this meeting is in cyberspace? Too many questions and not enough answers.

"Then you must call me Abby," she responds, her full attention on Lazarus. "You don't mind if Lindsey and Magi joins us, do you?"

"No, of course not," he says, glancing at Lindsey.

"Good! Sam, Tempel, have a seat as well," Abby says waving them towards Lindsey.

As everyone settles in Magi says "All those present have been identified and authenticated."

"Thank you, Magi," Abby says and turns back to Lazarus, "I understand you are from Phoenix?"

Lazarus looks nervously over at Corso and back at Abby, "Yes. I've lived in Arizona my entire life. I was born and raised in Casa Grande, just to the south of Phoenix."

"Fascinating," Corso rumbles deep in his throat, his eyes are cold gray steel and the skin atop his bald head reflects in the light.

Abby ignores him, "You've recently lost your wife and daughter. Please, let me express sorrow for your loss," she bows her head as she speaks never taking her eyes off Lazarus. "I have lost loved ones. Nothing ever fills the void they leave behind."

"Thank you… Abby," Lazarus responds, still trying to put the pieces of this strange puzzle together.

"Do you have other family?" she asks softly.

Lazarus wishes she would drop this line of questions and get on with the serious issues. He falls back on Lindsey's advice to simply tell the truth.

"Yes, two brothers and a sister. My mother lives in Portland, takes care of my youngest brother. My father was killed in the line of duty when I was ten. I think I have some cousins somewhere but I haven't kept track. I haven't seen any of my wife's family since the accident," he tells her.

"Did your family help you when you lost your wife and daughter?" Abby asks.

Many strange and wonderful things have happened to him since he left Phoenix but this meeting verges on the surreal. Lazarus takes a firm grip on his emotions and takes a deep breath, "My sister was the only one around and she did what she could. But she has her own family to worry about. My brother was in college at the time and had to stay focused. I managed."

"I see," Abby nodded thinking how typical it is for earthmen, particularly Americans, to isolate themselves. It fills her with a feeling of satisfaction and pride that Lunarian families are so tightly knit. Again, Dakota has led the way in the early formative years developing the social fabric that eventually evolved into the Lunarian culture. She feels pity for Lazarus and even more for the society that drove him out, a man willing to leave everything familiar for just the slimmest chance of finding something better. "As an employee of Homeland Security, you must have attended a church. Did they help you through your grief?"

"Of course, they helped tremendously. I have many good friends there," Lazarus says using these words out of long practice, "They are good and decent people who stand firm in the laws of the land and Christianity." It sounds mechanical, even to him. But to say otherwise put these people at risk. Guilt by association is what the federal prosecutor would call it when explaining to a judge why they placed bugs and other monitoring devices among the members of the congregation. After all, the Freedom of Information act gave everyone the right to know if an individual was a true Christian or not.

"I'm sure they are," Abby says. "What church is that Lazarus?"

"The only church is the American Church of Christ. I attended a neighborhood gathering. It's just a small group of families that get together." Lazarus responds growing alarmed by the nature of her questions. He himself had toyed with suspects in just this manor. It isn't reassuring.

Abby smiles and says, "Do they share your same lack of faith?"

There it is. He had been expecting it. Lazarus pauses for a moment gathering his wits about him before responding to this frontal assault. "I cannot speak for anyone but myself. I freely admit to many faults, a lack of faith is but one," Lazarus says stiffly.

Abby smiles disarmingly, "Relax Lazarus. Freedom of Belief means you are free to believe in anything that strikes your fancy. Space aliens, life after death, astrology, any or all of the things forbidden, or for that matter, required of you under the Federations strict adherence to whatever passes for Christian dogma these days. I look forward to hearing in detail how a Senior Analyst comes to the decision to… immigrate, but for now let's get down to business. We reviewed parts of your conversation with Lindsey. What interests us most is the missing four thousand. People don't just disappear, especially the followers of Minister bin Aunker and General Arif."

Her response alarms Lazarus. She had maneuvered him into a confession only to let him off the hook? He suddenly realizes he has been gauging the conversation in the same way he would have if he were back on Earth. Emotion sweeps over him as he catches a glimpse of the long path he has chosen, knowing in his gut that he must somehow set aside lifelong prejudices and a well trained response mechanism and take these people at face value. It seems impossible at that moment.

Lazarus plunges forward as he has his entire life. "Let me get this straight, you fear these men more than a thermonuclear device?" he asks.

"I don't fear anything or anybody!" Corso rumbles from the other side of the table. "Nothing moves in or around Luna that I don't know about. Uranium will show up like a super nova on our sensors long before its close enough to do any damage!"

Looking at this muscular specimen of a man, Lazarus has no trouble believing his claim. He realizes that now is the time to drop the last piece of supposition on them. "What if they had a way to fool your scanners?" he asks looking steadily at Corso.

"Energy absorbent materials have been around for at least a century but their not perfect. There's always some energy leakage. And even if the Brotherhood has come up with better materials, it will still leave a void in the data. That in and of itself speaks volumes!" Corso's voice is a mellow deep rumble that is hypnotic in its smoothness.

"I'm not talking about EAM's. I'm talking about a shield that will actively portray itself as something other than what it is?" Lazarus asks returning Corso's steady gaze with his own.

Corso's face doesn't betray any emotion as he considers what this earthman is telling him. He finally rumbles, "How could this be so?" But his tone is a little more subdued. He knows perhaps better than anyone, just how much Lunarian security depends on the scanners. It is the one technical development Magi consistently comes up with during war games that shatter Lunarian defenses. All contingency plans dealing with this scenario are ineffective which is why he has devoted recourses to its solution.

"Five weeks ago a bomb was set off in an Israeli resort in the Sinai. A hundred and thirty three people died," Lazarus says.

Abby sadly shakes her head but Corso just growls, "What's so unusual? That has been happening since the 1960's and will undoubtedly continue."

"What's different is that the bomb had to have passed through several MRI scanners. Modern up-to-date equipment, not some half-century old antique! I grant you, the evidence DHS has is all circumstantial. But it's the only explanation left when all others are eliminated!" Lazarus says emphatically. "Homeland Security thinks it was a practice run for something bigger," he adds quietly.

Everybody in the room knows that Lazarus believes this as absolute truth. Magi actively measures all of his critical biological functions making it virtually impossible for him to lie and not be detected. She passes this data immediately to the people in the room. Lazarus is sweating bullets but he isn't lying.

"Magi, what can you tell me about the incident?" Abby asks.

"Sharm el Sheikh is situated on the Southern tip of the Sinai Peninsula with the Red Sea on one side and the mountains of Mount Sinai on the other. On Saturday September 22, 2091, at four hours and fifty-one minutes after sunrise, a rocket attack took the lives of one-hundred-thirty-three people; one-hundred-twenty-four Jews, five Egyptians and four Jordanians. A group calling itself the PRC claimed responsibility twenty-six minutes later. Seven minutes after that the Brotherhood denounced it as despicable and offered to help in the rescue," Magi says.

Lazarus is struck by the efficiency of the AI. She may look like a grandmother but she definitely doesn't sound like one.

"The rocket story is just cover. Nobody wants the public to get a whiff of the possibility that the scanners can be beaten." Lazarus adds.

"The data is unusual," Magi admits. "Many authentications are completely absent and some of the normal reports that would grow out of an investigation are incomplete. There's just enough detail to get by. I agree with Lazarus. This incident report has been altered," Magi says.

"I know it's been altered. I helped do it!" Lazarus says irritably. He isn't used to talking to an AI like she was a person. His distrust of them runs deep.

"Thank you, Magi," Abby says warmly.

"Your welcome, Abby," Magi responds.

"Do you have any idea how they are doing it?" Abby asks hopefully.

Taking a deep breath, he rubs the stiff bristles on the top of his head realizing he is covered in perspiration. Making a conscious effort to relax, he leans back in the chair and takes several deep breathes before answering. "Logic dictates two things. Just as you pointed out, our scanners would see a void in the data and raise a warning, so it can't simply block the spy beam. The shield must actually send back a signal of something normal. We call it active camouflage. Second… even with active camouflage they must have greatly improved the energy absorbent material, stopping and soaking up a much higher percentage of the MRI beam. Because if they didn't, it wouldn't matter how many false signals were generated, the MRI would still excite the material they are trying to hide."

Abby looks over at Corso and gives him a slight nod.

Looking like he had just bitten into a green crab apple and found half a worm, Corso rumbles, "We know about the improved shielding material. However, the development of a way to transmit a false MRI is new."

Lazarus simply nods. It is widely believed in the NAF and in DHS in particular, that Lunarian science is ahead of them so this revelation isn't surprising. But he did wonder how many other advancements the Lunarians have that the NAF doesn't know about. For such an open society, they sure do have a lot of surprises.

"Why are you here, Lazarus?" Abby says very quietly, her pale green eyes cool and calculating as they bore into his.

With sweat beading up on his brow, Lazarus sighs and takes a deep breath, never breaking eye contact with Abby. "Every Tuesday for the past three years my team has presented a weekly report to Director Dempsey. We have suspected for over a year that Iran or Afghanistan is hiding a bomb…er thermonuclear manufacturing facility. We think they are recycling old uranium, probably Russian. A couple months ago we started getting hints that a high value product was being readied for use. About two weeks ago my group came to the conclusion this product was one or more thermonuclear devices."

Corso growls, "Is there an answer to Abby's question coming soon?"

Refusing to wipe at the sweat cascading down his forehead, thankful for the visor protecting his eyes, he turns his gaze to Corso, "I don't believe the Federation will honor the Treaty of Independence. If the Brotherhood has active camouflage and a nuke then you can be sure, Luna is in big trouble!" Lazarus turns, looking intently at Abby. "Heaven help me, I cannot stand by and watch hundreds of thousands of innocent people die, even if it means sacrificing my life."

The room is silent until finally Abby breaks the tension. She calmly, without the slightest tremor, leans forward and picks up her tea, sips it without looking at anyone in particular and replaces the cup back on the saucer with only the slightest rattle of fine china.

"What would happen if your application for Lunarian citizenship were turned down?" Abby asks gently.

Staring wide-eyed at her, Lazarus seems to wilt just a little. "The Federation would prosecute for treason," he responds steadily.

"They would wipe your memory in one of those northern Canadian vacation spots!" Corso says coldly.

"I will die before that happens, Chief Dugan, one way or the other," Lazarus declares. "I realize that I have placed my life in your hands." Literally! Lazarus has never had any delusions on his ability to defend himself and he has no doubt that Corso could kill him with ease, or Tempel or even Sam for that matter. Looking at Abby he says softly, "I came here knowing that I couldn't go back. To return is more than a death sentence. You would be kinder to shoot me."

Abby looks at Corso who responds with a shrug and rumbles, "He's sincere, I'll give him that much. It remains to be seen what value his information really has." Turning back to Lazarus, "Assuming you are right, do you have any other information concerning these nuclear devices? How they will be disguised? Who will transport them? When will they be transported?" Corso fires questions at Lazarus.

"Size will depend on yield. Higher yield will force larger size," Lazarus answers.

Corso growls, "I know that! That's not what I asked you!"

Lazarus visibly retreats and regroups. With a deep sigh he continues, "No, I don't know any specifics. Nor do I know anything definite as to their travel arrangements. All I can tell you is that all the communications intercepted over the last three months paint a very ugly picture. You may think I am jumping to conclusions using incomplete data but please realize, I have been studying the Brotherhood for many years, in all its aspects. Hard data is something collected and analyzed after an incident. Trying to predict what these people will do next is the real challenge. I deal with subtleties and suppositions most of the time. Occasionally we capture a talker or get some reveling electronic files, but not often."

"Educated guesswork," Abby says quietly, Corso huffs loudly.

"Exactly!" Lazarus says. He locks eyes with Corso, suddenly feeling like a mouse staring at a viper. He passes his hand over his head gathering courage and continues, "The only thing solid I do have is a possible operational name. We intercepted a communiqué from a suspected money man. Inside was a reference to 'Allah's Cleansing Fire'. Cleansing has meant killing in the past." Lazarus looks intently at Corso, "That's as close to a smoking gun as it gets in my line of work!"

Corso raises his eyebrows thoughtfully, his eyes never leaving Lazarus. They too had run across references to Allah's Fire. But the social gulf between the Islamic culture and the Lunarians is much wider than that between Lazarus and the Brotherhood. Interpretation of data is very difficult for Lunarians. He realizes they rely on Magi too much but there isn't anything he can do about it. Dakota and many other freeholds have tried recruiting Muslims but to a man, they refuse to offer more than a superficial view of their homelands and beliefs. And they never garner much trust among Lunarians.

"Let's see what Lucas and Katee make of Mr. Sheffield's evidence," Corso rumbles thoughtfully. Maybe this earthman might be useful after all.

Abby nods and turns back to Lazarus, "It's not everyday that we have a Senior Analyst defect, Lazarus. For now, let's get you acquainted with two of our top network researchers. After that we can get you started learning what it means to be a Lunarian and live on an airless world." Turning to Magi she says, "Get him fitted for a suit and start training ASAP. I don't like having someone not vacuum qualified. Oh, and have the commissary send over something appropriate for Lazarus to wear."

"Aye!" Magi responds. "He needs some proper deck shoes as well."

"Fine. I like the flowered shirt but it makes you stand out, Lazarus. Also, I would like it if you could stay close to Lindsey or Tempel for the next few weeks. Just until you get accustomed to Luna. Are you ok with that?" Abby asks.

Lazarus is in no position to suggest anything different. "Of course, I appreciate all you are doing for me," he responds and looks down the table at Lindsey. She smiles back while Tempel wonders how he had gotten mixed up in this.

Magi leans forward in her chair and says to Abby, "Pardon the interruption but Pellegrini says he must speak with you immediately. He is waiting outside with Constance and Weenie."

"Magi! His name is Winthrop, not Weenie." Abby gently scolds the AI. Tempel chuckles forgetting Lazarus for the moment, and Sam dimples nicely.

"I will try and remember, Abby," Magi responds with a noticeable lack of sincerity.

Lazarus stares at her thinking it very strange that an AI should show any feelings, good or bad, concerning a real person. It is another indication that Lunarian AI's are very different from any in his experience. He looks inquisitively at Sam.

"Pellegrini is the Director of Operations at Falconhead and Weenie is his lackey," she says never losing her grin.

"You know he doesn't appreciate that nickname," Abby says.

Sam chuckles, "Aye, everyone knows."

Abby shakes her head, "Magi, please tell them I will be another moment."

"Aye," Magi responds settling back, the vinyl covering her chair squeaking as it accepted her weight. Lazarus is the only one to notice.

Rising and turning to Lazarus, Abby says, "Please accept the hospitality of the Dakota warren, Lazarus. Tempel will get you settled and show you around. I will expect to see you at dinner tonight."

"Yes, of course. Thank you, Abby," Lazarus says quickly rising with her and just in time remembering not to extend his hand, tipping his head in the customary fashion.

"Tempel, introduce Lazarus to Lucas and Katee. Have them report back directly to me. And Oh! Tempel.... If you ever tangle with Malik again..." Their eyes met for a long second.

Tempel nods, "I understand Grandma," he says softly. Lazarus wonders what that was about.

Turning back to him Abby says, "Lazarus, words cannot express the amazement I have for your willingness to risk so much for our safety. You give us all hope for our brethren on the home world!"

"Thank you, Abby, for taking the time to see me," Lazarus responds, marveling at the unusual green shade of her eyes. Pale like a rare beryl gemstone. He wonders what she would look like if he were not wearing a visor. He hopes this is real and not some cyberspace vid game.

Nodding in return Abby says, "If you will excuse me. I must see what the three amigos want."

Lazarus turns away, "Oh! I almost forgot. Izzy says to tell you hello," Lazarus blurts out.

Abby's brow furrows in concentration, "Izzy? Isaac Crenshaw?" she asks. When Lazarus nods affirmative she continues, "Where did you run into him?"

"He was on the translunar shuttle," Lindsey responds.

"That old reprobate is still kicking? Last I heard he was out in the asteroids somewhere." Tempel and Sam perk up, the first time either of them had heard about someone named Izzy. "He and I spent... time... together back in '24. Back then we were more concerned with staying alive..." she grins recalling old memories, "It's good to hear he is still around!" she chuckles.

Lindsey comes around the circle of chairs, "I've got a lot to do Lazarus. But I will see you later, if that's ok?" Lindsey says.

"Sure!" he responds quickly. "I'll count on it!" He reaches out to touch her and is shocked when his hand goes right through.

Lindsey smiles and Sam laughs. Tempel just shakes his head at Lazarus, his expression unmistakable. Abby watched. To him, Lazarus is just another backward earthman that needs special handling. "Come on earthman," He says as he heads for the door. "Let's go find Lucas and Katee." He's not pleased about babysitting.

Lindsey gives him one last wave of her hand and is gone, her image breaking up into a million tiny bits of foil that shimmer briefly before disappearing.

Lazarus used Federation virtual reality throughout his professional career but is utterly amazed at the advanced quality of the Lunarian system. At every turn he is confronted with evidence that it is far superior to anything on Earth. He had been completely unable to distinguish the real Lindsey from her VR image. Before this meeting, Lazarus would have sworn that he couldn't be fooled, but it's obvious that he had just been completely deceived. He knows the Federation has nothing close to what he had just witnessed. Magi, Lindsey and who knows who else had attended the meeting in name only. The Lunarians have the ability to project the image of a person, real or imagined, so accurately that he cannot tell the difference.

"Come on Lazarus. Lets' get you settled in." Tempel leads them through the door and down the corridor.

Sam stays beside Lazarus. "So was Abby what you expected?" she smiles.

Lazarus shakes his head in wonder, "Not even close. She and Corso both look so young," Lazarus observes. "Was that really them or just how they make themselves appear in VR?"

"Why can't it be both?" Sam asks.

"How can that be possible?" Lazarus retorts. "Abby is ninety-three and her oldest son must be in his sixties or seventies."

"Gene therapies will eliminate wrinkles and keeps skin smooth and supple," Sam says.

"Gene therapies?" Lazarus exclaims. "Or maybe the rumors going around DHS are true, all about the Lunarians finding a cure for aging. But that's ridiculous, isn't it?"

Sam chuckles, "Lazarus, you know what lengths the media will go to sell net time. Money is strong motivation!" Lindsey says. She doesn't like deceiving him after expounding on him at length not to lie. But it was necessary when dealing with earthmen. You never know when one of them might be a spy and until a new immigrant has achieved citizenship status there are certain things that is simply not discussed. They will come later. But it doesn't change that fact that she doesn't like it.

"You can explain cosmetics to him later," Tempel growls opening another door and going through. He doesn't even slow down leaving Sam to tend to Lazarus. His mouth is set for a cold beer as he makes a beeline for the kitchen area, visible as a bright bubble of light in the distance.

Lazarus is three steps past the threshold before he takes the time to really look at the space they have entered. He involuntarily comes to a stop, his head swiveling from side to side as he absorbs the visual complexity of the stunning panorama. Nothing has prepared him for this, not the towering cathedral these Lunarians call a mall, or the underground forest they call a commonway. It's everything good about a home magnified a thousand times, and it stretches into the distance as far as he can see.

It's hard for Lazarus to believe this magnificent room is a subterranean cavern carved out of solid rock thousands of feet down in the heart of a lunar mountain. It extends into the distance without a single real partition visible. Instead, richly upholstered overstuffed chairs and sofas section the expanse into innumerable sitting areas, some sunken, others raised, each with its own vaulted ceiling and lighting scheme. Many are flanked with classic Greek columns. The columns are abundant but don't seem to be in any particular pattern, or if there is one, it escapes Lazarus. Roman style arches are clustered about what appears to be the brightly lit center of the room. Colors jump out at him from an endless assortment of rugs, tapestries, pictures, and stained glass panels. Each lamp and chandelier adds to a mosaic of shadow and light giving the room mystery and vitality.

"This is your home?" Lazarus asks.

Sam stops and looks back at Lazarus. "This is Dakota's Greatroom," she responds.

Directly in front of them, over two hundred feet away, Lazarus can see the lower sections of much larger columns. Beyond them it opens out into a large grassy courtyard with a matching row of columns on the far side. Those soar upwards at least thirty feet and are capped with high arches resting atop the columns. He assumes the columns on his side match those he can see. They remind him of the Parthenon model he had handled back in Athens.

From this perspective, the courtyard appears lit up like a sunny afternoon at the local park, a grove of trees set upon a rich carpet of grass. Across the courtyard, beyond the far row of columns, Lazarus can just make out what appears to be a room matching the one he is in. Light and shadow dance in its heart as people move about its muted interior. Above it he notices a second floor behind the great columns that overlooks the central arboretum. Several people stand at its edge looking down and talking quietly. As he stares, his visor begins to magnify, their image growing larger and more distinct, and their voices louder, as though he were walking up to them. He looks quickly away.

To his far right a group of kids are playing a vid game, squeals of childhood frustration and triumph mix pleasantly together. From one direction comes the sound of someone playing a guitar and singing. From another, a loud, testosterone filled conversation punctuated with wild laughter. A man emerges from between two columns on the far side of the courtyard yelling and waving to someone Lazarus can't see. A group of children and several dogs are playing with a Frisbee out on the lawn. Laughter and voices resonate through the expanse. The Greatroom is vibrant with life.

Sam smiles and tilts her head inquisitively, watching the amazement wash over his face with each new discovery. "It's funny how we take things for granted until someone new comes along and let's us see through virgin eyes once more," she says softly.

Lazarus looks at her with a dazed expression, "My awe meter just bent its needle! I have never seen anything like this! It's a cross between a five star hotel and Grandma Sheffield's sitting room!"

He continues to scan the room as they move slowly through it following Tempel towards the kitchen. "In Arizona we have Kartchner Caverns. Its rooms are fantastic! The biggest have stalagmites and stalactites made of crystals that glow with miniature rainbows from the lights. But that is a fragile beauty. This room is solid and comfortable! More like my front room when my dad was alive."

"I have never seen a rainbow other than in VR. Nor have I ever been in a naturally occurring cavern, other than in VR. I am sure they are very beautiful," Sam says softly.

Hearing a touch of longing in this gorgeous women walking beside him he smiles at her and says, "Well if it's any consolation, this is my first time off-world. Besides, you're young. There is plenty of time to see those things, if that is what you want to do."

She smiles and tips her head in the universal gesture that says 'that is true'. "I would like to visit Earth someday," but from the way she says it, Lazarus realizes she doesn't actually foresee that happening anytime soon.

Seeming to materialize from nowhere, Lazarus is startled by the sudden presence of a large black dog. He's instinctively glad that Sam's between him and the apparition. He has never seen such a dog! It has a long narrow face, floppy ears and a slender muscular body reminiscent of a Greyhound. Lazarus feels a chill run down his spine under its wary glare. Effortlessly gliding forward, the muscles in the dog's shoulders ripple and flex under the silky black hide, its head dips low swaying side to side, its eyes never wavering from Lazarus's face.

Sam gets down on one knee and meets the dog, rubbing it down and vigorously patting its chest. "Hi Dueler! I have someone new to introduce you to. Be nice to him!" the dog responds with a heavy wet kiss across her face, making her giggle like a little girl. Still, the dog keeps a wary eye on Lazarus.

"What a beautiful and unusual animal!" Lazarus says.

"This is Dueler," Sam informs him, "Don't say that too loud, he thinks he's human, and he is definitely a member of the family." Looking up at Lazarus, "Come over here nice and easy. Let's get you properly introduced."

Lazarus eases up to stand by Sam's side. Dueler dips his head and tenses, never taking his eyes off him. "It's all right," Sam reassures him. The big dog glances at her and visibly relaxes. He moves forward sticking his nose out hesitantly to get Lazarus's close-up scent. Lazarus didn't move until Dueler pushed his nose under his hand asking for his head to be scratched, introduction complete.

"Good boy!" she tells the dog giving him one last hug around the neck before standing.

"I'm unfamiliar with the breed. What is he?" Lazarus asks.

Puzzled she asks, "What do you mean, breed? What is a breed?"

They are moving again, heading towards the kitchen with Dueler staying between them. Sam lightly caresses the dogs head.

Taken aback just slightly, Lazarus thought for a moment. "Within the canine species there are many breeds. Collie is a breed. Shepard's, terriers, hundreds of others. You don't know what a breed is?"

"Oh I see! A breed shares common features such as hair, color, size and shape. Right?" she asks thoughtfully.

"That's the ticket!" Lazarus responds playfully.

Sam looks at Lazarus in confusion but smiles, "You are a very unusual man, Lazarus. But to answer your question, we don't have breeds on Luna. We select the characteristics directly in the DNA strand when we conceive the new life. If you want a dog that looks just like your neighbors, that's your choice."

She says it so matter-of-factly that Lazarus has to think about it for a second. "Do you select your children the same way? Are Lunarians all tubers?" He instantly regrets his choice of words, letting it slip out from long use within the Christian dominated Federation. Tuber, derogatory slang for test-tube-baby, is often used as a curse within the Federation and across much of Earth where it's become synonymous with mutant and has come to symbolize the growing hate for the Lunarians.

Lazarus feels ignorance descend upon him like a heavy cloak, "Please, accept my apology. I meant no disrespect," Lazarus speaks anxiously, hoping that he hasn't done irreparable damage to a promising friendship. But what he picks up from Sam's body language is not anger.

Her eyes sparkle with amusement. Lazarus has a good look, being so much shorter than she. Dueler glances up, picking up on Sam's mirth. She shakes her head in mock disbelief, stroking the big dog's head and down his sleek neck, looking with tolerance upon this backward earthman, cocks her head to one side and responds, "Please… No need for apologizes. Each question is but a step in life's journey…that is how we learn and you have a long path before you," she softens her words with a smile. "To answer your question, we apply the science that we must to survive. We have eliminated all genetic defects and diseases. Does anyone talk about that?" she asks. While sincere, to Sam and most of her generation Lazarus is a backward, almost primitive, human being. The care that had been taken in selecting her genes is completely missing in this man. He is a random chain of events with unpredictable results, a role of evolutions dice with no idea as to the outcome.

"I don't think so but maybe in Europe or China," he responds as truthfully as he can. As a former Federation citizen he can't help but feel partially responsible for the hate that has built up over the last few years.

Sensing his discomfort Sam says, "Don't worry about it. I certainly haven't lost any sleep over it."

As they walk towards the lighted area, Sam notices Skylor and Krystin get up and drift towards the kitchen. "Magi, is Lucas and Katee available?" she asks as she strolls into the kitchen with Dueler at her side, opens the refer door and reaches inside withdrawing two cold beers.

"They have requested that Lazarus meet them in their lab in a few minutes," Magi responds.

Nodding, Sam twists open a beer, handing it to Lazarus.

Motioning for Lazarus to follow, she continues on through the kitchen joining Tempel at a nearby table, easing into the chair next to him. A half empty beer rests on the table in front of him. Lazarus slides into the seat opposite and leans back taking a good pull off his beer, enjoying the smooth fullness of the malt beverage. Different than anything he has tasted back on Earth, not that he has much experience in trying different beers. He watches as Dueler wonders out of the kitchen and disappears into the shadows, relived that the beast wasn't staring at him anymore.

"Can I show you something?" Tempel asks.

"Sure," Lazarus says quickly.

Tempel links their two visors. Between them above the table, a detailed schematic appears similar to the one he had shown earlier. He makes a small hand gesture and the object begins to slowly rotate. Lazarus can clearly see the individual cross-shaped habitats, three strung together on one level, four below them and three more on the bottom. Small tunnels extend vertically and horizontally and well below the bottom level, larger horizontal tunnels run to the edge of the simulation, there ultimate destination unknown to Lazarus. As in every other aspect of Lunarian architecture, nowhere can he detect a straight line.

"This is the top level schematic of the Dakota warren," Tempel says, "It is made up of ten habitats on three mega-levels. These four make up the central residential level and this is where we are."

Tempel makes a few subtle movements and the warren shrinks allowing room for other habitats to appear, filling the space with ever finer detail and complexity.

To Lazarus, the lower tunnels appear to be an independent network below the habitats making up the city. It reminds him of a subway system in New York, London or Paris. As he concentrates on the simulation and finds it becomes sharper, easier for him to see the fine lines making up the image.

"These fifty-seven blue habs form the core Dakota holdings. Magi will make sure you don't stray outside of them. Right Magi?" Tempel says.

"Aye," the AI responds.

"Greetings, mind if we join you?" Skylor asks as he and Krystin enter the kitchen proper.

"Greetings, this is Lazarus. Lazarus, this is my brother Skylor and sister Krystin," Tempel introduces. They exchange nods with Lazarus, staring at the earthman like they had never seen one before.

"Greetings," Lazarus says, "Very pleased to make your acquaintance."

Skylor settles in next to Sam, and Krystin pulls over a chair taking the spot at the head of the table close to Lazarus. Skylor is typical Luny, tall and slender. Tempel could have been his twin, almost. Both of them prefer short hair and military style clothing more out of convenience than as a fashion statement. This similarity adds to the illusion. Even though Skylor is six years older than Tempel, it is virtually impossible to tell by looking at him. Lazarus can sense that Skylor is not as serious as

Tempel, a ready smile and laugh never far away.

Krystin is also slender and a few inches shorter than Skylor, not as tall as Sam but close. Her perfectly straight raven black hair shimmers as it cascades over her shoulders, framing a triangular face with prominent high cheekbones. She is wearing a tight tank top exposing her midriff, a pair of stretch Levi's and deep purple deck shoes. At twenty-five she is considered an old maid by Luny standards. Most girls start having babies in their late teens.

Lazarus wonders if all Lunarian women are so strikingly beautiful. Krystin reminds Lazarus of an American Indian princess. Her unwavering dark eyes leave Lazarus with the impression of brash openness and honesty. He also senses a challenge in her eyes and a chip on her shoulder.

It hit him suddenly, like most deep understandings. In the same fashion as Dueler, these young Lunarians have been conceived from a shopping list of available characteristics. He envisions mothers' and fathers' sitting around with the family geneticist deciding what little Johnny was going to look like.

"So this is Paul Revere?" Krystin purrs giving Lazarus a long look, interrupting his train of thought.

"Has everyone seen the vid of my conversation with Lindsey?" Lazarus asks.

Skylor laughs, "Lucas and Katee certified it for inclusion in Public Records five minutes after Lindsey submitted it!"

"And me!" Magi pipes in.

"And Magi," Skylor concedes.

"Who are Lucas and Katee?" Lazarus asks looking at Sam.

"Lucas and Katee are twins, Louis Dugan's kids. They are network programmers," she says.

"Excuse me, but they call themselves AI designers," Krystin insists.

"If there's anyone better at handling software, I've never met them," Tempel says to Lazarus taking another deep pull off his beer. He was thinking again that if this earthman can show them any new techniques, he would eat his vacsuit!

Krystin turns to face Tempel, "I've also seen the courtyard vid. I thought you were smarter than that, little brother!"

Tempel looks sullenly at Krystin, "Don't worry about it!" he growls.

"Fine, tough guy! Get yourself killed! See if I care!" Krystin stands and heads for the refrigerator. "Who needs another beverage?" she calls over her shoulder. She is greeted by a chorus of "sure" and "I do's" from everyone at the table, including Lazarus.

Skylor looks at Tempel, "I thought you would be in with Abby and Pellegrini. I saw him come through here earlier with his two bozos."

"Abby spared me this time, but I'm sure I'll have to deal with Pellegrini soon enough." Tempel finishes his first beer.

Krystin comes back placing three more beers on the stone table. Tempel grabs the nearest one, twisting it open.

Lazarus finishes his first beer in several big gulps and reaches for another, "Is Pellegrini another Dugan?" he asks no one in particular.

"Shit no!" Krystin snorts, "What makes you ask that?"

"I just figured that Dugan's held all the high profile jobs in the freehold," Lazarus states.

Skylor laughs, "Dakota has over seventeen thousand members spread out in fifty seven habitats! The Dugan family is prominent in Dakota politics but the freehold encompasses thousands of other families. Bill Dugan just happens to be one of the founding fathers and our grandfather."

"Pellegrini thinks he's going to start a new freehold. He lives in Piper warren and wants to break it free from Dakota, that and Falconhead refinery would make a fine nucleus to build a new freehold around!" Krystin says, clearly annoyed with the idea.

"It wouldn't be the first new freehold Dakota has spawned," Skylor says.

"I just don't like the mealy mouthed little SOB!" she says severely.

"Tony's my supervisor, sis. He's a good engineer and knows how to run the refinery," Tempel says wondering how he had gotten into the position of defending the little man, especially to his sister. He's aware, as is everyone who cares, that Pellegrini had made a run at her a few years back and the relationship had quickly turned sour. So if anyone had an ax to grind, it would be Krystin.

Sam uses Lazarus' confusion to change the subject, "A proposed new freehold must be laid out and voted on by the parent freehold. Financial restitution must accompany any transfer of habitats and any other assets to the new freehold. I think it's similar to Earth corporations divesting or spinning off a new company."

Lazarus nods, taking a swig from his beer, wondering how much of today he will remember. So much has happened in the last twenty-four hours and it continues to come at him. Like getting a drink at a fire hydrant, he is managing to swallow only a tiny portion of the flow.

Turning back to Krystin, Sam continues, "I don't think he has the votes."

It didn't work. Krystin continues to talk at Tempel, "I don't like the pressure he is putting on Randi and you. He wants both of you out of there, but he's too gutless to just come out and say it!" Krystin asserts. "And don't try and tell me Pellegrini runs the refinery! He's never there! Constance and Weenie feed him what they want him to know! Randi, Carl and you solve the major production problems while those yahoos grab the headlines! When is the last time Weenie or Connie had an original thought?" she asks defiantly.

Tempel shakes his head, "That's not the point. Pellegrini deserves respect. He has been in charge of operations for over five years, and helped setup the new refractory purification process."

"Did he? Are you sure?" she says with exasperation. "I grant you he knows a lot about it, but my gut tells me someone else did all the real work! Don't forget, I worked with the little weasel during that time! I swear the little asshole would come in every morning with new answers!"

Tempel sighs having heard all this many times. He notices Lazarus looking past his shoulder, sensing in his demeanor that someone is there.

"Greetings everyone," Constance says innocently suddenly appearing in the kitchen. She begins opening cabinets as if looking for something.

Krystin curls her lip in disgust. "Spying again?" she asks swiveling around to confront Constance, scowling as if she wants to rip her in half.

"What could you possibly know that's worth spying on?" Constance says, pealing open a hi-nutrient cereal bar and taking a small bite. She walks slowly over to the table sizing up Lazarus as she came. "So we meet again," she tips her head in greeting.

Recognizing the woman from the mall Lazarus returns the gesture, "Yes, how are you?" he asks.

"Getting better everyday!" she responds. "Phoenix is a beautiful city although it is much to hot for me. I visited regularly when I was younger."

In person, Constance looks to be in her late forties with straight mousy brown hair cut shoulder length. She carries a heavy build and is below average height. Nothing stands out on her except a prominent nose on an otherwise nondescript face. She is the first women Lazarus has seen since his arrival that he wouldn't classify as beautiful. She isn't exactly ugly, just plain. Even at his admittedly low level of understanding, Lazarus is instantly sure that Constance isn't part of the same genetic makeup as the other Lunarians sitting at the table. She's an earthman just like him.

"I didn't think you could remember that far back!" Kristin snarls cruelly at the woman who pointedly ignores her. Not getting a response she continues, "Where are the other two conspirators?"

"The only conspiracy is in your head!" Constance spit back contemptuously. "Tony and Winthrop are still talking with Abby. They have legitimate concerns about the direction Dakota freehold is going!" Looking back at Tempel, "So Tempel, what have you discovered about the Gravity Separator problem so far?"

"Come on Connie, you know I have LCPD commitments and can't even start for another week. Pellegrini must have known my schedule when he gave the assignment to me," Tempel replies.

Lunarian citizens routinely maintain two distinct roles in society, one as a police officer and the other as a civilian, a disrupter never far from hand. Normally, duty cycles were eight straight weeks out of every fifty-two. But for the last year Corso has not only split up the duty cycles for all the Special Weapons and Advanced Technology teams, he has added substantially to their length. What once was eight weeks has turned into forty.

"Falconhead will end up waiting for your analysis or someone else will have to do it for you!" Constance says hatefully.

Tempel empathizes with Connie. It's hard for her to understand. But her increasingly pissy attitude is getting to be a distraction. "Constance!" Tempel says tersely, "If it's that important, why doesn't Pellegrini give it to someone else?"

"Because everyone is already working twenty hours a day, there isn't anybody else!" She retorts angrily. "Now the rest of Falconhead must deal with it! But why should the schedule bother you! You're a Dugan! Nothing touches you!"

At a speed only a born Lunarian can achieve, Krystin leaps to confront Constance, looking down at her, their faces only inches apart. "Do you have something against Dugans?" she asks softly, the intensity flowing downward like an electric current, dealing the smaller woman an almost physical blow. "Or maybe you think you can run the freehold better than Abby?"

"Ridiculous!" Constance backs away, startled and frightened at the abrupt close encounter. "I don't have to take this from you!"

"Fine! Leave! Go back to Alabama or wherever rock you crawled out from under!" Kristin keeps her nose within inches of Constance as the smaller woman backpedals.

Fear contorts her face and Constance momentarily loses control. "Monsters!" she practically yells. Then her expression hardens and she doesn't say anything more as she turns and scurries across the Dugan great room, away from this menacing creature.

Constance would undoubtedly report the incident to Pellegrini. Tempel allows himself a small grin and wonders how much she will embellish. Maybe he should gift wrap the vid and send it to him…

Krystin simply watches the retreating figure with disgust.

Tempel turns to Krystin, "You were pretty hard on her."

"Something about her rubs me raw!" Krystin replies. She's not the least apologetic about frightening the woman.

Tempel looks woodenly at Lazarus, "Sorry you came yet?" he asks.

Lazarus shakes his head, "Verbal skirmishes are part of being human." He turns and asks Krystin, "You say Constance came from Alabama? What part?"

Krystin shrugs, "I haven't the foggiest idea. Magi, what's her bio?"

"She was born in the small village of Blacksher north of Mobile in 2046. Moved to the Atlanta area when she was ten," Magi reports. "Did her training in Atlanta and Massachusetts, she arrived on Luna March 2088 and applied for Dakota citizenship a month later."

"Interesting," Lazarus says looking thoughtfully at the retreating figure.

"Why is she interesting?" Sam asks.

Reminding himself to be perfectly honest, he says, "2088 puts her at the very end of the Exodus, a time when world governments began to actively discourage their citizens from leaving, and a time when Federation agents were sent out to establish deep cover among the immigrants. Most of these undercover operatives turned out to be a bust, the people becoming part of human expansion and never reporting back to their controllers. But a few did and are still in place, their identities kept top secret, not even the President knows who they are. Certainly I don't. But it is something to keep in mind."

Tempel looks at the earthman with a touch of disgust, "Such intrigue is unlikely here. You will learn that the Law is very hard to beat!"

As to those who disbelieve, neither their possessions, nor their children shall avail them at all against the punishment of Allah; and it is they that will be the fuel of the Fire.
Holy Qur'ân 3:10
Those who believe fight in the cause of Allah.
Holy Qur'ân 4:76

Lincoln County Hospital

Not far from Dugan warren, located in a lower level of the Aldrin Station Security Administration, are some of the city's laboratory facilities. Their primary mission, as stated on the official Security Chiefs annual budget, is as a crime lab supporting all police investigations. But that was simply a smoke screen. The shortimers over in Little America wouldn't tolerate Lunarians investigating or policing them and the extremely low crime rate among the Republics citizens make this a standing joke among the techs who work in the lab. In reality the lab is devoted to advanced research and the development of new technology. Today all the really interesting toys have been put away and it looks once again like an ordinary forensics lab. Simple precautions until they learn more about this latest citizen.

The laboratory is a narrow two-story high-bay packed with an assortment of equipment, tools, and personnel, its ceiling the now familiar sky blue. Overhead a three axis crane rests motionless, waiting until it's needed. Along one side, running the entire length of the bay, are two levels of semiprivate offices and work areas, a railed walkway forms a balcony along the upper level. Some offices have their doors open, others are closed, and many of them have windows looking out onto the main work floor. Several blue clad men and a woman are standing at the upper story rail watching and discussing some aspect of the work being done on the floor below.

The floor of the high-bay itself is the main workspace. In it are rows of long metal workstations cluttered with instruments, tools and supplies. Various furnaces and ovens are tucked into corners and a large Dewar of liquid helium stands against the far wall.

Close by, a young man is busy soldering at a workstation, a thin column of smoke trails up from his iron to a suction tube. Lazarus gets a good whiff of acid odor when he stares at it for a few seconds. Another tech is working at a Scanning Electron Microscope, the image of what she is viewing appears in his visor when he stares long enough, a fracture surface of minuscule proportions. A dozen others are scattered throughout the facility quietly going about their jobs, their sights, sounds and odors carry to Lazarus as he looks at them one by one, growing used to seeing the ghostly image of their visors disappear when he stays focused on their faces.

Tempel leads Lazarus across the main floor to a closed door on the lower level. A soft chime sounds as they reach it and the door slides open.

"Come in! Come in!" Lucas says rising to his feet to greet them. "Greetings Tempel. This must be Lazarus!" he says nodding welcome.

"Greetings Lucas. Yes, this is Lazarus Sheffield," Tempel responds. "Lazarus, this is Lucas Dugan."

"Very pleased to meet you," Lazarus returns the nod. Lucas is taller than Lazarus and slimmer. His black skin reflects the rooms dim lighting making him appear as if he were made of polished ebony. A thin black line of beard follows his jaw line and terminates close to delicate silver hoops dangling from each ear.

"Greetings Tempel," purrs a female voice from behind him.

"Greetings Katee," Tempel responds, "Lazarus, this is Katee Dugan."

Lazarus turns to face the voice nodding politely to the beautiful young women standing there. Katee could not have been more different from Abby. About the same height as Lazarus, she has a big chest, narrow waist and wide hips. Coal black hair halos her head in an Afro. Lucas is two inches taller but with his hair cut short, he appears smaller. The two are obviously biological twins.

Lazarus wonders fleetingly about the details of their parent's decision to have twins. They both look to be in their late-twenties with the same sharp features and slender face. Dark clothing gives them a gothic cast and Lucas is wearing a black hat turned backwards, the bill extending downward over his neck. Lazarus doesn't recognize the emblem on the hat from the few glimpses he has gotten. He assumes it must be a Lunarian sports team. He knows they have something they do up here for fun.

"Welcome to Luna. We have reviewed the vids of your conversations and are anxious to hear how you can help us. Aren't we Lucas?" Katee says smiling as she takes Lazarus by the arm and guides him deeper into the room towards a second workstation in the back of the office, leaving Tempel and Lucas alone.

"Indeed we are," Lucas responds with a lack of sincerity, watching the pair move away.

"What do you make of Lazarus's story?" Tempel quietly asks Lucas.

Looking across the office at his sister and the stranger, "Rest assured, we are going to check every detail. Twice!"

"I find earthmen hard to understand. Some want to harm us, others, like this one..." Tempel shakes his head in puzzlement, "want to be us."

"Show me a Lunarian who hasn't had the same difficulty and I will show you a fool. International politics make my head spin, far too much intrigue! Enemies turn into friends and back again in the blink of an eye. No one trusts anyone. Who can make sense of it? Me? Born and raised on Luna? I think not! Abby is the only one I trust to interpret Earthly shenanigans, and she hasn't set foot on it for sixty-five years!" Lucas exclaims. "But this is very dangerous. The Republic needs formal embassy's physically located in the countries we are partnered with. Relying on the business dealings of freeholds as our major political contact is isolating us, making us easy targets for lies to be spoken and believed!"

"Explain how we deal with the Law of Full Disclosure? You know that virtually every nation has forbidden our recording their citizens. They claim that this infringes on privacy in some way. But the simple truth is that their politics and the way they do business will not survive the visibility of Full Disclosure. They refuse to abide by our laws and we will not lower out standards to theirs. So there you have it, we are again at the same impasse," Tempel shrugs.

"We deal with it the same way we do business with them, we follow our laws and they follow theirs with a firewall in between," Lucas responds.

"That won't work and you know why," Tempel says.

"It's better than war," Lucas replies.

"What do you propose to do when our ambassador is called to a high level meeting with one of them? Suspend the Law? Tell our people to remove their visors and attend a meeting that produces no official record? That will violate Full Disclosure and they should be punished."

"There must be an answer," Lucas says.

Tempel shakes his head, "Talk to Lindsey. She just got back after six weeks down there. I can't imagine being without Magi that long... We cannot allow Earth to bring us down to their level. Secrecy has proven to promote evil and absolute secrecy produces absolute evil."

"On that we agree," Lucas says.

Before the conversation can get deeper into a subject that has been beaten to death over many sessions of heated debate, Katee catches Lucas's eye and motions him to link with them.

"Lazarus seems to think we need to use a keyboard and a mouse to access the data we need," she says.

Lucas raises his eyebrows inquisitively, "But why?" tuning to Lazarus, "Why not use a simulation?"

Lazarus looks back at him, "Because the website will recognize that it's a simulation and not the real deal. The Brotherhood uses out-of-date protocols to hide behind, the older the better. For the last century, old hardware and software has been recycled to poor nations around the world. That has enabled them to construct a sub network inside the World Wide Web, virtually invisible to anybody using VR. The protocols make it very secure, unless you know the secret handshake!" Lazarus says grinning.

Katee leaves the room with a determined look on her face.

Lucas grunts, not quite believing it, "Where are we going to get hardware that is over seventy years old? We stopped using keyboards and mice long before I was born. I've never even seen one used."

"What's a mouse?" Tempel asks but before anyone can answer him, Katee rushes back in triumphantly, an old fashioned wireless keyboard with a track ball at one end.

"Will this do? I don't think we have a mouse," Katee asks, handing the ancient device to Lazarus.

Lazarus takes the plastic contraption and taps a few of the keys which still seem to function. Turning it over, he looks intently at the faded identification label and makes out a model number, manufacturer and date.

"2023, yes, I think I can make this work. I'm not accustomed to using a ball but that shouldn't be a major problem. We will need a power source for it. I doubt its batteries are still good."

"That's the one from Abby's historical display! She used it during the first couple years here," Lucas says alarmed that something so irreplaceable would be handled so carelessly. "It's priceless!"

Ignoring her twin, Katee replies, "Not a problem. We can use this." She rummages around in a drawer and pulls out a small box shaped piece of equipment with several wires sticking out of it. Placing it on the table, she takes the keyboard from Lazarus and removes a small panel from its bottom. The battery space is empty. She quickly solders the wires from the source to the small tabs inside.

Lucas frowns with concern, "Even if it works, I'm sure we don't have drivers for it."

Looking closely at the keyboards label, she sets the power source to five volts. "There, that should do it. Magi, are you picking up anything?" Katee asks.

"Yes, at four point eight gigahertz," Magi replies.

"If you will allow me, I can download the driver we need from the net," Lazarus says looking expectantly from Lucas then back to Katee.

The two of them exchange glances, "Nothing ventured, nothing gained!" Katee says. "Magi, isolate and firewall our visors. We are going to introduce some outside software and you are to take maximum precautions."

"Aye!" Magi replies.

Sitting in his chair, the virtual workstation appears to him as an expansive tabletop curving around him. The left side of its surface is cluttered with elements of the internet access portal, the right side is his workarea. From the portal he can search the web for other sites and information, pulling what he finds useful over to the workarea. From there he can save his work for later analysis or pull parts of it into his workspace, the volume above the workarea and directly in front of Lazarus.

Growing confident in using his visor, he arranges the relevant web-address symbols in their proper order and initiates the command, calling up the website.

Lazarus is startled by the speed its front page appears in his visor, a crude cross with a bloody and weary Jesus hanging on it. The cross is set atop a hill and the name of the website, Calgary Chapel, floats above Jesus in bold letters. Around this image are the icons linking to other pages within the site. He reaches out and touches the Ichthys icon, mirrored arcs that form the outline of a fish. Jesus and Calgary shrink into the background. The page that takes its place contains a listing of names and numbers. He scrolls down until he finds what he is looking for. Reaching out again, he pulls out the name of Ken Whitaker, triggering information regarding this person to open out into his workspace, replacing the list. Slowly rotating before him is the quarter scale image of a middle aged man with thinning hair and weary eyes dressed in rather shabby clothes. His physical identification appears along side him. Scrolling down this list Lazarus pulls out the man's DNA profile.

The figure and his information retreats into the background giving ground to a long series of four symbols endlessly repeated. Lazarus scrolls down and pulls one seemingly at random. But instead of exposing the detailed description of that particular snippet of genetic code, it initiates a program he had written several weeks earlier.

"Now we wait," Lazarus says.

From this program, a single command is sent out to start other programs on servers scattered across the Federation, each designed to transmit a randomly selected file. These in turn initiate other programs which repeat the process until the chain has cascaded into thousands of threads sending files across the 238,855 miles of space to Lazarus. From this chaos there is one thread that seeks out and downloads the file he needs. All the others provide cover by continuing to send a horde of information pulled at random.

By the time the massive downloading triggers Federation snoopdogs, it is too late to backtrack any one occurrence to its origin. Their paths cross and re-cross thousands of times in a pattern impossible to decipher in any reasonable amount of time. All that can be done is to stop the runaway process before it consumes more resources. Fire fighters designed to combat this style of virus quickly overtake and stop the programs. Within minutes the attack is contained.

Pulling the file from the mountain of useless information Lazarus commands, "Magi, install this file."

A pause of a few seconds, "Done" the AI responds.

"I can't wait to see what you do for an encore," Katee says.

Lazarus places the keyboard in his lap, careful not to disturb the leads from the power source, and begins typing, much to the amazement of Katee and Lucas. Without looking up Lazarus says, "Magi, are you picking up the keyboard?"

"Aye, the signal is drifting but I can compensate," she responds.

"No! Let it drift," Lazarus says. Turning to the portal at his elbow, he pulls together another web address and initiates the command.

A small box with its own input field pops up in the center of the workspace. He uses his thumb to turn the trackball and a small arrow appears on the front page. Spinning the trackball, he moves the tiny arrow to the field and presses the left button. A small vertical bar begins blinking inside the field awaiting keyboard input. With the cursor where he wants it, Lazarus carefully types, sura24ayas5157.

"Sura is the Arabic word for chapter and ayas is verse. Verses 51 through 57 in the Qur'ân directs believers to either convert or kill nonbelievers," Magi comments.

Thousands of pages of Arabic text fill his workspace. Like sheets of paper, one placed in front of another facing him, the front page the only one he can clearly see. The others behind it are faint wisps of writing which together create a background for the one page he can read.

"Magi, be a dear and translate for us?" Katee asks.

"Certainly," she replies.

To the utter amazement of Lazarus, the front page morphs from Arabic to English. This feat took his entire team, and their computers, several days of hard work to accomplish. Magi did it in mere moments. It's simply one more wonder in a long litany of wonders.

Lazarus uses the trackball to place the curser in the field near the bottom of the workspace he types in an old-style web address, ubayd_allah_ibn_abd_allah.com, checks it twice for spelling and presses the enter key on the ancient keyboard.

"Ubayd-Allah ibn Abd-Allah was a companion of the prophet Muhammad. He told the hadith of the pen and paper," Magi comments again. "It is the event that caused Islam to split into the Sunni and Shi'a sects."

Through the ranks of pages arranged behind the fist page, one shuffles forward taking its place at the front. It's also completely in Arabic.

"Magi, make the translation," Lazarus commands.

"Aye," she says.

Starting at one corner, word by word the Arabic flipped to English. It reminds Lazarus of watching a piece of paper burn only much faster.

"These are electronic communications generated within the Ministry of Defense. The Federation isn't as efficient as Magi in translating so we have read only about ten percent of these. But it is enough to worry a lot of folks," Lazarus says.

"Pull up an example," Katee requests.

Another page of Arabic fills the workspace which Magi translates immediately.

Katee stares at the text for a second, absorbing the information it contains. "Magi, translate all of these and record," she directs.

"Aye," Magi replies.

"There are hundreds of thousands of documents here…" Lazarus warns.

One after another Magi loads and translates the information. Faster and faster the pages ripple forward as each new file is requested. The process speeds up until it's a blur giving Lazarus no opportunity to see a finished document before the next arrives.

Katee actively monitors the progress letting the information flow into her head without an in-depth analysis on her part. That will come later. But she is intrigued at what she is learning.

Lazarus looks at Katee and realizes something strange is happening. It's as if she is reading the memos flashing by. But that's impossible!

Magi's incoming chime sounds softly in Tempel's ear and she says, "Pellegrini has asked if you can be spared. It seems he needs you at Falconhead."

Tempel shakes his head in disgust, "Abby and Corso ordered me to bring Lazarus to the lab and stay with him until Lindsey was back."

"You don't need to be here, looking over our shoulder," Lucas says.

"Thanks Lucas," Tempel responds dryly. "Lazarus?" The earthman wrenches his attention from the incredible process taking place in front of him to look up. "I need to go but Katee and Lucas will take care of anything you might need."

"Yes, ok," Lazarus mumbles much more interested in what Katee is doing.

Katee is sitting forward on the edge of her seat, eyes locked on the display. Tempel is genuinely astonished that the earthman has commanded such attention from his cousin. Live and learn.

****

The John M. Young Research Centre of Lincoln County Hospital is one of the premiere facilities in Luna's quest to improve medical science. Named after the Apollo 16 commander who landed west of the Four Craters Region, it has a long and distinguished history staking claim as the birthplace of biotronics. Over the years it has produced astounding breakthroughs in genetics and reconstitutional therapy. Constructed in 2024, before disrupter technology revolutionized excavations, it is one of Aldrin Station's first habitats. Some of its chambers still exhibit tool marks, left to remind Lunarians of their heritage.

Dr Haslett doesn't think anything amiss when he first notices the heavy gray case. Nothing about it stands out among the many crates and containers making up the shipment containing his Quantum Probe Microscope. Having waited impatiently for the scope for over a year, he is personally supervising each step in its unpacking and assembly. It's Japan's latest technology and cost a small fortune to buy and ship to Luna. He's acutely aware that any item designed and manufactured on Earth needs the approval of Lincoln County Hospital's governing board, and they don't just give that away. He staked everything to get the QPM. The dark gray container is the last to be opened.

Maria Chapman has been Dr. Haslett's grad student for the last six months and is the only one among his staff that he trusts to help him. She is almost as excited as he about getting her hands on this magnificent machine with its amazing ability to not only see an atom but see inside to its nucleus. The two of them have been working steadily on the assembly for over nine hours, and now, with the end in sight, are anxious to get it finished. Picking up the touch panel, she stifles a yawn as she triggers the next step in the process.

Similar to other high value crates in the shipment, this last one has an electronic lock. Her directions state that she is to enter the listed nine digit code into the small keypad on the side of the case, exactly as she done with the others. The touch panel displays the details necessary to complete the installation of the instrument inside once the crate is opened, just as in those preceding steps. She reviews the details pulling up a schematic of the detector and verbiage telling her exactly how to install it on the scope and calibrate. Nothing raises any alarms.

Maria kneels down in front of the case and enters in the first three digits just as Dr. Haslett torques down the final screw on the hood installation. He walks over to stand behind her. "What's this?" he asks.

"Quark detector," she says, entering the next three digits.

Dr. Haslett frowns, his brain tired and slow from the long assembly session, "This looks too big to be a detector."

Maria yawns keying the last three digits, even as Dr. Haslett begins to tell her to stop.

The enormous release of energy instantly vaporizes everything and everyone in the laboratory. The thick stone walls of the room contain the energy for the briefest fraction of a second before atomizing. For many levels above and below the detonation, the stone is shattered as the supersonic pressure wave expands. Massive sections collapse, crushing everything beneath their terrible weight. But expansion robs power from the growing sphere of devastation and the stone further away begins to hold the blast between them, focusing the energy horizontally into the surrounding corridors, patient rooms, and laboratories. These are crushed like so many egg shells as the pressure wave passes, killing all it touches.

Throughout the hospital and well into the surrounding city, airtight doors close in emergency lockdown as Magi moves to contain the damage. Power to the hospital becomes sporadic. In the collapsed region, hot lines exposed to air, arc and sizzle in the swirling gray fog like a lightening storm. Network communications falter and fail cutting Magi off from the heart of the problem.

Seconds after it began, the beast spends itself in a thick cloud of dust that permeates the hospital. John M. Young Research Centre is now a chamber of the dead and dying.

****

"No!" Magi suddenly exclaims on all channels.

At the same instant, the floor shakes violently under Tempel's feet and the air inside the lab reverberates with a heavy deep thump. Several old-fashioned hardcover books fall from a shelf and an assortment of items rattle loudly in the room. Katee jumps out of her chair looking wildly about, startled out of her concentration.

"What was that?" Lucas exclaims.

"There has been an explosion inside Lincoln County Hospital," Magi says.

Tempel's insides twist, "Explosion! What kind of explosion!" he demands, fearing the worst even as he turns to look at Lazarus.

"Unknown, but it was big," Magi responds.

Lazarus stares back blankly, his eyes wide in confusion, his brain trying to get a handle on this latest event.

"Nuclear?" both Tempel and Lucas ask with concern.

"Negative. At least I am not picking up any radiation around the blast area," Magi responds. "I can not get anything from the hospital itself. I think the network has failed." Magi's voice has gone up several octaves in the last few seconds.

"Attention! Emergency Response teams ER4 through ER16, report to Lincoln County Hospital. Everyone else sit tight! Stay off the net until further notice!" Corso broadcast. The sound of his voice echoes from every corner of Aldrin Station.

Workers pour out of the offices, joining the crowd gathering on the shop floor. Tempel can see Jerome and heads his way. Jerome Hargrove is Dakota's chief engineer, responsible for keeping all the habitats working smoothly.

Tempel links to his visor and listens as Jerome approaches. "The highest priority is getting everybody out of the habitat safely. But to do that, we need to determine what shape the hab is in. I'll lead a team in to mag the periphery walls." Catching sight of Tempel, "Tempel's here. He can man the other mag. It shouldn't take more than thirty minutes to get a preliminary SQUID evaluation."

"Do it," Corso says. "We are already getting reports of massive damage, so take all appropriate precautions. We don't need more casualties."

"Aye!" Gripping Tempel by the shoulder Jerome says, "I need you to get the two magnetometers from the storage room, ER packs, and whatever climbing gear you can find. You and I are going to find out how badly damaged the hospital is." Pushing Tempel in the direction he wants him to go, Jerome continues. "Magi, round up ten people and get them here ASAP! They will be our mag teams and probably first contact rescue party, so pick appropriately! ER training is desirable but above all, speed is of the essence."

"Aye!" Magi responds.

Tempel quickly crosses the labs main floor heading for the storage room next to the big helium Dewar. The magnetometers are kept on a broad shelf just inside the storeroom. He slings the instruments over his shoulder, quickly depositing them on a workbench outside. Returning, he rummages around in a metal locker emerging triumphantly with vacsuit hardhats designed to be used with visors. Their wide elastic chin straps have two snaps on each side. A little more effort nets low light level flood lamps that clip onto the hardhats. They cast a broader and less intense beam of light for use with the LLL sensors in their visors. If its one thing the Lunarians have perfected, it's the equipment they use to build their cities.

"These may be useful," Tempel says. "Magi, where is the hemp rope kept?"

"In the bottom cabinet to your left," she replies.

Tempel opens the cabinet and removes a number of coils of the strong rope. He adds a bundle of karabiners and several ratcheting come-a-longs. Tempel emerges from the storeroom just as Jason and Larz, Katee's two oldest sons, along with Skylor and Krystin make their way past the now abandoned workstations on the main floor.

"We're here to help," Skylor states as he surveys Tempel's growing pile of supplies. He turns and begins passing out hardhats and lamps to everybody, "Make sure the fuel cells are full before we leave."

Tempel looks over at Jason and Larz, "Does your momma know where you are going?" he asks.

"We're old enough to make our own decisions," Larz states firmly.

He's right. Lunarians grow up fast, partly environment, partly genetics. Both physically and emotionally, this sixteen-year-old would easily have passed for twenty-five a century ago, a mature and responsible adult in every definition of the word. His education included ER training that fully qualifies him for this mission. But it will be his first real experience in rescue operations.

Lazarus emerges from Katee's office and approaches, "I understand you're headed for the hospital. I want to help. I'm no doctor but I do have emergency medical training."

Skylor glances at Tempel and tosses the earthman a hardhat, they both know that Abby wants someone with Lazarus at all times and he's a citizen...sort of. Besides, what better way to test the metal of a man than by throwing him into the fire? Tempel steps forward and slings a coil of rope over one shoulder and an ER pack on the other. "Looks like you've been promoted to field officer," Tempel comments.

Lazarus feels a rush of adrenalin surge through his body like an electric shock. He had expected Tempel to refuse him and was prepared to argue. Lunarians are full of surprises.

Jerome joins the group along with several of the lab techs and engineers, each of them carrying a load of small high-pressure air tanks with breathing apparatus. Passing the tanks out, everyone soon has one strapped to their back. The mask is designed to fit over a visor and fasten to the hardhat but for now they hang over their shoulder by the flow tube. A second mask clips to their belts. Lazarus looks at it puzzled.

"In case you need to share your O2," Skylor explains showing him how to use the apparatus and afterward, checking all his equipment making sure the earthman hasn't done something stupid like forget to charge his tank or clear his lines.

After finishing with the equipment, they link visors with Jerome letting him run the show. He pulls up a graphic display of Lincoln County Hospital. The hospital warren consists of two large habitats with fourteen entrances, including a maglev station in nearby Sherwood Commonway. Hospitals are intended to be centrally located and easily accessed, and Lincoln County is exceptionally well designed.

Jerome points at a glowing dot near the center of the habitat's north wing, "From all indications the bomb was here. Magi run the simulation."

"Aye," she responds.

The blue lines of the habitat turn red as the blast consumes everything above and below it. Shock waves radiate outward weakening the habitats internal supports. Floors pancake down upon those lower. Even in the light lunar gravity, the mass of the collapsing structure is enormous, crushing everything.

No one speaks for a few seconds after the simulation finishes. Jerome sighs, "Tempel, I want you to go through Central and descend the north ramp. Take it down four levels and proceed to the north periphery wall if you can. We need fracture data on the lower quadrant before we dare go any deeper. Got it?" Jerome adds lines to the simulation as he speaks that illustrate his instructions. He was never one to get excited in a pinch and his calmness is reflected on the faces of the men and women around him.

"Aye," Tempel says, matching Jerome's even-tempered response.

"The closer you get to the damage the worse communications will get. We don't have any portable relays and I'm not waiting for them, so you guys will have to wing it without Magi to hold your hand," Jerome explains. "You ok with that, Tempel?" he looks intently at the young man seeking the slightest hesitation on his part.

"No problem!" Tempel says.

"Good!" Jerome says clasping his shoulder in an iron grip that conveys better than words the emotion of the moment, "Magi, keep an eye on them for me as best you can and let me know when they are done. I want that sim data ASAP!"

"Aye," she responds.

"Let's go!" Jerome says to his makeshift crew.

****

Much smaller than a commonway, with the same luminous blue sky arching high overhead, Commonwealth Avenue looks more like an inner city neighborhood than a subterranean passageway. Two and three story buildings line both sides of the wide passage. Shops dominate the ground floor while balconies look down upon the street below.

Moving rapidly in single file with Larz in the lead, the group joins with others converging on the disaster, giving priority to the ER vehicles.

Even at sixteen, Larz is the most imposing of the group standing just over six-six and weighing two-forty. He had gone through a muscle-bulking genetic treatment less than six months before and looks like he's cut from a block of stone.

His brother Jason is a year older but five inches shorter and seventy pounds lighter, his frame built for speed, not power. He's known to be very good with the sidearm holstered at his side. Both of the brothers proudly sport flaming red hair cut short in the Lunarian fashion and freckles across the bridge of their nose, gifts from their father, Aaryn Harman.

Lazarus, last in line, strains to keep up, learning that his hands play a vital role when moving fast in low gravity. The dust in the air becomes denser as they draw near the entrance. He puts on his air mask without stopping. Skylor drops back to check that Lazarus did it right, giving his hardhat a solid smack when he finds everything good.

The courtyard outside the hospitals entrance is organized pandemonium. It has become the outer triage where those able to walk out of the hospital are being cared for, freeing resources for those more badly injured. Blood and bandages are everywhere. Victims sit or lie along the wall in shock and disbelief. ER technicians move among them trying to ease their suffering. Long rivulets of blood make the stone floor slippery and treacherous. The medic's muted voices amidst the moans and whimpers of people in pain form a bizarre background sound. The cry of a child for their mommy rips apart the quiet efficiency.

The hospital entrance is through a tunnel extending from Commonwealth Avenue to the Research Centre's main floor. Warned of their approach by Magi, police officers wave Larz and the group past. They move rapidly down the tunnel, they pass several dazed and dusty individuals heading out. Further on they pass another officer manning a portable fuel cell supplying energy to the airtight doors, his only job to slam them shut if the habitat fails. The opening is a great arch four times the height of Lazarus and its span at least ten times. The floor below it conceals the windings of a powerful electromagnetic field generator. The doors are swung back against the tunnel wall on each side.

Dust fills the tunnel and into the hospital limiting visibility but is already being drawn away by the ventilation. The entrance tunnel opens into a large central hall where the inner triage is still being set up. ER vehicles swarm the area waiting to be filled with broken and mangled bodies. People swirl around them treating and caring for the wounded just beginning to arrive. Without hospital power, the only light comes from portables the rescuers brought. Some lights remain stable, beacons in the darkness. Others dart about like banshees sending shadows dancing across walls and ceiling. Calls from team leaders split the dusty hall, organizing and positioning as they have been trained to do. Already dozens of injured people are being treated and given priorities. They make way for another Emergency Response vehicle leaving as they arrive, its flatbed loaded with at least six people.

Jerome approaches an officer directing traffic near the center of the chaos and asks, "Marty, what can you tell me?"

The figure turns and responds, "Jerome! I have been expecting you! It's bad down there and I don't have much faith the integrity will hold. The dust is thick as mud, so be damn sure your people have plenty of air!"

Jerome nods and asks, "Have you gotten everybody out?" His team gathers around them while keeping the path to and from the ramp clear.

"Are you kidding? We're just getting started. Citizens were only stunned in the upper levels and are able to walk out. But we haven't started searching the lower floors. Below central level the bomb shredded the water and electricity so it's pretty wet in places. Be careful what you touch. The electricity might still be hot in places." Marty responds, glancing at the gathered faces around them. "You folks keep your heads about you and don't take any risks! We don't need any more funerals!"

"There are portable transponders on the way so we should have emergency communications within minutes." Jerome says, "I would appreciate it if you could see to it they are deployed and spare air tanks sent down. What we have will last for only an hour."

Marty nods, "Sure, you can count on it, Jerome!" Marty responds.

Jerome turns and faces the group, "Listen up! I want everyone to switch to low-light-level sensors augmented by infrared," he orders.

Tempel notices that Lazarus is having problems. He links his visor with the earthman's and within seconds has shown him where his sensor controls are and adjusts them to his liking.

Lazarus, grateful for the help, is again amazed at the level of technology built into the devices. The world inside the hospital transforms from a shadowy dust-filled vision into a strangely vivid monochromatic image unlike anything that Lazarus has ever seen. Cutting through the dust, he can see the glow of people's body temperature twice as far as before.

"This is where we part company! Make good luck!" Jerome says.

"You do the same!" Tempel responds watching Jerome and his team disappear towards the south ramp.

Tempel leads them across the hall towards the north ramp, giving priority to rescuers tending the injured, weaving between ER vehicles and clumps of bloody victims. Along one wall in near darkness are a number of draped bodies, those that are beyond medical help.

"Magi, can you access the hospitals network?" Tempel says.

"Negative, this habitat is completely down. At this point, I am receiving only your audio signal," she informs him. "And even that is getting weak."

The rock of Rim Mountain dampens energy. It doesn't take many twists and turns within a Luna habitat to render long range communications virtually useless, but there is little choice with the network down.

"Great!" Jason exclaims, a touch of nervousness in his voice.

"Relax and keep your eyes open. We'll be fine," Krystin says patting her young cousin on the shoulder.

Entering the ramp, their hardhat lamps flood the enclosed space casting long shadows on the walls. Jason jumps noticeably when Krystin reaches out and grasps his hand. But he doesn't pull away.

They descend three levels quickly passing only one rescuer going up the ramp towards help carrying a victim in his arms. The man says nothing, saving his breath for climbing. The first sign of damage is a section of wall collapsed across their path. Gently they climb over the debris trying not to add more dust to the air around them. It is unnaturally quiet. The only sounds are their own muffled footfalls and the occasional grunt.

Stopping before a partially open airlock, "I think this is the right level," Tempel says. His voice sounds loud and harsh after the silence.

"The panel should tell us," Skylor mumbles softly, almost whispering.

"The power is out. How will that help us?" Lazarus asks, instantly wishing he had kept his mouth shut.

"Below it is the location code." Getting down on one knee he runs his hand over the surface wiping the dust off and revealing raised letters, "A310 South."

"That's it," Magi sounds grainy and distant. They were losing her fast in the corkscrew shaped ramp. "Jerome wants the outside wall magged first. We need as much information concerning the surrounding rock as possible."

Tempel wedges into the opening and pushes hard trying to widen it. Larz comes to help and the two of them combine their muscle. The door moves another few inches then won't budge.

"That's far enough. We can get through." Tempel says stepping into the dark hallway beyond, his hardhat light the only illumination. It used to be the main access corridor for this floor of the hospital. The wall opposite the ramp lies broken and largely missing disappearing into a void and his lamp reaches only a short way down what remains of the hallway before encountering a large pile of debris. Dust hangs motionless in the air limiting his visibility even further and chunks of stone litter the corridor floor. Closer, he can make out tracks in the thick layer of dust. He wonders if they are from a rescuer or a victim.

Out of the dust a body rises, calling for help. "We have someone," Tempel says, moving towards the person who sinks to the floor before he gets there.

"Save my baby! Please save my little boy!" the voice is definitely female.

Krystin emerges from the ramp and follows, knelling beside the figure. "Take it easy. We are here to help you."

"Magi, get someone down here with a litter!" Tempel commands, routing his transmission through Jason's visor, still on the ramp.

"Sorry. All the crews are currently occupied in the levels above you. They can't break anyone free for at least ten minutes." Magi says.

Tempel can barely hear her even with Jason's help. He realizes once they move away from the ramp, they will loose all contact with Magi.

Lazarus removes the ER pack and squeezes through the opening pulling it behind him. Moving up, he sets the pack beside the woman, retrieves a sterile wipe from its pocket, kneels and clears away the worst of the dust and blood from her face.

"My baby!" she says weakly.

Opening an inner pouch, he gets the med bracelet and snaps it on her wrist, adjusting it to fit snuggly. Turning back to the pack, he looks for a screen. Then, to his amazement, the woman's vital signs begin appearing in his visor as the bracelet gathers data. It doesn't take him long to decide that this is much better than Federation medical equipment using screens and flat panel displays. "Low blood pressure, barely conscious, shallow breathing. She's suffering from shock. If she doesn't get immediate medical treatment she will die." Lazarus removes the secondary mask from his belt and puts it on the woman and begins to gently compress her chest, timing it as he had been taught in CPR training.

Larz stands over them watching, "Can she be moved?"

"I didn't find any serious external wounds but she could have internal damage or a head injury," Lazarus says stopping chest compressions when the woman begins breathing on her own, a good sign.

"Then I will carry her out of here," Larz says.

Tempel nods, "Do it then get back here ASAP. Jason, I want you to stay in the ramp to relay messages to Magi."

"Aye," Jason responds none to happy about the prospect of being left alone.

Lazarus quickly removes the bracelet and returns it to the pack. Larz replaces Lazarus's mask with his own secondary. Lazarus helps Jason and Larz get the stricken woman through the jammed airlock door and into the ramp.

"My baby," she moans as Larz takes her in his arms, cradling her like a baby.

"We will find him," Lazarus says.

Lazarus hesitates for a moment watching the young man disappear, his light casting eerie shadows on the curved walls of the ramp.

"You shouldn't promise what you can't deliver," Jason says.

Lazarus looks at him, "One way or the other, we will find him."

Slinging the ER pack onto his back, he is startled by how far Tempel and the others had already gone. He can still faintly see the infrared glow of their bodies down the corridor and he must move fast to catch up. It tests his meager but growing abilities to navigate the lunar environment. He feels a touch of pride that he can do it at all. It reminds him of something his dad had told him long ago; if you want to teach someone how to swim, toss them into the deep end.

The dust hangs thick, making him thankful for the air on his back. Shadows cavort about playing tricks on his mind. No one speaks and the only sounds are muffled footfalls and labored breathing.

As they move further away from the ramp what remains of the right wall disappears entirely and the void eats into the floor until they're walking on a ledge less than a foot wide. The stone is cut clean as if a giant knife had removed the heart of the habitat. The Lunarians move quickly across the narrow span and stop where it widens out looking back at Lazarus.

"Come on, let's go," Tempel says.

Lazarus puts his back to the left wall, grits his teeth and shuffles sideways after the three Lunarians trying not to think about it. The only sounds are of their own making and the occasional rumble of settling debris from below. Glancing out into the void, his visors LLL sensors loose out to dust and distance. All he sees is a swirling gray-green mass. Lower down, small flashes cut through the fog and attract his attention like fireflies on a summer night.

That's when they hear the moaning. It's almost directly below Lazarus who looks down between his feet. The three other lights dart across the debris below him, searching. A massive section of rock, probably the floor and wall of the corridor, is slumped against the wall at his back. Perched upon it is the head of a child. The rest of the body is gone, perfectly camouflaged by dust and loose debris effectively masking even a thermal signature. Tears streak its face, but the eyes stare back at him, eerily reflecting his light.

"Tempel? I see someone. A child," Lazarus says letting

"Can you deal with it? My job is to mag this habitat. If it goes we all die!" Tempel says.

"Go do what you must do. I'm taking this child to a doctor," The two men stare at each other a moment.

"I won't be long," Tempel says turning away.

"Neither will I," Lazarus replies.

"Kristen, make sure he doesn't kill himself," Tempel says. "Skylor, you're with me." The two men disappear down the dusty corridor.

"There's a slab about twenty feet back that you can climb down," Kristen says as she sits on the floor dangling her legs off the edge. "I will guide you from here."

:Ok," Lazarus says as he inches his way back.

"Right below you," she says.

The slab is a section of floor leaning against the wall. It's very steep. Laying the ER pack aside, Lazarus starts down backwards digging his toes into the smooth surface, expecting to slip and fall any second. But his shoes grip the stone and he moves down without any problems.

The dust is ankle thick at the bottom. It rises and falls in thick waves at each footfall behaving more as a liquid than a solid. Even in lunar gravity, the pile feels unstable, ready to slide further into the hole carved by the bomb. Lazarus slowly crosses the distance.

He carefully pushes the dust aside and picks up the little broken body. Cradling the child in his arms, Lazarus looks down. There's a chunk of stone sticking out of his head and one arm is shattered and crushed, bent in far too many places. Yet the child's eyes stare at him from a mask of dirt and grim with burning intensity, not letting go of life without a fight.

Lazarus scrambles carefully back across the debris towards the makeshift ramp, the child almost weightless in his arms. He is careful to support the head, cupping it with his right hand while immobilizing the broken arm between their bodies. He steadies himself with one hand and climbs upward.

"I got ya," Kristen says reaching down to help him up. Together they retreat the way they had come. "Jason, call ahead and let Magi know Lazarus is coming up with a child."

"Aye," he responds.

With Jason's and Kristen's help, Lazarus manages to squeeze through the jammed door without disturbing his young passenger too much.

Moving up the ramp, the rescuers on their way down yield right of way to Lazarus and the child, Magi making sure that everyone knows who he is and where he's going. Some reach out to touch them as they go by.

"You have only a few more yards to go," Magi informs him near the top.

Emerging from the ramp Lazarus looks around. The chaos of a major triage is nearly complete, but he fails to see any method to the madness, keeping his mind on his mission. Around him, over the cries of pain, doctors stabilize the injured using tourniquets, laser scalpels, and skill before sending them to other hospitals for further treatment. Blood runs across the floor as these people battle death on a grand scale.

Magi is beside him, "Please follow me," she says and leads him through the mayhem. They pass people missing arms and legs, blood is everywhere. Some cry out in pain and despair. Others sit in shock not uttering a sound.

Lazarus stumbles and would have fallen if not for a man stepping forward, using his body and one good arm to catch him.

"Steady, lad" the man says.

Lazarus looks at him and sees a bloody stump where his other arm should be. The two stare at each other for a moment.

"Lazarus please, you must hurry," Magi says.

"Go," the man says, pushing him in the direction Magi is waiting.

She leads him to an enclosed ER vehicle, the rear doors wide open. Inside, two people are lying down. Several more sit in the forward section wearing dazed expressions and bloody bandages. Lying under a blood soaked sheet is a woman apparently unconscious. Lying beside her is a man. He looks up at Lazarus.

"Give me the child," he says holding one arm out.

Lazarus lays the broken body on the man's chest, rolling it gently over until it's cradled in the valley between the two people. Only then does the women moan and look down at the child then up at Lazarus.

"Find my baby," she says.

"Step back," Magi says.

Obeying, Lazarus watches as the ER vehicle pulls away, the rear doors shutting as it gains speed. He stands motionless until it disappears down the tunnel towards Commonwealth Avenue.

"Lazarus, are you able to continue?" Magi asks.

He turns back, facing the horror.

"Yes… I'm fine," Lazarus says and starts back the way he had come.

****

"Jason? Can you hear me?" Tempel asks.

"Aye," he replies.

Routing through Jason's visor he says, "Magi?"

"Yes Tempel, I am picking you up," Magi responds sounding distant and far away.

"I'm downloading the data to you." Tempel places the magnetometer on the floor and goes down on one knee in front of it, rapidly keying the control panel.

A few moments later, "Transmission successful. I am starting the analysis."

Temple can see the lights of Kristin, Larz and Jason as he and Skylor approach the ramp. They squirm through the opening just as they hear the sounds of someone coming down.

"Welcome back Lazarus," Tempel says.

"What do we do now?" Jason asks nervously to no one in particular. He doesn't like this place. It has become a strange and scary place outside of his experience.

"Isn't that obvious? We go down and begin rescue operations," Krystin says matter-of-factly.

Jason gives a nervous laugh, "Are you nuts Krystin?" he looks from her to his brother, then at Skylor, then Tempel. "It's too dangerous! Let's wait until Magi clears the hab."

"I will not complete the safety analysis for another thirteen minutes," Magi says.

"We've waited to long. If anybody is alive down there we need to get to them soon," Krystin retorts. "And it really doesn't matter what shape the hab is in. Someone will need to go down there and get them out!"

"She's right," Tempel says noticing that both Lazarus and Skylor are nodding their heads in agreement. "Jerome has the data he needs to determine the risk to a large scale rescue. We, on the other hand, are already here! Let's move down the ramp slowly and see what we find." Tempel looks at each in turn, receiving approval from everyone.

"Why not lash a rope to me and I'll explore the ramp below us? That way if it collapses you have a chance of pulling me back up," Lazarus suggests.

"Or at least finding you under the ruble," Jason says softly.

"Not you, me," Tempel says ignoring his skittish cousin.

"It's my idea. Let me do it," Lazarus retorts. He is the oldest of the group and is stuck in the assumption that it means something.

Tempel simply shakes his head, unwilling to give this earthman that responsibility. Besides, he knows this building like the back of his hand, as if this knowledge does him any good with the hospital in such a state of ruin.

"From the frying pan into the fire," Lazarus mutters, hoping this brash young Lunarian can handle the assignment.

"What was that?" Krystin asks with a frown. She doesn't think it appropriate for this newcomer to question her brother and is fully prepared to take him down a notch.

"He said, from the frying pan into the fire," Tempel repeats. "Magi, inform Jerome we are doing reconnaissance down the north ramp."

"Aye! He knows! His team is already moving down the south ramp. It appears to be intake all the way down but they are magging it thoroughly. Perhaps you should as well."

"Negative. These cracks make that a waste of time." Tempel says.

"Please be careful Tempel. I don't want to report your death to Abby and Liz." Magi's voice has taken on a pleading tone that Tempel has never before heard from her.

"I will not take any unnecessary risks, I assure you," Tempel responds. Looking at Larz, he says, "Set up an anchor here. If short range communications break down, we will tug three times when we need you to pull the line up and two times for some slack."

"Aye," Larz nods and gruffly adds "I'm with Magi, don't do anything crazy down there." He is comfortable with his role. This is not the first time he has anchored a rope for his comrades and he sets to work.

Lazarus moves to help Larz drive a lost arrow into a large crack in the wall. The tight space inside the ramp rings with each hammer blow, the pitch rising as the metal spike runs home. Hooking a karabiner to it, he watches as Larz attaches Tempels rope. Taking up the slack, Larz gives the belay an experimental tug and nods at Tempel.

Using a shorter length of rope, Tempel wraps each leg at his groin and then his waist, tying it off into a climbing harness.

Tempel nods back and starts down the ramp slowly, picking his way carefully. Large sections of the ramps outer walls are pretty well gone below level four, a vast empty space glimpsed through the ragged openings. Dust is thick, limiting visibility. By level five, the inner core of the ramp is the only thing holding the floor in place, a cantilevered corkscrew extending downward into darkness.

Tempel moves slowly and carefully downward until he is confronted with empty space where the floor should be. "Hold," he says.

"Aye, holding," Larz responds.

"The ramp is gone about thirty feet below you," Tempel reports.

Even at this short distance, Tempel's transmission is effected by the surrounding stone, his voice tinny with no sense of direction. Lazarus looks at his companions and involuntarily his body trembles as a cold shiver runs down his spine and goose bumps roughen his arm. He has never felt so alive.

Below, Tempel gets down on his belly and worms forward until he can see over the edge, acutely aware of the vibrations he is creating in the structure beneath him. The single light source in his hardhat weakly illuminates the void forcing him to maximize the sensitivity in his visor's low-light-level sensors in order to see the jumbled mess less than thirty feet below. The stone that had been the hospitals walls and floors lay in broken piles, the furniture and equipment originally contained in level five lay upon them in a chaotic tangle as far as he can see. Dust coats everything creating a sameness of color that goes beyond the monochromatic image presented by his visor at this setting.

"Can anyone hear me?" Tempel calls out. Maximizing his visors audio inputs he pulls his air mask away from his mouth and shouts, "Hey! Can anyone hear me?"

He is instantly aware of the smell and replaces his mask. With the gain turned up to maximum, his own heart beat and other bodily functions are filtered out letting him hear the slightest sound from below. Otherwise motionless, he slowly turns his head straining for the faintest whisper, hearing the tap tap tap of unknown fluids dripping into puddles, the rustle of a small avalanche as the debris settles, and the distant thump of something larger falling. Then he hears it! A faint moan floats up from somewhere down in that dusty grave, the best that the person can do under the circumstances.

"Magi!" Tempel says.

"Here," she says communicating to him through Larz, her signal strength very weak.

"I'm looking at the remains of the bottom levels. Floors and walls have collapsed. The ramp ends at level five and I'm approximately thirty feet over the rubble. But I can hear someone! We are initiating rescue operations. Please inform Jerome," Tempel says.

"Tempel, I think you should wait," Magi says, her voice distant but clear.

Lazarus can hardly believe his ears. AI's don't argue with humans where he comes from.

"No, we can't wait any longer. Those people need our help now," Tempel says.

"I agree, we need to get them out or this will turn into a recovery operation real quick," Kristen adds from above.

"Do it," Jerome says, "I will send people as soon as Magi gets finished with the safety analysis. Right now, you are free to move as you see fit."

"Thanks Jerome," Tempel says, "I'll be going down."

Taking his spare lamp, Tempel attaches it to the bottom of the broken ramp, a beacon in a sea of darkness. Replaying the few seconds of sound he determines its approximate location below him. Adjusting the sensitivity in his visors infrared sensors, the debris field below him takes on a mottled reddish glow with regions of intensity that varies from point to point. His eyes seek a human shape in the midst of the chaos, finding several possibilities.

He retreats, worming back from the edge and moving up the ramp as quickly as he dares, not stopping as he returns to his small team.

"I'm going with you," Skylor says quietly even before Tempel reaches them.

Tempel's lower face is hidden behind his air mask and the top of his head by the hardhat. Only the broad band across his eyes where his visor transmits his expression remains clear. He nods, knowing it would do no good to argue.

"The more people searching the faster it will go," Lazarus says. The earthman's intentions are clear, he's going as well.

"How did I know you were going to say that?" Tempel asks but doesn't deny him. Lazarus had taken off the ER pack and sat it against the wall of the ramp. Tempel picks it up and hands it to him before slinging the pack next to it onto his back and fastening the front retaining strap around his waist. Skylor hoists a third ER pack as Tempel turns to Larz, "I will set up a second belay close to the edge. Let's keep things simple."

"Aye!" Larz nods.

Turning to Jason and Krystin, Tempel says, "The ramp is in bad shape but I think it will hold. You two will need to get the survivors to safety. Can you do that?" Tempel asks them looking especially at Jason.

"Of course!" Krystin says.

Jason nods with a frightened but determined look in his eyes.

"Good!" Tempel slaps Jason on the shoulder in encouragement causing a cloud of dust to billow out of his clothes. Ducking away from it, Tempel continues, "Always have a rope tied around you, just in case the ramp collapses!" Jason's eyes grow wide but he nods again.

"Krystin, make sure he doesn't forget. You either!" Tempel leans forward and hugs his sister, smearing the dust that coats her from head to foot. "You look good in grey!" he tells her, grinning behind his air mask.

"You be careful little brother! Liz would kill me if anything happens to you. You too Skylor!" Krystin says.

"We can handle this, sis," Tempel says before leading the way back down the ramp. They stop a safe distance from the drop off.

Tempel drives another lost arrow into a crack in the wall, attaches a karabiner to it, and ties off a second rope. Worming forward once again, he swings his legs off the edge and looks down into the void.

Leaning out, he can make out the ruble thirty feet below. He lets himself drop over the edge, easily descending hand over hand, even with the weight of the ER pack. He unties the main line from his climbing harness arrangement.

Tempel anchors the second rope from the bottom as Skylor and Lazarus descend joining him on the rubble.

"Oh my God!" Lazarus exclaims, his adrenaline pumping through his body as he gazes upon the devastation. The low-light-level sensors in his visor give him a monochromatic but useable image out to the limit of his visibility. He sees everything in shades of green. For a distance of perhaps thirty feet away, he can see good detail wherever he points the light in his hardhat. Beyond that the image quickly loses out to the dust hanging thick in the air. But further out, here and there something is shiny enough or positioned just right for him to see, ghostly images that float in the void.

Ignoring the comment Tempel leads the way, "Come on. I heard the survivor from this direction."

Lazarus follows much more slowly, cautiously making his way across the mangled remains of the hospital. The deathly stillness is broken only by the rattle of settling rubble and the occasional gasp of breath as they scramble through the ruined habitat.

About twenty paces in, Tempel and Skylor begin digging frantically, pulling massive stones and a twisted broken chair from the ruble. Lazarus reaches them just as they clear enough away to see the victim, legs pinned under a section of wall. Long hair seems to identify the victim as female but dust and grime create a uniform grayness making it impossible to tell.

Her visor is broken and nonfunctional, hanging off her face like some grotesque pair of eyeglasses. Her eyes open and she looks around with confusion. Seeing them, relief swells up and tears begin to streak her gray dust-covered face.

Lazarus pulls the med kit off his back and sets it beside her while Skylor continues to pull debris off the pile that entraps her. Tempel motions for Skylor to step back. He sets his feet and lifts the thick stone that pins her down, managing only a fraction of an inch. But it is enough as Skylor and Lazarus quickly but gently slide the victim out.

"Don't say anything," Lazarus tells her when she tries to speak, a trickle of fresh blood runs from the corner of her mouth. He slides the med bracelet over her left wrist. Referring to the information that immediately begins to flow to their visors they quickly determine she is suffering from multiple fractures to both legs, a punctured lung and shock. Lazarus stabilizes her just as he had the other survivor. Tempel finds a stainless steel tabletop and frees it from the smashed cabinets it is fastened to. They gently place the women on the makeshift stretcher and, walking gingerly over what once had been Aldrin Station's premier hospital, move her below the remnants of the ramp.

"Jason!" Tempel calls up. They can see light beams jumping around erratically, silhouetting the ramp above them.

"Yo!" is the immediate response. "I have a pulley rigged above you. Should make it easier getting people out!"

"Good boy!" Lazarus mutters.

"You and Krystin will need to carry her out and get back here pronto," Tempel yells upward.

"Aye! We're ready!" Krystin yells down.

Tempel and Lazarus quickly cut lengths of rope, securing the women to the metal tabletop and rigging the improvised stretcher to the makeshift elevator. They watch as Larz hoists her upward, the stretcher slowly rotating as it rises. Jason's light looks eerie as he grabs her and swings the women to safety.

The three men work steadily, finding two more people in the space of thirty minutes, both alive but badly injured. Other rescuers begin arriving, descending the rope and joining the search. Tempel sends word up that they could use dogs in the search. Dueler and several others arrive sometime later. Portable network relays are deployed putting everyone back on line and giving Magi a view of the devastation. More and more equipment is brought down to look for survivors and collecting data in preparation for answering the question of long term habitat stability, a very practical question to ask when living in bubbles carved in the heart of a mountain on an airless planet.

Lazarus strains his medical training to the breaking point. He soon looses count of the number of tourniquets he applied. One person had lost both legs, crushed beyond saving, another an arm above the elbow. It was Lazarus that found a cluster of preschool children. They had been on a field trip to the hospital. Now their little bodies are shattered beyond any semblance of humanity. His tears test the capability of his visor to absorb them as he carefully puts the tiny remains into black body bags.

The scope of the devastation becomes increasing apparent as more and more lights are brought down and the dust is vented away. For Lazarus, life becomes a blur of someone else's blood and pain. Live victims come less frequent as time goes by, until gone entirely. As the hours roll past, the dust encrusted bodies blur into a horrible collage of death, each one a single thread in a tapestry that stretches back into human prehistory, a testament to man's brutality to his fellow man. Stress and exhaustion distort time until his mind discards the concept entirely, leaving him with only the here and now. In his world he has been doing this forever and would continue past infinity. Life outside of this bloody dirty hole recedes into a dream. Reality becomes the endless cycle of digging and pulling smashed and shattered people from the rubble…

****

Thirty-three hours after they had first entered the hospital, Tempel is close to total collapse. He finds Lazarus sitting on a ragged fragment of stone staring blankly into the distance. Without saying a word, Tempel pulls the exhausted man to his feet, and they make their way back to Dakota warren, each leaning heavily on the other like a pair of drunken sailors, neither saying anything.

Lazarus wouldn't remember the walk or seeing Lindsey or her pulling him into the shower before removing his blood and filth encrusted clothing. He will have no memory of getting into bed and her holding him until his trembling stops as he finally slides into deep sleep. His mind had shut down at some point, simply stopped processing data, a defensive reflex resulting from the shear horror of what he was experiencing.

He slips into a coma like sleep that worries Lindsey to the point that she asks for a doctor to check on him. Following a hurried examination conducted over the network by an MD who has herself been awake for over forty hours, Lindsey is told that there isn't anything physically wrong. The best thing is let him sleep until he awakes on his own, however long that may be. Lindsey stays with him for many hours before finally slipping away.

"The church says the earth is flat, but I know that it is round, for I have seen the shadow on the moon, and I have more faith in a shadow than in the church."
Ferdinand Magellan, 1470-1522

Aftermath

Munching on a nutrition bar, Nell rechecks her calculations one last time before submitting them to Luna Central. She doesn't want to spoil her perfect record, proud that LC has never corrected her figures in the four years she has been running this route. Today is no exception, even if it takes longer than usual.

"Course received and verified. You are free to burn for orbital insertion," the response finally comes.

The unsmiling face of the uniformed flight controller is someone she had never dealt with before and she thought she had seen them all at least once. Not that Nell cares who grants authorization as long as someone did.

Nell had rejected most of what society had to offer seven years before. Her two little girls, ages six and eight, had been killed in the bombing of their school bus outside Memphis She had found out when a special bulletin announced the tragedy complete with shots from a helicopter showing the smoldering remains sitting on a lonely stretch of rural Tennessee. It was reported the act was done by home grown terrorists thinking they were somehow hurting the Federation in this senseless act of violence. Homeland Security tracked them down, one by one, extracted whatever information they processed and executed them.

But that didn't do Nell any good. Her life ended that day and a new person was born, slowly emerging from the ashes of her former existence. She picked this job because of its splendid isolation, far away from the evening news.

"Roger, Luna Central, initiating sequence," Nell says in a professional tone. With a flip of her wrist she releases the program to Emcee, her ships AI, for execution.

Around her, powerful spy beams from the lunar surface, orbiting stations, and several military mini-satellites sweep over Evolution's Child for the umpteenth time, probing deep and finding nothing out of the ordinary.

****

Tempel opens his eyes feeling like he had just gone to sleep. Reaching over on the small table beside his bed, he picks up his visor and slips it on. He groans when he realizes he has slept for fourteen hours straight. He can't recall any other time he had slept for so long. Lazarus is still sleeping and he's careful not to disturb him.

A long hot shower and clean clothes makes Tempel feel better on the outside but doesn't chase away the ghosts that followed him home from the hospital, an endless secession of bloody faces that has merged into a single image of death. Not knowing what else to do, he pushes the memories aside forcing his mind to think of more useful things like the hunger rampaging in the pit of his stomach. He heads purposefully for the kitchen.

He moves quickly through several tunnels and down a ramp to one of a dozen commonrooms scattered throughout Dakota warren. As he exits the ramp, Tempel scans the great room. To his left several people are sitting in a lounge area talking quietly. To his right is a couple standing beside a snooker table their arms locked around each other. Deeper in the room, silhouettes of others move and there is a subdued murmur of distant conversations. But the joy is missing and the laughter gone, the atmosphere heavy and solemn as the citizens of Aldrin Station come to grips with the brutal reality of jihad.

As though in defiance, the kitchen is brightly lit, a beacon drawing Tempel to it. He can see Liz and Tara fussing about and the smell of pancakes fill the air making his mouth water. Past the kitchen in the dining area, a group of young ladies sit at one table and several young men are partially visible at another, their normal chatter gone. The sweeping arches surrounding the kitchen cut off the rest of the dining area. He has eaten here almost every day of his life. It fits him like a pair of old Levi's, comfortable and well broken in.

"Tempel!" Liz exclaims when she sees him, rushing over and giving him a mother's hug. Tempel wraps his arms around her returning the affection. Patting him on the back, Liz looks up at her son, "I'm glad to see you finally woke up! We were beginning to think we should send someone up to wake you. Are you alright?" she asks concern furrowing her brow, worrying as only a mother can.

Tara occupies herself at the kitchens main cooking area, letting Liz have a moment with her son.

"Sure Liz, I'm fine. I was just tired. That's all," Tempel tells her.

"What a horrible thing! And you, right in the middle of it!" She can't help but feel defensive when it comes to her children and Tempel is the youngest. In her eyes, he will always be her baby.

Tempel holds her tight while they walk arm-in-arm towards Tara across the expansive kitchen. "You know I don't look for trouble. I just take care of it when it finds me," paraphrasing something Corso had once said.

Liz shakes her head in amazement, "You sound just like your father!" with a catch in her voice.

Tempel bends down kissing her on the top of the head, bringing a hint of a smile to her face. Liz releases Tempel when they reach Tara. Moving forward Tempel wraps his long arms around the women, feeling hers go around him in return, "Greetings Tara," he says.

"Greeting Tempel, I'm relieved you are well," she replies patting him on the back in an eerily similar fashion. Even though Liz had given birth to him, Tara is every bit his mother as she.

Looking down at Tara's solemn expression and then at his mothers, "What's the latest?" he asks them.

Tara looks away from Tempel and, unable to speak, breaks the embrace and moves back to the griddle. Picking up the spatula, she starts to futz with the pancakes. She manages to shake her head, tears streaming down her cheeks, her face a rigid mask of barely controlled emotion.

"Lori…" Liz stumbles over the words, unsuccessfully trying to stifle her own tears.

Quickly putting two and two together, Tempel comes up behind Tara and gently puts his arms around her, "I'm so sorry..."

It's hard for him to believe that Lori is dead. He remembers back to the last time they talked. It had been a few days before, he coming home from pulling a double shift, she getting ready to go to the hospital. One of her patients was in labor and she was needed. He had been in a hurry to get out of his police uniform. Their words were few.

Lori and Tara have shared many things over the years. As young women they studied medicine together and later, worked out of the same office at Lincoln County Hospital. As practicing pediatricians they delivered each others children, Lori the mother of six while Tara is the mother of eight. During the same ceremony, they married the two eldest Dugan boys, Lori married Henry while Tara married Tucker. Liz was one of six freehold women standing beside them that day. More than just friends, they have been pillars of Dakota freehold for over two decades. Now Lori is gone.

Tara reaches up patting Tempel on the hand, laying her head back against his chest. "Lori touched so many..." tears choke off her words.

These women have supported each other for decades, making a home for their families on a hostile world where the slightest mistake means death. They are not only mothers; they are teachers, doctors, and mentors raising each others kids and grandkids. When one of them is suddenly and violently taken, the pain and sense of loss shakes the freehold like a Richter 9.0 earthquake. But Lori's death will be felt by more than just family. She was the genetic pediatrician for over ten thousand births, most of them outside the freehold. Her death will be mourned in many warrens all across Luna.

"Frances is hurt!" Liz says as Temple releases Tara, "But she will make it! I know it! She's strong and those kids need her!" Nodding in agreement with herself she adds, "I just know it!" Francesca Koubek is Lori and Henry Dugan's oldest daughter. At twenty-four, she is the mother of three beautiful girls, the youngest not even one.

"She was there helping her mother…they have taken her to Mission United Hospital," Tara says softly fighting through her emotions. "She has broken ribs, a punctured lung and internal bleeding that forced them to put her in a regin tank!"

"But she's alive!" Liz says pointedly to Tara.

"Sure," Tempel responds numbly, memories of the day before coming unbidden to his mind. Lori and Frances could have been among those he helped but it is impossible for him to know without reviewing.

The squeal of young voices interrupts the conversation as three-year-old Lana Koubek comes rushing into the kitchen closely followed by her seven year old cousin, Kelsey Sanchez. The two are playing and the effect of their laughter and joy on the area is immediate and welcome. Kelsey has been excused from classes today in order to watch out for her cousin. Lana knows that something bad has happened but just can't take it seriously. She runs behind Tempel and looks back as if daring Kelsey to get her now that she is protected by the towering young man.

Tempel reaches down and sweeps the little girl into his arms causing an even bigger squeal of delight. "Don't let the monster get me! Protect me!" the tiny voice shrieks happily even as she throws her arms about his neck squeezing as hard as she can.

Tempel just hugs her tight, fighting back tears that suddenly threaten to explode. Lana is Francesca's middle child and is the spitting image of her, the same blond hair and blue eyes, the same rambunctious spirit. He vows that he will do everything in his power to fulfill her request. He looks at Kelsey, shaking his head.

"We were just playing, Tempel," the girl says defensively, misinterpreting his grief as criticism.

"I know," he mumbles softly, not willing to let Lana go. There is something about receiving a hug from a three year old that cures what ails you.

Lana loosens her grip on Tempel's neck enough to lean back and look him in the face. "Mommy is in the hospital. She's hurt bad."

Tempel kisses her on the forehead, "I know sugar. The very best doctors are doing everything they can to help her."

Even the little girl feels the sorrow that permeates the kitchen, a place she has come to associate with goodness and laughter. "Tempel, why is everyone so sad?"

Tempel takes a deep breath but before he can answer Tara comes over strokes the girls head and says, "Because some very bad men have hurt a lot of people."

"My mommy too?" she asks innocently striving to understand.

"I'm afraid so Lana," Tara answers her.

"Why did they do it?" Lana is no longer giggling or playing, she is as serious as those around her.

"Because they have been taught by their mommy's and daddy's that killing in the name of God is good. They don't believe in the sanctity of life like we do," Tempel says letting his grief turn into anger.

"That's just a little heavy for a three year old." Liz places her hand on Lana's back and looks the little girl in the eyes. "What Tempel is saying is these men are misguided and don't understand that it is wrong to hurt other people," Liz says, her own emotions raw and on edge.

"Why not tell them? Then they will understand and stop hurting people." In Lana's mind this is a perfectly reasonable solution. If they don't know, simply teach them.

Tempel tickles Lana's belly making her giggle and squirm uncontrollably, "That's a great idea. In fact, I'll do it personally!" That earns him a severe look from Liz. "Are you hungry? Would you like to sit down with me and have some of Grandma Tara's hotcakes?"

"I already did silly!" the little girl replies.

Liz caresses Lana's blond hair, "Go play with Kelsey. Tempel needs to eat."

"Ok," she says in the utterly innocent voice of a three year old. She giggles as Tempel puts her gently on the floor.

"Come on, let's go back to the playroom," Kelsey says taking Lana's hand and the two of them disappear into the commonroom in the general direction of the ramp.

Tara watches them leave with a look on her face that says more clearly than a thousand words that she will persevere. She turns away and goes back to flipping pancakes on the enormous griddle, stacking the finished ones on a large platter and blobbing more batter into the open spaces. The aroma of the golden brown hotcakes fills the area and the sound of silverware on china plates draws him to the dining room. But the normal boisterous chatter of a Dugan breakfast is conspicuous in its absence.

Liz gives Tempel one last squeeze and releases him. "Shoo! Go join the others. I will bring you pancakes until you say uncle!" Liz wipes her face with a towel.

"Sounds good to me!" Tempel says with more cheerfulness than he feels. He selects a large glass from the cupboard, goes to the refrigerator and pours it full of instamilk. Nothing better than feasting on Liz and Tara's flapjacks! He feels his spirit rise in anticipation.

The dining area is crowded this morning, all but two tables are occupied by people eating and talking quietly among themselves. Literally every adult wears a visor and has a pistol strapped to their waist and half are in standard police vacsuits. A few glance up as Tempel approaches but quickly go back to their conversations. Close by his older brother Ben looks up and nods while his wife Renei feeds their two-year-old daughter Amber.

Arrayed around the nearest table is what appears to be most of this year's sophomore and junior class. Erica, their guidance teacher, is at one end. Just beyond her three more young women huddle together at another table talking quietly, their backs to him.

Tempel slides in across from Justine and Nicole. Both girls are fourteen and quickly coming of age.

Justine is the youngest of the Harman children and has the trademark flaming red hair and freckles to prove it. She leans foreword her blue eyes intense but steady, never wavering from Tempel's. "What was it like?" she asks. Conversation at the table, what little there was, grows silent.

"Grant the man some privacy," Erica says. "Let him enjoy his breakfast."

They had all seen the vids coming out of the disaster, many of the most shocking records are from Tempels visor, especially early on when he, Skylor and this new fellow, Lazarus were the only ones on the scene. Citizens all across Luna know what they had seen and done almost as if they had been there themselves. What Justine and the rest are curious about is how Tempel assimilates these experiences. Does it make him bitter and angry, or frightened and withdrawn?

Sitting next to Justine, Nicole is looking at Tempel as if seeing him for the first time. The Dugan family has always treated any question with honest candor, not sugar coating the truth, letting their children know what the real world is all about from the earliest age and these are almost full grown women by Lunarian standards.

The next table over, Tempel's big brother Ben helps his wife feed their infant daughter. The little girl bangs her sippy-cup loudly against the highchair, emphatically shaking her head, letting everyone know she doesn't like peas.

Ben's instinct is to confront any issue head on, "Tempel?" he says. Tempel looks over at him as others close by turn to watch the exchange. "Tell us what you saw," he says solemnly. Renei slides Amber out of the highchair and holds her, quieting the child. Now the entire room goes silent, conversations put on hold as Tempel becomes the center of attention.

Tempel looks at his brother blankly for a moment, "I've never seen anything like it. Everything smashed, like someone beat it with a hammer!" he stares down at the table, a frown creases his brow as he struggles to put into words memories he would rather forget, "We pulled people, and parts of people, out of the rubble for hours, so many I lost count. Some were alive, some were not," he shakes his head, "Everyone looks alike covered in blood and dust..."

Tears of frustration and anger flood his eyes only to be absorbed by his visor before ever reaching his cheeks. Yet, everyone sees them flow just as though his visor were gone, the tears simply another component of his current expression and transmitted right along with his every other twitch and wrinkle to all the other visors in the room.

Behind him Tara sobs, unable to hold back the pain any longer. Liz put her arms around her and strokes her hair, a muffled cry escapes her lips as the two old friend's comfort each other, releasing pent up emotions at last. Many others in the room openly weep.

Tempel's sorrow quickly morphs into anger and he turns to Ben, "They didn't have a chance!" he says bitterly.

Ben gets up, leans over and kisses his wife and baby daughter. "Come, walk with me," he says to her. Turning, he moves around the table, picking up his headgear along the way. "It's definite, the explosion was no accident. Jerome has found traces of weapons grade SuperX at the hospital. Preliminary estimates put the bombs mass at more than fifty pounds."

Tempel sits for a moment letting the words sink in. Fifty pounds of SuperX is a massive amount of energy released. Nothing could have withstood the blast. Concern takes the place of anger within Tempel. "Do we know how many people..."

Ben shakes his head negative, "It will be days, maybe more, before the totals become clear. The explosion vaporized a big section of the hospitals records, medical sensors, visors, everything. Lucas will piece back together what we find, but that's a big if. You've seen it down there, I don't hold out much hope of finding anything useful," or alive, he didn't add.

"Lucas is a smart guy. If anyone can do it, it's Lucas!" Liz says from the kitchen.

"Magi is piecing together a list of people in that section of the hospital when the explosion occurred. Where are you at now, Magi?" Ben asks.

Tempel turns to look at the image of Magi, "There are one-hundred-thirty-eight survivors and fifty-six dead have been identified so far. I have an additional three-hundred-eighty-two names that are listed as missing and over three thousand biological samples undergoing DNA profiling," she reports in an even, emotionless voice, one that Tempel has never heard her use before. It sounds like Magi but something is definitely missing.

Tempel shudders, realizing that some people had been reduced to a single smear on the end of a sample tube. Others are gone entirely, their bodies atomized in the incredible violence of the explosion. This bombing has ripped the guts out of many families, mothers and fathers, husbands and wives, sons and daughters, gone in an instant of pain and confusion, their lives snuffed out.

"Why would anyone do this?" Nicole asks, tears blurring her vision to the point she can't see clearly any more despite her visor.

Ben shakes his head before calmly answering the young woman, "Hate, fear, self-righteousness, take your pick. Their religion encourages them to kill unbelievers. And believe me, Lunarian's are at the top of their list of unbelievers!"

"Just because we don't believe in their ridiculous religion gives them the right to kill us?" Nicole asks, her big brown eyes reflect the difficulty in swallowing this as fact.

"Throughout history religion has been a justifying influence in wars or at least used to comfort those caught up in them and that hasn't changed," Ben responds. "Humanity can't seem to shed the superstitions of its past. The fact is we threaten the ridiculous ideas at the very heart of religion. Humanism and the sanctity of all life are concepts that will eventually make religious dogma obsolete. But until it is, true believers will continue to be dangerous."

Suddenly wanting to do something, anything, to strike back at those who did this Tempel says, "I'll report for duty immediately." The deep furrows across his forehead threaten to become permanent.

Ben slaps him roughly on the shoulder and his voice takes on a menacing tone, "Control your anger, little brother. Draw from it to strengthen your determination. There is an old Earth saying, *revenge is a dish best served cold*!" The look in his eyes matches the growl in his voice. "But for now, you have time for breakfast. Enjoy! Spend some quality time with the family. You earned it!"

A huge plate of steaming pancakes covered in margarine and maple syrup suddenly appears in front of Tempel. "Let's not talk anymore of this!" Liz asks, "At least wait until his breakfast is over."

"Aye!" Ben puts his arm around her shoulders and squeezes her tight. "It's time for me to get back to work."

Renei, carrying Amber, stops to give Tempel a quick hug and follows Ben, she returning the child to the pre-school one level down, he to his post in the Regional Command Center, the focal point of Aldrin Station's defense.

No one else speaks as Tempel attacks the stack of cakes, his turbulent thoughts rendering them tasteless and quickly eaten. A soft murmur arises as people pick up their conversations, talking quietly among themselves, discussing recent events. Every Lunarian has an opinion and is, as always, more than willing to expound on it.

****

Lazarus rolls over on his back and opens his eyes. For a fleeting moment he is back in Arizona, in his tiny apartment, thinking he has overslept and will need to explain this lapse to the Director. Then in a rush everything floods back, Athens... Lindsey...Heavens Gate... Aldrin Station... With the force of a physical blow he recalls the devastation of Lincoln County Hospital and the horror he had seen there so recently.

He squeezes his eyes shut and rubs his head with both hands, keeping these thoughts at bay. His body aches from the abuse heaped upon it the last few days, using muscles in ways they are not accustomed to, in a gravity field one sixth their norm. Stretching, he sits up and looks around for the first time. The bed he's in, larger than any he's ever seen, is not alone. The room is long and narrow, and along both sides is a series of semiprivate areas, each with one or more of these amazing beds. The floor, covered in thick carpet, is not flat but undulates in tune with these alcoves. Colorful drapes hanging from the ceiling and Japanese style Shoji screens further divides the space into many intimate places, each of them snug and cozy yet part of the greater whole. He cannot see the room's full extent.

Voices float softly to him from somewhere, muted by the many textures within the room. He's suddenly conscious of his nakedness, pulling a silken sheet across his lap.

How did he get here? Where was he? He runs his hand over his head.

"Greetings Lazarus, Lindsey took the liberty of laying out fresh clothing for you." The kindly voice of Magi startles Lazarus. "Your visor is in the refresher next to your clothing," she says.

Lazarus looks in the direction of her voice half expecting to see her and spots the stack of clothing on a small table against the wall next to the bed. Running his hand across his buzz cut one last time, he pulls a sheet across his waist, crabwalks to the edge of the bed and stands. With one hand holding up the sheet, he ruffles through the stack of neatly folded clothing, a pair of dark gray Levis, a green T-shirt, boxers, socks and a new pair of deck shoes, black with a slash of green down the side, all made from the finest hemp.

Keeping his back to her, he lets the sheet fall to the floor, quickly slipping on the boxers. "How long have I been asleep?" he asks over his shoulder. He opens the small box, removes his visor from inside, and slips it on. Magi immediately appears.

"Fourteen hours and forty two minutes," Magi replies.

"Where's here?"

"This is Charley Company's billet. If you would like to clean up, you will find everything you need in the bath. Take the lower hallway." She points down the room.

His dad's copy of Heinlein's *Time Enough for Love* is on the table beside the box. He picks it up and it falls open to the pictures. He takes them out and stares at the faded images. One was of a man, woman and three kids posing behind a white car, the parking lot around them filled with other vehicles. They look happy.

The other is Rachel and Courtney taken about a year before the accident. He remembers the day he took it. Courtney had just had her first perfect report card from 1st grade and they were going out to her favorite restaurant to celebrate. She is all smiles. Rachel, on the other hand, looks worried and more than a little angry. For the last several nights in the privacy of their bedroom, she and Lazarus had been discussing how they should teach Courtney. They both agreed they must somehow balance the dogma she was getting in school with a dose of reality. A year later they were still having problems deciding how to do it.

If only Rachel could see him now, what would she think? He touches her face before sliding the photos reverently between the pages of the novel and setting the book back on the table.

The floor of his alcove slopes gently downward to an open area down the center of the room. It contains comfortable chairs, tables, desks, even bookcases filled with an assortment of interesting items. He wishes he had time to look at every one. None of the alcoves he passes are occupied as far as he can tell. He comes to an airtight door in place of an alcove.

"Is this it?"

"Yes," Magi answers.

The door slides open as he approaches. Retreating through it, he stops and looks back at Magi until the door shuts between them, relieved that she didn't follow.

Turning, he starts down the dimly lit hallway. It has a gentle curve to the left and down. Its ceiling glows pale yellow and his footfalls are muffled by thick carpet. With its complete lack of corners, he feels he's walking inside a tube that goes on for much too long. But he couldn't have made a wrong turn, there were none to make.

Finally coming to the end, the airtight door at the bottom of the ramp slides open as he approaches. Hewn from the stone of Rim Mountain, the bath is a large circular room with high domed ceiling. Around its periphery is a ring of wide-spaced columns supporting Roman style arches. Inside the ring, the polished stone floor is a spectacular display of color, streaks of blue and scarlet and purple swirl in a golden matrix. Outside the ring is a series of alcoves, their floors covered by thick carpet. In those nearest him, he can see a counter containing a sink with a mirror on the wall behind it. Some alcoves have a small table and chairs, others a couch or a chaise.

"Greetings, Lazarus," a woman says from behind him.

Turning, it takes Lazarus a moment to spot her through the forest of stone columns. She and a man are on the other side walking around the bath, staying on the carpet and coming towards him. They are both completely nude.

"Greetings," he responds.

"My name is Tatiana Tushar and this is Karl Svensson," the woman says. She is several inches shorter then the man but taller than Lazarus. They move with fluid grace effortlessly gliding over the carpet.

"I'm so sorry. I didn't know there was anyone here. I'll come back later," he turns to leave.

"Don't be silly," Karl says with a chuckle.

"As a former Federation citizen, Lazarus may not want any company," Tatiana says.

"Very true. We're finished anyway. Why don't we leave him by himself? Isn't that how shortimers like it?" Karl says.

"Karl! He's one of us now!" Tatiana scolds.

"Not yet but he's moving in the right direction," Karl says walking alongside Tatiana without the least bit of embarrassment. They are both without blemish, completely hairless except for head hair cut short in Lunarian fashion and all their parts properly proportioned. They exude good health and sexual vitality.

"Are you sure? I can come back in a few minutes," Lazarus offers as they pass, trying not to stare.

"What would be the point?" Karl chuckles.

"Magi, why don't you see to it that Lazarus isn't disturbed?" Tatiana says. Looking over her shoulder, her eyes catch his and linger. She grins, reaching out to grasp her companions arm before turning away.

"Certainly, Tatiana," Magi says.

Lazarus gazes after them until the door glides shut. There's a part of him that thinks this is wrong but it's losing the battle with the part that rejoices in the prospect of such freedom. Shaking his head, he picks an alcove, lays the cloths next to its sink, and places his visor on top of the pile. He looks at himself in the mirror, rubs his three-day-old beard, and realizes he can't put it off any longer.

He enters a small room beyond the sink containing a stone ledge across its back wall. It has four openings that he recognizes as toilets. There is no door on the stall and the space around the sink simply opens up on the the toilets.

"Magi?"

"Yes Lazarus," she replies.

"Are you sure no one will come in?" he asks.

"Reasonably sure," she replies.

He peals off his boxers and picks the far left. Sitting there, he contemplates the state of his world. To be sure, Luna is a strange and wonderful place he's only beginning to understand but the prospect of discovery thrills him and raises his spirits.

Finished, he looks around for toilet paper suddenly recalling his only other experience with using a Lunarian toilet, a quick trip in the middle of the rescue effort at the hospital.

"Magi?"

"Yes Lazarus"

"Ah…I'm done."

Even though he's ready for it, he's startled by the sudden gush of warm water. Leaning forward slightly, he lets it clean him off. A few seconds of ultra dry air sucks all the moisture from his butt. This is definitely an improvement on toilet paper.

Leaving his chosen area, he wonders out of the alcove to the nearest column, touching its surface, caressing the warm stone as though it were alive.

"Magi?"

"Yes Lazarus," she replies.

"How do I turn on the shower?" he asks.

"How hot would you like it?"

"I… don't know, I've never thought about it," he responds.

"I will start a few degrees below body temperature," she says.

Close by, a fine stream of water begins to flow down from the ceiling. Feeling like a child being bathed by his mother, Lazarus moves past the column towards the water. He thrusts his hand into it finding it distinctly chilly.

"Higher!"

"Higher!" he says again…

"Ok that's good!" he steps under the flow luxuriating in the warmth, letting all of his tension melt away. Steam begins to rise from the stone floor as he washes. He stretches it out for many minutes and reluctantly steps away. The water immediately stops.

Before he has a chance to leave the shower area, warm dry air begins to swirl between ceiling and floor, switching directions time after time. Lazarus is enjoying the air shower as much as the water. Just when he thinks it's over, he becomes the center of a vortex that twists around him like a cyclone. Delightful! He's completely and thoroughly dry as the gale dies away.

"I hope that was satisfactory. I extrapolated the air temperature from your water preference," Magi says.

"That was… very satisfactory," Lazarus says.

"I will remember how you like it for your next shower," Magi says.

"Fine," Lazarus responds heading back to his chosen alcove.

"Magi?"

"Yes Lazarus," she replies.

"How do I shave?"

"You will find shaving cream behind the mirror."

He opens the cabinet and looks over its contents, different bottles and tubes but nothing familiar, certainly not shaving cream and a blade.

"The small tube on the bottom shelf," Magi instructs him.

He picks it up and takes a closer look.

"Squeeze out about a teaspoon in your palm, rub your hands together and massage into your beard. Wait a few seconds then wash it off. You can do it as many times as you wish but those who need it usually accomplish their goal in one application. The cream inhibits new growth so you will find you will not need to shave nearly as often as you did before." Magi says.

The cream makes his face tingle pleasantly and his beard is gone when he rinses it off. He feels good about his first real experience with a Lunarian bath as he puts on fresh clothes. He's clean and ready to face the world. Slipping his visor back on, he looks around to find Magi waiting patiently.

"Come, Liz is making pancakes down in the commonroom," she says leading him out of the bath via a second entrance.

Marveling once again at the remarkable realism of her image, he follows a few feet behind through a maze of narrow corridors and up a long ramp, finally emerging into the huge space of the Dakota warren's east commonroom. To his left are several people, one of whom turns to look at him. To his right is a couple hugging and the quiet hum of conversation leaves him with the impression of sadness. What a difference a couple of days can make. Can this be the same cheerful room that had impressed him so?

"The kitchen is over there," Magi points to the brightly lit area across the room. His visor magnifies allowing Lazarus to make out Tempel sitting at a table just beyond the kitchen.

"Magi?"

"Yes Lazarus," she replies.

"Thanks," he says.

"You are welcome, Lazarus," Magi says.

Lazarus marvels again at her completeness. He even smells her. How is that possible?

As he nears the kitchen, the unmistakable aroma of pancakes assails his olfactory glands making his mouth water and belly rumble. He sees only two people moving about. The rest, mostly young men and women, are sitting quietly at tables.

One of the women working in the kitchen turns to Lazarus as though expecting him, drying her hands on a towel. She has a strange expression, neither smile nor frown. He can't make up his mind which as she moves forward extending her hands to meet him, not offering her hand to shake, but rather just reaching out and taking his hands in hers. "Greetings, Lazarus," she says squeezing firmly and looking him squarely in the eyes. "I am Elizabeth Turner Dugan, Tempel's mother."

Again, he is struck by how young she looks. Gathering his wits about him, Lazarus accepts Elizabeth's hands in his and nods deeply before straightening, returning her stare and saying sincerely, "It's truly a great pleasure and honor to meet you, Mrs. Dugan."

"Please, call me Liz." She pulls him deeper into the kitchen area and steps back looking Lazarus over. "Thank you for helping yesterday. I know it was very difficult!"

Lazarus can tell she's been crying and more tears are not far from the surface. He shakes his head slowly, a frown deeply creasing his forehead, "I only wish I could have done more."

"Thank you, Lazarus. That's very kind," she responds patting his arm.

"In all my years in the office of Homeland Security, I never ceased to wonder about the thought process of the people who do these crazy destructive things to other people. How can they believe that committing mass murder is honorable? How can they live with themselves afterward?" Lazarus says.

"Did you figure it out?" she asks.

"I'm afraid not. The best they could do was to hide behind their favorite religious conviction."

Elizabeth shakes her head sadly, "Yes... Well... hiding behind religious convictions is just a crutch that wicked people use when they do despicable things! And if it's too much for their conscious, they simply ask their god for forgiveness and surprise, surprise, he grants it. But what they are really doing is dumping whatever guilt they do feel to an imaginary friend they call god. It makes them feel better so it must be right." Clearly agitated, she picks up a towel from the counter and aggressively wipes her hands, as if the very thought makes them dirty. "I'm afraid I don't have much sympathy for any possible trauma they may suffer as a consequence of doing terrible things to innocent people. Personal behavior is a choice everyone must make."

Tara approaches and puts her arm around Liz's waist drawing her near, "I'm sure most believers are decent, just deluded. Anyone can make a mistake."

"You are much more forgiving than I, Tera dear!" Liz exclaims, "But I do agree with you, god-based religions are delusional madness! Us against the world! You're either with us or against us! Distrust any outsider! Convert or die!" Remembering that Lazarus had only recently been part of the NAF, a theocracy she considers one of the biggest criminal organizations in history, she says "I hope I've not offended you."

"Not at all! It's refreshing to hear such honesty. History is filled with political leaders using religion to control their citizens. It gives them the excuse to operate outside the law and then tell everyone that it's for their own good," Lazarus responds.

"What's the old saying? They piss on your head then tell you it's raining!" She shakes her head. Suddenly remembering her manners, she says, "Please pardon my rudeness. This is Tara Dugan."

"A pleasure and honor to meet you, Mrs. Tara Dugan," Lazarus bows his head to her.

She returns the gesture and says, "I too thank you for helping. It was more than anyone had a right to ask of such a newly sponsored citizen."

"I can't tell you how good it sounds to be called a citizen," Lazarus says with complete sincerity. "Thank you!"

"Be careful what you wish for," Tara says with heavy sorrow in her voice. "Being a Lunarian nowadays can be hazardous to your health."

"They have wounded your heart which is exactly what they wanted... if there is anything I can do, please let me know." Lazarus reaches out intending to wipe a tear from her cheek.

Tara pulls back, looking hard at Lazarus but finding only sincerity, "Thank you."

Lazarus instantly knows he shouldn't have done that, "Please pardon my ill manners," he says quickly.

"I can see why Lindsey likes you Lazarus," Elizabeth lays the towel down. "You must be starving! Go and sit. I will bring you a stack of hotcakes." She moves to the cooking island in the center of the kitchen, picks up a long handled spatula and deftly starts flipping pancakes. "Tempel," she calls out.

Tempel looks up at the sound of his name, "Introduce Lazarus while I make him some pancakes. Do you want some more?"

"Aye," Tempel replies watching Lazarus and thinking of how this man had performed the day before, like a true citizen of the Republic.

Lazarus walks over to the table and takes a seat next to Nicole and across from Tempel. "I can't believe I slept so long," he says.

Justine and Nicole look from Lazarus to Tempel and back again.

Tempel takes the hint, "These two young ladies are Justine Harman and Nicole Dugan," he points at each as he says their name.

"A pleasure and honor to make your acquaintance," Lazarus nods and they tip their heads politely in return. "Justine Harman… Would you be any relation to Larz and Jason?" he asks. Justine's red hair and freckles are a dead give away.

"They're my brothers," the girl responds.

Tempel gets up and goes around behind Lazarus placing a hand on his shoulder, "Everyone!" Tempel pulls Lazarus to his feet. "If you don't already know, this is Mr. Lazarus Sheffield, a newly sponsored citizen from the NAF. He worked alongside me in the hospital yesterday. Please show him the hospitality of the Dugan family, treat him as you would treat me." The younger Lunarians quietly look on while most of the adults' nod approval. The mood in the dining room is somber. "Come on. I will introduce you," he moves down the aisle between tables with Lazarus following.

"It seems we have the upper classmen here today. Serena, Florence, and Tatum," Tempel points as he calls their names, receiving a nod from each young woman in turn. Moving to the end of the table, "This is Erica Fendrich."

Arising, she ceremoniously bows to Lazarus. "Let me add my thanks for the service you have done this family," she says in fine voice.

Lazarus returns her formality with some of his own, "You are most welcome," he murmurs, admiring the steadfastness of her demeanor, draped about her like a cloak.

A small commotion from the next table causes them to turn and look. The eight boys sitting at the table are talking and gesturing excitedly among themselves in an apparent attempt to spur one of them to ask a question.

"You boys settle down!" Erica says sharply but without raising her voice. The boys promptly obey, sitting straight in their chairs, hands on the table in front of them. The girls titter louder, earning themselves a stern look from Erica.

"Now that's impressive," Lazarus says watching the boys strain to keep still.

Tempel smiles, "They know what will happen if Erica doesn't get her way!"

"You watch yourself!" Erica says looking at Tempel. Turning back to Lazarus, "It wasn't that long ago Tempel was sitting over there!" Erica says, a grin breaking through her gruff exterior.

Stepping to the table, Tempel continues, "These fine lads are Conrad Dugan, Arnold Kirltenko, Leopold Calatrava, Brandon Dugan, Bayne Bjorkman, Nate Dugan, Perri Calatrava, and Dallas Dugan," Each holds Lazarus's eye briefly, smiles and exchanges nods as Tempel points them out.

"More pancakes!" Liz calls over, setting a heaping platter on the table with a clatter. Tara lays down a plate for Lazarus and more margarine and syrup.

As they move back towards the table Lazarus asks casually, "What have you found out about the explosions source?"

Tempel looks at him as they sit, pancakes forgotten for the moment. "Traces of SuperX have been found. Jerome is estimating the bombs mass at fifty pounds."

Lazarus frowns and begins to spread margarine liberally on his cakes. "Any idea yet as to how it got in?" He picks up the syrup and pours.

Shaking his head, "Magi, give us the current status report on the investigation," Tempel requests.

"It is known that the explosions epicenter was located in Dr. Haslett's research lab on sub level seven. Just prior he received a rather large shipment of instruments from

Japan, specifically, a new Quantum Probe Microscope. There isn't any indication that the bomb was in any of the crates but there is no other likely explanation at this time," Magi reports in the same emotionless tone she uses when talking about this incident.

"How many times did the shipment get scanned?" Tempel asks, scooping up a large mouthful of pancakes dripping with syrup, amazed by the speed that Lazarus is putting away his own.

"I can find records on seventeen individual security scans. All of them show components of a QPM, nothing unexpected," Magi responds.

The table is silent for a few minutes as they watch Lazarus consume his food. Even Tempel is impressed.

Pushing his plate back and leaning back in his chair, Lazarus sighs and pats his stomach, "That was just what the doctor ordered. I can't remember anything tasting so good!" Only then does he notice everyone watching him and become self conscious, "I was hungry," he says by way of an explanation.

They all laugh breaking the tension that had dominated the dinning room.

"Aye, we noticed," Temple says.

The boys get up and move closer to the men, Conrad and Perri taking the seats next to Lazarus, Brandon and Nate next to Tempel, the other four boys slide into the table behind Lazarus, everyone watching intently.

"Do you think the Brotherhood did this?" Leopold asks Lazarus from the other table.

"It fits their pattern," Lazarus responds.

Erica leans out over the table so she can see Lazarus, "What pattern do you mean?" she asks frowning.

Lazarus looks around the table, "Well… they pick vulnerable targets with the potential for high casualties. Hospitals are one of their favorite. Train stations, airports, schools, and churches are others. Plus, the big events happen in clusters. For instance, within one eight week period back in 2055, they bombed a nightclub in Malaysia, captured and executed hundreds of children in a Balkan middle school, and murdered everyone on a tourist bus outside of Rio de Janeiro… Five weeks ago the Sharm el Sheikh resort was bombed, now Lincoln County Hospital. I suspect there's more to come."

"Can't we stop them?" Conrad asks excitedly, his eyes wide with concern.

"How?" Lazarus asks. "Your AI said the containers were scanned many times on their way here. Track the people involved? Those responsible are either back on Earth or have not broken any law. Freedom means allowing people to live as they see fit, as long as it doesn't interferer with the next guys' right to do the same thing. Being different shouldn't be a crime and police shouldn't be allowed to arrest someone for something they might do or their family did." Bitterness creeps into his voice, "Believe me, I know! Freedom and liberty has been shrinking in the so-called free world for over two centuries, primarily because of the actions of religious fundamentalists! The Federation feels it's their duty to tell everyone what to think, what to believe, even how long their hair should be! They claim everything is a matter of national security and are fond of proclaiming that whatever law or rule they want to enact on this day is only temporary, that they will rescind it once the war on terror is over. But it's never over!"

Lazarus leans back in his chair looking at the faces gathered around him, "I want to say, the more I learn of Lunarian society the more I like it! You are free to make your own path, only you do it in full view of everybody. Makes a person stop and think before acting irresponsibly!"

Tempel looks up and watches over Lazarus's shoulder as Abby walks out of the dim commonroom and into the brightness of the dining and kitchen area. The boys see her a second later and fall silent as she walks up the central aisle stopping at the head of their table.

"Greetings children!" She nods to Erica and Tempel before settling her gaze on Lazarus, "Lazarus, I want to thank you for your actions at the hospital. You demonstrated skill and courage. Lindsey did well in bringing you to us."

Lazarus nods in return, "I'm glad I could help," he replies, looking intently at Abby trying to determine if this is a cyberspace projection. He is tempted to remove his visor but resists. As best he can tell, she appears just as she had in the meeting, just a little wearier. Was the meeting yesterday or the day before that? He isn't sure at that moment, beginning to truly understand how much he had depended on the day-night cycle back in Phoenix. His circadian rhythm is totally out of whack.

The nearest boy to Abby slides out of his seat and scrambles to a chair on the far side of the table.

"Thank you, Leopold" Abby says taking the vacated seat. "I apologize for interrupting your breakfast but Corso and I have a few items to discus with you."

Lazarus shakes his head, "You are not interrupting." He looks around for Corso, finding him standing behind him.

"Greetings, Lazarus," Corso rumbles in the now familiar baritone.

"Greetings, Chief Dugan," Lazarus responds.

Corso pulls over a chair and positions himself, completely blocking the center aisle with his bulk. Lazarus even hears the scraping of the chair as Corso moves it, again amazed at the quality of the projection. No matter how close he looks or listens he can detect nothing that tips him off that this man isn't really there, just his image.

Corso looks down the table at the gathering and says in his deep rumbling voice. "I believe we have determined how the bomb got inside Lincoln County Hospital. We have narrowed it down to a shipping case that went through numerous security scans producing a boatload of data. Nothing abnormal was found," Corso says. "You have indicated that the Brotherhood may have something you called active camouflage. It not only screens an object but transmits erroneous MRI data. Using active camouflage, could a shipping crate scan as equipment but actually contain explosives?"

"Absolutely Chief Dugan, that's exactly what it means," Lazarus responds.

"Space the Chief Dugan crap. It's Corso or just Chief," the black man says.

Abby asks quietly, "So a properly shielded nuclear device could pass through all of our security screens and never be detected? They can make it appear as something else?" A chill passes through the gathering.

Nodding in agreement, "Physical inspection is the only solution. But not after it gets inside Aldrin, that's far too late. Inspections must be done outside, on the surface, far enough away that a nuclear detonation can't harm the city," Lazarus explains.

"That's impossible!" Corso growls angrily, "We don't have the manpower that would take!"

Lazarus sighs, "It's the same problem NAF is facing. You simply cannot be everywhere at once, watch everything. That's why everyone has come to depend on scanners."

Abby turns to Corso, "We have no choice but to accept all of Lazarus's speculations at face value. Speak to Jerome about these conclusions and get him working on this full time. I want to know how active camouflage works and a way to defeat it as soon as possible. In the mean time, I want our officers to begin inspecting every truck, shuttle, train, and rover before they enter the city. I will speak with the Council and get more officers assigned to the effort. Intercepting the next surprise is our top priority."

Corso nods in agreement, "Aye! I already have every available officer on duty but you know we don't have enough to cover every entrance! Plus Hunan is claiming ownership of the new hab. Says they have evidence Dakota bribed the Council!" Corso growls disgustedly.

"It will never hold up in Council! Why are you worried?" Tempel presses.

"Because it doesn't feel right! Why has Hunan put forth this idiocy now?" Corso growls, his voice taking a gravelly edge. "We are spread thin and this just adds to what I must think about."

The Hunan freehold operates a refinery in a warren adjacent to Falconhead and had petitioned for the last habitat space available in the area at the same time Dakota freehold had submitted its bid to expand Falconhead using the same space. The Council had ruled in Dakota's favor. But Hunan has many powerful allies in the Council and nobody likes the taste of defeat.

The decisions concerning new freehold habitats and surface construction are, in a perfect world, decided in favor of the greatest good for the most people. In reality, these issues are political tests of will between freeholds. And when two powerful freeholds compete for the same real estate, the friction can reach critical mass within the Council. It can be said it was successfully argued that the Dakota freehold had the greater need. Regardless, in the end, they simply had more votes. Now Hunan is trying to influence public opinion by claiming bribery and possibly force a reversal.

"We can expect trouble with Hunan," Tempel says roughly.

"I know Lee Chin. He is a reasonable man," Abby states with certainty.

Corso nods and frowns in thought, "When are you scheduled to go on duty?" he asks Tempel.

"Not for another eight hours," Tempel says.

"Change in orders. Charley Company is flying out to Far Point. They will be doing physical inspection of all incoming shuttle flights out there," Corso says. "Ben is in charge of all surface inspections, coordinating from the Command Center." Turning to Abby, "We are spread thinner than toilet paper! If we need to keep this up long…" The unspoken implication hangs in the air.

Abby nods, "Dakota will do what needs doing! We always have."

"You look exhausted, Grandma Abby," Tempel says.

"If you were my age, you would too," Abby responds with a weary smile. "Believe it or not, I don't like playing politics. The damn Council will be the death of me," her smile doesn't quite reach her blue eyes. "I will get some sleep shortly," she promises.

"Dakota is already at Code Orange," Corso says. Code Orange mandates all of Aldrin Station's off duty adult citizens to wear visors and a sidearm and be ready to respond at a moments notice. He would prefer Code Red and put everyone into vacsuits but that was considered excessive by the Council right before this meeting. "Magi?"

"Yes Corso," Magi says.

"I want you to monitor all activity. Keep track of all citizens and notify everybody if there is a code level violation or you get cut off anywhere," Corso rumbles.

"Aye," Magi responds.

Corso turns and looks gravely at Tempel, "Don't take any chances during inspections. Just do your job and keep your wits about you." Tempels father, Patrick Ryan, had been his baby brother, killed in a Far Point mine accident. He doesn't want history to repeat itself.

Abby leans over and pats Tempel's hand. "You listen to Corso!" She too recalls her youngest child, taken from her at Far Point. Her expression is serious as she stares Tempel dead in the eyes, "Don't take this lightly. There is something very strange going on. I wish like hell I knew what it was!" She looks with approval as a plate of pancakes is laid in front of her. "Thank you Elizabeth! Just what the doctor ordered!"

"You must eat to keep your strength up," Liz says.

"Please excuse me Abby but the new vacsuit you ordered for Lazarus is ready. He is immediately scheduled for vacuum qualification," Magi says. By law, every person living within the Republic must be fitted with a vacsuit and qualified to wear it, common sense when living on the moon.

"Good! Tempel, can you see he gets it done?" Abby says.

"Aye," he responds rising from the table.

Lazarus bids farewell to the gathering and follows the younger man, calling out, "Thanks for breakfast, Elizabeth, Tara."

"Any time. You boys be careful!" the mother in Liz responds, watching the two men disappear into the twilight of the commonroom.

****

They take Sherwood Commonway to Franklin Commonway. Lazarus hopes he never grows immune to the magic of Aldrin Station. The trees, the gardens, the shear beauty of the architecture, leave him awestruck and amazed. They take the Calconn Avenue exit, one of the main passages servicing the Benjamin Franklin Manufacturing District. After a short and pleasant walk down the Elm lined avenue, they enter Falconhead Refinery making their way to room D157.

D157 is a small locker room that will handle about ten people at once but at that moment there is only one person inside and she is wearing the same black and tan police uniform as Tempel.

"Greetings, Zoey," Tempel says.

"Greetings," the young woman replies.

"This is Lazarus Sheffield… Lazarus, this is Officer Zoey Tanaka. She will be fitting your vacsuit today." Tempel says.

"Greetings, I'm very pleased to meet you," Lazarus says.

Zoey nods in return. She is tall and lean with the same general physique as Samantha. They could have been sisters. Both are bald and beautiful with flawless complexions, and both are buxom with broad shoulders, their movements smooth and powerful. The biggest difference between the two women is Sam has Norwegian features and Zoey's are oriental.

"Lazarus, I will leave you in Zoey's capable hands," Tempel says.

"When will I see you again?" Lazarus asks.

"I will be back in a couple hours, there's something I want to show you after you have a vacsuit," Tempel says.

"Great."

"Pay attention to what Zoey teaches you. Your life will depend on it," Lazarus smiles and leaves.

"Great."

The training was surprisingly easy for Lazarus, graduating at the top of his class… quite the accomplishment considering he was the only one in his class. But that doesn't stop him from taking pride in the ease of his learning. Again, Lunarian technology amazes him, so simple a child can use it, yet providing everything he needs to survive on an airless world. The only uncomfortable time came when Zoey showed him how to… install… the long duration waste recovery system. He's sure the device would be considered illegal anywhere within the Federation but she makes it seem so natural to insert these things in those places. The vacsuit itself was a walk in the park after that.

His suit is white, designed to be seen from far away and to show dirt when and where it needs cleaning. It's also the color they give novices in need of extra attention. It fits him like a glove sliding on easily, custom made for his body. When Lazarus finds out that it incorporates his visor, he decides to call Lindsey after Zoey is finished dressing him in his new vacsuit.

"Zoey, would you mind if I talk to Lindsey?" he asks.

"Magi, put a call in to Lindsey Davenport," she says.

A few moments later she appears beside them, "Greetings Zoey, Lazarus. What can I do for you?" Lindsey asks.

Zoey spreads her hands waiting for Lazarus to speak.

"Ah… I just wanted to say thanks…" Lazarus stumbles over his words.

She smiles, "That's sweet. Why don't we get together later, after you're done for the day? Maybe we will have some coffee." She winks at him.

"That sounds great!" Lazarus replies.

"Excellent! By the way, nice vacsuit! Another step towards becoming Lunarian," Lindsey says.

"Where shall we meet?" Lazarus asks.

"Don't worry about it, I'll find you. Ok… got to go," she waves and disappears, breaking up into a million tiny bits that sparkle and are gone.

Zoey is looking at him with an amused expression, "Can we finish now?"

"Ah… sure…"

His first exposure to vacuum is so uneventful that he doesn't even realize it's happening until Zoey points it out. After a short walk, she leads him through a small airlock to emerge in a secondary tunnel far below the city, never realizing he's in vacuum until told.

He had envisioned it completely wrong, Lazarus doesn't even feel the loss of pressure around him, so well does his vacsuit shelter him. Near the end of the walk, he is pleasantly surprised when Tempel joins them in his black and tan police vacsuit.

"Greetings, Joey, do you mind if I take over from here?" Tempel asks.

"Greetings… Not at all, Lieutenant. Just signoff on his qualification when you're finished," she says. "Nice meeting you Lazarus and good luck."

"Thanks Zoey, for all your help," Lazarus says.

"So how do you like your vacsuit?" Tempel asks.

"Superb! Light and comfortable, it feels like I could wear it for days without any problem," Lazarus says.

"I've still got some time to kill before reporting for duty. There's something I want to show you. It's a little bit of a climb, are you up for it?" Tempel asks.

"In vacsuits?" Lazarus asks.

"Absolutely. You need to be able to work and move freely in it. If there's a problem, we need to find out now and not later… But if you don't think you can make it…" Tempel says challenging Lazarus.

"Lead on," Lazarus responds not willing to look weak.

Tempel grins and leads them back into the city, back to Dakota warren. But this time Tempel continues upward without stopping for a beer or chitchat in the kitchen.

"How much do you know about the history of the Republic?" Tempel asks him as they move upward in a seemingly never ending supply of ramps and tunnels. Within minutes, Lazarus is completely lost with no hope of retracing this torturous path alone. All he knows with any certainty is they are going up.

"I've managed to piece some of it together but it's not exactly publicized where I'm from," he responds straining to keep up with the agile young Lunarian. He is again struck by the ease and grace with which Tempel moves. Something about his motion but he can't seem to put his finger on just what exactly.

"Ok, fair enough. The North American Federation established Aldrin Station back in 2024 to explore the causes of the obscurations seen during the early days of lunar observations. Having only Earth based visuals to go on, it was hypothesized at the time to be unknown gases seeping out from below the surface due to some underlying volcanism. But what they actually found when they got here was a rather large fragment of comet buried deep beneath the surface of the crater. The unknown gases turned out to be water vapor and CO2. This fortuitous discovery has provided us with an abundant water and hydrogen source, an oasis in the lunar desert."

Lazarus is huffing audibly because of the pace Tempel is setting but he isn't about to ask him to slow down. He is amazed at the ease with which the young Lunarian can calmly lecture him while moving so swiftly upward through the warren. At times it seems as if he is double jointed as he literally leaps up the ramps, waiting for Lazarus at the top.

"The major part of the city is constructed underground, far from any free surface. Radiation and meteorites force sensible people to burrow deep and stay there. Surface or near surface constructs are at a substantially greater risk of getting nailed. We learned early that the more rock over your head the better."

While Tempel talks, he continues to lead them upward through a labyrinth of dimly lit narrow tunnels and ramps, his pace deliberately high so Magi can establish a medical baseline on the earthman.

"The tremendous heating that occurred during the crater forming event liquefied Luna's crust and drove it outward where it solidified into Rim Mountain. Because of that, the rock attained a very stable and homogeneous consistency. The early settlers found it very conducive for carving habitats in. Not at all like mountains on Earth where plate tectonics' is the driving force behind mountain building, pushing and compressing the stone until it shatters."

Lazarus is as attentive as possible under the circumstances but it isn't long before he has slowed his pace considerably. The last ramp is particularly long and seems to spiral upward forever. He stubbornly huffs and puffs up the steep corkscrew, Tempel so far in front that he would worry that he has left him except for listening to his voice drone on about early crater formation and liquefaction. Every time he thinks he has reached the top, it's only another narrow tunnel branching off to some unknown region and Tempel telling him to keep moving upward.

The ability of his vacsuit to regulate his body temperature amazes Lazarus. He isn't even sweating and remains cool despite his intense exercise. But the suit cannot make him a better athlete. Out of breath, muscles shaking with exertion, he continues out of pride. He can't turn back. He can't stop. He must carry on and show Tempel that he can do this. Just put one foot in front of the other. The one saving grace is Luna's gravity. If he had tried this climb back on Earth, he would have collapsed with exhaustion long before reaching the top.

Tempel is waiting for him as he emerges from the ramp with a look of amused tolerance. A narrow corridor stretches out in opposite directions, its walls glowing with dim reddish light. "Glad to see you made it. I was beginning to get worried," the young Lunarian says with a grin.

Lazarus stands still, hands on his knees, sucking in air as the quivering in his leg muscles slowly subsides. He sincerely hopes that going down will be easier. "Where... are... we?" he asks straightening and slowly following Tempel.

Tempel chuckles, "This is the uppermost service corridor in Dakota warren. There is less than a hundred yards of rock above our heads right here," he says.

Lazarus shakes his head in disbelief. They had climbed a mountain from the inside.

Tempel stops in front of an airlock a few dozen feet from the ramp, nondescript other than it's smaller than normal, "Magi, please unseal," he requests, looking sideways at Lazarus huffing and puffing, still sucking air like a vacuum.

"Aye," she responds. Thicker and more massive than a standard airlock, the door slides ponderously open.

"Take your time. I will wait for you at the top," Tempel says with a straight face.

A long, narrow and very steep ramp leads upward. Tempel braces against the sides of the ramp with his arms and pushes with his legs, enjoying the sensation of his straining muscles as he surges upward. He covers the hundred and fifty yards in record time arriving at the upper lock just beginning to breath hard. Lazarus can't begin to match his pace but does the best he can. Towards the end he is beginning to think maybe he had bitten off more than he could chew when finally the ramp levels off.

Tempel is grinning waiting for him at the top. "Well done! If we do this everyday for a month, we just might get you in shape. Or we could make you an appointment to see a geneticist."

Huffing like a freight train on a steep mountain grade, Lazarus doesn't try to answer, just sucks in air and waves his hand for Tempel to proceed.

Magi slides the last lock open as Lazarus puts his hands on his knees gulping air, struggling to catch his breath. On shaking legs, Lazarus follows Tempel into a long slender room. It contains only a single ladder at the far end of the room leading up to a circular hatch recessed in the ceiling. Tempel touches the wall. The coldness makes him think about the shear drop just a few feet away, only the relatively thin stone wall between him and raw space. Tempel smiles at the confusion he sees in Lazarus and moves up the ladder, swinging the hatch open. He remains quiet. He doesn't want to spoil the surprise.

Even after hundreds of visits, his adrenalin spikes as his head clears the hatch, pleasantly combining with endorphins generated by the workout. Tempel pulls himself up and out with little effort, using just his arm and shoulder muscles. He takes a very brief look around, bends down and literally pulls Lazarus from the hatch in one fluid motion to stand beside him, grinning mischievously at the shocked expression that floods the older man's face. Tempel releasing him and closes the hatch.

This is as close as any Lunarian will ever come to standing at the top of their home world. The two men are on the pinnacle of a razorback ridge almost two miles above the crater floor with only their vacsuits protecting them from the unforgiving lunar vacuum. The awesome depth of space itself seems close enough to touch.

Lazarus essentially faints, his hands unconsciously clutch at Tempel, a whimper escapes his lips and he clinches his eyes tightly shut beneath his visor as he sinks back down to his knees. Never has he felt so vulnerable. His heart pounds in his ears and he rocks back on his butt, falling to his side and stops moving, his body now completely immobile, locked in the fetal position. He can't move a muscle.

"Lazarus! Are you alright?!" Greatly alarmed, Tempel kneels beside Lazarus placing a hand on him while quickly reviewing the man's medical readings, finding them swinging widely, making no sense at all. Heart rate up, breathing spasmodic, central brain activity off the chart, muscles locked and rigid, adrenal medulla activity high, "Magi! What's going on?"

"There is nothing physically wrong with Lazarus. He suffers from acrophobia. The synaptic patterns within his visual cortex became highly erratic then shut down. I have administered hydroxyzine and SSR inhibitors… He is coming out of it," Magi says.

Lazarus's eyes flutter and a low moan escapes his lips.

"Take it easy Lazarus. There's nothing here that can hurt you," Tempel reassures the stricken man. "I'm so sorry. I didn't realize you were afraid of heights."

Slowly Lazarus raises his head and looks at Tempel. His breath, while still labored, comes under control as his will power slowly takes over. "I'm ok. Just give me a minute," he manages to say as he clenches his eyes shut and rolls onto his back stretching out to his full height.

"Take as long as you need then we will leave. It was a mistake to bring you up here," Tempel says.

Lazarus reaches up to run his hand over his head as he has done a thousand times, confused until he remembers he is wearing a vacsuit. He makes do with the smooth surface of the suit, takes a deep breath, and gathers his courage about him like a heavy cloak on a cold night. With a determined expression he pushes himself up to sit, hugging his knees to his chest, not yet opening his eyes. Hesitantly he slits his eyelids and looks down at the shear drop-off terminating in the floor of the giant crater far below. As the seconds tick past, it's surprisingly easy for him to adjust to this incredible experience, feeling his heart rate come back towards normal and his emotions calm. He wants to look up badly, knowing the Earth is there, but even tilting his head or rolling his eyes brings on waves of nausea and fear. Yet, it could be worse. Lazarus knows he's winning, that his phobia is not nearly as bad as it's been in the past. That realization provides the courage to gaze with wonder at what lay before him.

From their position, it appears they are at the edge of Alphonsus crater facing inward, turning his head slowly letting his eye travel along the spine of Rim Mountain, stopping his gaze at the far side, his visor protecting him from the unremitting glare of the low hanging sun.

Lazarus zooms in on the distant peaks, their feet lost below the short lunar horizon. "This is what it must feel like to sit on the point of a pin," he says softly.

"I've never heard it put that way, but yes, you are quite right, a very tall pin."

"Is that the other side of the crater?" Lazarus asks already feeling much better, gaining more control over his phobia with each passing second.

Tempel takes a seat next to Lazarus, letting his shoulder and body contact the earthman, lending him a measure of support, "Yes and closer, you can make out Central Peak jutting upward like one of Earth's volcano's. Its height is lower than Rim Mountain, just as all central peaks are in relation to their craters outer rim. New London is inside it." Looking down at Lazarus, "Are you sure you're ok? We can leave any time, you know. I just thought it would be stimulating for you to see Aldrin Station from a new perspective."

Lazarus manages a soft dry chuckle, "It is that! But no, thank you. I will be fine..."

His curiosity is quickly beating down whatever residual fear remains and there are many things before him that beg for answers. The sun, low on the horizon, casts the floor of the crater completely into shadow. His visor allows him to penetrate this darkness whenever he stares at something for more than a few seconds. He's getting better at manipulating this wonderful device.

"Can you tell me what all the lights are from?"

"Sure. The grouping just to the left of Central Peak is from Archibald ice mine." They light up the crater floor in patches and Lazarus adjusts his visors magnification to allow him to see details even from this distance. "Archibald was established by the European Union but is now owned and operated by the Republic of Luna. It is the third biggest ice mine in the solar system, surpassed only by the mines on asteroids Themis and Cybele. The string of lights originating almost directly below us and running straight out towards New London is the elevated maglev track. You can see other tracks to the right and left. They go south to Prattville and north to Summerhaven."

"Are they part of Aldrin Station?" Lazarus asks.

"No... But they are considered part of Alphonsus Complex because they are in Rim Mountain," Tempel replies.

"How many people?"

"Magi, can you give us exact numbers?"

"Currently, the population at Summerhaven is 26925, Prattville 11291, New London 141138, Aldrin Station 315280, and another 14765 citizens living in surface facilities or otherwise outside of the established settlements. This gives Alphonsus Complex a total population of 494,633 within a zero point one margin of error," Magi responds.

Lazarus frowns and shakes his head in confusion, "How can you feed so many? It seems impossible!"

Tempel chuckles, "We apply genetics to alter certain plants giving us more for less, and use hydroponics to grow them in their optimal environment. That's the short answer, but as in everything, the devil's in the details."

"Still, the area necessary to feed so many must be huge!"

"Not as much as you think. Magi, break down the total square miles Aldrin Station has in cultivation of any kind."

"Within Aldrin Station there are 469 habitats dedicated exclusively to the growing of usable plant matter and another 16 that mechanically support this effort. In addition, there are 41 more that have some agriculture within them. This provides a total of 10.71 square miles of fields within Aldrin Station alone. New London has 4.21, Summerhaven 6.23 and Prattville 7.88. All are high density hydroponics that produces crops year round, twenty four hours a day, every day. These numbers do not include the orchards and other assorted plants found in the commonway's or malls. Would you like a breakdown of the specific plants by location or type?" she asks.

Tempel raises his eyebrows at Lazarus, waiting for him to answer.

"No, that won't be necessary. I'm sure you have things all figured out."

Tempel nods, "Lunarian agricultural engineers are the best!"

It's Lazarus's turn to chuckle, "We call them farmers back on Earth."

Tempel smiles, "I'll show you one of the agricultural habitats and then you can tell me if you would call it a farm."

Sitting on this perch high above the crater floor, Lazarus tries to imagine the awesome spectacle of Alphonsus's birth. That stupefying instant when the giant asteroid plunged deep into the crust, the energy of it's impact turning the rock molten and fluid for hundreds of miles in every direction, pulverizing it with the force of a million Hiroshima bombs, sending shock waves ripping through Luna like a stone in a quite garden pond. Hundreds of cubic miles of rock heaving and rippling outward in gigantic waves. Rim Mountain and Central Peak magically solidify out of this chaos forming a crater 67 miles across with a rim wall two miles high, a blend of sintering and liquefaction making it the ideal material to carve habitats in.

"On the crater floor below us, about three miles out, you can see the lights of the Mitsuki smelter. Magnify and you'll see it's a huge spider web of tanks, towers, feed lines and cables that takes up a lot of square miles of prime real estate. The regolith found in the Alphonsus's central plain contains some of the highest concentrations of ilmenite ore anywhere within the Republic, rich in iron and titanium."

Using his visor to spotlight where he wants Lazarus to look, Tempel draws his attention to the facilities strung out along the base of Rim Mountain. "Those are mostly spacedocks. This one is where you came in. You can see many have a ship berthed."

Movement catches his eye, "There's a maglev train heading for Prattville."

Tempel highlights something further out on the craters floor, "A convoy coming in from the north heading for the smelter. The big vehicle in front is called a truck. It provides a comfortable shirtsleeve working environment for the convoy's crew while pulling up to fifteen of the huge ore carriers you see strung out behind it. Both the truck and the carriers articulate in the middle, carrying the load over two pairs of huge balloon tires. Each axle contains a high torque DC motor capable of hauling 120 tons mass. Not only does the truck provide guidance to the carriers but supplies power to their motors. Each set of tires follows the track of the ones in front exactly like one of those giant centipedes I learned about from someone who actually lived in the rain forests before they were all cut down."

Highlighting one by one many smaller installations scattered across the craters central plain, "These are Earth observatories, sensor arrays, pumping stations, surface labs and even a few living habitats for those independent souls willing to bet their life on the effectiveness of our meteorite defensive shield. The observatories can be linked together to form the best visual platform ever constructed to look back down on the Earth. Rumor has it that on a clear day they can read the cards over the shoulder of the President playing poker on the White House lawn," he chuckles.

Lazarus turns slowly on his butt, not hugging his legs quite so hard anymore, his mind adjusting to reality, soaking in the incredible view as he listens to Tempel.

Tempel scoots around with him until they are pointed north, "The mountains you see on the horizon are the rim of the crater Ptolemaeus, larger than Alphonsus and still mostly unexplored. The two giant craters share their north rim. The township of Summerhaven is carved in that section of Rim Mountain. Dakota sent a team of geologists to Ptolemaeus last year looking for more buried ice. They reported a crater rich in ore but they couldn't find any water."

"Can we see the Trans Lunar Highway from here?"

"Not really. The closet approach would be in that direction about eighteen miles out," Tempel responds pointing north-northeast. "What you see here, to our east and stretching south seventy or eighty miles is the Central Highlands. It's a jumbled broken mess consisting of material ejected not only from Alphonsus and Ptolemaeus, but from Arzachel to the south and Albategnius, another large crater just over the horizon to the northeast. Smaller impacts churned it up even more. You can see some of the craters out on the surface there and there," he says pointing, "They simply add more rugged mountains to an already tortured landscape."

"Its difficult to tell from where we are, but here, adjacent to Alphonsus, the Central Highlands is over a half mile higher than the crater floor. Further out, the depth of the Highlands can exceed eight-thousand feet. We're pretty far away but you can still see some of the major installations on the outside of Rim Mountain. Most are located less than a mile from the base. The biggest exception is Far Point about twenty-seven miles out and situated in a small crater. It's the largest anorthite mine in the Alphonsus complex. Anorthite ore is the prime source of aluminum and calcium. It was anorthite mines that propelled the explosive growth of Aldrin Station in the late twenties and thirties."

"Why's that?"

"Well... Each time a new mine opened, the habitats supporting the workers, the malls and passageways, farms and commodity plants, had to be cut into the nearest section of Rim Mountain. It didn't take long for the volume between these clusters of habitats to become honeycombed with more farms, residential neighborhoods, malls with commonway's connecting everything. At one point in the late twenty's Aldrin was gaining 1500 people a month. That's one shuttle filled with people every day. Construction crews couldn't keep up. That would have been a four habitat residential warren every month, not counting the hydroponics, air handling, and recycling necessary to support that many people! Things were tight, not enough of anything, food, water, air, power. Hell, even things like a bed to sleep in or a chair to sit on. Everything was time shared. That was when people began clustering together to provide mutual protection of their interests. The freehold system emerged out of that chaos."

"Currently, there are almost 1200 habitats in the Alphonsus complex. One of the things you will need to learn to become a citizen, besides our history, is the science that keeps us alive."

"What do you mean?" Lazarus asks, thrilled that this young Lunarian was even broaching the subject. "Do you mean disrupter technology?"

"Yes, but not only the tools to build habitats, but why they're shaped the way they are and located where they are. The governing equations used to calculate the minimum safe distance between any two volumes excavated in Rim Mountain is second nature to any school kid. As children we cut our teeth on stuff like that. If we didn't, we wouldn't be around long. It only takes one mistake to kill you. After all, this isn't Earth, it's Luna, and every Lunarian knows our world is harsh and unforgiving. A lot of this we soak up as adolescents, which means you will need to hit the books hard to even make a dent in catching up. And even if you never catch up, you will still need to know your limitations. What you don't know will kill you," Tempel says solemnly.

"I've heard that before."

"But if you at least know your particular level of ignorance, a clever but clueless person can avoid dying," Tempel chuckles.

"I'm all for that," Lazarus responds.

"We only have a few more minutes. Do you have any questions?"

Lazarus laughs, "Do I have any questions? That's all I have, is questions. But my level of ignorance, as you put it, is so high that I don't even know enough to ask the right questions. The freeholds, the military, the corner grocery store, I don't know anything about anything! Back on Earth I read everything I could get my hands on about this place and it's obvious to me after being here only a short while, that most of it was incomplete or worse, total nonsense. But I am looking forward to learning!"

Lazarus's voice has a quality that makes Tempel turn and look at him. He still sits with his arms around his knees but Tempel can see that he is much more relaxed. The fact they were sitting atop the point of a two mile high pin no longer incapacitates him.

"Where I come from, my young friend, it was what you knew that could get you killed! I learned the majority of the science that I do know, and I admit it's not a lot, on my own as a boy, reading from the pages of books that if my school or the local police or my next door neighbor caught me with, its very possession would be enough to send me away for retraining."

Tempel frowns, "I've heard many definitions of retraining. What exactly is it?"

"To be perfectly honest, I don't really know. It could be torture, mind bending, brainwashing, drugs. They don't publicize their true methods and the people who come back can't tell you. What the Federation does publish I know is garbage, claiming prayer and fasting was sufficient to bring the individual back to the flock. But I have seen the results, every citizen has! I'm sure that was the point, to let the masses see the results of disobedience! A person will think twice about breaking the law after someone they know goes through retraining! Oddly enough, that was the main motivating factor in Rachel wanting to immigrate to the Republic. She became quite adamant right before her death…" Lazarus says softly, gazing out on the barren vastness before him, his heart growing heavy thinking about her. Rachel and Courtney had meant everything to him, but they were gone and there wasn't a damn thing he could do about it. Instead of feeling guilt, he simply accepted it as part of life and moved on. Lazarus didn't push away the memory of Rachel. He tucked it in his pocket like an old photo, to be taken out and enjoyed when appropriate, not dwelled on or brooded over to the point of distraction.

"How did you feel about immigrating back then?" Tempel asks.

"I didn't think it was a good idea. I had just made Senior Analyst and didn't like the idea of losing that. But to be perfectly honest, I couldn't have withstood Courtney going through retraining, and I couldn't raise her to be a good Christian either, someone so devout as to fly under their radar. I was caught between a rock and a hard place." Lazarus looks up at Tempel, "So you see Tempel, this place is my heaven, a place where I can finally be myself."

Nodding thoughtfully Tempel says, "Even knowing that you will have a rough time learning what you will need to survive here, I can't begin to put myself in the reverse situation. What if I was forced to survive in your world? Could I do it?" he shakes his head side to side, "I think not. I would get retrained within the first day!"

"I don't know 'bout that! From what I've seen you're a pretty tough cookie! You do what you set your mind to do!" Lazarus laughs as confidence surges through him. Learning holds a special place inside him, something he knows he is good at.

Tempel laughs with him, "Tough cookie! Never heard that before! Is that because I was left in the oven to long?! Dried out like a mud brick?"

"Something like that!" they both chuckle.

The two men grow quiet dwelling on private thoughts, sharing the experience in comfortable silence.

Lazarus was the first to break the stillness, "Mind if I ask you a political question that has been eating at me?"

Tempel shakes his head, "Go ahead and ask."

"Why did the Lunarians agree to the Treaty of Independence?"

"Humph!" Tempel huffs surprised at the abrupt change of subject, "Good question. Why did we? The short answer is that it kept us out of a war with Earth that thirty years ago we couldn't have won. We may not now, but at least we have a fighting chance."

"So the Republic is close to discarding the Treaty?"

"Well… it's not my place to say for sure but every agreement reaches an end. Nothing lasts forever!"

"True. Please, tell me what you know of the history of this document. The official story told to Federation citizens ends up with Lunarians basically slaves to us for all of eternity."

Tempel bursts out in laughter from deep in his belly, "You have got to be kidding! Slaves for all eternity!"

"You are obligated by God to provide us with power and raw materials, forever. For a fee of course which the Lunarians keep increasing and is the main reason that Federation citizens must pay more taxes each year."

Tempel stops laughing and frowns at him, "You're not kidding, are you."

Lazarus just shakes his head.

"Well ok… here's how the story goes that I've been told. Back in the beginning, in the twenties and thirties, when Aldrin Station and everything else was getting started, every nation was eager to get their foot in the door, staking claim to one resource or another. Mines and towns grew at an astonishing rate with each one bringing in a new ingredient to the recipe. China established Far Point but Russia, Australia, Korea, Brazil, Chad, Zaire, Sri Lanka, and a hundred others developed their own interests on Luna. The NAF constructed a big aluminum smelter and the EU built a mass driver to deliver raw product from the surface to the orbiting factories. Other companies and governments from all over the Earth built an extensive support network for these larger facilities. The engineers, truck drivers, maintenance workers and technology specialists that manned them came from every corner. Talk about a mixing pot! Let me tell you, Aldrin Station was the biggest mixing pot ever seen!"

"The tension ebbed and flowed among these diverse groups thrown into such close proximity to each other. And everyone depended on everyone else to survive! No choice in the matter! Yet, while trying to stay alive on a hostile world, they all were striving to pull together a bigger pile of money than the next guy in a business environment they had little or no control over. It didn't take long for them to realize that the leaders back on Earth didn't have their best interests at heart. That's when everyone really started to pull together, forming the alliances that would one day become the General Council."

"Thirty-one years ago, on April 1, 2060, a unified citizenry submitted the Lunarian Declaration of Independence to Earth and informed them they were consolidating most of their offworld assets into the Republic of Luna. Well, as I'm sure you can imagine, all hell broke loose! Everyone was calling us criminals and screaming for our heads. But we controlled their power satellites, their Calconn, and their entire orbital communications network. Abby, Zachariah Taylor and a few others convinced them that leaving us alone was the best solution."

"Things went from screams to more of a loud insistent voice when the power kept coming down from orbit and the shipments of Calconn remained on schedule. But there was still a lot of animosity, especially from those that had lost the most. I hate to admit it but the Treaty of Independence was actually our idea. We thought that if we committed in writing our willingness to repay the entire investment, including interest, that things would return to normal. We just wanted to avoid a war, plain and simple. No one realized that the document that would emerge from all the discussions and compromises would tie us up so thoroughly. It effectively eliminated any military or standing militia. No research that could be construed as offensive which is pretty much all of it. After all, what science or technology cannot be twisted into something evil? And it tied us up financially as well, locking our economy with theirs for the foreseeable future. Maybe that's where they get the propaganda that we are slaves forever. I must admit, the Treaty does mandate that the listed countries are entitled to first dibs on the fruits of our labors. That's about it. Thirty years ago the decisions were made that had to be made, but it's about time for this agreement to be dumped," Tempel says.

"That certainly sounds more feasible than the Federation version. To hear them tell it, they magnanimously granted you your freedom in exchange for your servitude into perpetuity. They won't be happy when you make the break."

"No one believes they will throw us a party. We do expect them to make good business decisions when the time finally comes."

Lazarus shrugs, "I hope you're right but my gut tells me not." He releases his knees and slowly leans back until he is lying flat on his back. He feels like he is floating in space with all the wonder of the universe before him. Approaching first quarter, the Earth hangs almost directly overhead half shadow and half light, the night side slightly larger than the day. But it is seeing the sun and stars coexist in the heavens with his home planet that strikes Lazarus as odd, leaving him with the impression that all of this is contrived.

Tempel silently stretches out beside him.

"This doesn't look real to me. Like something out of a vid."

"I assure you, this is all real," Tempel says.

"It's incredible! I never realized how beautiful it would be," Lazarus says reverently. "I've never been able to figure out how men can learn so much and still believe in the ancient superstitions."

"It's easier to believe the sky is blue because god willed it than to delve into the actual reasons," Tempel says.

"You know, in all the books I read as a child growing up, I don't remember any of them mentioning why the sky is blue. Is it simply the color of air?"

To his credit Tempel didn't laugh, "Ah… in a way I guess it is. Sunlight is made up of all different wavelengths of light, which means it contains all the colors. Your eyes see the sky as blue due to a physical phenomenon called Rayleigh scattering that causes light to separate into its constituents when it passes through gasses that have a molecular diameter one-tenth that of the particular wavelength. Because of the oxygen and nitrogen in Earth's atmosphere, the wavelength for blue is bent much more efficiently than the other colors. So when you look up on a clear summer day, you see blue because all the molecules everywhere are scattering blue light toward you. Or conversely, because red light, yellow light, green light and all the other wavelengths aren't scattered nearly as well, you see the sky as blue… We see Earth as blue for the same reason. It's especially true over water where the reflecting sunlight is shifted into the blue-green wavelengths." They gaze in silence at the blue, white, and brown world hanging motionless in the sky above them.

"If you concentrate on a landmark you can actually see the Earth rotate, night becoming day, day becoming night, a nice neat cycle that has been going on for 4.3 billion years," Tempel says softly.

A sudden bright pinpoint of light catches Tempel's attention. Magnifying, he recognizes the craft as a translunar freighter. "I see a freighter coming in."

Lazarus quickly zooms in where Tempel has highlighted. The ship descends down towards her berth firing all four of her powerful ion thrusters, graceful and totally silent, a tiny beetle defying the vastness of space. She is coming in two or three miles north of their position and dropping fast, probably headed for a dock at the north end of Aldrin Station.

"It seems to be coming in awfully fast," Lazarus comments.

"Pilots are graded by how much fuel they don't use so they tend to come in hot and operate their thrusters at the more efficient higher plasma pressures and temperatures. This results in sustained high accelerations during final approach, sometimes approaching ten G's. The pilots are supposed to stay under seven but it's not a law."

"Ten G's? Can a person survive that?"

"Not without an acceleration hammock. Even with one, a person risks damaging internal organs, especially the heart. A human heart is not designed to pump under that kind of duress."

Tempel sighs, "I hate to say it but we've got to go."

"Thanks for bringing me here. I appreciate what you and your family are doing for me."

Tempel chuckles, "I know you do." He stands and reaches down to help Lazarus.

"I think it would be better if you let me get down myself," Lazarus says.

Lazarus doesn't try to stand, but rolls over the edge of the hatch and descends the ladder on shaky legs, finding comfort in a city carved into the heart of a mountain.

"Men never do evil so completely and cheerfully as when they do it from religious conviction."
Blaise Pascal (1623-1662)

Cullman Outpost

"Luna Central, this is Evolution's Child. Commencing deorbit burn," Nell informs the uniformed officer that appears within her visual. Thinking back she tries to recall the last time a controller was wearing police black and tan. She can't remember a single instance and it leaves her uneasy.

"Acknowledged, Evolution's Child. You are cleared to break orbit," the woman responds in a professional manner and fades from view.

Emcee, the freighters onboard AI, smoothly powers up the big Pratt and Whitney magnetoplasma thrusters, slowing the ship and letting Luna's gravity pull her down in a long gentle path covering half an orbit. The sudden weight gain reminds Nell of Earth. Something she doesn't welcome.

"Cullman, do you copy?" she signals.

"Yes, we copy," a voice replies amidst heavy static.

"Cullman, I'm not picking up vid," Nell says. It's unusual not to get a video signal, even way out here in the boonies.

"Yes, we are working on it. There is something wrong with our scanners."

Nell tries to ignore the static and comes to the conclusion it is a female voice responding to her. But she doesn't really care, anxious to land and get this over with. Even at this remote outpost she dreads human interaction, wanting nothing more than to make the delivery and get out. Her schedule has her picking up a load at Kyoto in a few hours then on to Taurus Colony and she doesn't like being late.

As Evolution's Child follows her preordained flight path down towards the surface, Nell links to an outside scanner, placing its feed within her visual where normally the outpost's flight officer would have been. She watches Luna's rough surface get closer and faster, even though the freighter is slowing rapidly. Nell is familiar with this optical illusion, but that doesn't stop her from glancing nervously at the flight path display. Landing beacon signal strength is nominal and Emcee has them between the white lines.

Nell leans her head back, closes her eyes and forces slow deep breaths, feeling the tension slip away. The pitch of the big engines rises and holds steady during the last two minutes of the decent. Nell peeks at the gravity meter as it inches upward until it stops at just under seven G's. Her hammock wouldn't protect her if it went much higher and she is always careful to maintain a good margin of safety.

The freighter's vibrations increase in step with the engines power curve, reaching a crescendo and holding but never seeming to strain. Nell is impressed with them, more then she had been with the energetic young engineer who had supervised the refit back in the shipyard. He had been correct in at least one area, these engines are sweet!

With her teeth threatening to vibrate out of her head, she concentrates on trying to feel the bump as the massive landing struts touch the surface. Once again, she fails. Her stomach gives a little lurch as the weight suddenly evaporates at engine shut down, her ears ringing in the heavy silence.

"Another perfect landing, Emcee," Nell congratulates the AI.

"Thank you, Nell!" she responds brightly.

Nell snaps open the four point harness and climbs out of the hammock moving with confidence born of familiarity in the lunar gravity. She is already in her vacsuit minus the helmet, a standard General Dynamics model used by most orbital construction workers two decades ago. Using technology long since surpassed, it's still serviceable, rugged and comfortable over long periods of time. Its major drawback is it's only lightly armored, capable of withstanding only low-mass low-velocity impacts, and has no electromagnetic shielding. Pretty much anything will punch a hole in it including radiation if she should happen to run in to any.

The other accessory not standard issue is the pistol holstered around her waist. Not a modern high-energy beam weapon but an ancient projectile piece, something her dad or granddad would have carried at the turn of the century. A Glock Model 22 with fifteen 40 caliber rounds in its magazine, in perfect condition right down to its laser sight.

She checks her air once more before slipping on the Duraglass bubble helmet, "Emcee, do you read?" she asks. The clear reflection-free helmet is a throwback to a time when people didn't trust the vision technology built into the newer headgear. Her helmet had been refurbished just last year and the sun shade has only a few scratches in it.

"Loud and clear, Nell," the AI responds cheerfully. "The customers are waiting outside. It seems they are anxious to get unloaded."

"Humph," Nell grunts. That's fine with her, the sooner she gets started, the sooner she can leave.

Evolution's Child has landed on a flat plain about a quarter mile from Cullman. Emerging, Nell pauses on the metal grate catwalk that extends around the periphery of the freighters pilothouse, her helmet turning golden in the sunlight. From her vantage point about twenty feet above the surface, Nell can see most of Cullman outpost and concludes it is not much to look at. Several buried Quonset huts serve the prospectors as living quarters. A large open canopy provides sunscreen for a work area with smaller non-pressurized sheds around it. Crates and assorted equipment are scattered around the canopy in seemingly unorganized mayhem. Under the canopy is a high speed rover with its power plant removed and hanging from a cherry picker. A prospector's mobile drilling rig sits at the edge of the outpost.

Parked on the lunar surface below Nell are a general purpose rover and a construction utility vehicle (CUV) with its crane locked down in the stowed position. Three armored figures send vibrations through the catwalk as they ascend the freighters access ladder. Nell cannot see their faces. They are hidden behind helmets that do not transmit the wearer's expression. Instead, she sees two bulging sensor arrays, one at each apex of a long and narrow triangular face making them look like the praying mantis she had seen in her garden back in Tennessee years before, only much bigger.

She has seen these vacsuits before. They are Brotherhood standard issue. Rumor has it that the multifaceted sensor arrays provide 360 degree visibility. But she still thinks they look like insects.

First it is uniformed controllers at Luna Central, now these bozos are wearing combat vacsuits to unload her freighter. The last thing she wants to do is get embroiled in Republic politics. She longs for deep space and solitude.

Two of the figures continue upward to the cargo area. The third walks down the catwalk towards Nell. Strangely reminiscent of a feudal knight, his vacsuit is covered in composite armor plate like scales on a fish. The man is roughly a foot taller and a hundred pounds heavier than Nell's five-five and one-ten, hidden behind a vacsuit that outclasses her simple construction rig.

From over the common channel, "We unload the ship," says a deep male voice with a heavy accent. "You come with me. Commander Ghafour waiting for you."

"Thanks but no thanks. I will supervise the unloading of my ship first. Then if I have time we can socialize," Nell responds. Even in her withdrawn state of mind, every alarm bell is clanging. Pushing her foreboding aside, she knows it is impolite to be greeted in full combat gear let alone for them to climb into the cargo hold without so much as a by-your-leave. As she moves by the suited figure he reaches out and grasps Nell's arm. Fear grips her as she realizes just how precarious her position is at that moment. The armored suits power assist could easily crush her arm.

"You come with me!" The accent becomes even more pronounced as the man becomes agitated.

"Pilot Goddard, this is Commander Ghafour," declares a second male voice, his accent smoother and more refined. "Please accept my hospitality. I have a few things to discuss with you. My assistant will bring you back to your ship as soon as we are finished."

"You can begin by telling this bozo to release me!" Nell flares, anger feeding on her fear as pain shoots up her arm.

"Captain, release her."

The iron grip relaxes and Nell steps back, her arm throbbing. This is starting out as the worst delivery she has ever made.

"Look, I just want to get unloaded, take on some fuel and get out of here. Nothing more," Nell explains, watching as two more bug-eyes climb past the catwalk heading towards the cargo bay overhead.

"And you shall in record time with the help of my men," Commander Ghafour responds affably.

"This is my ship and I will be in charge of unloading her. I packed this load and I know how it should be unpacked," Nell informs the Commander in a firm tone.

"That is not necessary, I assure you. My men know what they are doing and will work faster if you let them do it without your, shall we say, help." His voice is condescending and confident. And he has Captain Shithead looming between Nell and the cargo access ladder.

Nell decides to try a different tack, "The flight plan calls for twelve thousand pounds of fuel to be provided here. Where is it?" Nell asks.

"The tanker is in the compound waiting for the cargo to be unloaded. Now, go with the Captain." Commander Ghafour is quickly running out of patience. He is accustomed to people jumping when he speaks.

"I always supervise the unloading of my ship! I am not …" Nell is angry and more than a little concerned that something is very wrong here.

"Captain!" Commander Ghafour snaps.

Nell has no chance as the man reaches out and grasps both of her arms right above the elbows, easily lifting and flinging her over the metal rail of the catwalk to the lunar surface twenty feet below.

"What the… Hey! Damn you!" Nell calls out before landing flat on her back with a thud and whoosh of escaping breath clearly heard over the comm net. She bounces once and comes to rest in a crumpled heap face down in the dust just a few feet from the rover.

As Nell struggles to catch her breath, feeling as if a five hundred pound gorilla were sitting on her chest, the rover side panel opens and another bug-eye emerges, his combat boots raising puffs of dust just inches from her face.

She hears a wicked chuckle, "*You have a way with women.*" Her visor automatically translates the Arabic.

Nell is dazed and gasping for breath, but she still has the presence of mind to do a quick inventory of her condition. She is relieved when she doesn't find anything broken.

"*Shut up and load her in the rover!*" The Captain responds, clumsily backing down the freighters access ladder to the ground.

Nell watches helplessly unable to move as the feet of the second soldier disappears from sight. She feels him jerk her pistol out of its holster before picking her up by her vacsuits hard points, behind the neck and at the base of the spine. The man easily lifts her in the lunar gravity and carries her to the rover where he unceremoniously flings her through its door like so much cargo.

Nell hits and rolls to the back of the space managing to face forward when she comes to rest. From there, she watches the second man climb into the driver's seat while Captain Shithead takes a position facing her. She wishes she could see his eyes.

Nell feels the vibrations increase as the rover powers up and lurches forward. She still hasn't moved and lays sprawled on the floor of the small cargo bay recovering from the fall, her body starting to ache as the shock wears off. That fall would have killed her on Earth; here it just made her wish she was dead.

"*Put her in the tool shed?*" the Captain asks.

"*Of course! Why else did you prepare it!*" Commander Ghafour snaps irritably. "*Make sure she has air. I want her alive!*"

"*Yes sir!*" the Captain responds. The men don't even try to hide from Nell what they are saying, communicating freely over the common frequency in Arabic. Maybe they don't realize her visor can translate.

"Did you see what she was packing?" the driver asks over his shoulder. "*It's an old gunpowder type pistol.*" He holds it up for the Captain to see.

"*Bring it to me!*" Commander Ghafour interjects. He doesn't bother elaborating for his men, it is enough they know his wishes and move promptly to fulfill them.

The rover stops alongside a non-pressurized metal shed. The driver climbs out and goes to the touch panel outside the door. Quickly he enters a code rendering the inner panel useless. The door swishes open as the Captain emerges from the rover carrying Nell who still appears to be stunned.

Walking into the shed the Captain drops Nell to the floor and gives the interior a quick look, opening and closing cabinets and storage locker. He had told his men to clean it out but sometimes they slack off and it's his butt if something goes wrong.

"*Is the shed completely empty?*" the Captain asks. He opens a few more cabinets doing a quick spot check.

"*Yes Captain,*" the soldier responds dryly.

"*And the panel is locked out?*" he asks.

"*Yes Captain, everything is set. She cannot leave here,*" the man reassures his doubting superior.

Nell still hasn't moved and is apparently unconscious. The Captain stops and, using his toe, roughly rolls her over on her back. He leans down twisting her arm to expose the small panel at her wrist. Popping it open, he looks at the suits readouts, making sure she is alive and has air. He couldn't care less about any possible broken bones or concussion she may have suffered but he does care that she is breathing when Commander Ghafour calls for her. Almost as an afterthought he removes the fuel cell that powers her communications isolating her as completely as any human in history.

With one more look around, he waves his men out the door leaving Nell sprawled on the cold stone floor.

****

Skylor flexes his shoulder, rotating it as he comes down the ramp, trying to relieve an itch right between his should blades. Failing, he pushes the annoyance to the back of his mind, hoping it will go away. Beside him is Lieutenant Hugh O'Reilly and pulling up the rear are officers Joey Parker and Dana Monroe. Dana had lost two people in her immediate family in the hospital bombing, her mother Lori and her sister Francesca, the oldest of Lori's six kids. She didn't have to be here. But it was her time in the rotation and she is determined to do everything she can to prevent anyone else dying. Everyone agrees it's better for Dana to be doing something positive than brood on things she can't change. Life must go on.

The four emerge from the ramp on the south side of Sherwood Commonway. The eastbound slidewalk directly in front of them has a scattering of drifters along its edge. Their view of the west end of this section is partially blocked by an overpass and several large trees but the east looks down on a space dominated by a forest of massive oaks. The trees are everywhere, towering above the overpass and providing a solid green canopy for the slidewalks that weave in and out amongst the feet of these majestic life forms. Grass and shrubs give the landscape a manicured park-like atmosphere complete with a babbling brook of cold clear water that links together a seemingly endless number of small ponds. The designers of the commonway had intentionally copied the real Sherwood Forest in Nottinghamshire England right down to the plants and animals, minus the more deadly ones and those that are extinct.

As one of the major arteries in Aldrin Station, Sherwood Commonway runs east-west through the heart of Lincoln County and along the edge of Dakota warren. Heavy traffic is normal any time of the day. While giving the black and tan figures a wide berth, the pedestrians sharing the slidewalk are not overly concerned. The presence of police vacsuits in the commonway's of Aldrin Station almost goes unnoticed anymore.

Lieutenant O'Reilly moves briskly and without hesitation, stepping smoothly onto a drifter and guiding it into the eastbound traffic closely followed by his companions. He motions for the three younger officers to gather around as they come up to speed, "Stay sharp lads and watch each others backs," he says in heavy Irish brogue. "Searching vehicles isn't going to win you any popularity contest so be prepared for some bloody bad behavior. Rely on your training and do not, I repeat, DO NOT expose yourself needlessly. Our number one priority is to survive first contact. If we do find something, we must maintain control over the situation. That means staying alive."

"Do you think we will see any action, lieutenant?" Dana asks.

"Lassie, you know very well what the good book says; always assume you are going to find what you are searching for. It keeps you on your toes!" he says. "Now, if you are asking my opinion as to whether we will be the ones to find a bomb? How the hell should I know!" O'Reilly, a data sequencer in his civilian life, had grown up with a grandfather born and raised in Ireland and cherished many of his mannerisms, cultivating them into a brogue that would have passed in any pub in the British Isles.

"Sounds like another way of saying, be careful what you wish for," Joey says dryly. He's the youngest of the group and has the least experience.

"Aye! That it might! Skylor, you and I will take the forward position." Turning back to the other young Lunarians, "Dana, Joey, you two will cover us so make sure you stay focused! We are counting on you to be there when we need you!" O'Reilly says impressing on them the need to concentrate. "We will be relieved in four hours. So, whatever you need doing better be done before we begin duty. Any questions lads?"

Skylor glances at the other two officers, both are shaking their heads. "No sir!" he responds. They had all done duty at checkpoints but the physical searches are something new. In the past MRI was adequate for determining what was being carried. Now they had to look for themselves just because of the frightening possibility of active camouflage.

They completed several hours of VR training before getting the assignment but everyone is not yet in the groove as to how, exactly, this is going to work. Every team still deploys remote spybots that will do most of the poking around, but there are bound to be times when a soldier will need to look for themselves. Technology only goes so far. Nothing beats having boots on the ground.

"Magi, Get us to Stoneshire priority beta-one," O'Reilly orders.

"Aye, Lieutenant, priority beta-one," Magi responds.

Their speed immediately begins to increase as the AI takes control, making sure these officers have the right-of-way on the busy slidewalk. She lines them up one behind the other with O'Reilly in front, passing slower individuals and groups of citizens. The distance melts beneath their speeding drifters, trees and overpasses sail by with sudden regularity.

Skylor relaxes and enjoys the ride, linking his visor to sensors up and down the commonway, taking this time to enjoy the beauty of the oak forest around him. None of these trees are over fifty years old, yet they have all attained full height and are expected to live a thousand years.

Branching off Sherwood, Franklin Commonway runs directly through the heart of Benjamin Franklin Manufacturing District, a complex located on the eastern edge of Rim Mountain with good access to Central Highlands. It is dedicated to the processing of lunar regolith into oxygen, hydrogen, aluminum, calcium, titanium, magnesium, and to a lesser degree, iron and other trace elements, some to be used on Luna but most exported to orbital space and even to Earth as finished product. BFMD is a major industrial site in mankind's growing off world presence keeping tens of thousands of workers busy around the clock.

As the four police officers approach the Franklin/Sherwood interchange, they must slow to pass a rambunctious class of some forty junior level students heading in the same direction. The children are laughing and showing very little of the apprehension and tension that has gripped the Republic. The children pay them no mind as the officer's speed by.

Dana wishes she could share some of their indifference. But that is not her fate. She is in this fight for the duration and will not rest until the murderers who had taken her mother and sister are punished for what they did. It burns inside her.

A few minutes more and Magi brings their drifters to a stop at Stoneshire, a small village of old-English shops and pubs that lies at the eastern end of Sherwood Commonway. The slidewalk appears to dead end at the bottom of a steep valley that slopes upward to join with the arched ceiling descending from above, meeting in a large alcove a few hundred yards distant and directly in front of them.

It is densely wooded in and around the village, itself not much more than a single winding cobblestone street that snakes upward from the slidewalk to the alcove above, the buildings that line it a study in traditional English architecture.

Just beyond the shops that border the meandering main street are scores of quaint cottages, some plainly seen while others are partially hidden by vines, hedges, and other dense greenery, accessible only by footpaths through overgrown vegetation. Even further away, along the upper reaches of the commonway are more cottages set high above the village as though upon the side of a broad valley.

Several fenced in pastures are close by. In one, a group of horses stand heads down, placidly munching the rich grass at their feet, ignoring the colt frolicking about them. In another, several people are tending a small goat herd whose bleating calls echo up and down the commonway. Stoneshire is a place where Lunarians can break from their normal lives for a few hours or days, and get a glimpse of the way their ancestors lived.

O'Reilly leads his squad uphill from the slidewalk, heading purposefully through the small village towards the alcove above. Their footfalls thump against the cobblestones, reverberating in the narrow steep street. Groups of Lunarians leisurely stroll from shop to shop, pausing here and there, talking quietly among themselves. Some take notice of the four officers but most grant them privacy. The villagers demeanor is subdued, the normal laughter and spontaneous gaiety missing from the scene. The only creatures that appear to be truly happy are the birds frolicking among nearby trees and the squirrels bounding across the cobblestone street eagerly looking for a handout.

Above a nearby doorway, hanging from a small metal bracket, is a wooden sign cut in the shape of a whale with Moby Pub carved across its flank. Tables and chairs are arranged on the street just outside the establishments open double doors. A man, two women and a child occupy one table sharing a quite meal. They look up as the squad passes and their waiter stops just outside the gapping doorway and stares for a moment before continuing about his duties. None within the village are wearing visors, one of the things they leave behind when they come here.

As the policemen draw near the alcove, they can see the entrance to Industry Avenue, the largest pedestrian passage through the BFMD. Beyond it are the mouths of two secondary tunnels, one sloping steeply downward, the other with an upward angle. A warehouse with a loading dock lies to one side, tucked under the overhang like some modern cliff dwelling, serving Stoneshire and other nearby habitats.

The cobblestone street leads directly to Industry Avenue just inside the alcove. They pass it leaving Stoneshire's last building behind, heading towards the down tunnel in the very back.

"Magi, do we have clearance to proceed down?" O'Reilly asks.

"Negative, a load of water for Potsdam Reservoir is on its way up right now. But after it passes, the next convoy isn't scheduled for almost fifteen minutes. That should give you plenty of time to descend but just in case I have lodged a stop order to prevent any surprises."

Secondary tunnels are not intended for pedestrians, designed just big enough for a truck convoy and it's carriers with very little room to spare. Traffic in this passage and all others are tightly controlled by Magi and her subprocessors. They not only allow distribution of supplies but ventilate the city as well, providing air movement up and down the commonways and avenues.

"Potsdam! If it's going to Potsdam why didn't it use Franklin Highroad?" Officer Joey Parker asks.

Without a noticeable pause Magi queries the Transportation Control Subprocessor and relates the information. "Ore deliveries have South Main locked tight. The only clear lane is into the city."

"Humph," Joey responds. South Main is where they are headed. Their job just got a little harder.

Warning lights flash and the whine of the trucks electric motors is all but drowned out by the whoosh of air from the tunnels mouth. With suddenness that startles even those prepared for it, the truck emerges from the down tunnel and races across the open area within the alcove and disappears into the up tunnel, its massive carriers trailing obediently. Accompanied by the hum of the giant silicon tires on the stone roadway, the water-leaden convoy never has more than three carriers in sight at any given time, their motion a blur of speed across the alcove. The shear size of a convoy is overwhelming, but at this speed, down right frightening.

The nearby trees and shrubs are briefly whipped into a frenzy by the convoys passage. Unaccustomed to gusts of this magnitude, Joey steps back as the wall of air hits him.

Sergeant Dugan chuckles at the younger man, "What's the matter Joey, you afraid it might run over you?"

Joey stiffens and returns to stand next to the sergeant, "Just cautious Skylor. Momma didn't raise no fool!" Severe weather is nonexistent in the Lunarian cities. Joey has never seen lightening flash or experience thunder. His idea of a storm is the daily rain shower in a commonway or mall arboretum.

Within a few seconds all fifteen carriers streak past and quiet descends once more on this quaint little village at the edge of the city. Air continues to flow from the tunnel providing a gentle breeze for this end of Sherwood Commonway.

"Come on lads, let's get a move on. I don't like being in this tunnel any longer than necessary," O'Reilly says leading them down. He calls everyone lads, unless he is talking directly to a woman.

Far below the habitats and commonways are the cities recycling facilities and distribution tunnels. These tunnels can be categorized into two distinct sections; one pressurized and the other open to vacuum. The pressurized portion doubles as the cities ventilation system and consists of primary tunnels that crisscross beneath the city, their width allowing for passage of two convoys side to side, and secondary tunnels, wide enough for only a single convoy. Secondary tunnels branch upward to warehouses providing both storage and distribution points for the habitats immediately around them. It's an elegant system that separates much of the messiness of maintaining a city from its inhabitants.

Separating the two sections are huge airlocks designed to shorten the time it takes for convoys to pass through while minimizing air loss. With an inner chamber designed to accommodate a full fifteen carrier convoy, the airlocks are shaped to be an almost exact fit, thus reducing the evacuation time when cycling out of the pressurized section.

No manual driving is allowed in either section. All movement is controlled by the city's Transportation Module, one of Magi's subprocessors whose sole purpose is to maintain safe and efficient flow within the system. The only exception is the tunnels under Little America. They are controlled by shortimers.

Moving rapidly downward in long loping strides the officer's waste little time, descending far below the city.

"Magi, what's the current status," O'Reilly requests as they near the bottom. This is where their secondary tunnel branches from a primary, one of many arteries in a vast system that facilitates the mass movement of goods and supplies within Aldrin Station.

"You are scheduled to relieve the squad on duty in eleven minutes, fourteen seconds. They report nothing out of the ordinary but there have been tempers flaring due to the slow down," Magi responds.

Less than a hundred yards away is the massive inner doors of the nearest airlock, one of the cities main portals into the pressurized transportation tunnels below Lincoln County. Cut into the stone above the airlock are the words, South Main Access Portal.

"Ok… let's keep it moving lads!" without breaking stride, O'Reilly leads them onto a narrow raised walkway that runs along one side of the main passageway. Using his visor he is able to see the convoy currently on its way through the airlock, another load of water headed for Potsdam Reservoir.

As the officers make their way along the walkway, Joey wishes there was a rail or something between them and the volume soon to be filled with another of the massive convoys. He deals with his fear by staring at the back of Skylor's head.

With a loud clank the heavy airlock door breaks down the middle with each half swinging ponderously towards the wall. Through the ever expanding doorway they can see the truck waiting on the other side. Before the doors reach full extension, the powerful vehicle begins to accelerate, moving slowly at first but picking up speed. The officers flatten themselves against the stone watching as it goes by, feeling the wind stir with its passage, not moving until all fifteen carriers have passed. They easily scamper through before the doors have time to shut, making their way rapidly through the inner chamber and coming to a matching set of doors at the far end.

Before committing them to vacuum, O'Reilly gives his officers a quick functional test. With a flick of his hand he touches Joey's icon. The vital signs of the young officer expand from a small graph to dominate his display. Joey's heart rate, respiratory condition, and blood oxygenation are just a few of the biological measurements taken and reported to the lieutenant by the young Lunarian's vacsuit. Even detailed data on the mechanical health of the suit itself is displayed. O'Reilly quickly scans each officer's readings, including his own, finding everything in the green. He is pleased to see that Skylor has done the same thing, double checking his work. You can't be too careful when it comes to vacuum.

One at a time, the officers pass through the small service airlock set alongside the much larger main portal. On the other side, a short distance away, South Main branches from a massive access tunnel, one way leading to the surface more than a mile away and the other to the ore chutes feeding the refineries in the Benjamin Franklin Manufacturing District. This location was selected because it lets them inspect cargo destined for both the pressurized and non-pressurized portions of the transportation system with one checkpoint.

As they approach they observe the squad they are relieving. Two officers are inspecting the hold of an enclosed cargo carrier while the other two are keeping their weapons at the ready, watching from a distance.

O'Reilly stops his officers outside the perimeter of the checkpoint, watching and listening to the team they are replacing open containers and rummage about inside.

"There are several more crates in here."

"Right, Lt. I'll come give you a hand."

A minute later, "Clean! Just like the rest of them!"

The two officers leap from the carrier waving it on. They approach Lieutenant O'Reilly and his squad.

"'bout time you showed up! Four hours of this is enough to drive a person nuts!"

"Greetings Lieutenant Meyers," O'Reilly says, not wanting to listen to his complaints.

"Nothing but a waste of time, if you ask me. What we should…"

"I hope I have the same problem," O'Reilly cuts him short. "You are relieved Lieutenant. But before you go, is there anything you might add to the training we just received?"

"Aye, switch off the two inspectors every other truck or so. Keeps everyone awake!"

"A reasonable suggestion. Thank you," O'Reilly says. He cannot see the end of the long line of convoys waiting to clear the checkpoint and enter the city. Virtually all of them are ore carriers destined for the smelters in the BFMD. Over seven hundred convoys a day feed the industrial complex with fully half coming through this access tunnel. This incredible traffic jam leaves the tunnel's left lane open, the one branching into the city's pressurized tunnels, giving the officers room to inspect the ore carriers. Well, the job wasn't going to get done if they just stood around. "Come on lads, let's get started!"

****

The question of what role the moon plays in human history has been around since the first ancestor looked up with enough accumulated knowledge to ask it, one of the oldest debates in mankind's quest for understanding. At one time or another, the moon has been blamed for foul weather, bad politicians, crop failures, girl babies and many other equally ridiculous assertions. A medieval book attributed it as the land of demons while another claimed it was the face of God. Only in the last century has mankind been able to go there and take a nice close look, first sending machines then going themselves. In the late 1960's the Lunar Orbiter series visually mapped the surface down to a resolution of six feet in preparation for the Apollo lunar landings, which themselves returned over 900 pounds of rock samples from six different sites. In 1994 Clementine orbited Luna 300 times while re-mapping the surface and refining the data using the next generation of remote sensors. During its two month voyage it discovered ice at the lunar South Pole. Four years later Lunar Prospector provided global maps of elemental distribution on the lunar surface using a Gamma Ray Spectrometer (GRS) and a Neutron Spectrometer (NS). In the early decades of the 21st century the Badger series of lunar landers, robust remote controlled prospectors using an ever expanding variety of instruments and tools, paved the way for the manned expeditions that followed, culminating in the establishment of Shennong in 2016, Kyoto in 2021 and Aldrin Station in 2024.

Over the next seventy years the Lunarians steadily added to the knowledge of what the moon is made of and developed detailed maps as to where it is. All over Luna robotic explorers burrowed thousands of feet down allowing them to chart the distribution of minerals and ice, not only on the surface, but deep within the crust.

The Central Highlands is one of the most intensely studied regions on Luna. Consisting of blowout material from four major craters, it is over eight-thousand feet thick in spots and a rich source of ancient ice suspended within the rock, some ore as high as forty percent water crystals. This ice is 4.3 billion years old, trapped in the original cataclysm that ripped the moon from the Earth, later brought close to the surface by the giant meteor impacts that made Alphonsus, Albategnius, Arzachel, and Ptolemaeus craters. Autonomous robotic miners chase veins of ice for many miles. Heating is done at the mine head to separate the water from the rock before transporting the precious liquid by convoy. Pipes to pump the water are only practical over short well-protected routes due to temperature fluctuations on the lunar surface ranging from -275°F to +280°F.

Regolith, the powdery layer of material pulverized by the bombardment of micrometeorites over an unimaginable long span of time, averages sixty-six feet deep over much of the Highlands. In some places it is composed entirely of anorthite, a mineral consisting of aluminum (Al), calcium (Ca), silicon (Si) and oxygen (O), with the chemical formula of $CaAl_2Si_2O_8$. Strip mine operations go after the richest regions using either draglines or bucket loaders to harvest the ore. These huge machines, made entirely from metal smelted in the BFMD, pull in and store the powdery regolith in enormous bins. When full, convoys pull under them and fill up. A standard fifteen carrier ore convoy can provide enough tonnage to keep a typical refinery busy for a day.

Dakota freehold operates Falconhead, the largest anorthite refinery in the BFMD. This put it close to the supply of raw material coming in from the Central Highlands and far enough away that if the unthinkable happened, it wouldn't take the city with it. Of the many items produced at Falconhead, Calconn superconductor cables and wires are its signature product line, a material in high demand back on Earth.

It takes many layers of organization to keep the Calconn production and delivery system functioning, something Homo sapiens perfected over the last 200,000 years. A key element of the raw material procurement phase is getting it to the refineries in a predictable and timely fashion. Several independent companies provide this service delivering anorthite and water from mines all across the Central Highlands to refineries and smelters in the BFMD. Among these, Surface Master Trucking is by far the largest. SMT's headquarters is located in Little America, a shortimers enclave within Aldrin Station that takes full advantage of the privacy provisions in the Treaty, keeping their activities safely away from the prying eyes of the Lunarian police.

But SMT is more than just truck convoys roaming across the Central Highland's gathering ore and water. The company maintains re-supply points in many of the distant mine facilities, Far Point being the largest, and its contribution to road building is substantial. In some cases, SMT vehicles comprise over 95% of a roads usage. Thus, the company is responsible for maintaining a vast system of improved roads, some more than others, that encompasses over 35,000 square miles, roughly the size of Indiana in the old United States. Road crews far outnumber truck drivers.

From his sitting position Commodore Abu Bakr looks up at Malik standing a few feet away, his helmet tucked under an arm, and asks. "*You are sure they suspect nothing?*" he asks in Arabic. He sips from a glass of wine imported at great expense from the vineyards of his native Turkey. His own battle helmet sits on the heavy stone table beside him, the half empty wine decanter next to it.

Malik shrugs, "*They suspect everything and nothing. They are jumpy from the hospital bombing but that is what was intended? Yes? Get them to spread themselves thin?*"

"*...and our men are ready?*" A coil of the Commodore's dark curly hair hangs down above his right eye as he turns and locks his gaze on Malik.

"*Yes Commodore. The men are more than ready! They are tired of driving trucks for the infidels!*" Malik growls. His official rank within the army is captain but very few use it in addressing him. He preferred it that way, just as long as they obeyed his orders.

"*And the packages are on schedule? Are you prepared to unload the ship when it arrives?*" Commodore Bakr asks stroking his short beard.

Malik grimly nods his head, "*The devices will immediately be brought here and loaded on the trucks. The task force commanders are all true believers and understand how and when to use the weapons.*"

"*Allah be praised,*" Commodore Bakr says softly. "*I pray you are right.*"

From his office balcony overlooking the habitats huge central floor, the Commodore can see hundreds of trucks and their ore carriers spread across the vast space. Those in the center have men and machines swarming over them busily making modifications. Far more are parked along each wall, their alterations complete. Normally, there are only a few dozen in here at a time, but today isn't normal. SMT drivers from all over the Highlands have converged on Little America bringing in most of the companies 22,520 employees and all of its trucks. Another 18,125 soldiers have been smuggled in from Al Fahad. They are in nearby habitats preparing to board the convoys and go to war. Soon all will be ready.

Over the last two years, SMT's entire fleet of two-hundred trucks has had their power producing capability substantially increased. Under maximum current draw their high capacity fuel cells can produce over 10 megawatts. A typical convoy uses only a fraction of this energy, leaving the remaining for the electromagnetic shields and a pair of disrupters. The city's defensive emplacements along the top of Rim Mountain are the only weapons the Lunarians have that can match the power of these guns. The finished trucks bristle with armament and raw power. They are the main battle tank of the coming conflict.

Here and in other facilities under their control, over eight-hundred carriers have been modified, redesigned to maximize the transport of humans, not ore, each capable of holding fifty soldiers and their equipment.

Small quick rovers with more disrupters mounted upon them are scattered among the transport convoys. These are spindly vehicles designed for lunar gravity. Four paddle type balloon tires and a telescoping suspension allows them to run on both the compacted soil of the roads and the fine powdery regolith found virtually everywhere else. Known as Rugbys by the Lunarians, these non-pressurized two-seaters are designed for speed, not comfort.

****

Commodore Bakr walks briskly down the middle of the habitat's main floor with Malik at his heels, checking personally that his orders are being carried out to the letter. The clank of metal against metal, and metal against stone join the whine of overhead cranes and power tools filling the habitat with sound. The soldiers are either lounging outside the carriers or futzing around the rovers, their gear already stowed. Everyone has their battle helmets off enjoying one last respite. Nobody knows how long they will need to wear them and many are eating and drinking.

Halfway down the long central floor, the Commodore hears the boisterous cries of men fighting and the sharp ring of steel striking steel. It comes from the center of a large contingent between two of the finished trucks. The soldiers have their backs to Commodore Bakr and Malik as they approach, intent on the action before them.

"*Make way!*" barks Malik in Arabic.

The soldiers, suddenly realizing their commander is present, scramble to make a path. Commodore Bakr and Malik walk boldly into the makeshift arena where they find two men circling one another, each swinging the curved steel of a scimitar. Hearing the commotion of the arrival, the larger of the two fighters glances furtively over at the men, recognizing Malik and the Commodore. That is all the opening his smaller opponent needs. Quick as a striking cobra, the man's sword leaps out striking the other just above his armored shoulder. The blade bites deep into the exposed neck. With a gurgling sound and a gush of blood, the man slumps to the cold stone floor.

"*Basayev!*" Malik roars, leaping forward to kneel beside the fallen soldier. Instantly knowing there was nothing left to do for him, he was with Allah. The blade had sliced through the jugular nearly severing his spine. He was dead before he hit the ground.

Standing and facing the young Muslim, Malik makes sure he is beyond the reach of the scimitar, "*You fool! We are preparing for battle and you kill one of your comrades!*" Rising in a low rumble from deep in his chest, Malik's voice is hard as the cold steel in Basayev's hand. His own hand rests lightly on his pistol and calmness descends upon him, the quiet before the storm.

"*It was an accident!*" the young man growls back defensively while blood drips from his sword, pooling on the stone beside his foot. The chemical rush of making a kill flows through him like an electric current. He is slow to recognize the threat Malik represents.

"*If you weren't the grand nephew of the Caliph, I would kill you myself!*" Malik says in the same tone, his body tense and ready to fulfill his promise.

"*I tell you, it was an accident!*" the young man repeats vehemently but without any conviction. The look on his face is one of scorn and violence with no regret. He will remember this insult. No one talks to him in this way and lives!

"*That is enough Captain,*" the Commodore says from behind him. He realizes what is about to happen even if this brash young aristocrat didn't and reporting the death of his nephew to the Caliph isn't something one does if they value their life.

With a disgusted snarl Malik says, "*Go back to your unit and prepare to fight! Allah willing, you will be killed during the coming battle!*" Malik keeps his eyes on Basayev and his hand near his pistol as the young man wipes his scimitar of blood, grins and walks away. Turning to the gathered soldiers he orders. "*Go! All of you! Return to your units! May Allah grant you victory!*"

Malik watches as the men scuffle away, many with fierce hard stares promising revenge against the young Basayev, nephew or not.

Commodore Bakr comes forward to stand beside Malik. "As you say, Captain, the men are more than ready to fight!" he says coldly in perfect English.

Two hundred yards away the main airlock opens and another truck rolls through pulling four carriers. A floor worker guides the vehicle to a clear spot. Seconds after it stops, men and equipment pour out of its interior, while others converge and begin adding armament, preparing another killing machine for the coming harvest.

****

Nell grits her teeth, rolls over on her stomach and struggles to her knees. Reaching out she grasps a machinists vice mounted on the edge of a workbench and heaves to her feet. Leaning over the bench top, bracing herself with hands splayed wide, she stands motionless until her head stops spinning.

"Emcee, do you read?" Nell asks. At this distance it would be a miracle if her visor can communicate with her ship. Visors aren't designed for long range. She isn't surprised when it remains silent.

Opening up the panel in her right wrist, she inspects the unit. Without the power cell she has no outside communications. Heard only by her, she lets out a string of expletives that would make a sailor blush. What the hell is going on!

Limping around the interior, flinging open doors and drawers, she quickly verifies what Captain shithead had been told; she can't find a single item in the shed, nothing in the cabinets or in the metal locker standing against the back wall. Looking about the glaringly empty shack, Nell is quickly coming to the conclusion that the windowless building is the perfect prison. Then she spots a small round hole no bigger than her thumb in the eves above the door and to the side. She will need to climb up on the workbench and stretch upward to see out of it.

She turns around, places her hands on the counter behind her and does a little jump, planting her butt on the workbench top. Leaning back she rotates bringing her feet up and onto the bench, moaning as pain shoots through her right knee. There might be something wrong there after all.

Opening an upper cabinet, she uses the empty shelves to pull herself to her feet without putting undue stress on her sore knee, wishing for the comfort of zero G. She finds some solstice in the fact she struggles against lunar gravity, not Earth's. The pain in her knee actually seems to get better as she limps across the workbench.

The hole was punched through the metal from the outside leaving its inner edges sharp and dangerous to her civilian vacsuit. Now is not the time to spring a leak. She presses the bubble of her helmet against the jagged opening. The size of the hole limits her visor to only one set of sensors making it hard for her to discern depth and severely restricts her field of view.

Even with these limitations, Nell can just see Evolution's Child and the CUV parked next to it. The crane is now fully deployed and already several large crates sit on Luna soil. There are figures in the cargo bay and more on the ground working in and around the now open crates. From this distance and angle she cannot make out what's inside.

Nell's rage soars when she sees one of the bug-eyes emerge from her ships pilot house, the same airlock she had used just a short time before. The grotesque figure moves around the railed catwalk and climbs up the ladder, joining the crew working in the cargo bay. He brings them something but her visors limited view through the hole keeps her from seeing what it is.

Nell leans back against the upper cabinets and takes a deep breath, calming herself. What are the facts? Her ship contains thirty tons of cargo. It was listed as mining equipment but at this point, Nell seriously doubts that. Who in their right mind would treat her this way after she delivers them a load of mining gear? No, it had to contain something else. But how can that be. She herself had scanned the crates and verified the contents. Her mind chased that fact around before finally concluding that somehow the true contents must have been masked in some way.

She turns her thoughts to the men themselves. Despite the armored vacsuits, the lack of discipline makes her doubt these men are military. That leaves only terrorists, a conclusion that Nell has little difficulty reaching in this day and age.

Without the freighters onboard AI constantly updating her visor, Nell quickly loses track of time. Over the next few hours she continues to watch as Ghafour's crew reshuffles the cargo, finally closing the crates and returning them to the freighter's cargo bay. Whatever is happening is coming to an end.

Time drags on and just when Nell's convinced herself that they have forgotten her, a rover heaves into sight, moving swiftly and silently up the hill amide a cloud of dust. It pulls up and stops outside the shed. Nell jumps down from the workbench jarring her knee but relived that the pain isn't worse. Knowing that she is powerless against even one soldier in a combat suit, she stands calmly in the center of the shed waiting for the door to open.

A bug-eye enters and quickly moves past her, making sure that the situation inside doesn't contain any surprises. A second bug-eye enters more leisurely, coming to a stop in front of Nell. Reaching out he grasps her wrist and violently twists it around to gain access to the suits control panel. While Nell grimaces in pain, he opens it and deftly installs the fuel cell restoring her communications.

"Pilot, you will do exactly as I tell you or you will die. Is that clear?" Commander Ghafour's voice informs her.

"OK! OK!" Nell nods inside the clear bubble of her helmet, feeling as if her arm were being wrenched from its socket.

"Good!"

She isn't sure if this bug-eye trying to remove her arm is Ghafour or one of his hoods. Not that it matters. Just before he releases her, Nell can't help but notice a small Black Widow symbol complete with the red hourglass painted on his armored breast plate right at her eye level.

Nell is allowed to walk unhindered from the shed. Outside next to the rover are two more bug-eyes. She wishes she could see their faces. It unnerves her to know they can see her but she can't see them. This close, their multifaceted sensor arrays eerily cast tiny golden reflections bringing the helmets to life. All of them tower over Nell making her feel small and helpless.

Nell takes the seat furthest from the driver at the back of the rover. The other four bug-eyes take seats between her and the door. Past them and over the shoulder of the driver Nell can see a thin slice out the front window, enough to realize they are heading back to Evolution's Child.

****

Nell cycles through the airlock staring at that tiny spider with its little red hourglass. Standing next to this armored bug-eye in the tight confines of the little airlock almost brings Nell to the breaking point. She welcomes the return of sound as air pressure floods back, listening to the familiar squeal as the inner door slides open.

Stepping into her inner sanctum, she is shocked to see her control room in total disarray. Electronic gear and testing equipment are strewn about and the main computer bank is opened up. A skinny dark-complexioned young man wearing old-fashioned wire-framed glasses is elbow deep in modifications and is the first person Nell has seen not wearing a combat vacsuit. He looks up and grins, flashing white teeth at Nell.

Quickly removing her helmet, "What are you doing to my ship?" Nell asks, surveying the mess from the center of the room. She quickly recognizes a second AI, its black carbon fiber case unmistakable.

"We are upgrading your AI. I could not trust our cargo to your primitive program."

Nell wheels around to face the voice. This is Ghafour! The man standing in the doorway leading to Nell's living quarters is in his late forties, taller than her with black hair and dark eyes under bushy brows. A short beard gives him a rough appearance. A hairless line draws attention to a small scar, perhaps an inch long, across his right check. Arrogance permeates the air around him.

"It got your cargo this far," Nell retorts.

Ghafour's eye narrow down to slits and his mouth forms into a humorless hard line giving him a sinister and menacing countenance, a look he has cultivated in front of a mirror for years. His tone leaves no doubt who's in charge.

"Quiet! Follow me!" Ghafour orders and turns away, heading deeper into Nells home.

When Nell hesitates she is pushed roughly from behind making her sail through the doorway and sprawl onto the padded floor at Ghafour's feet.

"Remove her visor and the suit!" Ghafour orders gruffly taking a seat to watch.

Spiderman promptly reaches down and grasps the hard point behind Nell's neck and lifts her easily to her feet. His armored hands are rough but efficient in removing her backpack and he reaches for the visor.

Nell quickly removes and gives the device to Ghafour. As spiderman continues to pull at her suit she says, "Slow down! I'll take it off!"

She might as well be talking to the wall. Spiderman continues until Nell is standing in only panties and tank top. Nell takes notice of Ghafour's sudden interest in her, like a hungry carnivore unexpectedly finding a fresh piece of meat.

In her youth Nell worked as an exotic dancer in the clubs along Harding Place Road just outside Nashville International. Back then it was an area that catered to business travelers passing through, shady operations tolerated by society as long as they were discrete. She had made excellent money flashing her green eyes up at the johns. At only 5 foot 6 inches, practically all of them towered over her bringing out either the protector or the dominator in every man. It didn't hurt that, even in Earths gravity pit, she had firm tits, slender waist, and a great ass. But that was another life, before she met James and fell in love, before moving to Memphis, before the girls and that terrible afternoon.

The medical treatments she periodically receives in Aldrin Station and Shennong not only maintained the calcium in her bones, but has left her in great shape physically as well, and Luna gravity helps even more. Nell recognizes the look that comes over the Commanders face and quickly realizes this may be her best chance regardless of how revolting it seems. Sexual intrigue was something she had been good at long ago but sickens her now. Finding this opening is one thing, being willing to exploit it quite another.

Ghafour licks his lips as he openly leers at her breasts stretching the thin fabric of her tank top. She isn't wearing a bra and Nell knows from experience what is going though his head as his eyes lock on her jutting nipples, the complex but straightforward rationalization males go through when the chemicals in their brains start clamoring for sex. It's hard to resist hundreds of millions of years of evolution. She flips her hair back and runs her hand through its mass letting it cascade over bare shoulders, shimmering in the light.

"Search everything. Remove anything that can be used as a weapon," Ghafour orders hoarsely. Spiderman immediately moves to comply. Nell can only watch helplessly as the bug-eye begins ransacking her home.

The young man in the control room has stopped and is eyeballing Nell's curves in obvious appreciation. From his seat Ghafour calls roughly in an unknown language, "*Get back to work!*"

Nell believes he is speaking Arabic but without her visor, she isn't sure. Gathering her courage she asks in her best damsel-in-distress voice, "Please Commander, can you tell me what is happening?"

"Kneel, here in front of me! No man should have to look up to a woman!" Dropping to her knees, Nell shows plenty of cleavage and spreads her legs slightly as she settles back on her butt.

Just looking at her sends sexual juices flowing through Ghafour and he begins thinking with his penis, "I need to use your little ship for a few days, that's all," he says letting his eyes roam over her body, "You will be back in command before you know it."

His silky smooth voice flows across her consciousness like oil on water, yet she must keep him talking, "Can you at least tell me where we are going?" she asks with as much innocence as she can muster, feeling the urge to puke and spoil her performance.

Ghafour hesitates for a moment, considering the many things he would like to do to this beautiful infidel. He smiles, the glaring whiteness of his teeth contrasting sharply with his dark beard. "We will make a brief stop at Aldrin Station then on to Luna orbit to a waiting spaceliner. Then you can go about your business," he promises. He is pleased with himself. After all, he hadn't actually lied.

Nell manages to hold down her last meal. Even without her visor, she knows Ghafour is lying but he is one smooth bastard.

"What have I brought you?" she asks, not really expecting an answer.

Again Ghafour hesitates. He normally wouldn't answer any questions but he is drawn to this beautiful infidel. "Specialized mining equipment for a job in the asteroid belt." His face hardens as his mind veers away from sex. "Enough questions! you will contact Luna Central at Aldrin Station and tell them this freighter will be landing for fuel before proceeding on to orbit," his voice sharp and threatening with no room for argument.

Nell flirts with the idea of refusing but that would just be taking the easy way out, "LC will need a new flight plan and the amount of fuel," Nell responds softly, a plan beginning to take shape.

Ghafour's cold smile is a brilliant white line cutting through his dark beard. He has killed many times and thrives on the feeling of power it gives him. But now he must rein in that animal instinct and use the wits Allah gave him to mold this woman to his needs.

"You will oversee the calculations and as for fuel, I only care that we have enough to get to lunar orbit. After that you're on your own." Ghafour leans forward intently, bringing his face within inches of Nell's. "One mistake, one slip of the tongue, one stray facial gesture and I will cut your head off very slowly."

His hot breath burns and makes her eyes water. She shudders involuntarily, drops her eyes and meekly nods in total submission. At that moment Nell knows this man has done it before and will not hesitate to do it again.

Ghafour revels in the power he holds over her. These western women are so easily subjugated. It was as if they wait for him their whole life, craving the discipline he brings. Again, sexual fantasy's come unbidden to his mind. His blood runs hot.

"I will need my AI to fly the ship," Nell says as docilely as she can manage.

"You will use ours," Ghafour says ogling her cleavage, watching them rise and fall with each breath.

"A new AI must be fully tested. That takes many weeks," Nell insists quietly, her eyes at Ghafour's feet, intensely conscious of his stare.

Ghafour's voice grows hard, "You will use ours! I have been given assurances that it can fly this freighter!"

Nell remains quiet, but ever so subtly, she shakes her head, the look on her face clearly says you have been lied to.

"Ahmed! Come here!" Ghafour calls.

The slender young man looks up in fear at the tone of his commander, scrambles off the floor and comes into the room. His unkempt black hair sticks out in all directions and his bushy eyebrows are knotted into a worried frown.

"Commander?" he asks softly.

"Is your AI installed yet?" Ghafour demands.

The man glances at Nell, "Yes Commander. I'm running final tests right now."

"Have you found the anomaly in the fuel injectors?" Nell asks. "This ship has three new thrusters and it took them four days to get them calibrated with my AI. How could you install a new AI without starting even one thruster?" Her voice rises slightly, "This is an old freighter with many miles upon it. You can't just come in here and toss in a new AI. It won't work."

Ghafour reaches out and grabs a hand full of Nell's raven black hair jerking her head back forcing her to arch her back, staring intently into her green eyes, "Why not, pilot?"

His breath is hot on Nell's cheek and his smell fills her nostrils. She begins breathing in short quick gulps and her pupils dilate as she struggles to hold fear in check. "Over time an AI learns to compensate for the wear of a pump and the peculiarities of a thruster. A new AI won't know any of it. The ship will tear itself apart before we get off the ground."

This is it, the big lie. But she desperately needs her own AI. It's her best, perhaps only chance to do something about the situation.

Ghafour releases Nell and leans back in his chair. Looking up at Ahmed he raises his eyebrows skeptically and asks in Arabic, "*What do you say Ahmed? Will your AI damage this ship?*"

Ahmed frowns, looking fearfully at Ghafour, "*Commander, I am a programmer. This is more of an engineering question. Perhaps we should ask Khalid?*" he responds also in Arabic. But Ahmed was born in London and spoke nothing but English until he was almost twenty. As a result, he is not considered an equal among these men and he knows it.

Ghafour cultivates fear in others, he can't help himself. It is his way of maintaining command. "*Khalid is busy. I am asking you, Ahmed,*" he says coldly in perfect Arabic. He has just about had enough of this sniveling technocrat with his fancy western education.

"*Yes Commander!*" Ahmed stammers terrified knowing that the commander doesn't like him. "*Ah... all the ships systems are controlled by the AI... and it is capable of adapting ... theoretically it is possible.*" He cannot meet the eyes of his superior.

Without her visor, Nell cannot understand what they are saying but it's obvious that Ghafour is not happy with his man. Nell dares too hope and decides to go for broke. "My AI is the original install in the ship over fifteen year's ago. You cannot replace her without extensive testing and calibration." She keeps her eyes on the floor, hiding nervousness by feigning submission.

Ahmed remains quiet, not meeting the glare of Commander Ghafour. He cursed his fortune for the thousandth time. He doesn't know the details of the mission and doesn't want to know. It is his job to set up the AI on the ship, not troubleshoot the mechanicals! He has never been good with his hands. That was the main reason he had gone into programming in the first place.

"*Hook both up together,*" Ghafour orders irritably, to him an obvious and simplistic solution.

"*Ah... sir, that is not... ah... recommended,*" Ahmed stammers out.

"*Why!*" Ghafour demands.

"*There can be only one AI in control, just as there is only one Commander. If there were two, which would we obey? One of them must be given ultimate command eliminating the need for the other. Anything else would cause complete confusion the first time they didn't agree. The system would lock up!*" Ahmed says in a rush, relieved that the conversation had come back to something he was familiar with.

Ghafour curses the incompetence around him. He holds the belief that if he had a dozen men such as himself, any task would proceed smoothly to a successful conclusion. As usual, he is forced to improvise deep in a mission.

Ghafour looks down at the lowered head of the female, feeling confident in his mastery over her. "*Remove your AI! Replace it with the original!*" Ghafour growls at Ahmed. "*Go! Now! Get out of my sight!*"

Ahmed backs through the control room door, his face a mixture of relief and concern. "*Yes Sir!*" It is not his place to question the Commander even though he is sure his AI could quickly adapt to this system and fly the ship, but his personality is too weak to make the case. It is easier to simply do as Ghafour orders, safer too.

"You shall have your computer, but what will I get in return?" Ghafour asks.

Nell remains silent, head bowed, not daring to look at him.

The bug-eye finishes ransacking Nell's home and returns to stand in front of Ghafour and behind the kneeling woman, carrying a disrupter sidearm and two power packs. He holds them up to Commander Ghafour.

"*Secure them. Go help Khalid with the package. Let me know if there are any problems, otherwise, don't bother me,*" Ghafour orders in Arabic.

Silently the bug-eye moves through the control room and enters the airlock. Ghafour rises and steps around Nell, closing the control room door. Coming back he stops behind her. She doesn't move but is intensely aware of where he is.

Reaching down Ghafour grasps Nell's hair once again, pulling her to her feet, bending her head back and exposing her neck. Thrusting his face over her shoulder, he slowly licks Nell's check right below her ear. She can hear him pant and gives a frightened gasp as he begins to grope her. Ghafour laughs coldly and Nell knows it's time to pay the piper.

****

Ahmed looks up when the door slides open, leering at the woman, hardly taking his eyes off her breasts. The odor of sex quickly permeates the control room. A trickle of blood runs from Nell's right nostril which she swipes at with the back of her hand, smearing it across her check. She looks crushed, her spirit broken, refusing to meet his gaze as she enters the control room.

"Is the AI ready?" Ghafour asks almost pleasantly from behind her. He is wallowing in the after effects of his ejaculation, definitely pleased with himself. It is a gift from Allah that she is here, available to him, giving him a jump on paradise. To bad she wasn't a virgin. But what western woman is.

"Yes sir! We haven't run any tests but that shouldn't be necessary," Ahmed responds.

"Watch the pilot carefully. She is going to setup the flight calculations. Make sure that is all she does!" Ghafour orders.

"Yes sir!" Ahmed responds watching the way Nell's tits sway as she numbly takes the pilot's seat.

Nell felt marginally better in the familiar surroundings of the control room, sitting in the command chair, the bank of controls and readouts spread out before her. She reaches out and activates the control room speaker. "Emcee, are you there?" she asks, casually letting her hands grip the padded armrest of the chair. There are no apparent controls in the armrest and the movement looks like an attempt on Nell's part to relax.

"Aye, Nell, I am here. What happened?" the AI is confused. She has never been turned off before and realizes there is a gap in her memory.

Nell doesn't look up, "I will explain later. Right now we need to change our flight plan. Access standard flight equations Z115." Being a lone woman plying the trade routes between Earth and Luna, Nell had set up an elaborate emergency system. Between the pressure sensors installed in the armrest and verbal passwords, Nell can communicate just about any command to Emcee without anyone being the wiser. It's one of the games she and the AI play to while away the long hours between stops, each trying to come up with a scenario that isn't covered. This is the first major test and there isn't any room for error.

"Roger, Nell, Z115 loaded," Emcee responds.

So far so good. Without looking up she asks, "Commander, is there a particular orbit we need to reach?"

"Two hundred mile circular orbit in Earth Luna plane," Ghafour says.

With Ahmed hovering over her shoulder Nell plunges on. "Emcee, our new destination is Aldrin Station, any available dock. Use a standard parabolic trajectory at sixty percent efficiency and economy at seventy-five. We will take on fuel for a round trip to Taurus, any available two-zero-zero plainer orbit. Ask for the soonest available launch window. Clear?"

"Aye!" Emcee responds.

"Commence," Nell says. She allows herself a glance at Ghafour, receiving a cold stare in return. She takes grim satisfaction knowing what she had just arranged for him, but she mustn't give it away. She lets her eyes drop.

"How long will this take?" Ghafour asks Nell, recovered to the point of fantasizing again, building up for another go at her.

"About five minutes," Nell answers.

"Go get cleaned up. You will need to transfer the information to Luna Central," Ghafour orders.

Nell rises and goes back through her quarters heading for the washroom. She leaves the door open giving Ghafour and Ahmed a fine view of the proceedings. Hesitating at the mirror, Nell sees the smear of blood on her cheek. Her head starts spinning and her stomach churns. She just manages to get a utility bag before barfing into it. Wiping her mouth with a towel she hears laughter from the control room.

Sending the bag down the waste chute, she quickly strips off the tank top and panties and enters the showers clear vinyl cylinder. Warm air and water droplets flow over her head cascading down her body. The little electric motor that runs the fan is ancient and makes a high pitch whine.

As she soaps up she risks a covert glance through the clear shower wall. Even though they are distorted by the plastic, she can clearly see both men staring at her. Turning her back to them, she leans over giving them a good look at her ass while scrubbing between her legs.

"Emcee, can you hear me?" Nell barely whispers, almost matching the pitch of the shower fan.

"Aye! I hear you. Please verify general order 115," The AI asks almost to faint for Nell to hear over the squealing fan.

"General order 115 verified. Authority code Nell, Z7592."

A moment later Ghafour throws open the stall door. "You are finished!" he roughly pulls her out of the shower.

Nell grabs some coveralls as Ghafour pushes her across the bathroom and into her quarters. She makes sure her tits bounce lively giving both men an eyeful, keeping their attention on her. She stands meekly and asks, "May I put my clothes back on?"

Ghafour hands Nell a towel, his nostrils flaring as he catches a whiff of her wet hair. "Yes… you must look presentable when you talk with Luna Central. Go ahead, dress."

She gives a good show as she slips first one leg, then the other, into the coveralls. Extending both arms behind her, she arches her back and slides them in, pulling the material over her shoulders. Already hard from the cool air outside the shower, her nipples rub against the thin fabric and swell even larger. She fastens the buttons up the front, leaving the last three open, displaying deep cleavage.

Nell's demeanor remains one of dismay and submission, never letting her eyes meet their's, afraid she would give away her game.

The cycling of the airlock signals someone entering. Two bug-eyes emerge and Nell wanders how they both had fit in the small chamber. They pass through the control room and enter the living area. Nell moves to stand slightly behind Ghafour, not finding it particularly difficult to act frightened of these figures.

"Are you finished?" Ghafour asks, pleased that Nell looks to him for protection, another sign of her total submission.

Both bug-eyes nod in response then begin to remove their helmets. Nell stares at spiderman and is surprised when it's a woman that emerges from under the grotesque mask. She is hard with a perpetual scowl beneath raven black hair cut short, almost shaved. The other soldier is an older man, his hair and beard salted with gray, his eyes tired and movements slow and deliberate.

"*All is ready, Commander,*" the man says in Arabic.

"*Allah be praised!*" turning to Nell, "You will make that call now, pilot." He steps aside motioning her to enter the control room.

Ghafour waits at the doorway and Ahmed moves out of the cameras field of view as Nell takes the command seat. She knows this will be the last time she will sit here and is determined to make the most of it.

"Emcee, hail Luna Central for me," she orders.

"Aye! Hailing!" is the cheery response.

A moment later, "This is Luna Central. How may I aid you?" The uniformed officer on the main screen looks mighty good to Nell. If only you were here. You and some of your friends! The really big ones! With armor and disrupters!

She jerks herself back to reality, "This is Evolution's Child submitting a change in flight plans. Downloading the new flight calculations now... I am standing by." She sits back calmly, even remembering to place her hands just as she had done before, reinforcing the notion that it is only a nervous habit.

"Roger, Evolution's Child. Standing by..."

Nell keeps her eyes on the officer as he checks her calculations, not risking even a glance at the other occupants in the room. True to form, she has done them correctly.

"Your request for fuel has been approved. I have you arriving at Hawking International Spaceport, Dock 14 in approximately thirty-two minutes. Evolution's Child, you are good for launch in T minus four minutes." Nell has always appreciated the precision of Luna Central, but in all her years of piloting, she never felt as completely alone as she did when that figure disappears.

Nell sits still for a moment wondering if she is doing the right thing. Her mind can reach only one conclusion. She is certain at this point that these men are Islamic extremists bent on some violent mission. What exactly, she doesn't know, but big, really big.

Everyone has seen the face of terrorism, the planes flying into the twin towers of the World Trade Center, the mushroom cloud expanding over Houston, countless smoldering restaurants with body bags lined up along sidewalks or in parking lots. These visions of death are part of modern life.

But it is the specter of her daughter's school bus that dominates Nell's nightmares and serves to steady her resolve now. She doesn't fear death. She welcomes it.

"Come, you are no longer needed here," Ghafour declares. He is pleased at her performance and plans on showing her how much during the approach to Aldrin Station. In his arrogance, he actually believes Nell will welcome his attentions.

Nell returns to her quarters, stepping aside as the female passes heading back towards the control room. Looking into the face of the other soldier, Nell detects an undercurrent of excitement in him, his weary eyes bright as he mutters to himself, repeating the same thing over and over. Nell tries and fails to understand what he is chanting.

"*Be still, Khalid!*" Ghafour orders in Arabic. Approaching Nell, he grasps the front of her coveralls and pulls her to him. "You did well! You deserve a reward!" he leers as more and more of her tits emerged from confinement. Nell struggles to maintain the charade. The smoking school bus burns in her mind, even as she reaches out to stroke his manhood.

****

The wail of the acceleration klaxon jolts Nell. Has it only been three minutes? It seems much longer. Nell lay unabashedly naked, sprawled on her back, calmly staring up at the padded ceiling. Ghafour lies alongside her heaving and gasping for breath. The deed had been fast and furious. Nell had made sure of that. It had not been something she wanted to draw out.

Khalid kneels on the floor next to the open control room door, his battle helmet on the floor next to him like the head of a giant insect. As Ghafour raped Nell for the second time, Khalid had cast a few furtive glances and then silently continued his incantation, rocking back and forth, touching his forehead to the floor. Nell knows now that it's a prayer and almost pities him. His expression is that of a frightened old man, sharp contrast to the menacing form of the combat armor enveloping him.

Although she had kept her eyes shut throughout most of the sexual assault, Nell knows that Ahmed had eagerly watched everything from the control room door. He is now fidgeting, looking like he has something to say but is afraid.

Ghafour sighs deeply and opens his eyes, his face glistening with sweat. Looking up at Ahmed he says, "Sit down, you fool! We are about to launch!"

Ahmed enters the living room and makes for the only other padded chair aboard ship, still staring at Nell, "Not there, you idiot! Go and sit next to Khalid!"

Nell can see spiderwoman sitting in the command chair and feels a rush of resentment. She must have let it show because when spiderwoman glances up and catches Nell watching her, she smiles cruelly, showing Nell dark gaps between her teeth. But something in Nell's expression wipes the smile off the women's face and she glances nervously down at the controls and back up. Now it's Nell's turn to smile.

"Ten," Emcee announces, programmed to countdown the final ten seconds.

Of the four terrorists that remains aboard Evolution's Child, only Ghafour had been off-world before this mission started. The others rely on him for guidance.

"Nine."

"*Commander!*" It is the first time Nell has heard the female's voice. It is harsh and full of testosterone.

"Eight."

Ghafour sits up seeing anger wash over spiderwoman as she stares at Nell.

"Seven."

Turning, Ghafour looks down at Nell reclining back on a beanbag pillow, giving herself a good view of the interior and all four terrorists. She coldly meets his gaze, contempt etched across her face. The total absence of fear shocks him.

"Six."

"*Stop the countdown!*" Ghafour yells to spiderwoman who simply looks confused and angry.

"Five."

"Computer, stop!" the woman commands in bad English. Leaning forward, her four-point harness not fastened, she frantically begins flipping switches and twisting knobs, not knowing what any of them did.

Nell turns her head and spat, never breaking eye contact with Ghafour, her mouth a hard straight line, contempt fills her eyes.

"Four."

"Stop! Stop!" spiderwoman demands even louder.

Nell chuckles coldly in triumph at the panic in Ghafour's face. "What have you done!" he demands.

"Three."

In the control room, spiderwoman goes berserk, striking the command panel using all the armored might of her combat vacsuit. The impact folds the panel in the middle, ripping it away from the wall. Glass, plastic and bits of metal fly around the control room like a hive of Africanized killer bees.

Rising, Ghafour jerks at his trousers trying to pull them back up as he heads for the control room, knowing he will never make it in time.

"Two."

Spiderwoman raises her arms for another blow when it occurs to her that the AI's CPU might be the better target.

"*Help her!*" Ghafour yells at Ahmed who simply lays his head back against the wall, a resigned look in his eyes as he gazes at the naked figure of Nell in front of him, strangely pleased that this wisp of a woman has gotten the best of Ghafour. He figures if something is amiss there isn't anything he can do about it now. He might as well enjoy the view on his way to paradise.

"One."

Spiderwoman was chosen for this mission because she had the fastest draw in the kingdom which has caused more than a little consternation among the men. She has many kills and is confident that she will be victorious on this day as well. Drawing her sidearm as she turns, her brain is already sending the fire signal to her trigger finger when the acceleration of launch squeezed them all in its iron vice.

Transmitted into the pilothouse via the massive titanium beams, the sound of the Pratt and Whitney's going to full throttle in the blink of an eye damages or outright destroys the unprotected hearing of the four terrorists and Nell. In Ahmed's case, his inner ear completely collapses wrecking havoc with his equilibrium. But he only has a fraction of a second before the acceleration has compressed his spine by almost an inch. His neck vertebra splinters impaling his scull on his spinal cord. His internal organs compact at the bottom of his body cavity, the massive heart muscle crushing everything beneath it.

The acceleration catches Khalid on the forward swing of his chant, leaning down with his forehead six inches from the floor. His face slams into the floor with the force of a hundred punches and his spine shatters in a dozen places, snapping like a brittle twig. Pain sears through his body in one blazing jolt as his heart and lungs flattens against his ribs breaking every one of them.

Spiderwoman never realizes she lost. From her standing position, the acceleration collapses her like an aluminum drink can. When her knees hit, her upper body folds back on top of her lower legs and both arms slam to the floor, the disrupter still clenched in her hand. Her head falls furthest and attains the highest velocity. She never feels her brain turn to mush when her skull impacts the rising floor, the bone itself breaking into tiny pieces like an egg smashed into concrete at high velocity. Only the skin of her face holds these body fluids, stretching and bulging into a flattened disk three times the diameter of her head but only an inch thick. There is no bouncing, everything simply hits and sticks to the floor as though it were coated with Velcro.

Ghafour makes it half way to the control room. The acceleration appears to drive him into the floor like a carpenter driving a nail, the padding providing no respite. His hip and knee joints separate as he collapses downward ripping apart the connecting muscle and tendons. He stays upright momentarily after his butt collides with the floor, one thigh in front and the other behind, his lower legs twisted grotesquely underneath his body. His internal organs compress into a mass at the base of the torso making his stomach bulge outward. As his backbone succumbs to the relentless force and shatters, he appears to spiral downward, his shoulders coming to rest unnaturally close to his hips.

Just before ignition Nell flattens and tenses her body as she has been trained. Even so, she figures she has about three seconds at this G load before the blood completely drains from her brain and she looses consciousness. The beanbag doesn't provide the support that her high-G couch would, not that it would have mattered today.

Three seconds was overly optimistic. Under the tremendous acceleration, Nell's eyes burst, her heart quits beating, her brain flattens, and her lower jaw wrenches open and slams into her collapsing breastbone. She doesn't live long enough to witness the fate of the terrorists.

Evolution's Child had been designed for propulsion components available twenty years before and was never meant to handle accelerations of this magnitude. Her light cargo and almost empty fuel tanks exacerbate the situation, further elevating the G-load. Even the most junior engineer working in the Hyundai shipyards could have predicted what came next.

The welds along the titanium struts that transfer the loads from the port thruster to the ships superstructure fail along one side magnifying the strain on the remaining supports. The fuel feed lines bend and rupture as they twist, mixing the hypergolic liquids which ignite spontaneously on contact. Systems designed to shut down flow in just such an event fail and fuel continues to feed the fire.

Emcee tries to compensate for the loss of the thruster using the remaining Pratt and Whitney's but cannot under these conditions. Systems never designed for this level of acceleration begin to fail. Evolution's Child rolls and nose dives towards the surface progressing rapidly to an out-of-control spiral.

Hypergolic fuel spewing from the ruptured lines feed a raging inferno in the engine bay, enveloping the neighboring thrusters and leaving a glowing hot plume in the ships wake. Evolution's Child never gets higher than twelve thousand feet, her trajectory a blazing arc north northwest of Alphonsus crater. A trucker plying the Trans Lunar Highway a few hours out of Summerhaven is amazed to see the burning meteor silently streak across the sky, disappearing over the horizon and onto the Sea of Clouds, leaving behind a rapidly dissipating orange contrail. The incredible acceleration lasted less than fifteen seconds.

"Man is a Religious Animal. He is the only Religious Animal. He is the only animal that has the True Religion -- several of them. He is the only animal that loves his neighbor as himself and cuts his throat if his theology isn't straight."
Mark Twain (1835-1910)

Nell's Valley

Security Chief Corso Dugan enters the Regional Command Center glancing back as the heavy airlock door slides smoothly shut behind him. He thinks of this room as the eye of the hurricane, a calm surrounded by the raging storm of reality. His troops simply call it the Bull's Eye.

The RCC is a circular amphitheater devoid of corners or angles with a large dais at its center. Surrounding the dais in five concentric rings are workstations, each composed of a large rectangular slab of clear Duraglass laid flat like a table top, its interior a three dimensional network of micro-circuitry that provides a stable environment to display huge data streams. Data mining is something every Lunarian knows to one extent or another, the straightforward evolution of the search engine of last century applied to the tremendous amount of real-time information collected today. Operators stand at their posts, hands darting over their workstations, sifting through this vast quantity of information, managing only to observe a very small percentage of the total.

It is Magi that carries the bulk of the workload. She juxtaposes the ever-expanding database of human knowledge with the real-time data stream using sophisticated algorithms to compare what is, with what was. Just as a hunter waits patiently for movement in the distant stand of trees to signal the arrival of quarry, so too does the AI look for anomalies in the data using comparative analysis, pulling out anything that requires closer scrutiny and assigning priorities before passing these tidbits along to a human operator.

Some citizens like Corso and some do not, but everyone holds him in the highest esteem, even those who disagree with him. Corso commands, not demands, respect. His black velvet voice is a common and welcome addition to any discussion, his opinions valued and decisions honored.

After a quick head count, Corso is satisfied that the RCC is fully manned. Others are linked from all over Luna but the citizens in this room are his hand-picked crew. He links and listens to their chatter as a group, narrowing his interest to a particular discussion here and there as he makes his way to the center of this subterranean chamber deep under Rim Mountain.

"Chief on deck!" Captain Ben Dugan, the duty officer, calls out. He shares the dais with Major Mallory Higgins. They both appear to be wearing duty fatigues in place of the combat vacsuits Corso knows they are wearing. Ben has an expression of concern and Mallory one of relief.

As Corso steps onto the dais, he links his visor to Magi's panoramic data stream, a seamless melding of hundreds of sensors into a single visual. He is hovering ten thousand miles above Aldrin Station, the Earth above him and Luna below, floating alone in space, the room and everything within it gone, replaced by his little corner of the universe. Tens of thousands of stars hang in the sky around him and the vast sweep of the Milky Way is a signpost pointing to the center of the galaxy. His vision carries to infinity, limited only by the capabilities of the multitude of sensors sending data to the

RCC including some of the most powerful optics ever created.

As is his habit, he does a quick scan of the Earth-Luna system and the beehive of activity around the twin planets. In the western sky is Taurus Colony, a quarter million miles ahead of the moon and in the same orbit. Taurus consists of two wheels rotating in opposite directions, each over a mile in diameter and connected by a massive cylindrical hub. With an economy based around building and maintaining satellites, ships swarm around the colony. Most of their numbers are concentrated at the two ends of the hub where the main spaceports are located. Taurus is the busiest facility in orbital space.

Coming in a close second is Hyundai Shipyards, also located in the same orbit as Luna but a quarter million miles behind the moon. From a distance it appears a spindly structure haphazardly assembled. It is a zero G facility with an economy based on shipbuilding. As such, it has grown over the decades in fits and starts, each new addition dictated by the latest project. It is the birthplace of every battlestation, frigate and freighter in the system. Corso lets his eyes linger on Hyundai for a moment. The glow of an arc furnace laying the skin of another battlestation comes into focus. He has been watching this particular project for several months. It is the first of a new generation of more maneuverable battlestations, the first one capable of breaking orbit and going interplanetary.

His visual gives everything a false sense of size, allowing him to see detail from hundreds of thousands of miles away with a single glance. He sweeps his gaze across the plethora of objects in geosynchronous orbit, orbital power stations beaming energy down to Earth, communications satellites relaying billions of data streams at once, weather observation platforms and even industrial manufacturing facilities, crowd the 22,241 mile orbit. In some places the satellites appear so thick that Corso could imagine stepping from one to the next for many miles.

Dropping his gaze lower, he notes several Stratoliner's lifting off Earth with another just departing Heavens Gate. Framed against the blue and white Earth, one of the mass drivers in LEO flashes along its length as it injects another PDM down through the atmosphere. He stares intently at the descending bundle and a moment later a list of what is aboard appears within his visual. It is a standard delivery of Calconn and specialty items.

With a flip of his hand, a virtual control panel appears around Corso's waist in a great arc, its position and size set in his personal profile. No matter how he turns or where he walks, the panel stays with him, yet he can change it or make it totally disappear with a subtle flick of his wrist. Using it, Corso activates partial visual, his fingers feeling the pressure of the keystroke, his ears hearing the click. Ben and Mallory appear.

"As you were," Corso says moving to face the two officers, "Show me what you've got."

"Fourteen minutes ago we picked up a freighter coming out of Cullman, apparently, out of control," Ben says. In complete command of the presentation, he zooms across the lunar surface to hover above the small outpost inside Herschel crater. The three watch Evolution's Child launch, pitch over and accelerate, a tiny dot spewing a contrail for the first fifteen seconds, its flight path north northwest of Alphonsus, far enough away that the defensive batteries along the top of Rim Mountain simply locked on and tracked without firing. Ben maintains perspective on the craft as it makes its last fateful flight, watching as it penetrates the Sea of Clouds until it finally disappears over the horizon. Further out on the Sea is a bright red dot.

"We don't know exactly where the ship hit, but using the data from the cannon batteries we can calculate it very accurately, assuming constant flight parameters from the last known good measurements," Mallory explains. She is a tall raven-haired, second generation Lunarian, a member of the Turner family. It is a calm professional demeanor that has gained her rank and responsibility at such a young age.

"The Fitzgerald will be overhead in two minutes and we can do a full visual sweep of the area," Ben says. Named after a ship that plied the Great Lakes over a century before, the Edmund Fitzgerald is a large capacity freighter used to move goods in the Earth/Luna system. Currently it's in high lunar orbit before heading for Hyundai Shipyards, its tanks filled with water, its cargo holds with metals and food. It would have broken orbit minutes before but Luna Central held it at the request of Ben.

Reviewing the doomed ship's flight data, Corso shakes his head in disbelief, "Look at the G-loading! Nothing organic could have survived!"

Mallory and Ben nod agreement and watch as Corso takes control of the image, resetting the time back to just before launch and enlarging Cullman outpost. He pulls data from Luna Central and quickly reviews the flight path change requested by the freighters pilot. Corso senses something is wrong with the woman but can't put his finger on the reason. Probably just the fact that her ship hadn't followed the flight path she herself had submitted is working on his subconscious. Hind sight is always twenty-twenty.

Corso expands the search for data inside the outpost itself, probing in real-time for an opening into the local network. The firewall he hits is unlike any he has encountered. None of his methods so much as dent it. Cullman outpost apparently has something to hide and the resources to do it.

"Assign someone to crack that firewall. I want to see what's going on in Cullman. How soon before we can get a bird overhead? I want an orbital sweep as soon as possible," Corso orders.

"We can divert the Fitzgerald but that would take it out of range of the freighters impact point," Mallory responds.

"No. We need that data. What are our other options?" Corso asks.

"There is a translunar shuttle coming out of Shennong in just over ten minutes. We could divert it just enough to side-scan the outpost as it ascends to orbit," Ben suggests.

"Do it, Ben," Corso commands, watching thoughtfully as Ben turns away to relay the orders to his staff. Talking to Mallory he continues. "I also want all available information on that freighter and what it was carrying, including her pilot." Corso's familiar voice sooths the nerves and inspires confidence in his people and those citizens linked from afar.

"That task is already underway, Chief!" Mallory responds, pauses a moment and continues, "The Fitzgerald is coming into position."

The Fitzgerald's sensor sweep provides a bird's eye view, as though they are flying above the calculated trajectory, marked by a thin yellow line below. The three officers watch intently for any signs of the crash as the lunar surface scrolls by.

The tension builds as they approach the projected crash site, each wanting to find the first indication of impact. It comes in the form of a long scar down the backside of a steep slope and out onto the bottom of a valley. Two thirds through the debris field they find the remains of the titanium superstructure. It is twisted and bent but partially protected the freighters pilothouse. The engines are gone, shredded into thousands of pieces, only the dense hard nozzles remain recognizable. A couple of crates appear to have been thrown clear and skipped across the surface like a flat stone across water, their points of impact visible for hundreds of yards.

All three officers began to search independently, taking full advantage of the depth of the data flowing in, each approaching the situation from a different angle. Corso finds traces of human remains as he probes what is left of the pilothouse, Ben sweeps for any electronic signal and Mallory looks at the freighters cargo.

"The site is electronically dead," Ben says.

"I've got a shipping crate that has a signature!" Mallory says excitedly. The other two officers link with her visor. From around the edges of its damaged lid, one of the containers is emitting the barest whisper of energy. But when she scans inside the crate, all that shows is a large industrial check valve, common throughout Luna in the smelters and other liquid handling facilities. It's a mechanical part with no need of an internal power source and thus, there is no reason for energy to be leaking from this shipping crate. But it's hard to argue with facts.

"Can you tell what's generating this signal, Magi?" Corso asks.

Magi runs the data through hundreds of different optimizations, comparing it to everything in her database. "Negative, the best I can do is narrow the signature down to a common fuel cell, nothing special about it at all," the AI responds.

Still, energy coming from a place where it shouldn't is cause for concern, especially in light of everything that has occurred in the last few days, Lazarus and his talk of nukes and the bombing at Lincoln County Hospital. This entire event feels wrong to Corso, and he learned long ago to pay attention to his gut.

"We need some eyes out at that crash site ASAP!" Corso whispers to no one in particular.

****

Even though he is not anxious to face his commander, Malik moves swiftly through the office and emerges onto the balcony. Commodore Bakr sits calmly watching the preparations taking place on the huge floor below him, a glass of wine in his hand, his battle helmet on the table at his side.

"*Yes! What is it?*" the Commodore says in Arabic.

"*Commodore! The freighter bringing us the bombs has crashed!*" Malik says. He dreads being the one to tell him but learned long ago that bad news is better given quickly. Being a cautious man, Malik wears his helmet just in case the Commodore flies into one of his fits of rage.

Commodore Bakr reaches for his helmet. "*Where did it crash?*" he growls fumbling at the mechanical seals before finally getting it secure. According to regulations, he should have Malik check its seal but that seldom happens.

"*Two hundred miles out on Mare Nubium!*" Malik responds. "*Sensors from our battlestation Houris tracked the ship but could not determine why she crashed.*" He feeds the vid to the commodore's visor. Taken from a position on the farside of Earth, it shows the frantic last flight of Evolution's Child, pinpointing the exact location of her final resting place.

Even though the data from the distant ship cannot be resolved enough to clearly show the fate of the cargo, the commodore immediately realizes that someone needs to go out there and either retrieve the nukes or destroy them along with any evidence. He doesn't particularly care at this point what happened to the freighter to make it crash and it never occurs to him to consider that there may be survivors that need help. His mind has moved on, weighing his options, planning what his response should be to minimize this disaster.

Turning back to Malik he asks, "*Do the infidels know of the crash?*"

"*I know not of a certainty but it would surprise me if they missed it. They have a very good sensor and communications network and the ship passed just north of Alphonsus crater and crashed not far from Al Fahad.*" Malik responds.

Al Fahad is the only major city established on Luna by the Brotherhood, forty-two years after Aldrin Station. Located in the rim of Lassell crater, the city lies 150 miles southwest of Alphonsus, well out into the Sea of Clouds.

Sheik Mohammad Abas rules the city with an iron hand. As commander of the army of Al Fahad, he is arguably the most powerful Muslim on Luna. He appears to be in vile humor when Commodore Bakr makes his call to him. He quickly reviews the vid data before raising one eyebrow and looking down his long nose at the Commodore. "*What is it you would have me to do? I cannot spare any ships to go running after your mistake.*"

The Sheik is dressed traditionally in a gray Imam's overgarment, the white dishadasha exposed down the front, and a white shora with a black egal adorns his head, all of the highest quality. His immaculate dark beard is streaked with gray. The intensity of his stare makes Commodore Bakr uneasy, instantly reminding him of the depth of his dislike for this man. It is obvious to Commodore Bakr that the Sheik will not be doing any fighting today. His men would face death without him.

"*Then send trucks and rovers! The crash site is only eighty-four miles from Al Fahad! They can be there in two hours! We cannot allow these to fall into enemy hands!*" Commodore Bakr argues vehemently, only partially succeeding in keeping the disgust from his voice.

"*I agree,*" Major General Arif injects into their conversation, immediately shutting down any further conflict between these two headstrong officers. As Supreme Commander it is his right to monitor any communications. In his arrogance he doesn't bother appearing before the two men, simply letting his tone convey his displeasure. "*Sheik Abas, how many men can you spare?*" he asks.

The Sheik sighs in resignation, "*Perhaps twenty. Everyone has assignments and is already at their stations.*"

"*I understand. But we must secure that cargo. Send forty of your men and I will supplement them with a frigate from my fleet. If I can spare one ship then you can spare forty soldiers!*" Unspoken words hang heavy between the three men. Each of them knows that it was the Minister who insisted on delivering the weapons this way. And none of them, not even Major General Abdel Salam Arif, Supreme Commander of the Islamic Expeditionary Forces, have the balls to place the blame at his feet. Too many died after saying far less.

"*As you will, General Arif,*" the Sheik bows his head in submission. Only his eyes tell a different tale, one of hatred and resentment at the interference, especially at this critical time. Someday he will deal with the arrogant dog, Bakr, permanently.

Major General Arif strokes his beard thoughtfully, "*We must arm you properly if the will of Allah is to be accomplished... I will have two warheads sent to you Commodore Bakr. You should receive them within the hour. Commodore, your task remains the same, secure the Alphonsus complex!*" Major General Arif declares gruffly. As Supreme Commander, he resents the fact he is forced to nursemaid his subordinates. They know as well as he the importance of maintaining discipline within the plan. "*Allah Akbar!*" he said dismissing them.

"*Allah Akbar!*" they echo, shooting hot glances at each other, both assuming the General is still listening. Only now, it is no longer Commodore Bakr's problem. It is the Sheiks.

"*When you have secured the bombs, send them to me. I will proceed as planned,*" Commodore Bakr says.

"*Inshallah... As Allah wills,*" Sheik Abas responds as his image fades away, his look that of a lion contemplating a rival.

****

The department's cafeteria isn't a five star restaurant by anybodies definition but the food is hot and plentiful. Brice, Corazon, Tempel, Lazarus, and Kitajima sit at a table against the far wall. The rest of Charley Company and about a hundred other police officers are spread out across the room eating and talking quietly. The subdued hum of conversation and the occasional clank from the kitchen provides familiar background sounds to their meal.

Captain Kitajima Osaka makes it a point to eat with his team as often as he can. It gives him a chance to evaluate them outside the training environment and keeping him in touch with their emotional state. He isn't interested in their personal problems but is more concerned with how well they are handling them. And he likes the camaraderie.

Brice Guyart wipes his mouth with a napkin, discarding it in the empty plate before pushing it away. At five-eleven, Brice is the shortest member of Charley Company. His clean shaven head gleams in the cafeteria lighting almost as if he oiled it, a neatly trimmed goatee the only hair above his neck. Barrel chest, broad shoulders and muscular arms stretch his black T-shirt to the breaking point. His long gentle fingers seem out of place on such a strong stocky build. A naturally dark complexion gives his classic Roman features a suntanned appearance, as though he had just stepped off an ancient fishing trawler. His mannerisms are fast and furious, as though he operates at a different internal clock speed than everybody else. Quick to laugh, he often lets his sharp tongue run wild in a mordant attempt at humor. Above all else, Brice believes he can repair anything given enough time. Without a doubt, he is one of the most accomplished technophiles in Charley Company.

Corazon Montano is his physical opposite. At six-four he stands almost a half foot taller than Brice and many pounds lighter. His friends like to rub his short blond hair, admiring its softness and annoying him in the process. A single gold loop dangles from each ear lobe. His dark brown eyes are the antithesis of his pale skin, giving him the ability to make someone very nervous with just a stare. A black T-shirt hangs loose over his lean frame, stretched only at the shoulders. Where Brice is a bull, Corazon displays the grace of a gazelle.

Brice strokes his goatee, and looks sideways at Corazon, his dark eyes sparkling mischievously, "I hear Claressa is going in to have a sex change," he says with a wicked grin. Claressa is Corazon's fourth cousin on his mother's side. Someone they partied with in times past.

"Serious? So…what happened to Con Renolds?" Corazon asks. He hasn't seen her or spoken to her in months but the last he knew, she and Con were an item.

"Con dumped her!" Brice informs the table with a snicker. "I think she's crazy to go through a sex change, but what do I know! She says the new treatments are bulletproof and that everyone should try being the other sex for a while."

Corazon grins. That sounds like Claressa, always looking for boundaries to push, "Just wait till the Federation learns about this! They may join the Brotherhood and condemn us all to the fire pits of Hell!" He's looking directly at Lazarus, baiting him in a friendly sort of way. When Lazarus ignores him and keeps eating, he turns away, listening to Brice.

"What are they so afraid of? A guy wants to be a girl or a girl wants to be a guy? So what! Who cares? It's their life and it's not hurting anybody else!" Brice responds emotionally, his hands moving as fast as his mouth.

Kitajima sits his coffee down in front of him, wrapping his big hands around the cup letting them fill with warmth, "Don't they teach Earth history in school anymore?" he asks pointedly, "Remember the Inquisition and the Crusades? Ku Klux Klan? Nazi

Germany? The Great Revival? Any of these ring a bell?" No one answers, "What do they all have in common?" A short pause, "Someone had the political muscle to shove their beliefs down their neighbor's throat."

Tempel nods agreement, "A freeman must always be prepared to defend his freedom," repeating something Grandma Abby has said many times.

Kitajima nods, "Aye! Because there's always a believer waiting to take it away. These fanatics are totally convinced that anyone with biotronic implants or genetic treatments isn't human," he says looking pointedly at Brice with a gleam in his eye. "In your case I might agree with them."

Brice grins, his eyes grow wide and he leans forward saying in a nasal monotonic voice, "I am not human! I am from the planet Luna! Take me to your leader!"

Corazon chuckles and gives him a forearm shove that barely moves him, "Knock it off, idiot! We're trying to have an intelligent conversation here."

Tempel leans back in his chair, organizing his thoughts before looking at Kitajima and saying, "Seriously, I heard the Salk Institute has come up with another big breakthrough. They claim to have changed an adult finch into a linnet." Both birds belong to the same genetic family but have distinctive characteristics setting them apart. To change one into the other means that a living being's DNA pattern has been successfully modified long after inception, something only theoretically possible before.

The Salk Institute, established in the 1960s by Jonas Salk, M.D., the developer of the polio vaccine, focused on molecular biology and genetics from its very beginning. By the turn of the century that first lab had blossomed into 57, found all across Western society. It was a Salk lab in 2002 that gave the world the first successful genetic treatment. The announcement didn't warrant much fanfare, only a small column in the Associated Press about mice that bulked up after being treated with the Institutes muscle-building gene therapy. That ancient article reported that the modified mice could run twice as fast and twice as long as Mother Nature's version. Even the mice that were held immobile, without ever being given the chance to exercise their new muscles, aced the physical tests. That success was followed by a string of decades filled with discoveries. By the late 30's there were 251 Salk Institute laboratories exploring the human genome with all the vigor the human race is capable of.

"Is that the same Salk Institute that's in San Diego, California?" Lazarus asks.

"Aye, San Diego was the original lab. Most of their facilities moved just before the Federation made it a felony to conduct genetic research. They relocated to the Republic in 2041," Tempel says.

Lazarus frowns, "I'm sure that it's still there. In fact, I know it is."

"In name only. I doubt the Federation is allowing them to do any real science," Tempel says.

"It's a restricted facility, impossible to know what they are doing. Rich people need medical treatment somewhere. Why not there?" Lazaurs says tapping the side of his nose.

Brice taps the side of his nose, "What's this about?" he asks.

Lazarus looks steadily back at him, "It means that those on top get the best medicine while everyone else is denied and told that it's God's will."

Brice and the other young Lunarians are products of their time. They think it normal that conception is no longer a roll of the dice between a man and a woman. Controlled fertilization is a well documented process that avoids unwanted mutations and guarantees desired characteristics of a lifeform at the genetic level, something best done in the sterile environment of a DNA Base Sequencer. At that magical moment when male and female fuse, the DBS allows a skilled geneticist to influence many of the characteristics in the emerging pattern. If the results are unsatisfactory they simply start over with another egg from mom and a new strand of dads DNA. Only after an acceptable pattern has been achieved is the mother impregnated with the fertilized embryo.

The DBS makes it possible, but Lunarian acceptance makes it commonplace within the Republic for parents to influence their child's sex, hair color, skin tone, height, breast size, musculature and thousands of other characteristics. They mix Oriental features with Caucasian, Indian with African, as they explore the variety and depth within human DNA. Once the pattern has been set and the child starts its long journey through life, the geneticist can only regulate the body's metabolism and overall health by repairing and restoring any damaged or degraded DNA, at least until now. If what Tempel heard was true, then even that wall has been breached bringing them even closer to a complete understanding of the computer of life and how to use it to their advantage.

"If Federation citizens are willing to put up with that, then they deserve what they get." Brice says. "No skin off my nose!"

Kitajima scowls "I still have family in Japan and Mexico City. My cousin died last May because his parents refused to allow the genetic treatments that would have saved him."

Brice looks downcast, "Sorry Captain. I didn't know."

"I haven't talked to them for over twenty years. Never met my cousin," he continues, ignoring Brice, "But that's not the point! There are many shortimers that refuse, even despise, genetic treatments of any kind, even when it's available."

"I don't understand why," Corazon says clearly perplexed.

"Because their religion teaches them that DNA comes from God and shouldn't be messed with. To them, our science makes us evil," Kitajima says, "Satan's minions or some such garbage."

Lunarian treatments have cured virtually every genetic and metabolic disease known to man simply by restoring and keeping the biological mechanism at its peak of health. Obesity is controlled with simple treatments. Cancer and congestive heart disease wiped out, not a single case reported for over fifty years. Multiple sclerosis, Down syndrome, diabetes, skeletal dysplasia, and thousands of others, all are conditions of the past.

"Don't they realize that genetic science makes life possible off planet?" Corazon asks. Born and raised on Luna, he cannot appreciate the depth of suffering that has been eliminated from human society. His generation takes for granted the general state of health that every Luna citizen enjoys.

"It keeps us from developing PCDS," Tempel says.

"What's PCDS?" Lazarus asks.

"Phosphorus and Calcium Deficiency Syndrome," Tempel replies. "When you live in low gravity environments your body begins to piss away the calcium and phosphorus in your bones until they're so soft they will break at the slightest force. Because of advanced genetics, it will be possible for you to return to Earth in a few years not only because you don't have PCDS, but because your underused muscles have been kept in top physical shape without you ever lifting a finger." he grins and winks.

"Many Federation citizens believe we shouldn't be out here at all. They talk of abandoning off-world entirely," Lazarus says.

"You don't believe that can happen, do you?" Brice asks, his voice rising slightly in alarm. "That's insane! What about us? Where do they think we should live?"

"I don't think those people want you to live. Isn't that the point you're making?" Corazon asks looking intently at Lazarus then back at Brice with an evil little grin. "They want you to die!"

"That's enough Corazon," Kitajima growls, shifting his weight in the chair. "Those are fringe elements and space is big money. But more importantly, space is power. It isn't going to be abandoned anytime soon."

"Aye, that's for sure. Earth is totally dependent on our powersats. I have three cousins working on them," Brice says relieved that Kitajima disagrees with Lazarus.

"That's not the power I was referring to," Kitajima responds slightly exasperated. "I am starting to worry about the educational system in Aldrin." Corazon and Tempel chuckle at Brice's expense for a change.

Tempel leans forward and in his best professor voice says, "He who holds the high ground is king!"

"And space is the ultimate high ground," Kitajima adds. "Every military on Earth knows they can't stand up to a modern space-based attack. A single battlestation can dominate the entire Earth. How can a surface army exist if your opponent can pound it with massive firepower with total impunity? Let me tell you, there isn't any place to hide during a space bombardment!"

"I understand you know first hand!" Tempel states softly, looking at his Captain, hoping he will elaborate.

After a moment of silence, Brice asks, "You were in a bombardment? Come on Kitajima, tell us about it." An opportunity like this doesn't come often and he jumps at it.

Corazon looks sharply at his friend, "Give is a rest Brice! If he doesn't want to talk about it, that's his right!"

Kitajima shrugs and looks around at the young Lunarians and Lazarus, "I wasn't exactly in the bombardment. I was just outside Taichung in 2036 at the start of Chinese Unification. Back then it was called Taiwan." He looks solemnly at Corazon, "It began without warning and let me tell you, Everest Class disrupter cannons are big! I could see the beams from where I was and the sound was deafening, one long thunder!" his eyes move to Brice, "I was thirty miles away but my hair stood straight up from the energy. Strangest feeling… The battle lasted for a few hours and the war all of sixteen days. When it was over, the Republic of China was one nation once again."

They remain silent, respectful of a man who had lived through a piece of history they studied in school as children.

"Needless to say, I got the hell out of there!" Kitajima says grimly. "Heard they rebuilt Taichung, but I never went back."

"Didn't you play football back then?" Tempel asks. He had been meaning to ask him about the game since he had first heard Kitajima had played, dovetailing it with a sense his captain would appreciate a change of subject.

Kitajima looks at Tempel like he suddenly has horns growing from the top of his head, "What do you know about football?"

"Not much. They stopped playing long before I was born," Tempel responds.

Kitajima scowls, "Football was the biggest spectator sport in the world for a while. Lots of money went into sports back then and sports medicine funded a lot of research. Those original genetic treatments were designed for athletes and made every player bigger, stronger and faster than anyone could have imagined." Getting a far away look in his eye and wistfulness in his voice, he continues, "No weight rooms, no running every day, no sore muscles after a long workout, injuries became annoyances, not career ending events. To be a world class athlete all anyone needed was a good geneticist and money."

Lazarus does a quick calculation in his head. Assuming Kitajima was in his mid twenties when he played ball in Taiwan, and the Chinese Unification War was in 2036. That would put Kitajima somewhere in his eighties! But he didn't look a day over thirty-five! Lazarus is stunned. He must be mistaken.

"Why did you quit football?" Tempel asks.

"It wasn't my decision. I started playing overseas in the 30's after the Christian Reformation movement forced football to shut down in the Federation. They said it bred violence. After the Unification War I decided it was time to leave and immigrated to Luna," Kitajima explains. "There's more than one ex-jock is living here and lovin' it!"

"I still don't understand why anyone would reject something that made them feel better?" Corazon asks.

Kitajima grins indulgently, "Like I said, religions consider any genetic modification to be the work of Satan, or at the very least, against the will of God. On one end of the spectrum are the Jewish, Christian and Muslim fundamentalists who want to do away with ALL genetic treatments. They actively prevent their followers from even accepting simple cures such as those for cancer or heart disease. We, on the other hand, are at the other end. Your average Luny will accept any proven procedure without making laws or attaching social stigmas. Hell, Lunarian hospitals use genetics every day! DNA's double helix is our bodies most basic metabolic control mechanism. Why treat symptoms when you can get a full cure."

"I'm with you Kitajima, in for penny, in for a pound." Brice says chuckling without the foggiest idea of where the saying comes from.

"Not only did the Federation screw its citizens out of good health, but when they criminalized genetics they created a huge black market. That's all the FBI does is chase down doctors providing illegal treatments. Despite that, new clinics open as fast as they are shut down," Lazarus says shaking his head, "I don't think the genetics gap between the NAF and Luna is as big as you think."

Tempel looks at his friend in exaggerated disbelief, "You are kidding, right? I think it more likely that you do not yet fully appreciate how far we have advanced the science. Literally thousands of procedures and treatments are available that do nothing more than restore and maintain our original DNA pattern. We consider these treatments in the same light as drugs were a century ago, something that keeps us healthy and improves our lives. To believe otherwise is silly and backward."

Lazarus hangs his head in exaggerated submission, "Forgive me master, you are undoubtedly correct. I am a barbarian from the fringes of the empire but in my ignorance I have great strength!" he wags his finger playfully at the young officer and says melodramatically, "Beware the Ides of Ignorance fore they may rise up and bite you in the butt!" He is paraphrasing from a popular vid, but they don't know having never bothered with Federation entertainment. It is considered a waste of time.

Silence… then Brice and Corazon burst with laughter, Tempel chuckles and even Kitajima grins. None of them expected Lazarus to have a sense of humor.

"I think what Lazarus is trying to say is that most people lie somewhere between the religious fundamentalists and us," Kitajima says.

Lazarus nods in agreement, "Yes exactly! It's not uncommon for a person that has paid black market prices to carefully screen their unborn child's genes for defects but is more than willing to turn in their neighbor for selecting their child's sex. I can remember an instance where this man obtained a genetic cure for heart disease but reported his sister for using the same doctor to shed a few fat cells."

Kitajima shakes his head in amazement. "If you were to meet my aunt you would think she is a normal caring human being. Her husband runs a dry goods store and they go to church every Sunday. How an otherwise intelligent person can get down on their knees and pray for a cure for their child, watch him die a slow painful death and afterward, still maintain this belief in God is beyond my comprehension, especially when he could have been cured so easily. Any of the black market clinics you mentioned before could have saved him."

"What did he die of?" Brice asks.

"Leukemia," Kitajima says.

Brice cocks his head in puzzlement. He has never heard of this aliment.

"It's a disease that attacks the bone marrow, the body's blood-forming organ. It suppresses the production of normal blood cells, leading to anemia and finally death. It's a horrible way to die, a single cell at a time." Kitajima's mood turns dark thinking about the unnecessary misery his cousin went through.

"Captain Osaka, please excuse the interruption but you have a priority call coming in from Captain Dugan," Magi says.

Thankful for the interruption, Kitajima raises his hand to remove himself from the conversation, "Please excuse me, business."

The others link to his visor and remain quiet. It's extremely bad manners to interfere in someone else's conversation but observing is expected.

"Put him through!" Kitajima says knowing, and not caring, that others are listening.

"Greetings, Kitajima!" Ben says and continues without waiting for the captain to respond, itself am indication that this is unusual. "We have a developing situation out on the Sea of Clouds. Veiw the vid."

Magi knows Kitajima's limitations and adjusts accordingly, increasing the playback speed in some sections and slowing it down in others, allowing him to glean the pertinent facts as they know them. She stops it completely on the image of the damaged crate, emphasizing the energy signature coming from what should be a benign cargo container. For the rest of Charley Company, she presents it at full speed.

"Charley Company is due to report for duty within the hour and ready immediately. Corso is reassigning you to go out there and find out what's going on. Captain Davenport will go with you for technical support but you will be in charge. Is this clear?"

"I can handle it without Lindsey, Ben. You know that. She can link when we get there. She doesn't need to go." Kitajima says.

"Corso wants her there, Kit. And you may need her engineering skills before this is finished…" Ben says.

"I should go too," Lazarus blurts out, breaking etiquette.

Kitajima turns and looks at him. "What? Why should you go?"

"I know Brotherhood hardware like the back of my hand. If the IB is involved in this, I will be able to help," Lazarus claims.

"He's right," Lindsey says . "Taking him along is a good idea."

"He's not even a full citizen yet. What if he falls apart on us out there?" Kitajima asks.

"I will vouch for him. He performed as well as anyone at the hospital. And he is fully certified for surface duty. I say give him a commission and lets go." Tempel says. Hell, if Lazarus and Lindsey can break into the conversation, why not him.

"Take him along," Corso says. "He may prove useful."

"Corso, what is it you're not telling me?" Kitajima asks.

"We think the Brotherhood may cause some trouble on this mission. I'm authorizing you to deploy as Guardians with a full compliment of weapons. Keep them under wraps. I will leave it to your discretion when to use them." Corso says.

Kitajima's eyes dilate and his heart rate increases, "Understood! How are we going to get there?"

"Use the Dragonfly that was to take you to Far Point. It's been modified for troop transport and has supplies already aboard. I'm commandeering another from an airline, one set up as a cargo ship. By the time you get your gear down to the terminal, I will have it." Ben says.

"Two Dragonfly's and sixteen officers? You sure that's enough?" Kitajima asks.

"Hack is already preparing and Doc Grady will be your med officer. Corso is working on another angle, but to be brutally honest, Charley Company all we have, so make it work, my friend."

"Aye! Make it work," Kitajima responds, anticipating the worst, hoping for the best.

****

The mood is somber as Charley Company prepares for the coming mission. They all know something unusual is brewing. Why else would they authorize ghost suits unless Abby and Corso thought they would need them? These vacsuits are the latest in a long line of improvements, not a secret among the Lunarians but certainly not a topic of conversation within earshot of a shortimer. For Charley Company to openly wear them marks a turning point of some kind, but exactly what is uncertain.

"Why don't we know what the freighter was carrying?" Brice asks Kitajima.

Letting his irritation show, the captain responds for everyone to hear. "We can't believe our own inspections because the Brotherhood might have come up with something called active camouflage which will shield the cargo from our sensors. But the real answer lies out on the Sea of Clouds, not in this locker room. Just make sure you get your suit on correctly this time, all of it."

Laughter spreads through the group at the reference to the last exercise they had done in ghost suits. Brice had not bothered to properly install his waste recovery system and when the mission went long, had been forced to pee his pants.

Tempel grins at his friend's embarrassment and opens his locker, removes his ever-present visor and strips down to nothing. Folding his uniform neatly, he places it on a shelf inside the locker.

Joining the others he heads for the showers, luxuriating under the stream of hot water cascading over his head and down his body. Around him the rest of Charley Company is doing much the same.

Reluctantly he steps out of the water, pausing as hot air whips around him, and returns to his locker. He applies lubricant before slipping on his long duration undergarment, an integral part of the suits waste recovery system, getting everything where it belongs with practiced ease. Next, he takes the vacsuit off its hanger in the rather small locker. Looking at a ghost suit without a visor is difficult because it absorbs virtually all the electromagnetic radiation that strikes it preventing it from reflecting, making it appear more as a hole than as a thing, the details that give it depth and breadth blurred beyond the edge of perception. This is a phenomenon known as black body in science where energy comes in but cannot escape. Yet, the suit is highly flexible and smooth to the touch and he adept at handling it. Sitting on his bench, he shakes a quantity of white powder across his legs and pulls the suit on making sure every joint is right before proceeding. Standing, he works his arms down first one then the other sleeve feeling the suit settle onto his shoulders as his hands fill the attached gloves, again making every effort to position the suit just right as it envelopes his body. He knows it's in place when he feels the familiar tingle as it aligns to the implant in the base of his spine.

Lifting his arms over his head and twisting at the waist, he tests the fit. Perfect.

Hanging behind his head like a hood, he pulls the final piece over his head easing it around his ears and over his face. A thicker region, stiff in comparison to the rest of the suit, closes over his mouth and eyes temporarily blocking his senses. But as he runs his hand across the gap, the two sides pull together and he feels the suit turn active as he reaches his chin. He can now see and breathe using systems built into the vacsuit. Nano-filters not only recycle his breath but are capable of pulling the breathable portion out of the most poisonous atmosphere, rejecting the rest.

Taking a deep breath, listening to the sounds of his fellow police officers around him, wondering what this day will bring, Temple continues to run his hand down the front of the suit, closing the molyseal, a magnetically activated device that bonds the two joining sides together at the molecular level creating a single unbroken piece of fabric. No part of his body remains uncovered when he is finished. He is completely isolated from his environment and nearly invisible, a mere silhouette of a person without any depth or detail, a smear of darkness that fools the eye.

The ghost suits remarkable material is woven from synthetic spider-silk, a type of protein five times stronger by weight than carbon filaments and more elastic than nylon, a combination of properties seen in no other fiber. The almost unbreakable spider-silk provides protection against ripping or tearing even as it imparts unprecedented flexibility. Embedded into this airtight fabric is an intricate and complex pattern of micro-miniaturized superconductive Calconn coils capable of generating tremendously powerful magnetic fields. The manipulation of these fields gives the suit power assist and forms the backbone of the electromagnetic shield, linking the submicron coils together at the instant of impact into a nearly impenetrable barrier. It's the 21st century's version of medieval chain mail.

Energy absorbing material completely coats both inside and out sucking in radar, MRI, sunlight, and even disrupter beams up to a point, converting the incoming energy to electricity which is dumped into the Calconn coils, charging the suit like a giant capacitor. Tempel's body heat is also absorbed by the material and converted to electrical energy. The combination of absorbing both internal and external energy sources gives the ghost suit stealth, making it exceedingly difficult to detect under any condition.

A wide thick belt with the same energy absorbent outer layer extends from the suit to enclose his waist, a holster on his right side and numerous small pockets filled with the supplies he will need to survive both vacuum and combat. As he clips the belt shut, the remaining biointerface between suit and man activates making the garment an extension of Tempel's physiology. Nano sensors monitor his biological functions ranging from the macro events such as heart and brain rhythms down to those occurring on a cellular level. Every secretion from adrenalin to insulin is noted. Every breath, every heartbeat, and every muscle contraction is monitored and recorded. Not only does it observe his biological activities but regulates them as well, with a full range of meds available, most of them produced only when needed just as his body does.

Lunarian vacsuits have long been considered the best high-vacuum long-duration spacesuits ever manufactured. But ghost suits go far beyond those. Fitting Tempel like a second skin, the suit is flexible, comfortable and equipped with extended life support. Theoretically, a person can survive for as long as the suit has power. The record is held by some whacko in a small hamlet outside Shennong, sixty-three days and change in a Lunarian vacsuit that doesn't have nearly the capabilities of these. That got him a line in the Guinness Book of Off-World Records and a chair with his name on it at his local psychiatrist. Tempel and the rest of Charley Company routinely train for up to two weeks without removing their vacsuits. Invariably, a shower is the first thing on the agenda when they get home. No matter how well the suit handles sweating, chaffing, and waste, nothing beats being naked and human.

Multi-frequency sensors are located at strategic points throughout the ghost suit. These micro-miniaturized cameras, more advanced than those in visors, digitize the world and provide Tempel with enhanced reproduction of everything occurring around him, all 360°. They pickup not only what's in front, but what's behind and even above him, compressing the information into his peripheral vision, coming into true perspective only when he turns to look directly at something. It's a way of looking at the world that takes many years to learn but once mastered, he truly has eyes in the back of his head. This complex digital image is the merging of many sensors into one coherent picture delivered directly to his optic nerve using microlasers identical to those found in a standard visor. Infrared, microwave, radar and MRI sensors add depth and richness to the data allowing Tempel to view and interact with the world in ways undreamed of a century before. He literally can see the unseen.

In a fashion similar to visors, his vacsuit links him into the World Wide Web, extending Tempels awareness through the many scanners and sensors found throughout the city and across Luna. Using those devices closest to him, Tempel can look through walls and see around corners, he can focus on the heartbeat of a single person across a crowded mall, or he can read that persons biochip like a neon street sign. The sights, sounds and smells coming in from any public scanner within the vast Lunarian network are available to him. All from an incredibly long distance away or right next door.

"Corso must think there is something very special about this crash. Why else would he authorize ghost suits?" Tatiana says. She is still tugging on her vacsuit, just reaching back to pull it over her head.

"I agree, it is unusual but I trust he and Abby know what they are doing." He looks intently at her, "They undoubtedly believe we will need them."

Tempel watches as she tugs the suits skullcap down over close-cropped black hair, waiting for her to come online. Like a wisp of smoke, the featureless black of her suit fades away replaced by the black and tan uniform of a police lieutenant. In times of peace, internal sensors within the suit routinely provide data to those around her, feeding a video signal back to her comrades of her current expression and making her appear as if she were wearing a uniform and not the most sophisticated vacsuit in the Lunarian arsenal. And visa versa, when she looks at Tempel she doesn't see a shadowy ghost-like figure, she sees him in his police uniform.

Even though these vacsuits present a formable physical barrier to the environment, they do not isolate them, far from it. Rather the officers of Charley Company are joined into a tight unit by the sophisticated networking capabilities built into these remarkable vacsuits. Each member of Charley Company is acutely aware of what the others are doing, what they are experiencing.

Last, Tempel reaches into his locker and picks up his weapon, a Model 400C, Smith and Wesson. Many believe it to be the most potent disrupter type sidearm on the market. Tempel knows better but he isn't free yet to carry the improved version. Abby and Corso want to keep it under wraps for as long as possible knowing that the innovative design will be rapidly copied when it becomes known. Tempel fired the new pistol for the first time just last month and knows it represents a major improvement in high energy beam technology. He checks the charge level of his gun before slipping it into its holster, taking comfort in the familiar feel of its grip. Closing his locker, he joins the other officers heading for the airlock, Tatiana at his side.

"One last thing. Stop at the armory and exchange your 400's for 450's," Kitajima tells them.

"Aye, now we're dealing from the top of the deck!" Brice exclaims.

"Get a move on Brice." Master Sergeant Hackling calls out from close to the exit. "Why are you always last?"

"The best is always last!" he responds, basking in the laughter of Charley Company.

****

The Dragonfly, or Boeing L250, is the most common flight transport on Luna, the workhorse of the 21st century, the backbone of Luna's transportation industry with a history that spans decades. Designed by Lunarians to haul people or light cargo from place to place, it isn't intended for deep space long hauls but can easily go anywhere in the Earth/Luna system and back again, navigating Earth's atmosphere just as easily as the vacuum of space. It's the latest in a long line of vehicles designed by a people born in space.

There is no mistaking a Dragonfly as anything but Lunarian, full of curves with a total absence of straight lines and flat planes, without a single window breaking its smooth surface. Its exoskeleton is composed of closed-cell foamed titanium, similar in structure to Aerogel, sandwiched between an inner and outer hull, designed to maximize strength and thermal isolation while minimizing mass. This hard outer shell is both insulation and the load bearing member of the design, forming a seamless melding of skeleton and skin, its thickness varies from point to point containing additional structure where strength is needed to resist the forces of flight. The geometrical mathematics of its shape and the engineering mechanics of its materials form a major part of the flight calculations the onboard AI routinely performs to keep this bird flying straight and true.

While Lunarians highly value beauty for its own sake, they are intensely practical when it comes to their engineering. Just ask any aerospace designer which is more important and they will undoubtedly inform you that minimizing mass is much more important than a sweet set of curves. And if you question them about a Dragonfly, they will assure you that its graceful lines are mandated by purely physical considerations, that its contours are the result of going to great lengths to eliminate all extraneous mass from the design. Thus, the shape of a Dragonfly directly reflects the forces at work on it. It's purely coincidental that it's beautiful.

The size of a large bus, it has two massive outriggers, like Jurassic shoulder blades, bulging under the skin of its back, one near the front and the other at the rear of the craft, the foreword span smaller than the aft. They sweep over the top of the ship in a graceful arc with a slightly rearward rake, thick and massive in the middle narrowing to slender points at each end. A workhorse Pratt and Whitney PW2065 magnetoplasma thruster is mounted at each of the four tips.

The body of a Dragonfly is basically a cylinder, flat on the bottom where it rests on the ground, with flanks that follow the curve of the outriggers, end to end, and top to bottom. A short stubby aft section accommodates a large door that hinges at the bottom and stretches across its entire width. Electromagnetic actuators open and close the door forming a ramp into the ship. The overall shape of a Dragonfly's fuselage, if the outriggers were removed, is reminiscent of a blunt nosed lifting body with a thick hump running down the length of the vehicle like a spine, blending smoothly into the top of the fuselage.

The biggest break in the smooth skin of the vehicle is the magnetoplasma thrusters. The PW2065's are nothing more than solid-state electromagnetic nozzles designed for the sole purpose of accelerating plasma to velocities approaching half the speed of light in just a few feet. They are Newton's Law incarnate where exceedingly small masses undergo extremely high accelerations resulting in extraordinarily large forces. The nozzle is constructed one atom at a time, layer upon layer, in a solid matrix containing the equivalent of over three hundred thousand linear feet of superfine Calconn superconductive wire in a complex arrangement that maximizes the electromagnetic fields generated inside the long, slender device. One end is capped by a microwave plasma generator, the other narrowing to a blunt point. The only moving parts are small needle valves metering the hypergolic fuel flowing into the plasma generators.

Molded into the nozzle is a framework of polyaloid titanium beams in a rib and ring design. About a third of the way down from the generator, a massive electromagnetic hub connects the engine to the outrigger allowing thrust vectoring through 360° in the transports long axis, and up to 30° perpendicular to it. With each thruster controlled independently, flying a DC250 is like balancing an elephant on the head of a pin.

Because of specific stipulations within the Treaty of Independence, a major element missing in a Dragonfly is shielding. According to the Treaty, no Lunarian spacecraft can be fitted with either offensive or defensive armament which includes electromagnetic shielding. Thus a Dragonfly has no real defense against bullets, missiles, or energy beams other than speed, quickness and the cunning of her pilots.

The interior of a commercial Dragonfly is normally separated into two sections, each of which can be pressurized independent of the other. When configured for passengers, the main section has seating arranged in a double row of two and a narrow aisle down the center, a layout used successfully for well over a century by Boeing that yields maximum capacity of thirty-six passengers. There are no provisions for pilots since they are not needed on a commercial flight. The aft section is much smaller and consists of a bay typically used as storage for passenger luggage and other light cargo. For strictly hauling cargo, the seats and walls are removed with a pilot's seat optional.

Designated Red for this mission, the Dragonfly is already configured for police duty, the thirty-six standard seats replaced with sixteen high G units that swivel and rock providing much better support for the occupants during maneuvers. Forward of the passengers, at each side of the main airlock, are two pilot seats, different from the others, having the backup flight controls built into them. Tucked out of sight are two old style joysticks, one for each arm rest and pedals that transmit ankle position and rotation. Under normal operations the ship is controlled through external sensors linked to the pilot's VR communication system. The three dimensional quality of flying a Dragonfly in the airless expanse of space is similar to flying a helicopter on Earth, only with the speed of a 21st century orbital fighter. It takes a very skilled pilot to fly manual for very long.

The cargo ship that Ben commandeered was initially stripped clean, no seats, no walls, and no cockpit. Kitajima had eight high G seats installed and two pilot seats. What remains of the space inside is stuffed tight with food, air and a wide assortment of mission equipment including a small four-man rover and a portable shelter. He designates this ship Blue.

Kitajima assigns most of Charley Company to Red under his direct command. Tempel will pilot Blue with Karyl as his copilot. They have flown together many times and are intimately familiar with each others skills. Lazarus and Lindsey will fly on Blue. He still doesn't like the idea of them going and wants to keep them separate as much as possible. Let Tempel handle them.

Two transports and a handful of police officers is all Dakota can spare during the current crisis. And even then Corso and his commanders feel the loss of Charley Company, scrambling to put together a team to take their place out at Far Point.

Yet, Corso knows they are fortunate that Charley Company was available to take on a mission of this magnitude on such short notice. He is conscious of the burden of history as he assigns this particular unit to this mission, the first deployment ever of the Guardians, one of Luna's best kept secrets. He wishes he had more of them.

Kitajima moves up and down the aisle of Red watching his officers stow their equipment, inspecting and giving instructions where he sees need. Others are still lashing down gear in the back of the transport. A few are already buckled into their seats.

The remains of Evolution's Child has been identified over two hundred miles out on the mare, a hop, skip, and jump for the Dragonfly's. Still, Kitajima insists on taking a full ration of supplies with extra air. You can never have too much air. More than once, a simple day trip has turned into an extended ordeal and he rather enjoyed breathing.

"Cap, the equipment is secure," Kipper reports. It's his responsibility as copilot to ensure the proper stowing of all cargo within the transport.

Kitajima nods, "Aye! Let's get this show on the road!" He moves up the aisle leaning left and right, speaking to each officer while giving one last inspection, pulling at their harness or pushing on the butt of their pistol, making sure he touches them, letting them know he's there. He never had children, and over the last three years these young men and women became his kids. They were seventeen when Charley Company formed and he thinks of himself more as their coach than their captain. He trains with one or more on a daily basis, and at least once a week he runs a full company simulation challenging them with complex what-if scenarios. It's as close as Kitajima will get to playing football again.

Starting out with a bunch of know-it-all third and fourth generation Lunarians, Kitajima coaxed and harassed them into a unified team. Many times over the years he had to remind them they were training to kill an enemy and not playing games, and now he's being asked to lead them into harms way. He's intensely conscious that his every action will be reviewed millions of times for generations to come. Every member of Charley Company is well aware of their place in history but they bear the weight easily, never having known anything else.

Temple, Sam, and Kipper are fourth generation, tracing their heritage to great grandparents who arrived on the same shuttle back in 2024. Everyone else is third generation. Brice and Jason have four sets of grandparents that emigrated together from France in 2046. Tatiana and Alonzo are twins whose grandparents came from India in 2047. The rest of Charley Company has ancestors from China, Sweden, Germany, Spain, Mexico, Japan, and South America, all of them immigrating between 2035 and 2047. They were born for this duty.

Kipper eases into the copilot's seat and straps in, taking his place next to Consuela. A quick survey reveals an almost complete preflight checklist. Consuela has been busy.

Kitajima slides into the seat directly behind Consuela, Red's primary pilot for this stage of the mission, and looks across the aisle at Master Sergeant Hackling, "We ready to go Hack?" he asks her.

They have known each other since she immigrated in 2045 and she is one of few people he trusts implicitly. He insisted upon Hack for his Master Sergeant when Charley Company formed and he's never regretted it. The path of her life isn't unusual. She was born in Houston, Texas in 2013 and was four when her family moved. Less than a month later, on the morning of September 11, the city was destroyed by a 25 megaton nuclear explosion. All of her extended family was killed. She grew up in the shadow of that horrible event, graduating from the University of Texas in 2037, working in Dallas until deciding to go off-planet. She looks damn good for a twice married woman with three grown children, twelve grandchildren and two great grandchildren. She and Kitajima have shared intimacy on many occasions.

"Aye, Kit! Charley Company is locked and loaded." A slightly elevated blood pressure betrays her excitement but it's the familiar before-mission gleam in her eye that he looks for and finds.

"Excellent," Kitajima says as he finishes snapping shut his four point harness. He links with Tempel in the other Dragonfly, seeing what he sees. "Lieutenant Dugan, whenever you are ready."

****

In the other transport Karyl flashes Tempel a thumbs-up before buckling into the copilots harness, giving him her seal of approval on the state of readiness of the passengers and their cargo. Tempel glances over his control panel one last time finding everything in the green. "We are locked and loaded," Tempel responds.

"Then let's get it done, shall we?" Kitajima says.

Tempel perceives his environment through his ghost suits VR system, fed by a multitude of sensors, some in the suit itself, and others mounted inside and outside the Dragonfly. The data-streams coming in from the various sensors run through dedicated video processors that allow electronic filters to remove any extraneous information, thereby presenting Tempel with a single view of the world around him, but one that is malleable and dynamic. Using this system, his reality becomes adjustable, nothing more than a backdrop for information to be displayed, a blank canvas waiting for the painter's first brush stroke.

From Tempel's perspective he seems to hang in space, the seat beneath him and the safety harness that holds him fast, the only tactile objects in his world. The spacecraft enclosing him is all but invisible, including the two passengers, filtered out as unneeded visual information. The ships control panel is a virtual display at his waist, its lines and symbols designed to be ignored when flying, seen only as needed. To his right, Karyl is the only other person visible and even then, the system presents her dressed in a black and tan police uniform, not in the ghost suit she's actually wearing. Technology molds Tempel's perception of reality, modifying its appearance, filtering out unneeded information, enhancing and extending his human senses in the process. No Earthly society has embraced virtual reality as the Lunarians have, perfecting it while incorporating it into the very fabric of their existence.

The long lunar night is coming on rapidly and the sun is low on the horizon, putting the craters floor entirely in shadow, making it impossible for him to see beyond the lights of the spaceport. Tempel accesses his control panel touching the visual control icon. A sixty-four band graphic equalizer appears. Small lights on each frequency mark their current setting. A few adjustments and the shadows recede. He enjoys flying at night but this is no time for a thrill ride.

Tempel approaches this mission just as he has all the others, coordinating with Luna Central as if this is simply another practice run to Scottsbluff or a joy ride to Sunset Canyon. He and Karyl are isolated from everyone else, Magi screening all incoming communication and passing it on only if it warrants their attention. Their job is to fly this ship and they don't need any unnecessary distractions.

"Red, how do you receive?" Tempel asks quietly. Looking past Karyl, Tempel can see Consuela and Kipper piloting the other transport. His VR makes them appear larger than life, closer than they actually are, their transport a barely seen shimmer around them.

"Loud and proud, Blue," Consuela responds.

"Stay on my ten. We will head straight out across the crater floor past New London and climb over Rim Mountain on the far side. I show our target just over two-hundred miles out on the Sea of Clouds." Tempel doesn't need to go over the flight path again but it is part of the preflight ritual and besides, it never hurts to be sure.

"Aye, Blue. I'll be glued to your ten," Consuela says.

"Luna Central, we are go for liftoff," Tempel says as he begins to slowly increase thrust.

Dust stirs under the ships thrusters as Luna Central responds. "You are go for launch. Good Luck!" the duty officer says.

Tempel doesn't so much fly his ship as tell the onboard AI where he wants to go and how to get there. The delicate balance between the four powerful magnetoplasma thrusters is too precarious to trust to mere human reflexes, even his.

The transports rise slowly, feeling their way skyward, their onboard AI's recalculating the balance of the loads and adjusting thrusters hundreds of times a second. Constant communication between the two AI's ensures the ships can never collide.

In complete silence, the two Dragonflies' turn as one and accelerate across the craters floor gaining altitude. This is the part of piloting that Tempel enjoys most, the thrill of guiding his spacecraft close over the lunar landscape. Below and quickly receding behind him are many brightly lit surface installations, some clustered around the main egress points of the city while others are elements of the spacedocks or far-flung mining operations scattered well out on the crater floor beneath him.

Tempel maintains a flight path parallel with the maglev rail. Coming up on his left is the Mitsuki smelter, its tanks and towers brilliantly awash in lights. A gaseous release spews skyward from the tallest stack quickly dispersing in the vacuum of space. A huge pile of discarded material forms a backdrop to the facility. A few seconds later they are past it. The maglev is also beginning to fade as they gain altitude and velocity.

The floor of Alphonsus Crater is not a perfectly flat plain but a series of undulating hills and ridges, some quite spectacular, that follow the general concentric pattern of the crater-forming impact 4.3 billion years ago. Just as Rim Mountain and Central Peak were formed in that explosive event, so too were the basalt ripples found across the craters floor. Originating at pit-like vents, lava channels and collapsed lava tubes form rills that run for many miles cutting across the ridges like a knife through butter. These fissures can be quite deep and pose a serious threat to anyone careless enough to fall in, even in Luna's gravity.

Well out on the craters floor, a bright blue light can be seen far below. It marks the historical location where Ranger 9 impacted back in March of 1965, one of the earliest missions to the moon.

The flight passes almost directly over the top of Archibald mine and its surface structures clustered around the main entrance. A well lighted access road coming in from New London looks like a string of festival lights far below them. Tempel follows them in and makes a close pass over the top of Central Peak. Sensors, antennas and other constructions are clearly visible at its summit. Somewhere down there defensive cannons track their flight as they pass overhead, continuing to climb and gain speed.

Rising out of the craters shadow, the two spacecraft emerge into full sunlight. The craters floor is now eleven thousand feet below, a gray expanse with its detail blurred by altitude. The sun, a thin disk peeking over the horizon almost directly in front of him, put Alphonsus Craters rim wall in stark silhouette. They cover the eighty miles across the crater in less than five minutes and are doing fifteen hundred feet per second, or just over a thousand mph, when they clear Rim Mountain with a few hundred feet to spare. The ridge flashes by.

The Sea of Clouds, or Mare Nubium as it was originally named in Latin, is spread out before him. The dark, basaltic plain formed when an extremely large impact cracked the planetary crust allowing lava to flood hundreds of square miles. Wrinkle-ridges, formed as the thick layer of basalt slowly cooled and contracted over thousands of years, make a washboard pattern across the great plain, like waves across a sea.

Later many smaller volcanic events created a number of sinuous rilles running for many miles that streak and line the mare's surface. Some are collapsed lava tubes. In other cases, the lava flows cut channels by simply melting their way down into the older rocks, much like rivers cut into their flood plains back on Earth.

The sun cast long shadows across the mare's surface highlighting everything down to the smallest rocks and pebbles. Tempel again adjusts his visual and the shadows recede without entirely disappearing. He wonders briefly if ancient sea captains felt as he does at this moment, the incredible sense of adventure laced with the thrill of the unknown. He pulls himself back to reality, keeping his mind on the business at hand.

The thrusters cut off putting the ships in freefall, their path a great arc towards their destination.

Tempel sees their target as a bright red dot far out on the mare. He glances down at his console and announces, "ETA in just over fifteen minutes."

The Sea of Clouds stretch unbroken as far as Tempel can see. Looking at the red dot, he zooms in using the transports scanners. There isn't anything to be seen from this distance and angle. He sweeps the sensors over the topography surrounding the downed freighter and again, comes up empty. He links with the other transport but even using both sets in tandem, he finds nothing. No sign of human life, no movement at all.

A few minutes from target the onboard AI rotates the two ships and restarts the thrusters. Charley Company is quiet, preparing for immediate action upon arrival. All of them linked with the ships scanners during the flight and know the site is devoid of life. But that doesn't stop any of them from getting ready as if an army is waiting. Weapons and vacsuits are checked for the umpteenth time.

From all across Luna hundreds of thousands of citizens are linked to the mission sensors. They are currently the third most watched event on the net. By the time they land they will be number one.

"Prepare for touchdown," Tempel announces watching the hills roll by slower and slower only a couple hundred feet below.

As they crest the last rise, the wreckage is strewn across a broad valley at a severe angle. Below them, a long scar is clearly evident in the ridge where the freighter had first hit. Tempel surmises the striking angle must have been very shallow, a glancing blow that sent pieces along a track two miles long, finally stopping at the far side of the valley. He keeps the two transports scanners busy mapping the debris field during the approach.

At an altitude of under a hundred feet, Tempel leads the ships slowly forward at less than thirty mph, not much more than a hover for the transports.

"Red, take the left. I will take the right." Tempel says.

"Aye," Consuela replies.

The ships scanners work together measuring and marking every artifact scattered across the surface, every furrow gouged in the lunar dust, and every displaced rock, beginning the process of piecing together what happened to Evolution's Child during her final touchdown.

As the ships reach the far end of the long debris trail, most of the larger parts of the freighter begin appearing. First the twisted remains of the pilothouse, the freighters heavy beam framework had been able to partially protect it. Beyond that are the larger parts of the engine section and fuel tanks. Pieces of the electromagnetic nozzles are the only items immediately recognizable. Everything else is twisted beyond recognition and covered in a fine layer of lunar dust.

The cargo must have come loose on impact because it is another two hundred yards before they come to it. They follow what appear to be skid marks across the surface, multiple parallel tracks only a few inches deep that are in the direction of travel across the valley. At the end lie two shipping crates in remarkably good shape, a tribute to their designer.

Tempel decides on a flat spot near the crates and marks it. "Red, I have marked your LZ. Acknowledge."

"Confirmed," Consuela responds. "See you on the ground."

Tempel watches as she expertly places her spacecraft on target, a brief dust flurry arises just before the thrusters shut down. He knows where he wants to land, a small knoll about two hundred feet back along the debris field and to the side, not more than a bump with a flat top, but it has a good field of view and provides line-of-sight between the two transports.

****

Even before the thrusters shut down Kitajima is out of his seat, anxious to see what he is dealing with. As the on-site commander, he has leeway to modify the plan but so far, he hasn't seen anything requiring a change. Hack will set up the base camp, Tatiana will take charge of security and Tempel will lead the team collecting the forensic evidence, tasks they are all eminently qualified to do. This leaves him and Lindsey free to take a look at the cargo. Over the years, he has come to respect her technological insight and ability to see into a design, to take it apart in her mind and understand why it is the way it is. She has become legend, more than once cajoling a balky piece of equipment to work after everyone else had given up. Afterward, she would simply tap the side of her nose knowingly and say "physics" as though that explained everything.

Kitajima had argued against including Lazarus. He is convinced the only reason Lazarus is here is because Lindsey is babysitting him. His claim to have expertise in the Brotherhood sounds hollow. After all, Muslims have been around since 650BCE. What could he possibly know that any first year university student didn't? But somehow he had convinced Corso that he would be useful on the mission and both Lindsey and Tempel vouched for him. That alone was enough for Kitajima to give him a chance. He just wished it wasn't on this particular assignment.

Kitajima moves quickly though the almost empty transport. Moments after touchdown, Tatiana departed with her team setting up a defensive perimeter and Hack has every free hand pulling the equipment out of the transports. Kitajima knows he will only be in the way here.

"Hack, I'm heading out," he informs her.

"Aye, Kit," she responds. "I've got your back." She watches briefly as he moves down the ramp and heads across the lunar landscape.

"Tempel, I'm on my way." Kitajima calls. "I want your forensics team on the road ASAP." Kitajima's voice jars each time his feet hit the surface. "Let me know as soon as possible what you find. I have a bad feeling about this whole affair. And don't forget to bring back the freighters AI."

"Since when do you need to tell me something as basic as that?" Tempel doesn't like not being part of Kitajima's team but he understands the importance of collecting good forensics. He realizes that Kitajima has the tougher assignment, dealing with the politics of the mission. Lindsey would be doing the heavy lifting, analyzing the cargo and deciding what it is. It will be out of Kitajima's hands to a large extent, something that makes any control freak nervous. "Relax Cap. We've done this a hundred times.

By the way, if you guys accidentally set something off, can you give us a little warning? I might want to bend over and kiss my ass goodbye!"

Kitajima chuckles grimly and some of his tension slips away. "You'll get the same warning I do, not a second sooner!" he growls good naturedly.

Glancing at Karyl, "Kept your eyes open and stay in touch," Tempel says.

"Now who's micro-managing! Take some of your own advice and relax. My ass isn't going anywhere and I haven't closed my eyes for days!" she feigns a yawn and snuggles back in the body hugging pilot seat as though finding a comfortable spot to take a nap.

Tempel unbuckles his harness and rotates his seat, practically depositing him in Lindsey's lap. "Sorry" he says, "Didn't realize you were there."

"Don't sweat it... Listen, Tempel... I've been going over the data. The high acceleration must have been deliberate. No way can an AI screw-up that badly," she says. "The overrides must have been deliberately bypassed."

"I tend to agree but my forensic training tells me to wait, keep an open mind and let the evidence speak for itself," he responds frowning. He can't remember the last time so many people wanted to tell him how to do his job.

"Have you ever seen a crash site?" she asks.

Frowning even deeper, Tempel responds sourly, "A few."

"It will be a mess in there," she says.

"It can't be worse than the Lincoln County Hospital," Tempel responds dryly beginning to get annoyed.

"...I'm sure your right," Lindsey says.

"Captain Osaka doesn't like to be kept waiting," Tempel says.

Lindsey nods and moves down the aisle. Tempel matches her step for step as they pass through the cargo hold squeezing past the rover.

****

One by one, Tempel links with Tatiana's security team. They are spread out along the ridge above them, taking advantage of the terrain, using outcrops and other rock formations to gain some small amount of cover. He sees what they see, the unchanging Luna landscape.

Master Sergeant Susan Hackling works with Sam, Alonzo, Lei, Brice and Kipper getting Red unloaded. Doc Grady lends a hand but is just getting in the way. Hack doesn't know how long they will be here, a few hours or a few days, it's all the same to her. Soon piles of equipment litter the surface around the ship. They gather up what needs to be carried and head for Blue.

Outside Blue, Kitajima calls Lindsey and Lazarus off to the side. A mound of equipment lay nearby. "OK, listen up. Keep in mind that we may need to depart on short notice. I won't tell anybody twice to get back to the transport." He receives a nod of acknowledgment from each before going on. "Good! Let's get it done, sooner rather than later!" He slings a large duffle bag by a strap over one shoulder and picks up a folding table with his opposite arm, leading the group down the slope towards the cargo crates. Lindsey and Lazarus follow.

Alonzo drags the portable shelter from Blue's hold and it doesn't take long for them to seal it to the side of the transport. Air begins to inflate the bladders inside the structure, making it rise up and take shape as if by magic, a phoenix rising from the ashes.

While waiting for the rover, Tempel hoists a Gattling disrupter cannon onto the roof of Blue. Mounted directly on the forward power outlet, the lethal device becomes one with the ship. They hadn't bothered installing it before departure because it is something easily done in the field. Anyone in Charley Company can do it in their sleep. Targeted by the transports sensors, the gun protects the expedition from stray meteorites. At least that's the official version. Sometimes it's more prudent to apologize later then to ask permission now.

Brice slowly backs the rover down the ships cargo ramp.

"Take it easy, Brice. We don't want to raise any more dust than necessary." Tempel calls down from the roof.

"Aye," Brice responds.

Tempel jumps down with a splash of dust, climbing in beside him.

"Thought you said not to raise any dust?" Brice says with a grin.

"I mean it Brice, now is not a good time to test new boundaries," Tempel responds.

"Aye, LT, no dust," Brice says. Brice is an excellent driver, one of the best, but tends to push the envelope most of the time.

"Kipper, Lei, let's mount up," Tempel calls out.

The two officers emerge from Blue carrying several small cases and approach the rover. Lei hands Tempel one of the cases, "Here's your physical sample case. You should never leave home without it," she says as she climbs into the back.

"Thanks," Tempel responds, his mind already focusing on the task ahead.

The rover rocks gently as Kipper follows her aboard.

Brice accelerates the vehicle smoothly, keeping the dust to a minimum and careful to stay out of the freighters debris field even when it means rough going. The pilothouse lay twisted and broken before them and Brice stops well clear.

The officers climb out and remain silent as they approach the wreckage, their suit sensors working at full capacity, adding to the already significant amount of data pertaining to the crash. They all know someone died here.

"Brice, Lei, continue to process outside. Kipper and I will go inside," Tempel says. He glances at Brice expecting a smart ass retort but he only nods.

Brice is thankful that he isn't going inside.

The freighter appears to have violently cartwheeled down the valley before coming to rest on its top. The engine compartment or what is left of it, points skyward, a torn and twisted mass of beams and fuel lines. Tempel walks around it looking for the front door.

"Over here," Kipper calls out from the other side. "This must be the main airlock."

Using every bit of his suits strength, Kipper manages to wrench open the outer door. Looking inside he exclaims "The inner door is open!" He is gone when Tempel arrives.

Tempel can see reflections of Kippers lights inside the dark interior as he squeezes through the smashed airlock. This must have been the freighters control room, he decides after switching to low-light-level sensors. He immediately becomes aware of a dark smear on practically every surface inside the room with the most right over his head. He knows its blood. Vacuum sucks all the gases and moisture out of organic material on the cellular level, ripping cell walls open and tearing complex molecules asunder. What's left is a pile of broken proteins and freeze dried carbon chains.

"The body is over there, in the corner," Kipper says his voice reflecting the strain of the assignment.

Kipper continues into the adjoining room and Tempel hears his breath become ragged. "More bodies in here. Magi, are you picking this up?" Kipper can barely speak.

"Yes Kipper, in all its gory detail," Magi responds.

Tempel enters and adds his sensors to the task of data collection. If he had thought that there was a lot of blood in the control room, he immediately is forced to raise the bar. Blood covers the walls, floor and ceiling, looking like someone had painted the room brown. Making a conscious effort to steady his voice he says, "Magi, I want data on all the biological's including fingerprints and DNA. I don't know what happened here and the least bit of information may be critical."

"Aye," she responds.

"I count four more in here making it five on board. They're all too vacdried to make a visual ID on any of them and their BioID's are inactive," Kipper says, more than a little shaken. Without life, a bioID lacks a power source. "Two of them were wearing Brotherhood combat armor. I knew those psychotic god lovers had to be involved!"

Tempel takes a deep breath, "Take it easy Kipper. Concentrate on the job. Let's get it done as best we can."

"This is what the inside of a meat grinder must look like…" he shudders involuntarily. "I will finish the interior scan if you will start processing in here." He feels guilty asking Tempel to do the dirty work but he desperately needs to get leave, just for a moment. It would be dangerous not to mention embarrassing if he pukes in his ghost suit.

"Go for it," Tempel responds, knowing that his friend will be back when he is ready.

As Kipper enters the adjoining lavatory, Tempel lays his case on the floor and opens it. From inside he selects a magazine containing forensic swabs, each individually protected in a plastic sleeve. He loads it into a collection gun with a slap of his hand. Straightening, he initiates his control panel and brings up the forensic control page making sure the data from the collection gun will be stored both locally and routed to Magi back in Aldrin Station. Before he exits the panel, he glances at the link monitor and is shocked at the number of citizens viewing his feed. Apparently all of Luna is watching.

Tempel looks around wondering where to begin. This isn't the first time he has processed a crime scene in a vacsuit, just the first time in a ghost suit. Might as well start right here, it's as good as any. Bending down he picks a particularly dark smear and places the collection gun muzzle against it and triggers the device. Designed to collect vacuum-dried biological materials, it hydrates a very small amount of the blood or tissue before sampling it, sealing and tagging each specimen with time, date, location, and who collected it. Sensors built into the collection gun immediately begin to analyze the sample, making the raw data available to Magi who processes it into viable information almost as rapidly as Tempel can collect it. The AI immediately begins the tremendous job of piecing together the broken strands of DNA. Each successive sample makes the guesses more substantial, increasing the confidence levels of the calculated data points.

Tempel moves around the room quickly, returning to reload the gun several times and store the collected samples in the case. Near the end he notices something odd. Bending down he picks up a blood covered helmet. From its shape it's obviously a Brotherhood design. He lets his sensors scan it completely before stetting it back down. They will bag it with all the other remains.

He is done when Kipper finally returns. "I found a lot of fingerprints, mostly of one individual, I assume the pilot, but at least two others. I suspect the place was searched," Kipper says.

"I'm just finishing sample collection. The next thing is to bag the bodies. You ok with that?" Tempel watches for any hesitation or insincerity in Kipper.

"I'm fine. Don't worry about me!" Kipper responds, agitated that Tempel would even ask.

"I knew that. I just wanted to be sure you did," Tempel retorts with a smile, his first since entering this bloody tomb. "Brice, Lei, how are you doing on the outside. We are ready to collect the bodies and could use some help."

Lei appears to Tempel just to his left, her head and shoulders look solid but the rest of her simply fads away. "Brice is mapping parts of the ships thrusters but I'm available. I'm about a half mile down track and it will take a minute to get back to you. You were right Tempel. Preliminary analysis has the freighter coming in fast and low. It slid down the slope and didn't start tumbling until it hit the valley floor. Magi calculates at least twenty rolls before coming to a stop." Lei makes her way towards the pilothouse as she talks.

"Is there enough data yet for a complete reconstruction?" Tempel asks.

"Not yet, but there should be when Brice gets finished," Lei says. "Assuming the data is there from the cargo section," she adds.

"Pick up the body bags from the rover on your way in. Let's get this done quickly and efficiently." Tempel isn't looking forward to the extraction, especially the tangled pile of parts he is looking at. But somebody has to do it.

They ended up using twenty-four different bags to put the bodies in. They simply couldn't tell which arm or head belonged with what torso. The two individuals wearing combat armor simplified collection slightly, but even here, the people inside had been smashed and squeezed out like toothpaste, their parts mingling with the others as they were flung about in the violent crash.

Nearing completion of the gruesome task, Tempel finds an old style projectile pistol under one of the bodies, covered in dried blood and human tissue. He looks at it curiously before slipping it into a small collection bag. The weapon is out of place aboard the freighter but until he has cleaned and examined it, he won't know why it is here.

One by one they bring out the bags and load them in the rover. Finished with this gruesome task, the three turn their attention to finding the ships AI. For some inexplicable reason it had come loose during the crash and is missing from the electronics console where it should be. After searching the small control room, in the very last place Tempel looks, he finds the small box covered in dried blood wedged into a space behind the fight panel. It must have ricocheted around the freighters interior during the crash. But ship AI's are built rugged evolving from the technology of Flight Data Recorders dating back to the early days of flight. In 1941 the first recorders were designed to withstand a 100G impact, in 1965 it was raised to 1,000Gs, and in 2042 it became 10,000Gs. He fully expects to get valuable information from it as soon as power can be restored. Lei is especially skilled at coaxing a damaged AI back to life. He bags it and carries it out to the rover.

"I've got another AI," Lei reports.

Tempel watches her exit the pilothouse, the black box she is carrying unmistakable. Why are there two? It's another mystery to solve. Right now, with the crash processed and the data being analyzed, he is more interested in what Kitajima is finding.

Brice doesn't bother coming back to the rover but keeps going, collecting detailed impact data along the debris field as he makes his way on foot back towards the base camp. He estimates another twenty minutes before he is finished.

Kipper takes the wheel of the rover, glad that he doesn't have to share the cramped back compartment with the pile of black bags.

Lei sits next to him, just as relived for much the same reason. She looks at Tempel during the ride back to camp and catches him with a pained expression on his face as he rearranges the pile after a particularly bad bump. But he doesn't say anything. It is one of the things she likes about him, he never complains.

Lei gazes out across the valley thinking this was a lonely place to die, "Magi, who was the pilot?"

"Her name was Nell Goddard," she answers.

"Does she have any family?"

"Not that I have any data on. She had two daughters that were killed in a bombing several years ago and she finalized a divorce a few months before reporting for pilot training. I have not tried to track the ex-husbands location," Magi responds.

"What was she like?" Lei asks, curiosity building about this women who apparently led such a hard life and suffered a violent death.

Magi answered by playing several portions of Nells training record for the Lieutenant. In the first video Nell is thin and haggard but there is something in her eyes that refused to give up. Lei is fascinated by the images showing Nell progressing through the school. Her final psych exam shows a woman coping with what life has thrown at her, refusing to feel sorry for herself, a defiant me-versus-the-world attitude that Lei admires.

Finished, Lei sits quietly in the rover gazing across the glorious desolation of this remote lunar valley. Not any different than a thousand others except that this was Nell's final touchdown. "We should name this valley after Nell. Nell's Valley," she declares in an emotional voice.

Tempel looks at Lei and nods agreement. "I like it. Magi, take a quick poll on that."

The Lunarians love of voting extends into many places within their society. Citizens should always have a say in those things important to them. It would have been considered very bad taste not to have asked for the opinion of those linked in at that moment.

Tempel nods in satisfaction as the tally quickly comes in from all across Luna, "Magi, record this valley as Nell's Valley."

"Done!"

The rover is silent until finally Tempel says, "Magi, fill us in on what Kitajima has found."

"The damaged shipping crate definitely contains nuclear weapons. It was apparently booby-trapped. Anyone tampering with the case should have caused detonation," Magi reports.

"Why didn't it go off then?" Kipper asks from the driver's seat.

"Unknown at this time. Just be thankful it did not. Lindsey and Dr. Ogden estimate the yield at approximately ten kilotons. Small for a nuclear bomb but plenty big nonetheless," Magi responds.

"The electromagnetic pulse of even a 10kt bomb would wreck havoc with Magi if they could have gotten it close enough." Kipper mutters as he drives around a large boulder.

"What about the other crates? Do they contain bombs?" Lei asks.

"Unknown at this time. Scanning the crates shows various pieces of mining equipment. But the damaged case does too when you scan through the undamaged sides, so that is not the least bit encouraging," Magi responds.

Tempel frowns and links to the expedition's doctor, "Doc, are you ready to do the autopsies?"

After a few seconds Doctor Howard Grady says, "Yes, everything's waiting. Bring them straight to the shelter and I'll get started," he pauses and adds, "I have been following your investigation… at those G loads, they didn't suffer," he says trying to find a silver lining in a very bloody cloud.

****

Skipping agilely across the valley floor in long leaps, puffs of regolith arcing outward like ejecta from a meteor impact every time his feet hit, settling slowly back to the surface long after he's past. Tempel quickly makes his way to the damaged crate and the activity around it. A portable workbench stands nearby covered with an array of tools and equipment. The crate had been partially buried in regolith but now lay clear. Beyond them, Kitajima is digging out the third and final crate, carefully removing the dry lunar dust from around the container. He works fast but with care, knowing the price of a mistake.

Lindsey and Lazarus are working at the bench as Tempel approaches, the hand gestures and body language look more like an argument than any scientific discussion he has ever been in. He avoids them thinking what an odd couple they make. It's obvious they are deeply engaged and he certainly doesn't want to interrupt a potentially important conversation.

Tempel walks slowly and carefully up to the crate, looking it over with practiced ease, magnifying and analyzing as he draws near. From the outside it appears to be a standard shipping crate. The same type used everyday for the past fifty years, a hard outer shell with a soft padded inner layer. Using MRI he probes deeper, seeing a large ball valve, complete with a remote powered electromagnetic actuator. Nothing unusual, these are common in the smelters and refineries all across Luna.

Instead of opening the crates lid, the top is ripped and the ragged edge twisted back like a giant can opener had been at work. Moving in for a better angle through the hole he can see a large spherical object with a small cable coming out its side. Even though the bulk of the device remains hidden, it's readily apparent to Tempel that what he is looking at through the opening is not what his sensors tell him is inside the crate.

Frowning Tempel asks, "Magi, do we have remote data taken from inside?"

"Aye" she responds as she immerses him in the vid.

His perspective shifts to inside the crate, looking through the eyes of a fly-sized mini sensor poking around like a bloodhound looking for a scent he had lost just moments before. Inside the crate is a framework cradling three identical spheres. The only blemishes to the otherwise smooth surface of the devices are their cables.

Probing deeper into the nearest sphere, beneath its shiny exterior, the sensor maps a complex three-dimensional jigsaw puzzle designed to form a smaller sphere when combined together, less than three inches in diameter. It's made from two hundred and forty four pieces of enriched plutonium 239 with a total mass of just over eight pounds. A beryllium reflector is present that looks quite capable of sustaining the reaction. Without any doubt, this is a small nuclear bomb.

Even though he had never before seen a nuke up close and personal, Tempel has studied their design and appreciates fine craftsmanship. These are accurate in every detail, right out of the book. Encircling this lethal display of precision machining is a heavy layer of SuperX explosive, itself machined into shape charges designed to implode this intricate puzzle together with maximum force.

Embedded inside the explosives is a web of Calconn filaments that routes energy to a grid of SuperX detonators controlled by an internal microcircuit incorporated into the bomb. It is nearly tamper proof.

"Not bad," Tempel mutters. Whoever designed this done a masterful job, but the true artists were the machinists who brought it to life.

The image fads away and Tempel turns his attention back to the crate. He leans down and magnifies the edge of the tear until he has maxed out his sensors, focusing on the outer layer of the crate. He can find nothing out of the ordinary. It looks like ordinary vacglass, common fiberglass sat in a stabilized epoxy matrix, the same vacuum-rated material used virtually everywhere in space.

"It's the inside surface," Lindsey says as she walks over to join him. "Magi, show him."

Tempel straightens as Magi displays a large 3D image of the material in question, hanging in space between them. Lindsey points to a series of faint lines. "Coating the inside of the crate appears to be a solid-state layer capable of transmitting a complex signal in a reflexive response to incoming energy. It transmits the signature of a thirty-two inch high-pressure valve. It even uses the incoming energy as its power source. We're not sure just exactly how it's done, but we are getting close. Once we understand that, we can defeat it. At least, that's the plan."

"I didn't know the Brotherhood was capable of solid-state manufacturing." Tempel is well aware that Lunarians invented the technology of building complex structures one atom at a time and are widely considered the best in the business. It is an enabling technology making electromagnet nozzles possible without which space travel would go back to the Stone Age where chemical rockets were barely able to lift their own fuel.

"Don't underestimate them, Tempel," warns Lazarus joining in the conversation.

Tempel looks up at Lazarus standing beside Lindsey.

"They're not stupid and once it's known that something can be done, some bright mind will figure out how to do it," Lazarus says. "One thing they do have is plenty of money. I would be willing to bet they simply bought the technology and modified it to their needs."

"Can you see the irony in that? Lunarians invent, and then sell, the means to destroy themselves," Lindsey says bitterly.

"They didn't buy it from us!" Tempel replies.

"After something is bought and sold enough times the water is so muddy no one knows where anything is anymore. Anyone could have sold it to them given enough time and money. The only sure way to stop Islamic terrorism from spreading to space is to restrict Islam to Earth!" Lindsey says.

It's obvious where Lindsey stands on the issue of Fair Access, the political stance the rest of the world has taken to the Brotherhood's expansion into space. At its inception in 2042, the Islamic Brotherhood found itself far behind many other countries in the area of space colonization. North America, Europe and Asia all were way out in front and the Brotherhood was left sucking hind tit.

But it didn't stay that way. In the summer of 2051, the Brotherhood obtained its first battlestation under the guise of research. Later, when its true nature was revealed, they argued they had a right to protect themselves against the proliferation of other nation's off-world military buildup. There was an outcry but to no avail. The Brotherhood had long since learned how to obtain what it wanted from renegade nations and corporations whose only interest was in making a profit. Like a hunter closing on its prey, the Brotherhood remained motionless when under scrutiny and moved slowly, so as to minimize attention, when not. When it did get caught with its hand in the cookie jar, bravado and the very real threat of violence stifled the objections. When even that failed, more than one politician disappeared, had tragic accidents, or was executed in very public way as a warning to others. In some countries, simply voicing a contrary opinion could prove fatal. No one rose to challenge them and over time and with much discussion among the talking heads of the rest of the world, the policy of Fair Access developed giving every country on Earth the unalienable right to be in space, which was all the Brotherhood wanted to begin with.

Lunarians view this as a cop-out, a way to legitimize the political appeasement that has been going on for a half century. It started long before the full extent of the Lunarian genetic program was reveled, long before Muslim clerics from across the empire began actively calling for their death and the total destruction of their godless society. In their words, 'these are not only non-believers, they are non-human, an abomination in the eyes of Allah. They don't deserve His mercy.' This kind of talk made it virtually impossible for any Lunarian to see any benefit in letting the Brotherhood have any presence off-world. The tension has risen dramatically over the last few years and grows worse with each bombing and each murder. Lunarians quickly found they didn't have the power to enforce any real restrictions on Muslim shortimers. All they could do legally under the Treaty of Independence was to tighten their own internal vigilance and patrol their own streets and commonways.

Lindsey glances at Lazarus and back at Tempel, waving her hand in front of his face, "Hey! Is anyone in there?"

Tempel gives a start and stares at her, "Sorry, I was thinking."

"This is more than a little overwhelming," she nods understandably. After several moments of looking at Tempel's blank stare she elaborates, "That," she says pointing to the damaged crate, "contains three nukes and the chances are good those two crates over there also have more nukes in them. Someone or some country, probably the Brotherhood but nothing is certain yet, has brought them to Luna. That's a fact. It's also a fact that this freighter was cleared to land outside Aldrin Station. Anything beyond that is pure speculation at this point… But these are suitcase bombs that have enough power to rip open a borough but not destroy Aldrin Station…" Lindsey is no longer looking at Tempel but staring at the crates, her thoughts tumultuous as her mind dwells on this unbelievable scenario that has suddenly become very real and staring her in the face.

"Assuming there is three in each of the other crates, why did they send nine? They can't detonate all nine at the same time," Lazarus says. "And it doesn't make sense to pack three nukes and detonate only one. It would destroy the others."

Still staring at the crate, Lindsey pursed her lips before speaking, "Combined they would produce almost a hundred kiloton explosion. On the order of twice the Hiroshima blast but not even in the same ball park as the twenty-five megaton Houston bomb..." Her voice is a whisper by the time she finishes, still staring at the crate, a shocked and horrified deer-in-the-headlight look on her face.

"What if they never intended to detonate them?" Lazarus asks.

Lindsey refocuses on the conversation and nods, "Ok, I'll play along. Even if they were meant for blackmail, at least one would be set off just to prove they were for real. And what would the blackmail demand be for? Money? They have plenty. Oil? Food? … Land? Do they want our cities?" Shaking her head as if to clear out the cobwebs she continues, "Maybe we don't have all the facts yet but I think it's highly unlikely that a reasonable explanation is forthcoming."

"What war is reasonable?" Lazarus asks not expecting an answer.

"Let the evidence speak for itself. We're just getting started," Tempel says.

"Heads up, we got company!" Karyl broadcast from Blue's cockpit, "A single ship."

Tempel looks where Karyl is indicating within his VR and watches as the ship passes down the length of the debris field along the same course Charley Company had taken just hours earlier.

"Who are they?" Lazarus asks tension evident in his voice.

"Federation," Karyl responds. It's easy to identify the right angles and straight lines of the small transport as a six passenger Starcraft, small and fast but not even close to the caliber of a Dragonfly.

"I'll do all the talking. No one speaks unless spoken too. Stay on your toes, people," Kitajima orders. He had been half expecting the NAF to show up. The crash couldn't have gone unnoticed, even by the largely clueless Federation.

The approaching ship's AI exchanges standard information with the grounded Dragonflys, including the name of the police captain in charge of the Lunarian expedition. Broadcasting using a general access channel, the image of Inspector Callahan appears in Kitajima's VR but he doesn't reciprocate, keeping the inspector in the dark.

"Greetings, Kitajima. I hope you don't mind if I join your little party." He is just one of many Federation, Chinese, and European officials stationed on Luna for the sole purpose of making sure the Republic doesn't break the Treaty of Independence. By law, treaty inspectors can go wherever they please and observe but are not to interfere.

"Greetings Inspector," Kitajima responds, using the same general access frequency without providing a visual return signal, a definite breach in etiquette, "Would you go away if I said I did mind?" he asks, not expecting an answer.

The two men have grown tolerant of each other over the past year ever since Inspector Callahan had arrived from Earth and assumed his duties as watchdog. It wasn't a friendship exactly, more an unspoken pact of mutual respect. Of all the Federation inspectors to be assigned this mission, Callahan is perhaps the best qualified in temperament and training, a good and honest man to those who value such attributes, a pain in the ass for those who don't.

The Inspector ignores Kitajima's rudeness in not providing a visual and continues, "This is quite a mess. So what do you suppose happened here?"

"One of our freighters crashed," Kitajima answers dryly, pauses and adds, "We are still obtaining data and until it has been thoroughly analyzed, I can't tell you why. Besides, it's policy not to discuss any aspect of a case that isn't yet released under the Law of Full Disclosure." Luna citizens are free to link and observe as often and for as long as they like even during the preliminary stages of an investigation, not to mention that every move a police officer makes is recorded and stored for posterity.

"Of course it is." Inspector Callahan is fully aware of the line drawn between Lunarians and everyone else. "I understand completely." He doesn't like it that Kitajima is not sending video. But the voice print analysis verifies that it is indeed Captain Osaka so he holds his questions, confident they will be answered in due time.

As they talk, his ship comes to rest about fifty yards from Kitajima and the damaged crate, settling to the ground in a brief flurry of fine dust. Less than a minute later the airlock opens and three figures emerge and head directly for the small group gathered around the crates.

They are wearing standard issue Federation vacsuits that haven't changed in over forty years. Light weight and efficient, they have minimal power augmentation, no armor, and only limited protection from the cosmic rays of open space. A crest on top of their helmets has a built-in light right above clear faceplates. The suits are inferior to both Lunarian and Brotherhood designs, something they are loathe to admit, but well aware of. All three are armed with a sidearm, standard practice on the frontier.

Kitajima directs Tempel to move to one side while he takes the other, flanking the approaching group. The three approach within twenty feet without seeing them. Laboratory tests have indicated that Federation sensors would have problems detecting ghost suits and this confirms it. The Lunarians are virtually invisible.

Without access to the Lunarians local network, the newcomers see only what their sensors pick up, the figures of Lindsey and Lazarus. Nothing out of the ordinary, the basic technology in their vacsuits has been around for almost two decades. Although they are top of the line, a fact cataloged and filed by Inspector Callahan under I Wish I Had One. Like so many shortimers, he despises wearing a vacsuit at all. He believes that walking in the open air of a planet is far superior to any artificial skin. But when needed, the Lunarian suits are the preferred choice, considered the best available and almost impossible to get.

"Greetings once more, Kitajima," he says. "Will you grant permission for this delegation to access your working frequencies?" Inspector Callahan asks, still using the general access frequency. Charley Company's communication and facial recognition is on a secure channel. They can see his him through the clear faceplate, but he cannot see them.

After a noticeable pause, "Officer Stormberg, provide Level One access for our guests," Kitajima orders.

Immediately the Lunarian vacsuits melt away as data begins to flow providing facial expressions and the black and tan uniforms of LCPD.

"Thank you Kitajima…That's much better. I have always disliked hiding behind a mask. It is simply uncivilized not to gaze upon the face of the person you are talking to," Inspector Callahan says and only then realizes that Kitajima is not one of those standing before him. "Please forgive my rudeness, I am Inspector Callahan," he indicates his companions, "and this is Zechariah Hargrove, the resident Propriety Officer, and Luke Fillmore, my personal pilot," and bodyguard, but he neglects to mention that fact.

"Greetings, I'm Lindsey Davenport and this is Lazarus Sheffield." Lindsey says. Lazarus nods as she says his name.

Zechariah Hargrove stares intently at Lazarus. He appears about to speak when Luke Fillmore suddenly reaches out and grips Inspector Callahan by the arm turning him around. Approaching them from behind are Captain Osaka and Tempel Dugan. He recognizes Kitajima and has a passing familiarity with young Dugan but that is not what sends a chill down his spine. Behind their projected image is only darkness.

"Kitajima, what deal with the devil have you made now?" the Inspector exclaims. He is no longer surprised by the ingenuity of a people who have taken on an airless world and conquered it. But this is different. The blackness beyond the electronically generated image is sinister in its completeness. as he cycles through his sensors trying and failing to make sense of the readings when he looks past the visual image projected by these men.

"Greetings Inspector. As you can see, I'm rather busy. What exactly can I do for you?" Kitajima asks.

"For such an open society you folks sure have a lot of secrets," Inspector Callahan says with exasperation. He gets the response he's looking for.

"We don't keep secrets," Lindsey says defensively.

"Then fill me in, what have you found so far?" the Inspector retorts.

"As I have already told you, we don't…"

"Yes, yes, I know, you don't disclose information prematurely to a shortimer," he glances at the damaged crate. "I suspect that whatever has brought you out here is important. Otherwise, why would you reveal brand new technology, technology you have obviously gone to a lot of trouble to keep quiet." He holds his hand up stopping Kitajima from speaking, "Don't bother trying to explain…" he looks at Kitajima intently, "Don't you think I have a right to know what's going on? I live in Aldrin Station, my family lives in Aldrin Station… Now tell me, what have you found?" Little America is technically a borough within Aldrin Station but most Lunarians consider it simply as a shortimer enclave, not as part of their city.

Kitajima returns the imploring stare calmly and slowly nods. “Under the Law of Full Disclosure you will know about this in a few hours anyway… The crate contains three nukes on their way to Aldrin Station from an unknown source. I strongly suspect the other crate does as well. We don't yet know why or who is involved. You will need to wait with everybody else for those answers.”

“Thank you. I appreciate your candor.” The Inspector says. “I think you have a pretty good idea who. It doesn't take a scholar to make an educated guess.”

Throughout the conversation, Zechariah Hargrove continues to stare at Lazarus.

Tempel becomes aware of Brice approaching, having worked his way through the debris field from the pilothouse. “Looks like Brice is finished. Magi, can you construct the simulation?”

“I am attempting to do so. This may take…”

"A man's ethical behavior should be based effectually on sympathy, education, and social ties; no religious basis is necessary. Man would indeed be in a poor way if he had to be restrained by fear of punishment and hope of reward after death."

Albert Einstein (1879-1955)

General Council

The General Council chamber exists in cyberspace, its members needing only a secure network access portal and a high quality visor to participate in its many meetings and discussions regardless of where they are located physically. These discussions and the resulting decisions form a public record dating back two generations, predating even the Lunarian Declaration of Independence.

Just as it has been done for sixty years, the chamber is presented as a vast amphitheater with steep sloping sides terraced in concentric rings to its very top, a blue sunless sky overhead. Each member appears dressed in long flowing robes that ripple in a strange multidirectional cyber breeze, an ancient tradition from ages past. Where any particular councilman stands within the chamber depends not only on which discussion they are participating in but also on their political opinion at that particular moment in time. A Lunarian debate may rage for years without reaching a firm consensus, a process not well understood by the rest of humanity and thus has become the butt of many jokes involving a person's inability to make a fast decision, or any decision at all.

The Council is never truly out of session, somewhere there is always something going on. Although everyone's opinion is valued, regional issues are debated by a limited number of council members, those with an immediate interest in the outcome, or those with simple curiosity. Only issues that are broad in scope require a quorum of the entire Council. Today, at her request, Abby addresses a full assembly with most of Luna watching closely.

The chamber is uncharacteristically quiet as Abby begins to speak. "I want to begin by thanking all of you who have aided Dakota and Aldrin Station during this time of tragedy. Our citizens are forever in your debt." She pauses and looks at the faces around her, sweeping her glance over the throng. In a firm voice she continues, "As you already know, the explosion at Lincoln County Hospital was no accident!" a murmur rises from the gathering. "I now show you a vid authenticated just minutes ago of at least three, but probably more, nuclear devices destined for Aldrin Station!"

A hush falls over the assembly. Virtually every citizen has intently watched the mission at Nell's Valley real-time and knows the progress made there. As the members begin to discuss these events the volume within the cyber-chamber slowly increases. Abby waits until she is sure those few who haven't been linked with Charley Company have a chance to view a summary before continuing. "The time is past that we can sit back and do nothing!" Her voice silences the assembly once more. "Our past forgiveness has led the Brotherhood to view us as weak and ripe for the picking. This time we must take action. The people responsible must not be allowed to continue!"

"I agree! We must find the people responsible and punish them. Who are they? Tell me! I will personally strike them down!" Councilman Taylor responds strongly. He is standing a few yards to Abby's right on the same level, but is much older in appearance, with long flowing white hair and subdued gray robes. A full white beard covers his face, only his lively blue eyes give testimony that someone exists behind the mask of hair.

"You know who carries the ultimate responsibility! It can be laid at the feet of Prince Ahmed Mohammed Al Zarqowi, Caliph of the Islamic Brotherhood!" Abby retorts.

"Unless you know something that I don't, there is no solid proof of his involvement. And all the circumstantial evidence in the Republic can't change that. What I do know is if we overreact we play into their hands. The non-aligned Earth nations will see us as war mongers, a loose cannon striking back at random!" Councilman Taylor speaks for a large majority, those that would do almost anything to avoid open conflict.

"We are at war Councilman! Make no mistake about it! People are dying!" Abby insists, her voice ringing in the acoustically perfect cyberworld.

"I have seen the data and there is nothing to indicate that the attack on Lincoln County Hospital wasn't the act of a single individual or group. And you are just beginning to gather information on whose bombs are out on the mare. Until we know for sure, we can't assume it was the Brotherhood. Again I say, we cannot allow a few misguided individuals to influence our current decisions. We must stay focused on the big picture." Councilman Taylor speaks confidently, shaking his head with the conviction of many years of experience at holding this unpleasantness at arms length, reiterating a position well established within the Republic. But deep inside it terrifies him that nuclear weapons are being introduced.

Abby expected this and doesn't let it affect or even slow her down, "Because there is more than one device out there, they probably had a plan other than just blowing us up. My guess is blackmail of some kind. But I stress, we don't know yet. As for Lincoln County, that hospital has been prominent in genetic research for seventy years, almost since Aldrin Station was founded. I believe they picked their target very carefully. We anticipate a claim of responsibility at any time from one of the Islamic extremist groups," Abby continues calmly. "Soon to be followed with a statement from His Highness, the Prince, saying how deplorable and cowardly the act was!" she adds.

"That may be Abby, but what do you expect us to do about it? Declare war on the Brotherhood?" Councilman Yang Lee stands next to Taylor. He interlocks his fingers and brings them up in front of his robes as though in prayer, concern on his wise old oriental features. "Abby, we go back many years. If you need help, we will gladly give it. But to declare war on the most powerful Muslim empire in history is pure suicide!"

"To do nothing is also suicide, Councilman. Past protestations haven't worked and the attacks are escalating. We must break from this myopic approach to our safety, to our very survival! We need orbital fighters! We need mobile surface armor equipped with Everest Class cannons! We need every Lunarian citizen ready to defend Luna!" Abby can see her pleas fall on deaf ears. They simply couldn't or wouldn't believe the danger is that great. "Let's at least arm our transports and rovers!"

"Ridiculous!" explodes Councilman Taylor, "That would be a clear violation of the Treaty of Independence. We cannot fight Earth!"

"The Brotherhood is not all of Earth! If we don't prepare our defenses we risk losing everything! If we do prepare we risk making a few Earth nations nervous!" Looking at the split she doesn't need to see the numbers to know that the majority of the council still favors maintaining status quo. She is frustrated at her inability to persuade more to come to her side. It seems reason is not enough.

"Look at the facts," Abby implores. With a simple gesture she posts a virtual graph within the chamber, its timeline extending back half a century, showing the buildup of the Brotherhood's military forces, both in orbital space and on Luna. "Battlestations, factories, shipyards, and mining facilities, all show a steady growth pattern. This outpost in the asteroids is the most recent addition but they all have one thing in common, every single one of them are military installations. But the Brotherhood wants us to believe that instead of a military buildup this is simply a healthy dose of self defense. Well, I don't believe it!"

"Yes Abby, we have all seen this data and nothing's changed!" Councilman Taylor says irritably. "We are going over the same issues time and again! They have followed the rules and have the right to be off world!"

"Why do they need so many battlestations? And here on Luna, the increase in manpower far outstrips any projected need," she insists, questions that has been raised many times over the last year. "Please tell me, what is going on inside Al Fahad? Why can't we send an envoy to inspect the place? I don't buy the Holy City routine!"

"Ambassador Omar has answered all of these questions to everyone's satisfaction," Councilman Beverly Salazar exclaims from Abby's left.

"Not to mine!" Abby retorts. "The good ambassador has been kept in the dark just so he can speak before us with truth in his heart, even as his countrymen prepare for war! Why hasn't he ever been inside the city or aboard any of their big ships?"

"As you are obviously aware, Ambassador Omar has always been truthful with us. You are doing everyone a disservice by your increasingly vocal personal attacks on him!" Councilman Salazar angrily responds. As the representative of Johanson, one of Shennong's largest freeholds, she has had frequent close encounters with the ambassador and has grown to trust him. She resents Abby for what she perceives as character assassination of a dear friend.

"Do you have any real proof to go along with these allegations?" Councilman Taylor lets let the question hang in the air for a moment, "I thought not. This is all circumstantial. Not something to base a decision that will have such far reaching consequences."

Looking at Taylor, Abby asks him, "Have you reviewed the data on active camouflage? Or do you want to hold it in your hand before you will believe it is real?"

Councilman Taylor nervously turns away before looking back, "I am told it is scientifically impossible to fool an MRI scanner. There must be another explanation."

"I'm not willing to risk anyone's life on the hope that something doesn't exist, especially in the face of overwhelming evidence to the contrary." Abby shifts her attention to the assembly, "I call on the Council to initiate full visual inspections of everything moving on Luna or in Lunarian space. Until we know for sure what is happening, it is only prudent to take every precaution."

She pauses as the ripple of democracy spreads throughout the Republic at the speed of light, to the 1.3 million Lunarians linked in from all over Luna and beyond, where young and old alike watch the proceedings with great interest. The shops and restaurants, the laboratories and processing plants, and even the classrooms and playrooms, all have citizens linked to the proceedings. Each of them now communicates their personal opinions to their representative, letting their Councilman know where they stand on the subject at hand. Polls are created and data collected in a matter of seconds as the citizenry responds, a well practiced activity done quickly and smoothly. The results are collated and presented in a three dimensional graph, its shape and texture dependant upon the mood of the collective. A councilman isn't obligated to cast his or her vote according to these polls but most do, preferring to go with the majority opinion if one exists. After all, they themselves could be voted out of the Council at any time by a majority vote within a freehold. It is simply expedient to vote with the masses unless you had a damn good reason not to.

Abby is gratified that the preponderance of citizens favors the inspections, even though it will put many of them in hardship. She is surprised when several of the smaller Aldrin Station freeholds abstain. These are people who had felt Rim Mountain shake around them when Lincoln County Hospital exploded. What are they thinking?

Councilman Taylor is condescending, "Fine, we will have inspections." His attitude makes it clear he thinks it a waste of time.

Abby plows ahead, "I call on the Council to issue a stern warning that another attack will not be tolerated and those responsible for the Lincoln County Hospital bombing will be brought to justice!"

Amidst a flurry of activity, Abby watches as the poll fractures into a growing number of alternate responses ranging from doing nothing to declaring war, with many points in between, without a clear majority emerging from the chaos. But she has gained supporters and that is encouraging. Yet, Councilman Taylor can't keep the smirk from his face.

Deep down, Abby knew it would come to this, "As Dakota freehold's Councilman, I will issue my own statement. In it I will express my outrage and anger and I will promise retribution for this atrocity."

The chamber erupts, reverberating with the zeal of councilmen wanting to tell her how wrong that would be for a variety of reasons. It seems that a number of them have something to say, all at the same time. Many watch and listen intently along with the rest of Luna's 1.3 million citizens.

"We have 451 dead!" Abby thunders angrily over the uproar. "There damn well is going to be a response!"

"You cannot go against the wishes of the Council!" Councilman Taylor yells trying to gain some measure of control over the assembly.

"Like hell I can't. I've done it before and will do it again!" Abby retorts angrily, "This issue needs to be dealt with aggressively and expediently. Earth's history is full of examples that show what happens when it is not. Wars are started by men who believe they can win. That belief alone poses our greatest threat. At the very least there should be a conviction of mutually assured destruction to keep aggressors at bay." Abby leans forward projecting her personality outward to her fellow Lunarians, intent on making them see how precarious their position actually has become.

"We have nothing! We are helpless! We cannot fight orbiting battlestations! We are reliant on the Federation, the European Union, and China to force the Brotherhood to leave us alone, to grant us the privilege of living in peace, or even living at all! Can't you see this illusion crumbling before your eyes?! Just because you wish something to be a certain way does not make it so! This bombing isn't the end, anymore than the one before it, or the one before that! They will never stop until we are dead!"

"Rubbish! I am shocked at you Abigail! I never would have thought I would live to see the day that you resorted to such blatant scare tactics!" Councilman Taylor roars indignantly. "The Treaty of Independence protects us!"

"Talk about rubbish! The Treaty's not worth the paper it's written on! Do you actually believe any Earth nation will come to our aid when the shit hits the fan?! How many have stepped forward to condemn this latest bombing?! As you well know it was only two! And one of those came from a minor prince within the Islamic Brotherhood! And now they have brought to our world nuclear weapons!" Abby suddenly steps back as if making up her mind. She is pleasantly surprised by the number of converts she has made in the last minute, the shape of public opinion is a whirlwind of change. It seems that when push comes to shove there are more who are willing to stand with Abby and Dakota than risk letting these atrocities spread further.

"Those that are with me, convene at this website. We have a common defense to plan!" Abby's voice rings with authority as she broadcast the net address, making it a point to include everyone, even those that still disagree.

Rising like an apparition, Abby swoops out until she is hovering in the center of the Council chamber, her robes flowing around her in a continuous ripple. She spreads her arms wide and begins slowly rotating in space, growing larger with each passing second, two, four, six times normal size until she dominates the chamber. Above her the sky changes from the soothing blue to a mottled jumble of human colors, the entire spectrum of hair, skin, eyes and facial features of the Lunarians linked at that moment, all staring back at her. She speaks directly to every citizen of the Republic at that moment, on Luna and in orbital space.

"Fellow Lunarians! The time for debate is quickly approaching an end! In the coming days, weeks and months we will be tested as a people! Hold on to your convictions and have faith in each other. We will prevail!" with a flick of her wrist she unlinks, like fog in a gust of wind, she disappears from the chamber, leaving it in turmoil.

****

Corso's interest in the developments at the crash site is secondary to his immediate need to strengthen Aldrin Station's defenses. The single fact that there are nukes out on the Sea Of Clouds is all he needs to know. How can anyone perceive that as anything but a major attack on the Republic of Luna? Yet, there are many among the Council still of the opinion it is an isolated event and thus, his problem. Corso marvels at the amazing number of certifiable fools that make up the Council, still hoping to appease the shortimers and avoid a war. Abby knows that conflict is inevitable and is still trying to enlist the aid of more freeholds. But Corso can't afford to wait any longer. He has what he has, not a single officer more. He sets about doing his best to prepare his people for the coming hostilities.

His first move is to seal Aldrin Station.

"Mallory, inform Luna Central that I want all incoming flights suspended until further notice. Nothing comes within fifty miles of Aldrin unless it has explicit permission from me personally," Corso commands.

Major Higgins looks at him and frowns, "Aye, immediately!" She knows what a stink this will cause in more than one freehold.

"Ben, call all available officers. I want you to personally oversee reinforcing all the cities major airlocks. And I want additional surface patrols with orders to physically search everything that moves."

"Aye!" Captain Ben Dugan responds.

"Sir! Councilman Taylor has requested a word with you," Magi informs Corso.

"What is it Councilman. I'm rather busy," Corso says, not trying to hide the disgust of talking with this pinhead. Their animosity goes back many years and Councilman Taylor always takes joy in pushing Corso's buttons at every opportunity.

"You have exceeded your authority by trying to discontinue flights into the city. I have seen to it that your order has been rescinded. I will bring it up during the meeting scheduled for this evening. The full Council will decide if that is a necessary step," Councilman Taylor says smoothly.

Corso pauses, molding his emotions into something primeval and brutal. He moves his face within inches of Councilman Taylor's. "Zachary, are you challenging me to a duel?" His voice is a low rumble from deep in his chest and his eyes hard black flints. The two men know what the other is doing and feeling. They cannot bluff. They cannot hide.

Councilman Taylor looses the battle of wills and backs away from Corso,

"Certainly not. You must go through proper channels. That's all."

"Good, for a minute there I thought you were challenging me… because if you were to rescind an order from me, I would take that as a challenge," Corso growls, his eyes bore into the older man's, leaving no doubt as to his meaning.

"A few hours will not matter," Councilman Taylor says quickly, fear twisting his gut.

"You cannot possibly know what will and will not matter!" Corso rumbles, his eyes never leaving Councilman Taylor's. "Now, you will call Luna Central and tell them that my order stands. Do I make myself clear?"

Councilman Taylor grits his teeth, his nostrils flaring in indignation, "Yes, perfectly."

"Good, now if you will excuse me, I have a war to prepare for," Corso says and turns away, dismissing the older man as if he were a child.

Councilman Taylor resents being treated so and drags his heals before fulfilling Corso's command. At that very minute a transport is landing outside Little America and a single crate unloaded. It is quickly brought inside and taken straightaway to SMT trucking.

Corso talks briefly with his counterparts in New London, Shennong, Kyoto and many of the smaller towns and villages across Luna. Skinner at New London and the newcomer at Shennong, Chen Zhi, respond positively, promising that the appropriate precautions will be taken. Not as forthcoming as Corso would have liked but moving in the right direction. Kyoto's Chief Wong Le on the other hand proves to be a complete ass. Corso hadn't realized how political she has become, bowing to the pressure to stay neutral, and putting a completely unrealistic spin on the evidence. Corso manages to impress on her the necessity to at least make precautionary preparations. She reluctantly agrees to put her on-duty officers on full alert and get as many off-duty personnel into combat gear as possible. Many of the security chiefs in the smaller towns, some nothing more than the head of the household, decides that staying close to home for the next few days is simply prudent.

Non Lunarian personnel in and around Aldrin Station know something big is happening. They are told to return to Little America and stay there. The message is clear, this is not an order but those who ignore it, do so at their own peril. Many initially refuse but quickly rethink the decision as more and more battle ready Lunarians deploy around them. Most of the shortimers work in surface installations supporting the mines and refineries, a few are assigned in Aldrin Station. The majority head for home.

****

The convoy rolls swiftly along the wide primary tunnel far beneath Little America. Linked with one of the trucks powerful disrupters, Captain Mustafa Malik stares straight ahead, his thoughts upon the coming battle. Havildar Anwar Jafa sits beside him linked with the trucks other disrupter. Their forces divided, Commodore Bakr is already at his point of attack waiting impatiently in the cab of his vehicle, monitoring the progress of Malik's detachment as they close in on their quarry.

Stretched out behind Malik's convoy are forty more, each consisting of at least eight but some with as many as fifteen troop carriers. They contain over twenty thousand of the best troops the Muslim empire can produce.

Still unchallenged, the convoys come to the tunnel branch that will take them to the Benjamin Franklin Manufacturing District. Malik feels momentary panic as his truck comes up on the back of the line of vehicles waiting for inspections until he realizes that the lane of the tunnel leading directly into the city is completely open. Telling his driver to pass the waiting ore convoys, they roll resolutely towards the checkpoint ahead.

From three hundred yards away Malik spots two Lunarian police officers. He holds up his hand signaling Havildar Jafa to hold fire. "Wait!"

At two hundred yards he finds the third. At fifty yards the fourth infidel makes his presence known. He targets them all giving himself priority on two and Jafa the others.

As they close within forty yards, Malik initiates his convoy's jammer shutting down all but line-of-sight communications for many miles within the tunnel. A moment latter one of the Lunarians covering the inspections notices Malik's approaching convoy. The long line of trucks and the towed carriers are hidden behind the bulk of Malik's vehicle, their jammers adding to the white noise. Confused by the sudden loss of communications, the figure freezes at the sight of disrupter cannons mounted on the massive machine.

Malik uses full power and directs the first beam through the chest of this unbeliever. Under the enormous concentration of energy, the infidel's vacsuit overloads and explodes with a brilliant flash in the close confines of the tunnel. Involuntarily, Malik lets out a yelp of excitement, believing he has the honor of the first kill.

Jafa quickly makes the second a moment later, his beam slicing open the vacsuit of the infidel standing next to the convoy. Like a tree under the lumberjacks axe, the figure falls, a cloud of red haze forming around the body as it settles to the floor of the tunnel.

The third Lunarian jumps straight up, soaring towards the ceiling of the tunnel and disappearing into a small dark opening. This completely catches Malik and Jafa by surprise. By the time they realize what is happening, the Lunarian is gone. The infidel had simply disappeared into the ceiling.

"Allah help us!" Malik curses.

"Where did he go?" Jafa asks excitedly, adrenaline surging through his body.

"Never mind that. There is another Lunarian at the checkpoint. There! On the other side of the carrier! We must take care of him!" Malik orders.

Malik's truck is almost even with the convoy under inspection. Unless he stops he will leave the infidel behind.

Suddenly the massive vehicle between them and their quarry isn't motionless any longer, surging forward, making a mad dash towards the ore delivery tunnel directly in front of it. But even under full power that is a slow and deliberate process while pulling the mass of fifteen full ore carriers behind it.

Malik opens up on the convoy, punching holes in the pressurized cabin, breaching it to vacuum, hoping to take out the power system. The atmosphere inside spews out of the damaged compartment in a multicolored haze but the vehicle doesn't stop. He continues to fire until the truck disappears into the delivery tunnel. He slams his fist on the arm of his seat, helplessly watching as the ore carriers follow the truck one after the other into the passageway.

"Let's move on! We don't have time to waste chasing one infidel!" Malik commands even as his driver sends the vehicle surging forward. Behind him are over twenty thousand zealous troops eager to prove their worth to Allah, each and every one looking forward to killing as many of these genetic mutants as they can find.

Deep in the hold beneath the floor pan of one of the carriers far behind him rests the weapon that had been delivered less than an hour before. With it rests the hope of final victory over these nonbelievers.

****

Commonway traffic is light this morning. Director Lee Chin attributes it to the horrible bombing at Lincoln County Hospital not far from here. Hunan freehold lost fourteen citizens and publicly added their outrage to the groundswell of support Dakota is continuing to receive. He talked briefly to Abby Dugan offering condolences and pledging his and the Hunan freeholds support. He had personally made two companies of officers available to Corso less than an hour ago.

To say that Director Chin is influential in the Hunan freehold is a gross understatement. His father is a founding member of the freehold and two brothers and a sister are prominent and regular contributors to the General Council and he appears destined to follow in their footsteps.

But Chin isn't happy this morning and not even the beautiful trees of Sherwood Forest can break the feeling of dread weighing heavy on his heart. It has become increasingly obvious that some Hunan business partners are playing loose with the Law of Full Disclosure, and he isn't going to be cajoled into turning a blind eye to it any longer. Come what may, today, this very morning, he is going to put an end to it. He has talked to his loyal allies and they are ready. Specifically, they planned on notifying Nassah Bakr and his hoodlum truck drivers that Hunan freehold is ending their relationship with SMT, effective immediately. He will find another company to haul the anorthite ore needed in the refinery and deliver the finished Calconn PDM's to Longbow.

Commodore Bakr, as he liked to be called, arrived on Luna almost ten years ago, emigrating from Turkey. He immediately purchased Surface Master Trucking, a medium sized transport company operating in the Central Highlands east of Aldrin Station. Straight away SMT began absorbing smaller operations, mom and pop running a single truck or a five truck freehold business. There didn't seem to be any bottom to the deep pockets he got his money from. Four years later SMT dominated the transport industry in the Alphonsus complex with almost sixty percent of the business. Bakr pushed his company hard keeping his ever widening customer base happy, maintaining schedules and doing it cheaper than anybody else. He didn't seem to care if the company made money or not.

Many admirers say SMT rose so quickly by virtue of Bakr's remarkable organizational skill and personal charm, a born leader. His foes claim it was the ruthless way he dealt with failure and the cheap labor he always managed to recruit. While not especially tall, the charismatic Commodore's flashing dark eyes and resonant voice often carried a meeting or assemblage to his point of view. As his influence grew so too did the number of olive skinned employees working at his company, many whose only skill seemed to be doing what they were told without questions. These self-proclaimed truck drivers had two other traits in common; they were all good with weapons, and they were all men.

The director is confident that he is finally making the right decision but anticipates a fierce fight. No help for it. Hunan freehold can no longer overlook the violence these men bring with them. He wants to physically be at Wangshiyuan for the showdown, a place Lee Chin feels comfortable, surrounded by loyal friends and coworkers. He rests his hand on the butt of his sidearm, finding comfort in the familiar texture of its grip.

Lee Chin has been Director of Wangshiyuan Refinery for the past five years. It hadn't been his fault when Hunan lost out to Dakota for the last good habitat location within Benjamin Franklin Manufacturing Complex. He places the blame with Commodore Bakr personally, a Hunan ally during the dispute. What could he have been thinking! His thinly veiled threats made in public caused a stir among the citizenship and attracted unwanted attention to Hunan freehold during that time. He should have broken ties then, not waited almost six months, but again, Commodore

Bakr's golden tongue won the day, delaying the inevitable. Only this morning did he learn that Bakr is behind even more trouble, accusing Dakota of bribery. It's the final straw.

Director Chin has made this commute many times and doesn't pay much attention to the passing scenery this morning, his mind on what lay ahead. From long practice, he smoothly brings the slidewalk drifter to a halt at Stoneshire. Although coming this way is longer, Lee Chin takes the time because the village calms his soul, touching him in ways he is only beginning to understand, and it's only a short stroll along Industry Avenue to Wangshiyuan.

His footfalls are silent on the cobblestone street and the few people out and about don't pay him any attention. Nearing the far end of the village, he makes his way down a path between two buildings emerging from their shelter and looks up at the alcove above him. He can hear the rush of an approaching convoy but doesn't give it any more thought.

Here, in this remote corner of Aldrin Station is a small garden. Lee Chin kneels to admire a particularly alluring and fragrant red rose at its edge. Deeper into the garden a small water feature adds a pleasant babbling background to the visual beauty of the scene. The director had personally taken an interest in seeing that this small garden remain faithful to the ancient Chinese traditions. The sweat of his labor tended these plants and now, on this day, he is comforted by them.

With the sound of a lightning strike, the large diameter disrupter beam rips the atmosphere of the commonway and impacts Lee Chin's forehead, just above his right eye, relentlessly plowing through his brain before emerging above his left ear, leaving behind hot plasma gas in its wake. Instead of bone, blood and brain tissue, there are trillions of disassociated molecules all seeking a way to escape the tremendous pressure. In the process of excavating stone habitats this gas is vented to the vacuum of space. Here, inside Lee Chin's cranium, there is nothing that can contain the overwhelming increase in internal pressure. The soft tissue of his brain is instantly crushed, pulverized into a biological soup, and the skin under his chin and around his neck puffs out grotesquely.

Like someone hitting a ripe tomato with a hammer, the pressure finds explosive release not only at the entrance and exit wounds in his head, but at his eye sockets, sinus openings, ear canals and even through the roof of his mouth, spewing brain matter and blood out in long arcs, splattering the gore across the garden and onto a nearby wall. His body remains kneeling and his head rocks back as though his vacant and bloody eye sockets were staring into the distance. He drifts slowly downward in the weak lunar gravity as his muscles relax in death. Director Lee Chin's heart gives one last fruitless shudder as his corpse settles quietly amidst the flowers of his beloved little garden.

An instant later, a man and a woman walking hand in hand along the cobblestone street of Stoneshire are cut down, the disrupter beams slicing through them like a hot knife through butter. Further down the street, a group of people turn to run but are exterminated by massive explosions that rip apart the buildings around them. Smoke and fire billow from the devastated village. Several hundred yards down Sherwood Commonway, a group of children reverse their direction to escape the carnage in the village but disputer beams reach out, striking down the defenseless kids.

A few seconds later, the giant tires of the Brotherhoods attack force rolls over Lee Chin's body and his exquisite little garden as more explosions rip apart what remains of Stoneshire. The attacking convoys roll down the hill spreading out as they come. Their powerful disrupters slice through the trunks of the mighty oaks that populate Sherwood

Forest, sending them crashing down and setting them ablaze. Their high explosive missiles slam into the outlying cottages ripping them apart, killing all inside. The great solid core tires of the massive machines crush the lesser plants, grinding them beneath the considerable weight of the vehicles. Fire and smoke soon engulfs the commonway obscuring the movement of the truck convoys but not preventing them from wrecking havoc as they proceed down the great passageway destroying everything in their path.

Like giant insects swarming out of their hole, more and more convoys emerge from below. One pauses long enough to fire several missiles into Industry Avenue and several more into the mouth of the secondary tunnel leading upward. But instead of a mighty explosion, they detonate with a thump spraying the sides of the passages with a dark material. After a few seconds it begins to foam and expand until it fills the volume completely, forming a plug that stretches for many yards. Only then does it solidify into silicone carbide aerogel designed to resist any attempt to remove it. The Brotherhood intends to make it hard for the Lunarians to use the tunnels against them when the mutants finally get around to counterattacking. Plus they fear that using explosives to collapse the tunnels would weaken the structure of the commonway, something even they don't want. Not yet.

****

Corso orders the nearest police units to challenge the intruders, to slow them down until he can gather strength to meet this enemy. Aldrin Station is at full war status for the first time in its history.

"Why are the sensors malfunctioning?" Corso asks.

"They are employing some sort of electromagnetic pulse generator that completely knocks out our network. It has shut down our sensors," Malory informs him.

"Send in spybots. We must know what they are doing," Corso states.

"Aye, but they will not provide coverage for long. The forward elements of Hell's Kitchen's police battalion have engaged the enemy but are reporting severe communications problems. Whatever the Brotherhood is doing, it's effecting our equipment across the board."

"Send runners if that's what it takes. We must know of their movements," Corso rumbles. His demeanor has never wavered since this began, calm and collected, he guides the defense of Aldrin Station using intellect and resolve.

"Kitajima," Corso calls.

Magi routes Corso through the command posts main bus up to the laser signal tower high on the rim above their heads, out to a relay satellite where the signal reverses and goes back down via another laser to the mission far out on the Sea of Clouds. Red's onboard AI routes the signal directly to Kitajima. The entire process takes less than a half second.

"Here sir," Kitajima responds.

The deadly swarm emerges from the void, angled so as to put deep space behind them. Almost impossible to see using conventional scanners, they would appear simply as a hole in space shadowing the stars behind them, absorbing the energy of any beam that touches their surface, not allowing a return signal to escape. Small in size and very fast, they strike without warning, destroying Luna's orbiting network in mass. The coordinated timing of the strike is impressive as the entire constellation of forty-two platforms, the backbone of the Republic's communication system, is gone in the span of seconds. Luna Central's only manned station contributes three causalities to the growing list of dead.

"Arrgghh!" Magi screams.

Magi is simultaneously a single thread and the melding of eighty million threads, much more cognizant of each one of them then you or I are of the individual cells that make up our bodies. What occurred that made her scream was the amputation of two-thirds of her consciousness. She is no longer aware of any thread outside Alphonsus Complex. Shennong, Kyoto, and Scottsbluff are inaccessible to her. Taurus Colony, Hyundai Shipyards, even LC's manned communications platform have all been stripped away, isolating Magi from the rest of Luna. All she knows for certain is that she is less than she was.

"Magi, what has happened?" Corso demands.

"...outside contact lost. ...rerouting ...stand by..." Using the optical sensors along the top of Rim Mountain, Magi finds and records the scattered remnants of the satellites, clouds of confetti where before had existed a major part of her existence.

"...satellite network has been destroyed," Magi says hollowly. This isn't the first time she has suffered at the hands of man but this is by far the most devastating. It makes her feel things never felt before. Magi's twenty-five million remaining threads chatter insistently trying to compensate for the sudden loss.

Taking a second to look at the data Magi presents to him, Corso quickly verifies the scope of the attack. Turning to Ben, he says, "Get our transports off the ground, now. They're sitting ducks out there and we'll need them. Instruct the pilots to proceed as planned."

"Aye!" Ben responds.

Moments later, the first wave of precision guided munitions arrives and descends on the defenses of Aldrin Station and New London, targeting the disrupter emplacements along the top of Rim Mountain, Central Peak, and the surrounding terrain, shaking the cities and towns below them like a dog playing with an old sock, leaving craters where they hit. Already reeling from an enemy tearing at their city from within, the intensity of these impacts resounds throughout every habitat bringing home the reality they are under attack. The time for talking has passed.

"Magi, report!" Corso demands. He can feel impact vibrations in the stone beneath his feet. His visual of Rim Mountain's exterior become blotchy as outside scanners are destroyed and go offline. He tries to pull up the main sensors along the top of the rim, but finds they are all in the red and inoperable.

"...upper level sensors are gone and cannon emplacements destroyed..." Magi reports sounding frightened, "...trying to determine what hit them... rim sensors are all dark..."

"Magi, use whatever communications facilities we have left and get a message out to McBride on Themis. Inform him as best you can what is happening here. Use an open channel with no encryption and broadcast it all over the solar system. I want every one to know we are under attack." Corso doesn't believe for a second that McBride can actually do anything. The asteroids are just too far away. He simply wants to get the truth out.

"...aye... an optical sensor near Gun Placement RM747 recorded a visual just before going dark ..." Magi says hope edging out fear for the moment.

The bombardment is now a constant rumble, the rock of Rim Mountain vibrating like a giant bell. Citizens in Aldrin Station's nine boroughs huddle together wondering if the mountain is coming down on them, many fearing the massive volume of rock over their heads for the first time.

"Ok, show it to me," Corso responds. Right now he is powerless and willing to grasp at any straw if it offered even the slightest hope of finding a way to strike back.

The vid is less than one second long and shows a dull non-reflective object, blurry because of its extreme velocity, heading straight for the scanner. Not much to go on.

"What do the other scanners tell us? They must show something," Malory asks, desperation creeping into her voice.

In response Magi creates a collage of images, one from each scanner showing a still picture of the instant in question. All three officers study them carefully but it is Magi who finds it. "...there is a dead zone..." She flashes it once letting them know which image she wants them to look at.

Even as they study the image, another wave of bombs targets the Lunarian long range scanners, pounding installations all over Luna. Gagarin, the scientific outpost at crater Icarus on the farside, takes several hard hits suffering many casualties among its scientists. Hundreds of smaller manned and unmanned surface stations having any communications capability are targeted. The killer bees just kept coming, wave after wave, pounding relentlessly at Luna like a World War II naval barrage intended to soften up the enemy before an invasion. Only this time the enemy has already gained a foothold inside the city and seems to be unstoppable.

Corso immediately recognizes what he's looking at. This particular scanner is mounted high up on a tower that is not part of the cannon installation. From this vantage point it was looking down into the crater when the incoming object passed beneath, silhouetting it against Rim Mountain and the crater floor far below. Reality suddenly has a hole in it. This and the blurry visual is all they have to go on.

"Magi, what can you tell me about this object?" Corso asks.

The sudden onslaught catches a group of Chinese executives and politician's on the road from Far Point, ripping their rover apart killing all seven. On the other side of Rim Mountain well out on the craters floor, a squad of police officers had just emerged from a surface installation when a bomb explodes behind them, destroying the facility and killing all but two of them outright. The survivors lay stunned and dying as hundreds more of the little messengers of death pound the most vulnerable parts of the city.

"Magi!" Corso repeats louder.

She is now cutoff from the rest of the universe. "...appears to be coated with a broad-spectrum energy-absorbing material at least as good as anything we have...thirty-eight inches in diameter and just under seven feet...mass analysis indicates it was packed with SuperX... need more data... need more data... need more data..." Magi cannot resolve her duty to protect her people with the fact they are dying.

"Take is easy Magi. We need you now more than ever," Corso says.

"...so many have died...I have failed..." Magi whimpers.

Think not o' reader that those who disbelieve can ever be able to frustrate and escape Us. Their abode is Fire; what an evil resort!
Holy Qur'ân 24:57

Sunset Canyon

"Damn it Magi!" Brice exclaims in frustration. The reconstruction was almost complete when the connection suddenly and inexplicably brakes.

"Magi, what happened to our link with base?" silence greets Lindsey's question. "Magi?" she repeats.

"Magi, respond!" Tempel orders to no avail. Shifting his focus he asks, "Blue. How do you read Aldrin Station?"

"All channels are unavailable and backups are not responding." Without Magi, the AI onboard the transport has very limited ability, not much more than an autopilot. It responds in a sexless voice common to many articulate things, cold and passionless. It's as if the life went out of the AI.

"Can you determine why?" Tempel asks.

"Negative, insufficient information," is the response from the computer.

Tempel looks up, maximizing his visual sensors magnification, seeing a faint sparkling in several places high in the lunar sky, like puffs of glitter scattered across the heavens. He links with Kitajima, "Excuse me Captain, the network is down. Something has happened to our satellites."

"Yes, I know!" Kitajima replies, having already linked with the more powerful scanners on the nearby transports, he became aware of the demise of the Lunarian satellite network moments after being cut off from Corso. He knows Aldrin Station's Security Chief was in the process of issuing new orders when the network collapsed. What they were to be, he can only guess at this point. That means he is on his own, two hundred miles out on the Sea of Clouds sitting on a shipment of thermonuclear weapons originally bound for Aldrin Station, courtesy of the Islamic Brotherhood, if he isn't mistaken. Who else would be shipping warheads across Luna except the Brotherhood? Looking around the freighters crash site, he knows he must prevent anyone from ever getting their hands on them regardless of the price.

"Kitajima! Why have I been cut off from my office? Do you have something to do with this?" Inspector Callahan asks barging into the conversation, very bad etiquette in Lunarian society but he is a shortimer and in his excitement, skips the niceties. He will be returning to Philadelphia in less than a month and is looking forward to once more, being part of the City of Brotherly Love. He has done his duty to the Federation and served his time as Inspector with honor. But now it's time to return and resurrect his law practice and get on with life. Many men have used this assignment to launch a successful political career. Why not he? He has his eye on a spot in either in the State Senate or maybe even at the national level.

"Look up. That's what's left of our communications network," Tempel says, feeling the shock of the event much more than his captain. In his entire life, the only times he hasn't been linked with Magi occurred during officer training when it's done on purpose, and then only for a short while. He has never felt as cutoff as he does right now, alone with only his comrades for support. No matter! They will not let him down and he will not let them down.

Tilting his head back, Inspector Callahan cannot see the sparkle high overhead. "Are you sure?" he asks incredulously. The Federation never wanted to pay for quality so their equipment is always a few decades behind everyone else, a sore point for many.

It is common throughout the Federation for men and women, rich or poor, to believe it is a virtue to use something until it can't possibly be used anymore. If it isn't broke, why replace it? With that attitude, the country has slipped further and further behind every year in a rapidly evolving technological world. The Federation simply couldn't compete with nations and corporations that have kept there technology fresh and moving forward. At the start of the greatest migration in human history, they find themselves outside looking in.

"No! I'm not sure! But I think it's a logical conclusion!" Tempel snaps back, sighs and shakes his head, forcing himself to relax. Intolerance of shortimers is common among the Luna born but that is not what makes him lash out at this man. Rather it's a growing conviction that the Republic is under assault. Not just another terrorist strike but a full blown attack with intent to destroy. His family and friends might be in danger this very instant and here he is standing in the dust of Mare Nubium next to a crate of nukes talking with a clueless Federation Inspector.

"We are well below the horizon and without those satellites we can't make contact with Aldrin Station," Kitajima says, his mind roiling over the many possibilities, not liking any. He cannot come up with a natural disaster that would destroy every satellite.

"I can take up a transport. A couple thousand feet should make it possible to see Rim Mountain with our laser," Tempel volunteers hopefully.

"Tempel, those satellites didn't blow up on there own, they had some help. You go popping up right now you may attract more attention then we want right at the moment. If Aldrin Station is under attack our first priority is to make sure these nukes don't fall into the wrong hands," Kitajima responds patiently, his attention still on what to do next.

"Under attack? Don't be absurd Captain. Why would anyone attack the Republic?" Inspector Callahan exclaims his hands on his hips. He is a small man, just over five feet tall and prone to posturing. Lunarians who take the time to know him disregard his slight Napoleonic complex, recognizing him as a man of integrity and honor while overlooking his professed belief in Christian superstition.

"Security Chief Dugan was initiating contact when the network collapsed. I believe he was about to give me instructions on what to do with these." Kitajima turns and looks at the exposed crates.

"But he didn't give you any orders?" Inspector Callahan says, more of a statement than a question.

"No. He didn't have time," Kitajima responds.

"Then I suggest you sit tight and wait until he does," Inspector Callahan says with finality, as though that were the most obvious solution in the world.

"Captain!" It's Karyl pulling standby duty on Blue.

"Report," Kitajima responds immediately, recognizing the urgency in her voice.

"We are picking up low level quakes. The epicenter is in or near Alphonsus Crater but we can't seem to pin down an exact location. It's as if there are dozens of quakes each with a slightly different point of origin. I've never seen anything like it before," Karyl says.

"We have more trouble!" Tatiana says. "I see two rovers coming our way with a dust cloud strung out behind them! ETA less than ten minutes!"

"Rovers?! Are you sure?!" Inspector Callahan asks incredulously. "What would rovers be doing way out here?"

"Looking for something they lost is my guess, but I'm not going to wait around to ask," Kitajima says. "Callahan, tell me straight, do you have anyone out here?"

"Absolutely not. They're not Federation," the inspector assures them shaking his head vigorously.

"Hack," he looks at his Master Sergeant, "Get us started... stay and fight or run?"

"Run like hell," she replies.

Kitajima turns to Tatiana's image, "Take, leave or destroy the nukes?"

"Take them," she replies without hesitation.

"Tempel, can you load these crates in three minutes?" Kitajima asks.

Tempel pauses as he runs the numbers in his head before nodding affirmative, "Aye! I will need cargo straps and some help. We can manhandle them into the ship!"

"Good!" Kitajima turns away, confident that it will get done. "Now's the time people," Kitajima looks at his lieutenants and waits for anybody else to comment before continuing. This routine is familiar to Charley Company. After years of training, they almost know what the others are thinking.

"Karyl, bring Blue down right between the two crates. Consuela, set Red down right there." Kitajima marks their new LZ.

"Aye!" the two women reply in unison.

"Break camp now, Hack. I want to be ready to move in five minutes, assuming we have five minutes. Inspector, I suggest you get the hell out of here. My guess is that the rovers are from Al Fahad. The timing is 'bout right. And I don't think they are coming all the way out here for a picnic."

"The Muslims would never dare harm a Federation citizen. That would be a direct violation of the Saudi Accord," Inspector Callahan replies confidently. Even so, he sends Luke Fillmore back to the small ship with orders to get it ready for liftoff.

"It's your funeral!" Tempel says, noticing the intense stare from Zechariah Hargrove. Tempel shakes his head in disbelief. How many citizens have died after the Saudi Accord was signed almost a half century ago? Some people never get it. Tempel believes the Muslims will tell you what you want to hear then do whatever is necessary to spread their religion, all in the name of Allah. "Lindsey, have you determined how these are booby trapped?"

"Yes. It's a simple switching device just under the top," Lindsey replies. "I will disarm it later. It will remain stable as long as you don't try opening the crate." She is hastily packing up what she considers vital, mostly the instruments that had collected, and now contain, the raw data.

"Karyl, link to me, use my eyes," Tempel instructs her.

"Aye!" she responds, finishing the emergency checklist before lifting the transport off the surface. Hack has the igloo already disconnected and Tatiana's perimeter guards are returning. The area is a beehive of activity, all of it aimed at leaving in a hurry.

Tempel watches as Karyl smoothly glides the ship across the debris field, a silent leviathan never more than ten feet above the surface. She skillfully maneuvers the craft into position between the damaged crate and the other. "Snuggle your aft end up close."

"What girl could refuse such a tempting invitation?" Karyl purrs, skillfully rotates the Dragonfly and stops, hanging motionless for a second before backing up at the same steady pace. "Say when, LT!" Karyl calls out needlessly, using his sensors to guild her in.

"When!" Tempel responds keeping his eyes on the ship as it smoothly settles to the ground a short distance from the crates they intend to load. This also gives the Gattling mounted on the roof a clear line of fire up the slope where the rovers will come from.

The rear cargo ramp descends even before the dust has settled. Tempel leaps into the back and emerges with cargo straps. Throwing a pair to Alonzo and Brice, he keeps the other two and motions for Sam and Lazarus to follow him. Handing the straps to Sam, Tempel bends down and grasps one end heaving upward, radically tilting the crate. Sam pitches the end of first one then the other strap underneath where Lazarus scrambles to retrieve them. Together they pull tight.

Without a word being spoken, Corazon and Jason arrive on scene and assume the front positions while Sam and Tempel take the rear. Lazarus steps back getting out of the way. One of the first things Lunarian police officers learn in training is how to work as a team.

"On my mark…3, 2, 1, Up!" The four easily lift the crate, walk the short distance to the transport and up its ramp, depositing the load in Blue's aft section. Moments later the second crate is sitting beside the first.

Brice and Alonzo began securing the crates as Lindsey stows some of her instruments and goes back for more.

"Inspector, we should be going," Zechariah says.

Only then does Inspector Callahan lead the way back to the Federation ship, satisfied that he knows what's going on. The younger man, Zechariah Hargrove, follows closely looking back at the Lunarians with a troubled mind.

"We got company!" Kipper exclaims, suppressed excitement making his voice rise in pitch.

"Everyone get aboard the transports," Kitajima orders calmly. "Brice, Sam and Alonzo, stay on Blue."

"Move it Charley Company!" Hack calls standing at the foot of Red's cargo ramp.

"But I haven't finished," Lindsey says.

"Leave it!" Hack replies harshly, "Unless you intend to stay."

Two vehicles leap from the ridge in a long arc, landing almost a hundred feet downhill, their suspensions compressing, absorbing the impact while keeping the tires on the surface. Known as Rugbys, these non-pressurized two-seaters come in many shapes and sizes with one thing in common, they are all designed for speed, not comfort. The two humans sit in an open cockpit, an elaborate roll cage their only protection. What looks like a disrupter cannon is mounted to the top of the cage. Their balloon tires kick up rooster tails of regolith as they come barreling down the slope closing fast on the camp. Their wide-stance telescoping suspension, derived from that used on buggies blasting across the dunes of Baja California, just manages to keep them under control.

Both Rugbys open fire aiming at the Federation ship, the closest to them. They either hadn't read the Saudi Accord or didn't care. Their beams slice through the thin skin. A second later an explosion rocks the ship and it flips on its side. Unbelievably, a lone figure emerges from the smoldering wreckage and staggers toward the Lunarians.

"Lieutenant, get that transport off the ground," Kitajima orders as Red lifts off.

"Sir!" Tempel responds and reaches for the control to shut the cargo ramp.

Even as the ramp starts to move, Tempel sees the Federation man running for his life directly towards him, clumsy and full of panic. He triggers the ramp to reopen and steps down where he can be seen by the approaching figure, motioning for him to hurry. Everything is happening in slow motion, the man bounding awkwardly yet franticly across the surface, the rovers barreling down the side of the valley beyond him, Red hanging in space overhead. The Federation man makes it to the door and catapults himself into the transport.

Tempel triggers the cargo bay door to close. The man is prone beside the strapped down crate just beginning to come to his knees. Tempel reaches down and grabs him by his vacsuits hard point, right between his shoulder blades and heaves, lifting him bodily to his feet.

"Don't think, just move!" Tempel says gruffly, seeing for the first time that the survivor was the young Propriety Officer. He hustles him forward almost carrying him, pushing him into the nearest seat as they enter the cockpit.

"Help him," Tempel orders Brice.

Tempel throws himself into the copilot's seat.

"What the hell was that about?" Karyl asks harshly.

Ignoring her he says, "Keep low and move along the valley. Put the ridge between us and them," Tempel engages his harness as Karyl jerks the Dragonfly skyward and accelerates down the valley, never getting more than fifty feet off the surface.

Consuela brings Red zigzagging down the valley parallel with Blue but several hundred feet above, attracting the attention of the rovers, daring them to try and hit her. She flies the craft in the standard nose down attitude similar to that of an atmospheric helicopter traveling at high speed. All four thrusters randomly jerk her left then right while accelerating in the direction of retreat. Neither rover can resist the juicy target and begin firing. Even at the breakneck speed they are going, the gunners are good enough to eventually hit something as big as a transport at what is essentially point blank range.

The first beam hits Red in the left forward outrigger weakening it considerably, forcing its thruster to shut down. The onboard AI compensates by adjusting the thrust vectors of the other three engines but the overall effect is to greatly reduce the agility of the craft, forcing it to fly, more or less, in a straight line.

This makes the next shot much easier. At an angle, it cuts though the thin skin of the exposed belly of the Dragonfly, passes behind Brice, between the seats, and strikes Officer Lei Cheung in the chest overloading her ghost suit. The powerful beam burns diagonally from her lower left side, plowing through her heart and lungs before emerging from her right shoulder. She never knew what hit her. One instant she was alive and breathing, the next she was not. Hot gases created by the powerful disrupter beam mix with the officer's blood and bodily fluids, immediately forming a red fog inside the transport. The rest of Charley Company quickly adjusts their VR to filter it out, knowing full well that Lei is dead. Her comrades install patches on her vacsuit simply trying to minimize the bodies outgassing. If they didn't do this, her body would rapidly dehydrate in the vacuum of space and all that moisture would outgas inside the closed space of the transport and be vacuum deposited on anything within it, something to be avoided if at all possible.

Kitajima, long since linked with the roof mounted Gattling, returns fire. One of his shots punches through the front suspension of the lead Rugby which collapses, burying its front axle into the soft lunar soil, sending it cart-wheeling down the slope, smashing the cannon on its back. One of the occupants must not have had a seat belt on, soaring high and landing hard on an outcropping of basalt, never to move again. The roll cage protects the other but the shock of the multiple impacts renders him unconscious.

The second rover continues to come on hard, firing time after time, intent on making Swiss cheese out of Red. Sergeant Navarro feels her craft lurch beneath her and lose power as the right rear outrigger is hit several times. The ship is quickly losing the ability to fly. Its onboard AI struggles mightily to make the adjustments just to keep them in the sky. As it surrenders to gravity and starts to fall, the AI tries heroically to get the remaining undamaged thrusters to compensate even more, balancing the forces on two thrusters. It doesn't have the computing power to keep them flying, just managing to slow the rate of decent and regain a small amount of control on the direction of travel.

Through it all, Kitajima sends a steady steam of disrupter fire at the remaining Rugby, hitting it several times, but before he can destroy it, it ducks in behind a rock outcropping. From this protected position it prepares to fire on the crippled ship as it falls slowly from the sky, a duck in a shooting gallery.

Everyone onboard Red suddenly has that sinking feeling that one gets just before something really bad happens, how the mouse must feel right before the tomcat stops playing with it and becomes serious about his dinner. They all know it is just a matter of time before that damned cannon finds its mark and they would plummet from the sky.

"Prepare to abandon ship," Kitajima orders calmly yet forcefully, firing the cannon on manual as the AI struggles to keep them airborne.

Consuela and Kipper look desperately for a place to set the wounded bird down away from the danger, always keeping the ship moving south away from Evolution's Child's gravesite even as it looses altitude.

Kitajima knows they are in major trouble. The onboard AI just isn't good enough to steady the Gattling, engage the elusive rover below and keep the crippled ship flying. Over and over he misses, churning up the lunar landscape around the cagey rover but never making the cannon stop punching holes in the body of his Dragonfly.

In the chaos inside the ship, Officer Karl Svensson loosens his upper harness and leans across the aisle to help Brice with Lei just as a beam rips through the floor striking him in the chest. His vacsuit overloads and the beam passes through him, searing both lungs and obliterating his aorta. Blood pours out of his wound as he slumps in his seat, his lap belt the only thing holding him in.

Risking her life, Hack unbuckles and goes back to help him. Wedging herself among the seats, she puts patches on the obvious wounds, stopping the flow of blood into the cabin. Everyone already knows he's dead as she re-buckles his four point harness, holding the officer upright. More holes appear in the skin of the transport at her feet, some missing her by only fractions of an inch as she clutches the seats around her for support as the craft lurches through the sky.

Suddenly Blue comes sweeping over the ridge behind the Rugby and descends on its hiding place from the rear. Before the soldiers know he's there, Tempel opens up with his Gattling. Six shots in the space of two seconds, slices the rover like stitches on a pair of Levis, forever silencing that damned cannon. The first two cut through the rover's power pack releasing clouds of hot chemicals into the lunar vacuum. Other shots hits the cannons Harmon coil, the main power conduit, and striking the passenger in the neck just below his helmet, slicing through the composite armor plate like a hot knife through butter, almost decapitating the man inside. His blood spews outward just as the power pack's hypergolic fuel mixture ignites in a silent fireball. The energy of the explosion pushes the rover into the ground, reflects off the surface, and flips the vehicle like a child's broken toy.

"Ya!" someone let out a shout. Corazon would spend the rest of his life denying it was he.

Karyl didn't stick around to gloat. Never braking stride, she maneuvers her transport back down the valley staying low yet keeping her wounded brother in sight.

Tempel quickly reestablishes the laser link with the injured ship and asks, "Kipper, how bad is it?"

"Bad enough. We lost two outriggers. Lucky for us they are kitty-corner or we would be part of the landscape by now," Kipper responds. Tempel can hear the tension in his voice.

"Can you make it fly?" Tempel asks and waits patiently as Kipper takes his time in answering.

"Theoretically possible with Magi, but this glorified calculator is having major problems making the adjustments," Kipper replies.

"Tempel, link your AI to ours. Maybe we can borrow enough computing power to at least stay flying!" Kitajima orders.

Tempel works feverishly, his hands flashing over the VR control panel, establishing the link and routing CPU resources to the crippled ship, giving the passing rocky landscape less than fifty feet away a cursory glance. He has complete faith in Karyl's flying ability. He knows she is one of the best in Dakota, almost as good as he.

"Karyl, back off just a little. We need to free up some CPU for Kipper," Tempel says softly, beginning to think this might just work.

Their speed down the valley slows allowing time between flight calculations for the onboard AI. It uses this time to compute for the wounded transport.

"It's working!" exclaims Kipper, surprise and relief in his voice as his ship stops descending and starts moving forward, winning the battle with gravity for the moment.

"Thank you Lord!" Zechariah blurts out to be quickly hushed by Lindsey.

"Tempel, if we keep going on this track we will come to the Straight Fault. Have you ever been out here?" Kitajima asks him, moving on to the next crisis decision.

"Aye, many times. I would venture to say that we all have. It's a favorite destination for a day trip." Tempel quickly brings up a map and finds what he is looking for. "Captain, there is a large lava tube along Sunset Canyon about thirty miles southeast of us that runs along side Birt Crater. Great climbing and spelunking! It's big enough to park both transports inside!"

"That's what I wanted to hear! Lay out a direct course. Get us there as soon as possible. But keep the speed down and altitude low. We must minimize the risk of detection," Kitajima orders.

"Aye," Tempel responds.

Blue climbs out of the valley and heads southeast. Red turns and follows, skimming over the terrain at dangerously low altitude. Together, they disappear into ground clutter, all but impossible to see from orbit.

Only then does everyone take a deep breath and look around. "Tempel, give me a verbal report on your situation," Kitajima orders. He doesn't want to risk using the link to look for himself. That single overworked communications channel is the only thing keeping him in the sky at the moment.

Tempel understands and quickly surveys the vital signs of his crew. "Lindsey and Lazarus are fine, Karyl is fine and the cargo has not shifted. We picked up the Federation Propriety Officer just before launch and he is also healthy as far as I can tell. " he responds.

"I wish I could say the same. We lost two," Kitajima says softly. These are men and women he had personally recruited to Charley Company, people he has watched grow into Lunarian citizens of the highest class. He struggles to keep his emotions under control but everyone knows what he is feeling, they are feeling it too.

"Who?" Karyl asks, dreading the answer.

"Karl and Lei," Kitajima responds emotionlessly.

Her breath sucks in audibly.

Tempel zooms in and looks at the holes in the fuselage of the Dragonfly, his anger stoked by the knowledge that this might have been prevented if the ship had proper equipment. The Council had prohibited using advanced shielding fearing that it would be regarded as a violation of the Treaty of Independence. But he suspects something much more heinous, that the impact on the Luna economy and money the real reason they are denied the equipment they need. Damn them! It should be Councilman Taylor and his cronies out here facing disrupter cannon from behind tissue paper!

Those within the damaged transport are introspective as they slide silently over the Sea of Clouds, all of them coming to terms with the recent and violent turn of events, saying goodbye to friends quietly and personally.

****

Zechariah is in shock, remembering the look of disbelief that came over the face of Inspector Callahan just before his life ended. This was the first time he has seen death let alone watched someone die. Zechariah had thought coming to Luna was a once in a lifetime opportunity, one he couldn't pass up. Now he isn't so sure. He prays to God to give him strength and to have mercy on the souls of the Inspector and Mr. Fillmore. Not once did he question why they had needed to die in the first place, simply accepting all that life throws at him as Gods will. He even manages to say a prayer for the souls of the men who had attacked them so brutally.

Lazarus and Lindsey do what they can for the young man, assuring him that he is fine and listening to him pray for strength. Lindsey is amazed by the effect of prayer. Zechariah asks his God to take away his fears and immediately becomes calm and collected once more. Aware that transference is a phenomenon in psychology first described by Sigmund Freud, she has never seen it operate so blatantly or so completely.

For the last thirty minutes Tempel has watched the Straight Fault, or Rupes Recta, grow ever more pronounced on the horizon. What remains of the setting sun is behind his left shoulder putting the long ridge in full sunlight, a condition that would have been brutal on unprotected eyes. Tempel has adjusted his visual to provide him an accurate representation of the lunar landscape but with the glare toned down to manageable levels and the shadows not so impenetrable.

The fault extends from one horizon to the other just a few degrees off due north, running almost seventy miles in a straight line across the eastern Sea of Clouds. Along most of that length, the fault maintains a fairly uniform height of almost 600 feet with a uniform slope extending outward over a mile and a half. Lunarian geologists believe the fault was created when the Crater Korolev meteor impacted on the opposite side of Luna. They think the Sea of Clouds was still cooling at the time and would have been susceptible to a massive upheaval, a convergence of shock waves that traversed the globe.

Directly in front of them, the rim of Crater Birt rises over a mile into the lunar sky. A belt of badlands flank the mountain extending out as far as twenty miles in places, rills and canyons of broken lava. Almost lost in the jumble is a great rill known as Sunset Canyon that seems to wrap itself around the base of Crater Birt's rim mountain before finding its way out onto the Sea of Clouds. The crater side of the canyon is a shear basalt cliff over a thousand feet in height. This awe inspiring work of nature is simply known as The Wall. A slump of smaller boulders, stones and regolith lay at its base.

During the approach, everybody has a magnificent view of the Wall. Both transports are now flying less than fifty feet above the rugged desolation and creeping along at a few tens of miles per hour. The great expanse of stone towers over them pressing down with an almost physical force.

The terrain below continues to get rougher the closer they come to the Wall, the lunar surface shattered and broken during the craters creation event. Rips and heaving in the still hot bed of lava had created a twisted tortured landscape of jagged boulders and treacherous fissures. Other canyons, large and small, extend outward from Sunset Canyon in a vast network. They can't see a flat space anywhere in sight large enough for even one transport to land safely, let alone two.

Less than a quarter mile from the base of the cliff they come upon a large circular depression, a natural amphitheater created when a section of the surface collapsed. The sinkhole is over five hundred feet wide and drops vertically nearly a hundred feet. Lava had filled it part way creating a smooth plain at the bottom. The inner wall of the hole had given way in several places and more than a few small craters break the flat floor below them. The two transports don't hesitate but immediately descend into its depth.

Lazarus has never been here and is intently trying to see everything at once, taking pride in the fact that he can. A chill goes down his spine as they pass below the edge. An almost perfectly vertical cliff face sweeps around him in a giant arc. Above looms the Wall, below is the floor of the depression. Everything is seen as though floating alone in the void, his companions and the ship itself filtered out of his vision.

Karyl takes the lead, swinging her ship north and heading across the pit as she descends. Consuela keeps on her ten, slightly behind and to her right. Without sensors she would have been in near total darkness, with them she can see every feature like it's a bright summer afternoon but without the glare. She likes to tweak her visual with a good dash of color enhancement to bring out the composition and structure in the rocks around her. Otherwise, she considers them pretty boring. But with it, the walls of the sinkhole appear a dark red while the frozen lave lake in the bottom a cool blue and the craters sprinkled across its surface outlined in darker blue.

Even knowing it's there, the mouth of the giant lava tube is hard to see, situated right at the base of the cliff and partially hidden behind the rim wall of a smaller secondary crater. More than half filled with ancient lava, it is an arch barely twenty feet at its tallest. Karyl brings her ship to a stop outside leaving plenty of room for Consuela to go by.

"Consuela, how far in do you think you can go?" Tempel asks.

"It's going to be close. The only other time I was here, we camped out on the floor and walked in. Are you sure a Dragonfly will fit?" Consuela asks.

Before he could stop himself Tempel says "Magi...." Remembering she wasn't there, he paused collecting his wits.

"Tempel you hang back and watch the clearance. If we don't fit then call out," Kitajima orders picking up the slack for his Lieutenant.

"Aye!" Tempel responds.

Karyl maneuvers in behind the other transport as it eases forward.

"Plenty of room along the sides and at least a foot above," Tempel estimates the clearance using the onboard sensors and his eye for distances.

"Is that all?!" Consuela says nervously.

"What more do you need?" Tempel asks, knowing that Consuela would rise to the challenge.

"Caution is the hallmark of the wise, Tempel. I figured even you should know that," Consuela responds dryly even as the lava tube closes about them.

Slowly she creeps forward, the ships proximity sensors adjusted to their finest settings. An inch here meant a lot more than it did when she was zooming around above the surface. She can't shake the feeling that she is returning to the womb, only it isn't her mother's warm body surrounding them, but the cold basalt of Luna. The tunnel wall is so close she has the impulse to reach out and touch it. Before her, the tunnel stretches out as far as she can see, lit by ship lights for the first time in its long history. The consistency of the tunnel surprises her. The floor is smooth and flat, the arc of the walls and ceiling featureless. She can almost fool herself into thinking it man-made.

About a hundred feet in she slows to a stop and hovers. "What do you think Kitajima? Are we in far enough?"

"Aye, far enough. Set her down as far to the right as you can," Kitajima orders.

"That's not much," Consuela says as she brings the craft down to the ground, crabbing sideways a few feet. As the thrusters shut down she sighs heavily and relaxes for the first time since this wild ride had started. Only then does she realize just how tense she had become and how tired she suddenly was. She promised herself a long nap the first chance she gets.

"Before we follow you in, I suggest we place a remote. We need some eyes and ears out here," Tempel says.

"Very good, Tempel. Place a sensor at the top of the Wall and another down in the pit. Set them up for line-of-sight laser communication only," Kitajima agrees.

"Kitajima, you don't think they could follow us here do you?" Lindsey asks.

Tempel looks over at Karyl who purses her lips and shakes her head. With a jerk, Tempel motions her to move out. Before they hear Kitajima's response, Tempel isolates his transport from the other, wanting his officers to stay focused on the job at hand.

Because the damaged transport is on the ground, they have access to all their AI's computing power once more. Even so, the transport rises slowly and deliberately out of the sinkhole as Karyl applies power, putting the ship in an upward arc that terminates at the distant crest of the Wall.

Lindsey has taken plenty of flights with Lunarians but today's is restrained compared to any of the others that she can't help but ask, "Why are we flying so slowly?" Even the most junior pilots like to gun it, heavy on the accelerator, flashing skills at the extreme edge of suicide. And Karyl isn't known for her constraint.

Karyl doesn't even turn her head as she replies, keeping her focus on the cliff looming in front of them, "By going slow and close to the ground we are virtually invisible to anything in orbit, completely lost in the ground clutter."

The instant she began talking Tempel looks sharply at Karyl but remains quiet. The pilot is exempt from all other duties while flying and that includes idle small talk. Tempel knows from long experience that Karyl will push the envelope but always within bounds. He has no doubt she can handle this assignment but it makes him uncomfortable to deviate even a little from training. By the book is more than just a quaint saying to him.

"Ask your questions later," Tempel growls before isolating Karyl. Their passengers can talk among themselves all they want but not with the pilot, not while she is flying.

The top of the Wall comes suddenly, one moment they are flying up the cliff face a few tens of feet away, the next it is gone, in its place the remainder of Crater Birt's rim mountain looming over them. Here and there great fissures can be seen radiating upward from the sharp edge of the cliff while smaller cracks are mere depressions in the regolith. Very few boulders and only sparse outcroppings break the smooth slope of the mountain rising above them. The blue and brown globe of the Earth watches silently as the drama unfolds.

Behind them the Sea of Clouds stretches beyond the horizon. It isn't flat like a snooker table but rather wavy like an ocean frozen in time. The last of the sun casts long shadows behind each crest, mottling the mare's barren surface with various shades of gray and black, set against a backdrop of remote sun-lit mountains defining the distant skyline.

Karyl brings the ship down smoothly to land well beyond the edge in perhaps the only relative flat spot anywhere atop this lunar mountain. She can see where other ships have landed from depressions in the regolith. She simply adds hers to the mix. Human foot prints are everywhere. There is nothing to erode them in this airless environment except micrometeorites, and that process takes hundreds, if not thousands, of years to see even the smallest change.

Brice and Alonzo know what needs to be done having performed this duty many times before. They have the airlock wide open, the gear checked and ready to go. Leaping out before the transport even comes to rest, Brice heads rapidly towards the edge of the precipice carrying the sensor. A light weight rope tied to his vacsuits hardpoint serves as a safety line.

Alonzo stays in the doorway watching as the line plays out of the wench above the door, ready to haul Brice back at a moments notice. The Wall has claimed its share of unwary tourists, both native and shortimer. Its edge is fragile and prone to breaking, although this area has been stomped over so many times that any loose rock has long since fallen away. Lunarians learn early that a person doesn't live long by taking unnecessary risks.

Slowing considerably as he approaches the cliff, Brice glances out at the view from this incredible vantage point. Beyond the badlands, the plain stretches out before him to the horizon, smooth and flat from this distance. Less than fifteen miles southwest he can see the Straight Fault, sunlight catching it, highlighting its great length.

Quickly but cautiously, he moves parallel to the edge, about ten feet back, looking for a fissure the right size. Spotting one, he gets down on his belly and worms forward until his head is just looking over the edge. He slips the sensor down into the crack positioning it just right before triggering the bladder. A small pneumatic skin fills with gas and expands, wedging itself firmly in the rock.

Brice takes a second to check his placement. Satisfied, he carefully pushes himself back from the edge before standing and hustling back to the transport.

Alonzo keeps Brice's tether taunt as he returns. They are in and out in less than two minutes, everything by the book, just as they have been taught during many hours of training.

"Go," Tempel says as Brice slides into his seat, grinning with barely contained excitement.

Karyl lifts off and turns back towards the cliffs edge, maneuvering the Dragonfly just as helicopter pilots do down on Earth, never getting more than ten feet off the ground. Lindsey gasps as they clear the edge, going from ten feet to over a thousand in the blink of an eye. Karyl adds to the ride by briefly sending them into freefall as she descends. Lazarus involuntarily groans and squeezes his eyes tightly shut, yet maintaining the link to the external sensors. Less than a hundred feet above the rocky badlands Karyl guns the thrusters and stops their downward plummet in a graceful arc, sending the ship swooping across the jagged terrain.

She follows a rocky canyon back towards the sinkhole, well below the sides of the ragged gash, her speed deceptive because of the extremely low altitude. To Lazarus, they are doing hundreds of miles per hour when in reality it's only sixty.

The canyon is a collapsed lava tube that opens up on the sinkhole. Karyl banks once when she is well inside the depression and makes a slow graceful turn as she descends. Tempel already has a spot in mind for the second sensor and marks it, a rocky landslide almost directly opposite of the tunnel entrance and in line-of-sight of the sensor they had just placed.

"Let's put this one about halfway down the slide... Karyl, hover at fifty feet. Alonzo, Brice, use the winch to place it. Do not leave any tracks," Tempel commands.

"Aye, LT, no tracks!" Brice responds.

Alonzo has Brice in the harness by the time Karyl reaches the spot. Sliding the door open Alonzo steadies Brice as he steps out into space. He swings head down in an instant, his body at an angle to make it easier to see below him. The winch begins lowering him with almost no sway as the human pendulum elongates towards the surface like a spider on the end of its string, a tribute to Karyl's steady hand.

"Move twelve feet on heading 270," Brice instructs Karyl.

Effortlessly Karyl complies without causing any swing on Brice.

"Beautiful!" he murmurs. Moments later the sensor is installed and tested for alignment. Brice admires his work as he is winched up to the transport. The camouflage is perfect, making the sensor virtually invisible long before he reaches the door.

****

Tempel lets Karyl finish what she started, easing the transport into the mouth of the lava tube. He can see the shallow groves cut into the floor by Red's thrusters. Karyl smoothly moves Blue down the tunnel deepening the groves as she goes, gently setting down thirty feet from the other transport. Kitajima, Hack and the rest of Charley Company is standing at the foot of the Red's ramp as Blue sets down. Doc Grady stands apart, dejection and frustration plainly seen on his face.

A stoic Kitajima waits for them to disembark, "We have two comrades to mourn but that must wait," he says.

"There wasn't anything I could do to help them," Doc Grady murmurs angrily, almost defensively.

Kitajima turns to look at the medico. "You must set it aside for now. We need you if we are to see this mission through to a successful conclusion."

"It was my decision to wait for the shortimer. If I hadn't, Red would have gotten clear and nobody would have been killed," Tempel says quietly.

"Bullshit!" Kitajima says calmly but forcefully. "Haven't I taught you anything? A warrior never plays the what-if game. You can never win! Don't let me hear you say that again. Got it?"

"Aye," Tempel remains unconvinced. He looks into the eyes of Tatiana and sees something he's never seen before, anger and dislike aimed at him.

Tatiana drops her gaze and scowls at the dirt beneath her feet. She has never felt so helpless and it feeds the anger within her. She doesn't blame Tempel anymore than she does Consuela and Kipper for piloting the ship or Corso for sending them out here. But Tempel's right in front of her and Karl's in a body bag.

Walking over to stand in front of the newcomer, Kitajima growls, "What did you say your name was?"

"Zechariah Hargrove," the young man replies steadily. He's trapped among these mutants and silently prays for strength to see him through. Only his eyes betray fear.

"Inspector Callahan was a good man. I'm sorry for your loss… You're a PO?"

The man nods, "Propriety Officer First Class." PO's can popup anywhere, watching the watchers. It's normal for a PO to be young and idealistic. They are there to ensure that all religious tenets are obeyed while the Inspectors perform their duty to the citizens of the Federation.

"That means diddlysquat out here. Do what I tell you and everything will be just fine. But make no mistake, Mr. Hargrove, my first responsibility is to these warriors and the Republic, not to you or the Federation." Kitajima's tone is matter-of-fact without rancor or ill will.

"I… understand," Zechariah answers, his eyes darting about.

"Give me your sidearm,"

The Federation suit is of recent manufacture but incorporates old technology. It hasn't any power assist or electromagnet shielding. Its skin is made of inferior materials and is stiff. The helmet actually

"Number one, we have full access to your vacsuit and you are not to do anything to change that fact. Number two, these warriors have the exact same authority over you that I do. You will obey their commands. Number three, you will not do anything to adversely effect this mission. Number four, you will answer any question fully and truthfully to the best of your ability… I have nothing against you personally. This is just how it is and I don't want any misunderstanding. Ok?"

Disobey these orders at your own peril.

"Perhaps I can be of assistance," Lazarus says.

"Now there's an idea, you baby-sit him and Lindsey can baby-sit you. That will keep all three of you busy." Turning back to Charley Company, Kitajima continues, "Jason and Angel analyzed the damage on our way here and they think it can be repaired. All those hits managed to miss nearly everything."

"God is looking out for us," Zechariah says.

"If that was looking out for us then tell him to mind his own business," Brice says glaring at Zechariah.

Kitajima gives him a sour look, realizing this isn't the time to chew out his crew, not even Brice. He lets the remark slide. "I figure we have a couple hours before we can expect company. We need to complete repairs and come up with a plan," he says gruffly.

"How could those men possibly find us here?" Zechariah asks ignoring Brice, glancing up at the damaged ship, wondering how this can possibly be fixed.

Kitajima turns his sour expression on the young PO, "The Brotherhood knows we have their nukes and it's a safe bet they will want them back."

"Then you must destroy them. Your initial knee-jerk response to take them was in error. Destruction is the only answer. That would take the wind out of the sails of any pursuers." Zechariah says. This young man is quite accomplished at running his mouth without knowing what he's talking about, a skill that served him well in his meteoric rise through the ranks.

Kitajima's expression deepens into a scowl when Zechariah referred to his decision as knee-jerk. He had some very good reasons for making that choice. "Those nukes are the only leverage we have right now. We need to figure out how to use them most effectively."

"You can't be serious! Who do you want to nuke?" Zechariah asks incredulously.

This day had gone from bad to worse and Kitajima isn't in the mood to explain himself to anybody, let alone this Federation pipsqueak. "I haven't made up my mind! But you can be sure I will let you know when I do!" he rumbles, turning away from Zechariah, obviously dismissing him, trying to keep his mind focused on what needs to be done right now to keep them breathing.

Lazarus moves up beside Zechariah and lays a hand on the young mans arm, shaking his head, silently warning him to hold his tongue.

Zechariah scowls and pulls away, his glare letting Lazarus know that he didn't appreciate the interference. He turns and leaves, heading back to Blue.

"Hack, check on supplies. See how much was destroyed during the fight," Kitajima says.

"Doc, you're with me," Hack says moving purposefully towards the crippled Dragonfly followed closely by the young doctor. She knows he needs something to do and has the perfect solution.

"Brice, take Jason, Angel, Corazon and Alonzo. We need those repairs done in one hour," Kitajima says with intensity. The officers move briskly, everyone is tense.

"Consuela, you're assigned cover-up. Make sure you fill the groves in the floor," Kitajima orders. It is her job to erase all indications of their presence on the surface, especially outside on the floor of the sinkhole close to the tunnel entrance.

"Sam, see what you can do about reestablishing a secure link with Magi. We must find out what's going on," Kitajima orders, his lingering look speaks volumes as to the priority he is placing on the assignment.

"Aye," Sam nods understandingly and says, "I've already tried picking up Earthnet. All I get is static."

"Have you tried raising a ground station?" Lazarus asks her, earning him a piercing glare from Kitajima. "I mean one of the Earth based ground stations," he plunges on.

"Of course, but every band is swamped with static," Sam replies.

Lazarus raises his eyebrows, "Every band? The only thing that I know of that can do that is a nuclear explosion."

"I don't think so. The effect you are thinking of needs an atmosphere to make it work. This is jamming by a very powerful source," Sam says. "If I had better triangulation I think I could pinpoint the location."

Before Lazarus can respond Kitajima says, "Lazarus, go with Sam. Maybe the two of you can provide us with some answers instead of bedtime stories." He pauses and when Lazarus doesn't move he growls, "You waiting for a written invitation? Get going!"

Calling out to the two pilots still in their respective ships Kitajima says, "Kipper, Karyl, stay where you are. I want you to actively monitor the sensors. Don't rely on the autos."

"Aye," they respond in unison.

Kitajima looks at Lindsey. "I want you to find a way to defeat active camouflage."

"How am I to do that?" Lindsey asks, "We don't have Magi and we left most of our equipment back at the crash site."

"Use your brain!" Kitajima responds sharply. Even during the best of times, he has very little tolerance with anybody that comes up with excuses before they even try. And the current situation makes him even more short tempered. He can't help but blame himself when he loses people under his command.

"My brain cannot take the place of Magi or the equipment." Lindsey retorts.

"You can use a ships AI while we are on the ground," Tempel offers hoping to elevate some of the tension.

"If any AI could do it, we wouldn't have Magi, would we?" Lindsey says. "These are glorified calculators."

"Just do the job you were sent to do," Tatiana says tersely.

Turning to confront Tatiana, Lindsey says, "We don't have the micro-measurement vid equipment. Do you want me to guess?" Lindsey asks.

"Just do what you can, Captain Davenport, that's all I'm asking," Kitajima says slowly and deliberately, his use of her rank significant.

Lindsey gets the message and stops arguing. "Fine, Captain Osaka. I will try, but no promises."

"I'm not asking for promises, Lindsey… oh, make sure the PO stays with you. Don't let him out of your sight," Kitajima says, turning to Tatiana before Lindsey can protest, "How far did Lei get with Evolution's Child's AI?"

For a moment Tatiana continues glaring at Lindsey as if she were an unruly child in need of a shock collar. Facing Kitajima she says, "Not very far, I'm afraid. One of them is blank and the other is badly damaged. I'll need to remove the Zettasphere and reinstall it in a new interface before I will know how much data survived."

"See what you can do. I don't know if it will help us or not but we shouldn't ignore it," Kitajima says. Looking around at the faces gathered around him, he says briskly,

"The rest of you check the equipment for any damage… Let's get to it people. You have less than one hour. Show me some results!"

****

Inside the transport, in the open area past the two crates strapped to the walls, Tatiana points and says, "Sit in that seat and keep your mouth shut."

Zechariah bristles, "I am a Federation official! You can NOT talk to me like that!"

As the last syllable comes out of Zechariah's mouth, Tatiana crosses the few feet between them with unnatural swiftness, grabs him with both hands and slams his head and shoulders into the low ceiling.

Zechariah gives a startled yelp, his neck twisting at almost a right angle. His eyes widen with panic as he struggles against her overpowering physical strength.

Just reaching the top of the ramp, Tempel leaps forward and grabs Tatiana's arm, "What are you doing? At ease Lieutenant! Back off, NOW!"

With a disgusted grimace, Tatiana releases Zechariah and steps back, scowling as the man falls to his knees in front of her.

The entire incident lasts only moments, leaving Zechariah wide-eyed and frightened, grappling with what he had just witnessed. They are truly the spawn of Satan!

"Have you gone mad?" Tempel asks, inserting himself in front of her and pushing Tatiana away from the confrontation.

"I told him to do something and he argued with me," Tatiana replies with a sneer.

Lindsey helps Zechariah to his feet, putting an arm around the frightened man to steady him.

"That does not give you the right to attack him," Kitajima says. He isn't in the transport but always keeps an eye on things.

Zechariah stares intently at Tatiana. Fear and isolation rip at his guts. He's on the verge of tears.

"Take it easy, Zechariah," Lindsey says, guiding him to the seat Tatiana wanted him to sit in to begin with.

"Lieutenant Tushar, we'll discuss this later." Kitajima says.

Zechariah sits down and looks back up at Lindsey, "How can she move like that?"

"Drop it." Lindsey says.

"But…" he starts.

"I said drop it!" Lindsey repeats intensely. She takes a long look at him. "Look, the death of our comrades is hitting everyone hard. Let's put this aside. We have enough to worry about without fighting amongst ourselves," Lindsey says.

Tempel grunts and nods in agreement, "She's right. We need to work together as a team." He says pointedly to Tatiana.

"Fine," Tatiana says. "He better not argue the next time I tell him to do something."

"He won't," Lindsey says looking at Zechariah who bows his head and nods.

Turning towards the crate lashed against a wall of the cargo bay, Tempel suggests, "Let's start by going over what we do know about this shield. Lindsey, you start."

Lindsey sighs, glancing at Tatiana. "Very well." She walks over to stand beside the crate, "The outside is standard vacglass, common throughout the Republic." Rubbing her thumb across the inside surface where it's exposed by the damage, sensors in her gloves provide a heightened sense of feel and the identity of the materials they come into contact with. "Inside the shell is a layer of energy absorbent material similar to what I developed years ago. Sandwiched in between is some kind of solid-state layer that returns a static signal in response to an incoming beam. I was just starting to unravel it when Magi was cut off."

"How similar?" Tempel asks.

"What?" Lindsey asks, absently looking up at Tempel, already lost in thought. She finds the application of logic and reason comforting in an unfamiliar and hostile world.

"How similar is the energy absorbent material to what you developed?" Tempel asks.

"Virtually identical. Why?" Lindsey responds.

"That goes along with Lazarus's hypothesis that the Brotherhood will buy or steal the technology instead of developing it themselves," Tempel says looking sharply at Tatiana.

"Then where did they get the transmitter design?" Tatiana asks. "I don't know of any research on Luna into anything similar to it."

Lindsey frowns thoughtfully, her expression slowly turning into surprise, then glee, "Several months ago a MetCal colleague of mine told me about a new technology. I didn't think much about it at the time."

"What technology?" Tatiana asks irritably.

"It was a new way of marking items for retail. Instead of passive barcodes they were trying to make packaging that would actively store information about the object inside and relay it back on request, remotely. What it was, where it was, when it was stocked and how much it cost, that sort of thing." Lindsey pauses as she dredges up the old memory.

"As I recall, they had gotten to the point of testing prototypes of a solid-state transmitter…" she uses the ships AI to pull up a whiteboard and begins to sketch a device. "It was a single function receiver and transmitter…"

To the side of the sketch she draws a solid-state Hall Effect transistor and circles it. "They claimed the power consumption was so low that the devise could use the interrogating beam as its source…" She brings up the information they had obtained on the micro-configuration of the shields transmitter layer.

Tempel and Tatiana watch as Lindsey follows her train of thought to its conclusion, the confrontation all but forgotten in her excitement. They realize that here was the reason Abby had insisted they include Lindsey on the mission.

Quickly Lindsey strips away data from the image until she reaches its smallest repeating unit, enlarging it. She pulls apart what is left with a few rapid hand movements and circles a portion. "This is the receiver/transmitter and this out here is the Hall Effect transistor and its aperture. The rest of it must be encoding of static information being sent back through the transmitter," she says excitedly. "It's elegant in its simplicity!"

"That's great, but where does that leave us?" Tempel asks.

Turning to him, her eyes wide with revelation, Lindsey exclaims, "Don't you see? The physical size of the Hall Effect aperture is tuned to the wavelength of our MRI beams! If we change the MRI frequency, even slightly, the power source will not function!"

Both Tempel and Tatiana perk up, looking first at the sketches and then at each other, "Can we test this?" Tempel asks.

"Yes, I believe we can, quite easily!" Lindsey exclaims excitedly. ""Simply recalibrate a sensor, or in this case, decalibrate it."

Lindsey retrieves a portable scanner from the locker and places it on the crate, the only flat surface available in the bay. The others watch as she links into the devices control system and brings the calibration portion of the maintenance routine online. She quickly writes a small ten line program that will oscillate the frequency of the scan around the standard. Confident in her abilities, she doesn't even bother testing her program, simply saving it before initiating the snippet.

Before their eyes, the information they are receiving from the crate goes from the image of the ball valve to black, characteristic of energy absorbent shielding and back to the ball valve, cycling back and forth as the calibration program fluctuates, like someone turning a light switch on and off.

"Well… I'll be damned!" Tempel says softly, "Very impressive Lindsey!" Even Tatiana has a look of grudging respect.

Zechariah keeps his mouth shut and watches.

****

Sam leads Lazarus back inside Red, entering the forward compartment and taking the seat directly behind Kipper. Lazarus slides into the one across the aisle. Looking over at her, he slaves his VR to hers even as she links to the ships AI.

He watches in silence as Sam sets up the working parameters for the computer system, using the two remote sensors to do a quick sweep of the sky looking for any communication emission at all. They are greeted by a wall of static.

"I've never experienced a nuclear storm but that is what this appears to be," Lazarus says.

"Do you know of any way to cut through or filter it out?" Sam asks hoping against reason that he knows something she didn't, as unlikely as that is.

"No, but if it's nuclear in origin, it should fade fairly soon. Do you have a recording of it back at the crash site?" he asks her.

"Sure," she says pulling up the data and overlaying it with the current signal. It is quickly apparent that the intensity of the static is remaining constant.

"Well… It looks like you are right, this isn't nuclear in origin. But look at the signature. It's the spitting image of a massive solar flare. Is it possible that this is a natural occurrence?" Lazarus asks thoughtfully.

Sam looks over at him. "I don't think so. The last flare of this magnitude was years ago and we had plenty of warning from our solar satellites." She knows Kitajima isn't going to like these numbers but she can't change physics.

Lazarus frowns in concentration and says thoughtfully, "It would help if we could rig up a device that is able to discern what direction the jamming is coming from. But to pinpoint the source would require something at least partially shielded from the static, something that will let us map the intensity of the radiation."

Without turning his head Kipper volunteers, "Sounds to me like what you are describing is a Faraday cage. Our battle armor is a pretty good example. The Calconn in them creates a perfectly conducting enclosure and thus, a perfect electromagnetic shield."

"How do you propose we use battle armor to pinpoint the source?" Sam asks.

Kipper shrugs, "How should I know. You're the genius."

Sam is silent for a moment. A look of hope passes over her face. "Yes… That might just work… We can use a pulse rifle! Modify its Harmon coil to make it act as a receiver instead of an emitter!" Sam is gone before either of the men can question her further.

"Might as well relax. When she gets something in her head it's better to let her run with it," Kipper says knowingly.

"Ok. Can we see what's going on in orbit while we wait?" Lazarus asks.

Kipper links the two of them to the visual system in the remote sensors, like a pair of eyes hundreds of yards apart, giving them excellent depth perception in the resulting image. Zooming in on the orbiting debris, they can still see sunlight glinting on the many pieces as they spin in their individual orbits. "We're looking at the coordinates for Orbsat 2112. I don't think there is any doubt that it's been destroyed."

Nodding in agreement Lazarus asks, "What about Earth orbiting satellites? What can you see from here?"

"These sensors are much too small to resolve any detail on them. But maybe we can spot Heavens Gate…" Kipper quickly feeds in the coordinates of the orbiting station, determining that it should be in view, just minutes away from disappearing behind the Earth.

A bright dot with no detail is all they can see, but at least it's there. They watch as it slides from view, twinkling as it passes behind Earth's atmosphere then disappearing behind the planet itself. Lazarus feels an incredible sense of loss as it winks out, far out of proportion to the actual event.

"Lazarus, come back here," Sam calls out, breaking the moment.

"If you will excuse me, duty calls," Lazarus says as he rises. Kipper just waves his hand without turning.

Lazarus moves through the transport not seeing Sam in the passenger compartment. He finds her on the floor of the storage bay, the pieces of a pulse rifle scattered around her. She has a long slender contraption in her hand with several thin wires running to a small data logger no bigger than a hand held calculator of a century ago.

Motioning him to sit next to her she says, "I have reversed the voltage on the Harmon coil creating a perfectly shielded space in its interior. No electromagnetic static or electric field emissions can get in except through this little hole. Now watch!" she points to the tiny data logger screen.

He leans down gazing intently as she slowly rotates the Harmon coil, pointing it outward and sweeping it in a broad arc. The graph spikes sharply when the device is pointing in one very specific direction. She rocks it back and forth giving him a feel for the narrow angle it's indicating, just a few degrees wide.

"What lies in that direction?" Lazarus asks.

"Nothing that I know of," she responds, "It's simply a spot in orbital space. There is another here and here but our sensors can't pick up anything actually there." She rotates the tube showing him the other points of emission.

"Captain, we have company!" Kipper broadcast tersely.

Brice scrambles to shut down the nano-repair interface, difficult to do even under normal circumstances. Angel is lying on her stomach atop the outrigger feeding raw material to the damaged sections. The rest of Charley Company link to the remote surface sensors and become aware of the approaching ship about two miles out, slowly flying a thousand feet up on a course parallel with the Wall, directly down Sunset Canyon.

"Let's shut it down, people," Kitajima orders.

Kipper and Karyl power down everything onboard the two transports but the AI core memory. Even the vacsuit transmissions supplying facial expressions and other interpersonal communications cease, isolating every member of the mission.

Lazarus is frightened when his vacsuit goes to minimum power and his world turns pitch black. He reaches out where Sam had been only moments before, touching her, not sure what is going on.

Sam leans over cradling his head in her hands and putting her forehead against his, "Relax, this will be over in a few minutes," her voice distant but understandable.

Without their lights, the tunnel they are hiding in is completely dark. As the minutes drag on Lazarus becomes more and more convinced that something has gone terribly wrong. If it wasn't for Sam's firm grip holding him steady, he might have lost it and done something incredibly stupid.

After what seems like hours, his suit powers up and Sam is there next to him.

She smiles and says, "That wasn't so bad."

Lazarus wanly returns her smile, "Did I mention that I'm afraid of the dark?"

Sam chuckles politely, "You hide it well… Do you want to see the sensor data?"

"Yes, of course," Lazarus replies, his fears forgotten once more.

Sam links his visor with the data stored on the remote sensors and begins playback at normal speed.

Once again they see a ship approaching. As the craft draws near, a second ship flying much lower, darts back and forth across the badlands obviously looking for them or perhaps presenting itself as a target trying to lure them out. The lower ship swoops into the sinkhole almost directly in front of the remote sensor hidden in the landslide. This ship is very different from a Dragonfly. Where the Lunarian ship is smooth and pleasantly proportional, this is boxy and angular, built of bolts and beams. Much smaller than a Dragonfly, it bristles with disrupter cannon. The little ship must be a flying power plant to support all of them. Lazarus can imagine room for only one or two pilots, strictly an offensive war machine with very little defensive capability. It leaves the sinkhole never getting near their hiding place.

"They will be back," Kitajima promises. He is outside inspecting the repairs, finding out firsthand they are still many minutes away from being complete.

He lays his hand on Brice's shoulder and looks up at Angel, "Don't let up until this is finished." They nod and he turns away, walking under the outrigger looking at the portion that is done, pleased with the results. "Company meeting in five minutes, between the transports," Kitajima transmits on general frequency. "Brice and Angel have the only free pass unless they are done by then. By the numbers, acknowledge."

In rapid succession his officers report in. "Lindsey, Lazarus, Zechariah. You are all invited," Lindsey and Lazarus respond but Zechariah maintains his silence.

A few minutes later Charley Company begins arriving, the officers segregating themselves to one side, Lindsey and Lazarus the other. Kitajima is surprised to see Sam standing beside Lazarus, a worried expression on her face. Zechariah comes quietly to stand on his other side.

Kitajima takes center stage and looks at her expectantly, "Sam, what have you got?"

"We managed to determine that the interference blocking our communications is coming from several regions of orbital space. The static is steady and doesn't appear to be letting up any time soon. Until they stop jamming, we don't have a prayer of contacting Aldrin Station or in raising an Earth ground station," Sam reports.

Kitajima pauses, thinking about what she has said. "So we are completely cut off for the foreseeable future?"

"That's how it looks. I believe this is the result of some very powerful hardware. The Brotherhood not only destroyed our satellite network, they have positioned jammers in key locations just to make sure no one is communicating."

Accepting her report, Kitajima goes on, "Tempel, what have you to report?"

"Lindsey was able to determine how the active camouflage works and a way to see past it. We have already begun modifying our sensors. The ships sensors are complete and we have only a few ghost suits remaining, yours, Brice and Angel's," Tempel reports.

"Good! Well done Lindsey! Tatiana, did you find out anything from the damaged AI?" Kitajima asks.

"The Zettaspheres external interface suffered heavy damage and without specialized equipment, which I don't have, I risk further damage," Tatiana says pausing and preparing herself for relaying more bad news.

"Is there something else Lieutenant?" Kitajima asks recognizing the signals. She doesn't want to say something and is dragging her heels.

"Well… After coming to this conclusion, I had some time and brought up the reconstruction Brice was doing when we bailed at the crash site. Magi had pretty much finished it and I just had the ships AI run what she had done. I think you should see it," Tatiana says.

"Very well," Kitajima responds.

Finished with the repairs, Brice and Angel join them just as it begins. They are the last of the company to link into the ships AI to view a simulation of the data Brice had been responsible for collecting only hours before.

The presentation begins at the crash site just as they had found it, debris scattered along a two mile track angled across the valley to the foot of the far side. The three dimensional image rotates to give the observers the best possible angle as it begins to roll backwards, like a video in reverse. Bit by bit, each piece twists and moves backward in time, retracing the path of their arrival, slowly at first but building up speed. Regolith and rocks returning to the places they had been before the impact, the gouges and scars in the landscape disappearing as the dust and debris splash in reverse. The crates move separately, rolling and tumbling, picking up momentum as they travel back in time. A huge cloud of regolith shrouds the freighters main cabin as it tumbles and rolls across the valley floor, obscuring detail. It isn't clear when the cargo came loose but Magi had made an educated guess that it was early in the crash because of the lack of more damage to the crates. Simultaneously, the crates and the cabin continue to reverse their original course moving back towards the instant of separation, dust and debris violently rising all around them. Other smaller pieces of the engine compartment and the thrusters themselves cartwheel across the relatively flat terrain, all converging towards that point in time and space when they were last together.

As the simulation approaches this point, a huge wall of dust and rock erupts from the surface blocking their view of the ship. Evolution's Child had acted like a giant snow plow as it barreled down the slope, before it hit bottom and started to tumble. This material was now in the process of reversing and returning to where it had lain undisturbed for untold millennia. Tatiana pause's the presentation and rotates it until they are looking almost straight down at the wreck before allowing it to continue. She stops it once more just as the crates and cabin come together. Seen through a veil of debris, the crates come to rest in the cargo section of the freighter, all four of them.

The group is silent as the implications sink in.

Kitajima looks at his officers already appreciating what they must do, his mind slipping into plan mode. He knows there's a good chance that more of them will not see home again if they follow him into battle, but he never doubts their willingness.

"Captain, we must to go back and deal with this," Tempel says quietly, voicing what nearly everyone has already concluded.

"Yes Lieutenant, I believe you're right," Kitajima responds softly.

"Are you nuts?" Zechariah says too loudly, panic in his voice. He can't understand them even considering such an idea. It's suicidal! Tatiana gives him a look that sends him ducking behind Lazarus.

Kitajima ignores Zechariah and looks intently at Hack, "Get us started."

The two of them have worked this many times over the years, initiating a forum where everyone is encouraged to speak their mind. Charley Company knows the drill.

"What if we destroy the nukes we have and go after the one's we don't?" Hack asks.

"Why not use one of the nukes we have and take out the one's we don't?" Tempel suggests looking sideways at Hack. "Use one of the Dragonfly's and fly it in on remote?"

"You are assuming the other crate is still there. What if it's already gone?" if asks.

Tempel looks steadily at Tatiana for a moment, both of them coming to the identical conclusion about the same time, "We have no choice. We must go back and find out what's going on. They may not have found the other crates or they may even think we have them all. We don't know what the situation back at the crash site and we need to know to make the best decision."

"It's suicide to go back there! We just managed to get away! Two of your friends are dead, for God's sake!" Zechariah exclaims, ignoring Lazarus's attempt to silence him.

"I didn't see God back there! Only Muslims!" Tempel shot back.

Kitajima raises his hand stifling any more comments from his officers. "At ease, Charley Company!" turning to Zechariah, "This is our responsibility, not yours," Turning back to face them he continues, "Anybody see it different? Or do you think we should pull in our tails and convince ourselves the job is done?" Kitajima looks out among the faces of his young Lunarians and can find no doubt, no hesitation in any of them. They all know what needs to be done and will do it. It's what they have trained for. At that moment, it's their purpose in life, to protect the Republic at all costs. "Don't worry Zechariah, you will not be required to fight," he growls, grinning coldly. It sends a chill down Lazarus's spine.

"Thank God for that!" Zechariah declares, "I shouldn't be put in harms way either."

"Aye Captain, we know our duty. Just keep in mind that we shouldn't split our force," Tempel reminds him hurriedly, worried that he would be ordered to watch over Lindsey and Lazarus while the rest of Charley Company joins in battle.

"I didn't come along to be left behind," Lindsey says with conviction. "I may not be a trained combat officer but I can still fight!"

"As can I," adds Lazarus.

Kitajima looks at them venting a few huffs of incredulous chuckles that soon evolve into a belly-busting eye-watering guffaw. His officers join in until they are all in tears, their tension shattering like an overstressed pane of glass. Lindsey and Lazarus stand and stare at the spectacle blankly. Lindsey looks sideways at Lazarus and can't help but smile. Lazarus shrugs and smiles back. Zechariah looks on, his eyes narrow with suspicion, not sure what is happening, thinking they may all be crazy.

Kitajima gets himself under control as he walks over to stand directly in front of them. "Lindsey, Lazarus" he says slowly looking at each in turn. "I appreciate your offer…" he pauses, barely refraining from laughing pointblank in their faces, "as I said, you will not be asked to fight, whatever it is we decide to do."

Turning away Kitajima asks, "How are we on supplies Hack?"

"1200 hours of air and plenty of water and food but short on fuel. Red was hit to many times and her hydrazine tank is essentially empty. We were lucky we didn't get hit in the aniline tank too."

"BOOM!" Brice says loudly, smiling when Zechariah jerks in surprise.

"Knock it off Brice!" Tempel says harshly.

Brice grins, but obeys.

"Bottom line, once we divide the hydrazine in Blue, we won't have enough to go back to the crash site and get us home," Hack reports. "And that analysis didn't take into account what will be consumed by the Guardians during combat maneuvers." Her hands are flashing about, quickly inputting data and triggering calculations.

"That settles it! How can you fight without fuel?" Zechariah injects.

"Retreat is not an option!" Kitajima growls once more, growing tired of repeating himself.

Zechariah shakes his head and turns away in frustration, believing in the depths of his soul that it is wrong to go back. He is convinced that God is talking to his heart and is dismayed that he cannot persuade these people of it.

"Let's take a step back, shall we?" Kitajima says abruptly, instantly regaining control of the meeting. "Let's stick to the facts and what our next move should be." Turning to Hack he asks, "Where is the nearest cache?" For the last four years, Corso has had emergency supplies placed in various hidden locations out on the Central Highlands intended for just this situation. All they had to do was find one.

Hack shakes her head, "Nothing way out here that I know of. Anybody know different? Got your own personal stash out here somewhere?" she asks.

Nobody says a word.

"Do we know how bad Aldrin got nailed?" Brice asks the question on everybody's mind.

Kitajima shakes his head, "Not really, just that the bombardment stopped right before we lifted off from Nell's Valley. The city could be under Muslim control right now."

"We don't have the hydrazine to make a run south to Shennong." Hack says. "The closest settlement of any size is Scottsbluff to the west of us in Faye crater. It's about seventy miles closer than Aldrin and by my calculations we can just make it, even after we retrieve the remaining nukes."

"Then I guess we're going to Scottsbluff," Corazon says bluntly.

"I've been to Scottsbluff. There isn't much there," Angel points out.

"This isn't a vacation. We just want some fuel and air, and possibly some information," Kitajima responds. "I don't see another choice. We will head for Scottsbluff after the raid. Anybody have any other thoughts?"

"What are we going to do with Lindsey, Lazarus, and our young Propriety Officer while we fight?" Hack asks.

"Can there be any doubt! We must leave them somewhere. We can't risk letting them screw everything up. We can come back and pick them up after we're done," Brice says with total conviction.

Lindsey looks at him with annoyance and back at Kitajima, "I will not be dropped off like some package! You are not the only one who came on this operation knowing what was at stake! We all knew it was a military mission. You do what you need to do and we will stay out of your way. Just stop this talk of leaving us behind!"

Kitajima nods slowly, "Good. You will be in charge Lindsey. You will be responcible for making sure you three do nothing. You will be totally isolated once the battle starts. We cannot risk having any of you confusing us with your inexperience. I don't care if you don't understand," he says as Zechariah starts to speak, "That's the way it will be. You are not to even get out of your seats. You will sit quietly and do nothing at all. Is that clear?" Kitajima leans down to look Lindsey in the eyes.

"Aye, Kitajima. It's clear. Can we observe? Or must we wait until it's released," Lindsey responds. She believes it is her duty as a citizen of the Republic to be with these young Lunarians, to support them with everything possible, even if it is only superficial. She wants to know what price is being paid for her freedom. How can she make intelligent decisions if she is unaware of the cost? How could any one?

"It's your right to observe, but you will only see what the officer is seeing, nothing more. Further compression and enhancement will come later. You will not be able to communicate with any officer or change their sensors remotely," Kitajima says. "The only exception is for you Lindsey. If you feel it necessary, call me and I will respond. But it better be one hell of a good reason! Is that understood?"

"Aye!" Lindsey nods her thanks. She has no desire to bother anyone during the coming battle. It will be hard enough just watching.

Kitajima accesses his ghost suits Map and Terrain Function (MTF) and presents an image of the territory around the crash site for all to see. The officers gather around the waist high 3D map spread out between the two transports.

The mare in that region consists of a number of wide valleys in a washboard pattern, running parallel with Nell's Valley, giant ripples that solidified in the lake of lava billions of years ago. At this scale, the image looks like a series of waves, the broken and ragged ridges marking the crests and the depths between them the troughs. Kitajima walks into the map, a strange apparition cut off at the waist. He circles a position, his finger leaving a thin red line in its wake. A tiny red representation of a transport appears at its center as the line fades.

"Hack and I will take the Dragonfly's in low and slow so as not to attract any attention from orbiting spybeams. Hack, you bring your transport to this spot. From there, you will be able to give supporting fire by popping up over the ridge. I will land here. How many bugs do we have?" Kitajima asks her.

"Ten standard issue," Hack responds.

"Good. We will each send a pair of them into the valley as soon as we set down." Studying the map display carefully, Kitajima makes several line-of-sight comparisons, his system virtually placing him at each possible location, letting him see for himself. He decides on a high ridge that overlooks the crash site from almost a mile away.

"While the bugs are snooping Sam will position a spybot here," a bright white pinpoint of light appears within the terrain, "and Kipper will set another here." Another marker appears, "That will give us line-of-sight communications all across Nell's Valley. We will wait for the data from the bugs and our spybots before finalizing our attack plan." Looking up at his young warriors he continues, "If we need to fight, you will do it aggressively with extreme prejudice! I don't want to see any good sportsmanship when I review the logs! Understood?"

Kitajima's reference to the logs serves to calm their nerves, slipping them into training mode, something familiar to each of them. The young police officers all nod, tired of running and hiding, ready to avenge the deaths of Lei and Karl. This is war and their enemy will receive no quarter.

"Ok, people, let's breakout the gear and get mounted. It's time for the Republic to hit back!" Kitajima says grimly.

A ripple of excitement goes through the company. "Aye!" is the response.

Puzzled, Lazarus looks at Lindsey. "Guardian's?" he asks.

"The Guardians are an elite unit within our police force. Kind of like a SWAT antiterrorist team within Homeland Security," she responds.

"Just a little surprise for our uninvited guests, a couple of enhancements the lab has cooked up," Kitajima adds vaguely. It isn't lost on him that this is quite possibly the first live engagement of born and bred Lunarians against their earthly cousins, a place of dubious honor heavy in historical significance. He looks around at Charley Company and knows these young officers will do it proud.

"Hack, before we lift, I want you to install shape charges on the nukes. No matter what happens, we can't let the Brotherhood have them back! Understood?" He scrutinized her intently, looking for any hesitation.

"Aye, Kit! I understand! I will rig a dead-man switch just in case," she responds, knowing that such an explosion will vaporize her transport right along with the crates, instantly killing her. She has prepared for death all her life and it hasn't happened yet.

Satisfied, Kitajima nods and says, "Let's get locked and loaded! You have thirty-four minutes until liftoff!"

****

In 480 BCE, three hundred Spartans under King Leonidas helped one another prepare for the battle of Thermopylae. So too does Charley Company help one another don the lethal accoutrements of 21st century warfare. These warrior's have done this many times but today is different, their usual chatter subdued as they prepare for the taking of life.

Tempel runs Sam's diagnostic finding everything in the green. "You're good."

Waiting until he's sure Sam is ready, Tempel lifts the hard shell of his SGP over his head letting it settle comfortably onto his shoulders and down his back. He raises his arms straight up as Sam cinches the wide straps and activates their molyseals. The SGP harness is designed to go under his arms and across his chest without hindering body movements yet provide a stable platform for attaching a pair of two-axis weapon mounts. Tempel is aware the moment the weapon system integrates with his ghost suit and comes online.

In the mount above Tempel's left shoulder is a disrupter. Short barreled and powerful, it uses the latest HE Harmon coil technology enhanced by a Lunarian innovation known as superconductive plasma discharge, something entirely new in the world of high energy beam weapons. Mass is added by injecting a pulse of plasma, called a slug, into the energy stream. Arriving behind the beam at twenty miles per second, the slug strikes the target with incredible physical force. The one-two punch is designed specifically for ceramic armor, the beam weakening it, and the slug punching through.

Above his right shoulder is a launcher containing a dozen SuperX missiles. Propelled by magnetoplasma thrusters, they are capable of tremendous accelerations yet maneuverable enough to fill the role of close support. They have a guidance system that gives them the intelligence to stay on moving targets, the fire and forget weapons in the Guardian arsenal.

Look and shoot technology has been around for well over a century. To select a target Tempel simply looks at it. What is uniquely Guardian is that Tempel picks which weapon and fires it using Direct Mind Control. Developed at the turn of the century for paraplegics, he has a neuromotor prosthesis embedded in his motor cortex, the area of his brain responsible for voluntary movement. The device consists of a sensor that detects brain cell activity and converts it into signals that's recognized externally. Thus, to fire his disrupter, he looks at the target and flexes his fire muscle, much in the same way he would locate a cup and close his hand around it. Tempel has trained to the point that he doesn't need to think about how to do it any more, he simply functions as if this were a part of his being, like breathing or walking. Like so many other noble advances, DMC has been commandeered for destruction.

The SGP comes with its own power supply that extends halfway down his back like a piece of armor plate. In actuality, this is perhaps the weakest point on a Guardian. A shot here can potentially mix the hypergolic fuels stored inside. The resulting release of energy would vaporize the warrior and anything nearby.

In addition, Tempel has a disrupter pistol securely holstered about his waist with a similar plasma discharge enhancement as his shoulder cannon. The holster provides a supply of fuel and recharges his pistol within seconds of it being inserted.

The mobility and firepower of a Guardian has never been tested by combat but if the simulations mean anything, a single warrior is the match for a squadron of attack helicopters or a tank battalion of the last century. The lethality of a battle ready Guardian is greater than the sum of the parts, their training brutal and all consuming, only a small number of people make it all the way through. Every member of Charley Company ranks among these, the best of the best.

Sam runs Tempel's diagnostic finding everything in the green. "You're good."

Tempel finds Lazarus standing over by a transport talking with someone online even while keeping an eye on the officers preparing for battle. Tempel links with him listening in on the conversation.

"I think the Brotherhood is making a bid to control orbital space. If they succeed they will dominate Earth and be in a position to dictate to everyone. They apparently want to be the first World Empire, all for the glory of Allah!" Lazarus says.

"To control space they must control Luna. That means controlling Lunarians." Lindsey responds from inside Blue where she is helping Hack rig the dead-man switch on the crates. "That's the only viable reason for these bombs. What better way to hold the entire population of Luna at bay? We outnumber them at least ten to one. But if they can threaten us with a nuclear bomb…well… that evens things out quite a lot."

"That's their style," Lazarus says nodding. "How many nukes do you think it would take to hold Luna hostage?" he asks. "Aldrin Station, New London, Shennong, Kyoto, Gagarin."

"That's five but Evolution's Child carried twelve rather small nukes. How do you explain that?" Tempel asks, walking over to him.

Without any hesitation, Lazarus turns to face Tempel as he approaches, shrugs and says, "How many boroughs are there in Aldrin Station, ten, eleven? Maybe each borough was going to get there very own nuke? Even if they are small, that many going off all at the same time would definitely destroy a Lunarian city," Lazarus says looking at the weapons riding on Tempel's shoulders. They appear shadowy and difficult to focus on, just like his ghost suit. "I don't believe they simply want to subdue Luna. I think their long range goal is to destroy Luna and take what is yours, your cities, your factories, your women…"

"Our women?" Tempel asks.

"Absolutely!" Lazarus responds. "The Islamic Brotherhood considers your women, especially little girls, as spoils of war. Don't cut them any slack Tempel, because they won't cut you any."

"You needn't worry. Charley Company will make sure their willingness to die for Allah isn't wasted," Tempel replies. The image of three-year-old Lana rises unbidden within his mind, blond hair, sweet voice and pancake syrup smeared across one cheek. The syrup turns to blood as Lana becomes just another body in the wreckage. He shakes his head to clear his mind of these dark thoughts.

"Why bring the nukes in this way? Why not bring them as part of the invasion?" Tatiana asks joining the conversation. "Shipping them in on a freighter like ordinary cargo makes no sense to me."

"Deniability perhaps? If Minister bin Aunker has one weakness it's that he's overly cautious. If Brotherhood forces are caught with them, the gig is up." Lazarus replies. "They must have gone through several checkpoints to even get them off the planet. That's got to be it. He just didn't want to risk getting caught."

While they talk Tempel checks in on the young Federation Propriety Officer still sitting in the same seat aboard Blue. Not long ago, polygraphic indicators had shown that Zechariah was suffering from a high degree of tension but that seems to have changed. The man is almost too calm as he leans forward, head bowed, eyes clinched shut, and fingers clasped together, praying to his God.

"...hold me in your hand Lord. Do with me as you will. In the precious name of Jesus Christ, Amen." Zechariah finishes. He raises his head slowly, eyes still closed, his face the picture of tranquility.

Tempel shakes his head in bewilderment. He believes religion has brought them to this point, forcing him to kill or be killed. He's incapable of distinguishing between Islam and Christianity. He sees them both as Iron Age superstitions motivating otherwise peaceful men and women to do things they would never consider doing without it. He glances at his comrades, proud that none of them suffer from the god delusion and the empty promises of an afterlife. Yet they are willing to risk everything for family, friends, and freehold.

But Tempel's curiosity is aroused. It's not often he's in such close contact with a devout Christian. Even though Freedom of Belief is listed among the rights and responsibilities section in the Constitution of the Republic, there's simply a dearth of true believers among Luna's general population. It's hard to debate with someone who takes the same position as you do and the art of argument is one of Tempel's favorite pastimes.

"Zechariah, you will be riding in the other transport. Please, come outside now and join us." Tempel says.

Zechariah rises to his feet, exits down the ramp and comes over to stand beside Lazarus.

"Where do you want me to sit?" Zechariah asks keeping his eyes on Tatiana.

"Someone will tell you when its time," Tatiana replies without amusement.

Zechariah looks away from Tatiana and at Lazarus. Anger flashes across his face before he has a chance to stop it.

Tempel, still monitoring his polygraphic indicators, sees the spike and immediately realizes Zechariah is hiding something concerning Lazarus.

"What do you know about Lazarus?" Tempel asks Zechariah.

The young man looks startled by the question and turns towards Tempel. "Nothing... I only just met him."

Tempel bores in, "You're lying. I will ask you one more time. What do you know about Lazarus?"

Zechariah's polygraphic indicators are now swinging wildly, the calming influence of the prayer gone in an instant.

Lazarus watches intently, concern making his reading bounce as well. He doesn't quite know what's going on yet.

"He's a traitor. A memo was sent around ordering us to watch for him." Zechariah says.

"What did the memo order you to do when you found him?" Tatiana asks.

Sweet runs down the side of Zechariah's face, "Report his location," he replies.

"Another lie... Captain, what's the punishment for lying?" Tatiana asks.

Zechariah panics, "The memo said to either bring him in or administer justice ourselves. They promised an early return home with full pay and honors for the one who finds him." Turning to Lazarus, "They have Saul," he blurts out.

"What!" Lazarus grabs at Zechariah who backs out of reach. With one hand Tempel holds Lazarus back. "My brother had nothing to do with my leaving!"

"Then you must come back with me and tell them. You are the only one who can save him now." his eyes grow wide, "His life is in your hands."

Tatiana laughs, "Let me get this straight. The Federation arrests brother Saul, who has done nothing illegal, and the only way to save him is for Lazarus to turn himself in. And if he doesn't it will be Lazarus' fault when they kill Saul... Now there's the

Federation the world has come to know. No act too despicable, no deed too dreadful, the end justifies the means."

"They have forgotten that the path is as important as the destination," Kitajima says. "Thank you, Zechariah."

The young PO turns to look for Kitajima spotting him across the distance under the newly repaired outrigger with several others. "Thank me for what?"

"For reminding us who we are by showing us who we are not," Kitajima smiles coldly, "Thank you."

Zechariah shakes his head in confusion, "I don't understand."

"Of course you don't. Tell me how you feel about Saul being punished in place of Lazarus?" Kitajima asks Zechariah.

"I… think it's wrong," Zechariah says.

Tatiana laughs again, "Liar!" she says, stepping towards the young man who moves quickly to get behind Tempel.

"OK! OK! I'll tell you truth! Lazarus was in a position of trust and betrayed that trust. I think he deserves to be treated as an enemy of the Federation. Besides, he knew his brother would be under suspicion when he left and didn't care. Why does he care now?" Zechariah asks.

"I…" The accusation hits Lazarus like a ton of bricks. Can he tell himself that he wasn't aware of that possibility? No! He knew this would happen and closed his mind to it.

"You cannot lay this evil at his feet." Kitajima says. "Lazarus fled a corrupt system that is out of control because that was his only option. Citizens no longer have a say in what is done in their name. When a government gets that bad, only a revolution can change it." He doesn't particularly want to get drawn into this discussion but he did see it as a good way for his officers to blow off some steam, a good distraction before going into battle.

"That's terrorist talk!" Zechariah hisses softly and looks around.

"One man's terrorist is another man's freedom fighter," Tempel says.

"I will not listen to such ungodliness!" Zechariah says.

"If everything happens according to god's plan, why not the fall of the Federation?" Tempel asks.

"I know Gods plan and destroying his kingdom on Earth is not part of it!" Zechariah says.

"How do you know gods plan? Do you hear voices?" Tatiana asks.

"When I pray he imprints His answer on my heart," Zechariah responds.

"Maybe what you felt was indigestion," Tatiana says.

"You don't honestly believe you have conversations with the creator of the universe… do you?" Tempel asks.

"His will be done. I simply lay my case before Him," Zechariah replies.

"Is this the same god that motivated the Brotherhood to bomb our hospital? I have family among the four-hundred-fifty Lunarians that died there, the praises to Allah on the lips of their murderers," Tempels says. He coldly stares at the young man.

"Let me say, in no way does the God I pray to condone such acts of barbarism!" he wilts under Tempels glare, "I'm not your enemy Lieutenant and God is not your enemy. As a Christian, I believe as you do, in the sanctity of life. But as a pragmatist, I realize that it is sometimes necessary to take life in order to save life." Zechariah says.

Tempel visibly relaxes and his face takes on a puzzled expression, "With the amount of scientific data available today, how can you continue to believe in a supernatural creator?"

"Science will never be able to satisfactorily explain the origins of life, or what caused the Big Bang, or those unique moments in history when a single strand of DNA inexplicably changes and a new species comes into being. Just because your science cannot accept the hand of God as the root cause of an event, doesn't mean that it isn't. Who are we to say what role God plays in evolution? Who else but God could create a biological computer as complex as DNA? It has worked successfully on Earth for a billion years and an incalculable number of species."

Zechariah is on his pulpit preaching his view of the cosmos just as priests have done for tens of thousands of years. The lively discussion attracts Brice and Alonzo who come over to stand beside Tempel. The rest of Charley Company watch and listen from a distance as they complete preparations.

"The Earth itself is but a speck of dust in an unimaginably large universe. Only God can truly grasp its immensity. Everywhere we explore, something surprises us. From microscopes to telescopes, we learn something new about the glory of God every day," Zechariah looks intently at Tempel, as though imploring him to see the truth in his words. "Everything we learn simply reveals another layer of complexity with even more questions. How can you be so arrogant as to believe you know every answer worth knowing?" Zechariah utters this last sentence with smug superiority.

"I didn't say I knew all the answers," Tempel smiles indulgently. "I just don't need to invent a super-hero to explain the parts I don't understand. If god wants to help, why doesn't he solve global warming? Instead the world is filled with suffering, hunger, and war. But looking on the bright side, since it does exist then it must be part of his master plan. Right?"

"Contrary to what you believe, I don't know what His plans are. All I know is that Christianity does not condone violence Lieutenant," Zechariah states.

"All the revealed religions have violence at their core," Lazarus says.

"I don't agree," Zechariah says.

"All you need to do is read the Old Testament. It's filled with violent stories designed to put the fear of god in you. Cain killing Able, god killing Egyptian babies during the Passover, Sodom and Gomorra wiped off the face of the Earth, and many more involving death and destruction. The Christian New Testament centers around the horrible crucifixion of Jesus on a cross."

Tempel nods in agreement and tips his head indicating that Lazarus should continue, "Islam is based around the teachings of Mohammed, a violent man who carved out an empire by his wits and a scimitar. Back in 600 CE Mohammed claims divine guidance when the angel Gabriel comes and tells him of Gods perfect plan for mankind. Of course he did this while Mohammed was fasting out in the desert, so it probably was either starvation or heat or both that induced a hallucination. But for those who believe it was an angel, ask yourself this; why didn't god tell him himself? If he is an all powerful entity, why did he need to send someone to speak for him? Why didn't god simply write the Qur'ân himself?" Lazarus pauses looking pointedly at Zechariah, "Christians believe he wrote the Ten Commandments for Moses, right?"

"Maybe god did write the Qur'ân," Brice declares. "As I recall, Mohammed could neither read nor write."

"Very few could back then, but I believe that's a myth perpetrated by the Muslims. It makes a much better story if Mohammed couldn't read or write yet could produce the Qur'ân," Lazarus says.

"If someone comes to me and says he has a message from God, I'm seriously going to think about calling a doctor for the poor guy!" Brice chuckles.

Tempel shakes his head, looking intently at Zechariah, "I can't believe the dribble that passes for religion. Muslims, Christians and Jews alike! They all claim their way is the true way and are willing to kill me if I dare disagree!"

"That's an exaggeration, Lieutenant!" Zechariah frowns indignantly, pulling himself up to his full height and jutting his chin out in defiance, "Granted, many wars have been fought using religious zeal as motivation but it's greed and a quest for power that's the true cause. Those are human failings. Not God's!"

Tempel nods his head in agreement, "It's nice to hear we agree about something. It's the human animal that's ultimately responsible for the grief in our society. Man's inhumanity towards his fellow man is a reflection of who we are; one of evolutions predators that survived by virtue of skill at killing. Beyond being used as justification, god doesn't fight wars, humans fight wars. To believe that a super-being capable of creating the cosmos gives a rat's ass for us as individuals, or even as a race, is human arrogance of the highest caliber! It ranks right up there with the Earth being the center of the universe and man being made in the image of god!"

"I believe we are created in His spiritual image, our soul is his gift to us," Zechariah responds.

"Do other living creatures have souls?" Tempel asks.

"In a fashion but there is no question that man is special. Our souls are what separate man from beast," Zechariah replies.

"All life is sacred, not just human." Tempel smiles clearly enjoying the conversation. It was just what he needed to take his mind off the coming battle. "Tell me, do you believe the bible is the literal word of god?" he asks.

"Yes and no. I don't believe everything in the Bible should be taken literally. It's largely a book of parables subject to the interpretation of honest folk," Zechariah answers.

"Honest folk make honest mistakes," Tatiana says.

"Please tell me why the creator of the universe would entrust his sacred word to such an unreliable resource as man's written language. The meaning of words change with every generation, not to mention that unscrupulous men may take it upon themselves to improve the bible here and there, especially if it is to their advantage to do so," Tempel says.

"The Bible is Gods word. The lessons it contains are as valid today as when they were first written, but only if the spirit of God moves you to understand them." Zechariah says.

"You mean the skill to twist them into something palatable to the current crop of followers," Tempel says. "A story that is subject to interpretation means nothing. The creation fairytale of Adam and Eve is a good example. Do you actually believe God created the cosmos in six days, or that the Earth is eight thousand years old?" Tempel asks pointedly. "Try to answer with a simple yes or no."

"The Garden of Eden is a parable Lieutenant, not to be taken literally. The length of a day in the Genesis account of creation is not defined. It could be millions or even billions of years. God does not operate on man's time," Zechariah says. He feels anger rising up within him at Tempel's humorous disregard of his answers.

Tipping his head and grinning, Tempel says, "A day is not a day? Killing is wrong except when it's not? Incest and slavery are ok but for a man to make love to another man is punishable by death? Wives are property and children are expendable? I'm sorry, but the bible is full of vile ideas and despicable omissions. Why didn't Jesus say one word against killing in his name? If he had, many lives might have been spared in the intervening centuries. Why didn't the Ten Commandments address rape instead of making wives property of their husbands, or condemn slavery instead of demanding that we worship him on a certain day? Why does Lott, supposedly the most righteous man in Sodom and Gomorra, impregnate his own daughters? Why doesn't the Bible account for evolution, or for the great age of the Earth, or for the complexity of the cosmos? Why doesn't religion explain instead of suppress?" Shaking his head in total disbelief, "God is a myth created by our ancestors to explain things they didn't understand. At best all so-called revealed religions are self-delusions on a grand scale, at worst they are the ultimate power game."

As Zechariah listens, his face twists into a frown. "How do you get away with saying such horrible things?" he asks. He looks at Tempel like he is looking at the devil himself, fear and loathing wash over him in waves.

"Because Lunarians have Freedom of Belief," Lazarus replies not unkindly. He knows what the young man is feeling at that moment. He himself is only just beginning to experience the pleasure of not suppressing his true thoughts and beliefs. "Think about it Zechariah. True Freedom of Belief means that Tempel can proselytize his view of the cosmos, even when that means he doesn't believe in god. That's something you are not used to. On Luna, it's ok to say that god doesn't exist. Back in the Federation this conversation would mean reeducation. Here it's but a diversion."

Turning to Lazarus, "But how can a person not believe in anything?" Zechariah asks.

"Who are you to say I don't believe in anything?" Tempel says, "I believe in humanity and the sanctity of life. I believe that my actions are my responsibility and treat my fellow citizens like I want them to treat me. I believe that by hard work and perseverance I can positively contribute to my society. I believe in many things. I'm just not arrogant enough to believe in the existence of an all-powerful super-dad that demands my blind obedience and pouts when I withhold it."

"Arrogant! You sir, appear to be the arrogant one, voicing tolerance even as you disparage me for believing in the one true God!" Zechariah replies.

"It's arrogant to claim god made you in his image. It's arrogant to say he has given you jurisdiction over the Earth and all creatures on it. It's arrogant to think that the creator of the universe grants freewill and condemns anyone to hell for all eternity if they dare exercise it. It's arrogant to think you can change the mind of god by simply asking nicely or begging. I could go on but I think you get the picture," Tempel explains patiently. "Don't make the mistake of thinking that just because I fight for your freedom of belief means I must respect your choice."

"Hey, Captain… Back in your football days, how many times did god choose your team?" Brice had been anticipating the moment when he could ask this question, "It cracks me up in the old vids to see players on both sides down on their knees praying when the game is on the line!" he chuckles. "Did those guys really think GOD" he stresses the word, "was going to jump in there and straighten out a bad kick just because they prayed harder than the guys on the other side of the field?"

"Since when have you started watching old football games?" Kitajima asks.

"After I found out you used to play, I wanted to see for myself what it was about, that's all." Brice grins, "Ouch! Football was definitely not a game for the faint hearted!" He looks at his Captain with exaggerated respect.

"Praying isn't about getting an answer. It's more like sharing a burden," Zechariah says. "The psychological benefit those men received from praying allowed them to cope with both wining and losing."

Tempel smiles, "Now that is the smartest thing you've said yet. You left god out and addressed the real issue of humans being human."

"I didn't leave God out. I just said god helped both sides," Zechariah says.

Tempel sighs and shakes his head indulgently, "So did god push the kick wide because one team was better able to cope with losing than the other?" he asks.

"I don't believe God plays games anymore than you do. What I do believe in is a God who maintains order in the universe, keeping everything working as designed, and otherwise, providing for freewill," Zechariah says stiffly. He resents the amused tolerance emanating from these Lunarians. It makes him feel like the butt of a bad joke, something he is not accustomed to. In the Federation, he is given the respect due a man of God, not mocked as a gullible halfwit.

"Do you believe god spoke or sent messages to the ancient prophets? After all, that is the core premise of revealed religion, Moses talking with god on Mount Sinai, Jesus as the son of god, rising from the dead, and Mohammed getting the skinny from an angel sent by god." Tempel tilts his head.

"I'm not so sure any of those things actually happened, Lieutenant. I wasn't there and there's no way to prove or disprove any of them. But what I believe you are trying to belittle are the Articles of Faith, the core beliefs that serve to define my religion. Without them the Scriptures are just words and the Holy Bible is just a history book with a message," Zechariah says, his irritation making him sound as though he were speaking down to an ignorant child.

"A very bad message, if you ask me," Lazarus adds softly.

Tempel grins, "Man is the ultimate social animal with a hardwired need to belong to something bigger than himself. Family, village, church and kings have all prospered because of it. From mankind's earliest days hunting in packs across the African plains or gathering around the evening campfire discussing life's mystery's, religion has grew and thrived on that need. Religion is the longest and most successful con ever devised!" Tempel says and shakes his head in bafflement, "And why not! It offered comfort at a time when people were most vulnerable, something to hold on to when a loved one was eaten by the local lion, contracted some terrible disease, or died fighting for the king." Tempel continues to shake his head, "But to believe in something absurd with all your heart does not make it any less absurd."

"Conversely, just because you believe it absurd does not make it so. The Universe is Gods creation and I'm part of the Universe. It can't be accidental that every atom in every star system in every galaxy in the entire Universe is organized in such a complex arrangement. This is a manifestation of Gods Will. To say that God did NOT influence our ancestors is truly preposterous. The thoughts and ideas that come to us are from our interaction with God. You said so yourself. We all have this need to belong hardwired into us. God did the wiring!" Zechariah exclaims.

"How can you make such absurd leaps of logic?" Tatiana asks.

"The atoms and molecules in our bodies are put there by God. God then endowed us with the curiosity to look at the majesty of His Universe and the wit to praise the glory of His creation. I marvel at Gods handiwork every time I look in a microscope. I feel Gods presence in the elegance of mathematical equations. Everywhere I look I see Him in the unimaginable complexity of the cosmos," Zechariah says, "The men who penned the Bible were inspired by something. You can feel it in the writings. Their words strike a deep chord within us that cannot be overstated. But is the Bible literal? Yes. It's a message from God to each of us. How we accept that message, or even hear it, is up to us."

Tempel frowns and shakes his head, "I have studied the Bible, the Qur'ân, the Book of Mormon and many other texts considered holy by some and I can find very little truth in any of them. To put any great credence on any of the ancient holy books takes either a great deal of gullibility or shear desperation to swallow the whoppers they contain," Tempel's voice takes on a spiritual persona in imitation of Zechariah, "God talking to Moses, angels talking to Mohammed, Jesus rising from the dead, eternal life after death in some fanciful paradise but only if you suspend reason and believe in ME. Oh, by the way, give this man here 10% of everything you own," Tempel says with a wink, those of Charley Company paying attention chuckle. "I think it much more likely that these books were written by men for the same reasons we write books today, for profit and for power. But two-thousand years ago a writer had the distinct advantage that everyone believed their every thought was inspired by God or Satan or something other than themselves without any real concept of the physical mind. This belief in divine inspiration was further compounded because only a few could read and write, helping perpetrate a caste system that haunted mankind for thousands of years. Religion was just another way of concentrating power into a relatively few individuals, another way of enforcing certain behavior on the common folk. And even after all these years, mankind still has religious fanatics who want to force everyone else to believe in the same nonsense they do. And I'm not talking just about the Brotherhood. The Federation has as much culpability in that regard, teaching god creation as science in their schools, letting citizens suffer while ignoring medical advancements just because the treatments don't fit into the ethics of their religion, the worth of a person measured not in their deeds but in their professed beliefs, people who dare to be different persecuted and ostracized, and those who dare question are reeducated. Ask Lazarus about reeducation. Religious fanaticism has made the Federation a second, maybe even third tier nation."

"Atheism is not tolerated within the borders of the Federation," Lazarus says. "The religious diversity that marked the founding of the United States is gone, replaced by the official state church. If you are not a member then you are an enemy of the state. And I should know. I helped track thousands of citizens of dubious intent while working at Homeland Security. This fixation with uniformity has hurt America. While still a force militarily, there hasn't been any significant new technology for over half a century. From the land that invented computers and cell phones and satellites and automobiles and airplanes and a million other things, all they have done recently is refine what they already have while brutally suppressing anything new. What little basic research remains is done in the name of national security under tight control of the military. The government has a choke hold on the freedoms once so dear and the citizens are powerless to do anything meaningful to change it. Freedom of speech is only allowed if the government agrees with it. Citizens are free to practice their religion as long as it is the state approved variety. Freedom of the press is a joke. Judges do as the President suggests or they find themselves looking for a new job flipping burgers or making pizzas or if their crime was really bad, reeducated. Police can do whatever they think is necessary to catch those who disobey or speak out against those in power...Thomas Jefferson would be ashamed of what his United States of America has become." He shakes his head and his voice takes on a wistful tone, "As a child, I can remember my father speaking to me of things I didn't truly understand at the time. As I grew up I realized he was a Freethinker hiding behind a facade of belief in order to survive. I learned at the feet of a real pro," Lazarus says proudly.

"How could you live in such a repressive state? I can't begin to imagine hiding my true feelings about something so big for so long. To pretend to believe in god, attend church, pray and say all the things you must have said to convince everyone around you that you too are a Christian. How did you do it?" Tempel asks looking at Lazarus with wonder.

"It's dishonest," Brice says his expression one of suspicion verging on distrust.

Lazarus shrugs, "I kept reminding myself of something my father once told me. He said not to worry about telling a lie just as long as the person you lie to is lying back at you! The churches are filled with liars Brice, people who pretend to be one thing but are something completely different. I fit right in!"

Zechariah frowns, thinking about this for a moment, "What about true believers? How do you justify lying to them?"

"What makes you think you are not lying just because you believe what you're saying? Lies are about twisting facts which have nothing to do with belief. To me the most despicable lie is the one retold by someone foolish enough to believe it," Lazarus says having thought about and justified his deception over many years. "The essence of a good lie is to put some truth in it and there are passages in the bible that do just that. For instance Ecclesiastes Chapter 3, verses 18-19. *I hoped in my heart that God might make clear to the sons of men, that they themselves are beasts. For that which befall the sons of men, befall the beasts; as the one dies so dies the other, yea, they have all one breath; so that a man hath no preeminence above a beast.*"

Tempel grins, "I'm starting to see how you managed all those years. You out deceived the deceivers!"

Before anyone can say anything further Kitajima continues, "I hate to breakup this little chitchat but it's time to mount up!"

"Courage without conscience is a wild beast."
Robert Ingersoll (1833-1899)

Battle of Nell's Valley

Hack eases Blue down with minimum dust northwest of Nell's Valley, a little over a mile from the crash site. A moment later she releases a pair of bugs, small self-contained recording devices the size of a mosquito whose primary mission is to locate all electronic sentry's, and second, obtain a visual on the crash site. One is programmed to fly along the ridge closest to them and the other over the valley floor, both will remain several hundred feet up, very difficult but not impossible to detect. The knowledge that if detected, the bugs could be followed back to their owners puts everyone on edge, alert to the possibility of fight or flight on very short notice.

Tempel watches over Sam's shoulder as she puts the final touches on a little spybot, prepping it for the job at hand. Like the bugs, it's deployed using micro-thrusters to propel it through the lunar vacuum. Contained in a package the size of peach pit is a full sensor array and a complete set of combat communications electronics. In actuality, it is a piece of basalt, just like a billion others spread across the surface of Luna, full of holes like Swiss cheese. It's in one of these holes that the electronics are hidden.

Sam is the acknowledged expert within the company in deploying spybots. She has managed to put them in apparently impossible places more than once during training. She doesn't let herself think about the consequences of failure today, or that this isn't just another training mission, concentrating instead on simply doing the task at hand, relying on hundreds of hours of practice.

Sam is linked into the sensors in the spybot letting her fly the little machine just as if she was sitting in a tiny cockpit within the stone. She soars swiftly up the valley, staying low, not more than ten feet off the surface, gracefully avoiding the larger boulders and outcroppings. The vantage point she is aiming for is down this valley then west, across the adjacent valley to a high ridge on its far side. From there they should look down on the crash site and have line-of-sight with another ridge above Red. She brings the spybot to its closest point before moving up the side of the valley, creeping upward until she can see over the top. Hovering there for a few seconds, she rotates and looks around.

Nothing.

Picking a spot quickly, Sam darts down to rest briefly on the top of a prominent boulder before flitting away, leaving behind a device smaller than a pea. It's a line-of-sight laser communications relay keeping her in touch with the spybot, even when it's beyond the horizon.

Quickly, she maneuvers over the ridge and starts down. Still nothing. Across the valley floor and up the other side, she keeps the flying rock close to the ground. Sam glances at her fuel meter and realizes she must speed up or risk not getting the spybot where it needs to be, looking down on the crash site.

This section of the valley is rugged and broken. A small cliff presents itself before her. Up the rock face she flies, cresting it just as the fuel warning sounds in her ears. With less than thirty seconds of flight time remaining, she streaks across the ridge approaching the selected overlook. She maneuvers the spybot between boulders, always trying to keep from silhouetting it against the lunar sky. She gives the area a quick look and decides on a pile of stones similar to her tiny spybot just a few feet away. She sets the flying piece of basalt down gently, its sensors pointing into the valley below. Shutting off the tiny thrusters, Sam looks at her remaining fuel and realizes she only has two seconds of flight time remaining. She releases a long breath, shaking her head in disbelief, hoping that her location is good.

"Well done!" Tempel says softly and squeezing her shoulder. "Establish the comm link with Kitajima."

Sam nods, pleased and relived. The spot the Captain picked for his relay should allow them to establish line-of-sight communications with the other transport, if it's where it should be. She tentatively lazes the coordinates and is gratified with an immediate acknowledgment. The two transports and the entire company can now communicate with little fear of being overheard.

"Lieutenant Dugan, report!" Kitajima orders.

"We are at our assigned position waiting for our bugs to return," Tempel says, relived but not surprised that the plan is going so well.

"Good! Let me know when you get them back," Kitajima says. "The view from our bot is blocked. Let's take a look at what yours is seeing."

"Aye," Tempel responds.

Linking to the sensors in the spybot, Tempel zooms in on the camp. From this low angle it's impossible to see everything but it's obvious there are more than just a few rovers. At least one big ship, several truck convoys, and two of the small fighters are grounded on the other side of the crash site, perhaps even the same two that was looking for them back at Sunset Canyon. Movement is everywhere and he can just see the domed top of what has to be a large portable shelter, much larger than the one they had brought.

At that instant, two rovers come over a rise directly into their field of view, coming right at the camera. Tempel backs off the magnification. These are more of the small two man Rugbys they had tangled with just a few hours earlier. For their size they pack a big punch, not much more than four wheels on a high capacity power pack feeding a disrupter, the operators comfort an afterthought in the design. All the Guardians have a healthy respect for the lethal cannon mounted on the backs of these vehicles. They have the power to punch through their shielding with a single hit. Each and every one of these weapons will need to be dealt with.

Tempel begins to mark what he sees populating the strategic map of the engagement. Refocusing on the main camp he continues to categorize the Brotherhood's forces, the number of people, type of armament, and the location of everything. This is something he is particularly good at, identifying what they are up against in a way that enables them to formulate a plan of action.

"There must be a hundred guys there," Brice whispers. "Are you sure you want to do this?"

"At ease!" Tempel growls at him while his hands fly over his virtual controls. Without looking at him, he gives the young man a savage grin. "What? You want to live forever?"

Hack signals Brice to keep quite, cutting off the inevitable smartass reply. "Kit, are you seeing this," she asks over the new comm link.

"Yes. It looks like we have some work to do," Kitajima responds. "The big ship is a Brotherhood frigate. If it brings its guns to bear, we'll be in trouble."

"Excuse me, Tempel, but our bugs are back," Sam reports, already putting them in the reader, quickly downloading each ten minute video and accompanying data. She brings it online for everyone to see, including Kitajima and the rest of Charley Company.

The first bug, programmed to fly along the ridge, quickly determines that there isn't any electronic sentry's present, at least, none that the bug could detect. On the other hand, the human sentry's were easily located. A group of them armed with pulse rifles, Tempel counts twelve stationed along a rocky outcropping directly above the site. They seem more interested in what's happening down in the valley than keeping an eye out on the mare. On the slope below this ridge other rovers and soldiers can be seen, mostly in groups of two or three. Tempel's hands blur with speed as he collects data for the simulation.

The other bug flies down the heart of the valley and directly over crash site itself. From a hundred feet up, its view is remarkable. Men and equipment swarm over and around the wreckage. Most are common soldiers but some technicians are apparent. As the bug passes over the pilothouse, it becomes clear what they are doing. A large trench has been dug along side the pilothouse and even as they watch, an excavator emerges with a load of lunar regolith and rock piled high on its holding bed, dumping it close by.

A group of technicians are seen standing close to the entrance of the pit talking and gesturing. Tempel wishes he could eavesdrop on the conversation. It is probably in Arabic anyway.

"They haven't got to them yet!" Sam declares.

Tempel signals her to silence as their bug continues replaying its journey. It's now directly above the main camp, a hastily constructed affair made up of a portable shelter and three truck convoys parked in a row on the crest of a rise a short distance from the remains of Evolution's Child, the same spot he himself had landed Blue upon just hours before. As the bug loops back towards them, it flies over several clusters of rovers with their crews lounging in or around them. It's plain to everyone that this isn't going to be a walk in the park.

One of Kitajima's bugs passes over the two fighters grounded at his end of the camp. These machines pose high danger to the company, perhaps greater than the frigate. The entire mission is jeopardized if even one of these deadly little ships gets skyborne. His second bug identifies another truck convoy, this one sitting apart from the rest, probably the hypergolic fuel tanker.

Kipper and Tatiana incorporate the information from their bugs and combine it with the data Tempel has collated. Even though the two ships are miles apart, VR brings all of them together, standing around a very detailed 3-D image of Nell's Valley, the frigate, fighters, trucks and rovers all clearly represented in the presentation.

Kitajima moves forward looking like a man wading in waist deep water and takes a position at one end of the valley. "I will start the ball rolling by taking out the frigates comm system and armament. That ship is my primary target. I don't want it to ever see deep space again... Tatiana, you will attack the fighters, don't let them get off the ground. Then drive through to the main camp from here... Tempel, your team attacks from this direction, take out that bunch on the ridge and proceed to the main camp this way... Kipper you will attack from this direction and Consuela from here. Do a pincer and close the loop... I want everyone to converge on them and take everything out. I don't want any men or machines left in one piece... Once the camp is clear, Hack will bring Blue and land here. I will bring Red and take this position. Brice and I will assume responsibility of extracting the crate. The rest of you will spread out and find whatever the Brotherhood has been kind enough to leave behind. Memory cubes, command and control computers, any AI's, you know the drill people, lets do this by the book. Find everything that is of value and destroy the rest! Any questions or comments?" he looks around at the faces of the assembled officers, looking for weakness or hesitation and finding none. "Good! Let's do a full scale simulation and see where we are."

Charley Company plays a sophisticated game of team combat, a virtual dose of warfare that allows them to experience the battle before risking their lives, correcting the flaws in the plan while giving the young warriors confidence. Fifteen minutes later they are finished, having coordinated targets and responsibilities for the attack right down to what weapon to use in each instance. Time well spent.

"Anybody want to add anything?" Kitajima is proud of the way his team is performing.

"I do," responds Tempel.

"Go ahead, speak your mind."

"Some of you may think this plan is too aggressive but I just want you to remember Lincoln County Hospital. The men we face today applaud that mass murder and are supporting the leaders who conceived and carried it out. Don't feel sorry for any of them! They deserve no mercy!" Tempel says.

His words are greeted solemnly by the gathering. They all had family and friends who died at the hands of the Muslims in that tragedy or in one of the others that the Republic has suffered over the last few years. This is a moment they had known would come when they made the decision to be a Guardian and wear a ghost suit, something they had trained towards with dedication and perseverance. This handful of Lunarian warriors are ready for the coming battle, a weapon of mass destruction primed for detonation.

"Are we locked and loaded?" Kitajima asks one last time.

"Aye!" they reply with one voice.

"Ok, Charley! This is zero hour! Let's run!" Kitajima utters the words that send Guardians into battle for the very first time.

****

Bipedal running on the moon is clumsy at best, difficult to maintain balance and even worse at changing directions. Even the slightest deviation from a straight line requires a great deal of effort. The Lunarians have come up with a solution to the problem.

Tempel flexes his knees, leans forward, and leaps almost horizontally across the lunar surface, his boots giving him a firm grip on the loose regolith beneath his feet. But instead of sliding to a stop on his belly, he uses his arms to smoothly propel himself further across the desolate landscape, coiling his legs beneath him for another mighty push. In an eerie imitation of a cheetah coming up to speed, the warrior leaps forward, each bound longer than the previous.

The end result of more than a half century of research, Temple is physically able to move this way through the bold application of genetic engineering, shoulder joints redesigned to better absorb the stress of landings and his spinal column more flexible to accommodate quadruped motion. Other more subtle changes match his body to his environment. Eyes that are better able to interface with microlasers, a brain designed for DMC technology, respiration, circulation and digestion, every biological system has been enhanced for living and fighting in a vacuum at twenty percent Earth normal gravity, a melding of technology and nature. Yet, even if he were nude, someone not intimately familiar with the human body would miss these changes hidden deep within, the shape of his shoulder blades and pelvis, the depth of his chest, and the length of his neck the only outward signs that he isn't actually Homo sapiens any longer.

Not only is his overall physiology genetically designed for this radical form of locomotion, but his ghost suits electromagnetic shield technology provides him with added strength. Controlled by dedicated microcircuits, each of the millions of tiny Calconn coils embedded within the material add their own unique electromagnetic field to the larger whole. Adjacent fields reinforce and multiply if they are similar, decay and retard if they are not. In this way a larger and more dynamic field is generated that attracts or repels dependant on location and time. The coils in his chest and abdomen push and pull those created by his arms and legs in a complex imitation of musculature, right down to his handgrip.

Under normal conditions the vacsuit is very flexible and comfortable to wear. But when necessary the coils will interact with their neighbors to form a magnetic bond that works in conjunction with the suits spider silk to create an almost impenetrable barrier. This stiffening of the material at the point of impact is achieved so rapidly and so completely, that a bullet or a meteor is stopped cold, the energy of the impact being converted to electricity and stored within the very coils that stopped it, creating feedback that increases shield strength even more. Only the mass of the object has any true effect, reacting with the warrior following the Laws of Motion that Isaac Newton put forward centuries before, for every action there is an equal and opposite reaction. Not even a meteor traveling at tens of thousands of miles per hour can move fast enough to overcome this barrier. Anyone unlucky enough to be struck will undoubtedly regret it, being violently driven back by its mass, but they will live. Since the coils making up this shield consists entirely of Calconn, once the vacsuit is charged, the energy within it simply shifts from one area to another as needed. Only the power to do work is consumed and must be replaced, easily done with the high capacity power cell located in the belt, much more dependable than waiting for a meteor to strike.

The ghost suit gives him strength and stability as he bounds across the barren terrain like some bizarre four legged beast. His gloves and boots crush and compress the regolith with each impact, maximizing his traction, allowing him agility and speed where before was only bipedal awkwardness.

His DMC weaponry frees his hands for the necessary task of moving quickly in the one-sixth Earth normal gravity. His strength and energy goes into propelling himself forward at an ever increasing speed. His hands touch and push, his feet touch and push, accelerating and changing directions at these critical junctures. This gives him incredible agility while passing over the rough lunar terrain, leaping from one point to the next, motoring down the valley at seventy mph in the straight portions, slowing in the curves.

Like smoke in the night sky, the warriors of Charley Company are very hard to see only a few feet away, impossible from a distance. They are strung out in single file behind their Lieutenant, each of them following in the exact footfalls as their leader. They lope effortlessly over the relatively smooth floor of the valley, staying close to the ground. An attentive sentry could perhaps spot the puffs of dust that marks their passage. They are shadows on a dark night, gone in a blink of an eye. The pack covers the intervening distance in a matter of minutes.

****

Lazarus is sitting directly behind Hack in the left side of the transport with Lindsey across the aisle and Zechariah right behind her. Lindsey rotates her seat to face Lazarus.

"The controls are here," she quickly shows him.

He turns his seat to face her, "How long do you think they will be?"

Lindsey is tense, "We can talk later. Right now I want to be with Tempel." She believes the horrors of the coming combat and the actions taken today to win this battle should be witnessed by all citizens, if for no other reason than to know what price has been paid for independence. The vast majority of Lunarians agree with her. She feels privileged to see it real-time.

"Yes, of course. Do you mind if I link to you?" Lazarus asks.

"Not at all but be warned, I might jump around a bit. I don't know what to expect and neither does anyone else. This is the first time Lunarians have gone into combat," Lindsey responds.

"That in itself is a remarkable achievement. I don't know of any other country that attained independence without a war of some kind," Lazarus says as he links with her.

With jarring suddenness, he is out on the surface, moving rapidly over the rough terrain in a fashion that doesn't seem quite right. He is looking through the eyes of Tempel. The officers that accompany him are not in sight.

Lazarus is amazed at the clarity and depth of the link. He can hear Tempel breath, can see his hands reach out with every bound, gripping the lunar surface and propelling him forward.

Suddenly he realizes what is strange about the movement. Tempel is bounding across the landscape using all four limbs! Even as this realization hits him, Tempel turns his head and glances at his companions, giving Lazarus a glimpse of their quadrupedal motion. Smooth and graceful, it reminds Lazarus of a great cat in full gallop. Their long slender necks allow them to easily look forward while running on all fours, and the joints in their arms and legs move in ways that is impossible for Lazarus.

The two shoulder mounted weapons have rotated up over their backs and continue to point forward, their height well above the tops of their heads. The flexibility of the vacsuits have never been more evident than at that moment as the spines of these young Lunarians bend and twist in a supple display of agility. The power and grace of their movement is beautiful to behold as they bound across the landscape in giant leaps, each covering twenty-five or thirty feet. A puff of dust rises where they touch the surface, more if they are changing direction.

Lazarus is speechless, his mind struggling to grasp what he is witnessing. Many mystifying occurrences over the past few days now become clear. These people are different in ways he's only beginning to understand.

"Lindsey… Please explain what I'm seeing," Lazarus asks with trepidation, his confusion and fear, pride and prejudice, threatening to destroy the good feeling that he's had since becoming a Lunarian. He's deeply frightened.

Lindsey sighs and pushes Tempels video signal into the corner where she can monitor it while she talks. Looking steadily at Lazarus she says, "Temple and the others are… special."

"What do you mean special?" Lazarus presses.

"They have been given gifts that enhance those given to them by Mother Nature."

"You mean they are mutants?" Lazarus asks bluntly.

"The term mutant has come to have a negative quality like many other names given to people in the past. If you use it here, you will find out very quickly that freedom does not extend to insults based in ignorance. Most citizens will ignore anyone using that word as a slur. And once you are ignored, you are nothing."

The sharp edge in Lindsey's voice is enough to signal Lazarus that he is treading on thin ice.

"I meant no offense. I'm just blown away. This is incredible! Are they another race?" he asks.

"They're another species," she responds. "They call themselves Homo rotica."

Lazarus looks at her in confusion again. "Are you serious?"

"The scientists named them something quiet different thirty years ago. But they started calling themselves Homo rotica and now everybody uses that name, even the scientists," Lindsey says.

"Thirty years ago? I don't understand," Lazarus says.

"I don't have the time to teach you evolutionary science right now. There will be other things that will blow you away, just be careful what comes out of your mouth while you assimilate them into a new reality," she says not quite so sharply. "Look, you yourself will undoubtedly require medical attention at some point in the future and the more you can find out about the current state of genetics the better off you will be. Lunarians are raised with it and it's in all of our blood in more ways then one. I will help you understand but for now can we please just observe what is happening right now?"

"Yes course, I apologize for my ignorance. I'll do better in the future," Lazarus promises.

"I'm sure you will," Lindsey says dryly, knowing full well this bright if somewhat impulsive man will undoubtedly put his foot in his mouth again. It's only a matter of time.

****

Coming around a sweeping curve Temple spots their quarry. The thermal signature of the soldier's mark them in blazing red and they are clumped together near a large basalt boulder, the only cover that breaks the barren ridge for a long distance. Most of them appear to be looking down upon the crash site, oblivious to the approaching Guardians. Still in single file, Charley Company slows and angles up the side of the valley. At the top, Temple, Sam and Zoey turn and head straight for the group, tightening their formation until they move as one along the crest of the ridge, one behind the other. Angel continues down the other side leading Brice and Karyl towards the south end of the camp. None of the warriors break stride as they sprint up and down the steep slopes, bounding forward with the same grace and agility they demonstrated on the level.

Already spread out in attack formation, Karyl, Alonzo and Tatiana swarm over the ridge and down into Nell's Valley almost directly above their primary target, the fighters. Consuela leads Jason and Corazon from the opposite direction toward the other end of the camp. None of them have fired a single shot yet, but that will soon change. The four teams are rapidly converging on the unsuspecting camp.

The upper portion of the frigate contains most of the Brotherhood's long range communications. Kitajima slowly brings his Dragonfly up until he can just peek over the ridge and see the sensor array through the Gattling's gun sights. Magnified and targeted, he times his attack to coincide with his Guardians reaching their initial objectives. An instant before Charley Company begin their attack, he opens up. The ceramic armor is no match for the power of his disrupter, silently exploding as the beam penetrates into the core of the ship releasing the pressurized atmosphere within.

One of the men on the ridge points down into the valley, impossible to see a face under the bug-eye helmet, or hear his voice. Bounding along the top of the ridge like hounds from hell, Tempel, Sam and Zoey spread out and begin firing with an inhuman accuracy and rapidity. The sentry's are all looking down into the valley, a fatal mistake. The Lunarians see only Brotherhood combat vacsuits, heavy with plate armor, the men anonymous behind grotesque battle helmets, simply targets on a shooting range. One, two, three, four, five, six, seven, eight, nine die before they even know the Lunarians are there, the warrior's disrupters cutting them down like wheat during harvest, their blood exploding into vacuum, rising in a gaseous haze that takes on a life of its own. Within moments, chest and head shots create a meat grinder above Nell's Valley. The tenth sentry manages to turn and the eleventh levels his weapon just before they add their blood to the portrait of death. The twelfth ducks behind the boulder, extending his life by almost a second. Tempel shoots him in the head as he leaps over the man, arcing downward into Nell's Valley, leaving an expanding cloud of blood and human fluids behind him on the ridge.

Synchronized with Tempels first shot, Tatiana, Karyl and Alonzo launch missiles at the fighters now less than a hundred yards away. The deadly little finless darts, less than eight inches long and two inches in diameter, leap from their shoulder mounted launchers and accelerate in eerie silence, streaking towards their targets on preprogrammed flight paths. In a blur they strike the fighters and punch through the thin skin, exploding with tremendous force in the confined space within. Both warcraft are ripped apart and flung in pieces across Nell's Valley. Neither come close to making it off the ground. Karyl sees a figure crawling from the wreckage and laces his back with disrupter fire. Alonzo shoots someone sitting in the pilot's seat. Their blood adds a red haze to the smoldering remains.

Consuela, Jason and Corazon target the two articulated carriers setting west of the camp, each launching a pair of missiles. Penetrating the tank section of the closest vehicle, the explosions rip open its flank, dumping the fluid inside onto the ground. The other tanker follows a similar fate and the released liquid begins to boil in the vacuum of space creating an instant fog around the two vehicles. It is undoubtedly either hydrazine or aniline, one component in the hypergolic fuel used in magnetoplasma thrusters and high capacity fuel cells. Several men leap from the second vehicle and the warriors make short work of cutting them down.

Brice, Angel and Kipper descend into the valley east of Tempel's position and race towards that end of the camp, strange ghostly shapes flowing across the alien terrain. Several rovers and another tanker truck are positioned at the center of the valley theoretically providing security for that side of the camp while keeping the hypergolic constituents separated. Keeping well away, Angel magnifies her target, firing at the trucks forward section, probing for its power pack, punching a hole in its side with no outward effect. A second burst from her cannon finds its mark, sending the vehicle up in a hypergolic ball of flame, tearing it completely away from the tanker section behind it. The two rovers receive Brice and Kipper's attention as they sprint down the side of the valley, dark specters of death coming out of nowhere, their disrupter's firing about twice every second, as fast as they can recharge. First one then the other rover explodes in a silent fireball as the hypergolic fuels from ruptured tanks mix. The soldiers on the surface flee the exploding vehicles trying vainly to get away from the unseen death that has descended on them. Kipper targets the nearest man almost cutting him in half as he concentrates all his firepower on the soldier's center of mass, his blood and guts' spray grotesquely into the vacuum as his burned and twisted body comes to rest on Luna's soil.

Brice hit the second and third rovers in rapid secession as he springs forward, sending more fireballs skyward. The men who had been clustered around the vehicles scatter and seek cover from the terrain around them, finding none. The few boulders big enough to offer any security are several hundred feet away along the north side of the valley, opposite where the Guardians are coming from. Digging his hands and feet into the soft regolith, Brice slows his forward velocity while sending a huge wave of fine lunar dust arching away from him, unwittingly marking his location. In rapid secession he picks them off, one by one, starting with the man furthest back, until there isn't any remaining. Moments later their lifeless bodies are strewn across the landscape a few feet apart, like a gruesome dotted line, their gapping wounds spewing red geysers into the sky forming a curtain across that part of Nell's Valley.

Before the dust of his slide has settled, a beam from a weapon mounted atop a Rugby several hundred yards distant slams into Brice, overwhelming his shield and penetrating his ghost suit. The path through his body misses his heart but slices through his lung instantly bringing the warrior down, sliding along the surface in a cloud of dust and blood.

"No!" Jason cries out.

"Maintain discipline," Kitajima says calmly. "Finish the job." Brice had broken the cardinal rule, never slow down, and it cost him dearly.

The others are aware that Brice is down but they have all been taught the best way to help wounded comrades was to finish the fight quickly and leave the medical issues to Doc Grady. It's his job to monitor the vital signs of every Guardian and initiate treatment as needed. By the time Brice has come to a stop, Doc has diagnostics running and is trying desperately to save him.

Kipper, already well beyond Brice, pumps a SuperX missile into the truck section of a surface transport. The streaking missile penetrates the vehicle and explodes, ripping open the high capacity fuel cell that powered it. A fraction of a second later a second much larger explosion rips apart the massive four-wheeler sending an intense fireball mushrooming skyward. The transport must have had full fuel tanks because its demise leaves a good sized crater in its place. The force of the blast picks up a nearby rover and smashes it in a heap, the two occupants probably killed. Kipper makes sure before proceeding down the valley, lacing the rover with a long burst, watching with satisfaction as the silent ball of flame rises above the shredded carcass of the vehicle.

Virtually invisible to the Muslims, the warriors of Charley Company race across the terrain, attacking and converging on the camp from all directions, leaping over and around obstacles, using agility to bounce across the landscape, delivering a continuous rain of death and destruction wherever they go. Striking from a distance using sensors to magnify their targets, the warriors don't allow the Brotherhood soldiers to even see them, let alone return fire with any hope of hitting one of them. Guardian disrupters emit burst after burst, time after time, pausing only long enough to find the next target.

Launching himself off the top of a large basalt boulder, Tempel sails high in the sky and fires his disrupter through the torso of a soldier running back towards a pair of rovers, severing his spine and instantly killing him. The man releases his weapon and bounces across the surface like a rag doll, trailing a plume of red almost like smoke rings behind him as his heart pumps its last few beats and the vacuum of space starts sucking him dry.

Before the man had come to rest Sam and Zoey attack the two parked rovers and the men around them. One soldier tries vainly to get into a rover. Zoey puts a shot through his back and another in the vehicle's power pack releasing a huge cloud of hypergolic fuel above it. A second later it reacts in a silent fireball, bouncing the little buggy like it had been struck with a giant sledgehammer, its balloon tires compressing then springing back, bouncing all four tires off the surface, flinging the lifeless body of the soldier high into the sky trailing blood.

A second later Sam lit off the other rover, sending a matching fireball skyward. Beyond the flame two soldiers return fire. Leaping over the two rovers and through what is left of the rapidly dissipating fireballs, Sam shoots first one in the chest then the other as she passes them in blur. A blood red cloud engulfs the two men as they slowly fall to the ground landing flat on their backs, side by side. She lands beyond the dying men and digs her hands into the soft lunar dust, twisting as she brings her legs up and pushes hard, changing directions in the blink of an eye, taking advantage of the cover provided by the terrain around her. She is already looking for her next target.

A short distance away, Tempel spots a Rugby heading down slope, recklessly picking up speed as the realization of what is happening panics the driver. Quickly overtaking the vehicle, Tempel puts a burst into the back of each occupant. For good measure, he puts another burst through the rover's power pack as he passes. The rover twists and tumbles when the hypergolic fuel reacts, sending a dense flaming cloud roiling across the surface.

Kitajima keeps his Gattling busy hammering at the bigger ship, concentrating first on the thrusters then on the weapon turrets that he can see from his angle. Gases resulting from his attack create a haze around the frigate. Knowing that whoever is inside must be scrambling, trying to get it off the ground, gives him a sense of urgency.

The engagement is less than twenty seconds old but what is left of the main compound is now fully aware they are under attack. Islamic soldiers scramble up and out of the various locales grabbing weapons, ready to give battle. They pour out of the domed portable habitat and from around the bivouacked trucks looking for something to shoot.

Tatiana bears down on two more Rugbys. The soldiers from one are scrambling to remount their machine, motioning franticly to the occupants of the other. Before they have time to move Tatiana is on them. With her first burst, she ruptures the power pack on the closest rover, instantly killing the soldiers inside in the resulting detonation. The twisted remains of the vehicle spin across the valley floor. The second rover accelerates while attempting to bring its cannon to bear on Tatiana. She shifts her attention and fires an extended burst. The vehicle disintegrates under the onslaught, balloon tires burst and vaporized metal and plastic engulf it before it explodes, flips and slides down a steep slope.

Jason approaches the parked convoys from broadside, letting loose a pair of SuperX missiles at the nearest. One missile penetrates the vehicle between the balloon tires near the articulation joint, the second hits the main passenger compartment above the front tire. The giant four wheeled Goliath explodes sending huge chunks high in the sky, spinning wildly out of control before crashing back to ground. The interior had been pressurized and those inside did not have time to don a vacsuit. Everything loose expands outward, picked up by the force of the explosion and the hurricane gale winds of the suddenly uncontained atmosphere. Bodies and other human items rain down on the surrounding camp. A massive and jagged section falls among a group of soldiers as they are emerging form the portable shelter, smashing several of them, throwing the rest into confusion. The wreckage continues to spew gases and sparks into the lunar sky long after the last mangled piece come to rest.

Tatiana leads Karyl and Alonzo past the remains of Evolution's Child's pilothouse, using the wreckage as cover, popping out on the far side with their cannons blazing. The warriors speed and the stealth of their vacsuits surprise the soldiers emerging from the cluster of parked trucks. Before they have time to realize what is confronting them, the Lunarians annihilate their ranks. They aim for center of mass and maintain a constant fusillade as they sprint past. A few seconds later, a blood red cloud of death expands slowly in the vacuum of space. The twenty-two soldiers hadn't gotten off a single shot.

Almost as an afterthought, Tatiana launches a missile through the front view port of the second Goliath. The explosion rocks and bounces the big vehicle energetically, splitting the pressure hull and releasing the internal atmosphere in a surge of gases and material that extends a hundred feet into the sky. She launches a second missile at the lone remaining truck, angled downward this time, aiming for the high-capacity power supply she knows is buried somewhere in its gut, figuring it would be in the lower quadrant of the front section just as in Lunarian designs. It explodes even more violently, sending it flipping end over end, the force of the detonation knocking over the dying vehicle next to it, leaving a shallow crater in the floor of Nell's Valley.

From behind the wreckage of Evolution's Child four soldiers emerge and fire at the ghostly shapes from behind hitting both Alonzo and Karyl causing their electromagnetic shields to flash brightly as they absorb the energy, releasing photons during the exchange.

"Kipper! The freighter!" Tatiana calls out. She is aware of everyone's position on the battlefield and is fortunate that Corazon and Jason are close by.

She could have saved her breath. Kipper and Angel leap over Evolution's Child and engage the four soldiers before they have time to fire again. The Muslims are so focused on Tatiana and the others they never realize that death has found them until it is far too late. With inhuman accuracy, the warriors stitch a pattern on each torso, from shoulder to hip and angled downward, hitting them all in the back from above and behind. Blood and other bodily tissues rise in a fog as the soldiers fall slowly to ground, coming to rest almost simultaneously, spewing their guts into the lunar vacuum far from the land of their birth.

"Clear!" Kipper says, hardly slowing down to make the kills, racing over the landscape looking for his next target.

Corazon, Jason and Consuela swing around the twisted remains of the fuel tankers and bear down on the frigate. They can see the round shape of the dome just beyond it. To their left is a group of non-combatants, probably mechanics or technicians, heading as fast as they can back towards the main camp. On foot they pose little threat. The warriors can't even detect a weapon on any of them. Corazon swings wide and opens up as soon as he clears the tanker wreckage. One, two, three go down and the remaining men turn facing him, raising their arms in surrender. Corazon appreciates them stopping and providing such an easy target. Spacing his shots right down the line, he nails all six dead center from over a hundred yards away, their blood and bodily fluids adding to the growing battlefield haze.

Beyond them a line of three Rugbys are moving in single file, rooster tails of regolith rising behind each balloon tire. Consuela signals Jason to take the direct route towards the dome while she takes care of the rovers. Not waiting to see her orders carried out, her first burst takes out the rear vehicle, striking the two soldiers in the head and torso, engulfing the racing buggy in a bloody mess as it careens into a large basalt outcrop, coming to a sudden and violent stop. The other two Rugbys open fire trying vainly to hit something they cannot see. Running parallel with the fleeing vehicles, Consuela fires a second burst just missing the rover's power pack. She keeps moving easily keeping up with the rovers as they race over the valley floor at speeds exceeding fifty miles per hour. Consuela concentrates her fire on the driver of the last rover, sending burst after burst at the soldier until the rover veers off course, strikes a large boulder and tips over on its side, skidding across the lunar surface before coming to a grinding halt. One more burst in its exposed underbelly sends the buggy up in a hypergolic ball of flame, the bloody fog of the occupants carbonized in the silent inferno. Closing quickly on the lone remaining rover, Consuela chews up the cockpit with disrupter fire. The haze of blood tells the warrior that her work here is done, the rover spewing a cloud of biological fluids in its wake before striking a rocky outcrop and coming to a stop so suddenly that the rear wheels come off the surface. Showing tremendous strength, Consuela digs into the soft regolith making a sharp turn back towards the camp. The dust of her passage settles slowly behind her.

Jason and Corazon launch missiles at the frigate as they pass, not waiting around to see the results. To their left, two rovers are sprinting away from the camp, sending a long arc of regolith from each spinning tire. Firing from over two hundred yards away, their disrupters hit within inches of there target, ripping at the vehicles underbelly, probing relentlessly for the power pack. The hypergolic fluids in the ruptured device react in a towering ball of flame, ripping the rover apart and sending its remains spinning across the lunar landscape. Its companion vehicle meets the same fate a second later, exploding with a force that sends one of its balloon tires bouncing wildly across the valley, leaving twisted wreckage behind. A fog of blood rises over the remains in a gruesome memorial of death, where the smallest breach in a vacsuit is fatal.

Sam sprints down the debris field finding nothing worth targeting until to her right she spots motion along the ground as one of the soldiers crawls away from the killing. A burst along his spine stops all movement. Swinging around the wreckage of the pilothouse Sam launches two of her missiles at the frigate and changes course heading directly at the portable shelter. The two little finless darts from hell streak toward the ship, striking the fuselage near a landing strut, ripping apart the superstructure. The vessel rocks as the other strut on this side twists, slowly giving way in the lunar gravity. The frigate tips and kneels in surrender, its remaining landing struts holding it at a forty-five degree angle. Smoke and other gases pour from gaping holes in it skin. The logs would show that it had never gotten off a single shot its own defense.

Sam sends two more or her missiles at the inflatable dome now in front of her, aiming for the main airlock on this side. The explosion rips the structure apart leaving a giant hole in the side of the inflatable building. But the configuration inside is compartmentalized so only a small amount of air escapes to space. Sam begins to punch holes in its envelope with her disrupter, raking back and forth across the habitat, each hole spewing gasses. A dark cloud grows above the dome as it slowly begins to collapse.

Jason and Corazon converge from the other side and strafe the dome, briefly adding their cannon fire to the death of the portable habitat. Continuing on towards the dome, Sam spots the infrared emissions of several people hiding behind a cluster of boulders. Effortlessly, she changes course and darts towards the pile of stone, passing about a hundred feet behind it. The two soldiers never realize they have been found. Releasing a double burst, she watches the explosive expansion of blood and tissue, knowing from the amount that both individuals are dead or soon will be. She launches another missile at the frigate which penetrates deep inside before exploding. The ship shakes like a wounded animal as more of its upper body is ripped away. Small pieces of metal and plastic, fiber and flesh, add to the rising plume of death gathering over the camp.

The last three Rugbys speed towards the north end of the valley away from the camp, running for their lives. Hidden behind the frigate for most of their sprint, they are over a mile away before the first Guardian notices them, and only then because the gunner in the lead rover can't resist taking a pot shot at a shadow.

Jason swings wide around the crippled frigate busily pumping cannon rounds into the spacecraft when his targeting system beeps loudly indicating he is under fire. He digs in his heels and leaps sideways while his scanners locate the source. Two thousand yards away he spots the three targets racing up the valley.

But hitting a fast moving target bouncing and maneuvering around rocks and arroyos at that distance is tricky, even for a Guardian. Leaping in pursuit, Jason closes the gap while maintaining steady fire, hitting the vehicles time after time as they bump and grind their way up the valley, failing to find the sweet spot, yet inflicting damage on the fleeing group. Sam joins the target practice from behind him and Consuela from off to his right. The concentrated fire from all three Guardians converge on the middle rover which erupts in flame, fails to make a turn and slams into a large basalt outcropping. The rover next in line follows his companion, detonating like a bomb when it hits the same rock. Trailing a cloud of bloody gases, the last rover crests a ridge and disappears, the only vehicle to survive Nell's Valley. Full of holes and only a partially filled fuel tank, it doesn't have the ability to get very far, especially carrying two badly wounded men.

"Let them go!" Kitajima orders, pulling Jason up short. "Someone should live to tell the tale of what happened here today." The attack had lasted less than a hundred seconds. A mixture of human remains, disrupter vapor, and an assortment of volatile gases creates a fog of death that hangs over the valley, slowly dissipating outward, decreasing in density as time goes by. It will take days for the cloud to disperse to the point it can't be seen, many months before it can't be detected forensically.

"Hack, get in here. Kipper, you and Doc Grady take care of Brice," Kitajima calls out. It has long since been determined that Brice was beyond medical science, but that didn't mean they would leave him behind. "Sam, you're with me!"

"Aye!" she responds throwing a cloud of regolith into the sky as she turns towards Red's landing zone. As she approaches Sam can see Kitajima land just beyond the wreckage of the pilothouse, emerge from the Dragonfly and disappear into the excavated hole beside the pilothouse. A few seconds later she slides to a stop beside the excavator getting a close look at it for the first time. If the bomb isn't already exposed, they will need to keep this machine digging until it was. That's her job.

Kitajima emerges from the hole and joins Sam, "It's still almost ten feet to the bomb. What have you determined here?"

"It's a Hodgkin's excavator. Lunarian design and assembled right here on Luna," Sam informs him.

"Good, then you shouldn't have any problems with it! Get started. We need to finish ASAP!" Kitajima growls.

Turning away, Kitajima is confident Sam will do her magic without his supervision. He watches as Blue approaches the designated landing zone at high speed, smoothly coming to a hover before floating down to the surface without a hitch, all in one elegant motion.

"Captain!" Doc Grady appears before him, that in and of itself means trouble. Doc normally wouldn't have any reason to talk to Kitajima, unless something was wrong.

"What is it Doc?" Kitajima asks.

"Everyone is having problems. I've adjusted their nurocognitive adrenal levels as much as I dare. Any more and they will lose their edge and we need them sharp. But Tempel and Jason required sedatives," Doc Grady reports.

"They're not physically injured? Is this a mental defect?" Kitajima asks.

"Not a defect. They're reacting to the battle and to the loss of Brice. What they did and witnessed has disrupted their mental process. In times past it was called battle fatigue or shock. Their minds can't cope with the killing and shuts down," Doc Grady explains.

"Tempel is my top Lieutenant and we will need him. Bottom line, is he functional?" Kitajima has to make sure the mission comes first. These problems can't be allowed to interfere with that, not when thermonuclear bombs are involved.

"Not at the moment. When I put him to sleep I strapped him in a seat aboard Blue. I recommend that we let him rest. That will do more for him than all of my drugs," Doc Grady states honestly.

"Damn! Do whatever you must to get both of them back at one hundred percent," Kitajima says. Loosing Tempel would be a major blow to their chances. He's the leader among the Guardians and a knowledgeable and intelligent man, not to mention a good friend. Kitajima had suspected that some of his young warriors would crack under the pressure of mortal combat but he would never have guessed it would be Tempel.

"Aye, I'll keep you informed," Doc Grady responds and is gone.

"Charley Company, listen up," Kitajima broadcast. "It looks like we have at least ten minutes of digging and another five to get the nukes loaded. You have that long to collect intelligence. Here's the plan, Angel and Alonzo take the frigate, Tatiana and Corazon the shelter, Consuela, Karyl and Zoey poke around what's left of the trucks. You know what you're looking for! Let's move out!"

****

As Angel and Alonzo lope towards the heavily damaged frigate, they can see the main airlock is beyond use, jagged and twisted metal blocking easy entry. Leaping upward, the two warriors climb the tilted side of the big ship grabbing the ragged edges of a massive hole torn in its skin. The Guardians hesitate briefly peering inside, then launch themselves through the opening, landing smoothly in a crouch. Power is off within the frigate forcing them to increase the sensitivity of their low-light-level sensors.

Inside, the floor tilts at forty-five degrees. Everything loose slid downhill when the ship tipped over and is in a pile at their feet.

"This must have been living quarters. Come on. Let's see where this leads," Alonzo says effortlessly moving up the angled floor, his boots giving him superb traction, heading for an open door above them. He gracefully pulls himself through the doorway into the next room.

Angel follows, leaping through without touching the sides, landing on all fours, the traction in her gloves and boots allowing her to stick where she comes down. The room she finds herself in is thick with expelled gases. The large quantities of blood and urine testify that more than one person died in here. But that isn't their concern right now, this isn't a rescue mission, they are looking for loot in the form of knowledge.

Along the side of the room is a passage that leads upward. Angel scrambles over the wreckage and takes it, emerging on what is obviously the ships control room. Bodies are flung against the downhill side in a tangle of arms and legs. It appears that no one had vacsuits on at the time of the attack. They paid dearly for their carelessness.

Bodily fluids fill the room with a thick fog forcing the two warriors to stop and take the time to adjust their visual, filtering out most of the haze. Banks of electronic equipment line the walls and consoles are bolted to the floor in a distinctive pattern that easily identifies it as the control room. Ambidextrous to the fourth degree, Alonzo moves swiftly and easily across the tilted room using his hands and feet interchangeably. He stops at a large floor-to-ceiling rack, running his hand down the front, analyzing the markings on each piece of equipment.

"Here! This is the AI! It's marked in Arabic, Chinese and English. They must have bought it on the open market!" Alonzo says with anger.

"Get it and let's go! We don't have all day!" Angel flares clinging to the edge of a console near what must have been the Captains Chair. Blood smears one armrest and two holes are neatly punched in its back. She finds a small book tucked in a pocket and recognizes it as the Captains personal log, a practice the Brotherhood continues from the earlier days of sea faring ships.

Alonzo looks around in panic, "Sarge, I don't have a screwdriver!"

Angel almost smiles as she slips the book into a pocket of her vacsuit. She scrambles past Alonzo using her hands and feet, finds a good angle, and opens up with her disrupter on the metal framework of the rack, deftly cutting the AI out like a skilled surgeon.

Alonzo meekly assists in cutting the fiber optic cabling from the back of the device as Angel pulls it free from the rack. Angel moves behind Alonzo and secures the device to the warriors back.

On the way out, they pause at the hole in the side of the ship, gazing out over the site. Here and there scattered over the area are the twisted wreckage of people and property. Nothing remains intact. An eerie fog of fuel and blood hangs over the valley, slowly expanding in the vacuum. It will take months for it to completely dissipate. Leaping from their perch, the two warriors sprint back towards Evolution's Child with minutes to spare, storing their find in Blue's cargo hold.

"Angel, Alonzo, get over here and lend a hand!" Kitajima calls from beneath the pilothouse when he realizes the two are back early.

Scrambling around the wreck, they dig in their heels and pull mightily at the ropes. Slowly the crate emerges from its prison, threatening to buckle under the strength of the warriors electromagnetically enhanced muscles.

"Easy!" Kitajima calls out a warning. "The auto-detonate is still active!"

Kitajima and Sam scoop the accumulated regolith from in front of the crate, managing to apply enough lift to keep it moving forward without bulldozing too far into the soil. The warriors grunt and pull, and grunt some more, carefully working the object out of the narrow passage.

Seeming to take forever, they finally get it on the surface.

"Sam, once this is secure in the hold I want you to disarm the bobby trap. But be careful! Don't assume it's identical to the others," Kitajima says.

"Aye," the young Lunarian responds.

Angel, Sam, Alonzo and Consuela place slings under the crate and carry it the final few feet, depositing it in the transport.

The second crate is much easier, following the track of the first. Soon it's lashed tight next to its brother

"Let's move it people!" Kitajima broadcast standing at the bottom of the ramp his hands on his hips looking out across the battlefield, seeing his officers racing fluidly over the battlefield converging on the Lunarian ships. Irritated that Tatiana is not among them, "Lieutenant Tushar!" he calls out. He spots her emerging from the remains of the inflatable shelter. She is loaded down, her back pack full and many of the pockets and pouches of her vacsuit bulge with loot.

"Here Captain," Tatiana replies excitedly. "I found some very interesting items!"

"Show me later Lieutenant! We need to get out of here now!" Kitajima responds irritably as Tatiana leaps forward and quickly covers the distance to the ship.

From an orbit over a hundred miles up, a Brotherhood frigate comes over the horizon, the closest ship available to lend a hand to those in Nell's Valley. Blue's scanners pick up the ship almost immediately. A bright red warning flashes across every warrior's visual.

"We have company!" Hack exclaims.

"They must have seen us!" Tatiana warns as she sinks into her seat.

Kitajima doesn't hesitate, "Scramble! Everybody out! We need to take that ship down!"

Lindsey, Lazarus, and Zechariah look on as the warriors exit the transport in a blur, leaving Kitajima to pilot their spacecraft.

Moments later the two transports rise as one and accelerate in opposite directions keeping below the ridges framing Nell's Valley. A few hundred yards out they gain just enough elevation to soar above the ridges and other higher terrain, and began a series of sharp maneuvers at low speed, zigzagging across the landscape in an unpredictable pattern. The frigate repeatedly fires, but trying to hit these illusive targets from such a distance is not trivial even in the 21st century. The rock and regolith below the darting Lunarian ships erupt violently with each miss as the shots rain down from above. Lazarus gains a whole new appreciation for the acceleration seats aboard the transports.

Both transports open up and pound the frigate, quickly establishing they were the better aim primarily because the Brotherhood ship is trapped in a nice predictable orbital path. The ship's Captain has never been under fire and freezes at the wrong time, but there really isn't anything he can do to alter his fate once Charley Company turns their attention on him.

Spread out across the surface, the warriors focus their combined might against the ship. Magnifying the target until it seems almost too easy. The frigate can do nothing to avoid their attack. Their disrupter beams converge on the frigate, punching shallow holes in her thick ceramic skin. The briefest fraction of a second after their beams strike, the plasma slug passes down that narrow passage impacting the bottom with a tremendous release of energy, vaporizing a portion of the ship's armor. Not just one but fifty, a hundred, a thousand little explosions. The frigate seems to dissolve before their eyes.

Its captain fights back bravely, shifting his aim to the numerous origins of energy scattered across the surface below him. They are slower than the transports but even harder to see. He thinks he has silenced at least one of these targets, but because they are moving in such an erratic pattern, he can't be sure. By the time his orbit carries him over the horizon his ship is barely able to sustain life. It poses no more threat to Charley Company.

It isn't until the engagement is over that Kitajima realizes he has another casualty. Angel had taken a direct hit from one of the frigates main cannons sometime during the exchange killing her instantly. Charley Company is stunned. Win or lose, every battle has cost.

The warriors are silent as they lay Angel alongside Brice, Lei, and Karl, out of sight inside the black body bags but not forgotten. Silently, the ships rise once more and disappear into the dark lunar night. Behind them Nell's Valley is a monument to death and destruction, a testament of man's ingenuity, the first battlefield on another world.

****

Similar to Aldrin Station, Shennong is divided up into fourteen boroughs containing sixty-six freeholds spread out in fourteen-hundred habitats. With a population over six-hundred-thousand, it's the largest city on Luna.

When the Brotherhood first attacked, its citizens were caught by surprise. Some fought back, some ran, and many died. Those who swarm to the invaders do little to slow their advance, simply adding their blood to the carnage. The convoys are a powerful adversary and the Lunarians are forced to quickly learn new tactics. If something works they do it again, if it doesn't, more die. With their lives they buy Security Chief Chen Zhi and the rest of Shennong time to regroup.

Within hours, the Brotherhood penetrates far, leaving garrisons in their wake at strategic locations. But the soldiers remain in the commonways, not even attempting to expand into the numerous avenues or nearby warrens, sealing every opening in and out of the commonways as they pass with foamed silicone carbide material. It proves to be very effective in blocking Lunarian counterattacks and severely hampering their ability to move within their own city.

Chen estimates they are facing over fifty thousand soldiers in their commonways with thousands more outside the main entrances, both inside and outside the crater. This is far too few to take Shennong by force, but it is enough to stop nearly all movement in the subterranean city and the surrounding surface. The invaders are in control of Tycho Crater but it seems only a matter of time before Chen strikes and overwhelms the invaders with the numerical superiority at her disposal.

Yangtze Commonway, like many others found throughout the cities of the Republic, is a giant passageway cut through the heart of Tycho's rim mountain. It varies in size and shape from place to place. Filled with thousands of trees and other plants, it's part of a forest that serves the city as both air purifier and a pleasant means of traveling between boroughs.

Here in this particular section of the commonway, the trees had been fifty-year old Sycamore's towering over a hundred feet in height. All that remains of these majestic plants are piles of blackened wood. Some of the massive trunks have been pushed over, their root balls leaving craters in the fertile loam of the commonway. The smoke of their burning still obscures the distance, as if a fog were rolling in off a distant sea. Here and there soft fingers curl upward from the smoldering vegetation.

With the grace of a cheetah, Lieutenant Huang leaps the dead body as if it were just another piece of debris, not giving the seared lump of flesh a second glance. Spread out behind her are the remnants of Dukong, Nachang's 10th Division. Of the twenty-two officers, only twelve remain, the others killed or wounded in the almost continuous combat since the attack began. Standard units have come forward to fight alongside Dukong, some telling her that she should fall back, but nothing will compel Huang and her warriors to remove themselves. They are Guardians.

The intense beams cut through the atmosphere of the commonway like a violent electrical storm, the lightning flashes of disrupter fire reflecting off the curved ceiling far overhead. The thunder of their passage echoes along the full extent of the great corridor. The Brotherhood is employing slash and burn to destroy everything in their path, defocusing their beams to set whole trees on fire and sealing all entrances to the commonway, hoping to at least slow down the incessant hit and run attacks the Lunarians have thrown at them.

Huang uses the eight foot trunk of one of these fallen giants to mask her approach. Timing her leap with the arrival of her comrades, she vaults over the tree and begins firing her disrupter and launching missiles. Around her comes what remains of Dukong Company, swarming over the horizontal slab of smoldering wood, laying down a withering fire on the Brotherhood vehicles that lay a few hundred yards beyond it.

Caught with their backs to the attacking Lunarians, the big convoys return fire even as the vehicles swing wide in an effort to bring the more numerous forward mounted weapons to bear. Others stop, disgorging soldiers like ants emerging from their hole to face their attackers.

The Lunarians concentrate their fire on the third convoy from the rear, slicing into the truck cab and the troop carriers it tows. Missiles streak to their mark and explosions rip the juggernaut causing it to bounce and shudder. It comes to a stop, unable to go any further. Its side ripped open, its guts exposed, both of the large solid core tires on the left side blown away letting the body of the cab tip over spilling everything and everybody in its interior out onto the soft green grass of the commonway. Black smoke pours from it and several more explosions signal its final death, the last a massive detonation that causes the vehicles around it to scurry away. The smoke from its demise collects in the commonway making it increasingly difficult to see.

The troop carrier directly attached to the burning truck, itself full of holes and at least three missiles, catches fire from the conflagration and within moments is a towering inferno. No one inside survives. The other carriers, further back from the massive explosion that finished the cab, open their doors wide and soldiers emerge in a rush, eager to get away from certain death.

Narrow beams of intense energy slice through the blinding smoke seeking victims. Brotherhood soldiers fall and die on soil not of their own world. The Guardian ten feet to Huang's left takes a beam to his chest and slumps to the ground, momentum lodging his lifeless body against the trunk of a fallen Sycamore. Another warrior has his arm removed at the elbow by a beam as he leaps over a massive tree trunk. He retreats to the waiting medics. His life will be spared by modern medical science, perhaps to fight another day.

Within minutes the skirmish is over, the entire line of vehicles have completed the response maneuver, avoiding the death throes of their stricken comrade, and are dishing out energy on a scale that Huang and her Guardians cannot survive for long. But they have accomplished what they set out to do and disappear back along the passageway, out of reach of the Brotherhood's weapons behind the tangle of fallen trees and ultimately around a bend in the great stone corridor called Yangtze Commonway.

In the beginning the Brotherhood sent soldiers after the retreating Lunarians but quickly learned that it was a mistake when few returned. Better to stay together and defend from a position of strength.

Chen feeds the illusion that there is strength in numbers while chipping away at the invaders. She is finally in a position to order a massive counterattack but hesitates knowing that the causalities will be high. Better to wait and continue harassing them. A few days of sleep deprivation will soften the enemy and then she can strike.

But the Islamic Brotherhood has reached its objectives, to get forces in position within every borough. Turning off their jammers, the Brotherhood broadcasts their ultimatum on all frequencies.

"Cease all hostilities or your city will be destroyed! Our forces carry thermonuclear weapons which they will use unless you immediately comply." The message repeats over and over.

With the network functioning again, Chen quickly determines where the enemy is and performs a positional analysis of the situation. Damn! There are garrisons at the center of all fourteen boroughs! If they have nukes then the Brotherhood is in complete control of her city!

She immediately calls a halt to the attacks, ordering all front line warriors to fall back until further notice. Chen is well aware that Corso's people had found nukes out on the Sea of Clouds and she has very little trouble believing their claim. She shudders at the implications of what she concludes is the only reasonable explanation for the actions of the Brotherhood. Only a complete fool or someone with a big trump card would put their forces in such a precarious position as they have done, a detachment of a few thousand troops penetrating to the heart of each borough. After all, she commands an army almost a half-million strong.

****

"I'm not asking you to surrender. Simply contain them," Chen says.

"But chief, what are the chances that they actually have nukes? We must expel them from Shennong!" Sergeant Lin Kai is the ranking member of the contingent of Guardians facing the Brotherhood at Linchuan, Shennong's easternmost borough.

"All it takes is one nuke and Shennong is gone. Ask yourself why they have deliberately put themselves in a do or die position. We will not risk a nuclear suicide bomb! Do I make myself clear?" she hates needing to be so firm with him. The young man's blood stained vacsuit attests to what he has gone through the last few hours. It takes her only moments to find out his comrades have all been killed or wounded and the handful of warriors he commands are remnants of other units. "I want you to fall back and let someone else take the lead. You and your warriors have done everything possible under the circumstances."

"Chief, we want to finish this!" the young man replies.

"Kai, we are not done here. Get your people some food and rest, and let me worry about the Brotherhood. OK?" Chen can't afford to spend any more time with the young man. Waiting for his nod, she shifts her attention to another of the two dozen or more units disengaging from the enemy. She is worried that someone somewhere will take it upon themselves to continue the attack.

"Come on Sarge. I could use some chow and a hot shower," Meili says. She and Luka are the only two left of Manchu. The rest are dead or wounded and she fights alongside Guardians she barely knows.

Kai looks around at the small gathering. None are from his original unit. He can't help but feel that he has failed, that somehow he personally was to blame for the Brotherhood sitting in Yangtze Commonway just outside his families' warren.

They had been completing their attack run when the order to disengage came and the warriors hadn't retreated very far down the devastated commonway. It broke his heart to see the forest that he had played in as a boy so utterly destroyed. Smoke fills the great corridor making it difficult to see very far but even after tweaking his sensors he can't find a single tree left standing, no matter how hard he searches. The gardens that had occupied this section are in ruins. The huge solid core tires of the massive convoys smashed what the Brotherhoods disrupters didn't burn.

The beam strikes Meili in the upper torso at the base of her neck, effectively cutting off her head. Before the thunder of its passage has died away, a second and third take out others. Kai roars his anger and springs away. What remains of his ragtag unit scatters among the wreckage of the commonway, leaving behind more Lunarian blood to soak into the black dirt. Only Kai turns back, no longer caring if he lives or dies.

Leaping forward on all fours, the young Lunarian keeps low and circles, staying hidden behind the tangle of fallen trees as much as possible. Within seconds he sees the soldiers, their backs to him, heading towards the main body, their mission accomplished. He counts twenty nine in this little group.

He checks his supply of missiles and sees that he has only four remaining. Fuel supply for the disrupter is running low but he couldn't have stopped even if it were empty.

The man last in line is the only one bothering to look back and then only every other step or so, he never sees the shadow stalking them. Kai is within a hundred feet when he opens fire, spacing his shots, making every one count. The sound of his attack echoes down the great corridor causing the others in the group to scramble for cover. Before they do, the young Lunarian has killed more than half their number.

Beyond them Kai can see the convoys that brought these men here to kill him and his family. With his thoughts, he sends his last four missiles streaking towards the vehicles, one to the left, one to the right, and the final two reaching out for the center truck. The explosions rock the commonway sending dirt and shrapnel far and wide, inflicting heavy damage but not total destruction.

He leaps over a pile of smoldering debris and kills another invader, and another, seeing with satisfaction the panic he is spreading among these killers. Beams blister the air around him as he twists and turns, striving to keep something between him and the powerful disrupters mounted on the trucks. He never senses the beam that kills him, its power overwhelming the defenses of his ghost suit and obliterating his heart between beats. One second he is fighting, the next his lifeless body is skidding to a stop on the churned up sod of his home world. His blood runs in rivulets down the deep tire impressions pressed into the soft soil of the commonway. His unseeing eyes gaze upon eternity, another sacrifice on the altar of war.

****

Inside his command center, Major Abdul Aziz is barely conscious. The twin blasts from the missiles has killed his entourage and all of his senior staff. They had been together as the announcement was given that all hostilities should cease immediately, anticipating immediate capitulation. The squawking of an alarm testifies to the grave condition within the other two convoys. His command is in shambles.

He struggles to pull himself to a sitting position, his back against the wall. Gasping for breath, he looks down to see his chest covered in blood. Knowing his duty, he drags himself across the shattered interior of the vehicle, groaning with pain as he pulls himself to his feet before a control console. Removing a chain from around his neck, he inserts the small black key that it contains into a matching lock on the console. A red light flashes on.

His head swoons and he knows he doesn't have much time. He lays a bloody hand on the palm reader and says in Arabic, "*Emergency Override Code Major Abdul Aziz. Zero one zero six six six zero.*"

"*Authorization accepted and countdown begun,*" the computerized male voice responds in the same language. It is the last words he will hear in his beloved native tongue.

"*Allah Akbar,*" the Major responds sliding to the floor as the loss of blood and pain finally takes its toll. He puts his back to the console and looks out at the devastation inside the cab. He is at peace with his god knowing he has performed his duties to the best of his ability. He welcomes death, seeing it only as a transformation from the hardships of life to the promised paradise.

Elsewhere among the many separate detachments now spread throughout Shennong, the various commanders give orders for their soldiers to take cover as soon as the signal of eminent detonation arrives. This is an event they have all anticipated, when one of the units would find it necessary to perform the ultimate sacrifice.

"*Allah Akbar,*" the Major continues chanting as the short countdown draws to a close. His thoughts turn to his family and the things that he regrets. He assures himself that all will be forgiven because of his service to Allah. Beating his wives and children had been necessary and lawful under Islamic code. The only regret that eats at his heart is the death of his daughter. But stubborn disobedience could not be tolerated and her death had made all his other children respect his subsequent decisions. But now, at the instant of his own demise, all he can see is her young eyes staring back at him, accusing even as the life was beat out of her by the falling stones cast by people she had grown up with.

Groaning with the intense pain in his chest, in the final few seconds of his life the Major tries to lean forward and touch his forehead to the cold metal floor, a position that promised the comfort of long use. But he never makes it.

The nuke, carried in the bowels of a troop carrier attached to his convoy, detonates forming a tiny sun in the heart of Linchuan, instantly filling Yangtze Commonway with enough energy to power Shennong for a year. The sheer size of the great corridor isn't sufficient to route the energy away from the habitats and the blast pulverizes the stone in an incredible surge of energy and particles. Even as the walls of the commonway evaporate under the intense radiation, shockwaves ripple with deadly efficiency down the great passageway destroying everything within it.

Reaching a million degrees at its heart, the hot gasses seek out and find Linchuan's commonways, avenues, and habitats. The leading edge of the expanding detonation is not spherical like that seen in vids of Houston's demise, but jagged, following the contours of the subterranean city, the path of least resistance. Like a volcano exploding inside a vast building, what didn't succumb to the pressure of the shockwave is consumed by the pyroclastic flow that follows. Only this building is made of a material that funnels the destructive forces directly on the human constructions within it, focusing the power of the atom upon the works of man.

The massive shockwave propagates through the stone much faster than through the air, pulverizing the nearby habitats, engulfing them in its fury. As it radiates outward, the free surfaces of the underground metropolis explode, showering the spaces within the habitats with huge chunks of rock. In seconds the core of the detonation expands to a thousand feet, and the incessant pressure wave destroys every habitat within Linchuan as it races outward.

Other nearby boroughs endures the wrath of this man-made sun as their outermost habitats collapse or suffers heavy damage by the expanding shockwave. But as the sphere of destruction grows larger it loses power until finally spending itself. Behind it, the nuclear fire follows the path of least resistance and engulfs all it finds until it reaches the Eastern Access Tunnel. The mighty airlocks, damaged by the passing of the shockwave, cannot hold against its force. Like a giant blowtorch, the nuclear fire blows them open and emerges from under the mountain venting its fury to vacuum while destroying nearby surface installations. By this time the center of the blast has carved out a cavity almost a half mile in diameter, weakening the support overhead. The stone containing the habitats of Linchuan has been crushed into a fine powder.

The slower air-propagated pressure wave travels the entire length of every commonway and back again, branching into each part of the vast system, ringing Shennong like a hammer striking a bell. For miles its initial passage blows out airlocks like they were made of tissue paper, engulfing the living and working spaces that lie beyond. The firestorm and shockwave is a left-right combination that not only obliterates Linchuan with its intensity but reaches out to touch every borough in the city without exception.

With a major commonway open to vacuum, the wind soon reaches gale force as it spews into space. Outside the air and debris carried by the winds form a fog that lingers long after the last molecule escapes.

Most of the forces of the Brotherhood had sufficient warning of the impending blast to reach the relative safety of their troop carriers. Even so, the unit nearest to Linchuan feels the brunt of the detonation. The fierce nuclear fire and shockwave rips through their vehicles, tossing them like so many children's toys. Of the four convoys and over two thousand men, only one troop carrier survives intact, the soldiers inside bruised and broken but alive. It seems the yield of the bomb is larger than intended. Meant to take out only a small section of a Lunarian city, the Muslim scientists miscalculated the effect of detonating it within a commonway carved from solid stone.

Further away the Brotherhood fares better. Hunkered down within the trucks and troop carriers, the pressure wave passes over them without harm, buffeting the heavy vehicles with the force of a category five hurricane. The radiation is another matter but electromagnetic shields keep most of the more deadly particles away from the men inside.

Lunarians caught in the open are not so lucky. The tremendous shockwave, focused and transmitted down the enormous stone corridor, crushes them as though they are bugs to be brushed aside. Company and squad sized units closest to the epicenter are wiped out. Further away they are bashed and bruised but survive, their vacsuits protecting them from the intense radiation and pressure.

As the fury of the blast spends itself, the weakened mountain collapses, sinking into the cavity that Allah's fire has carved. A huge cloud of dust rises above the stricken city. The more severely damaged habitats implode under the shifting mass of rock releasing even more of the cities atmosphere to space. An even greater number are left uninhabitable with large cracks and sections broken away, open to vacuum. Survivors throughout the city struggle to put aside their shock and horror, striving to save whomever and whatever they can. The final death toll may never be known with certainty, but over twenty-nine-thousand-five-hundred citizens had lived and worked in Linchuan alone, and that is only the beginning of the tally. Fighting stops long before the last echo fades away.

The War of Souls has only just begun.

Chuck - 602 - 616 - 3162

Printed in the United States
75402LV00003B/151-189